MW00785891

SUE GRAFTON

THREE COMPLETE NOVELS
M,N,O

M IS FOR MALICE

N IS FOR NOOSE

O IS FOR OUTLAW

Also by Sue Grafton from Wings Books®

SUE GRAFTON: THREE COMPLETE NOVELS

"A" is for Alibi

"B" is for Burglar

"C" is for Corpse

SUE GRAFTON: THREE COMPLETE NOVELS

"D" is for Deadbeat

"E" is for Evidence

"F" is for Fugitive

SUE GRAFTON: THREE COMPLETE NOVELS

"G" is for Gumshoe

"H" is for Homicide

"I" is for Innocent

SUE GRAFTON: THREE COMPLETE NOVELS

"J" is for Judgment

"K" is for Killer

"L" is for Lawless

SUE GRAFTON

THREE COMPLETE NOVELS
M,N,O

M IS FOR MALICE

N IS FOR NOOSE

O IS FOR OUTLAW

WINGS BOOKS
NEW YORK

This edition contains the complete and unabridged texts of the original editions.

The contents of this omnibus were originally published in three separate volumes under the titles:
"M" is for Malice, copyright © 1996 by Sue Grafton
"N" is for Noose, copyright © 1998 by Sue Grafton
"O" is for Outlaw, copyright © 1999 by Sue Grafton

This 2008 edition is published by Wings Books, an imprint of Random House Value Publishing, a division of Random House, Inc., New York, by arrangement with Henry Holt and Company, Inc.

Random House
New York • Toronto • London • Sydney • Auckland
www.valuebooks.com

Printed and bound in the United States of America

A catalog record for this title is available from the Library of Congress.

ISBN: 978-0-517-23076-3

10 9 8 7 6 5 4 3 2 1

CONTENTS

M
IS FOR MALICE

For my good friends . . .

Barbara Brightman Jones and Joe Jones

and

Joanna Barnes and Jack Warner

The author wishes to acknowledge the invaluable assistance of the following people: Steven Humphrey; John Mackall, attorney-at-law, Seed, Mackall & Cole; Sam Eaton, attorney-at-law; B. J. Seebol, J.D.; William Tanner, Tanner Investigations; Dan Deveraux, plant manager, Granite Construction; Marcia and David Karpeles, The Karpeles Manuscript Library; Captain Ed Aasted, Detective Sergeant Don F. Knapp, Detective Jill Johnson, Detective Roger Aceves, Detective Lieutenant Nicholas Katzenstein, and Lieutenant Richard Glaus, Santa Barbara Police Department; Dana Motley; Melinda Johnson, Santa Barbara Newspress; and Lucy Thomas, Reeves Medical Library, Cottage Hospital.

M

IS FOR MALICE

1

Robert Dietz came back into my life on Wednesday, January 8. I remember the date because it was Elvis Presley's birthday and one of the local radio stations had announced it would spend the next twenty-four hours playing every song he'd ever sung. At six A.M. my clock radio blared on, playing "Heartbreak Hotel" at top volume. I smacked the Off button with the flat of my hand and rolled out of bed as usual. I pulled on my sweats in preparation for my morning run. I brushed my teeth, splashed water on my face, and trotted down the spiral stairs. I locked my front door behind me, moved out to the street where I did an obligatory stretch, leaning against the gatepost in front of my apartment. The day was destined to be a strange one, involving as it did a dreaded lunch date with Tasha Howard, one of my recently discovered first cousins. Running was the only way I could think of to quell my uneasiness. I headed for the bike path that parallels the beach.

Ah, January. The holidays had left me feeling restless and the advent of the new year generated one of those lengthy internal discussions about the meaning of life. I usually don't pay much attention to the passing of time, but this year, for some reason, I was taking a good hard look at myself. Who was I, really, in the scheme of things, and what did it all add up to? For the record, I'm Kinsey Millhone, female, single, thirty-five years old, sole proprietor of Kinsey Millhone Investigations in the southern California town of Santa Teresa. I was trained as a police officer and served a two-year stint with the Santa Teresa Police Department before life intervened, which is another tale altogether and one I don't intend to tell (yet). For the last ten years, I've made a living as a private investigator. Some days I see myself (nobly, I'll admit) battling against evil in the struggle for law and order. Other days, I concede that the dark forces are gaining ground.

Not all of this was conscious. Much of the rumination was simmering at a level I could scarcely discern. It's not as if I spent every day in a state of unremitting angst, wringing my hands and rending my clothes. I suppose what I was experiencing was a mild form of depression, triggered (perhaps) by nothing more complicated than the fact it was winter and the California sunlight was in short supply.

I started my career investigating arson and wrongful-death claims for California Fidelity Insurance. A year ago, my relationship with CFI came to an abrupt and ignominious halt and I'm currently sharing space with the law firm of Kingman and Ives, taking on just about anything to make ends meet. I'm licensed, bonded, and fully insured. I have twenty-five thousand dollars in a savings account, which affords me the luxury of turning down any client who doesn't suit. I haven't refused a case yet, but I was strongly considering it.

Tasha Howard, the aforementioned first cousin, had called to offer me work, though the details of the job hadn't yet been specified. Tasha is an attorney who handles wills and estates, working for a law firm with offices in both San Francisco and Lompoc, which is an hour north of Santa Teresa. I gathered she divided her time just about equally between the two. I'm normally interested in employment, but Tasha and I aren't exactly close and I suspected she was using the lure of business to insinuate herself into my life.

As it happened, her first call came on the day after New Year's, which allowed me to sidestep by claiming I was still on vacation. When she called again on January 7, she caught me off guard. I was at the office in the middle of a serious round of solitaire when the telephone rang.

"Hi, Kinsey. This is Tasha. I thought I'd try you again. Did I catch you at a bad time?"

"This is fine," I said. I crossed my eyes and pretended I was gagging myself with a finger pointed down my throat. Of course, she couldn't see that. I put a red eight on a black nine and turned up the last three cards. No play that I could see. "How are you?" I asked, perhaps a millisecond late.

"Doing well, thanks. How about you?"

"I'm good," I said. "Gee, your timing's uncanny. I was just picking up the phone. I've been making calls all morning and you were next on my list." I often use the word *gee* when I'm lying through my teeth.

"I'm glad to hear that," she said. "I thought you were avoiding me."

I laughed. Ha.Ha.Ha. "Not at all," said I. I was about to elaborate on the denial, but she plowed right on. Having run out of moves, I pushed the cards aside and began to tag my blotter with a little desktop graffiti. I block-printed the word *BARF* and gave each of the letters a three-dimensional cast.

She said, "What's your schedule like tomorrow? Can we get together for an hour? I have to be in Santa Teresa anyway and we could meet for lunch."

"I can probably do that," I said with caution. In this world, lies can only take you so far before the truth catches up. "What sort of work are we talking about?"

"I'd rather discuss it in person. Is twelve o'clock good for you?"

"That sounds fine," I said.

"Perfect. I'll make reservations. Emile's-at-the-Beach. I'll see you there," she said, and with a click she was gone.

I put the phone down, set the ballpoint pen aside, and laid my little head down on my desk. What an idiot I was. Tasha *must* have known I didn't want to see her, but I hadn't had the nerve to say so. She'd come to my rescue a couple of months before and though I'd repaid the money, I still felt I owed her. Maybe I'd listen to her politely before I turned her down. I did have another quick job in the works. I'd been hired to serve two deposition subpoenas in a civil case for an attorney on the second floor of our building.

I went out in the afternoon and spent thirty-five bucks (plus tip) on a legitimate salon haircut. I tend to take a pair of nail scissors to my own unruly mop about every six weeks, my technique being to snip off any tuft of hair that sticks out. I guess I must have been feeling insecure because it wouldn't ordinarily occur to me to pay real bucks for something I can do so handily myself. Of course, I've been told my hairstyle looks exactly like a puppy dog's backside, but what's wrong with that?

The morning of January 8 inevitably arrived and I pounded along the bike path as if pursued by wild dogs. Typically, I use my jog as a way to check in with myself, noting the day and the ongoing nature of life at the water's edge. That morning, I had been all business, nearly punitive in the energy I threw into the exercise. Having finished my run and my morning routine, I skipped the office altogether and hung around my place. I paid some bills, tidied up my desk, did a load of laundry, and chatted briefly with my landlord, Henry Pitts, while I ate three of his freshly baked sticky buns. Not that I was nervous.

As usual, when you're waiting for something unpleasant, the clock seems to leap forward in ten-minute increments. Next thing I knew I was standing at my bathroom mirror applying cut-rate cosmetics, for God's sake, while I emoted along with Elvis, who was singing "It's Now Or Never." The sing-along was taking me back to my high school days, not a terrific association, but amusing nonetheless. I hadn't known any more about makeup in those days than I do now.

I debated about a new outfit, but that's where I drew the line, pulling on my usual blue jeans, turtleneck, tweed blazer, and boots. I own one dress and I didn't want to waste it on an occasion like this. I glanced at the clock. It was 11:55. Emile's wasn't far, all of five minutes on foot. With luck, I'd be hit by a truck as I was crossing the street.

Almost all of the tables at Emile's were occupied by the time I arrived. In Santa Teresa, the beach restaurants do the bulk of their business during the summer tourist season when the motels and bed-and-breakfast establishments near the ocean are fully booked. After Labor Day, the crowds diminish until the town belongs to the residents again. But Emile's-at-the-Beach is a local favorite and doesn't seem to suffer the waxing and waning of the out-of-town trade.

Tasha must have driven down from Lompoc because a sassy red Trans Am bearing a vanity license plate that read TASHA H was parked at the curb. In the detective trade, this is what is known as a clue. Besides, flying down from Lompoc is more trouble than it's worth. I moved into the restaurant and scanned the tables. I had little appetite for the encounter, but I was trying to stay open to the possibilities. Of what, I couldn't say.

I spotted Tasha through one of the interior archways before she spotted me. She was seated in a small area off the main dining room. Emile had placed her by the front window at a table for two. She was staring out at the children's play equipment in the little beach park across the street. The wading pool was closed, emptied for the winter, a circle of blue-painted plaster that looked now like a landing pad for a UFO. Two preschool-age children were clambering backward up a nearby sliding board anchored in the sand. Their mother sat on the low concrete retaining wall with a cigarette in hand. Beyond her were the bare masts of boats slipped in the harbor. The day was sunny and cool, the blue sky scudding with clouds left behind by a storm that was passing to the south of us.

A waiter approached Tasha and they conferred briefly. She took a menu from him. I could see her indicate that she was waiting for someone else. He withdrew and she began to peruse the lunch choices. I'd never actually laid eyes on Tasha until now, but I'd met her sister Liza the summer before last. I'd been startled because Liza and I looked so much alike. Tasha was cut from the same genetic cloth, though she was three years older and more substantial in her presentation. She wore a gray wool suit with a white silk shell showing in the deep V of the jacket. Her dark hair was streaked with blond, pulled back with a sophisticated black chiffon bow sitting at the nape of her neck. The only jewelry she wore was a pair of oversized gold earrings that glinted when she moved. Since she did estate planning, she probably didn't have much occasion for impassioned courtroom speeches, but she'd look properly intimidating in a skirmish nonetheless. Already I'd decided to get my affairs in order.

She caught sight of me and I saw her expression quicken as she registered the similarities between us. Maybe all the Kinsey girl cousins shared the same features. I raised a hand in greeting and moved through the lunch crowd to her table. I took the seat across from hers, tucking my bag on the floor beneath my chair. "Hello, Tasha."

For a moment, we did a mutual assessment. In high school biology, I'd studied Mendel's purple and white flowering peas; the cross-breeding of colors and the resultant pattern of "offspring." This was the very principle at work. Up close, I could see that her eyes were dark where mine were hazel, and her nose looked like mine had before it was broken twice. Seeing her was like catching a glimpse of myself unexpectedly in a mirror, the image both strange and familiar. Me and not me.

Tasha broke the silence. "This is creepy. Liza told me we looked alike, but I had no idea."

"I guess there's no doubt we're related. What about the other cousins? Do they look like us?"

"Variations on a theme. When Pam and I were growing up, we

were often mistaken for each other." Pam was the sister between Tasha and Liza.

"Did Pam have her baby?"

"Months ago. A girl. Big surprise," she said dryly. Her tone was ironic, but I didn't get the joke. She sensed the unspoken question and smiled fleetingly in reply. "All the Kinsey women have girl babies. I thought you knew."

I shook my head.

"Pam named her Cornelia as a way of sucking up to Grand. I'm afraid most of us are guilty of trying to score points with her from time to time."

Cornelia LaGrand was my grandmother Burton Kinsey's maiden name. "Grand" had been her nickname since babyhood. From what I'd been told, she ruled the family like a despot. She was generous with money, but only if you danced to her tune—the reason the family had so pointedly ignored me and my aunt Gin for twenty-nine years. My upbringing had been blue collar, strictly lower middle-class. Aunt Gin, who raised me from the age of five, had worked as a clerk/typist for California Fidelity Insurance, the company that eventually hired (and fired) me. She'd managed on a modest salary, and we'd never had much. We'd always lived in mobile homes—trailers, as they were known then—bastions of tiny space, which I still tend to prefer. At the same time, I recognized even then that other people thought trailers were tacky. Why, I can't say.

Aunt Gin had taught me never to suck up to anyone. What she'd neglected to tell me was there were relatives worth sucking up to.

Tasha, likely aware of the thicket her remarks were leading to, shifted over to the task at hand. "Let's get lunch out of the way and then I can fill you in on the situation."

We dealt with the niceties of ordering and eating lunch, chatting about only the most inconsequential subjects. Once our plates had been removed, she got down to business with an efficient change of tone. "We have some clients here in Santa Teresa caught up in a circumstance I thought might interest you. Do you know the Maleks? They own Malek Construction."

"I don't know them personally, but the name's familiar." I'd seen the company logo on job sites around town, a white octagon, like a stop sign, with the outline of a red cement mixer planted in the middle. All of the company trucks and job-site Porta Potti's were fire engine red and the effect was eye-catching.

Tasha went on. "It's a sand and gravel company. Mr. Malek just died and our firm is representing the estate." The waiter approached and filled our coffee cups. Tasha picked up a sugar pack, pressing in the edges of the paper rim on all sides before she tore the corner off. "Bader Malek bought a gravel pit in 1943. I'm not sure what he paid at the time, but it's worth a fortune today. Do you know much about gravel?"

"Not a thing," I said.

"I didn't either until this came up. A gravel pit doesn't tend to produce much income from year to year, but it turns out that over the last thirty years environmental regulations and land-use regulations make it very hard to start up a new gravel pit. In this part of California, there simply aren't that many. If you own the gravel pit for your region and construction is booming—which it is at the moment—it goes from being a dog in the forties to a real treasure in the 1980s, depending, of course, on how deep the gravel reserves are and the quality of those reserves. It turns out this one is on a perfect gravel zone, probably good for another hundred and fifty years. Since nobody else is now able to get approvals . . . well, you get the point I'm sure."

"Who'd have thunk?"

"Exactly," she said and then went on. "With gravel, you want to be close to communities where construction is going on because the prime cost is transportation. It's one of those backwater areas of wealth that you don't really know about even if it's yours. Anyway, Bader Malek was a dynamo and managed to maximize his profits by branching out in other directions, all building-related. Malek Construction is now the third-largest construction company in the state. And it's still family owned; one of the few, I might add."

"So what's the problem?"

"I'll get to that in a moment, but I need to back up a bit first. Bader and his wife, Rona, had four boys—like a series of stepping-stones, all of them two years apart. Donovan, Guy, Bennet, and Jack. Donovan's currently in his mid-forties and Jack's probably thirty-nine. Donovan's the best of the lot; typical first child, steady, responsible, the big achiever in the bunch. His wife, Christie, and I were college roommates, which is how I got involved in the first place. The second son, Guy, turned out to be the clunker among the boys. The other two are okay. Nothing to write home about, at least from what Christie's said."

"Do they work for the company?"

"No, but Donovan pays all of their bills nonetheless. Bennet fancies himself an 'entrepreneur,' which is to say he loses great whacks of money annually in bad business deals. He's currently venturing into the restaurant business. He and a couple of partners are opening a place down on Granita. Talk about a way to lose money. The man has to be nuts. Jack's busy playing golf. I gather he's got sufficient talent to hit the pro circuit, but probably not enough to earn a living at it.

"At any rate, back in the sixties, Guy was the one who smoked dope and raised hell. He thought his father was a materialistic, capitalistic son of a bitch and told him so every chance he could. I guess Guy got caught in some pretty bad scrapes—we're talking criminal behavior—and Bader finally cut him off. According to Donovan, his father gave Guy a lump sum, ten grand in cash, his portion of the then-modest family fortune. Bader told the kid to hit the road and not come back. Guy Malek disappeared and he hasn't been seen since. This was March 1968. He was twenty-six then, which would make him forty-three now. I guess no one really cared much when he left. It was probably a relief after what he'd put the family through. Rona had died two months before, in January that same year, and Bader went to his attorney with the intention of rewriting his will. You know how that goes: 'The reason I have made no provision for my son Guy in this will is not due to any lack of love or affection on my part, but simply because I have provided for him during my lifetime and feel that those provisions are more than adequate—blah, blah, blah.' The truth was, Guy had cost him plenty and he was sick of it.

"So. Fade out, fade in. In 1981, Bader's attorney died of a heart attack and all of his legal files were returned to him."

I interrupted. "Excuse me. Is that common practice? I'd assume all the files would be kept by the attorney's estate."

"Depends on the attorney. Maybe Bader insisted. I'm not really sure. I gather he was a force to be reckoned with. He was already ill by then with the cancer that finally claimed him. He'd also suffered a debilitating stroke brought on by all the chemo. Sick as he was, he probably didn't want to go through the hassle of finding a new attorney. Apparently, from his perspective, his affairs were in order and what he did with his money was nobody else's business."

I said, "Oh, boy." I didn't know what was coming, but it didn't sound good.

" 'Oh, boy' is right. When Bader died two weeks ago, Donovan went through his papers. The only will he found was the one Bader and Rona signed back in 1965."

"What happened to the later will?"

"Nobody knows. Maybe the attorney drew it up and Bader took it home for review. He might have changed his mind. Or maybe he signed the will as written and decided to destroy it later. The fact is, it's gone."

"So he died intestate?"

"No, no. We still have the earlier will—the one drawn up in 1965, before Guy was flung into the Outer Darkness. It's properly signed and fully executed, which means that, barring an objection, Guy Malek is a devisee, entitled to a quarter of his father's estate."

"Will Donovan object?"

"He's not the one I'm concerned about. The 1965 will gives him voting control of the family business so he winds up sitting in the catbird seat regardless. Bennet's the one making noises about filing an objection, but he really has no proof the later will exists. This could all be for naught in any case. If Guy Malek was hit by a truck or died of an overdose years ago, then there's no problem—as long as he doesn't have any kids of his own."

"Gets complicated," I said. "How much money are we talking about?"

"We're still working on that. The estate is currently assessed at about forty million bucks. The government's entitled to a big chunk, of course. The estate tax rate is fifty to fifty-five percent. Fortunately, thanks to Bader, the company has very little debt, so Donovan will have some ability to borrow. Also, the estate can defer payment of estate taxes under Internal Revenue Service code section 6166, since Malek Construction, as a closely held company, represents more than thirty-five percent of the adjusted gross estate. We'll probably look for appraisers who'll come up with a low value and then hope the IRS doesn't argue too hard for a higher value on audit. To answer your question, the boys will probably take home five million bucks apiece. Guy's a very lucky fellow."

"Only nobody knows where he is," I said.

Tasha pointed at me. "That's correct."

I thought about it briefly. "It must have come as a shock to the brothers to find out Guy stands to inherit an equal share of the estate."

Tasha shrugged. "I've only had occasion to chat with Donovan and he seems sanguine at this point. He'll be acting as administrator. On Friday, I'm submitting the will to the probate court. In essence, all that does is place the will on record. Donovan's asked me not to file the petition for another week or so in deference to Bennet, who's still convinced the later will will surface. In the meantime, it makes sense to see if we can determine Guy Malek's whereabouts. I thought we'd hire you to do the search, if you're interested."

"Sure," I said promptly. So much for playing hard to get. The truth is, I love missing-persons' cases, and the circumstances were intriguing. Often when I'm on the trail of a skip, I hold out the prospect of sudden riches from some recently deceased relative. Given the greediness of human nature, it often produces results. In this case, the reality of five million dollars should make my job easier. "What information do you have about Guy?" I asked.

"You'll have to talk to the Maleks. They'll fill you in." She scribbled something on the back of a business card, which she held out to me. "This is Donovan's number at work. I wrote the home address and home phone number on the back. Except for Guy, of course, the 'boys' are all still living together on the Malek estate."

I studied the back of the card, not recognizing the address. "Is this city or county? I never heard of this."

"It's in the city limits. In the foothills above town."

"I'll call them this afternoon."

2

I walked home along Cabana Boulevard. The skies had cleared and the air temperature hovered in the mid-fifties. This was technically the dead of winter and the brazen California sunshine was not as warm as it seemed. Sunbathers littered the sand like the flotsam left behind by the high tide. Their striped umbrellas spoke of summer, yet the new year was just a week old. The sun was brittle along the water's edge, fragmenting where the swells broke against the pilings under the wharf. The surf must have been dead cold, the salt water eye-stinging where children splashed through the waves and submerged themselves in the churning depths. I could hear their thin screams rising above the thunder of the surf, like thrill seekers on a roller-coaster, plunging into icy terror. On the beach, a wet dog barked at them and shook the water from his coat. Even from a distance I could see where his rough hair had separated into layers.

I turned left onto Bay Street. Against the backdrop of evergreens, the profusion of bright pink and orange geraniums clashed with the magenta bougainvillea that tumbled across the fences in my neighborhood. Idly, I wondered where to begin the search for Guy Malek. He'd been gone for eighteen years and the prospects of running him to ground didn't seem that rosy. A job of this kind requires ingenuity, patience, and systematic routine, but success sometimes hinges on pure luck and a touch of magic. Try billing a client on the basis of *that.*

As soon as I got home, I washed off my makeup, I changed into Reeboks, and traded my blazer for a red sweatshirt. Downstairs in the kitchenette, I turned on the radio and tuned the station to the Elvis marathon, which was moving right along. I lip-synched the lyrics to "Jailhouse Rock," doing a bump and grind around the living room. I pulled out a city map and spread it on my kitchen counter. I leaned on my elbows, backside still dancing while I located the street where the Maleks lived. Verdugo was a narrow lane tucked between two parallel roads descending from the mountains. This was not an area I knew well. I laid Donovan's business card on the counter beside the map, reached for the wall phone, and dialed the number printed on the front.

I was routed through the company receptionist to a secretary who told me Malek was out in the field but due back at the office momentarily. I gave my name and phone number, along with a brief explanation of my business with him. She said she'd have him return the call. I'd just hung up when I heard a knock at the door. I opened the porthole and found myself face-to-face with Robert Dietz.

I opened the front door. "Well, look who's here," I said. "It's only been two years, four months, and ten days."

"Has it really been that long?" he asked mildly. "I just drove up from Los Angeles. Mind if I come in?"

I stepped back and he moved past me. Elvis had launched into "Always On My Mind," which, frankly, I didn't need to hear just then. I reached over and turned off the radio. Dietz wore the same blue jeans, same cowboy boots, the same tweed sportscoat. I'd first seen him in this outfit, leaning against the wall in a hospital room where I was under observation after a hit man ran me off the road. He was two years older now, which probably put him at an even fifty, not a bad age for a man. His birthday was in November, a triple Scorpio for those who set any store by these things. We'd spent the last three months of our relationship in bed together when we weren't up at the firing range doing Mozambique pistol drills. Romance between private eyes is a strange and wondrous thing. He looked slightly heavier, but that was because he'd quit smoking—assuming he was still off cigarettes.

"You want some coffee?" I asked.

"I'd love some. How are you? You look good. I like the haircut."

"Forty bucks. What a waste. I should have done it myself." I put a pot of coffee together, using the homey activity to assess my emotional state. By and large, I didn't feel much. I was happy to see him in the same way I'd be happy to see any friend of long standing, but aside from mild curiosity, there was no great rush of sexual chemistry. I felt no strong joy at his arrival or rage that he'd shown up unannounced. He was a man of impulse: impatient, restless, abrupt, reticent. He looked tired and his hair seemed much grayer, nearly ashen along his ears. He perched on one of my kitchen stools and leaned his forearms on the counter.

I flipped on the coffeepot and put the bag of ground coffee back in the freezer. "How was Germany?"

Dietz was a private eye from Carson City, Nevada, who'd developed an expertise in personal security. He left to go to Germany to run antiterrorist training exercises for overseas military bases. He said, "Good while it lasted. Then the funding dried up. These days, Uncle Sam doesn't want to spend the bucks that way. I was bored with it anyway; middle-aged man crawling through the underbrush. I didn't have to get out there with 'em, but I couldn't resist."

"So what brings you back? Are you working a case?"

"I'm on my way up the coast to see the boys in Santa Cruz." Dietz had two sons with a common-law wife, a woman named Naomi who had steadfastly refused to marry him. His older son, Nick, was probably twenty by now. I wasn't sure how old the younger boy was.

"Ah. And how are they?"

"Terrific. They've got papers due this week so I said I'd hold off until Saturday and then drive up. If they can get a few days off, I thought we'd take a little trip somewhere."

"I notice you're limping. What's that about?"

He gave a pat to his left thigh. "Got a bum knee," he said. "Tore the meniscus during night maneuvers, stumbling on a pothole. That's the second time I've injured it and the docs say I need to have a knee replacement. I'm not interested in surgery, but I agreed to give the knee a rest. Besides, I'm in burnout. I need a change of scene."

"You were burned out before you left."

"Not burnout. I was bored. I guess neither one is cured by doing more of the same." Dietz's gray eyes were clear. He was a good-looking man in a very nonstandard way. "I thought I might stay on your couch for four days if you don't object. I'm supposed to stay off my feet and put ice on my knee."

"Oh, really. That's nice. You drop out of my life for two years and then you show up because you need a nurse? Forget that."

"I'm not asking you to make a fuss," he said. "I figure you're busy so you'll be off at work all day. I'll sit here and read or watch TV, minding my own business. I even brought my own ice bags to stick in the freezer. I don't want anyone hovering. You won't have to lift a finger."

"Don't you think this is a tiny bit *manipulative,* springing it on me like this?"

"It's not manipulative as long as you have the option of saying no."

"Oh, right. And feel guilty? I don't think so," I said.

"Why would you feel guilty? Turn me down if it doesn't suit. What's the matter with you? If we can't tell the truth then what's the point in a relationship? Do as you please. I can find a motel or I can drive on up the coast tonight. I thought it'd be nice to spend a little time together, but it's not compulsory."

I regarded him warily. "I'll think about it." There was no point in telling him—since I was barely willing to admit it to myself—how flat the light had seemed in the days after he left, how anxiety had stirred every time I came home to the empty apartment, how music had seemed to whisper secret messages to me. Dance or decline. It didn't seem to make any difference. I'd imagined his return a hundred times, but never this way. Now the flatness of it was inside and all of my past feelings for him had shifted from passionate involvement to mild interest, if that.

Dietz had been watching me and his squint showed he was perplexed. "Are you *mad* about something?"

"Not at all," I said.

"Yes, you are."

"No, I'm not."

"What are you so mad about?"

"Would you *stop* that? I'm not mad."

He studied me for a moment and then his expression cleared. He said, "Ohhh, I get it. You're mad because I left."

I could feel my cheeks brighten and I broke off eye contact. I lined up the salt and pepper shakers so their bases just touched. "I'm not mad because you *left.* I'm mad because you came back. I finally got used to being by myself and here you are again. So where does that put me?"

"You said you *liked* to be alone."

"That's right. What I don't like is being taken up and then abandoned. I'm not a pet you can put in a kennel and retrieve at your convenience."

His smile faded. " 'Abandoned'? You weren't *abandoned.* What's that supposed to mean?"

Just then the telephone rang, saving us from any further debate. Donovan Malek's secretary said, "Miss Millhone? I have Mr. Malek on the line for you. Can you hold?"

I said, "Sure."

Dietz mouthed *Did not.*

I stuck my tongue out at him. I'm very mature that way.

Donovan Malek came on the line and introduced himself. "Good afternoon, Miss Millhone . . ."

"Call me Kinsey if you would."

"Thanks. It's Donovan Malek here. I just spoke to Tasha Howard and she said she talked to you at lunch. I take it she filled you in on the situation."

"For the most part," I said. "Is there some way we can get together? Tasha wants to get moving as soon as possible."

"My attitude exactly. Listen, I've got about an hour before I have to be somewhere else. I can give you some basic information—Guy's date of birth, his Social Security number, and a photograph if that would help," he said. "You want to pop on out here?"

"Sure, I can do that," I said. "What about your brothers? Is there some way I can talk to them, too?"

"Of course. Bennet said he'd be home around four this afternoon. I'll call Myrna—she's the housekeeper—and leave word you want to talk to him. I'm not sure about Jack. He's a little harder to catch, but we can work something out. What you don't get from me, you can pick up from them. You know where I am? On Dolores out in Colgate. You take the Peterson off-ramp and turn back across the freeway. Second street on the right."

"Sounds good. I'll see you shortly."

When I hung up the phone, Dietz was checking his watch. "You're off and running. I've got to touch base with an old friend so I'll be out for a while. Are you free later on?"

"Not until six or so. Depends on my appointment. I'm trying to track down a guy who's been gone eighteen years and I'm hoping to pick up some background from his family."

"I'll buy you dinner if you haven't eaten, or we can go out and have a drink. I really don't want to be a burden."

"We can talk about it later. In the meantime, you'll need a key."

"That'd be great. I can grab a shower before I take off and lock up when I leave."

I opened the kitchen junk drawer and found the extra house key on a ring of its own. I passed it across the counter.

"Are you okay with this? I know you don't like to feel crowded. I can find a little place on Cabana if you'd prefer peace and quiet."

"This is fine for now. If it's too much, I'll say so. Let's just play it by ear," I said. "I hope you like your coffee black. There's no milk and no sugar. Cups are up there."

He put the key in his pocket. "I know where the cups are. I'll see you later."

Malek Construction consisted of a series of linked trailers, arranged like dominoes, located in the cul-de-sac of an industrial park. Behind the offices, a vast asphalt yard was filled with red trucks: pickups, concrete mixers, skip loaders, and pavers, all bearing the white-and-red company logo. A two-story corrugated metal garage stretched across the backside of the property, apparently filled with maintenance and service equipment for the countless company vehicles. Gas pumps stood at the ready. To one side, against a tangle of shrubs, I could see six bright yellow Caterpillars and a couple of John Deere crawler dozers. Men in hard hats and red coveralls went about their business. The quiet was undercut by the rumble of approaching trucks, an occasional shrill whistle, and the steady *peep-peep-peep* signal as a vehicle backed up.

I parked in the side lot in a space marked VISITOR beside a line of Jeeps, Cherokee Rangers, and battered pickups. On the short walk to the entrance, I could hear the nearby freeway traffic and the high hum of a small plane heading for the airport to the west. The interior of the office suggested a sensible combination of good taste and practicality: glossy walnut paneling, steel blue wall-to-wall carpet, dark blue file cabinets, and a lot of matching dark red tweed furniture. Among the male employees, the standard attire seemed to be ties, dress shirts, and slacks without suit coats or sports jackets. Shoes looked suitable for hiking across sand and gravel. The dress code for the women seemed less codified. The atmosphere was one of genial productivity. Police stations have the same air about them; everyone committed to the work at hand.

In the reception area where I waited, all the magazines were work-related, copies of *Pit & Quarry*, *Rock Products*, *Concrete Journal*, and the *Asphalt Contractor*. A quick glance was sufficient to convince me that there were issues at stake here I never dreamed about. I read briefly about oval-hole void forms and multiproperty admixtures, powered telescopic concrete chutes, and portable concrete recycling systems. My, my, my. Sometimes I marveled at the depths of my ignorance.

"Kinsey? Donovan Malek," he said.

I looked up, setting the magazine aside as I rose to shake hands with him. "Is it Don or Donovan?"

"I prefer Donovan, if you don't mind. My wife shortens it to Don sometimes, but I make a rare exception for her. Thanks for being so prompt. Come on back to my office and we can chat." Malek was fair-haired and clean shaven, with a square, creased face and chocolate brown eyes behind tortoiseshell glasses. I judged him to be six feet tall, maybe two hundred twenty pounds. He wore chinos and his short-sleeved dress shirt was the color of café au lait. He had loosened his tie and opened his collar button in the manner of a man who disliked restrictions and was subject to chronic overheating. I followed him out a rear door and across a wooden deck that connected a grid of double-wide trailers. The air conditioner in his office was humming steadily when we walked in.

The trailer he occupied had been subdivided into three offices of equal size, extending shotgun style from the front of the structure to the back. Long fluorescent bulbs cast a cold light across the white Formica surfaces of desks and drafting tables. Wide counters were littered with technical manuals, project reports, specs, and blueprints. Sturdy metal bookshelves lined the walls in most places, crammed with binders. Donovan didn't seem to have a private secretary within range of him and I had to guess that one of several women up front fielded his calls and helped him out with paperwork.

He motioned me into a seat and then settled into the high-back leather chair behind his desk. He leaned sideways toward a bookshelf and removed a Santa Teresa high school annual, which he opened at a page marked by a paper clip. He held out the annual, passing it across the desk. "Guy, age sixteen. Who knows what he looks like these days." He leaned back and watched for my reaction.

The kid looking out of the photograph could have been one of my high school classmates, though he preceded me by some years. The two-by-two-inch black-and-white head shot showed light curly hair worn long. Braces on his teeth gleaming through partly opened lips. He had a bumpy complexion, unruly eyebrows, and long, fair sideburns. His shirt fabric was a wild floral pattern. I would have bet money on bell-bottom trousers and a wide leather belt, though neither were visible in the photograph. In my opinion, all high school annuals should be taken out and burned. No wonder we all suffered from insecurity and low self-esteem. What a bunch of weirdos we were. I said, "He looks about like I did at his age. What year did he graduate?"

"He didn't. He got suspended six times and finally dropped out. As far as I know, he never even picked up his GED. He spent more time in Juvie than he did at home."

"Tasha mentioned criminal behavior. Can you tell me about that?"

"Sure, if I can think where to start. Remember the rumor that you could get high off aspirin and Coca-Cola? He went straight out and tried it. Kid was disappointed when it had no effect. He was in the eighth grade at that point. Discounting all the so-called 'harmless pranks' he pulled back then, I'd say his first serious transgressions dated back to high school when he was busted twice for possession of marijuana. He was into dope big time—grass, speed, uppers, downers. What did they call 'em back then? Reds and yellow jackets and something called soapers. LSD and hallucinogens came in about the same time. Teenagers didn't do heroin or cocaine in those days, and nobody'd ever heard of crack. I guess that's been a more recent development. For a while he sniffed glue, but said he didn't like the effect. Kid's a connoisseur of good highs," he said derisively. "To pay for the stuff, he'd rip off anything that wasn't nailed down. He stole cars. He stole heavy equipment from Dad's construction sites. You get the picture, I'm sure."

"This may sound like an odd question, but was he popular?"

"Actually, he was. You can't tell much from the photograph, but he was a good-looking kid. He was incorrigible, but he had a sort of goofy sweetness that people seemed to find appealing, especially the girls."

"Why? Because he was dangerous?"

"I really can't explain. He was this shy, tragic figure, like he couldn't help himself. He only had one buddy, fellow named Paul Trasatti."

"Is he still around somewhere?"

"Sure. He and Jack are golfing buddies. Bennet pals around with him, too. You can ask when you talk to him. I don't remember any other friends offhand."

"You didn't hang out with Guy yourself?"

"Not if I could help it," he said. "I was busy keeping as much distance between us as possible. It got so I had to lock the door to my room so he wouldn't walk off with everything. You name it, he'd boost it. Stereos and jewelry. Some stuff he did for profit and some was just plain raising hell. After he turned eighteen, he got kind of crafty because the stakes went up. Dad finally flat told him he'd hang him out to dry if he fucked up again. Excuse my bad language, but I still get hot when I think about this stuff."

"Is that when he took off?"

"That was when he shifted gears. On the surface, he cleaned up and got a job out here, working in the maintenance shed. He was clever, I must say. Good with his hands and he had a good head on his shoulders. He must have seen this place as the answer to his prayers. He forged checks on Dad's accounts. He used the company credit card to charge stuff and then sold the goods. Dad, God bless him, was still covering. I begged him to blow the whistle, but he just couldn't bring himself to do it. Guy strung him along, telling lie after lie.

"What can I tell you? Dad wanted to believe him. He'd talk tough. I mean, he'd act like he was really cracking down this time, but when it came right down to it, he always gave in and offered him 'one more chance.' Jesus, I got sick of his saying that. I did what I could to close the loopholes, but I could only do so much." Donovan tapped his temple. "Kid had a screw loose. He was really missing some essential sprocket in the morals department. Anyway, the last stunt he pulled—and this didn't come out until he'd been gone a couple months—was a scam where he cheated some 'poor old widder woman' of her nest egg. That was the last straw. Dad had already kicked his ass out, but we were still stuck with the mess."

"Where were you at that time? I take it you were working for your father."

"Oh, yeah. I'd graduated by then. I'd been in and out of Vietnam, and I was working here as a mining engineer. I got my degree at Colorado School of Mines. My dad's degree was civil engineering. He started Malek Construction back in 1940, the year I was born, and bought his first gravel pit in forty-three. We were a construction outfit first and ended up owning all our aggregate sources. In fact, we built the business around that because it gives us a competitive edge. There's a lot of companies around here that do construction that don't own their aggregate sources and they end up buying from us. I'm the only one of the kids who went into the family business. I didn't get married till I was thirty-five."

"I understand your mother died the year Guy left," I said.

"That's right. She'd been diagnosed with lung cancer maybe ten years before. Fought like an alley cat, but she finally went under. I'm sure the uproar didn't help. Dad never remarried. He didn't seem to have the heart for it. All he cared about was the company, which is why I was so surprised about the will. Even in 1965, I can't believe he wanted Guy getting so much as a nickel from his estate."

"Maybe someone will come across the second will."

"I'd like to think so, but so far I've turned the house upside down. There was nothing like it in the safe deposit box. I hate to consider what's going to happen if Guy shows up again."

"Meaning what?"

"He'll cause trouble of some kind. I can guarantee it."

I shrugged. "He might have changed. People sometimes straighten out."

Donovan gestured impatiently. "Sure, and sometimes you win the lottery, but the odds are against. That's how it is and I guess we'll have to live with it."

"You have any idea where he might be?"

"No. And I don't lie awake at night trying to figure it out either. Frankly, it makes me crazy to think of him coming home to roost. I understand that by law he's entitled to his fair share of the estate, but I think he ought to be a brick about it and keep his hands to himself." He picked up a piece of paper and slid it in my direction. "Date of birth and his Social Security number. His middle name is David. What else can I tell you?"

"What about your mother's maiden name?"

"Patton. Is that for ID purposes?"

"Right. If I find him, I'd like to have a way to confirm it's really Guy we're dealing with."

"You're picturing an impostor? That's hard to imagine," he said. "Who'd want to be a stand-in for a loser like him?"

I smiled. "It's not that far-fetched. The chances are remote, but it's been done before. You don't want to end up turning money over to a stranger."

"You got that right. I'm not all that thrilled to give the money to *him.* Unfortunately, it's not up to me. The law's the law," he said. "At any rate, I leave this to you. He was a hard-livin', hard-drinkin' kid before the age of twenty-one. As to his current whereabouts, your guess is as good as mine. You need anything else?"

"This should do for the time being. I'll talk to your brothers and then we'll see where we stand." I got to my feet and we shook hands across the desk. "I appreciate your time."

Donovan came around the desk, walking me to the door.

I said, "I'm sure Tasha will have the proper notices published in the local paper. Guy may get wind of it, if he hasn't already."

"How so?"

"He might still be in touch with someone living here."

"Well. That is possible, I suppose. I don't know how much more we're obliged to do. If he never turns up, I guess his share of the estate gets placed in an escrow account for some period of time. After that, who knows? The point is, Tasha insists we get it settled and you don't want to mess with *her.*"

"I should think not," I said. "Besides, closure is always nice."

"Depends on what kind you're discussing."

3

I stopped by the office and opened a file on the case, recording the data Donovan had given me. It didn't look like much, the merest scrap of information, but the date of birth and Social Security number would be invaluable as personal identifiers. If pressed, I could always check with Guy Malek's former high school classmates to see if anybody'd heard from him in the years since he left. Given his history of bad behavior, he didn't seem like a kid others would have known well or perhaps cared to have known at all, but he might have had confederates. I made a note of the name Donovan had given me. Paul Trasatti might provide a lead. It was possible Guy had turned respectable in the last decade and a half and might well have come back to his reunions from time to time. Often the biggest "losers" in high school are the most eager to flaunt their later successes.

If I had to make an educated guess about his original destination on the road to exile, I'd have to say San Francisco, which was only six hours north by car, or an hour by plane. Guy left Santa Teresa when the Haight-Ashbury was at its peak. Any flower child who wasn't already brain-dead from drugs had gravitated to the Haight in those days. It was the party to end all parties, and with ten grand in his pocket his invitation would have been engraved.

At three-thirty, I locked up my office and went down to the second floor to pick up instructions for service on the two deposition subpoenas. I retrieved my car and headed to the Maleks' place. The house was at the end of a narrow lane, the fifteen-acre property surrounded by an eight-foot wall intersected by an occasional wooden gate. I'd grown up in this town and I thought I knew every corner of it, but this was new to me, prime Santa Teresa real estate dating back to the thirties. The Maleks must lay claim to the last section of flat land for miles. The rear portions of the property must have tilted straight uphill because the face of the Santa Ynez Mountains loomed above me, looking close enough to touch. From the road, I could pick out individual patches of purple sage and coyote brush.

The iron gates at the entrance to the property stood open. I followed the long, curved driveway past a cracked and neglected tennis court into a cobblestone turnaround tucked into the L of the main residence. Both the house and the wall that encompassed the grounds were faced with dusky terra-cotta stucco, an odd shade of red halfway between brick and dusty rose. Massive evergreens towered above the grounds and a forest of live oaks stretched out to the right of the house as far as the eye could see. Sunlight scarcely penetrated the canopy of branches. Near the front of the house, the pine trees had dropped a blanket of needles that must have turned the soil to acid. There was little if any grass and the damp smell of bare earth was pervasive. Here and there, a shaggy palm tree asserted its spare presence. I could see several outbuildings to the right—a bungalow, a gardener's shed, a greenhouse—and on the left, a long line of garages. The driveway apparently continued on around the rear of the house. A Harley-Davidson was parked on a gravel pad to one side. There were flowerbeds, but even the occasional suggestion of color failed to soften the somber gloom of the mansion and the deep shade surrounding it.

The architectural style of the house was Mediterranean. All of the windows were flanked with shutters. A series of balustrades punctuated the stark lines of the facade and a lovers' stairway curved up along the left to a second-story veranda. All the trim was done in dark green, the paint color chalky with age. The roof was composed of old red tile, mottled with soft green algae. The poured concrete urns on either side of the front door were planted with perennials that had died back to sticks. The door itself looked like something that had been lifted from one of the early California missions. When I pressed the bell, I could hear a single resonating note strike within, tolling my presence to the occupants.

In due course, the door was opened by a white woman of indeterminant age in a gray cotton uniform. She was of medium height, thick through the middle, her shoulders and breasts slumping toward a waist that had expanded to accommodate the gradual accumulation of weight. I pegged her in her early forties, but I couldn't be sure.

"Yes?" Her eyebrows needed plucking and her blond hair showed dark roots mixed with gray. This was a woman who apparently whacked at her own hair with some kind of dull instrument, a not-unfamiliar concept. Her bangs had been cut slightly too short, curling across her forehead unbecomingly. Maybe forty dollars for a haircut wasn't too much to pay.

I handed her my business card. "Are you Myrna?"

"That's right."

"I'm Kinsey Millhone," I said. "I believe Donovan called to say I'd be stopping by this afternoon. Is Bennet at home?"

Her expression didn't change, but she seemed to know what I was talking about. She was plain, her nose maybe half a size too big for her face. Her lips were antiqued with the remnants of dark lipstick, probably eaten off at lunch or imprinted on the edge of her coffee cup. Now that I'd become an aficionada of drugstore cosmetics, I was acting like an expert. What a laugh, I thought.

"He just got in. He said to put you in the library if you arrived before he came down. Would you like to follow me?"

I said, "Sure." I loved the idea of being "put" in the library, like a potted plant.

I followed her across the foyer, toward a room on the right. I took in my surroundings surreptitiously, trying not to look like a mouth breather in the process. In the homes of the rich, it doesn't do to gape. The floor was dark parquet, a complicated herringbone pattern with the polished wooden chevrons blending together seamlessly. The entrance hall was two stories high, but little if any light filtered down from above. Tapestries were hung along the walls at intervals, faded depictions of women with high waists and faces shaped like hard-boiled eggs. Gents in cloaks rode on horseback, trailed by hunting dogs on chains. Behind them, a merry band of woodcutters toted a dead stag that had spears sticking out of its torso like Saint Sebastian. I could tell right away that theirs was a world devoid of animal-rights activists.

The library had the look of a private men's club, or what I imagine such a place would look like if women were allowed in. Several large red Oriental carpets had been laid side by side to form a continuous floor covering. One wall was paneled in dark walnut and there were floor-to-ceiling bookshelves on the other three. The windows were tall and narrow, diamonds of leaded glass admitting more chill air than afternoon light. There were three groupings of ripped red-leather club chairs and an enormous gray stone fireplace with a gas starter, its inner hearth blackened by countless fires. The room smelled of charred oak and book mold and suggested the kind of dampness associated with poorly laid foundations. For a family that had amassed a fortune in the construction business, they really ought to think about pumping money into the place. Failing major home improvements, a quick trip to Pier I would have done wonders.

For once, left to my own devices, I didn't bother to snoop. Guy Malek had been gone for eighteen years. I wasn't going to find a copy of his outbound bus schedule or a drawer filled with personal diaries he'd kept as a lad. I heard someone walking on the second floor, the ceiling creaking as the steps passed from one side to the other of the room above. I circled the library, glancing out of every window I passed. The room was a good thirty feet long. At the far end, a solarium looked out on the rear lawn, a large expanse of dormant grass with a murky-looking koi pond in the center. The surface of the water was choked with lily pads.

I moved back toward the door and heard someone come down the stairs and traverse the hall. The door opened and Bennet Malek came in. He was four years younger than Donovan with the same fair hair. Where Donovan's was glossy, Bennet's was coarse, and he kept it cut short to discourage a visible tendency to curl. He'd apparently given up his battle to stay clean shaven and a blond beard and mustache now defined the lower portion of his face. He was heavyset, looking beefy across the shoulders and thick through the chest. He wore jeans and a navy sweatshirt with the sleeves pushed up along forearms densely matted with hair. Tasha had tagged him as a man who invested and lost sums of money on various faulty commercial ventures. I wondered how I might have responded to him if I hadn't been told in advance of his poor business sense. As it was, I found myself disregarding the hearty confidence he was at pains to project. Belatedly, I noticed that he carried the last half inch of a drink in his right hand, gin or vodka over ice with a twist. He set the drink on the end table closest to him.

He held out his hand and shook mine with unnecessary strength. We weren't about to arm wrestle so what was the point? His fingertips were icy and faintly moist to the touch. "Bennet Malek, Miss Millhone. Nice to meet you. Don said you'd be coming. Can I offer you a drink?" He had a big booming voice and made solid eye contact. Very manly, I thought.

"Thanks, but I'm fine. I don't want to take any more time than I have to. I know you're busy."

"Fair enough. Why don't you have a seat?" he said. His attentiveness seemed feigned, a salesman's maneuver for putting the customer at ease. I'd been in this man's company thirty seconds or less and I'd already developed an aversion to him.

I perched on the edge of a club chair with a wide, sunken seat. The leather surface was slippery and I had to fight a tendency to skid backward into the depths. As a child, I used to polish the trailer park sliding board to lightning-fast speeds by vigorous rubbings with sheets of Cut-Rite waxed paper. The glossy leather cushion had the same slick feel to it. To avoid losing traction, I had to keep my weight pitched forward, feet together and flat on the floor.

Bennet settled into the chair to my left with a series of creakings. "I understand you're a private investigator," he said.

"That's right. I've been licensed for ten years. I was a police officer before that. What about you? What sort of work do you do?"

"I'm into venture capital. I look for promising little companies with cash-flow problems."

And drain them dry, no doubt. "Sounds like fun," I remarked.

"It's gratifying. Let's put it that way." His voice had dropped into a confidential tone. "I take it you met with Don?"

"That's right. I talked to him earlier this afternoon."

He shook his head almost imperceptibly. "Did he mention the missing will?"

"Tasha told me about that when she was briefing me at lunch," I said. Vaguely, I wondered why he was raising the subject. The existence of a second will was really not my concern. "I guess your brother lucked out," I said.

He snorted. "I'll tell you what bugs me. I remember when Dad signed the second will. I can picture the day just as clear as I'm sitting here. Dad's attorney and two witnesses came out to the house."

"Well, that's interesting. Do you remember who they were?"

"The witnesses? Two women. I remember that much. I assumed they worked for the attorney, but I may have made that up. They weren't personal friends of Dad's as far as I know. The four of them came in here and emerged maybe half an hour later."

"Have you told Tasha about this?"

"I mentioned I was here the day the second will was signed. I can't remember now if I mentioned witnesses or not."

"I'd tell her, if I were you. She may find a way to determine who they were. From what I've heard, no one disputes the fact that a second will was drawn up, but was it signed in your presence? Were you apprised of the provisions?"

"Well, I wasn't in the room with him if that's what you're getting at. Dad referred to it later, but he never spelled it out. The question is, what happened to it?"

I shrugged. "Your father could have changed his mind. He could have torn it up and tossed it out."

Bennet stirred restlessly. "So everyone says, though I'm not convinced. It's an interesting issue, if you think about it. I mean, look at the facts. The will comes up missing and the black sheep of the family makes out like a bandit. Dad signed it in March and Guy left within days."

"You're saying your brother stole it?"

"I'm saying, why not? I wouldn't put it past him. He stole everything else."

"But what good would that do? Even if he snitched a copy, the attorney probably kept the original. Once Guy was gone, he had no way of knowing your father wasn't going to turn around and make another will just like it. Or write a third will altogether. From what Donovan's told me, your father was good at talking tough and not so good when it came to follow-through."

He shook his head and his expression was patronizing. "True enough. That's why I'm going back through all of Dad's personal papers. It's not that we want to deny Guy any monies he may be entitled to, but this is bullshit in my opinion. He collected his share once. Dad had the second will drawn up with every intention of eliminating Guy's claim. That's why he gave him the cash to begin with—to pay him off in full. I heard him allude to it many times over the years. As far as he was concerned, the ten grand he gave my brother was the end of it."

"Well, I wish I could help, but this is really not my turf. Tasha's the expert. I suggest you sit down and talk to her."

"What about my father's deal with Guy?" he went on argumentatively. "It was a verbal agreement, but doesn't that count for anything?"

"Hey, you're asking the wrong person. I have no idea. No one knows where Guy is, let alone what kind of bargain he made the day he left."

His smile flickered and I could see him curb a desire to continue arguing the point. "You're right, of course," he said. "So what can I tell you about Guy?"

"Let's start with the obvious. Did he say anything to you about his plans before he left?"

"I'm afraid Guy wasn't in the habit of discussing anything with me."

I shifted the subject slightly. "Could he have headed up to San Francisco? Donovan says he was into drugs in those days and the Haight might have been a draw."

"It's always possible. If that's where he went, he never said a word to me. I should probably warn you, the two of us weren't close. I don't mean to seem uncooperative, but I don't have much to offer in the way of information."

"Did you ever hear him mention a possible career? Did he have any personal passions?"

Bennet's smile was thin. "He made a career out of doing as little as possible. His passion was getting into trouble, making life miserable for everyone else."

"What about his employment? What kind of jobs did he have?"

"None significant. When he was still in his teens, he worked in a pizza place until he got caught skimming cash. He also got a job doing telephone sales. That lasted two days. I don't remember his ever doing much else until he started working for Dad. He pumped gas for a while so I suppose he might have become a career gas station attendant."

"What kind of car did he drive?"

"He drove the family Chevy until he was involved in a hit-and-run accident and his license was suspended. After that, Dad refused to let him use any of the family vehicles."

"Do you know if his license was ever reinstated?"

"If it wasn't, he probably drove without. He never cared much about life's petty little rules and regulations."

"Did he have any hobbies?"

"Not unless you count smoking dope and getting laid."

"What about his personal interests? Did he hunt, or fish? Did he skydive?" I was floundering, casting about in an attempt to develop a sense of direction.

Bennet shook his head. "He was a vegetarian. He said nothing should ever have to die so that he could eat. He was petrified of heights so I doubt he ever jumped out of airplanes or climbed mountains or bungee-jumped."

"Well, at least we can eliminate that," I said. "Did he have medical problems?"

"Medical problems? Like what?"

"I don't know. I'm just trying to find ways to get a bead on him. Was he diabetic? Did he have allergies or any chronic illnesses?"

"Oh. I see what you're getting at. No. As far as I know, his health was good—for someone so heavily into drink and drugs."

"Donovan says he had one good friend. Somebody named Paul?"

"You're talking about Paul Trasatti. I can give you his telephone number. He hasn't gone anywhere."

"I'd appreciate that."

He recited the number off the top of his head and I made a quick note in the little spiral-bound notebook I carry.

I tried to think about the areas I hadn't covered yet. "Was he a draft dodger? Did he protest the war in Vietnam?"

"He didn't have to. The army wouldn't take him. He had bad feet. Lucky him. He never gave a shit about politics. He never even voted as far as I know."

"What about religion? Did he do Yoga? Meditate? Chant? Walk on hot coals?" This was like pulling teeth.

He shook his head again. "None of the above."

"What about bank accounts?"

"Nope. At least he didn't have any back then."

"Did he own any stocks or bonds?"

Bennet shook his head again. He was beginning to seem amused at my persistence, which I found irritating.

"He must have cared about something," I said.

"He was a fuckup, pure and simple. He never lifted a finger for anyone except himself. Typical narcissist. The girls couldn't get enough of him. You figure it out."

"Look, Bennet. I understand your hostility, but I can do without the editorializing. You must have cared about him once."

"Of course," he said blandly, averting his gaze. "But that was before he became such a pain in the ass to all of us. Besides, he's been gone for years. I suppose at some level I have some kind of family feeling, but it's hard to sustain given his long absence."

"Once he left, none of you ever heard from him?"

His eyes came back to mine. "I can only speak for myself. He never called me or wrote. If he was in touch with anyone else, I wasn't told about it. Maybe Paul knows something."

"What sort of work does he do?"

"He's a rare-book dealer. He buys and sells autographs, letters, manuscripts. Things like that." He closed his mouth and smiled faintly, volunteering nothing unless I asked point-blank.

I wasn't getting anywhere and it was probably time to move on. "What about Jack? Could Guy have confided in him?"

"You can ask him yourself. He's right out there," Bennet said. He gestured toward the windows and I followed his gaze. I caught a glimpse of Jack as he crossed the back lawn, heading away from the house toward a slope to the left. The rear of the property picked up just enough sun to foster a mix of coarse, patchy grasses, some of which were dormant at this time of year. He had a couple of golf clubs tucked carelessly under one arm and he carried a bucket and a net in a blue plastic frame.

By the time we caught up with him and Bennet had introduced us, Jack was using a sand wedge to smack golf balls at the net he'd set up twenty yards away. Bennet withdrew and left me to watch Jack practice his chipping shots. He'd swing and I could hear the thin whistle as the club cut through the air. There'd be a whack and the ball would arc toward the net, with an unerring accuracy. Occasionally, a shot would hit the grass nearby, landing with a short bounce, but most of the time he nailed the target he was aiming for.

He wore a visor with PEBBLE BEACH imprinted on the rim. His hair was light brown, a shock of it protruding from the Velcro-secured opening at the back. He wore chinos and a golf shirt with the emblem for St. Andrew's stitched on the front like a badge. He was leaner than his two brothers and his face and arms were tanned. I could see him measure the trajectory of the ball as it sailed through the air. He said, "I hope this doesn't seem rude, but I've got a tournament coming up."

I murmured politely, not wanting to break his concentration.

Whistle. Whack. "You've been hired to find Guy," he said when the ball landed. He frowned to himself and adjusted his stance. "How's it coming?"

I smiled briefly. "So far all I have are his date of birth and his Social Security number."

"Why did Donovan tell you to talk to me?"

"Why wouldn't I talk to you?"

He ignored me for the moment. I watched as he walked out to the net and leaned down, gathering the countless balls, which he tossed in his plastic bucket. He came back to the spot where I was standing and started all over again. His swing looked exactly the same—time after time, without variation. Swing, whack, in the net. He'd put the next ball down. Swing, whack, in the net. He shook his head at one shot, responding to my comment belatedly. "Donovan doesn't have much use for me. He's a Puritan at heart. It's all work, work, work with him. You have to be productive—get the job done. All that rah-rah-rah stuff. As far as he's concerned, golf isn't worthy of serious consideration unless it nets you an annual income of half a million bucks." He paused to look at me, leaning lightly on his golf club, as if it were a cane. "I don't have any idea where Guy went, if that's what you're here to ask. I was finishing my senior year at Wake Forest, so I heard about it by phone. Dad called and said he'd told Guy to hit the road. They'd had a quarrel about something and off he went."

"When was the last time you saw him?"

"When I was home for Mother's funeral in January. When I came home again for spring break, he'd been gone maybe three days. I figured the whole thing would blow over, but it never did. By the time I graduated and came home in June, the subject was never mentioned. It's not like we were forbidden to refer to him. We just didn't, I guess out of consideration for Dad."

"You never heard from Guy at all? Not a call or a postcard in all these years?"

Jack shook his head.

"Didn't that bother you?"

"Of course. I adored him. I saw him as a rebel, a true individual. I hated school and I was miserable. I did poorly in most classes. All I wanted was to play golf and I didn't see why I had to have a college education. I would have gone off with Guy in a heartbeat if he'd told me what was going on. What can I tell you? He never called. He never wrote. He never gave any indication he gave a shit about me. Such is life."

"And nobody outside the family ever reported running into him?"

"Like at a convention or something? You're really scraping the bottom of the barrel on that one."

"You think you'd have heard *something*."

"Why? I mean, what's the big deal? People probably pull this shit all the time. Go off, and nobody ever hears from them again. There's no law says you have to stay in touch with people just because you're related."

"Well, true," I said, thinking of my own avoidance of relatives. "Do you know of anyone else who might help? Did he have a girlfriend?"

Jack smiled mockingly. "Guy was the kind of fellow mothers warn their little girls about."

"Donovan told me women found him attractive, but I don't get it. What was the appeal?"

"They weren't women. They were girls. Melodrama is seductive when you're seventeen."

I thought about it briefly, but this seemed like another dead end. "Well. If you have any ideas, could you get in touch?" I took a card from my handbag and passed it over to him.

Jack glanced at my name. "How's the last name pronounced?"

"*Mill*-hone," I said. "Accent on the first syllable. The last rhymes with bone."

He nodded. "Fair enough. You won't hear from me, of course, but at least you can say you tried." He smiled. "I'm sure Don was way too cool to mention this," he said mildly, "but we're all hoping you won't find him. That way we can file a petition asking the court to declare him dead and his share can be divided among the three of us."

"That's what 'diligent search' is all about, isn't it? Tell Donovan I'll call him in a day or two," I said.

I walked back across the grass toward the house. What a bunch, I thought. Behind me, I could hear the whistle of Jack's swing and the sound of the clubhead on impact. I could have knocked at the front door again and asked the housekeeper if Donovan's wife, Christie, was at home. As an old college chum of Tasha's, she might at least be gracious. On the other hand, she wasn't married to Donovan at the point when Guy departed, and I couldn't believe she'd have anything of substance to contribute. So where did that leave me?

I got in my car and started the engine, shifting into first. I eased down the long drive toward the street beyond. At the front gate, I paused, shifting into neutral and letting the car idle while I considered the possibilities. As nearly as I could tell, Guy Malek hadn't been a property owner in Santa Teresa County, so there wasn't any point in checking the tax rolls or real property records. From what his brothers had indicated, he'd never even rented his own apartment, which meant I couldn't consult with a past landlord, or query the water, gas, electric, or phone companies for a forwarding address. Most of those records aren't kept for eighteen years anyway. What else? At the time he'd left Santa Teresa, he had no job and no significant employment history, so there wasn't any point in checking with the local labor unions or with Social Security. He didn't vote, own a car or a gun, didn't hunt or fish, which probably meant he didn't have any permits or licenses on record. He'd probably acquired a driver's license and a vehicle by now. Also, using past behavior as a future indicator, he probably had a criminal history in the system somewhere, certainly with the National Crime Information Center. Unfortunately, I didn't have access to that information and, offhand, I couldn't think of anyone who'd be willing to run a computer check. A law enforcement officer with proper authorization has all sorts of databases available that I couldn't tap into as a licensed private eye.

I put the VW in first gear, hung a left, and drove over to the Department of Motor Vehicles. It was just shy of closing time and the place was clearing out. I filled out a form, asking for a records' search. Often, DMV records will be out of date. People move, but the change of address won't show up in the DMV computers until a driver's license or a vehicle registration is renewed. In this case, if Guy Malek had left the state, all the data might well be years out of date, if it showed up at all. At the moment, however, it seemed like the quickest way to get a preliminary fix on the situation. Since I didn't have his driver's license number, I picked up an ANI Multiple Record Request Form, filling in his full name and date of birth. The

Automated Name Index file would either show no record for the criteria given, or would show a match for last name, first name, middle initial, and birthdate. As soon as I got back to the office, I'd put the form in the mail and ship it off to Sacramento. With luck, I could at least pick up his mailing address.

In the meantime, since the office was nearly empty, I asked one of the DMV clerks to check the name through her computer.

She turned and gave me her full attention. "Are you nuts? I could get fired for doing that," she said. She turned the monitor on its swivel so I couldn't peek at the screen.

"I'm a PI," I said.

"You could be the Pope for all I care. You'll have to wait to hear from Sacramento. You get nothing from me."

"It was worth a try," I said. I tried a winsome smile, but it didn't get me far.

"You got a nerve," she said. She turned away with a reproving shake of her head and began to pack away her desk.

So much for my powers of persuasion.

4

I returned to the office, typed up the envelope, wrote a check to the state, attached it to the form, affixed a stamp, and stuck the packet in the box for outgoing mail. Then I picked up the phone and called Darcy Pascoe, the secretary/receptionist at California Fidelity Insurance. We chatted briefly about the old days and I caught up on minor matters before making the same request to her that I'd made to the DMV clerk. Insurance companies are always running DMV checks. Darcy wasn't actually authorized to inquire, but she knew how to bend the rules with the best of them. I said, "All I need is a mailing address."

"What's your time frame?"

"I don't know. How about first thing tomorrow?"

"I can probably do that, but it'll cost you. What's this kid's name again?"

• • •

When I got home, lights were on in the apartment, but Dietz was still out someplace. He'd brought in a soft-sided suitcase that he'd placed beside the couch. A quick check in the closet showed a hanging garment bag. In the downstairs bathroom, his Dopp kit was sitting on the lid to the toilet tank. The room smelled of soap and there was a damp towel hung across the shower rod. I went back to the kitchen and turned on the radio. Elvis was singing the final chorus of "Can't Help Falling In Love."

"Spare me," I said crossly and turned the thing off. I went up the spiral stairs to the loft where I kicked off my Reeboks and stretched out on the bed. I stared up at the skylight. It was well after five o'clock and the dark had fallen on us like a wool blanket, a dense, leaden gray. Through the Plexiglas dome, I couldn't even see the night sky because of the overcast. I was tired and hungry and strangely out of sorts. Being single can be confusing. On the one hand, you sometimes yearn for the simple comfort of companionship; someone to discuss your day with, someone with whom you can celebrate a raise or tax refund, someone who'll commiserate when you're down with a cold. On the other hand, once you get used to being alone (in other words, having everything your way), you have to wonder why you'd ever take on the aggravation of a relationship. Other human beings have all these hotly held *opinions*, habits, and mannerisms, bad art and peculiar taste in music, not to mention mood disorders, food preferences, passions, hobbies, allergies, emotional fixations, and attitudes that in no way coincide with the correct ones, namely yours. Not that I was thinking seriously of Robert Dietz in this way, but I'd noticed, walking into the apartment, an unnerving awareness of the "otherness" of him. It's not that he was intrusive, obnoxious, or untidy. He was just *there*, and his presence acted on me like an irritant. I mean, where was this going? Nowhere that I could tell. I'd no more than get used to him than he'd hit the road again. So why bother to adjust when his company wasn't permanent? Personally, I don't consider flexibility that desirable a trait.

I heard a key turn in the lock and I realized, with a start, I'd drifted off to sleep. I sat up, blinking fuzzily. Below me, Dietz was turning on additional lights. I could hear the crackle of paper. I got up and moved over to the railing, looking down at him. He turned on the radio. I put my fingers in my ears so I wouldn't have to listen to Elvis sing soulfully about love. Who needs that shit? Dietz was a big country music fan and I was hoping he'd flip the station to find something more twangy and a lot less to the point. He sensed my presence and tilted his face in my direction. "Good. You're home. I didn't see your car outside," he said. "I picked up some groceries. You want to help me unload?"

"I'll be there in a minute." I made a quick detour to the bathroom, where I ran a comb through my hair, brushed my teeth, and availed myself of the facilities. I'd forgotten how domesticated Dietz could be. When I thought about the man, it was his personal-security expertise that came foremost to mind. I padded down the stairs in my sock feet. "How'd you know what we needed?"

"I checked. Surprise, surprise. The cupboards were bare." He had the refrigerator open, placing eggs, bacon, butter, lunch meats, and various other high-fat, high-cholesterol items in the bins. On the counter was a six-pack of beer, two bottles of Chardonnay, extra-crunchy peanut butter, canned goods and assorted condiments, along with a loaf of bread. He'd even remembered paper napkins, paper towels, toilet paper, and liquid detergent. I put the canned goods in the cabinet and turned off the radio. If Dietz noticed, he said nothing.

Over his shoulder, he said, "How'd the interview go?"

I said, "Fine. I haven't made a lick of progress, but you have to start someplace."

"What's the next move?"

"I'm having Darcy run a DMV check through the insurance company I used to work for. She hopes to have something early tomorrow morning. Then we'll see what's what. I have other lines of pursuit, but she's my best bet so far."

"You're not working for California Fidelity these days?"

"Actually, I'm not. I got my ass fired because I wouldn't kiss someone else's. I rent an office in a law firm. It works out better that way."

I could see him toy with other questions, but he must have decided that the less said the better.

He changed the subject. "Can I talk you into eating out?"

"What'd you have in mind?"

"Something in walking distance where we don't have to dress."

I looked at him for a moment, feeling strangely unwilling to cooperate. "How's the old friend?"

Dietz surpressed a smile. "He's fine. Is that what's bothering you?"

"No. I don't know. I think I've been depressed for weeks and just now got in touch with it. I'm also nervous about the job. I'm working for my cousin Tasha, which I probably shouldn't be doing."

"A cousin? That's a new one. Where did she come from?"

"God, you *are* out of date."

"Grab a jacket and let's go. You can talk about it over dinner and bring me up to speed."

We walked from my apartment to a restaurant on the breakwater, three long blocks during which little was said. The night was very chilly and the lights strung out along the harbor were like leftover Christmas decorations. Over the softly tumbling surf, I could hear the tinkle of a buoy, the tinny sound mixing with the gentle lapping of water against the boats in the marina. Many vessels were alight and the occasional glimpses of the live-aboards reminded me of a trailer park, a community of small spaces, looking cozy from outside. Dietz's pace was rapid. He had his head bent, his hands in his pockets, heels clicking on the pavement. I kept up with him, my mind running back over what I knew of him.

His upbringing had been a strange one. He'd told me he was born in a van on the road outside Detroit. His mother was in labor and his father was too impatient to find an emergency room. His father was a brawler and a bully who worked the oil rigs, moving his family from one town to the next as the mood struck. Dietz's granny, his mother's mother, traveled with them in the vehicle of the moment—a truck, a van, or a station wagon, all secondhand and subject to breakdown or quick sale if the money ran low. Dietz had been educated out of an assortment of old textbooks while his mother and granny drank beers and threw the cans out the window onto the highway. His dislike of formal schooling was an attribute we shared. Because he'd had so little experience with institutions, he was fiercely insubordinate. He didn't so much go against regulations as ignore them, operating on the assumption that the rules simply didn't apply to him. I liked his rebelliousness. At the same time, I was wary. I was into caution and control. He was into anarchy.

We reached the restaurant, the Tramp Steamer, a cramped and overheated gray-frame establishment located up a narrow flight of wooden stairs. A modest effort had been made to give the place a nautical feel, but its real attraction was the fare: raw oysters, fried shrimp, peppery chowder, and homemade bread. There was a full bar near the entrance, but most of the clientele preferred beer. The air was saturated with the smell of hops and cigarette smoke. Between the honky-tonk jukebox, the raucous laughter, and conversations, the noise was palpable. Dietz scanned the room for seating, then pushed through a side door and found us a table on the deck, overlooking the marina. Outside, it was quieter and the chill air was offset by the red glow of wall-mounted propane heaters. The briny scent of the ocean seemed stronger up here than it had down below. I took a deep breath, sucking it into my lungs like ether. It had the same sedative effect and I could feel myself unwind.

"You want Chardonnay?" he asked.

"I'd love it."

I sat at the table while he moved back inside to the bar. I watched him through the window in conversation with the bartender. As he waited for the order, his gaze moved restlessly across the crowd. He crossed to the jukebox and studied the selections. Dietz was the sort of man who paced and tapped his fingers, subterranean energy constantly bubbling to the surface. I seldom saw him read a book because he couldn't sit still that long. When he did read, he was out of commission, utterly absorbed until he was finished. He liked competition. He liked guns. He liked machines. He liked tools. He liked climbing rocks. His basic attitude was "What are you saving yourself for?" My basic attitude was "Let's not jump right into things."

Dietz wandered back to the bar and stood there jiggling the change in his pocket. The bartender set a mug of beer and a glass of wine on the counter. Dietz peeled off some bills and returned to the deck, trailing the smell of cigarette smoke like a strange aftershave. He said, "Service is slow. I hope the food's good." We touched glasses before we drank, though I wasn't sure what we were drinking to.

I opened a menu and let my eyes trace the choices. I wasn't really that hungry. Maybe a salad or soup. I usually don't eat much at night.

"I called the boys," he remarked.

"And how are they?" I asked. I'd never met his two sons, but he spoke of them with affection.

"They're fine. The boys are great," he said. "Nick turns twenty-one on the fourteenth. He's a senior at Santa Cruz, but he just changed his major so he'll probably be there another year. Graham's nineteen and a sophomore. They're sharing an apartment with a bunch of guys this year. They're smart kids. They like school and seem to be motivated. More than I ever was. Naomi's done a good job, without a lot of help from me. I support 'em, but I can't say I ever spent much time on the scene. I feel bad about that, but you know how I am. I'm a rolling stone. I can't help it. I could never settle down and buy a house and work nine to five. I can't behave myself in a situation like that."

"Where's Naomi?"

"San Francisco. She got a law degree. I paid her tuition—I'm good about that end—but all the hard work was hers. The boys say she's getting married to some attorney up there."

"Good for her."

"How about you? What have you been up to?"

"Not a lot. Mostly work. I don't take vacations so I haven't been anywhere that didn't somehow involve a stakeout or a background check. I'm a bundle of laughs."

"You should learn how to play."

"I should learn how to do a lot of things."

The waitress approached, moving toward us from a table in the angle of the deck. "You two ready to order?" She was probably in her late twenties, a honey blond with her hair in a boy-cut and braces on her teeth. She wore matching black shorts and tank top as if it were August instead of January 8.

"Give us a minute," Dietz said.

We ended up splitting a big bowl of steamed mussels, nestled in a spicy tomato broth. For entrées, Dietz had a rare steak and I had a Caesar salad. We both ate as though we were racing against the clock. We used to make love the same way, like some contest to see who could get there first.

"Tell me about the depression," he said when he had pushed his plate aside.

I gestured dismissively. "Forget it. I don't like to sit around feeling sorry for myself."

"Go ahead. You're allowed."

"I know I'm allowed, but what's the point?" I said. "I can't even tell you what it's about. Maybe my serotonin levels are off."

"No doubt, but what's the rest of it?"

"The usual, I guess. I mean, some days I don't get it, what we're doing on the planet. I read the paper and it's hopeless. Poverty and disease, all the bullshit from politicians who'd tell you anything to get elected. Then you have the hole in the ozone and the destruction of the rain forests. What am I supposed to do with this stuff? I know it's not up to me to solve the world's problems, but I'd like to believe there's a hidden order somewhere."

"Good luck."

"Yeah, good luck. Anyway, I'm struggling for answers. Most of the time, I take life for granted. I do what I do and it seems to make sense. Once in a while I lose track of where I fit. I know it sounds lame, but it's the truth."

"What makes you think there are any answers?" he said. "You do the best you can."

"Whatever that consists of," I remarked.

"Therein lies the rub." He smiled. "What about the job? What scares you about that?"

"I always get amped on the eve of a big one. One of these days I'm going to fail and I don't like the thought. It's stage fright."

"Where'd the cousin come from? I thought you didn't have any family."

"Don't I wish," I said. "Turns out I have a bunch of cousins up in Lompoc, all girls. I'd prefer not to have anything to do with them, but they keep popping up. I'm too old to cope with 'togetherness.' "

"Such a liar," he said fondly, but he let it pass.

The waitress came by. We declined dessert and coffee. Dietz asked for the check, which she produced from a sheaf tucked in the small of her back, taking a few seconds to total it out. Her yellow socks and black high-tops really gave the outfit some class. She placed the bill facedown on the table slightly closer to Dietz's side than to mine. This was probably her tactic for playing it safe in case we were a twosome whose roles were reversed.

She said, "I can take that anytime you want." She moved off to deliver ketchup to another table. She must have the metabolism of a bird. The cold wasn't even producing goose bumps.

Dietz glanced at the check briefly, recalculating the total in the blink of an eye. He leaned sideways to extract his wallet and pulled out a pair of bills that he slid under his plate. "Ready?"

"Whenever you are."

We took the long way home. It seemed easier talking in the dark without looking at each other. The conversation was superficial. I'm an expert at using words to keep other people at bay. When we got home, I made sure Dietz had everything he needed—sheets, two pillows, an extra blanket, a small alarm clock, and a fresh towel—all of life's little amenities, except me.

I left him below and headed up the spiral stairs. When I got to the top, I leaned over the rail. "With your bum knee, I take it you won't be jogging with me in the morning."

"Afraid not. I'm sorry. It's something I miss."

"I'll try not to wake you. Thanks for dinner."

"You're welcome. Sleep well."

"Use your ice pack."

"Yes ma'am."

As it turned out, I slept a lot sooner than he did. Dietz was a night owl. I'm not sure how he occupied himself. Maybe he polished his boots or cleaned his handgun. He might have watched late-night television with the sound turned down. I sure never heard him. Once in a while, in turning over, I realized the light was still on in the living room. There was something so parental about his being on the premises. One thing about being single, you don't often feel protected. You tend to sleep with your mental shoes on, ready to leap up and arm yourself at the least little noise. With Dietz on guard duty, I got to cruise through a couple of rounds of REM, dreaming right up to the split second before the alarm went off. I opened my eyes, reached out, and caught it just before it blared.

I did my morning ablutions behind closed doors so the sound of running water wouldn't carry. Shoes in hand, I crept down the stairs in my stocking feet and tiptoed out the front door without waking him. I laced up, did a quick stretch, and set off at a fast walk to get warmed up. The night had shifted from pitch black to charcoal gray and by the time I reached Cabana, the darkness was beginning to lift. Dawn painted the early-morning sky in pale watercolor hues. The ocean was silver blue, the sky washing up from a smoky mauve to soft peach. The oil derricks dotted the horizon like clusters of iridescent sequins. I love the sound of the surf at that hour, the squawk of seagulls, the soft cooing of the pigeons already strutting along the path. A platinum blond and a black standard poodle were heading in my direction, a pair I saw most of the mornings I was out.

The run was good. Often three miles just feels like a pain in the ass, something I do because I know I must. For once, here I was feeling grateful to be physically fit. I wouldn't do well with an injury like Dietz's that prevented exercise. I'll never be any kind of champ, but for lifting a depression there's really nothing better. I did the turn at East Beach and started back, picking up my pace a bit. The sun was coming up behind me, sloshing rivulets of yellow light across the sky. Walking home again, winded and sweating, my mood was light and I was feeling good.

Dietz was in the shower when I got in. He'd brought in the paper and set it on the kitchen counter. He'd tidied the bedcovers and folded up the sofa bed, tucking the pillows out of sight somewhere. I put on a pot of coffee and then went upstairs, waiting until I heard him turn off his shower before I started mine. By 8:35, I was dressed, I'd finished breakfast, and I was gathering up my jacket and my car keys. Dietz was still sitting at the kitchen counter with his second cup of coffee and the morning paper spread out before him.

"See you later," I said.

"Have a good one," he replied.

On the way downtown, I stopped off at a nearby condominium with the two subpoenas in hand. I served both without incident, though the fellow and his girlfriend were hardly happy with me. Occasionally, I'll have someone who goes to absurd lengths to avoid service, but for the most part people seem resigned to their fates. If someone protests or turns ugly, my response is usually the same: "Sorry, pal, but I'm like a waitress. I don't cook up the trouble, I just serve it. Have a nice day," I say.

For a change, I parked in the public lot across from the courthouse and walked the two blocks to work. My current office is the former conference room for the law firm of Kingman and Ives, located in downtown Santa Teresa. From my apartment, the drive takes about ten minutes, given the usual traffic conditions. The Kingman building appears to be a three-story stucco structure, but the ground floor is an illusion. Behind a fieldstone facade, complete with barred and shuttered windows, there's actually a small parking lot, with twelve assigned spaces. Most of the office staff and the lesser tenants in the building are forced to scrounge parking elsewhere. The surrounding blocks aren't metered, but parking is restricted to ninety minutes max and most of us receive at least one ticket a month. Some mornings, it's comical watching us pass and repass, trying to beat one another to the available spaces.

I climbed the two flights of stairs, forgoing the pleasures of the elevator, which is small and takes forever, often giving the impression it's on the verge of getting stuck. Once in the office, I exchanged pleasantries with the receptionist, Alison, and Lonnie Kingman's secretary, Ida Ruth. I seldom see Lonnie, who's either in court or working doggedly behind closed doors. I let myself into my office, where I paused to make a note of the date, time, and a brief physical description of the couple to whom I'd served the subpoenas. I typed up a quick invoice, then picked up the telephone, leaning back in my swivel chair as I tossed the paperwork in my out box. California Fidelity didn't open until nine, but Darcy usually came in early.

"Hey, Darcy. It's me," I said when she answered on her end.

"Oh hi, Kinsey. Hang on a minute. I'm not at my desk." She put me on hold and I listened to leftover Christmas carols while I waited, feeling mildy optimistic. I figured if she hadn't found anything she'd have said so.

Half a minute passed and then she clicked back in. "Okay. Guy David Malek doesn't have a current driver's license in the state of California. His was surrendered in 1968 and apparently it's never been reissued."

"Well, shit," I said.

Darcy laughed. "Would you just *wait?* You're always jumping to conclusions. All I said was he doesn't drive. He has a California identification card, which is where I picked up the information. His mailing address is Route 1, Box 600, Marcella, California, 93456. That's probably the same as his residence. Sounds like a ranch or a farm. You want to see the picture?"

"You have a current *picture* of him? This is great. I don't believe it. You're a wizard."

"Hey, you're dealing with a pro," she said. "What's your fax number?"

I gave her Lonnie's fax number while I reached for the telephone book. "Are you sure he's in Marcella? That's less than a hundred miles away."

"According to DMV records. That should make your job easy."

"Ain't that the truth. What do I owe you?"

"Don't worry about it. I had to fake out some forms to make the request look legitimate, but nobody's going to check. Took less than a minute."

"You're a doll. Thanks so much. I'll be in touch and we'll have lunch. I'll pay."

Darcy laughed. "I'll take you up on that."

I put the phone down and paged through the telephone book, looking up the area code for Marcella, California. It was actually in the 805 area, the same as Santa Teresa. I tried directory assistance, giving the operator Guy Malek's name. There was no telephone listed at the address I'd been given. "You have any other listing for Guy Malek in the area? G. Malek? Any kind of Malek?"

"No ma'am."

"All right. Thanks."

I trotted down the hall to the fax machine just in time to see a copy of Guy Malek's photo ID slide out. The black-and-white reproduction had a splotchy quality, but it did establish Guy David Malek's SEX:

M; HAIR: BLND; EYES: GRN; HT: 5-08; WT: 155; DOB: 03-02-42. He looked ever so much better than he had in his high school annual. Three cheers for him. I confess I felt smug as I sat down at my desk, the little show-off in my nature patting herself on the back.

I called Tasha's office and identified myself to her secretary when she picked up. She said, "Tasha's in a meeting, but let me tell her it's you. She can probably take a quick call if it's important."

"Trust me, it is."

"Can you hold?"

"Sure." While I waited, I laid out a hand of solitaire. One card up and six cards down. In some ways, I was sorry everything had come together so fast. I didn't want Donovan to think he was paying for something he could have done himself—though in truth, he was. There's a lot of information available as a matter of public record. Most people simply don't have the time or the interest in doing the grunt work. They're all too happy to have a PI do it for them, so in the end everybody benefits. Still, this one was almost too easy, especially since I wasn't sure the family would believe their real interests had been served by my discovery. I turned the next card up on the second pile and placed another five cards down.

Tasha clicked on, sounding terse and distracted. "Hi, Kinsey. What's up? I hope this is important because I'm up to my ass in work."

"I have an address for Guy Malek. I thought I'd better let you know first thing."

There was half a second's silence while she processed the information. "That was fast. How'd you manage?"

I smiled at her tone, which was the perfect blend of surprise and respect. "I have my little ways," I said. Ah, how seductive the satisfaction when we think we've impressed others with our cleverness. It's one of the perversities of human nature that we're more interested in the admiration of our enemies than the approbation of our friends. "You have a pencil?"

"Of course. Where's he living?"

"Not far." I gave her the address. "There's no telephone listed. Either he doesn't have phone service or it's in someone else's name."

"Amazing," she said. "Let me pass this along to Donovan and see what he wants to do next. He'll be delighted, I'm sure."

"I doubt that. I got the impression they'd all be happier if Guy turned up dead."

"Nonsense. This is family. I'm sure things will work out. I'll have him give you a call."

Within fifteen minutes, my phone rang. Donovan Malek was on the line. "Nice work," he said. "I'm surprised how quick it was. I thought the search would take weeks."

"It's not always this easy. We got lucky," I said. "You need anything else?"

"Tasha and I just had a chat about that. I suggested we have you go up there in person. She could contact him by letter, but people sometimes react oddly getting mail from an attorney. You feel threatened before you even open the envelope. We don't want to set the wrong tone."

"Sure, I can talk to him," I said, feeling puzzled what the right tone would be.

"I'd like a firsthand report about Guy's current circumstances. Are you free sometime in the next two days?"

I checked my calendar. "I can go this afternoon if you like."

"The sooner the better. I want this handled with kid gloves. I have no idea if he's heard about Dad's death, but even with the estrangement, he could be upset. Besides, the money's a touchy issue. Who knows how he'll react."

"You want me to tell him about the will?"

"I don't see why not. He's bound to find out eventually."

5

I glanced at my watch. Since there was nothing on my schedule, I thought I might as well hit the road. It was just now nine-thirty. A round-trip to Marcella would take a little more than an hour each way. If I allowed myself an hour to track down Guy Malek, I'd still have plenty of time left to grab a quick lunch and be back mid-afternoon. I opened my bottom desk drawer and took out my map of California. According to the legend, Marcella was maybe eighty miles north, with a population of less than fifteen hundred souls. I didn't think it would take even an hour to locate him once I hit town, assuming he was still there. The conversation itself probably wouldn't take more than thirty minutes, which meant I might get this whole job wrapped up by the end of the day.

I put a call through to Dietz and let him know what was going on. I could hear the television in the background, one of those perpetual news broadcasts riddled with commercials. At the end of the hour, you know more about dog food than you do about world events. Dietz indicated he had no particular plans. I wasn't sure if he was angling for an invitation to accompany me, but since he didn't ask the question, I didn't answer it. I didn't want to feel responsible for his entertainment anyway. I told him I expected to be back by three and would bypass the office and come straight home. We could figure out what to do about dinner when I finally rolled in.

I gassed up my VW and headed north on 101. The sunshine was short-lived. Where the highway hugged the coastline, the fog had rolled in and the sky was now milky white with clouds turning thick at the edge. Along the road, the evergreens stood out against the horizon in a variety of dark shapes. Traffic moved steadily, mostly single-passenger cars with an occasional horse van, probably heading to the Santa Ynez valley just north of us. We hadn't had much rain and the hills looked like dull hay-colored mounds with an occasional oil rig genuflecting in a series of obsequious bows toward the earth.

The road turned inland and within the hour, the clouds had burned off again, fading back into a sky of pale blue, streaked with a residual haze as wispy as goose down. Just outside Santa Maria, I took 166 east and drove for ten miles on the two-lane road that paralleled the Cuyama River. The heat from the January sun was thin up here. Through the valleys and canyons, the earth smelled dry and a string of bald brown hills rose up in front of me. Rain had been promised, but the weather seemed to flirt, teasing us with high clouds and a hint of a breeze.

The town of Marcella was situated in the shadow of the Los Coches Mountain. Driving, I was aware of the unseen presence of the great San Andreas Fault, the 750-mile fracture that snakes up the California coastline from the Mexican border to the triple junction near Mendocino, the Pacific and North American plates grinding against each other since time began. Under the thin layers of granite and marine sediment, the crust of the earth was as cracked as a skull. In this area, the San Andreas Fault was intersected by the Santa Ynez

Fault with the White Wolf and the Garlock not far away. It's speculated that the mountains in this part of the state once ran north-south like other mountains along the coast. According to theory, the southern tip of this chain was snagged by the Pacific plate many millions of years ago and dragged sideways as it passed, thus shifting the range to its current east-west orientation. I'd been driving my car once during a minor quake and it felt like the VW had suddenly been passed by a fast-moving eighteen-wheeler. There was a lurch to the right, as if the car had been sucked into a sudden vacuum. In California, where the weather seems to change so little, we look to earthquakes for the drama that tornadoes and hurricanes provide elsewhere.

At the junction of two roads, I caught sight of a discreet sign and turned southward into the town of Marcella. The streets were six lanes wide and sparsely traveled. An occasional palm or juniper had been planted near the curb. There were no buildings over two stories high and the structures I saw consisted of a general store with iron bars across the front windows, a hotel, three motels, a real estate office, and a large Victorian house surrounded by scaffolding. The only bar was located in a building that looked like it might have been a post office once, stripped now of any official function. A Budweiser sign was hanging in a window. What did the citizens of Marcella do for a living, and why settle here? There wasn't another town for miles and the businesses in this one seemed weighted toward drinking beer and going to bed soon afterward. If you wanted fast food or auto parts, if you needed a prescription filled, a movie, a fitness center, or a wedding gown, you'd have to drive into Santa Maria or farther north on 101 to Atascadero and Paso Robles. The land surrounding the town seemed barren. I hadn't seen anything that even halfway resembled a citrus orchard or a plowed field. Maybe the countryside was devoted to ranches or mines or stock-car races. Maybe people lived here to escape the hurly-burly of San Luis Obispo.

I found a gas station on a side street and stopped for directions. The youth who emerged was about seventeen. He was skinny, had pale eyes, hair shaved very close up to his ears, and a tangle of teeth, all reminiscent of someone in an early episode of *The Twilight Zone.* I said, "Hi. I'm looking for a friend of mine named Guy Malek. I think he lives on Route 1 somewhere, but he didn't give me directions." Well, okay. I was fudging, but I didn't outright *lie.* I *would* be Guy's friend when he heard the news about the five million bucks.

The youth said nothing, but he pointed a trembling finger like the Ghost of Christmas Past.

I glanced over my shoulder. "Back that way?"

"That's the house."

I turned to stare with astonishment. The property was enclosed by chain-link fencing. Beyond a rolling chicken wire gate, I could see a small house, a shed, a large barn with corrugated metal siding curling away from the seams, an old yellow school bus, a single gas pump, and a sign too faded to read at any distance. The gate was open. "Oh. Well, thanks. Do you know if he's home?"

"No."

"He's not?"

"No, I don't know. I didn't see him today."

"Ah. Well, I guess I'll go knock."

"You could do that," he said.

I pulled out of the station and drove across the road. I nosed the VW through the open gate and parked on a length of raw dirt that I took for a driveway. I got out. The surface of the yard was white sand with a rim of brown grass around the edge. The house was frame, painted once-upon-a-time white, one story with a wooden porch built across the front. A trellis that shielded the windows on the left sported only one bare vine, which twisted through the latticework like a boa constrictor. A matching trellis on the right had collapsed under its burden of dry, brown vegetation. Various wires extended from the roofline, connecting the occupants to telephone, cable, and electricity.

I climbed the wooden stairs and knocked on the dilapidated screen. The front door was shut and there were no signs of life. There was a fine dusting of soot everywhere, as if the structure were downwind of a smelting plant. The porch floor began to tremble in a way that suggested that someone was traversing the wooden floor inside of the house. The door was opened and I found myself face-to-face with the man I took to be Guy Malek. Aside from a three-day growth of beard, he didn't look anywhere near his age. His hair looked darker and straighter than it had in his high school yearbook, but his features were still boyish: khaki green eyes fringed with dark lashes; a small, straight nose; and a generous mouth. His complexion was clear and his color was good. Age had sketched in fine lines around his eyes and the flesh along his jaw was beginning to sag, but I'd have pegged him in his mid-thirties. At fifty and sixty, he'd no doubt look just the same, the years making only moderate adjustments to his good looks. He wore denim overalls on top of what looked like a union suit. He was in the process of putting on a blue jeans jacket when he answered the door, and he paused to straighten the collar in the back before he said, "Hey."

As an adolescent, Guy Malek had been as dorky looking as the rest of us. He was the bad kid, lawless and self-destructive, one of life's lost souls. He must have been appealing because he was so in need of rescue. Women can't resist a man who needs saving. Now his good angel had apparently taken up residence, bestowing on his countenance the look of serenity. It seemed odd that his brothers had matured so differently. Already, I liked this man better than his siblings. Aside from the scruffiness, he didn't look like he was snorting, sniffing, or mainlining illegal substances.

"Are you Guy Malek?"

His smile was hesitant, as though I might be someone he had met before whose name he wished he remembered. "Yes."

"My name is Kinsey Millhone. I'm a private investigator from Santa Teresa." I gave him a business card. He studied the card, but didn't offer to shake hands. His were as soiled as an auto mechanic's. I could see a muscle work in his jaw.

His eyes came up to mine and his entire body became still. The smile faded. "My family hired you?"

"Well, yes," I said. I was about to launch into a diplomatic account of his father's death when I saw tears rise in his eyes, blurring the clear green of his gaze. He looked upward, blinking, and took a deep breath before he brought his attention back to mine. He dashed at his cheeks, laughing with embarrassment.

He said, "Whoa," pinching at his eyes with the fingers of one hand. He shook his head, trying to compose himself. "Sorry. You caught me by surprise. I never thought it would matter, but I guess it does. I always wished they'd send someone, but I'd about given up hope. How'd you find me?"

"It wasn't that hard. I ran a DMV check and came up with your California identification card. I tried directory assistance, but they didn't have you listed. I take it you don't have a phone."

"Can't afford one," he said. "You want to come in?" His manner was awkward and he seemed unsure of himself. His gaze fell away from mine and then came back again.

"I'd like that," I said.

He stepped back to allow me entrance and I passed into a room that was about what you'd expect. The interior construction was crude and featured wide, unfinished floorboards and windows that didn't quite shut. Various pieces of old furniture had been moved into the space, probably cadged from the city dump . . . if there was one in this town. Every surface was piled high with soiled clothes and books and magazines and utensils, pots and pans and canned goods and tools. There were also what looked like farm implements whose functions were unclear. There was a tower of used tires in one corner of the room and a toilet that didn't seem connected to much of anything. Guy caught my puzzlement. "I'm holding that for a fellow. I have a real bathroom in there," he said, smiling shyly.

"Glad to hear that," I said and smiled back at him.

"You want a cup of coffee? It's instant, but it's not bad."

"No, thanks. Were you on your way out?"

"What? Oh, yeah, but don't worry about that. I have to be someplace shortly. Have a seat." He pulled out a handkerchief and paused to blow his nose. I could feel anxiety stir in my chest. There was something touching about his openness. He gestured toward a frayed, lumpy couch with a spring sticking through the cushion. I perched on the edge, hoping not to do serious damage to my private parts. My discomfort was related to the fact that Guy Malek apparently thought his family had hired me to conduct the search out of sentiment. I knew their real attitude, which was actually hostile if the truth be known. I did a quick debate with myself and decided I'd better level with him. Whatever the outcome of our conversation, it would be too humiliating for him if I let him harbor the wrong impression.

He pulled up a wooden chair and sat facing me directly, occasionally mopping at his eyes. He didn't apologize for the tears that continued to spill down his cheeks. "You don't know how hard I prayed for this," he said, mouth trembling. He looked down at his hands and began to fold the handkerchief in on itself. "The pastor of my church . . . he swore up and down it would come to pass if it was meant to be. No point in praying if it isn't God's will, he said. And I kept saying, 'Man, it seems like they'd have found me by now if they cared enough, you know?' "

I was struck by the fact that his circumstances were oddly reminiscent of mine, both of us trying to assimilate fractured family connections. At least he welcomed his, though he'd misunderstood the purpose of my visit. I felt like a dog having to set him straight. "Guy, as a matter of fact, it's more complicated. I have some bad news," I said.

"My father died?"

"Two weeks ago. I'm not sure of the date. I gather he'd had a stroke and he was also struggling with cancer. He'd been through a lot and I guess his body just gave up on him."

He was silent for a moment, staring off into space. "Well. I guess I'm not surprised," he said. "Did he . . . do you know if he was the one who asked for me?"

"I have no idea. I wasn't hired until yesterday. The probate attorney is getting the process underway. By law, you're required to be notified since you're one of the beneficiaries."

He turned to me, suddenly getting it. "Ah. You're here on official business and that's all it is, right?"

"More or less."

I watched as the color rose slowly in his cheeks. "Silly me," he said. "And here I thought you were sent by someone who actually gave a shit."

"I'm sorry."

"Not your fault," he said. "What else?"

"What else?"

"I'm wondering if you have any other news to impart."

"Not really." If he'd picked up on the fact that he was due to inherit money, he gave no indication.

"I don't suppose there's any chance my father asked for me."

"I wish I could help, but I wasn't given any details. It's possible, I'm sure, but you may never know. You can ask the attorney when you talk to her. She knows a lot more than I do about the circumstances of his death."

He smiled fleetingly. "Dad hired a woman? That doesn't sound like him."

"Donovan hired her. She went to school with his wife."

"What about Bennet and Jack? Are they married?" He said the names as if the sounds hadn't been uttered for years.

"No. Just Donovan. I don't think he and Christie have any kids as yet. He runs the company, which I understand is now the third-largest construction firm in the state."

"Good for him. Donnie was always obsessed with the business," he said. "Did you talk to the other two?"

"Briefly."

The character of his expression had completely changed as we spoke. What had started out as happiness had shifted to painful enlightenment. "Correct me if I'm wrong, but I get the impression they're not really interested in me. The attorney said they had to do this so they're doing it. Is that it? I mean, the three of them aren't burdened by a lot of warm, gooey feelings where I'm concerned."

"That's true, but it probably stems from the situation when you left. I was told you were in a lot of trouble, so their memories of you aren't that flattering."

"I suppose not. Nor mine of them if it comes right down to it."

"Besides, nobody really believed I'd find you. It's been what, eighteen years?"

"About that. Not long enough, apparently, from their perspective."

"Where'd you go when you left? Do you mind if I ask?"

"Why would I mind? It doesn't amount to much. I went out to the highway to hitch a ride. I was heading for San Francisco, zonked out of my head on acid. The fellow who picked me up was a preacher, who'd been hired by a church about a mile from here. He took me in. I was tripped out so bad I didn't even know where I was at."

"And you've been here all this time?"

"Not quite," he said. "It wasn't like I cleaned up and got straight, just like that. I screwed up more than once. I'd backslide . . . you know, get drunk and take off . . . but Pete and his wife always found me and brought me back. Finally, I realized I wasn't going to shake 'em off. Didn't matter what I did. They were sticking to me like glue. That's when I took a stand and found Jesus in my heart. It really turned my life around."

"And you never got in touch with your family?" I said.

He shook his head, his smile bitter. "They haven't exactly been clamoring for me, either."

"Maybe that will change when I talk to them. What else can I tell them? Do you work?"

"Sure, I work. I do maintenance at the church and, you know, general handyman jobs around town. Painting and repairs, plumbing, electrical. About anything you need. Mostly minimum wage, but I'm the only one does it, so I stay busy."

"Sounds like you've done all right for yourself."

He looked around him. "Well, I don't have much, but I don't need much either. Place isn't mine," he said. "The church provides my housing, but I make enough to take care of the basics. Food and utilities, that sort of thing. I don't drive, but I have a bike and that gets me most places in a town this size."

"You've changed quite a lot."

"I'd be dead otherwise." He glanced at his watch. "Listen, I don't mean to rush you, but I probably ought to get myself on over to the church."

"I won't keep you then. I appreciate your time. Can I give you a lift?"

"Sure. We can talk on the way."

Once in the car, he directed me back to the highway. We turned right onto 166, heading east again. We drove for a while in companionable silence. He slid a look in my direction. "So what's your assignment? Find me and report back?"

"That's about it," I said. "Now that we have a current address, Tasha Howard, the attorney, will be sending you notice of the probate."

"Oh, that's right. I forgot. I'm a beneficiary, you said." His tone had turned light and nearly mocking.

"That doesn't interest you?"

"Not particularly. I thought I needed something from those people, but as it turns out, I don't." He pointed at an upcoming junction and I took a right-hand turn onto a small side road. The roadbed had been downgraded from blacktop to loose gravel, and I could see the plumes of white dust swirling up in my rear window as we drove. The church was situated at the edge of a pasture about a half mile down. The sign said: JUBILEE EVANGELICAL CHURCH.

"You can pull up right here," he said. "You want to come in and see the place? If you're paid by the hour, you might as well have the full tour. I'm sure Donnie can afford it."

I hesitated slightly. "All right."

He cocked his head. "You don't have to worry. I won't try to convert you."

I parked and the two of us got out. He didn't issue a proclamation, but I could tell from his manner that he was proud of the place. He took out a ring of keys and let us in.

The church was small, a frame building, little more than one room. There was something about its plain appearance that spoke of goodness. The stained glass windows were not elaborate. Each was divided into six simple panels of pale gold with a scripture written across the bottom. There was an unadorned wood pulpit at the front, positioned to the left of a raised and carpeted platform. On the right, there was an organ and three rows of folding chairs for the choir. Last Sunday's flowers consisted of a spray of white gladiola. "Place was destroyed by fire about ten years back. Congregation rebuilt everything from the ground right on up."

I said, "How'd you get on track? That must have been hard."

He sat down in one of the front pews and I could see him look around, perhaps seeing the place as I saw it. "I give credit to the Lord, though Pete always says I did the work myself," he said. "I grew up without much guidance, without values of any kind. I'm not blaming anybody. That's just how it was. My parents were good people. They didn't drink or beat me or anything like that, but they never talked about God or faith or their religious beliefs, assuming they had any, which I don't guess they did. My brothers and I . . . even when we were little kids . . . never went to Sunday school or church.

"My parents disliked 'organized religion.' I don't know what that phrase meant to them or what their perception was, but they took pride in making sure none of us were ever exposed to it. Like a disease of some kind. I remember they had a book by this guy named

Philip Wylie. *Generation of Vipers*. He equated the church teachings with intellectual corruption, the stunting of young minds."

"Some people feel that way," I said.

"Yeah, I know. I don't get it, but it's something I run into out there in the world. It's like people think just because you go to church you're not all that bright. I mean, just because I'm born-again doesn't mean I lost IQ points."

"I'm sure you didn't."

"Thing is, I was raised without a moral compass. I couldn't get a sense of what the rules were so I just kept pushing. I kept crossing the line, waiting for somebody to tell me where the boundaries were."

"But you were getting into trouble with the law from what I heard. You must have known the rules because every time you broke one, you ended up in court. Donovan says you spent more time in Juvenile Hall than you did at home."

His smile was sheepish. "That's true, but here's what's weird. I didn't mind Juvie all that much. At least I could be with kids as screwed up as I was. Man, I was out of control. I ran wild. I was a maniac, freaked out about everything. It's hard to think about that now. I have trouble relating to myself and who I was back then. I know what happened. I mean, I know what I did, but I can't imagine doing it. I wanted to feel good. I've thought about this a lot and that's the best explanation I've been able to come up with. I felt bad and I wanted to feel better. Seemed to me dope was the quickest way to get there. I haven't touched drugs or hard liquor for more than fifteen years. I might have a beer now and then, but I don't smoke, don't play cards, don't ballroom dance. Don't take the Lord's name in vain and don't cuss . . . all that much. Stub my toe and I can turn the air blue, but most of the time, I avoid swear words."

"Well, that's good."

"For me, it is. Back then, I was always teetering on the brink. I think I was hoping my parents would finally draw the line and mean it. That they'd say, 'Here, this is it. You've finally gone and done it this time.' But you know what? My dad was too soft. He waffled on everything. Even when he kicked my ass from here to next Tuesday, even when he threw me out of the house, he was saying, 'Give this some thought, son. You can come back when you've figured it out.' But like what? Figured what out? I didn't have a clue. I was rudderless. I was like a boat going full throttle but without any real direction, roaring around in big circles. Know what I mean?"

"Sure I do. In high school, I was a screwup myself. I ended up as a cop before I did this."

He smiled. "No kidding? You drank and smoked dope?"

"Among other things," I said, modestly.

"Come on. Like what?"

"I don't know. Kids in my class were all clean-cut, but not me. I was a wild thing. I ditched school. I hung out with some low-life dudes and I liked that. I liked *them*," I said. "I was the odd one out and so were they, I guess."

"Where'd you go to high school?"

"Santa Teresa High."

He laughed. "You were a low-waller?"

"Absolutely," I said. Low-wallers were the kids who quite literally perched on a low wall that ran along the back of the school property. Much smoking of cigarettes, funky clothes, and peroxided hair.

Guy laughed. "Well, that's great."

"I don't know how great it was, but it's what I did."

"How'd *you* get on track?"

"Who says I am?"

He got to his feet as if he'd come to a decision. "Come on out to the parsonage and meet Peter and Winnie," he said. "They'll be in the kitchen at this hour setting up supper for the Thursday night Bible study."

I followed him up the center aisle and through a door at the rear. I could feel the first stirrings of resistance. I didn't want anyone pushing me to convert. Too much virtue is just as worrisome as wickedness in my book.

6

The parsonage was situated on the property adjacent to the church and consisted of a rambling white frame farmhouse, two stories tall, with green shutters and a shabby green shingled roof broken up with dormers. Across one end was a wide screened-in porch distinctly tilted, as though an earthquake had pulled the concrete foundation loose. Behind the house, I could see a big red barn with a dilapidated one-car garage attached. Both the house and the barn were in need of a fresh coat of paint, and I noticed sunlight slanting through the barn roof where it was pierced with holes. Metal lawn chairs were arranged in a semicircle in the yard under a massive live oak tree. A weathered picnic table flanked with benches was set up close by where I pictured Sunday school classes and church suppers during the summer months.

I followed Guy across the yard. We went up the back steps and into the kitchen. The air was scented with sautéed onions and celery. Peter was a man in his sixties, balding, with a wreath of white hair that grew down into sideburns and wrapped around his jaw in a closely trimmed beard linked to a matching mustache. Pale sunlight coming through the window illuminated a feathery white fuzz across his pate. He wore a red turtleneck with a ribbed green sweater over it. He was just in the process of rolling out biscuit dough. The baking sheets to his right were lined with rows of perfect disks of dough ready for the oven. He looked up with pleasure as the two of us came in. "Oh, Guy. Good, it's you. I was just wondering if you were here yet. The furnace over at the church has been acting up again. First it clicks on, then it clicks off. On then off."

"Probably the electronic ignition. I'll take a look." Guy's posture was self-conscious. He rubbed his nose and then stuck his hands in his overall pockets as if to warm them. "This is Kinsey Millhone. She's a private detective from Santa Teresa." He turned and looked at me, tilting his head at the minister and his wife as he made the introductions. "This is Peter Antle and his wife, Winnie."

Peter's complexion was ruddy. His blue eyes smiled out at me from under ragged white brows. "Nice to meet you. I'd offer to shake hands, but I don't think you'd like it. How are you at homemade biscuits? Can I put you to work?"

"Better not," I said. "My domestic skills leave something to be desired."

He was on the verge of pursuing the point when his wife said, "Now, Pete . . ." and gave him a look. Winnie Antle appeared to be in her late forties with short brown hair combed away from her face. She was brown-eyed, slightly heavy, with a wide smile and very white teeth. She wore a man's shirt over jeans with a long knit vest that covered her wide hips and ample derriere. She was chopping vegetables for soup, a mountain of carrot coins piled up on the counter next to her. I could see two bunches of celery and assorted bell peppers awaiting her flashing knife. She was simultaneously tending a stockpot filled with vegetable cuttings boiling merrily. "Hello, Kinsey. Don't mind him. He's always trying to pass the work off onto the unsuspecting," she said, sending me a quick smile. "What brings you up this way?"

Peter looked at Guy. "You're not in trouble, I hope. You have to watch this man." His smile was teasing and it was clear he had no real expectation of trouble where Guy was concerned.

Guy murmured the explanation, apparently embarrassed to be the recipient of such bad news. "My father died. Probate attorney asked her to track me down."

Peter and Winnie both turned their full attention on Guy, whose earlier emotions were well under control. Peter said, "Is that the truth. Well, I'm sorry to hear that." He glanced over at me. "We've often talked about his trying for a reconciliation. It's been years since he had any contact with his dad."

Guy shifted his weight, leaning against the counter with his arms crossed in front of him. He seemed to be directing his comments at me, his tone wistful. "I don't know how many letters I wrote, but none of them got sent. Every time I tried to explain, it just came out sounding . . . you know, wrong, or dumb. I finally let it be till I could work out what it was I wanted to say. I kept thinking I had time. Mean, he wasn't old, by any stretch."

"It must have been his time. You can't argue with that," Peter said.

Winnie spoke up. "If you don't feel like work today, you go ahead and take off. We can manage just fine."

"I'm all right," Guy responded, again with discomfort at being the center of attention.

We spent a few minutes going through an exchange of information; how I'd managed to locate Guy and what I knew of his family, which wasn't much.

Peter was shaking his head, clearly regretful at the news I was bringing. "We think of Guy as one of our own. First time I ever saw this boy, he's a sorry sight. His eyeballs were bright red, sort of rolling around in his head like hot marbles. Winnie and me, we'd been called to this church and we'd driven all the way out to California from Fort Scott, Kansas. We'd heard all sorts of things about hippies and potheads and acid freaks, I think they called 'em. Kids with their eyes burned out from staring at the sun completely stoned. And there stood Guy by the side of the road with a sign that said 'San Francisco.' He was trying to be 'cool,' but he just looked pitiful to me. Winnie didn't want me to stop. We had the two kids in the backseat and she thought sure we'd be turned into homicide statistics."

"It's been a lot of years since then," Winnie said.

Pete looked over at Guy. "What are you thinking to do now, Guy, go back to Santa Teresa? This might be time to sit down with your brothers and talk about the past, maybe clean up some old business."

"I don't know. I suppose. If they're willing to sit down with me," Guy said. "I guess I'm not quite ready to make a decision about that." He glanced at me. "I know they didn't send you up here begging me to come back, but it seems like I might have *some* say in the matter. Would it be all right if I called you in a day or two?"

"No problem. In the meantime, I need to head home," I said. "You've got my card. If I'm not in the office, try that second number and the call will be forwarded automatically." I took out a second business card and jotted down Tasha Howard's name. "This is the attorney. I don't remember her phone number offhand. She has an office in Lompoc. You can call directory assistance and get the information from them. She's not that far away. If nothing else, you might make an appointment to have a chat with her. You'll need advice from an attorney of your own. I hope everything works out."

"I do, too. I appreciate the fact you made the trip," Guy said. "It's a lot more personal."

I shook hands with him, uttered polite noises in the direction of Peter and Winnie Antle, and made my getaway. I cruised down the main street of Marcella again, trying to get a feel for the place. Small and quiet. Unpretentious. I circled the block, driving along the few residential streets. The houses were small, built from identical plans, one-story stucco structures with flat rooflines. The exteriors were painted in pastel shades, pale Easter egg colors nestled in winter grass as dry as paper shreds. Most of the houses seemed shabby and dispirited. I saw only an occasional occupant.

As I swung past the general store, heading out to the main road, I spotted a sign in the window advertising fresh sandwiches. On an impulse, I parked the car and went in and ordered a tuna salad on rye from the woman at the deli counter in the rear. We chatted idly while she busied herself with the sandwich preparations, wrapping my dill pickle in a square of waxed paper so it wouldn't make the bread all mushy, she said. Behind me, two or three other customers went about their business, guiding small grocery carts up and down the aisles. No one turned to stare at me or paid me the slightest attention.

I let her know I'd just been over at the church. She exhibited little curiosity about who I was or why I was visiting the pastor and his wife. Mention of Guy Malek produced no uneasy silences nor any unsolicited confidences about his past history or his character.

"This seems like a nice town," I said as she passed my lunch across the counter. I handed her a ten, which she rang into the cash register.

"If you like this kind of place," she remarked. "Too quiet for my taste, but my husband was born here and insisted we come back. I like to kick up my heels, but about the best we can manage is a rummage sale now and then. Whooee." She fanned herself comically as if the excitement of used clothing was almost more than she could bear. "You want a receipt?" she said, counting out seven ones and change.

"I'd appreciate it."

She tore off the register receipt and handed it to me. "You take care of yourself."

"Thanks. You, too," I said.

I ate while I drove, steering with one hand as I alternated bites of dill pickle and tuna sandwich. The price had included a bag of potato chips, and I munched on those, too, figuring I'd cover all the necessary food groups. I'd forgotten to ask Guy his mother's maiden name, but the truth was, I had no doubt he was who he said he was. He reminded me of Jack, whose coloring and features were quite similar. Donovan and Bennet must have favored one parent while Guy and Jack looked more like the other. As cynical as I was, I found myself taking at face value both the reformation of Guy Malek and his current association with Jubilee Evangelical. It was always possible, I supposed, that he and the minister were singularly crafty frauds, who'd cooked up a cover story for any stranger who came calling, but for the life of me I didn't see it and I didn't believe anything sinister was afoot. If bucolic Marcella was the headquarters for some cult of neo-Nazis, Satanists, or motorcycle outlaws, it had sure escaped my notice.

It was not until I had passed Santa Maria, heading south on 101, that I realized Guy Malek had never asked how much his share of the estate would be. I probably should have volunteered the information. I could have at least given him a ballpark figure, but the question had never come up and I'd been too busy trying to evaluate his status for my report to Donovan. His emotional focus was on his father's death and the loss of his opportunity to make amends. Any profit was apparently beside the point as far as he was concerned. Oh, well. I figured Tasha would be in touch with him and she could give him the particulars.

I arrived in Santa Teresa without incident at two P.M. Since I was home earlier than I'd thought, I went into the office, typed up my notes, and stuck them in the file. I left two phone messages, one for Tasha at her office and one on the Maleks' home machine. I calculated my hours, the mileage, and miscellaneous expenses, and typed an invoice for my services to which I affixed the receipt for the tuna sandwich. Tomorrow, I'd include it with the typed report of my findings, send a copy to Tasha and one to Donovan. End of story, I thought.

I retrieved my car, unticketed, from an illegal space and drove home, feeling generally satisfied with life. Dietz fixed supper that night, a skilletful of fried onions, fried potatoes, and fried sausages with liberal doses of garlic and red pepper flakes, all served with a side of drab, grainy mustard that set your tongue aflame. Only two confirmed single people could eat a meal like that and imagine it was somehow nutritious. I handled the cleanup process, washing plates, flatware, and glasses, scrubbing out the frying pan while Dietz read the evening paper. Is this what couples did any given night of the week? In my twice-married life, it was the drama and grief I remembered most clearly, not the day-to-day stuff. This was entirely too domestic . . . not unpleasant, but certainly unsettling to someone unaccustomed to company.

At eight, we walked up to Rosie's and settled into a back booth together. Rosie's restaurant is poorly lighted, a tacky neighborhood establishment that's been there for twenty-five years, sandwiched between a Laundromat and an appliance repair shop. The chrome-and-Formica tables are of thrift-shop vintage and the booths lining the walls are made of construction-grade plywood, stained dark, complete with crude hand-gouged messages and splinters. It's an act of reckless abandon to slide across the seats unless your tetanus shots are current. Over the years, the number of California smokers has steadily diminished, so the air quality has improved while the clientele has not. Rosie's used to be a refuge for local drinkers who liked to start early in the day and stay until closing time. Now the tavern has become popular with assorted amateur sports teams, who descend en masse after every big game, filling the air with loud talk, raucous laughter, and much stomping about. The regulars, all four bleary-eyed imbibers, have been driven to other places. I rather missed their slurred conversation, which was never intrusive.

Rosie was apparently gone for the night and the bartender was someone I'd never seen before. Dietz drank a couple of beers while I had a couple of glasses of Rosie's best screw-top Chardonnay, a puckering rendition of a California varietal she probably bought by the keg.

I freely confess it was the alcohol that got me into trouble that night. I was feeling mellow and relaxed, somewhat less inhibited than usual, which is to say, ready to flap my mouth. Robert Dietz was beginning to look good to me, and I wasn't really sure how I felt about that. His face was chiseled in shadow and his gaze crossed the room in restless assessment while we chatted about nothing in particular. Idly, I told him about William and Rosie's wedding and my adventures on the road, and he filled in details about his stay in Germany. Along with the attraction, I experienced a low-grade sorrow, so like a fever that I wondered if I were coming down with the flu. At one point, I shivered and he looked over at me. "You okay?" he asked.

I stretched my hand out on the table and he covered it with his, lacing his fingers through mine. "What are we doing?" I asked.

"Good question. Why don't we talk about that? You go first."

I laughed, but the issue wasn't really funny and we both knew it. "Why'd you have to come back and stir things up? I was doing fine."

"What have I stirred up? We haven't done anything. We eat dinner. We have drinks. I sleep down. You sleep up. My knee's so bad, you're in no danger of unwanted advances. I couldn't make it up those stairs if my life depended on it."

"Is that the good news or the bad?"

"I don't know. You tell me," he said.

"I don't want to get used to you."

"A lot of women can't get used to me. You're one of the few who seems remotely interested," he said, smiling slightly.

Here's a word to the wise: In the midst of a tender discussion with one woman, don't mention another one—especially in the plural. It's bad policy. The minute he said it, I had this sudden vision of a long line of females with me standing not even close to the front of the pack. I could feel my smile fade and I retreated into silence like a turtle encountering a dog.

His look became cautious. "What's wrong?"

"Nothing. I'm fine. What makes you think there's anything wrong?"

"Let's don't talk at cross-purposes," he said. "You obviously have something to say, so why don't you say it?"

"I don't want to. It doesn't matter."

"Kinsey."

"What."

"Come on. Just say it. There's no penalty for being honest."

"I don't know how to say it. You're here for four days and what am I supposed to do with that? I'm not good at being left. It's the story of my life. Why get enmeshed when all it means is I get to have my heart ripped out?"

He lifted his eyebrows, shrugging with his face. "I don't know what to tell you. I can't promise to stay. I've never stayed in one place for more than six months max. Why can't we live in the present? Why does everything have to have a guarantee attached?"

"I'm not talking about guarantees."

"I think you are," he said. "You want a lien against the future, when the fact is you don't know any more than I do about what's coming next."

"Well, that's true and I'm not arguing that. All I'm saying is I don't want to get involved in an on-again-off-again relationship, which is what this is."

Dietz's expression was pained. "I won't lie. I can't pretend I'll stay when I know I won't. What good would that do?"

I could feel my frustration rise. "I don't want you to pretend and I'm not asking you to promise. I'm just trying to be honest."

"About what?"

"About everything. People have rejected me all my life. Sometimes it's death or desertion. Infidelity, betrayal. You name it. I've experienced every form of emotional treachery there is. Well, big deal. Everybody's suffered something in life and so what? I'm not sitting around feeling sorry for myself, but I'd have to be a fool to lay myself open to that shit again."

"I understand that. I hear you and believe me, I don't want to be the one to cause you pain. This is not about you. It's about me. I'm restless by nature. I hate to feel trapped. That's how I am. Pen me in and I'll tear the place apart trying to get out," he said. "My people were nomads. We were always on the move. Always on the road. We lived out of suitcases. To me, being in one spot is oppressive. You want to talk about death. It's the worst. When I was growing up, if we stayed in one town for long, my old man would get busted. He'd end up in county jail or in the hospital or the local drunk tank. Any school I attended, I was always the new kid and I'd have to fight my way across the school yard just to stay alive. The happiest day of my life was the day we hit the road again."

"Free at last," I interjected.

"That's right. It's not that I might not want to stay. It's that I'm incapable of it."

"Oh, right. 'Incapable.' Well, that explains it. You're excused," I said.

"Don't be so touchy. You know what I mean. God almighty, I'm not proud of myself. I don't relish the fact that I'm a rolling stone. I just don't want to kid myself and I don't want to kid you."

"Thank you. That's great. In the meantime, I'm sure you have ways of amusing yourself."

He squinted. "Where did that come from?"

"This is hopeless," I said. "I don't know why we even bother with this. You're addicted to wandering and I'm rooted in place. You can't stay and I can't leave because I love where I am. This is your biennial interlude and I'm here for the duration, which means I'm probably doomed to a lifetime of guys like you."

" 'Guys like *me?*' That's nice. What does that mean?"

"Just what it says. Emotionally claustrophobic. You're a basket case. So as long as I'm attracted to guys like you, I can bypass my own—" I stopped short, feeling like one of those cartoon dogs, skidding on a cartoon floor.

"Your own what?"

"None of your business," I said. "Let's drop the conversation. I should have kept my mouth shut. I end up sounding like a whiner, which is not what I intend."

"You're always so worried about sounding like a whiner," he said. "Who cares if you whine? Be my guest."

"Oh, *now* you say that."

"Say what?" he said, exasperated.

I assumed an attitude of patience that I scarcely felt. "One of the first things you ever said to me was that you wanted—how did you phrase it—'obedience without whining.' You said very few women ever mastered that."

"*I* said that?"

"Yes, you did. I've tried very hard ever since not to whine in your presence."

"Don't be ridiculous. I didn't mean it that way," he said. "I don't even remember saying it, but I was probably talking about something else. Anyway, don't change the subject. I don't want to leave it on this note. As long as the issue's on the table, let's get it settled."

"What's to settle? We can't settle anything. There's no way to resolve it, so let's drop the whole business. I'm sorry I brought it up. I've already got this ongoing family nonsense. Maybe I'm upset about that."

"What nonsense? You're related to these people, so what's the problem?"

"I don't want to get into it. Aside from whining, I hate to feel like I'm repeating myself."

"How can you repeat yourself when you never told me to begin with?"

I ran a hand through my hair and stared down at the tabletop. I'd been hoping to avoid the subject, but the topic did seem safer than discussing our relationship, whatever that consisted of. I couldn't come up with any rational defense of my reluctance to engage with this newfound family of mine. I just didn't want to do it. Finally, I said, "I guess I don't like to be pressured. They're so busy trying to make up for lost time. Why can't they just mind their own business? I'm not comfortable with all this buddy-buddy stuff. You know how stubborn I get when I'm pushed."

"Why did you agree to work for that attorney then? Isn't she your cousin?"

"Well, yes, but I didn't *intend* to agree. I intended to turn her down, but then greed and curiosity got the better of me. I have a living to earn and I didn't want to refuse out of perversity. I know I'll regret it, but I'm into it now so there's no sense beating myself up."

"Sounds harmless enough on the face of it."

"It's not harmless. It's annoying. And besides, that isn't the point. The point is, I'd like for them to respect my boundaries."

"What boundaries? She hired you to do a job. As long as you get paid, that's the end of it."

"Let's hope. Besides, it's not her so much as the other two. Liza and Pam. If I give an inch, they'll invade my space."

"Oh, bullshit. That's California psychobabble. You can't live your life like a radio talk show."

"What do you know? I don't notice you all cozied up to your family."

I could see him flinch. His expression shifted abruptly to one of injury and irritation. "Low blow. What I say about my kids, I don't want you throwing back in my face."

"You're right. I'm sorry. I withdraw the remark."

"Withdraw the knife and the wound's still there," he snapped. "What's the matter with you? You're so bristly these days. You're doing everything you can to keep me at arm's length."

"I am not," I said, and then I stared at him, squinting. "Is that true?"

"Well, look at your behavior. I haven't even been here two days and we're already fighting. What's that about? I didn't travel all this way to pick a fight with you. I wanted to see you. I was excited we'd have time together. Hell. If I'd wanted to fight, I could have stayed with Naomi."

"Why didn't you? I don't mean the question in a mean-hearted way, but I'm curious. What happened?"

"Oh, who knows? I have my version, she has hers. Sometimes I think relationships have a natural lifespan. Ours ran out. That's all it was. The explanations come afterwards when you try to make sense of it. Let's get back to you. What's going on in your head?"

"I'd rather fight than feel nothing."

"Those are your only two options?"

"That's what it feels like, but I couldn't say for sure."

He reached out and gave my hair a tug. "What am I going to do with you?"

"What am I going to do with *you?*" I replied.

7

When we returned to the apartment at ten-fifteen, Henry's kitchen light was on. Dietz said his knee was killing him, so he let himself into the apartment where he intended to take a couple of pain pills, prop his feet up, and put his ice pack to work. I said I'd be along momentarily. Our conversation at Rosie's hadn't really gone anywhere. I couldn't bear to continue and I couldn't bear behaving as though the subject hadn't been broached. I didn't know what I wanted from him and I wasn't sure how to say it anyway, so I just ended up sounding needy. My general policy is this: If your mind isn't open, keep your mouth shut, too.

I knocked on Henry's backdoor, waving at him through the window when he looked up at me. He was sitting in his rocking chair with the evening paper and his glass of Jack Daniel's. He smiled and waved back, setting the paper aside so he could let me in. He had the heat turned up and the inside air was not only warm, but deliciously scented with yesterday's cinnamon rolls.

"This feels great. It's really cold out there," I said. The kitchen table was covered with old black-and-white photographs sorted into piles. I glanced at them briefly as I pulled out a kitchen chair and turned my attention to him. From my point of view, Henry Pitts is perfection—smart, good-natured, and responsible—with the cutest legs I've ever seen. He's been my landlord for five years, since the day I spotted the ad for the apartment in a Laundromat. Henry was looking for a long-term tenant who was clean and quiet; no children, loud parties, or small, yapping dogs. As a lifelong mobile-home inhabitant, I was addicted to compact spaces, but ready to limit contact with a lot of close, unruly neighbors. Trailer-park life, for all its virtues, entails an intimate acquaintance with other people's private business. Since I make a living as a snoop, I'd just as soon keep my personal affairs to myself. The converted single-car garage Henry was offering was better than my fantasies and affordable as well. Since then, the place had been bombed and rebuilt, the interior fitted out in teak and as cleverly designed as a ship's.

From the outset, Henry and I established just enough of a relationship to suit us both. Over the years, he's managed to civilize me to some extent and I'm certainly more agreeable now than I was back then. Little by little, we forged the bond between us until now I consider him the exemplary mix of friend and generic family member.

"You want a cup of tea?" he asked.

"No, thanks. I just stopped to say hi before I hit the sack. Are these family pictures?" I asked, picking one at random.

"That's the claim," he said. "Nell sent me those. She came across two boxes of old family photographs, but none are labeled. No names, no dates. She hasn't any idea who these people are and neither do the other sibs. What a mess. Take my word for it. You should mark all your photographs, even if it's just a quick note on the back. You might know who's who, but nobody else will."

"Do they look familiar to you?"

"A few." He took the print I was looking at and squinted as he held it to the light. I peered over his shoulder. The woman in the picture must have been in her twenties, with a broad, bland face and hair drawn back in a bun. She wore a white middy blouse, with a calf-length skirt, dark stockings, and flat, dark shoes with a bow across the instep. Standing beside her was a glum-faced girl of eight with a drop-waist sailor dress and ankle-high lace-up shoes. "I believe this is a picture of my mother's younger sister, Augusta, taken in Topeka, Kansas, back in 1915. The child's name was Rebecca Rose, if memory serves. She and her mother both died in the big influenza epidemic of 1918." He picked up another one. "This is my mother with my grandfather Tilmann. I'm surprised Nell didn't recognize them except her eyesight's fading. Now that I think of it, I'm not sure why it matters. None of us have children, so once we're gone, it won't make any difference who these people are."

"Well, that seems sad. Why don't you put 'em in an album and pass them on to me? I'll pretend they're mine. What was his first name?"

"Klaus. My mother's name was Gudrun." The man staring fixedly at the camera must have been in his late seventies, the daughter beside him in her fifties by the look of her. I said, "What's the name Tilmann. Is that German? I somehow imagined you were all Swedes or Finns."

"Oh no, we're not Scandinavian. They're gloomy sorts, in my opinion. The Tilmanns were good German stock. Headstrong, autocratic, vigorous, and exacting. Some would say impossible, but that's a matter of interpretation. Longevity is genetic and don't ever let anybody tell you otherwise. I read those articles about folks who live to be a hundred. They all try to take credit, claim it's because they smoke or don't smoke, eat yogurt, take vitamins, or a tablespoon of vinegar a day. What nonsense. War and accidents excepted, you live a long time because you come from other people who live a long time. You have to take responsibility. You can't subject yourself to any kind of gross mistreatment. My mother lived to be a hundred and three and I imagine the remaining five of us will live that long as well."

"You certainly seem to be in good shape. Nell's what, ninety-six? And you have your eighty-sixth birthday coming up on Valentine's Day."

Henry nodded, making a motion as if to knock on wood. "We're healthy, in the main, though we're all shrinking down to some extent. We've talked about this and it's our contention that the shrinkage is nature's way of assuring you don't take up so much space in your coffin. You lighten up, too. Feels like taking air into your bones. Makes it easy on the pallbearers. And, of course, your faculties shut down. You get blind as a bat and your hearing fades. Charlie says it sounds like he's got a pillow on his head all the time these days. Get old, you might as well not worry about your dignity. Anybody talks about dignity for old folks has never been around one as far as I can tell. You can keep your spunk, but you have to give up your vanity early on. We're all in diapers. Well, I'm not, but then I'm the baby in the family. The rest of them leak any time they cough or laugh too hard.

"Nell says one reason she misses William so much now he's moved out here is because they can't play bridge like they used to. Have to play three-handed, which isn't as much fun. Lewis was thinking about asking a cousin to move in, but Nell won't tolerate another woman in the house. She says she's had her brothers to herself now for sixty years and she's not about to change. Nell says once she 'goes' they can do anything they want, depending on who's left."

"I can't believe they're still willing to endure the winters in Michigan. Why don't they all move out here? You could play all the bridge you want."

"There's talk of that. We'll just have to see. Nell has her ladies' luncheon group and she hates to leave them." Henry put the photo down and took his seat again. "Now then, how are you? I had a nice chat with your friend Dietz. He says you picked up some work."

"Actually, I finished it. One of those quickies you remember fondly when the tough ones come along," I said. I took a few minutes to fill him in on the search for Guy Malek.

Henry shook his head. "What's going to happen? Do you think he'll get his share of the estate?"

"Who knows? I don't always hear the end of it, but Tasha thinks they'll be able to work something out."

"How long will Dietz be here? I thought I'd have the two of you over for supper one night."

"Probably not long. He's on his way up to Santa Cruz to see his sons," I said.

"Well, let me know if he's still going to be here Saturday and I'll cook something special. We'll invite William and Rosie and Moza Lowenstein, if she's free."

By the time I let myself into my place, Dietz had fallen asleep in his underwear, slouched down in his chair, snoring lightly. The television set was on, the volume low, the channel tuned to a nature show about underwater shark attacks. Dietz had his leg propped up on the edge of the sofa bed, a blanket pulled up across his chest and shoulders. The partially melted ice pack had toppled to the floor. I put that ice pack in the freezer and took out a second one, laying it carefully across his knee without waking him. His kneecap was swollen, the bare flesh looking pale and vulnerable. I left him as he was, knowing he'd wake long before morning. He sleeps in fits and starts like an animal in the wild, and I knew from past experience he seldom manages to make it through the night without getting up at least twice.

I eased off my shoes and made my way up the spiral stairs. From above, I stared down at him. His lined face looked alien in sleep, as if sculptured in clay. I seldom saw him at ease. He was restless by nature, perpetually in motion, his features animated by the sheer force of his nervous energy. Even as I watched, he stirred himself awake, jerking upright with a look of disorientation. I could see him wince, reaching for the ice pack balanced on his distended joint. I stepped away from the loft rail and went into the bathroom, where I washed my face and brushed my teeth. It was no doubt the proximity to all that testosterone, but I could feel the murmur of sexuality at the base of my spine. I grabbed an oversized T-shirt from a hook on the bathroom door. I usually sleep in the nude, but it seemed like a bad idea.

Once ready for bed, I turned out the light and slipped under the quilt. I reached out and set my alarm, watching the digital clock flip from 11:04 to 11:05. Below, I could hear Dietz get up and move into the kitchen. The refrigerator door opened and closed. He took down a glass and poured himself a drink—wine, orange juice, or milk—something liquid at any rate. I heard him pull out a kitchen stool, followed by the rustle of newspaper. I wondered what he was thinking, wondered what would happen if I heard him climbing the stairs. Maybe I should have pulled on a robe and gone down to join him, thrown caution to the wind and to hell with the consequences, but it was not in my nature. Being single for so long had made me cautious about men. I stared up at the Plexiglas skylight above my bed, thinking about the risks involved in reaching out to him. Passion never lasts, but then what does? If you could have it all, but only briefly, would the rush of love be worth the price in pain? I could feel myself sinking into sleep as though weighted down with stones. I didn't rise again until 5:59 A.M.

I pulled on my sweats, preparing for my run as usual. Dietz was in the shower when I left the house, but I noticed with a pang he was in the process of packing. He'd laid the soft-sided suitcase open on the floor near the sofa bed, which he'd folded away. The blanket had been refolded and placed across one end. He'd piled the sheets he'd used near the washer. Maybe he felt his exodus would address my issues with him, minimizing the chances of my forming an attachment. What I noticed, perversely, was that, having felt nothing on his arrival, I was now afflicted with a stinging sense of loss at his departure. He'd been with me for two days and I was already suffering, so maybe I'd been smart not to take things any further. I'd been celibate for so long, what was another year without sex? I made an involuntary sound that might have been a whimper if I allowed myself such things.

I closed the door quietly behind me, breathing deeply as though the damp morning air might ease the fire in my chest. Having passed through the front gate, I paused while I stretched, keeping my mind a blank. In the last several years as a private investigator, I've developed a neat trick for shutting off my feelings. Like others who work in the "helping" professions—doctors and nurses, police officers, social workers, paramedics—emotional disconnection is sometimes the only way to function in the face of death with all its tacky variations. Originally, my detachment took several minutes of concentrated effort, but now I make the shift in the blink of an eye. Mental-health enthusiasts are quick to assure us that our psychological well-being is best served by staying in touch with our feelings, but *surely* they're not referring to the icky, unpleasant ones.

The run itself was unsatisfactory. The dawn was overcast, the sky a brooding gray unrelieved by any visible sunrise. Gradually, daylight overtook the lowering dark, but the whole of it had the bleached look of an old black-and-white photograph. My gait felt choppy and I never really hit my stride. The air was so chilly I couldn't even generate a decent sweat. I dutifully counted off the miles, feeling gratified to be doing it in spite of myself. Some days the discipline is an end in itself, a way of asserting the will in the face of life's little setbacks. I walked the half block home, carefully brushing aside any slovenly sentiment.

Dietz was sitting at the counter when I got in. He'd put on a pot of coffee and set out my cereal bowl. His bowl was already washed, rinsed, and drying in the dish rack. His suitcase, fully zipped, was waiting by the door along with his garment bag. Through the open bathroom door, I could see he'd tidied the basin of all his personal possessions. The scent of soap mingled with his aftershave, a damp male perfume permeating everything.

"I thought it might be easier if I took off," he said.

"Sure, no problem. I hope you're not doing it on my account."

"No, no. You know me. I'm not that good at staying put," he said. "Anyway, you probably have a lot of work to do."

"Oh, tons," I said. "You're heading up to Santa Cruz?"

"Eventually, yes. I'll drive on up the coast, maybe spend a day in Cambria. With this knee, I have to break up the trip, anyway. You know, get out and stretch every hour or so. Keep it warm and loose. Otherwise, it locks up."

"What time are you taking off?"

"Whenever you leave for work."

"Well, great. I'll just grab a shower then and you can hit the road."

"Take your time. I'm in no hurry," he said.

"I can see that," I remarked, as I headed up to the loft. This time he didn't ask if I was mad. This was good because, in truth, I was furious. Under the fury was the old familiar pain. Why does everyone end up leaving me? What did I ever do to them? I went through my morning routine as efficiently as possible, flung on my clothes, and ate my cereal without pausing to read the paper. To demonstrate my indifference to his abrupt departure, I took out fresh sheets and asked him to help me remake the sofa bed. I hoped the implication was that some other guy was lined up for bed space as soon as he left. Neither of us said much and what we said was transactional. "Where's the other pillowcase?" About like that.

Once the sofa was redone, he took his suitcase to the car and came back for the garment bag. I walked him out to the curb and we exchanged one of those insincere kisses with the sound effects attached. *Mmch!* He fired up his Porsche and I dutifully waved as he roared off down the street. You little shit, I thought.

I went into the office, ignoring a faint tendency to tear up for no reason. The day yawned in front of me like a sinkhole in the street. This was just what it felt like when he left before. Now how does this happen to someone of my rare spunk and independence? I played a few rounds of solitaire, paid some bills, and balanced my checkbook. Anxiety whispered in my gut like a stomachache. When the phone finally rang just before lunch, I snatched up the receiver, absurdly grateful at the interruption.

"Kinsey. This is Donovan. How are you?"

"Gee, I'm just fine. How are you?"

"Well enough. Uh, listen, we got your message and we'd like to compliment you on a job well done. Tasha had to fly back to San Francisco this morning, but she said she didn't think you'd mind giving us the information firsthand. Could you stop by the house for a drink late this afternoon?"

"Well, sure. I could do that. I was going to type up my report and put it in the mail, but I can give you a rundown in person if you'd prefer."

"I'd appreciate that. I expect Jack and Bennet will want to be there as well. That way, if they have questions, you can fill us all in at the same time and save yourself the repetition. Would five-thirty be convenient?"

"Fine with me," I said.

"Good. We'll look forward to seeing you."

After I hung up, I could feel myself shrug. I had nothing against an informal report as long as I didn't somehow get sucked into the family drama. Aside from Guy, I wasn't crazy about the Malek brothers. I happened to believe Guy had changed his wicked ways, so maybe I could do him a service and convince the others. Not that it was any of my business how the monies were distributed, but if there were any lingering questions about his "worthiness," I certainly had an opinion. Besides, with Dietz now gone, I didn't have anything better to do.

I skipped lunch and spent the afternoon cleaning my office. Lonnie Kingman had a maintenance crew that serviced the premises weekly on Friday afternoons, but it felt therapeutic to get in there and scrub. I even spent twenty minutes dusting the artificial ficus plant someone had once mistaken for real. The space I occupied had originally been a conference room with a full "executive" bathroom attached. I found a plastic bucket, sponges, cleansers, a toilet brush, and mop and entertained myself mightily killing imaginary germs. My method of coping with depression is to take on chores so obnoxious and disgusting that reality seems pleasant by comparison. By three o'clock, I smelled of sweat and household bleach and I'd forgotten what I was so unhappy about. Well, actually, I remembered, but I didn't give a shit.

Having sanitized the suite, I locked the door, stripped off my clothes, hopped in the executive shower, and scrubbed myself. I dressed again in the same jeans, pulling on a fresh turtleneck from the ready supply I keep handy for sudden travel. What's life without a toothbrush and clean underpants? I typed up the official version of my encounter with Guy Malek, tucking one copy in my office files, another in my handbag. The third I addressed to Tasha Howard at her San Francisco office. The end. Finito. Done, done, done. This was the last job I'd ever take from her.

By 5:25, dressed in my best (and only) wool tweed blazer, I drove through the entrance to the Malek estate. It was close to dark by then, the winter-shortened days still characterized by early twilights. My headlights swept in a forlorn arc across the stucco wall surrounding the fifteen-acre property. Along the rim of the wall, three strands of rusted barbed wire had been strung years ago, broken now in places and looking singularly ineffective. Who knows what intruders were anticipated back then? A chilly wind had picked up and the darkened treetops swayed and shivered, whispering together about things unseen. There were lights on in the house, two upstairs windows illuminated in pale yellow where much of the first floor was dark.

The housekeeper had neglected to turn on the outside lights. I parked in the turnaround and picked my way across the cobblestone courtyard to the shadowy portico that sheltered the entranceway in front. I rang the bell and waited, crossing my arms for warmth. The porch light was finally flipped on and Myrna opened the door a crack.

"Hi, Myrna. Kinsey Millhone. I was here the other day. Donovan invited me for drinks."

Myrna didn't exactly break into song at the news. Apparently, advanced classes in Housekeeper's Training School cautioned the students not to give expression to sudden bursts of joy. In the two days since I'd seen her last, she'd renewed the dye job in her hair and the whole of it was now a white blond that looked like it would be cold to the touch. Her uniform consisted of a gray top worn over matching gray pants. I would have bet money the waistband was unbuttoned underneath the tunic. "This way," she said. Her crepe-soled shoes squeaked slightly on the polished parquet floor.

A woman called down from somewhere above our heads. "Myrna? Was that the front door? We're expecting someone for drinks." I glanced up, following the sound of her voice. A brunette in her late thirties was leaning on the stair rail above our heads. She caught sight of me and brightened. "Oh, hi. You must be Kinsey. You want to come on up?"

Myrna veered off without another word, disappearing into the rear of the house as I climbed the stairs.

Christie held out her hand when I reached the upper landing. "I'm Christie Malek. Nice to meet you," she said as we shook hands. "I take it you've met Myrna."

"More or less," I said. I took her in at a glance, like an instant Polaroid. She was a fine-featured brunette with shiny dark hair, worn shoulder length. She was very slender, wearing jeans and a bulky black-ribbed sweater that came down almost to her knees. She had the sleeves rolled back and her wrists were thin, her fingers long and cool. Her eyes were small, a dark penetrating blue, beneath a lightly feathered brow. Her teeth were as perfect as a mouthwash ad's. The absence of eye makeup gave her a recessive, slightly anxious air, though her manner was friendly and her smile was warm enough. "Donovan called to say he'd be a few minutes late. Jack's on his way home and Bennet's around some place. I'm just going through Bader's papers and I'd love some company."

Still talking to me, she turned and moved toward the master bedroom, which I could see through an open doorway. "We're still looking for the missing will, among other things. Ever hopeful," she added wryly.

"I thought Bennet was going to do that."

"This is how Bennet does things. He loves to delegate."

I hoped there was a touch of irony in her tone. I couldn't be sure so I kept my mouth shut.

The suite we entered was enormous; two substantial rooms separated by a pair of doors that had been pushed into their respective wall pockets. We passed through the outer room, which had been furnished as a bedroom. The walls were padded fabric, covered in rose-colored silk with a watered sheen to the finish. The carpet was off-white, a dense, cut pile. Pale, heavy drapes had been pulled back to reveal the leaded glass windows that looked out onto the cobblestone entrance at the front of the house. There was a marble fireplace on the wall to the left. Two matching sofas were arranged on either side of it, plump, upholstered pieces covered in a subdued floral chintz. The four-poster bed had been flawlessly made, not a ripple or a wrinkle in the snowy-white silk coverlet. The surface of the bed table seemed unnaturally bare, as if once-personal items had now been hidden from sight. It might have been my imagination, but the room seemed to harbor the lingering scent of sickness. I could see that closets were being emptied, the contents—suits and dress shirts—packed into large cardboard boxes supplied by the local Thrift Store Industries downtown.

"This is gorgeous," I said.

"Isn't it?"

Beyond the sliding doors, a home office had been set up, with a large walnut desk and antique wooden file cabinets. The ceilings in both rooms were twelve feet high, but this was by far the cozier of the two. A fire had been laid in a second marble fireplace and Christie paused to add a log to an already snapping blaze. The walls here were paneled in walnut as dark and glossy as fudge. I could see a copier, a fax machine, computer, and a printer arranged on the built-in shelves on either side of the fireplace. A paper shredder stood on one side of the desk, its green On button lighted. I could see printed acknowledgments stacked up waiting to be addressed to those who'd sent flowers to the funeral.

Christie returned to the desk where she'd emptied the contents of two drawers into banker's boxes that she'd labeled with a black marker. There were two big plastic garbage bags bulging with discarded papers. Thick files were stacked on the desktop and a number of empty file folders were strewn across the carpet. This was the kind of task I knew well, classifying the odds and ends left behind by the dead. Below, in the courtyard, we could hear a motorcycle cruise in, the engine being revved once more before it was silenced.

Christie cocked her head. "I hear the Harley. Sounds like Jack's home."

"How's it going so far?"

Her expression was a wry mix of skepticism and despair. "Bader was supremely organized for the most part, but he must have lost his enthusiasm for jobs like this. Look at all this stuff. I swear, if I'm ever diagnosed as terminal, I'm going to clean out my files before I get too sick to care. What if you kept pornographic pictures or something like that? I'd hate to think of someone sorting through my private affairs."

"Nothing in my life is that interesting," I said. "You want help?"

"Not really, but I could use the moral support," she said. "I've been in here for hours. I have to look at every single piece of paper and figure out if it's worth saving, though most aren't as far as I can tell. I mean, what do I know? Anything I'm not sure about, I put in one pile. The really junky stuff, I go ahead and shove in a garbage bag. I don't dare shred a thing and I'm afraid to toss much. I know Bennet. As sure as I pitch something, he tears in here and wants to know where it is. He's done that to me twice and it was just dumb luck the trash hadn't been picked up. I'm out there in the dark, like a bag lady, pulling crumpled papers out of the garbage can. This third pile is everything that looks important. For instance, here's something you might like." She picked up a file from the stack on top of the desk and handed it to me. "Bader must have put this together back in the early sixties."

A quick glance inside revealed a collection of newspaper clippings related to Guy's past misbehavior. I read one at random, an article dating back to 1956 detailing the arrest of two juveniles, boys ages fourteen and thirteen, who were believed to be responsible for a spree of graffiti vandalism. One of the teens was booked into Juvenile Hall, the other released to his parents. There must have been twenty-five such snippets. In some cases, the authorities withheld the names because the boy or boys arrested were still minors. In other articles, Guy Malek was identified by name.

"I wonder why Bader kept clippings. It seems odd," I said.

"Maybe to remind himself why he disinherited the kid. I figure Bennet will want 'em for ammunition if it comes down to that. It's exhausting just trying to make these decisions."

"Quite a job," I said and then shifted the subject matter. "You know, it occurred to me that since the two wills were drawn up only three years apart, the two witnesses for the first might have been witnesses for the second will, too. Especially if they were paralegals or law clerks working in the attorney's office."

She looked at me with interest. "Good point. You'll have to mention that to Donovan. None of us are anxious to see five million bucks flying out the window."

There was a tap at the door and we both turned to see that Myrna had reappeared. "Donovan's home. He asked me to serve the hors d'oeuvres in the living room."

"Tell him we'll be down in a second, as soon as I wash my hands. Oh, and see if you can round up the other two."

Myrna took in the request, murmured something inaudible, and withdrew from the room.

Christie shook her head, lowering her voice a notch. "She may be on the glum side, but she's the only person in the house who doesn't argue with everyone."

8

Lights were on and Donovan was in the living room when Christie and I came downstairs. He'd changed out of his work clothes, pulling on a heavy cream-colored knit sweater over casual pants. He'd exchanged his dress shoes for a pair of sheepskin slippers that made his feet look huge. A fire had been laid and he was poking at the logs, turning a bulky wedge of oak so that its uppermost side would catch. Donovan picked up another piece of wood and thunked it on top. A shower of sparks flew up the chimney. He replaced the fire screen and wiped his hands on his handkerchief, glancing over at me. "I see you've met Christie. We appreciate your coming over. Keeps it simpler all around. Can I make you a drink? We've got just about anything you'd want."

"A glass of Chardonnay would be fine."

"I'll get it," Christie said promptly. She moved over to a sideboard crowded with liquor bottles. A bottle of Chardonnay had been chilling in a cooler beside a clear Lucite ice bucket and an assortment of glasses. She began to peel the foil from the neck of the wine bottle, with a look at Donovan. "You having wine?"

"Probably with dinner. I think I'll have a martini first. Gin is Bennet's winter drink," he added as an aside to me.

Ah, the seasonal alcoholic. What a nice idea. Gin in the winter, maybe vodka in spring. Summer would be tequila and he could round out the autumn with a little bourbon or scotch. While she opened the wine, I took a momentary survey.

Like the bedroom above, this room was immense. The twelve-foot ceiling was rimmed with ten-inch crown molding, the walls papered in a narrow blue-and-cream stripe that had faded with the years. The pale Oriental carpet had to be seventeen feet wide and probably twenty-five feet long. The furniture had been arranged in two groupings. At the far end of the room, four wing chairs faced one another near the front windows. Closer to the center of the room, three large sofas formed a U in front of the fireplace. All of the side pieces—an armoire, an escritoire, and two carved and inlaid wooden tables—were the sort I'd seen in antique stores, heavy, faintly fussy, with price tags that made you squint because you thought you'd read them wrong.

Christie returned with two glasses of wine and handed one to me. She took a seat on one of the sofas and I sat down across from her with a murmured "thanks." The blue floral pattern was faded to a soft white, the fabric threadbare along the arms and the cushion fronts. There was a large brass bowl filled with fresh flowers and several copies of *Architectural Digest* lined up on the square glass coffee table in the crook of the U. There was also an untidy stack of what looked like condolence cards. While I was thinking about it, I took out my typed report and placed it on the table in front of me. I'd leave it for Donovan so he'd have a copy for his files.

I heard footsteps in the hall and the sound of voices. Jack and Bennet came into the living room together. Whatever they'd been discussing, their expressions were now neutral, conveying nothing but benign interest at the sight of me. Bennet wore a running suit of some silky material that rustled when he walked. Jack looked as if he'd just come in off the golf course, his hair still disheveled from the imprint of his visor. He wore a bright orange sweater vest over a pink short-sleeved golf shirt and his gait tended to a lilt as if he were still wearing cleats. Jack poured himself a scotch and water as dark as iced tea while Bennet made a pitcher of martinis that he stirred with a long glass wand. I made note of his vermouth-to-gin ratio—roughly two parts per million. He poured one for himself and one for Donovan, adding olives to both. He brought the martini pitcher over to the coffee table and set it down within range.

While drinks were being poured, various pleasantries were exchanged, none of them heartfelt. As with tobacco, the rituals of alcohol seemed to be a stalling technique until those assembled could get themselves psychologically situated. I had an odd sensation in my chest, the same itch of anxiety I'd felt before a third-grade dance recital in which I played a bunny, not a specialty of mine. My aunt Gin was ill and unable to attend, so I'd been forced to do my hippy-hopping in front of countless alien adults, who didn't seem to find me winsome. My legs were too skinny and my fake ears wouldn't stand up. The brothers Malek watched me with about the same enthusiasm. Donovan took a seat next to Christie on the couch across from me while Jack sat facing the fireplace with Bennet on his left.

It was interesting to see the three brothers in the same room together. Despite the similarities in their coloring, their faces were very different, Bennet's the more so because of his beard and mustache. Donovan and Jack were built along finer lines though neither was as appealing as their errant brother, Guy. Jack leaned forward and began to sift idly through the sympathy cards.

I thought Donovan was on the verge of asking for my report when Myrna came into the room with assorted edibles on a serving tray. The tray itself was the size of a manhole cover, very plain, probably sterling silver, and distinctly tarnished along the edges. The hors d'oeuvres, in addition to what looked like Cheez Whiz on saltines, consisted of a bowl of peanuts and a bowl of unpitted green olives in brine. No one said a word until she'd departed, closing the door behind her.

Jack leaned forward. "What the fuck is this?"

Bennet laughed at the very moment he was swallowing a mouthful of martini. He made a snorting sound as he choked and I saw gin dribble out his nose. He coughed into his handkerchief while Jack shot a smile in his direction. I bet as children they'd paused in the midst of dinner, opening their mouths to one another to exhibit masticated food.

Christie flashed them a look of disapproval. "It's Enid's night off. Would you quit with the criticism? Myrna's a nurse. She was hired to look after Dad, not to wait on the two of you. We're lucky she stayed on and you bloody well know it. Nobody else lifts a finger around here except me."

"Thanks for setting the record straight, Christie. You're a fuckin' peach," Jack said.

"Knock it off," Donovan said. "Could we hold off on this until we hear from her?" He grabbed a handful of peanuts, eating one at a time as his focus returned to me. "You want to fill us in?"

I took a few minutes to detail the means by which I'd managed to locate Guy Malek. Without mentioning Darcy Pascoe or California Fidelity Insurance, I played out the steps that led to the information on his identification card. I'll admit I stretched it out, making it sound more problematic than it had actually been. "As nearly as I can tell, your brother's cleaned up his act. He's working as the custodian for the Jubilee Evangelical Church. I gather he doubles as a handyman for various people in Marcella. He says he's the only one in town doing home maintenance, so he earns decent money, by his standards. His lifestyle is simple, but he's doing okay."

Donovan said, "Is he married?"

"I didn't ask if he was married, but he didn't seem to be. He never mentioned a wife. His housing's provided by the church in exchange for his services. The place is pretty funky, but he seems to manage all right. I grant you these are superficial judgments, but I didn't really stop to investigate."

Bennet shaved an olive with his teeth and placed the pit on a paper napkin. "Why Marcella? That's a dirt bucket of a place."

"The pastor of this fundamentalist church picked him up hitchhiking out on 101 the day he left home. Essentially, he's been in Marcella ever since. The church he joined seems pretty strict. No dancing, card playing, things like that. He did say he had a beer now and then, but no drugs. That's been for the better part of fifteen years."

"If you can believe him," Bennet said. "I don't know how much you could tell from the brief time you spent. You were there for what, an hour?"

"About that," I said. "I'm not exactly an amateur. I've dealt with addicts in the past and believe me, he didn't look like one. I can spot a liar, too."

"No offense," he said. "I'm skeptical by nature when it comes to him. He always put on a good show." He finished his martini, holding the glass by the stem. The last vestiges of the gin formed a distinct scallop along the rim. He reached for the pitcher and poured himself another drink.

"Who else did you talk to?" Donovan asked, reasserting his presence. He was clearly running the show and wanted to make sure Bennet remained aware of it. For his part, Bennet seemed more interested in his martini than the conversation. I could see the lines of tension in his face smooth out. His questions were meant to demonstrate his control of himself.

I shrugged. "I made one stop in town and mentioned Guy in passing to the woman who runs the general store. There couldn't be more than five or six hundred residents and I figure everyone there knows everybody else's business. She didn't bat an eye and had no comment about him one way or the other. The pastor and his wife seemed genuinely fond of him and spoke with some pride of the distance he's come. They could have been lying, putting on a show, but I doubt it. Most people aren't that good at improvising."

Jack picked up a cracker and lifted the dollop of Cheez Whiz off the surface like he was licking the filling from an Oreo. "So what's the deal? Is he born-again? Has he been baptized? Do you think he's accepted our Lord Jesus in his heart?" His sarcasm was offensive.

I turned to stare at him. "You have a problem with that?"

"Why would I have a problem? It's his life," Jack said.

Donovan shifted in his seat. "Anybody else have a question?"

Jack popped the cracker in his mouth and wiped his fingers on a napkin while he munched. "I think it's great. I mean, maybe he won't want the money. If he's such a good Christian, maybe he'll opt for the spiritual over the materialistic."

Bennet snorted with annoyance. "His being a Christian has nothing to do with it. He's penniless. You heard her. He's got nothing. He's flat broke."

"I don't know that he's broke. I never said that," I interjected.

Now it was Bennet's turn to stare. "You seriously think he's going to turn down a great big whack of dough?"

Donovan looked at me. "Good question," he said. "What's your feeling on the subject?"

"He never asked about the money. At the time I think he was more interested in the idea that you'd hired someone to find him. He seemed touched at first and then embarrassed when he realized he'd misunderstood."

"Misunderstood what?" Christie said.

"He thought I'd been asked to locate him because of family interest or concern. It became obvious pretty quickly that the point of the visit was to notify him of his father's death and advise him he was a possible beneficiary under the terms of Bader's will."

"Maybe if he thinks we're all kissy-kissy, he'll give up the money and opt for love instead," Jack suggested.

Donovan ignored him. "Did he say anything about talking to an attorney?"

"Not really. I told him to get in touch with Tasha, but she's the attorney for the estate and she's not going to advise him about that aspect of the situation. If he calls her, she'll refer him to a lawyer unless he already has one."

Donovan said, "In other words, what you're saying is we don't have any idea what he'll do."

Bennet spoke up. "Of course we do. There's no mystery. He wants the *money*. He's not a fool."

"How do you know what Guy wants?" Christie responded with a flash of irritation.

Bennet went right on. "Kinsey should have asked for his signature on a quitclaim. Get him signed off. Make a settlement before he has a chance to think too much."

Donovan said, "I asked Tasha about that. I suggested we draw up a disclaimer, thinking Kinsey could take it with her. Tasha nixed that. She said a disclaimer would be meaningless because he could always maintain later he wasn't properly represented or he was unduly influenced, overcome by the emotions of the moment, shit like that, which would make it useless. I thought her point was well taken. Tell the man his father's dead and then whip out a quitclaim? It's like waving a red flag in front of a bull."

Christie spoke up again, saying, "Kinsey had a good idea. She pointed out that since the two wills were drawn up just three years apart that the witnesses for the second will might have been the same as the ones for the first. If we can track down the witnesses, it's always possible one of them was aware of the provisions."

"Like a secretary or a paralegal?" Donovan asked.

"It's possible. Or maybe the clerk/typist acted as a witness. *Somebody* had to be involved in the preparation of that document," I said.

"If there was one," Jack said.

Donovan's mouth pulled down as he considered the point. "Worth a try."

"To what end?" Jack asked. "I'm not saying we shouldn't make the effort, but it probably won't do any good. You can be a witness to a will without being aware of what's in it. Besides, what if the second will left everything to Guy? Then we'd really be screwed."

Bennet was impatient. "Oh come on, Jack. Whose side are you on? At least the witnesses could testify the second will was signed. I heard Dad say half a dozen times Guy wasn't getting a thing—we all heard him say that—so wouldn't that make a difference?"

"Why should it? Dad had the will. He kept it in a file right upstairs. How do you know he didn't revoke it in the end? Suppose he tore it up before he died? He had notice enough. He knew his days were numbered."

"He would have told us," Bennet said.

"Not necessarily."

"Jesus, Jack. I'm telling you, he said Guy would get nothing. We've been over this a hundred times and he was adamant."

"It doesn't matter what he said. You know how he was when it came to Guy. He never stuck to his guns. *We* might have been forced to toe the mark, but not him."

Donovan cleared his throat and set his glass down with a sharp tap. "All right. Knock it off, you two. This is getting us nowhere. We've been through enough of this. Let's just see what Guy does. We might not have a problem. We don't know at this point. Tasha said she'd contact him if he doesn't get in touch with her first. I might drop him a note myself and we'll take it from there."

Bennet sat up straight. "Wait a minute. Who put you in charge? Why can't we discuss this? It concerns all of us."

"You want to discuss this? Fine. Go ahead," Donovan said. "We all know your opinion. You think Guy's a slimeball. You're completely antagonistic and with *that* attitude, you'll be pushing him right to the wall."

"You don't know any more about him than I do," Bennet said.

"I'm not talking about him. I'm talking about you. What makes you so sure he wants the money?"

"Because he hated us. That's why he left in the first place, isn't it? He'd do anything to get back at us and what better way than this?"

"You don't know that," Donovan said. "You don't know what went on back then. He may not harbor any ill will towards us at all. You go in there punching and he's going to go on the offensive."

"I never did anything to Guy. Why would he hate me?" Jack said blithely. He seemed amused at the fireworks between his two brothers and I wondered if he didn't habitually goad them.

Bennet snorted again and he and Jack locked eyes. Something flashed between them but I wasn't sure what.

Donovan intervened again with a warning look at both. "Could we stick to the subject? Anybody have something new to contribute?"

"Donovan runs the family. He's the king," Bennet said. He looked at me with the slightly liquid eyes of someone who's had too much to drink. I'd seen him suck down two martinis in less than fifteen minutes and who knew what he'd consumed before he entered the room? "The man thinks I'm a dick. He may pretend to be supportive, but he doesn't mean a word of it. He and my father never actually gave me enough money to succeed at anything. And then when I failed—when a business went under—they were quick to point out how I'd mismanaged it. Dad always undercut me and the notion that Guy can come along now and insist on his share is just more of the same as far as I'm concerned. Who's looking out for our interests? It ain't *him*," he said, jerking a thumb at Donovan.

"Wait a minute. Hold it! Where's that coming from?"

"I've never really stood up and asked for what's mine," Bennet said. "I should have insisted a long time ago, but I bought into the program, the story you and Dad cooked up. 'Here, Bennet, you can have this pittance. Do the best you can with this pathetic sum of money. Make something of yourself and there'll be more where that came from. You can't expect us to underwrite the whole venture.' Blah blah blah. That's all I ever heard."

Donovan squinted at him, shaking his head. "I don't believe this. Dad gave you hundreds of thousands of dollars and you pissed it all away. How many chances do you think you get? There isn't a bank in this town that would have given you the first *dime*—"

"Bullshit! That's bullshit. I've worked like a dog and you know it. Hell, Dad had a lot of business failures and so have you. Now suddenly I have to sit here and fuckin' justify every move I make—just to get a little seed money."

Donovan looked at him with disbelief. "Where's all the money your partners put in? You blew that, too. You're so busy playing big shot, you're not tending to business. Half of what you do is outright fraudulent and you know it. Or if you don't, more's the pity because you'll end up in jail."

Bennet pointed a finger, poking the air repeatedly as if it were an elevator button. "Hey, I'm the one taking risks. I'm the one with my ass on the line. You never put yourself out there on the firing line. You played it safe. You were Daddy's little boy, the little piggy who stayed home and did exactly what Daddy said. And now you want credit for being such an all-fired success. Well, fuck that. To hell with you."

"Watch the *f* word. Ladies present," Jack said in a singsong tone.

"Shut up, you little piss. No one's talking to you!"

Christie cast a look in my direction and then raised a hand, saying, "Hey, fellas. Couldn't we postpone this until later? Kinsey doesn't want to sit here and listen to this. We asked her to have a drink, not a ringside seat."

I took my cue from her and used the opportunity to get to my feet. "I think I should leave you alone to discuss this, but I really don't think you need to worry about Guy. He seems like a nice man. That's the bottom line from my perspective. I hope everything works out."

A paragraph of awkward verbiage ensued: apologies for the outburst, hasty explanations of the strain everyone was under in the wake of Bader's death. Personally, I thought they were a bunch of ill-mannered louts and if my bill had been paid I might have told them as much. As it was, they assured me no offense was intended and I assured them, in turn, that none had been taken. I can fib with the best of them when there's money at stake. We shook hands all around. I was thanked for my time. I thanked them for the drink and took my leave of them.

"I'll walk out with you," Christie said.

There was a moment of quiet as we left the living room. I hadn't realized I was holding my breath until the door closed behind us and I could suck in some fresh air.

"Let me grab a jacket," Christie said as we crossed the foyer. She made a detour to the closet, pulling on a dark wool car coat as we passed into the night air.

The temperature had dropped and a dampness seemed to rise up from the cobblestones. The exterior lights were now on, but the illumination was poor. I could see the dim shape of my car, parked on the far side of the courtyard, and we headed in that direction. The lighted front windows threw truncated panels of yellow on the driveway in front of us. In the living room, the three Malek brothers were more than likely engaged in fisticuffs by now.

"Thanks for getting me out of there."

"I'm sorry you had to see that. What a zoo," she said. She shoved her hands in her pockets. "That goes on all the time and it drives me insane. It's like living in the middle of a giant preschool free-for-all. They're all three years old. They're still slugging it out over the same toy truck. The tension in this house is unreal half the time."

"Bennet's drinking doesn't help."

"It's not just that. I came into the marriage thinking I was going to be part of a loving family. I never had any brothers and I thought the idea was keen. They seemed close at first. I mean, they sure fooled me. I guess I should have figured out that three grown men still living together under Daddy's roof didn't exactly speak of mental health, but what did I know? My family's so screwed up, I wouldn't know a healthy one if it leapt up and bit me. I wanted kids. Looks like I got 'em," she remarked in a wry aside. "I hate sitting around watching these 'boys' bicker and connive. You ought to see them operate. They fight over absolutely everything. Anything that comes up, they all instantly take the most disparate positions possible. Then they all take sides and form these temporary coalitions. It'll be Donovan and Jack against Bennet one day. The next day, Bennet and Jack form a team against Donovan. The allegiances vary according to the subject matter, but there's never accord. There's never any sense of all for one and one for all. Everybody wants to be right—morally superior—and at the same time, everybody feels completely misunderstood."

"Makes me glad to be an orphan."

"I'm with you on *that* one." She paused with a smile. "Or maybe I'm just annoyed because none of them are ever on my side. I live with a perpetual stomachache."

"You don't have any kids?"

"Not yet. I keep trying, but of course I can't seem to get pregnant in this atmosphere. I'm coming up on forty so if something doesn't happen soon, it's going to be too late."

"I thought women were having babies into their fifties these days."

"Not me. Forget it. Life's hard enough as it is. I mean, what kid would volunteer to come into a house like *this?* It's disgusting."

"Why do you stay?"

"Who says I'll stay? I told Donovan last fall, I said, 'One more round, buddy, and I'm outta here.' So what happens next? Bader up and dies. I don't feel I can walk out when things are such a mess. Also, I suppose I still harbor the dim hope that things'll work out somehow."

"I'm sure my finding Guy couldn't be a help," I said.

"I don't know about that. At least now maybe the three of them will gang up against *him.* In the end, that might be the only issue they agree on."

I glanced toward the lighted windows of the living room. "You call *that* 'agreement'?"

"Oh, they'll get around to it. There's nothing like the common enemy to unify the troops. The truth is, Guy's the one I feel sorry for. They'll take him to the cleaners if they have half a chance and from what you say, he's the best of the lot."

"Donovan seems okay," I said.

"Ha. That's what I thought, too. He puts up a good front, but that's all that is. He's learned how to function in the business world so he's got a little more polish. I'm sure nobody said so, but I know they were impressed with the job you did."

"Well, I appreciate that, but at this point, these people don't need a PI—."

"They need a referee," she laughed. "Tasha didn't do you any favors when she got you involved in this. I'm sorry you had to see 'em at their worst. Then again, at least you can appreciate what I have to live with."

"Don't worry about it. It's finished business," I said.

We said our good-nights and I slid in behind the wheel, taking a few minutes to get my car warmed up. The residual tension had left me feeling icy cold and I drove home with the VW heater level pulled to maximum effect. This consisted of a thin tongue of warm air licking at the bottoms of my shoes. The rest of me was freezing, a cotton turtleneck and wool blazer providing little in the way of insulation. As I turned onto my street, I gave brief consideration to having dinner up at Rosie's. I hadn't managed to eat so much as an unpitted olive at the Maleks' during the cocktail hour. I'd pictured sumptuous canapés that I could chow down instead of dinner, but the uproar had made even the Cheez Whiz seem less than appetizing. At the back of my mind, I knew I was avoiding the idea of going home to an empty apartment. Better now than later. It was only going to get worse.

I parked my car close to the corner and hoofed my way back to Henry's driveway. A dense fog had begun to blow in from the beach and I was heartened by the fact that I'd left a light on in my living room. At least letting myself in wouldn't feel so much like breaking and entering. I passed through the squeaky gate with my house key at the ready, unlocked my door, and tossed my handbag on the kitchen counter. I heard the downstair's toilet flush and a thrill of fear washed over me. Then the bathroom door opened and Robert Dietz walked out, looking as startled as I was. "I didn't hear you come in," he said. "I forgot to give back your key."

"What are you doing here? I thought you left."

"I got as far as Santa Maria and had to come back. I was halfway down the street and I missed you like crazy. I don't want us leaving each other on a bad note."

I felt a pain in my chest, something fragile and sharp that made me take a deep breath. "I don't see a way to resolve our basic differences."

"We can be friends without resolution. I mean, can't we?"

"How do I know?" I tried to shut down, but I couldn't quite manage it. I had an inexplicable urge to weep about something. Usually good-byes do that, tender partings in movies accompanied by music guaranteed to rip your heart out. The silence between us was just as painful to me.

"Have you had dinner?"

"I hadn't decided about that yet. I just had drinks with the Maleks," I said faintly. The words sounded odd and I wanted to pat myself on the chest as a way of consoling myself. I could have handled the situation if only he hadn't come back. The day had been hard, but I'd survived it.

"You want to talk?"

I shook my head, not trusting my voice.

"Then what? You decide. I'll do anything you want."

I looked away from him, thinking about the fearful risks of intimacy, the potential for loss, the tender pain implicit in any bond between two creatures—human or beast, what difference did it make? In me, the instinct for survival and the need for love had been at war for years. My caution was like a wall I'd built to keep me safe. But safety is an illusion and the danger of feeling too much is no worse than the danger of being numb. I looked back at him and saw my pain mirrored in his eyes.

He said, "Come here." He made a gesture with his hand, coaxing me to move closer.

I crossed the room. Dietz leaned into me like a ladder left behind by a thief.

9

Dietz's knee was so swollen and painful he couldn't make it up the stairs, so we unfolded the sofa bed. I brought the duvet down from the loft. We turned off the lamp and crawled naked beneath the comforter's downy weight like polar bears in a cave. We made love in the puffy igloo of the quilt while around us streetlights streamed through the porthole window like moonlight on snow. For a long time, I simply drank in the musky scent of him, hair and skin, feeling my way blindly across all his textured surfaces. The heat from his body thawed my cold limbs. I felt like a snake curling up in a patch of sunlight, warmed to the depths after a long unforgiving winter. I remembered his ways from our three months together—the look on his face, the hapless sounds he made. What I'd forgotten was the smoldering response he awakened in me.

There was a brief time in my youth when my behavior was both reckless and promiscuous. Those were the days when there seemed to be no consequence to sex that wasn't easily cured. In the current marketplace, you'd have to be a fool—or suicidal—to risk the casual encounter without a lot of straight talk and doctors' certificates changing hands. For my purposes, celibacy is my habitual state. I suppose it's a lot like living in times of famine. Without hope of satiation, hunger diminishes and the appetite fades. With Dietz, I could feel all my physical senses quicken, the yearning for contact overcoming my natural reticence. Dietz's injury required patience and ingenuity, but somehow we managed. The process entailed considerable laughter at our contortions and quiet concentration during the moments between.

Finally, at ten, I flung the covers aside, exposing our sweaty bodies to the arctic temperatures surrounding us. "I don't know about you, but I'm starving," I said. "If we don't stop and eat soon, I'll be dead before morning."

Thirty minutes later, showered and dressed, we found ourselves sitting up at Rosie's in my favorite booth. She and William were both working, he behind the bar and Rosie out waiting tables. Ordinarily, the kitchen closed down at ten, and I could see she was just on the verge of saying as much when she noticed the whisker burn that had set my cheeks aflame. I put my chin in my palm, but not before she caught sight of my sex rash. The woman may be close to seventy, but she's not unperceptive. She seemed to take in at a glance both the source of our satisfaction and our avid interest in food. I thought the application of my makeup had successfully disguised my chafed flesh, but she was visibly smirking as she recited the meal she intended to prepare for us. With Rosie, there's no point in even pretending to order. You eat what she decides will be perfect for the occasion. In honor of Dietz's return, I noticed her English was marginally improved.

She parked herself sideways to the table, wiggling slightly in place, refusing to look directly at either of us after that first sly glance. "Now. Here's what you gonna get and don't make with the usual face—like this—while I'm telling you." She pulled her mouth down, eyes rolling, to show Dietz my usual enthusiasm for her choices. "I'm fixing Korhelyleves, is also called Souse's Soup. Is taking couple pounds of sauerkraut, paprika, smoked sausage, and some sour cream. Is guaranteed to perk up tired senses of which you look like you got a lot. Then, I'm roasting you little cheeken that I'm serve with mushroom pudding—is very good—and for efter, is hazelnut torte, but no coffee. You need sleep. I'm bringing wine in a minute. Don't go way."

We didn't leave until midnight. We didn't sleep until one, wound together on the narrow width of the sofa bed. I'm not accustomed to sleeping with someone else and I can't say it netted me any restful results. Because of his knee, Dietz was forced to lie on his back with a pillow supporting his left leg. This gave me two choices: I could lie pressed against him with my head resting on his chest, or flat on my back with our bodies touching along their lengths.

I tried one and then the other, tossing relentlessly as the hours ticked away. Half the time, I could feel the sofa's metal mechanism cut across my back, but if I switched to the other position with my head on his chest, I suffered from heatstroke, a dead arm, and a canned left ear. Sometimes I could feel the exhalation of his breath on my cheek and the effect drove me mad. I found myself counting as he breathed, in and out, in and out. In moments, the rhythm changed and there'd be a long pause in which I wondered if he were in the process of dropping dead. Dietz slept like a soldier under combat conditions. His snores were gentle snuffles, just loud enough to keep me on sentry duty, but not quite loud enough to draw enemy fire.

I slept finally—amazingly—and woke at seven energized. Dietz had made coffee and he was reading the paper, dressed, his hair damp, a pair of half-glasses sitting low on his nose. I watched him for a few minutes until his gaze came up to mine.

"I didn't know you wore glasses."

"I was too vain before this. The minute you were out the door, I put 'em on," he said with that crooked smile of his.

I turned on my side, folding my right arm under my cheek. "What time will the boys be expecting you?"

"Early afternoon. I have motel reservations at a place close by. If they want to spend the night, I'll have room."

"I'll bet you look forward to seeing them."

"Yes, but I'm nervous about it, too. I haven't seen them for two years—since I left for Germany. I'm never quite sure what to talk about with them."

"What do you talk to anyone about? Mostly bullshit."

"Even bullshit requires a context. It gets awkward for them, too. Sometimes we end up going to the movies just to have something to talk about later. I'm not exactly a fount of paternal advice. Once I quiz them about girlfriends and classes, I'm about out of conversation."

"You'll do fine."

"I hope. What about you? What's your day looking like?"

"I don't know. This is Saturday, so I don't have to work. I'll probably nap. Starting soon."

"You want company?"

"Dietz," I said, outraged, "if you get in this bed again, I won't be able to walk."

"You're an amateur."

"I am. I'm not used to this stuff."

"How about some coffee?"

"Let me brush my teeth first."

After breakfast, we went down to the beach. The day was cloudy, the marine layer holding in the heat like foam insulation. The temperature was close to seventy and the air soft and fruity, with a tropical scent. Santa Teresa winters are filled with such contradictions. One day will feel icy while the next day feels mild. The ocean had a slick sheen, reflecting the uniform white of the sky. We took off our shoes and carried them, scuffling along the water's edge with the frothy play of waves rolling across our bare feet. Seagulls hovered overhead, screeching, while two dogs leaped in unison, snapping at the birds as if they were low-flying Frisbees.

Dietz took off at nine, holding me crushed against him before he got in the car. I leaned on the hood and we kissed for a while. Finally, he pulled back and studied my face. "If I come back in a couple of weeks, will you be here?"

"Where else would I go?"

"I'll see you then," he said.

"Don't worry about me. Any old day will do," I remarked, waving, as his car receded down the block. Dietz hated to be specific about dates because it made him feel trapped. Of course, the effect of his vagueness was to keep me feeling hooked. I shook my head to myself as I returned to my place. How did I end up with a man like him?

I spent the rest of the morning getting my apartment tidied up. It didn't really take much work, but it was satisfying nonetheless. This time I wasn't really feeling depressed. I knew Dietz would be coming back, so my virtuous activity had more to do with reestablishing my boundaries than warding off the blues. Since he'd done the grocery shopping, my cupboard was full and my refrigerator stocked, a state that always contributes to my sense of security. As long as you have sufficient toilet paper, how far wrong can life go?

At lunchtime I spotted Henry sitting in the backyard at a little round picnic table he'd picked up in a garage sale the previous fall. He'd spread out some graph paper, his reference books, and a crossword key. As a pastime, Henry constructs and sells crossword puzzles for those wee yellow books sold near grocery store checkout lanes. I made a peanut-butter-and-pickle sandwich and joined him in the sunshine.

"You want one?" I asked, holding out my plate.

"Thanks, but I just had lunch," he said. "Where'd Dietz disappear to? I thought he intended to stick around."

I filled him in on the "romance" and we chatted idly while I ate my sandwich. The texture of the peanut butter was a sublime contrast to the crunch of the bread-and-butter pickles. The diagonal cut exposed more filling than a vertical cut would and I savored the ratio of saltiness to tart. This ranked right up there with sex without taking off any clothes. I made a sort of low moan, nearly swooning with pleasure, and Henry glanced up at me. "Give me a bite of that."

I let him have the plump center portion, keeping my fingers positioned so he couldn't take too much.

He chewed for a moment, clearly relishing the intense blend of flavors. "Very weird, but not bad." This is what he always says when he samples this culinary marvel.

I tried another bite myself, pointing to the puzzle he was working on. "How's this one coming? You've never really told me how you go about your business." Henry was a crossword fanatic, subscribing to the *New York Times* so he could do the daily puzzle, which he completed in ink. Sometimes, to amuse himself, he left every other letter blank, or filled in the outer borders first in a spiral moving toward the center. The puzzles he wrote himself seemed very difficult to me, though he claimed they were easy. I'd watched him construct dozens without understanding the strategy.

"I've actually upgraded my technique. My approach used to be haphazard. I'm better organized these days. This is a small one, only fifteen by fifteen. This is the pattern I'm using," he said, indicating a template with the gridwork of black squares already laid in.

"You don't devise the format as well?"

"Usually not. I've used this one several times and it suits my purposes. They're all symmetrical and if you'll notice, no area is closed off. The rules say the black squares can't exceed more than one sixth of the total number. There are a few other rules tossed in. For example, you can't use any words of fewer than three letters, stuff like that. The good ones have a theme around which the answers are organized."

I picked up one of his reference books and turned it over in my hand. "What's this?"

"That book lists words in alphabetical order from three through fifteen letters. And that one's a crossword finisher that lists words in a complicated alphabetical order up through seven letters."

I smiled at the enthusiasm that had crept into his voice. "How'd you get into this?"

He waved dismissively. "Do enough of 'em and you can't help it. You have to have a go at it yourself, just to see what it's like. They even have crossword championships, which started in 1980. You ought to see those puppies go. The puzzles are projected on an overhead screen. A real whiz can answer sixty-four questions in under eight minutes."

"Are you ever tempted to enter?"

He shook his head, penciling in a clue. "I'm too slow and much too easily rattled. Besides, it's a serious business, like bridge tournaments." His head came up. "That's your phone," he said.

"It is? Your hearing must be better than mine." I hopped up from the table and made a beeline for my place, picking up the receiver just as my answering machine did. I reached for the Off button as my voice completed its request for messages. "Hello, hello. It's me. I'm really home," I sang.

"Hey," a man's voice said mildly. "This is Guy. Hope you don't mind my calling on a weekend."

"Not at all. What's up?"

"Nothing much," he said. "Donovan called me at the church. I guess last night the three of them—him and Bennet and Jack—had a meeting. He says they want me to come down for a few days so we can talk about the will."

I felt my whole body go quiet. "Really. That's interesting. You going to do it?"

"I think so. I might, but I'm not really sure. I had a long talk with Peter and Winnie. Peter thinks it's time to open up a dialogue. He's got a prayer meeting in Santa Teresa tomorrow, so it works out pretty good. They can bring me down after church, but he thought it'd be smart to talk to you about it first."

I was silent for a moment. "You want the truth?"

"Well, yeah. That's why I called."

"I wouldn't do it if I were you. I was over there last night and it all seems very tense. It's nothing you'd want to be exposed to."

"How so?"

"Feelings are running high and your showing up at this point is only going to make things worse."

"That was my first reaction, but then I got to thinking. I mean, Donovan called me. I didn't call him," he said. "Seems to me if the three of them are offering a truce, I should at least be willing to meet 'em halfway. It can't hurt."

I suppressed an urge to start shrieking at him. Shrieking, I've discovered, is really not a sound method for persuading other people to your point of view. I'd seen his brothers in action and Guy was no match. I wouldn't trust those three under any circumstances. Given Guy's emotional state, I could see why he'd be tempted, but he'd be a fool to go into that house without counsel. "Maybe it's a truce and maybe not. Bader's death has brought up all kinds of issues," I said. "You go in unprepared and you'll end up taking on a whole raft of shit. You'd be walking into a nightmare."

"I understand."

"I don't think so," I said. "Not to criticize your brothers, but these are not nice fellows, at least where you're concerned. There's a lot of friction between them and your appearance is only going to add fuel to the fire. I mean, honestly. You can't imagine the dynamic." I noticed the pitch and volume of my voice going up.

"I have to try," he said.

"Maybe so, but not *that* way."

"Meaning what?"

"You're going to find yourself in exactly the same position you were in when you left. You'll be the fall guy, the scapegoat for all their hostility."

I could hear him shrug. He said, "Maybe we need to talk about that then. Get it out in the open and deal with it."

"It's out in the open. Those three aren't shy about anything. The conflicts are all right out there in front of God and everyone and believe me, you don't want their venom directed at you."

"Donovan doesn't seem to bear me any ill will and from what he says, Bennet and Jack don't either. The truth is, I've changed and they need to see that. How else can I persuade 'em if it isn't face-to-face?"

I could feel my eyes cross while I tried controlling my impatience. I knew I'd be smarter to keep my mouth shut, but I've never been good at keeping my opinions to myself. "Look, Guy, I don't want to stand here and try to tell you your business, but this isn't about you. This is about their relationship to each other. It's about your father and whatever's been going on in the years since you left. You'll end up being the target for all the anger they've stored up. And why put yourself through that."

"Because I want to be connected again. I screwed up. I admit that and I want to make it up to them. Peter says there can't be any healing unless we sit down together."

"That's all well and good, but there's a lot more at stake. What if the subject of the money comes up?"

"I don't care about the money."

"Bullshit. That's bull. Do you have any idea how much money we're talking about?"

"Doesn't make any difference. The money doesn't matter to me. I don't need money. I'm happy as I am."

"That's what you say now, but how do you know that won't change? Why create problems for yourself later on? Have you talked to Tasha? What's she say about this?"

"I never talked to her. I called the office in Lompoc, but she'd already left for San Francisco and after that, the secretary said she was taking off for Utah on a ten-day ski trip."

"So call her in Utah. They have phones up there."

"I tried that. They wouldn't give me her number. They said if she called in, they'd give her my name and number and she'd call if she could."

"Then try someone else. Call another attorney. I don't want you talking to your brothers without legal advice."

"It's not about legalities. It's about mending the breach."

"Which is exactly what's going to make you a sitting duck. Your agenda has nothing to do with theirs. They don't give a shit about forgiveness, if you'll pardon my French."

"I don't see it that way."

"I know you don't. That's why we're having this argument," I shrieked. "Suppose they try to pressure you into making a decision?"

"About what?"

"About anything! You don't even know what's in your best interest. If your sole aim is to make peace, you're only going to get screwed."

"How can I get screwed if I don't want anything? They can keep the money if that's the only thing standing between us."

"Well, if *you* don't want the money, why not give it to the church?" The minute I said it, I wanted to bite my tongue. His motives were clean. Why introduce the complication?

He was silent for a moment. "I hadn't thought about that. That's a good point."

"Forget it. Just skip that. All I'm saying is don't go in there alone. Get help so you don't do something you'll regret."

"Why don't you go?"

I groaned and he laughed in response. Going with him was the last thing I wanted to do. He needed protection, but I didn't think it was appropriate for me to step in. What did I have to offer in the way of assistance? "Because it's not my place. I'm not objective. I don't know the law and I don't have any idea what your legal position is. You'd be foolish to come down here and have a conversation with them. Just wait for ten days until Tasha gets back. Don't do anything yet. There's no reason you have to hop-to the minute Donovan whistles. You should be doing this on your terms, not his."

I could hear his reluctance to accept what I was saying. Like most of us, he'd made up his mind before he asked. "You know something? This is the truth," he said. "I prayed about this. I asked God for guidance and this was the answer I got."

"Well, try Him again. Maybe you misunderstood the message."

He laughed. "I did that in a way. I opened my Bible and put my finger on the page. Know what the passage was?"

"I can't imagine," I said dryly.

" 'Be it known unto you therefore, men *and* brethren, that through this man is preached unto you the forgiveness of sins: And by him all that believe are justified from all things, from which ye could not be justified by the law of Moses.' " Like many of the faithful, he could recite Bible verses like song lyrics.

This time the silence was mine. "I can't argue that. I don't even know what it means. Look, if you're determined to do this, you'll do it, I'm sure. I'm just urging you to take someone with you."

"I just did. I asked you."

"I'm not talking about me! What about Peter and Winnie? I'm sure they'd be willing to help if you asked and they'd do a much better job. I don't know the first thing about counseling or mediation or anything else. Aside from that, all this family-related stuff gives me the willies."

I could hear Guy smile and his tone was affectionate. "Strange you should say that because somehow it feels like you're part of this. I don't know how, but it sure seems like that to me. Don't you have some kind of issue around family yourself?"

I held the phone away from me and squinted at the handset. "Who, me? Absolutely not. Why would you say that?"

Guy laughed. "I don't know. It just came to me in a flash. Maybe I'm wrong, but it feels like you're connected."

"My only connection is professional. I was hired to do a job.

That's the only link I see." I kept my tone casual to demonstrate my nonchalance, but I was forced to put a hand against the small of my back, where an inexplicable drop of sweat was trickling down into my underpants. "Why don't you have a talk with Peter again. I know you're eager to make amends, but I don't want you walking into the lion's den. We all know how the lions and the Christians came out."

He was silent for a moment and then seemed to change the subject. "Where's your apartment?"

"What makes you ask?" I was unwilling to be specific until I knew where he was headed.

"How about this? Maybe we can do this another way. Donovan says everyone's gone tomorrow until five o'clock. Peter'll give me a lift into town, but his schedule's too tight to do much more than that. If he drops me off at your place, could you give me a ride the rest of the way? You don't have to stay. I understand you don't want to be involved and that's fine with me."

"I don't really see how that addresses the point."

"It doesn't. I'm just asking for a ride. I can handle everything else if you can get me over there."

"You're not going to listen to me, are you," I said.

"I did listen. The problem is I disagree."

I hesitated, but really couldn't see any reason to refuse. I was already feeling churlish because I'd put up such resistance. "That sounds all right. Sure. I can do that," I said. "What time would you get here?"

"Three? Somewhere around then. I don't mean to be a bother. Peter's meeting is downtown, at that church on the corner of State and Michaelson. Is that anywhere close? Because I could walk over to your place and we could go from there."

"Close enough," I said, feeling crabby and resigned. "Look, why don't you give me a call when you get in. I'll swing by the church and pick you up."

"That'd be good. That's great. Are you sure this is okay?"

"No, but don't press your luck. I'm willing to do this much, but don't go asking for reassurance on top of it."

He laughed. "I'm sorry. You're right. I'll see you then," he said. He disconnected on his end.

As I hung up the phone, I was already having doubts. Amazing how quickly someone else's problems become yours. Trouble creates a vacuum into which the rest of us get sucked.

I found myself pacing the living room, inwardly refuting his ridiculous claim about the relevance of his situation to mine. His conflict about family had *nothing* to do with me. I sat down at my desk and made some notes to myself. In case Tasha asked, I thought it might be wise to keep a record of the discussion we'd just had. I hoped he wasn't going to get a bug up his butt about giving all his money to the church. That was really going to cause a problem if he got greedy on behalf of Jubilee Evangelical. I omitted any reference to a charitable donation, thinking if I didn't write it down, the subject wouldn't exist.

I picked up the phone again and put a call through to the Maleks. Myrna picked up and I asked to speak to Christie. I waited, listening as Myrna crossed the foyer and bellowed up the stairs to Christie. When Christie finally picked up the phone on her end, I filled her in briefly on my conversation with Guy. "Will you keep me informed about what's going on?" I asked. "I'll drop him off, but after that he's on his own. I think he needs protection, but I don't want to get into my rescue costume. He's a big boy and this is really none of my business. I'd feel better if I knew there was someone in your camp keeping an eye on him."

"Oh, right. And leave the rescue to me," she said, her tone of voice wry.

I laughed. "Not to get trivial, but he *is* cute," I said.

"Really? Well, that's good. I'm a big fan of cute. In fact, that's how I vote for a presidential candidate," she said. "Personally, I don't think you have anything to worry about. After you left last night, the three of them talked long and hard. Once they got done ripping each other apart, they settled down into some meaningful conversation."

"I'm glad to hear that. I was actually a bit puzzled why Donovan had called him. What's their inclination? Do you mind if I ask?"

"I guess it depends on what he says to them. Ultimately, of course, this is probably something for the lawyers to discuss. I think they want to be honorable. On the other hand, five million dollars might distort anyone's notion of what's fair."

"Ain't that the truth."

10

I pulled over to the curb in front of the Faith Evangelical Church the next afternoon at three. Guy had called me at 2:45 and I'd left the apartment shortly thereafter, taking a few minutes to put gas in my car. The sun was out again and the day felt like summer. I wore the usual jeans and a T-shirt, but I'd traded my Reeboks and sweat socks for a pair of openwork sandals in honor of the sudden heat. The grass on the church lawn had been recently cut and the sidewalk was littered with fine green at the edge. The turf itself featured a pale dun-colored haze where the cut blades had browned in the sun. A number of gullible daffodils had taken these balmy temperatures as an invitation to pop their green shafts into view.

There was no sign of Peter, but Guy was standing on the corner with a backpack at his feet. He spotted my car and pretended to hitchhike, holding his thumb out with a smile on his face. I confess when I saw him I could feel my heart break. He'd had his hair cut and his face was so freshly shaved he still sported a dot of toilet paper where he'd nicked himself. He wore a navy blue suit that didn't fit well. The pants were baggy in the butt and slightly too long, the backs of his trouser cuffs brushing the sidewalk. The jacket was wide across the chest, which made the shoulder pads look as exaggerated as a 1940's zoot suit. The garment had probably been donated to a church rummage sale or maybe he'd bought it from someone weighing forty pounds more. Whatever the explanation, he wore his finery with a self-conscious air, clearly unaccustomed to the dress shirt and tie. I wondered if my own vulnerability had been as apparent during my lunch with Tasha. I'd approached my personal grooming with the same insecurity, perhaps netting myself the same sorry results.

Guy reached for his canvas backpack, clearly happy to see me. He seemed as innocent as a pup. There was a softness about him, something guileless and unformed, as if his association with Jubilee Evangelical had isolated him from worldly influences all these years. The reckless element in his nature was now tamed to a gentleness I'd rarely seen in a man.

He slid into the front seat. "Hey, Kinsey. How are you?" He held his backpack on his lap like a kid on his way to day camp.

I smiled in his direction. "You're all spiffed up."

"I didn't want my brothers to think I'd forgotten how to dress. What do you think of the suit?"

"The color's good on you."

"Thanks," he said, smiling with pleasure. "Oh. By the way, Winnie says hi."

"Hi to her," I said. "What's the deal on your return? When are you planning to go back to Marcella?"

Guy looked away from me out the car window on his side, the casualness of his tone belying its content. "Depends on what happens at the house. Donovan invited me to stay for a couple of days and I wouldn't mind that if everything works out all right. I guess if it doesn't work, it won't make any difference. I got money in my pocket. When I'm ready to leave, someone can give me a ride to the bus."

I was on the verge of volunteering my services and then thought better of it. I glanced over at him, making a covert study of his face in profile. In some lights, he looked every one of his forty-three years. In other moments his boyishness seemed a permanent part of his character. It was as if his development had been arrested at the age of sixteen, maybe twenty at the outside. He was scanning the streets, taking in the sights as if he were in a foreign country.

"I take it you don't get down here that often," I said.

He shook his head. "I don't have much occasion. When you live in Marcella, Santa Teresa seems too big and too far away. We go to Santa Maria or San Luis if we need anything." He looked over at me. "Can we do a quick tour? I'd like to see what's going on."

"I can do that. Why not? We have time."

I circled the block, coming back out onto State Street. I turned left, heading downtown, a short three blocks away. The business district wasn't much more than twenty blocks long and three or four blocks wide, terminating at Cabana Boulevard, which parallels the beach. For many years, the stores along upper State attracted the bulk of the downtown shoppers. Lower State was considered the less-desirable end of town, the street lined with thrift stores, third-rate eateries, a movie theater that smelled of urine, and half a dozen noisy bars and run-down transient hotels. Lately, the area had undergone a resurrection, and the classy businesses had begun to migrate southward along the thoroughfare. Now it was upper State that featured deserted storefronts while lower State had captured all the tourist trade. In warm weather, pedestrians drifted up from the beach, a ragtag parade of sight-seers in shorts, licking ice-cream cones.

"It's grown," he remarked.

With a population of eighty-five thousand, Santa Teresa wasn't big, but the town had been flourishing. I tried to see it as he did, cataloging in my mind all the changes that had taken place in the last twenty years. Time-lapse photography would have shown tree trunks elongating, branches stretching out like rubber, some buildings erected while others vanished in a puff of smoke. Storefronts would flicker through a hundred variations: awnings, signs, and window displays, the liquidation sales of one business flashing across the plate glass before the next enterprise took its place. New structures would appear like apparitions, filling in the empty spaces until no gaps remained. I could remember when the downtown sidewalks were made wider, State Street narrowing to accommodate the planting of trees imported from Bolivia. Spanish-style benches and telephone booths had been added. Decorative fountains had appeared, looking like they'd been there for years. A fire had taken out two commercial establishments while an earthquake had rendered others unfit for use. Santa Teresa was one of the few towns that looked more elegant as time passed. The strict regulations of the Architectural Board of Review imposed an air of refinement that in other towns was wiped out by gaudy neon, oversized signage, and a hodgepodge of building styles and materials. As much as the local residents complained about the lengthy approval process, the result was a mix of simplicity and grace.

At Cabana, I drove out along the wharf, wheels thumping along the length. I turned at the end until we were headed back toward town. I motored north on State, seeing the same sights again from the reverse perspective. At Olive Grove, I turned right, driving past the Santa Teresa Mission and from there into the foothills where the Malek estate was tucked. I could sense Guy's interest quicken as the road angled upward. Much of the terrain in this area was undeveloped, the landscape littered with enormous sandstone boulders and prickly cactus with leaves as large as fleshy Ping-Pong paddles.

The Malek estate sat close to the borders of the backcountry, an oasis of dark green in a region dense with pale chaparral. At irregular intervals, fires had swept across the foothills in spectacular conflagrations, the blaze advancing from peak to peak, sucking up houses and trees, consuming every shred of vegetation. In the wake of these burns, species of native plants known as fire followers appeared, dainty beauties emerging from the ashes of the charred and the dead. I could still see the occasional black, twisted branches of the manzanitas, though it had been five or six years since the last big fire.

Once again, the iron gates at the entrance stood open, the long driveway disappearing around a shaded curve ahead. Somehow the Maleks' evergreens and palms looked alien set against the backdrop of raw mountains. Entering the estate, I sensed how the years of careful cultivation and the introduction of exotic plants had altered the very air that permeated the grounds.

"You nervous?" I asked.

"Scared to death."

"You can still back out."

"It's too late for that. Feels like a wedding where the invitations have gone out—you know, it's still possible to cancel, but it's easier to go through with it than make a fuss for everyone else."

"Don't turn all noble on me."

"It's not about 'noble.' I guess I'm curious."

I pulled into the courtyard and eased the VW around to the left. The garages at the end of the drive were all closed. The house itself looked deserted. All the windows were dark and most of the draperies were drawn. The visage was scarcely welcoming. The silence was broken only by the idling of my engine. "Well. This is it, I guess. Call if you need me. I wish you luck."

Guy glanced at me uneasily. "You have to leave already?"

"I really should," I said, though the truth was I had nothing else to do that afternoon.

"Don't you want to see the place? Why don't you stay a few minutes and let me show you around."

"I was just here for drinks. It hasn't changed since Friday night."

"I don't want to go inside. I have to work up my nerve. Why don't I show you the place. We could walk around outside. It's really beautiful," he said. He reached out impulsively and touched my bare arm. "Please?"

His fingers were cold and his apprehension was contagious. I didn't have the heart to leave him. "All right," I said reluctantly, "but I can't stay long."

"Great. That's great. I really appreciate this."

I turned off the engine. Guy left his backpack on the front seat and the two of us got out. We slammed the car doors in two quick, overlapping reports, like guns going off. At the last moment, I opened my door again and tossed my handbag in the back before I locked the car. As we crossed the courtyard, Myrna opened the front door and came out on the porch. She was wearing a semblance of uniform; a shapeless white polyester skirt with a matching overblouse, some vague cross between nursiness and household help.

I said, "Hi, Myrna. How are you? I didn't think anyone was here. This is Guy. I'm sorry. I don't remember anyone ever mentioning your last name."

"Sweetzer," she said.

Guy extended his hand, which flustered her to some extent. She allowed him one of those handshakes without cartilage or bone. His good looks probably had the same effect on her that they had on me. "Nice to meet you," he said.

"Nice to meet you, too," she replied by rote. "The family's back around five. You're to have the run of the house. I imagine you remember where your room is if you want to take your things on up."

"Thanks. I'll do that in a bit. I thought I'd show her the grounds first if that's okay with you."

"Suit yourself," she said. "The front door will be open if you want to come in that way. Dinner's at seven." She turned to me. "Will you be staying on as well?"

"I appreciate the invitation, but I don't think I should. The family needs time to get reacquainted. Maybe another time," I said. "I do have a question. Guy was asking about his father and it just occurred to me that you might know as much as anyone else. Weren't you his nurse?"

"One of them," she said. "I was his primary caregiver the last eight months. I stayed on as housekeeper at your brothers' request," she said, looking at Guy. Her delivery was staunch, as if we'd challenged her right to remain on the premises. From what I'd seen of her, she tended to be humorless, but with Guy she'd now added a grace note of resentment, reflecting the family's general attitude.

Guy's smile was sweet. "I'd like to talk to you about my dad sometime."

"Yes sir. He was a good man and I was fond of him."

There was an awkward moment, none of us knowing how to terminate the conversation. Myrna was the one who finally managed, saying, "Well, now. I'll let you go on about your business. I'll be in the kitchen if you should need anything. The cook's name is Enid, if you can't find me."

"I remember Enid," he said. "Thanks."

As soon as the door closed behind her, Guy touched my elbow and steered me off to the right. We crossed the courtyard together, heat drifting up from the sunbaked cobblestones. "Thanks for staying," he said.

"You're full of thanks," I remarked.

"I am. I feel blessed. I never expected to see the house again. Come on. We'll go this way."

We cut around the south side of the house, moving from hot, patchy sunlight into shade. To me, it felt like another sudden shift in seasons. In the space of fifty feet, we'd left summer behind. In the gloom of heavy shadow, the drop in air temperature was distinct and unwelcome, as if the months were rolling backward into winter again. Vestiges of the hot dry winds blew down the mountainside behind us, tossing restlessly across the treetops above our heads. We rambled beneath a canopy of shaggy-smelling juniper and pine. A carpet of fallen needles dampened our footsteps to a silence.

Near the house, I could see evidence of the gardeners—raked

paths, the trimmed shape of bushes, a profusion of ferns ringed with small perfect stones—but the larger portion of the property was close to wilderness. Many of the plants had been allowed to grow unchecked. A violet-colored lantana tumbled along the terrace wall. A salmon pink bougainvillea climbed across a tangled stretch of brush. To our right, a solid wash of nasturtiums blanketed the banks of an empty creek bed. In the areas of bright sun, where the dry breezes riffled across the blossoms, several scents arose and mingled in an earthy cologne.

Guy seemed to scrutinize every square foot we traversed. "Everything looks so much bigger. I remember when some of these trees were just planted. Saplings were this tall and now look at them."

"Your memories sound happy. That surprises me somehow."

"This was a great spot to grow up. Mom and Dad bought the place when I was three years old. Donovan was five and the two of us thought we'd died and gone to heaven. It was like one great big playground. We could go anywhere we wanted and no one ever had to worry. We made forts and tree houses. We had sword fights with sticks. We played cowboys and Indians and went on jungle expeditions in the wilds of the sticker bushes. When Bennet was a little guy, we used to tie him to a stake and he'd wail like a banshee. We'd tell him we were going to burn him if he didn't shut up. He was younger than us and he was fair game."

"Nice."

"Boy-type fun," he said. "I guess girls don't do that."

"How could your parents afford a place like this? I thought your father made his money later, in the years since you left."

"Mom had some money from a trust fund. The down payment was hers. Actually, it wasn't that much money even for the time. The house was a white elephant. It was on the market for nearly ten years and it was empty all that time. The story we heard was that the previous owner had been murdered. It's not like the house was haunted, but it did seem tainted. Nobody could make a deal work. We were told it fell out of escrow five or six times before my parents came along and bought it. It was big and neglected. The wiring was bad and the plumbing was shot. Daylight was showing through big holes in the roof. Tree rats ran everywhere and there was a family of raccoons living in the attic. It took 'em years to pull it all together. In the meantime, Dad's plan was to buy adjacent properties if they came up for sale."

"What is it now, fifteen acres?"

"Is that right? The original parcel was six. There probably isn't a lot more land available in this area."

"Is this city land or county?"

"We're right at the upper edges of the city limits. Lot of what you're looking at up there is part of the Los Padres National Forest." The term *forest* was a misnomer. The arching mountain range above us was overgrown with nettle, ceanothus, pyracantha, and coastal sage scrub, the soil too poor to support many trees. In the higher elevations, a few pines might remain if the wildfires hadn't reached them.

We passed the tennis court, its surface cracked and weedy along the edges. A tennis racket had been tossed to one side, exposed to the elements long enough to warp, its nylon strings sprung. Beyond the tennis court, there was a glass-enclosed structure I hadn't seen from the drive. The lines of the building were low and straight, with a red-tile roof that had altered with time until its color was the burnt brown of old bricks.

"What's that?"

"The pool house. We have an indoor pool. Want to see it?"

"Might as well," I said. I trailed after him as he approached a covered flagstone patio. He crossed to the building's darkened windows and peered in. He moved to the door and tried the knob. The door was unlocked, but the frame was jammed and required a substantial push before it opened with the kind of scrape that set my teeth on edge.

"You really want to do this?" I asked.

"Hey, it's part of the tour."

To me, it felt like breaking and entering, a sport I prefer to get paid for. The sense of trespass was unmistakable, nearly sexual in tone, despite the fact that we'd been given permission to roam. We entered an anteroom that was used to store an assortment of play equipment: badminton rackets, golf clubs, baseball bats, a rack lined with a full set of croquet mallets and balls, Styrofoam kickboards for the pool, and a line of fiberglass surfboards that looked as if they'd been propped against the wall for years. The gardener was currently keeping his leaf blower and a riding mower in the space to one side. While I didn't see any spiders, the place had a spidery atmosphere. I wanted to brush my clothes hurriedly in case something had dropped down and landed on me unseen.

The pool was half-filled and something about the water looked really nasty. The decking around the pool was paved with a gritty-looking gray slate, not the sort of surface you'd want to feel under your bare feet. At one end of the room was an alcove furnished in rattan, though the cushions were missing from the sofa and matching chairs. The air was gloomy and I could hear the sound of dripping water. Any hint of chlorine had evaporated long ago and several unclassified life-forms had begun to ferment in the depths.

"Looks like it's time to fire the pool guy," I remarked.

"The gardener probably does the pool when he remembers," Guy said. "When we were kids this was great."

"What'd you and Donovan do to Bennet down here? Drown him? Hang him off the diving board? I can just imagine the fun you must have had."

Guy smiled, his thoughts somewhere else. "I broke up with a girl once down here. That's what sticks in my mind. Place was like a country club. Swimming, tennis, softball, croquet. We'd invite dates over for a swim and then we'd end up making out like crazy. Girl in a bathing suit isn't that hard to seduce. Jack was the all-time champ. He was randy as a rabbit and he'd go after anyone."

"Why'd you break up with her?"

"I don't remember exactly. Some rare moment of virtue and self-sacrifice. I liked her too much. I was a bad boy back then and she was too special to screw around with like the other ones. Or maybe odd's the better word. A little nutsy, too needy. I knew she was fragile and I didn't want to take the chance. I preferred the wild ones. No responsibility, no regrets, no holds barred."

"Were your parents aware of what was going on down here?"

"Who knows. I'm not sure. They were proponents of the 'boys will be boys' school of moral instruction. Any girl who gave in to us deserved what she got. They never said so explicitly, but that's the attitude. My mother was more interested in being everybody's pal. Set limits on a kid and you might have to take a stand at some point. She was into unconditional love, which to her meant the absence of prohibitions of any kind. It was easier to be permissive, you know what I mean? This was all part of the sixties' feel-good bullshit. Looking back, I can see how much she must have been affected by her illness. She didn't want to be the stern, disapproving parent. She must have known her days were numbered, even though she survived a lot longer than most. In those days, they did chemo and radiation, but it was all so crudely calibrated they probably killed more people than they cured. They just didn't have the technology or the sophisticated choice of treatments. It's different today where you got a real shot at survival. For her, the last couple of years were pure hell."

"It must have been hard on you."

"Pure agony," he said. "I was the child most identified with her. Don't ask me why, but Donovan and Bennet and Jack were linked to Dad while I was my mother's favorite. It drove me wild to see her fail. She was faltering and in pain, going downhill on what I knew would be her final journey."

"Were you with her when she died?"

"Yes. I was. The rest of 'em were gone. I forget now where they were. I sat in her room with her for hours that day. Most of the time she slept. She was so doped up on morphine, she could hardly stay awake. I was exhausted myself and laid my head on the bed. At one point, she reached out and put her hand on my neck. I touched her fingers and she was gone, just like that. So quiet. I didn't move for an hour.

"I just sat by the bed, leaning forward, with my head turned away from her and my face buried in the sheets. I thought maybe if I didn't look, she might come back again, like she was hovering someplace close and might return to her body as long as no one noticed she'd left. I didn't want to break faith."

"What happened to the girl you broke up with?"

"Patty? I have no idea. I wrote to her once, but never heard back. I've thought of her often, but who knows where she is now or what's happened to her. It might be the best thing I ever did, especially back then. What a bastard I was. I have a hard time connecting. It's like somebody else was doing it."

"But you're a good person now."

He shook his head. "I don't think of myself as good, but sometimes I think I come close to being real."

We left the pool house behind, moving temporarily onto the sunny stretch of lawn where I'd watched Jack hit golf balls. We were on the terrace below the house, shadows slanting toward us as we crossed the grass.

"How do you feel? You seem relaxed," I said.

"I'll be fine once they get here. You know how it is. Your fantasies are always stranger than reality."

"What do you picture?"

He smiled briefly. "I have no idea."

"Well, whatever it is, I hope you get what you need."

"Me, too, but in the long run, what difference does it make? You can't hide from God and that's the point," he said. "For a long time, I was walkin' down the wrong road, but now I've turned myself around and I'm goin' back the other way. At some point, I'll meet up with my past and make peace."

We had, by then, reached the front of the house again. "I better scoot," I said. "Let me know how it goes."

"I'll be fine."

"No doubt, but I'll be curious."

As I got into my car and turned the key in the ignition, I watched him head toward the front door with his backpack. I waved as I passed and then watched him in my rearview mirror as I eased down the drive. I rounded the curve and he was gone from view. It's painful to think of this in retrospect. Guy Malek was doomed and I delivered him into the hands of the enemy. As I pulled through the gates, I could see a car approach. Bennet was driving. My smile was polite and I waved at him. He stared at me briefly and then glanced away.

11

At ten o'clock Monday morning I received a call that should have served as a warning. Looking back, I can see that from that moment on, troubles began to accumulate at an unsettling rate. I'd gotten a late start and I was just closing the front gate behind me when I heard the muffled tone of the telephone ringing in my apartment. I did a quick reverse, trotting down the walkway and around the corner. I unlocked the front door and flung it open in haste, tossing my jacket and bag aside. I snatched up the receiver on the fourth ring, half expecting a wrong number or a market survey now that I'd made the effort. "Hello?"

"Kinsey. This is Donovan."

"Well, hi. How are you? Whew! Excuse the heavy breathing. I was already out the door and had to run for the phone."

Apparently, he wasn't in the mood for cheery chitchat. He got straight to the point. "Did you contact the press?"

It was not a subject I expected the man to broach at this hour or any other. I could feel a fuzzy question mark forming over my head while I pondered what he could possibly be talking about. "Of course not. About what?"

"We got a call from the *Dispatch* about an hour ago. Somebody tipped off a reporter about Guy's return."

"Really? That's odd. What's the point?" I knew the *Santa Teresa Dispatch* occasionally struggled to find noteworthy items for the Local section, but Guy's homecoming hardly seemed like a big-time news event. Aside from the family, who'd give a shit?

"They're playing it for human interest. Rags to riches. You know the tack, I'm sure. A lowly maintenance worker in Marcella, California, suddenly finds out he's a millionaire and comes home to collect. It's better than the lottery given Guy's personal history, as you well know."

"What do you mean, as *I* well know? I never said a word to the press. I wouldn't do that."

"Who else knew about it? No one in the family would leak a story like that. This is a sensitive issue. The last thing we need is *publicity*. Here we are trying to hammer out some kind of understanding between us and the phone hasn't stopped ringing since the first call came through."

"I don't follow. Who's been calling?"

"Who hasn't?" he said, exasperated. "The local paper for starters and then the L.A. *Times*. I guess one of the radio stations got wind of it. It'll go out on the wire services next thing you know and we'll have six friggin' camera crews camped in the driveway."

"Donovan, I swear. If there was a leak, it didn't come from me."

"Well, someone spilled the beans and you're the only one who stands to benefit."

"Me? That makes no sense. How would I benefit from a story about Guy?"

"The reporter who called mentioned you by name. He knew you'd been hired and he was interested in how you'd gone about finding

Guy after all these years. He as good as told me he intended to play that angle: 'Local PI locates heir missing eighteen years.' It's better than an advertisement for all the work you'll get."

"Donovan, stop it. That's ridiculous. I'd never blab client business under any circumstance. I don't need more work. I have plenty." This was not entirely true, but he didn't need to know that. The bottom line was, I'd never give client information to the media. I had a reputation to protect. Aside from ethical considerations, this was not a profession where you wanted to be recognized. Most working investigators keep a very low profile. Anonymity is always preferable, especially when you're inclined, as I am, to use the occasional ruse. If you're posing as a meter reader or a florist delivery person, you don't want the public to be aware of your true identity. "I mean, think about it, Donovan. If I'd actually given him the story, why would he be quizzing you about my methods? He'd know that already so why would he ask you?"

"Well, you might have a point there, unless he was looking for confirmation."

"Oh, knock it off. You're really stretching for that one."

"I just think it's damn suspicious that you got a plug."

"Who's the reporter? Did you ask where he got his information?"

"He never gave me the chance."

"Well, let me put in a call to him. Why don't we just ask him? It might be something simple or obvious once you hear. You remember his name?"

"Katzensomething, but I don't think it's smart for you to talk to him."

"Katzenbach. I know Jeffrey. He's a nice man."

Donovan plowed on, not wanting to yield his ground. "I'm telling you, lay off. I don't want you talking to him about anything. Enough is enough. If I find out you're behind this, I'll sue your ass from here to next Tuesday," he said and banged down the receiver on his end.

The "screw *you*" I offered snappishly came half a second too late, which was just as well.

The minute he'd broken the connection my adrenaline shot up. My mouth was dry and I could feel my heart begin to pound in my ears. I wanted to protest, but I could see how it looked from his perspective. He was right about the fact that I was the only one outside the family who knew what was going on. More or less, I thought, pausing to correct myself. Myrna could have tipped the paper, but it was hard to see why she'd do such a thing. And of course, Peter and Winnie knew what was going on, but again why would either one of them want to make the matter known? I had a strong impulse to pick up the phone and call Katzenbach, but Donovan's admonition was still ringing in my ears. Once in touch, I was worried the reporter would start pumping me for information. Any comment I made might be quoted in a follow-up and then my credibility would be shot for sure.

Dimly, I wondered if Guy could have tipped off the paper himself. It seemed unlikely, but not impossible and I could see a certain canny logic if the move was his. If the issue of his inheritance became public knowledge, his brothers would have a hell of a time trying to screw him out of it. The problem with that notion was that Guy had never demonstrated much interest in the money and he certainly hadn't seemed concerned about protecting his share. Could he be as devious and manipulative as his family claimed?

I snagged my jacket and my handbag and headed out again. I tried to shake off my anxiety as I walked the short distance to my car, which was parked half a block down. There was no way to convince the Maleks of my innocence. Accused of the breach, I found myself feeling apologetic, as if I'd actually been guilty of violating the family's trust. Poor Guy. In the wake of my denial, they'd probably turn on *him.*

By the time I reached the downtown area, I'd managed to distract myself, wondering if I'd find a parking space within a reasonable radius of Lonnie Kingman's building. I tried the spiral approach, like a crime scene investigation, starting at the inner point and working outward. If nothing opened up, I could always use the public parking lot, which was three blocks away.

The second time I circled, I saw a van pull into the stretch of red-painted curb in front of the building. The door on the passenger side slid back and a fellow with a camcorder swung himself out on the walk. The slim blond who anchored the six o'clock news hopped down from the front seat and scanned the numbers on the building, verifying the address from a note on her pad. Coming up from behind, I couldn't see the logo on the side of the van, but it had an aerial on top that looked fierce enough to receive messages from outer space. Oh, shit. As I passed the van, I could see KEST-TV painted on the side. I resisted the urge to speed away as the woman threw a glance in my direction. I peered to my left, turning toward the building across the street. I waved merrily at someone emerging from the Dean Witter office. Maybe the press would mistake me for a cruising mogul with some money to invest. I kept driving, eyes pinned on my rearview mirror as the cameraman and his companion went into the entranceway.

Now what? I didn't like the idea of skulking in the bushes like a renegade. Maybe I was being paranoid and the crew was on its way to cover something else. I drove several blocks before I spotted a pay phone on the corner. I left my car at the curb, dropped a quarter in the slot, and dialed Lonnie's private line. He must have been in court because Ida Ruth picked up, thinking it was him. "Yessir?"

"Ida Ruth, this is Kinsey. Did a TV crew show up looking for me?"

"I don't think so, but I'm back here at my desk. Let me check with Alison up front." She put me on hold for a moment and then clicked back in. "I stand corrected. They're waiting for you in reception. What's going on?"

"It's too complicated to explain. Can you get rid of them?"

"Well, we can get 'em out of here, but there's no way we can keep them from hanging around on the street outside. What did you do, if I may be so bold?"

"Nothing, I swear. I'm completely innocent."

"Right, dear. Good for you. Stick to that," she said.

"Ida Ruth, I'm serious. Here's the deal," I said. I filled her in briefly and heard her cluck in response. "My, oh my. If I were you, I'd lay low. They can't stay long. If you tell me how to reach you, I'll call you when they're gone."

"I'm not sure where I'll be. I'll check back in a bit." I put the receiver down and scanned the street corner opposite. There was a bar on the corner that appeared to be opening. I could see a neon light in the window blink on. As I watched, a fellow in an apron opened the front door and kicked the doorstop into place. I could always hang out in there, drinking beer and sniffing secondhand smoke while I figured out what to do next. On the other hand, come to think of it, I hadn't *done* anything so why was I behaving like a fugitive. I fished around in the bottom of my bag and came up with a second coin. I put a call through to the *Dispatch* and asked for Jeffrey Katzenbach. I didn't know him well, but I'd dealt with him on a couple of occasions in the past. He was a man in his fifties, whose career had been stalled by his appetite for cocaine and Percocet. He'd always been sharp if you caught him early in the day, but as the afternoon progressed, he became harder to deal with. By nightfall, he could still function, but his judgment was sometimes faulty and he didn't always remember the promises he'd made. Two years ago, his wife had left him and the last I'd heard, he'd finally straightened up his act with the help of Narcotics Anonymous. Guy Malek wasn't the only one who'd undergone personal transformation.

When I got through to Katzenbach, I identified myself and we exchanged the usual pleasantries before getting down to business. "Jeffrey, this is strictly off the record. The Maleks are my clients and I can't afford to be quoted."

"Why? What's the problem?"

"There isn't any problem. Donovan's pissed off because he thinks I called you and spoiled the family reunion."

"Sorry to hear that."

"How'd you get wind of it? Or is this a 'confidential source'?"

"Nothing confidential about it. There was a letter on my desk when

I got in last night. We've always encouraged our subscribers to get in touch if they think there's a story we might not've heard about. Sometimes it's just trivia or crank stuff, but this one grabbed my attention."

"Who sent the letter?"

"Some fellow named Max Outhwaite with an address on Connecticut out in Colgate. He thought it was an item worth bringing to our attention."

"How'd he hear about it?"

"Beats me. He talked like he'd known 'em all for years. Basically, the letter says a search was conducted and Bader Malek's son Guy was located after an absence of eighteen years. That's correct, isn't it? I mean, tell me I'm wrong and I'll eat my Jockey shorts."

"You're correct, but so what?"

"So nothing. Like he says, here's this fellow working as a janitor in some backwater town, finds out he's inheriting five million bucks. How often does that happen? He thought the community would be interested. I thought it sounded like a winner so I put a call in to the Maleks. The number's in the book, it didn't require any red-hot detective work. I talked to Mrs. Malek—what's her name, Christie—who confirmed the story before I even got to Donovan. Sure enough, that's the deal unless there's something I missed."

"And I was mentioned by name?"

"You bet. It's one of the reasons I figured it was on the up-and-up. I tried to reach you last night, but all I got was your answering machine. I didn't bother to leave a message. I figured you were on your way over there to help 'em celebrate. How'd you find the guy? Outhwaite's letter says you got a lead on him through the DMV."

"I don't believe this. Who is this man and where's he getting his information?"

"How do I know? He acted like he was maybe a friend of the family. You never talked to him yourself?"

"Jeffrey, knock it off. I didn't call so you could pump me. I'm trying to persuade the Maleks I didn't leak this thing."

"Too bad you didn't. You could have filled in the details. I went back to check with Outhwaite and the guy doesn't exist. There's no Outhwaite in the phone book and no such house number anywhere on Connecticut Avenue. I tried a couple of other possibilities and I came up with blanks. Not that it matters as long as the story's legitimate. I got confirmation from the family."

"What about the L.A. *Times*? How did they get wind of it?"

"Same way we did. Outhwaite dropped 'em a note—almost like a press release. It's been a slow week for news and we're always on the lookout for human-interest stuff. This was better than a little lost kitty-cat trapped in a well. I thought it was worth pursuing, especially when I saw you were involved."

"I wished you'd done some fact checking with me along the way."

"Why? What's the problem?"

"There isn't any *problem*," I said, irritably. "I just think the family might appreciate a little privacy before the whole world rushes in. By the way, Jeffrey, I've heard you tippy-tapping on your keyboard ever since we started this conversation. I told you this is off the record."

"What for? It's a nice story. It's a great fantasy. What's the deal with the Maleks? Why're they so pissed with the coverage? We did front page, second section when Bader Malek died. He was an important figure in the community and they were happy to have the tribute. What's so hush-hush about Guy? Are they trying to cut him out of his inheritance or something?"

I rolled my eyes skyward. The man couldn't help but press for information. "Listen, buddy, I'm as clueless as you. What about the letter? What happened to it?"

"It's sitting right here."

"You mind if I have a copy? It would go a long way toward restoring my credibility. I feel like a fool having to defend myself, but I have a reputation to maintain."

"Sure. I can do that. I don't see why not. We're interested in Guy's perspective if you can talk him into it."

"I'm not trading—but I'll do what I can."

"Terrific. What's your fax number?"

I gave him the number of Lonnie Kingman's machine and he said he'd fax the letter over. If I located Max Outhwaite, Jeffrey wanted to talk to him. Fair enough. I said I'd do what I could. It didn't cost me anything to profess my conditional cooperation. I tried not to be too profuse in my thanks. It's not like I planned to take the letter straight to Donovan, but I was curious about the contents and thought it made sense to have a copy for my files. At some point, Katzenbach would extract something from me in return, but for now, I was fine. I didn't believe Guy would agree to an interview, but maybe he'd surprise me.

I got back in my car and drove over to the public parking lot. From there, I hoofed it to the office on foot. There was no sign of the KEST-TV van out front. I took the stairs two at a time and entered Kingman and Ives through an unmarked door around the corner from the main entrance. In the back of my mind, I was mulling over the possibility that maybe Bennet or Jack had taken the letter to the *Dispatch*. I couldn't see what it would net either of them, but *someone* had an interest in seeing Guy's homecoming splashed across the news and it was someone who knew more than I was comfortable with. Again, I could feel the faint nudge of uneasiness. Darcy Pascoe's computer search had been a bit of a fudge. I hoped she wasn't going to find herself in trouble as a result of my request. I checked the fax machine in Lonnie's office and found the copy of Max Outhwaite's letter sitting in the slot as promised. I went to my office, reading as I went.

Dear Mr. Katzenbach,

Thought you'd be interested in a Modern-Day ''Cinderfella'' story taking place right here in Santa Teresa! As I recall, your the reporter, who wrote about Bader Malek's death last month. Now, word around town has it that his Probate Attorney hired a Private Investigater (a ''Female'' no less) to locate his missing son, Guy. If you've been around town as long as me, you'll remember that as a youngster, Guy Malek was caught in a number of scrapes, and finally disappeared from the local scene, nearly twenty years ago. You'd think finding someone like that after all this time would prove daunting, but Milhone (the aforementioned ''Female'' Detective) ran a DMV check, and turned him up in less than two days!! Seems he's been up in Marcella ever since he left, and he's working as a <u>janiter</u> in a church up there! He's one of those ''Born-Agains,'' who probably didn't have two nickles to rub together, but his father's death has turned him into an instant millionnaire!! I think people would be heartened to hear how he's managed to turn his life around, threw his Christian Faith. Folks might also enjoy hearing what he's planning to do with his new-found riches. With all the bad news that besieges us from day to day, wouldn't this story give everyone a nice lift? I think it would be a wonderfull inspiration to the Community! Let's hope Guy Malek is willing to share the story of his ''good fortune'' with us. I look forward to reading such an article and know you'd do a fine job of writing it! Best of luck and God Bless!

Sincerely yours,
Max Outhwaite
2905 Connecticut Ave.
Colgate, CA

I noticed I held the letter by the corners, as if to avoid smudging prints, a ridiculous precaution given the fact that it wasn't even the original. The note was neatly typed, with no visible corrections and no words XXX'd out. Granted, there were spelling errors (including my name), an excessive use of commas, a tendency toward the emphatic, and a bit of Unnecessary Capitalization! but otherwise the intentions of the sender seemed benign. Aside from alerting the press to something that was nobody else's business, I couldn't see any particular attempt to meddle in Guy Malek's life. Maximilian (or perhaps Maxine) Outhwaite apparently thought subscribers to the *Santa Teresa Dispatch* would be warmed by this story of a Bad Boy Turned Good and the Resultant Rewards! Outhwaite didn't seem to have an ax to grind and there was no hint of malice to undercut his (or her) enthusiasm for the tale. So what was going on?

I set the letter aside, swiveling in my swivel chair while I studied it covertly out of the corner of my eye. As a "Female" Detective, I found myself vaguely bothered by the damn thing. I didn't like the intimate acquaintance with the details and I couldn't help but wonder at the motivation. The tone was ingenuous, but the maneuver had been effective. Suddenly, Guy Malek's private business had been given a public audience.

I placed the letter in the Malek file, turning it over to my psyche for further consideration.

I spent the rest of the morning at the courthouse, taking care of other business. As a rule, I'm working fifteen to twenty cases concurrently. Not all of them are pressing and not all demand my attention at the same time. I do a number of background checks for a research and development firm out in Colgate. I also do preemployment investigations, as well as skip traces for a couple of small businesses in the area. Periodically, I'm involved in some fairly routine snooping for a divorce attorney down the street. Even in a no-fault state, a spouse might hide assets or conceal the whereabouts of communal items, like cars, boats, planes, and minor children. There's something restful about a morning spent cruising through the marriage licenses and death records in pursuit of genealogical connections, or an afternoon picking through probated wills, property transfers, and tax and mechanics' liens at the county offices. Sometimes I can't believe my good fortune, working in a business where I'm paid to uncover matters people would prefer to keep under wraps. Paper stalking doesn't require a PI to slip into a Kevlar vest, but the results can be just as dangerous as a gun battle or a high-speed chase.

My assignment that Monday morning was to probe the financial claims detailed in a company prospectus. A local businessman had been approached to invest fifty thousand dollars in what looked like a promising merchandising plan. Within an hour, I'd found out that one of the two partners had filed for personal bankruptcy and the other had a total of six lawsuits pending against him. While I was about it, I did a preliminary search for Max Outhwaite, starting with voter registration and working my way through local tax rolls. I crossed the street to the public library and tried the reference department. Under that spelling, there were no Outhwaites listed in the local phone books and none in the city directories going back six years. This meant nothing in particular as far as I could see. It did suggest that "Max Outhwaite" was a nom de plume, but under certain circumstances, I could relate to the maneuver. If I wanted to call an issue to the attention of the local paper, I might conceivably use a fake name and a phony address. I might be a prominent person, reluctant to have myself associated with the subject in question. I might be a family member, eager to get Guy in trouble, but unwilling to take responsibility. Writing such a letter was hardly a crime, but I might feel guilty nonetheless and not want the consequences blowing back on me.

For lunch I bought a sandwich and a soft drink from a vending machine and sat on a stretch of lawn out behind the courthouse. The day was hot, the treetops buffeted by dry winds coming off the desert. The branches of the big evergreens planted close to the street seemed to shimmer in the breeze, giving off the scent of pitch. I leaned back on my elbows and turned my face up to the sun. I can't say I slept, but I gave a good impression of it. At one o'clock, I roused myself and went back to the office where I began to type up my findings for the cases I'd worked. Such is the life of a PI these days. I spend more time practicing my skills with a Smith-Corona than a Smith & Wesson.

12

My run that morning had been unsatisfactory. I'd done what needed doing, dutifully jogging a mile and a half down the bike path and a mile and a half back, but I'd never developed any rhythm and the much-sought-after endorphin rush had failed to materialize. I've noticed on days when the run isn't good, I'm left with an emotional itch that feels like anxiety, in this case compounded by mild depression. Short of drink and drugs, sometimes the only remedy is to exercise again. I swear this is not a compulsion on my part so much as a craving for relief. I drove over to Harley's Beach and found a parking spot in the shelter of the hill. The lot was nearly empty, which surprised me somehow. Usually, there's an assortment of tourists and beachcombers, joggers, lovers, barking dogs, and parents with small children. Today, all I spotted was a family of feral cats sunning themselves on the hillside above the beach.

I staggered across an expanse of loose, dry sand until I reached the hard pack at the water's edge. I would have pulled off my shoes and socks, rolling up my pant legs so I could jog in the surf, however someone had recently given me a small book about tide pools. I'd leafed through with interest, imagining myself in the role of inquisitive naturalist, poking among the rocks for tiny crabs and starfish (though their undersides are completely disgusting and gross). Until I read this colorful, informative pamphlet, I'd had no idea what strange, ugly beasties existed close to shore. I'm not the kind of person who sentimentalizes nature. The outdoors, as far as I can see, is made up almost entirely of copulating creatures who eat one another afterward. To this end, almost every known animal has developed a strategy for luring others within range. Among life-forms in the sea—some quite minuscule—the tactic involves thorny parts or pincers or tiny three-jawed mouths or trailing stingers or vicious suckers with which they latch on to one another, causing painful death and dismemberment, all in the name of nourishment. Sometimes the juice is slurped out of the victim long before death occurs. The starfish actually takes out its own stomach, enfolds its live prey, and digests it outside its body. How would you like to put your bare foot down on that?

I ran in my shoes, splashing through the surf when the waves came close. Soon my wet jeans clung to my legs, the heavy fabric cold against my shins. My feet were weighted as though with stones and I could feel the sweat begin to soak through my shirt from the labor of the run. Despite the damp breeze coming off the ocean, the air felt oppressive. For the third day in a row, Santa Ana winds were blasting in from the desert, blowing down the local canyons, pulling moisture from the atmosphere. The mounting heat collected, degree by degree, like a wall of bricks going up. My progress felt slow and I forced myself to focus on the sand shimmering ahead of me. Since I had no way to measure distance, I ran for time, jogging thirty minutes north before I turned and jogged back. By the time I reached Harley's Beach again, my breathing was ragged and the muscles in my thighs were on fire. I slowed to a trot and then geared down to a walk as I returned to my car. For a moment, I leaned panting against the hood. Better. That was better. Pain was better than anxiety any day of the week and sweat was better than depression.

Home again, I left my soggy running shoes on the front steps. I padded upstairs, peeling out of my damp clothes as I ascended. I took a hot shower and then slipped into a pair of sandals, a T-shirt, and a short cotton skirt. It was now close to four and there was no point returning to the office. I brought in the mail and checked for phone messages. There were five: two hang-ups; two reporters who left numbers, asking me to get back to them; and a call from Peter Antle, the pastor of Guy's church. I dialed the number he'd left and he picked up so fast I had to guess he'd been waiting by the phone.

"Peter. I got your message. This is Kinsey in Santa Teresa."

"Kinsey. Thanks for being so prompt. Winnie's been trying to call Guy, but she can't seem to get through. The Maleks have the answering machine on and nobody's picking up. I don't know what Guy's plans are, but we thought we'd better warn him. There are reporters camped out at the gas station across from his place. We have people knocking on the church door and a pile of messages for him."

"Already?"

"That was my reaction. Frankly, I don't understand how this got out in the first place."

"Long story. I'm still in the process of looking into it. I know the family was contacted by the local newspaper first thing this morning. The reporter here had had a letter delivered to him at the paper. I guess something similar was sent to the L.A. *Times.* I haven't seen the news yet, but I have a feeling it's going to get bigger before it goes away."

"It's even worse up here. The town's so small, none of us can manage to avoid the press. Do you have a way to get in touch with Guy? We're here for him if he needs us. We don't want him to lose his footing in the stress of the situation."

"Let me see if I can find a way to get through. I guess this is his fifteen minutes of fame, though frankly, I can't understand why the story's generating so much attention. Why should anyone give a fat rat's . . . aa . . . ah . . . ear? He doesn't even have the money yet and who knows if he'll ever see one red cent."

I could almost see Peter's grin. "Everyone wants to believe in something. For most people, a big windfall would literally be the answer to all their prayers."

"I suppose so," I said. "At any rate, if I reach him, I'll have him give you a call."

"I'd appreciate that."

After we hung up, I flipped on the TV set and tuned in to KEST. The evening news wouldn't air for an hour, but the station often ran quick promos for the show coming up. I suffered through six commercials and caught the clip I'd suspected would be there. The blond anchorwoman smiled at the camera, saying, "Not all news is bad news. Sometimes even the darkest cloud has a silver lining. After nearly twenty years of poverty, a Marcella maintenance man has just learned he'll be inheriting five million dollars. We'll have that story for you at five." Behind her, the camera showed a glimpse of a haggard-looking Guy Malek, staring impassively from the car window as Donovan's BMW swung through the gates of the Malek estate. I felt a pang of guilt, wishing I'd talked him out of coming down. Given his bleak expression, the homecoming wasn't a success. I picked up the phone again and tried the Maleks' number. The line was busy.

I called the number every ten minutes for an hour. The Maleks had probably taken the phone off the hook, or maybe their message tape was full. In either event, who knew when I'd get through to him.

I debated with myself briefly and then drove over to the house. The gate was now closed and there were six vehicles parked along the berm. Reporters loitered, some leaning against their car fenders, two chatting together in the middle of the road. Both men were smoking and held big Styrofoam coffee cups. Three camera units had been set up on tripods and it looked as if the troops were prepared to stay. The late-afternoon sun slanted between the eucalyptus trees across from the Malek property, dividing the pavement into alternating sections of light and shadow.

I parked behind the last car and went on foot as far as the call box near the front gate. All activity behind me ceased and I could feel the attention focus on my back. No one answered my ring. Like the others, I was going to have to hang around out here, hoping to catch sight of one of the Maleks exiting or entering the grounds. I tried one more time, but my ringing was greeted with dead silence from inside the house.

I returned to my car and turned the key in the ignition. Already, a dark-haired woman reporter was ambling in my direction. She was probably in her forties, with oversized sunglasses and bright red lips. As I watched, she fumbled in her shoulder bag and pulled out a cigarette. She was tall and slender, decked out in slacks and a short-cropped cotton sweater. I marveled she could bear it with the heat sitting where it was. Gold earrings. Gold bracelets. A daunting pair of four-inch heels. For my taste, walking in high heels is like trying to learn to ice-skate. The human ankle does not take readily to such requirements. I admired her balance, though I realized when she reached me that in bare feet she'd probably be shorter than I. She made a circling motion, asking me to roll down my car window.

"Hi. How are you?" she said. She held up the cigarette. "You have a light for this?"

"Sorry. I don't smoke. Why don't you ask one of them?"

She turned, her gaze sliding back to the two men standing in the road. Her voice was husky and her tone was dismissive. "Oh, them. That's the boys' club," she remarked. "Those two won't even give you the time of day unless you have something to trade." Her eyes flicked back to me. "What about you? You don't look like a reporter. What are you, family friend? An old sweetheart?"

I had to admire the placid way she eased right into it, casual, unconcerned. She was probably wetting her pants, hoping I'd provide a little tidbit so she could scoop her competition. I started rolling up my window. Quickly, she raised her handbag and turned it sideways, inserting it into the space so the window wouldn't close all the way. There was now a seven-inch gap where her leather bag was wedged.

"No offense," she said, "but I'm curious. Aren't you that private investigator we've heard so much about?"

I turned the key in the ignition. "Please remove your bag." I cranked the window down about an inch, hoping she'd pull the bag free so I could be on my way.

"Don't be in such a hurry. What's the rush? The public has a right to know these things. I'm going to get the information anyway so why not make sure it's accurate? I heard the kid spent a lot of time in jail. Was that here or up north?"

I cranked the window up a notch and put the car in gear. I pushed my foot down lightly on the gas pedal and eased away from the berm. She held on to the bag by its strap, walking beside the car, continuing the conversation. I guess she was accustomed to having the driver at her mercy once she used the old handbag trick. I increased my speed sufficiently to force her into a trot. She yanked the strap, yelling "Hey!" as I began to accelerate. I couldn't have been driving more than two miles an hour, but that's a tough pace to maintain when you're wearing heels that high. I inched my foot down on the gas. She released the bag and stopped where she was, watching with consternation as I pulled away. I passed the two guys in the road who seemed to enjoy the rude comment she was yelling after me. I couldn't hear the words, but I got the drift. In the rearview mirror, I saw her flip me the bird.

She removed a high heel and flung it at my rear window. I heard a mild thump on impact and saw the shoe bounce off behind me as I picked up speed. The long strap of the handbag dangled and flapped against the car door. About a hundred yards down the road, I paused long enough to roll down my window and give the bag a shove. I left it there in the road, curled like a possum, and drove to my apartment.

There were two newspapers on the sidewalk when I got home. I picked up both and left one on Henry's back doorstep before I let myself in. I turned on some lights and poured myself a glass of wine, then sat at the kitchen counter and spread the paper out in front of me. The story was in the second section and the tone was odd. I'd expected a fairy-tale version of Guy's life to date, his estrangement from the family and his subsequent spiritual transformation. Instead, Jeff Katzenbach had patched together, in excruciating detail, an inventory of all the sins from Guy's youth: countless episodes of reckless driving, vandalism, drunk and disorderly conduct, assault and battery. Some charges dated back to his juvenile record and should have been purged or remained sealed by the courts. Where had Katzenbach gotten his information? Some of it, of course, was a matter of public record, but I wondered how he'd known to look. He'd obviously been tipped off by Max Outhwaite's reference to Guy's earlier scrapes. I thought back uneasily to the file of news clippings Bader Malek had kept. Was there any way he could have seen that? This would have been a second leak of sorts. The first was the fact of Guy's return; the second, this detailed criminal history. I noticed Katzenbach had couched his revelations in typical journalistic fudgings. The word *alleged* appeared about six times, along with *confidential sources, informants close to the family, former associates,* and *friends of the Maleks who asked to remain anonymous.* Far from celebrating Guy's good fortune, the public was going to end up resenting his sudden wealth. Reading between the lines, you could tell Katzenbach considered Guy Malek an undeserving scoundrel. Somehow his current church affiliation looked self-serving and insincere, the convenient refuge of a culprit hoping to make himself look good in the eyes of the parole board.

For supper, I made myself a hot hard-boiled egg sandwich with lots of mayonnaise and salt and perched at the counter eating while I scanned the rest of the paper. I must have been more absorbed than I thought because when the telephone shrilled, I flung my sandwich sideways in response. I snatched up the receiver, heart thumping as though a gun had just been fired in my ear. If this turned out to be a reporter, I was going to hang up. "Yes."

"Hey."

"Oh shit. Guy, is that you? You scared the hell out of me." I leaned down and gathered up the remains of my sandwich, popping the crust in my mouth while I licked at my fingers. There was mayonnaise on the floor, but I could tend to that later.

"Yeah, it's me. How are you?" he said. "I tried calling a while ago, but you were out, I guess."

"Thank God you called. I was just over at the house, but I couldn't get anyone to answer my ring. What's happening?"

"We just finished dinner. Have you seen the news?"

"I have the paper in front of me."

"Not so good, huh."

"It's not that bad," I said, hoping to cheer him up. "It does look like somebody's really got it in for you."

"That's my assumption," he said lightly.

"Are you all right? Peter called earlier. He's been trying to get in touch, but all he's managed so far is the answering machine. Did you get his message?"

"No, but why would I? Everybody here is pissed at me. They think I notified the paper, trying to get attention. There's a powwow on for later, after Donovan gets home. He's got a meeting until nine. The delay's making me sick. Reminds me of that old business, 'You wait until your father gets home and he'll give you the what for.' "

I found myself smiling. "You want me to come get you? I can be there in fifteen minutes."

"Yes—no—I don't know what I want. I'd like to get out of here, but I don't dare take off with things as they are."

"Why not? The damage is done. Whoever spilled the beans, made it look as bad as they could. If *you'd* leaked the news, you'd have put a different spin on it."

"How would I manage that? You can't put a different spin on the truth."

"Of course you can. It's called politics."

"Yeah, but I did all those things. This is just payback time. I told you I was bad. At least, now you know the worst."

"Oh stop that. I don't care about that stuff. All I care about is getting you out of there."

"You want to come for a visit? I could sneak out for a few minutes. Jack and Bennet are downstairs and Christie's in the office, going through some of Dad's old papers."

"Sure. I can pop back over there. What do you want me to do? Shall I ring from the gate?"

"No, don't do that. I'll meet you out on Wolf Run Road," he said. "If the side gate's locked, I can scale the wall. I'm an expert at getting out. When I was a kid I used to do it all the time. That's how I managed to get in so much trouble back then."

"Why don't you bring your backpack and let me spirit you away," I said. "I'll drive you to Marcella and you can hire an attorney to handle your interests from here on."

"Don't tempt me. Right now, all I need is civilized conversation. Park in that little grove of trees just across from the gate. I'll be out there in fifteen minutes."

I took a few minutes to tidy up the kitchen and then I changed into jeans, a dark shirt, and my Reeboks. The evening air felt uncharacteristically warm, but I wanted to be prepared for night maneuvers if need be. Once at the Maleks', I took a quick swing by the front gate. There were now two more news crews and the gathering had taken on the feel of a vigil outside a prison. Portable lights had been turned on and a man with a microphone spoke directly to a camera, making gestures toward the house. I saw the dark-haired reporter, but she didn't see me. She seemed to be bumming a light for her cigarette from a poor unsuspecting "source."

I followed the wall, circling the property as I turned left on Wolf Run. I spotted the gate, a dark blot in an otherwise unbroken expanse of wall. I pulled off onto the berm across the road, gravel crackling under my wheels. I shut down the engine and sat there, listening to the tick of hot metal and the murmur of the wind. There weren't any street lamps along this section of the road. The high night sky was clear, but the moon had been reduced to the merest sliver, a frail curve of silver in a sky pale with stars. The dust in the air was as fine as mist. In the ambient light, the pavement was a dull, luminous gray. The stucco wall enclosing the Malek property had been robbed of its pink luster and stretched now like a ghostly band of drab white. June and July were traditionally dry and I associated the Santa Ana winds with the end of summer—late August, early September, when the fire danger was extreme. For years, January had been the rainy season, two weeks of rain that we hoped would fill our annual quota. Yet here we were with the dry wind tossing in the treetops. The bend and sway of tree boughs set up a hushed night music, accompanied by the rustling percussion of dry palm fronds, the occasional snap of tree limbs. By morning, the streets would be littered with dead leaves and the small withered skeletons of broken branches.

The gate opened without a sound and Guy emerged, head down. He wore a dark-colored jacket, his fists shoved into his pockets as though he were cold. I leaned over and unlocked the door on the passenger side. He slid into the seat and then pulled the door shut without slamming it. He said, "Hey. Thanks for coming. I thought I'd go crazy without a friendly face. I'd have called you before, but they were watching me like a hawk."

"No problem. I don't know why you don't break and run while you can."

"I will. Tomorrow. Or maybe the day after that. I told you we're supposed to have another meeting tonight just to talk about some things."

"I thought you already talked."

"Well, we did. We do. Every time I turn around, we have another chat."

"That's because you haven't knuckled under yet," I interjected.

"I guess that's it." He smiled in spite of himself. His tension was contagious and I could have sworn I smelled alcohol on his breath. I found myself with my arms crossed, one leg wound around the other as if to protect myself.

"I feel like we're having an affair," I said.

"Me, too. I used to meet girls out here in the old days when I was grounded. I'd slip over the wall and we'd screw in the backseat of a car. There was something about the danger set me on fire, and them, too. Made most of 'em seem more interesting than they were."

"I know this is none of my business, but have you been drinking?" I asked.

He turned and looked out the passenger window, shrugging. "I had a couple of drinks last night before all this shit came down. I don't know what got into me. Don't get me wrong—they were being nice at that point, but you could tell they were nervous and so was I. I'm ashamed to say this, but the alcohol did help. It mellowed us out and smoothed the conversation. Tonight was pretty much the same except everybody's mood was different. Cocktail hour comes along and those guys really hit it."

"Bennet and his martinis."

"You bet. I figure that's the only way I'll get through. Peter wouldn't be too happy with me, but I can't help it. I can feel myself sliding back to my old ways."

"What'd you think of Christie?"

"She was nice. I liked her. I was surprised at Bennet—at the weight he'd put on, but Jack seemed the same, still nuts about golf. And Donovan hasn't changed."

"What've they said to you so far?"

"Well, we talked some about the money, what else? I mean, the subject does come up. It's like Donovan says, we can't just ignore the issue. It's like this big dark cloud hanging over us. I think we were all uncomfortable at first."

"Have you resolved anything?"

"Well, no. Nothing much. At first, I think they were wondering, you know, generally, about my attitude. Now, anything I say and everybody jumps right on in. Tell you the truth, I'd forgotten what they're like."

"How do they seem to you?"

"Angry. Underneath it all, they're pissed. I keep feeling the anger coming up inside me, too. It's all I can do to keep a lid on it."

"Why bother? Why not blow? The three of them certainly don't hesitate."

"I know, but if I flip my lid that's only going to make matters worse. I'm trying to show 'em I've changed and then I find myself feeling like I always did. Like I want to smash lamps, throw a chair through a window, get stoned or drunk or something bad like that."

"That must be a trial."

"I'll say. I mean, literally. All I can think about is maybe this is some kind of test of my faith."

"Oh, it is *not,*" I said. "It may be a test of your patience, but not your faith in God."

He shook his head, pressing his hands down between his knees. "Let's talk about something else. This is making me so tense I could fart."

I laughed and changed the subject. For a while we chatted about inconsequential matters. Hunched there in the front seat, I was reminded of the occasional dates I had in high school where the only hope of privacy was remaining closed away in some kid's car. On chilly evenings, the front windshield would fog up even if all we did was talk. On warm nights like this, we'd sit with the windows rolled down, radio tuned to some rock and roll station. It was Elvis or the Beatles, clumsy moves and sexual tension. I don't even remember now what we talked about, those lads and I. Probably nothing. Probably we drank purloined beer, smoked dope, and thought about the incredible majesty of life.

"So what else's going on? Aside from interminable meetings?" I asked. Like a rough place on a fingernail, I couldn't resist going back to it. Apparently, Guy couldn't resist it either because we fell right into the subject again.

This time he smiled and his tone seemed lighter. "It's nice to see the house. I found some letters of my mother's and I read those today. She's the only one I ever missed. The rest of 'em are a waste."

"I don't want to say I told you so, but I did predict this."

"I know, I know. I thought we could just sit down like grown-ups and clean up some old business, but it doesn't really happen like that. I mean, I keep wondering if there isn't some kind of defect in me because everything I do just seems to come out wrong. Whatever I say seems 'off,' you know? They look at me like I'm speaking in tongues and then I see them exchange these looks."

"Oh, I know that one. Jack and Bennet are big on flicking looks back and forth."

"That's the easy part, but there's worse."

"Like what?"

"I don't even know how to describe it. Something under the surface. Something slides right by and no one owns up to it, so then I start questioning my own thought process. Maybe I'm nuts and it's not them after all."

"Give me an example."

"Like when I told 'em I'd like to give something to the church? I honestly don't want the money for me. I mean that. But Jubilee Evangelical saved my life and I want to give something back. To me, that doesn't seem so wrong. Does it seem wrong to you?"

"No, not at all."

"So, I say that and all of a sudden we're in the middle of a power play. Bennet's saying how it really doesn't seem fair. You know how he talks with that slightly pompous air of his. 'Our family's never been religious. Dad worked for the good of us all, not for the benefit of some church he never heard of.' He says it all in this completely rational tone and pretty soon I wonder if what I want to do is right after all. Maybe they have a point and *my* values are screwed up."

"Sure they have a point. They want you to relinquish all claim so they can divide up your portion among themselves. They know perfectly well you're entitled to a quarter of his estate. What you do with your share is none of their business."

"But how come I end up the magnet for all that rage?"

"Guy, stop. Don't do that. That's the third time you've said that. Don't get into self-blame. The gamesmanship has obviously been going on for years. That's got to be why you left in the first place, to get away from that stuff. I swear they were behaving the same way before you showed up."

"You think I should leave?"

"Well, of course I do! I've said it all along. You shouldn't take their abuse. I think you should get the hell out while you have the chance."

"I wouldn't call it 'abuse.' "

"Because you're used to it," I said. "And don't get sidetracked. Your brothers aren't going to change. If anybody goes down for the count, it's going to be you."

"Maybe so," he said. "I don't know. I just feel like I have to stay since I've come this far. If I cut and run, we're never going to find a way to work this through."

"I can tell you're not listening, but please, *please,* don't agree to anything without talking to an attorney first."

"Okay."

"Promise me."

"I will. I swear. Well, I gotta go before somebody figures out I've escaped."

"Guy, you're not sixteen. You're forty-three years old. Sit here if you want. You can stay out all night. Big whoop-dee-do. You're an adult."

He laughed. "I *feel* like I'm sixteen. And you're cute."

He leaned over quickly and brushed my cheek with his lips. I could feel the soft scratch of his whiskers against my face and I caught a whiff of his aftershave.

He said, "Bye-bye and thanks." Before I could respond, he was out of the car, shoulders hunched up against the wind as he moved to the gate. He turned and waved and then he was swallowed up by the dark.

I never saw him again.

13

Guy Malek was killed sometime Tuesday night, though I didn't actually hear about it until Wednesday afternoon. I'd spent most of the day over at the courthouse sitting in on the trial of a man accused of embezzlement. I hadn't been associated with the case—undercover cops had nailed him after seven months of hard work—but some years before, I'd done surveillance on him briefly at the request of his wife. She suspected he was cheating, but she wasn't sure with whom. Turned out he was having an affair with her sister and she broke off relations with both. The man was dishonest to the core and I confess I found it entertaining to watch the legal system grind away at him. As often as I complain about the shortage of justice in this world, I find it infinitely satisfying when the process finally works as it should.

When I got back to the office after court adjourned, there was a message from Tasha waiting on my machine. I noticed, in passing, it was the Maleks' number she'd left. I called, expecting to have Myrna pick up. Instead Tasha answered as if she'd been manning the phones. The minute I heard her, I realized how irritated I was that she'd gone out of town just as Guy arrived. If she'd been doing her job, she might have steered the family off their campaign of pressure and harassment.

Smart mouth that I am, I launched right in. "At long last," I said, "it's about time you got back. All hell's broken loose. Have you heard what's going on? Well, obviously you have or you wouldn't be there. Honestly, I adore Guy, but I can't stand the rest of 'em—"

Tasha cut in, her voice flat. "Kinsey, that's why I called. I cut my trip short and flew back from Utah this afternoon. Guy is dead."

I was silent for a beat, trying to parse the sentence. I knew the subject . . . *Guy* . . . but the predicate . . . *is dead* . . . made no immediate sense. "You're kidding. What happened? He can't be *dead.* When I saw him on Monday he was fine."

"He was murdered last night. Somebody smashed his skull with a blunt instrument. Christie found him in bed this morning when he didn't come down for breakfast. The police took one look at the crime scene and got a warrant to search the premises. The house has been swarming with cops ever since. They haven't found the murder weapon, but they suspect it's here. They're still combing the property."

I kept getting hung up about two sentences back. "Somebody killed him in bed? While he *slept?*"

"It looks that way."

"That's disgusting. That's awful. You can't be serious."

"I'm sorry to spring it on you, but there isn't any nice way to put it. It *is* disgusting. It's terrible. We're all numb."

"Has anybody been arrested?"

"Not at this point," she said. "The family's doing what they can to cooperate, but it doesn't look good."

"Tasha, I don't believe this. I'm sick."

"I am, too. A colleague called me in Utah this morning after

Donovan called him. I left everything behind and got myself on a plane."

"Who do they suspect?"

"I have no idea. From what I've heard, Jack and Bennet were both out last night. Christie went to bed early and Donovan was watching TV upstairs in their sitting room. Myrna's apartment is off the kitchen in back, but she says she was dead to the world and didn't hear anything. She's currently down at the station being interviewed. Christie came in a little while ago. She says the detectives are still talking to Donovan. Hang on."

She put a hand across the mouthpiece and I heard her in a muffled discussion with someone in the background. She came back on the line, saying, "Great. I just talked to the homicide detective in charge of things here. He wants to keep the phone line open, but says if you want to come over, he'll tell the guys at the gate to let you in. I told him he ought to talk to you since you were the one who found Guy in the first place. I told him you might have something to contribute."

"I doubt that, but who knows? I'll be there in fifteen minutes. Do you need anything?"

"We're fine for the moment. If no one's at the gate, the code is 1-9-2-4. Just punch the number in at the call box beside the drive. See you shortly," she said.

I grabbed my blazer and my handbag and went out to my car. The day had been mild. The high winds had moved on, taking with them the unseasonable heat. The light was waning and as soon as the sun set, the temperatures would drop. I was already chilled and I shrugged into my blazer before I slid beneath the wheel. Earlier in the day, I'd tried to use my wipers and washer fluid to clean the dust off my windshield and now it was streaked in a series of rising half moons. The hood of my car was covered with the same fine layer of dust, as pale as powder, and just as soft by the look of it. Even the seat upholstery had a gritty feel to it.

I put my hands together on the steering wheel and leaned my forehead against them. I had absolutely no feeling. My interior process was held in suspended animation, as if the Pause button had been pushed on some remote control. How was it possible Guy Malek was gone? For the past week, he'd been such a presence in my life. He'd been both lost and found. He'd occupied my thoughts, triggering reactions of sympathy and exasperation. Now I couldn't quite remember his face—only a flash here and there, the sound of his "Hey," the whiskery brush of his chin on my cheek. He was already as insubstantial as a ghost, all form without content, a series of fragmented images without permanence.

What seemed so odd was that life just went *on.* I could see traffic passing along Cabana Boulevard. Two doors away, my neighbor raked brittle leaves into a pile on his lawn. If I turned on the car radio, there'd be intervals of music, public service announcements, commercials, and news broadcasts. Guy Malek might not even be mentioned on some stations. I'd lived my entire day without any intuition that Guy had been murdered, no tremor whatsoever in my subterranean landscape. So what's life about? Are people not really dead until we've been irrefutably informed? It felt that way to me, as though Guy had, just this moment, been jettisoned out of this world and into the next.

I turned the key in the ignition. Every ordinary act seemed fraught with novelty. My perceptions had changed, and with them many of my assumptions about my personal safety. If Guy could be murdered, why not Henry, or me? I drove on automatic pilot while the street scenes slid past. Familiar neighborhoods looked odd and there was a moment when I couldn't recall with any certainty what town I was in.

Approaching the Maleks', I could see that traffic had increased. Cars filled with the curious cruised by the estate. Heads were turned almost comically in the same direction. There were cars parked on both sides of the road out front. Tires had chewed into the grass, plowing down bushes and crushing the stray saplings. As each new car appeared, the assembled crowd would turn, craning and peering to see if it was someone of note.

My car didn't seem to generate a lot of interest at first. I guess nobody could believe the Maleks would drive a VW bug, especially one like mine, with its dust and assorted dings. It was only when I pulled up at the gate and gave my name to the guard that the reporters surged forward, trying to catch a glimpse of me. They seemed to be fresh troops. I didn't recognize anyone from my earlier trip over.

Somehow the national media had already managed to get camera crews assembled, and I knew that by seven the next morning, someone closely associated with the Maleks would be seen in a three-minute interview. I don't know how the major networks make arrangements so quickly. It was one of the miracles of technology that less than twenty-four hours after Guy Malek's death, somebody would do a close-up of a tear-stained face, maybe Christie's or Myrna's or even Enid's, the cook I'd yet to meet.

There was a black-and-white patrol car parked to one side, along with a vehicle from a private firm. I spotted the security guard pacing along the road, trying to keep the crowd from moving in too close. A uniformed police officer checked my name on his clipboard and waved me in. The gate swung inward by degrees and I idled the engine until the gap was sufficient to ease through. In that brief interval, there were strangers knocking on my car window, yelling questions in my direction. With their various handheld mikes extended, they might have been offering gimcracks for sale. I kept my eyes straight ahead. When I pulled forward through the gate, two male reporters continued to trot alongside me like cut-rate Secret Service agents. The security guard and the cop both converged, cutting off their progress. In my rearview mirror, I could see them begin to argue with the officer, probably reciting their moral, legal, and Constitutional rights.

My heart rate picked up as I eased up the driveway toward the house. I could see five or six uniformed officers prowling across the property, eyes on the ground as if hunting for four-leaved clovers. Light tended to fade rapidly at this hour of the day. Shadows were already collecting beneath the trees. Soon they'd need flashlights to continue the search. There was a second uniformed officer posted at the front door, his face impassive. He walked out to meet my car and I rolled down my window. I gave him my name and watched him scan both his list and my face. Apparently satisfied, he stepped away from the car. In the courtyard to my left, there were already numerous cars jammed into the cobblestone turnaround. "Any place in here all right?"

"You can park in the rear. Then come around and use the front door to go in," he said, and motioned me on.

"Thanks."

I pulled around to the left and parked my car at the far end of the three-car garage. In the diminishing light, a cluster of three floods, activated by motion sensors, flashed on to signal my presence. Except for the kitchen on this end of the house and the library on the other, most of the windows along the front of the house were dark. Around the front, the exterior lighting seemed purely decorative, too pale to provide a welcome in the accumulating gloom.

The uniformed police officer opened the door for me and I passed into the foyer. The library door was ajar and a shaft of light defined one pie-shaped wedge of the wood parquet floor. Given the quiet in the house, I was guessing the technicians were gone—fingerprint experts, the photographer, the crime scene artist, coroner, and paramedics. Tasha appeared in the doorway. "I saw you pull in. How're you doing?"

I said "Fine" in a tone that encouraged her to keep her distance from me. I noticed I was feeling churlish, as much as with her as with circumstance. Homicide makes me angry with its sly tricks and disguises. I wanted Guy Malek back and with some convoluted emotional logic, I blamed her for what had happened. If she hadn't been my cousin, she wouldn't have hired me in the first place. If I hadn't been hired, I wouldn't have found him, wouldn't even have known who he was, wouldn't have cared, and would have felt no loss. She knew this as well as I did and the flicker of guilt that crossed her face was a mirror to mine.

For someone who'd flown back from her vacation in haste, Tasha was flawlessly turned out. She wore a black gabardine pantsuit with a jacket cropped at the waist. The slim, uncuffed trousers had a wide waistband and inverted pleats in front. The jacket had brass buttons and the sleeves were trimmed with a thin gold braid. Somehow the outfit suggested something more than fashion. She looked crisp, authoritative, and diminutive, the dainty MP of lawyers here to keep matters straight.

I followed her into the library with its clusters of dark red cracked leather chairs. The red Oriental carpets looked drab at this hour. The tall leaded glass windows were tinted with the gray cast of twilight, as chilly as frost. Tasha paused to turn on table lamps as she crossed the room. Even the luster of the dark wood paneling failed to lend coziness to the cold stone hearth. The room was shabby and smelled as musty as I remembered it. I'd first met Bennet here just a week ago.

I left my handbag beside a club chair and circled the room restlessly. "Who's the chief investigator? You said there was someone here."

"Lieutenant Robb."

"Jonah? Oh, terrific. How perfect."

"You know him?"

"I know Jonah," I said. When I'd met him, he was working Missing Persons, but the Santa Teresa Police Department has a mandatory rotation system and detectives get moved around. With Lieutenant Dolan's retirement, there was an opening for a homicide investigator. I'd had a short-lived affair with Jonah once when he was separated from his wife, a frequent occurrence in the course of their stormy relationship. They'd been sweethearts since seventh grade and were no doubt destined to be together for life, like owls, except for the intervals of virulent estrangement coming every ten months. I suppose the pattern should have been evident, but I was smitten with him. Later, not surprisingly, she crooked her little finger and he went back to her. Occasionally now, the three of us crossed paths out in public and I'd become an expert at pretending I'd never dallied with him between my Wonder Woman sheets. This probably accounted for his willingness to have me on the scene. He knew he could trust me to keep my mouth shut.

"What's the story?" she asked.

"Nothing. Just skip it. I feel bitchy, I guess, but I shouldn't take it out on you."

I heard footsteps on the stairs and looked up as Christie came in. She wore bulky running shoes and a warm-up suit in some silky material, the blue of the fabric setting off the blue in her eyes. She wore scarcely any makeup and I wondered if this was the outfit she was wearing when Guy's body was discovered. The library, like the living room, was equipped with a wet bar: a small brass sink, a minirefrigerator, an ice bucket, and a tray of assorted liquor bottles. She moved over to the fridge and removed a chilled bottle of white wine. "Anybody want a glass of wine? What about you, Kinsey?"

I said, "Alcohol won't help."

"Don't be absurd. Of course it will. So does Valium. It doesn't change reality, but it improves your attitude. Tasha? Can I interest you in a glass of Chardonnay? This is top of the line." She turned the bottle so she could peer at the price tag on the side. "Nice. This is $36.95."

"I'll have some in a bit. Not just yet," Tasha said.

Mutely, the two of us watched while Christie cut the foil cap from a wine bottle and used a corkscrew. "If I smoked, I'd have a ciggie, but I don't," she said. She poured herself some wine, the bottle clinking clumsily on the rim of the Waterford crystal. "Shit!" she said, pausing to inspect the damage. A jagged crack ran down the side. She dumped the contents in the sink and tossed the glass in the trash. She picked up a second glass and poured again. "We need a fire in here. I wish Donovan were home."

"I can do that," I said. I moved over to the hearth and removed the fire screen. There were six or seven hefty pieces of firewood in a brass carrier. I picked up one and chunked it onto the grate.

"Make sure you don't destroy any evidence," she said.

I looked up at her blankly.

"Ted Bundy killed one of his victims with a hunk of wood," she said, and then shrugged with embarrassment. "Never mind. Not funny. What a day," she said. "I can't figure out how to handle it. I've felt drunk since this morning, completely out of control."

I stacked two more logs on the grate while she and Tasha talked. It was a relief to be involved in a task that was basic and inconsequential. The wood was beautifully seasoned oak. Most of the heat would go straight up the chimney, but it would be a comfort nonetheless. I flicked on the electric match, turned the key in the gas starter, and listened to the comforting *whunk* as the jets ignited. I replaced the fire screen, pausing to adjust the height of the flame. Belatedly, I tuned into their conversation.

Tasha was saying, "Did you ask to have an attorney present?"

"Of course I didn't ask for an attorney. I didn't *do* anything. This was just routine," Christie said irritably. She remained standing behind the bar, leaning against its leather surface. "Sorry. What's the matter with me? I'm completely frazzled."

"Don't worry about it. Who's still down there?"

"Jack and Bennet, I think. They kept everybody separated like they did here. So absurd. What do they think, Donovan and I aren't going to discuss it in detail the minute we can put our heads together?"

"They don't want to risk your influencing one another," I said. "Memory's fragile. It's easily contaminated."

"None of us have anything much to report," she said. "I drank too much at dinner and fell asleep by nine. Donovan was watching TV in the sitting room off our bedroom."

"What about Guy?"

"He went up to bed about the same time I did. He was drunk as all get-out thanks to Bennet's martinis." She caught sight of her fingertips and frowned to herself. She turned away from us and ran water in the sink. "They took prints for comparison."

Tasha directed a brief comment to me. "After the body was removed and the fingerprint techs were finished, the homicide investigator had one of the Maleks' housecleaning crew come over and walk through Guy's room with him describing the usual position of furniture, lamps, ashtrays, that sort of thing."

"Did they find anything?"

"I have no idea. I'm sure she was cautioned to keep her mouth shut. I know they tagged and bagged a bunch of items, but I don't know exactly what or why they were significant. Now they've brought in additional officers and started a grid search of the grounds. Apparently, they spent a lot of time down in the pool house earlier."

Christie broke in. "I could see them from up in my room checking perimeter gates, any point of entrance or exit."

"They're still out there on the property. I noticed that when I came in. But why check the exterior? It almost had to be someone in the house."

Christie bristled. "Not necessarily. What makes you say that? We have people all over. Maybe fifteen a week, with the gardeners and the car washers, housecleaners, and the woman who takes care of the plants. We have no idea where those people come from. For all we know, they're convicted felons or escapees from a mental institution."

I wasn't going to speak to her flight of fancy. If the notion gave her comfort, let her hang on to it. "It's always possible," I said, "but I'm assuming none of them have access to the house at night. I thought you had an alarm system."

"Well, we do. The police were interested in the system as well, but that's the problem," she said. "With all the high winds we've had here the past couple of days, windows were blowing open and the alarm kept going off. It happened twice Monday night after we'd all gone to bed. Scared the shit out of me. We finally turned it off so it wouldn't happen again. Last night, the system wasn't on at all."

"When do they think Guy was killed?" I asked.

"Around ten, I gather. Between ten and eleven. The detective didn't actually say that, but I noticed that was the period that seemed to interest him. Bennet and Jack were both out until late."

A woman in a housekeeper's uniform, with an apron tied over it, peered in at the door. She was short and round, and looked like someone whose eating habits had long ago outstripped any fat-burning activities. She was probably in her mid-forties, with dark hair pulled back neatly under a red-and-white bandanna she'd wrapped around her head. I wasn't sure if the purpose was ornamental or meant to keep falling hair from seasoning the food. "Excuse me. I'm sorry to interrupt, but I'm wondering what time you want dinner served."

Christie made a face. "My fault, Enid. I should have talked to you. Donovan's not back yet and I'm not really sure about Jack and Bennet. What are we having? Will it hold?"

"Baked chicken breasts. I stopped off at the market on my way in to work. I went ahead and changed the menu, so there's plenty if you're having extra people. I did up some oven-roasted potatoes and a casserole of sweet-and-sour cabbage. I can wait and serve if you like." Somehow she managed to indicate without a word that waiting around to serve dinner was the last choice on her list.

"No, no, no. I don't want you to do that. Just leave things in the oven and we can help ourselves. As soon as you're ready, go ahead and take off. I know you were in early."

"Yes, ma'am. Myrna called me. I came as soon as I heard."

"Have the police talked to you? I'm assuming they have. They talked to everyone else."

Enid picked at her apron uncomfortably. "I talked to Lieutenant Bower shortly before you did, I believe. Do you want me tomorrow at the usual time?"

"I don't know yet. Call me in the morning and we'll see what's going on. I may want you here early if that's all right with you."

"Of course."

As soon as she withdrew, Christie said, "Sorry for the interruption.

That's Enid Pressman. She's the cook. I guess I could have introduced you. I didn't mean to be rude. Tasha's met her before."

"That's perfectly all right," I said. I made a quick mental note to have a chat with Enid at some point. She'd neatly avoided relating much in the way of information.

Tasha said, "Maybe I will have that drink. Here, let me get it. You look exhausted. We need to sit."

Christie had put the wine bottle in a cooler and now grabbed two more glasses. Tasha moved over to the bar and took the cooler from her, setting it down on a table between two chairs. Christie quizzed me with a gesture, asking if I was ready to have wine.

"I'm fine for now, but go ahead," I said.

Christie curled up in one of the leather chairs. She tucked her legs under her and crossed her arms.

I took the chair closest to the fireplace while Tasha perched on the arm of the chair next to Christie's. Tasha said, "What about Bennet? Where was he last night?"

"I'm not really sure. You'd have to ask him about that."

"And Jack?"

"Over at the country club with a hundred other fellows. There's a pro-am tournament coming up this weekend. Practice rounds start on Thursday. He went to the pairings' party with a friend of his."

"That should be easy enough to verify," Tasha said.

"Would you quit talking like that? He didn't kill Guy and neither did I."

"Christie, I'm not accusing you. I'm trying to analyze your position here. Given the situation, suspicion's bound to fall on one of you. I don't mean you specifically, so don't take offense. Other people may have access to the property, but who'd have a better motive than the family? There's a lot of money at stake."

"But Tasha, that's ridiculous. If one of us were going to kill him, why do it here? Why not somewhere else? Make it look like an accident or random violence."

I raised my hand like a student. "Think of the convenience. If you kill a man in his sleep, you don't have to worry about him putting up a fight."

Jonah Robb appeared in the doorway, his gaze fixed on Christie. "We'll be taking off shortly. The bedroom's still sealed pending the coroner's report. It's strictly off-limits until you hear from us. We'll be here early tomorrow morning to finish things up."

"Of course. Will there be anything else?"

"I understand your brother-in-law received some mail . . ."

"We gave that to the other detective, Lieutenant Bower."

Jonah nodded. "Fine. I'll check with her."

"Do you have any idea what time we can expect my husband? When I left the station, he was still being interviewed."

"I'll have him call if he's there when I get back to the station. With luck, he'll be done and on his way home."

"Thanks."

Jonah's gaze came to rest on mine and he tilted his head. "Can I see you out here?"

I got up and crossed the room. He held the door open and we went into the hall.

He said, "Donovan tells us you were the one who located Guy on behalf of the estate."

"That's right."

"We're going to want to talk to you in the morning, picking up background information."

"Of course. Glad to help. I can stop by at nine on my way into work," I said. "What's this business about the mail?"

"I haven't seen it yet," he said obliquely, meaning *none-of-your-beeswax.* We looked at each other for perhaps half a moment longer than was absolutely essential. I'd always thought Jonah was good looking. Black Irish, I think they call them. Blue eyes, coal black hair. He looked worn-out and tense, his eyes surrounded by a lacework of fine lines, his skin looking coarser than I remembered. Perhaps as a side effect of my renewed sexuality, I found myself sizing up the men in my life. With Jonah, there was a dark radiance in the air. I felt like a fruit fly, wondering if the pheromones were mine or his.

"How's Camilla?"

"She's pregnant."

"Congratulations."

"It's not mine."

"Ah."

"What about you? You involved with anyone these days?"

"Could be. It's hard to know."

His smile was brief. "See you in the morning."

That you will, I thought.

14

Once Jonah was gone, I found myself reluctant to return to the library. I could hear Christie and Tasha talking together companionably, their voices light, the conversation interspersed with nervous laughter. The subject had obviously changed. The ego is ill-prepared to deal with death for long. Even at a wake or a funeral, the topic tends to drift to safer ground whenever possible. I scanned the empty foyer, trying to get my bearings. Across from the library was the living room. I'd been in there, but I'd never seen the rest of the ground floor.

I passed under the stairs to an intersecting corridor that branched off in both directions. I caught a glimpse of a powder room across the hall. I saw two doors on the right, but both were closed. Under the circumstances, I thought it unwise to snoop indiscriminantly. In the unlikely event I encountered a cop, I was roaming in the guise of someone looking for the kitchen so I could offer my help.

Before, the house had felt comfortable despite the touches of shabbiness that appeared throughout. Now I was acutely aware of the imprint of Guy's murder. The very air seemed heavy, the gloom as languorous as a dense fog drifting through the rooms.

I took a left, moving toward the unhappy scent of cooked cabbage at the end of the hall. In a sudden glimpse of the future, I could envision the day when this house would be sold to a private boys' school and the smell of cruciform vegetables would overpower all else. Young lads in hard shoes would clatter through the halls between classes. The room where Guy had been bludgeoned to death would be turned into a dormitory where adolescent boys would abuse themselves surreptitiously after lights out. Always, there would be rumors about the pale apparition gliding down the corridor, hovering on the landing at the turn of the stairs. I found myself walking quickly, anxious for human company.

Beyond the dining room and butler's pantry, the swinging door to the kitchen stood open. The room looked vast to me, but then my entire culinary kingdom would fit in the rear of a moderately priced station wagon. The floors were pale, glossy pegged oak planks stretching out in all directions. The custom cupboards were dark cherry and the counters were topped with mottled green marble. There were sufficient cookbooks, utensils, and small appliances in view to furnish one small section of a Williams-Sonoma retail outlet. The stove top looked bigger than the double bed in my loft and the refrigerator had clear doors with all the contents on view. To the right, there was the equivalent of a little sitting area; and beyond, there was a glassed-in porch that extended the entire length of the room. Here the lush scent of roast chicken and garlic overrode the odor of cooked cabbage. Why does someone else's cooking always smell so much better than your own?

Myrna had come back from the police station. She and Enid were standing together near one of the two kitchen sinks. Myrna's face looked puffy and the prickle of red around her eyes suggested she'd been crying, not within the last few minutes, but perhaps earlier in the day. Enid had pulled on a poplin raincoat and the yards of tan fabric gave her the hapless form and shape of a baked potato. She'd removed her bandanna. Bareheaded, she had a wiry bird's nest of hair that was dark strands streaked with gray. Tea mugs in hand, they must have been having a few last words about the murder because both looked up guiltily as I came in. Given their proximity to events, the two of them must have been privy to just about everything. Certainly, the family wasn't shy about airing their conflicts. God knows they'd squabbled in front of me. Enid and Myrna must have picked up on plenty and probably compared notes.

Enid said, "Can I help you?" She was using the same tone museum guards take when they think you're about to reach out and touch something on the far side of the rope.

"That's what I came to ask," I said. "Can I do anything to help?" Little Miss Goody Two-shoes working on a Girl Scout merit badge.

"Thanks, but everything's under control," she said. She emptied her mug in the sink, opened the dishwasher, and set it in the top rack. "I better go while I can," she murmured.

Myrna said, "I can walk you out if you want."

"I'll be fine," Enid replied. "I can turn on the lights in back." And then with a look at me, "Can I fix you a cup of tea? The water's hot. I'm just on my way out, but it won't take but a minute."

"I'd like that," I said. I'm not that fond of tea, but I had hoped to prolong the contact.

"I can do it," Myrna said. "You go on."

"Are you sure?"

"Absolutely. We'll see you tomorrow."

Enid reached out and patted Myrna on the arm. "Well. Bye-bye. I want you to talk to my chiropractor about that bursitis and you call if you need me. I'll be home all evening." Enid took up a wide canvas tote and disappeared through the utility room, moving toward the backdoor.

I watched Myrna plug in the electric tea kettle. She opened a cabinet nearby and took down a mug. Wincing, she reached for a canister and removed a tea bag that she placed in the mug. Meanwhile, outside, I could hear a car door slam shut and moments later, the sound of Enid starting her car.

I moved over to the counter and perched on a wooden stool. "How're you doing, Myrna? You look tired," I said.

"That's my bursitis flaring up. It's been bothering me for days," she said.

"The stress probably contributes."

Myrna pursed her lips. "That's what my doctor says. I thought I'd seen everything. I'm used to death. In my job, I see a lot of it, but this . . ." She paused to shake her head.

"It must have been hellish around here today. I could hardly believe it when Tasha told me," I said. "You've worked for the Maleks, what . . . eight months?"

"About that. Since last April. The family asked me to stay on after Mr. Malek died. Somebody had to take responsibility for running the house. Enid was tired of doing it and I didn't mind. I've managed many a household, some of 'em a lot bigger than this."

"Couldn't you be making a lot more money as a private-duty nurse?"

She took down a sugar bowl and found a creamer that she filled from a carton of half-and-half in the refrigerator. "Well, yes, but I needed some relief from all the terminal illness. I become attached to my patients and where does that leave me when they pass? I was living like a Gypsy, moving from job to job. Here I have a small apartment of my own and the duties are largely supervisory. I do light cooking occasionally on Enid's nights off, but that's about it. Of course, they complain. They're hard to please sometimes, but I don't let it bother me. In some ways, I'm used to it. The sick are often difficult and it doesn't mean anything. I let it roll right off me."

"I take it you were here last night."

The tea kettle began a hoarse whisper that rapidly turned into a shriek. She paused to unplug it and the shrill sound subsided as though with relief. I waited while she filled the mug and brought it over to me. "Thanks."

I could see her hesitate, apparently debating with herself about her next comment. "Is something bothering you?" I asked.

"I'm not sure what I'm allowed to say," she hesitated. "The lieutenant asked us not to talk to the press . . ."

"Not surprising," I said. "Have you seen 'em out there?"

"Like vultures," she remarked. "When I came back from the station, they were all yelling and vying for my attention, pushing microphones in my direction. Made me want to pull my jacket right up over my face. I felt like one of those criminals you see on the television."

"It's probably only going to get worse. This started out as a minor human-interest story. Now it's big news."

"I'm afraid so," she said. "But to answer your question, yes, I was here, but I didn't hear anything. I've had trouble sleeping lately with this arm of mine. Ordinary analgesics don't begin to touch the pain, so I'd taken a Tylenol with codeine and a prescription sleeping pill. I don't do that often because I dislike the effect. Leaves me feeling logy the next morning, like I never quite wake up. Also, I find the sleep so deep it's almost not restful. I went to bed about eight-thirty and didn't stir until nearly nine this morning."

"Who discovered the body?"

"I believe it was Christie."

"What time was this?"

"Shortly after ten. I'd made myself a cup of coffee and I was back here in the kitchen, watching the morning news on that little TV set. I heard all the commotion. They were supposed to meet for breakfast to talk about the will, and when Guy didn't come down, I guess Bennet got furious. He thought Guy was playing games, at least that's what Christie told me later. Bennet sent her upstairs to fetch him.

Next thing I knew they'd dialed 9-1-1, but I still wasn't sure what was going on. I was just on my way out there when Donovan came in. He looked awful. He'd lost all his color and was white as a sheet."

"Did you see the body?"

"I did, yes. He asked if I'd go up. He thought there might be something I could do, but of course there wasn't. Guy must have been dead several hours by then."

"There's no doubt?"

"Oh, none. Absolutely. He was cold to the touch and his skin was waxen. His skull had been crushed and there was blood everywhere, most of it dried or congealed. Given his injuries, I'd say death must have been quick, if not instantaneous. Also, messy. I know the police have been puzzled by that aspect of the murder."

"Which aspect?"

"What the killer did with his own clothes. Not to be gross about it, but there would have been quite an area of splatter. Blood and brain material. There's no way you could leave the premises without attracting attention. The detectives were interested in a number of articles of clothing. They asked for my help since I take items to the cleaners."

"Did they find anything significant?"

"I don't know. I gave them everything that was going out today. They talked to Enid at length, but I'm not sure what they wanted with her."

"You have any idea what the weapon was?"

"I wouldn't hazard a guess. That's not an area where I feel qualified to comment. There was nothing in the room, at least as far as I could see. I did hear one of the detectives say the autopsy was scheduled first thing tomorrow morning. I imagine the medical examiner will have an opinion," she said. "Have you been hired by the family to investigate?"

I could feel the lie form, but then thought better of it. I said, "Not yet. Let's hope it doesn't come to that. I can't believe anybody in the family is going to turn out to be responsible."

I expected her to pipe up with protests and reassurances, but the quiet that followed was significant. I could sense a desire to confide, but I couldn't imagine what. I let my gaze rest on hers with an expression I hoped appeared trustworthy and encouraging. I could almost feel my head tilt like a dog trying to decipher the direction of a high-pitched whistle.

She'd become aware of a dried speck on the counter and she worked at it with her fingernail, not looking at me. "This is really none of my business. I had only respect for Mr. Malek . . ."

"Absolutely."

"I wouldn't want anyone to think badly of me, but I can't help but hear things while I'm going about my business. I'm paid well and God knows, I enjoy the work. Or at least I did."

"I'm sure you're only trying to help," I said, wondering where she was going with this.

"You know, Bennet never agreed to share the money. He wasn't convinced that was Bader's intention and neither was Jack. Of course, Jack sided with Bennet in just about everything."

"Well, maybe they weren't convinced, but given the missing will, I don't know what choice they had, short of court action. I gather nothing was settled."

"Not at all. If they'd settled their business, Guy would have gone home. He was miserable here. I could see it in his face."

"Well, that's true. When I talked to him on Monday, he admitted he'd been drinking."

"Oh, especially last night. They started with cocktails and went through four or five bottles of wine with dinner. And then, port and liqueurs. It was still going on when I went off to bed. I helped Enid with the dishes and she could see how exhausted I was. Both of us heard them quarreling."

"Bennet and Guy quarreled?"

She shook her head, lips moving.

I cupped a hand to my ear. "Excuse me. I didn't hear that."

She cleared her throat and raised her voice half a notch. "Jack.

Guy and Jack quarreled before Jack went off to his country club. I told the lieutenant about it and now I'm wondering if I should have kept my mouth shut."

"The truth is the truth. If that's what you heard, you had to tell the police."

"You don't think he'll be mad?" Her tone was anxious, her expression almost childlike in its apprehension.

I suspected the entire family would have fits when they heard, but we all had an obligation to cooperate with the police investigation. "Maybe so, but you can't worry about that. Guy was *murdered* last night. It's not up to you to protect anyone."

She nodded mutely, but I could see she remained unconvinced.

"Myrna, I mean this. Whatever happens, I don't think you should feel responsible."

"But I didn't have to volunteer the information. I like Jack. I can't believe he'd hurt anyone."

"Listen, you think I'm not going to end up in the same position? The cops are going to talk to me, too. I have to go down there tomorrow and I'm going to end up doing exactly what you did."

"You are?"

"Of course. I heard them quarrel the night I came here for drinks. Bennet and Donovan were going at it hammer and tongs. Christie was the one who told me they did it all the time. That doesn't make 'em killers, but it's not up to us to interpret the facts. You have to tell the cops what you heard. I'm sure Enid will back you up. Nobody's going to be arrested on that basis anyway. It's not like you saw Jack coming out of Guy's room with a bloody two-by-four."

"Not at all. Of course not." I could see some of the tension begin to leave her face. "I hope you're right. I mean, I can see what you're saying. The truth is the truth. All I heard was a quarrel. I never heard Jack threaten him."

"Exactly," I said, with a glance at my watch. It was nearly six by then. "If you're through for the night, I better let you go. I probably ought to get on out of here myself, but first I want to have a little chat with Christie."

Anxiety flickered in her eyes. "You won't mention our conversation?"

"Would you quit *worrying?* I won't say a word and I don't want you saying anything either."

"I appreciate that. I believe I would like to go wash my face."

I waited until Myrna had disappeared through the utility room, moving toward her apartment. My tea was untouched. I emptied my cup and left it in the sink. Despite Enid's good example, I've never owned a dishwasher and don't know the first thing about loading one. I pictured one false move and every dish would go flying, crashing in a heap of rubble. I returned to the library. Christie and Tasha had turned on the television set. Christie held the remote and she was switching from channel to channel to see if she could catch the news. She pressed the Mute button when I came in, turning to look at me. "Oh, there you are. Come in and join us. Tasha thought you were gone."

"I'm on my way," I said. "I went out to the kitchen to see if I could help out there. Could I ask you a question before I take off? I heard you mention the mail when you were talking to Lieutenant Robb. Can I ask what that was?"

"Sure. Uhm, let's see. I guess late Monday afternoon someone put an unsigned letter in the mailbox. The envelope had Guy's name on it, but there was no return address. He left it on the hall table when he went to bed last night. I thought the police might want to take a look."

"Was it typed or handwritten."

"The envelope was typed."

"Did you read the letter?"

"Of course not, but I know it bothered Guy. He didn't say what it was, but I gather it was something unpleasant."

"Did he ever mention a Max Outhwaite? Does the name mean anything to you?"

"Not that I remember." She turned to Tasha. "Does it ring a bell with you?"

Tasha shook her head. "What's the connection?"

"That's how the reporter first heard Guy was back. Someone named Max Outhwaite dropped off a letter at the *Dispatch,* but when Katzenbach checked it out, there was no one by that name and no such address. I double-checked as well and came up blank."

"Never heard of him," Christie said. "Is there any chance he's connected to one of Guy's old sprees? Maybe Outhwaite was somebody Guy mistreated back then."

"Possible," I said. "Do you mind if I check Bader's file upstairs?"

"What file?" Tasha asked.

Christie answered before I did. "Bader kept a folder of newspaper clippings about Guy's various arrests and his scrapes with the law. It goes back quite a way."

"I'll tell you something else crossed my mind," I said. "This Outhwaite, whoever he is, certainly put Jeff Katzenbach on the trail of Guy's criminal history. I'm not sure Jeff would have known about it otherwise. The minute I saw the letter, I remember wondering if it was really Bennet or Jack who tipped him off somehow."

"Using Outhwaite's name?"

"It seems possible," I said.

"But why would either of them do that? What's the point?"

"That's the problem. I don't know. Anyway, I could be off base on this one," I said. "I do like the idea that Outhwaite's someone Guy sinned against in the old days."

"Take the file if you want. It was still on the desk in Bader's office last I saw."

"Let me pop upstairs and grab it. I'll be right back."

I moved out of the library and crossed the foyer. Maybe when I talked to Jonah, he'd level with me about the letter. I went up the steps two at a time, studiously avoiding a look down the hall. I had no idea which room Guy had been in, but I didn't want to go near it. I took a hard left at the head of the stairs and went straight to Bader's room, where I opened the door and flipped on the overhead light. Everything seemed to be in order. The room was cold and smelled slightly musty from disuse. The overhead illumination was dim and the pale colors in the room looked flat. I passed through to the office beyond, hitting switches as I went. Bader's life force was being systematically erased. Closets had been emptied, all the personal items removed from his desktop.

I surveyed the surrounding area. I spotted the folder with all the newspaper articles about Guy's past behavior, relieved that the cops hadn't swept through and taken it. On the other hand, the search warrant probably wasn't that broad. The list of property to be seized might have been directed only toward the murder weapon itself. I leafed through the clippings, speed-reading for content, looking for the name *Outhwaite* or anything close. There was nothing. I checked through some of the stray folders on the desk, but found nothing else that seemed relevant. One more dead end, though the idea was sound—someone with a grudge making Guy's life difficult. I pressed the file under my arm and left the room, turning off the lights as I went.

I pulled the door shut behind me, pausing in the hallway outside the master suite. Something felt wrong. My first urge was to scurry down the stairs toward the lighted rooms below, but I found myself slowing. I could hear a crackling sound and I peered to my left. The far end of the corridor was enveloped in shadow, except for an X of crime scene tape across three doorways. As I watched, the tape seemed to become nearly luminous, vibrating audibly as if rattled by wind. I thought for a moment the tape would break free, clicking and snapping as though a current were moving through it. The air on the landing was chilly and there was the faint scent of something animal—wet dog or old fur. For the first time, I allowed myself to experience the horror of Guy's death.

I began to descend, one hand on the railing, the other clutching the file. I pivoted, reluctant to turn my back on the darkness behind me. For a moment, I scrutinized the stretch of corridor I could see.

Something hovered in my peripheral vision. I turned my head slowly, nearly moaning with fear. I could see sparkles of light, almost like dust motes materializing in the stillness. I felt a sudden flush of heat and I could hear ringing in my ears, a sound I associated with childhood fainting spells. My phobia about needles had often inspired such episodes. When I was young, I was often subjected to a typhoid inoculation, a tine test for tuberculosis, or a periodic tetanus injection. While the nurse took the time to pooh-pooh my fears, assuring me "big girls" didn't put up the fuss I did, the ringing would begin, building to a high pitch and then silence. My vision would shrink, the light spiraling inward to a tiny point. The cold would rush up and the next thing I'd know, there'd be anxious faces bending over me and the sharp scent of smelling salts held under my nose.

I leaned back against the wall. My mouth flooded with something that tasted like blood. I closed my eyes tightly, conscious of the thudding of my heart and the clamminess in my palms. While Guy Malek slept, someone had crept along this hallway in the darkness last night, toting a blunt object of sufficient brute matter to extinguish his life. Less than a day ago. Less than a night. Perhaps it had taken one blow, perhaps several. What troubled me was the notion of that first bone-crushing crack as his skull shattered and collapsed. Poor Guy. I hoped he hadn't wakened before the first blow fell. Better he slept on before the last sleep became final.

The ringing in my ears went on, mounting in intensity like the howling of wind. I was weighted with dread. Occasionally in nightmares, I suffer from this effect—an overpowering urge to run without the ability to move. I struggled to make a sound. I would have sworn there was a presence, someone or something, that hovered and then passed. I tried to open my eyes, almost convinced I'd see Guy Malek's killer passing down the stairs. My heartbeat accelerated to a life-threatening pitch, thrumming in my ears like the sound of running feet. I opened my eyes. The sound ceased abruptly. Nothing. No one. The ordinary noises of the house reasserted themselves. The scene before me was blank. Polished floor. Empty hall. Incandescent light from the chandelier. Glancing back down the corridor, I could see that the X's of crime scene tape was simply tape again. I sank down on the stairs. The whole of the experience had surely taken less than a minute, but the rush of adrenaline had left my hands shaking.

Finally, I roused myself from the step where I'd been sitting for God knows how long. From somewhere downstairs, I could hear a mix of male and female voices, and I knew without question that Donovan, Bennet, and Jack had returned from the police station, arriving while I was still in Bader's office. Below me, the library door stood open. Tasha and Christie must have gone to join them. Faintly, from the direction of the kitchen, I could hear the clatter of ice cubes and the clink of bottles. Drink time again. Everybody in the house seemed to need alcohol along with extended psychiatric care.

I completed my descent, anxious to avoid encountering the family. I returned to the library, peering in with caution, relieved to see the room empty. I grabbed up my handbag and shoved the file down in the outside pocket, then headed for the front door, heart still pounding. I pulled the door shut behind me, careful to soften the sound of the latch clicking into place. Somehow it seemed important to slip away undetected. After my experience on the stairs—whatever it was—I was incapable of making superficial conversation. It didn't seem unreasonable to suppose that someone in this household had murdered Guy Malek and I'd be damned if I'd make nice until I knew who it was.

15

Back in my neighborhood, parking spaces were at a premium and I was forced to leave my VW almost a block away. I locked the car and trotted to my apartment. It was fully dark by then and a chill shivered in the trees like wind. I crossed my arms for warmth, clutching the strap of my handbag as it bumped against my side. I used to carry a handgun as a matter of course, but I've given up that practice. I moved through the gate, which gave its usual welcoming squeak. My place was dark, but I could see the lights on in Henry's kitchen. I didn't want to be alone. I headed for his backdoor and rapped on the glass.

He emerged moments later from the living room. He gave a half wave when he saw me and crossed to let me in. "I was just watching the news. The murder's on all channels. Sounds bad."

"Awful. It's vile."

"Have a seat and get warmed up. It's gotten nippy out there."

I said, "Don't let me interrupt. I'll be fine sitting here."

"Don't be silly. You look cold."

"I'm freezing."

"Well, wrap up."

I put my bag down and grabbed his afghan, folding its weight around me like a shawl as I slid into his rocking chair. "Thanks. This is great. I'll be warmer in a minute. It's mostly tension."

"I'm not surprised. Have you eaten supper yet?"

"I think I had lunch, but I can't remember what I ate."

"I've got beef stew if you want. I was just about to have a bowl myself."

"Please." I watched as Henry adjusted the flame under the stew. He took out a loaf of homemade bread, sliced it thickly, and placed it in a basket with a napkin folded over it. He assembled bowls and spoons, napkins, and wine glasses, moving around the kitchen with his usual ease and efficiency. Moments later, he set bowls of stew on the table. I left his rocking chair and shuffled over to the kitchen table still wrapped in his afghan. He pushed the butter in my direction as he settled in his chair. "So tell me the story. I know the basic details. They've been blasting that across the TV screen all afternoon."

I began to eat as I talked, realizing how hungry I was. "You may know more than I do. I'm too smart to stick my nose in the middle of a homicide investigation. These days it's hard enough to put a case together without an outsider interfering."

"You're not exactly an amateur."

"I'm not an expert either. Let the techs and forensic specialists give it their best shot. I'll keep my distance unless I'm told otherwise. My stake's personal, but it's really not my business. I liked Guy. He was nice. His brothers piss me off. This is great stew."

"You have a theory about the murder?"

"Let's put it this way. This is not a case where some stranger broke in and killed Guy in the middle of a robbery. The poor man was asleep. From what I heard, everybody'd been drinking, so he more than likely passed out. He wasn't used to hard liquor, especially in massive quantities, which is how the Maleks go at it. Somebody knew where his room was and probably knew he was in no condition to defend himself. I tell you, with the possible exception of Christie, I've developed such an aversion to that family I can hardly bear to be under the same roof with them. I feel guilty about Guy. I feel guilty about finding him and guilty he came back. I don't know what else I could have done, but I wish I'd left him in Marcella where he was safe."

"You didn't encourage him to return."

"No, but I didn't argue that strenuously either. I should have been more explicit. I should have detailed their attitude. I thought the danger was emotional. I didn't think anyone would go after him and bludgeon him to death."

"You think it was one of his brothers?"

"I'm tempted by the idea," I said reluctantly. "It's a dangerous assumption and I know I shouldn't jump to conclusions, but it's always easier to pin suspicion on someone you dislike."

By eight-thirty that night, I was back in my apartment with the door locked. I sat at the kitchen counter for what felt like an hour before I worked up the courage to call Peter and Winnie Antle, who'd been following the story on the Santa Maria news station. The entire church congregation had come together earlier that evening, shocked and saddened by the murder. I hoped to cushion their loss, though in reality their faith provided them more comfort than I was able to offer. I told them I'd do what I could to keep in touch, and I broke the connection feeling little or no solace. Once the lights were turned out, I lay in my bed with a stack of quilts piled over me, trying to get warm, trying to make sense of what had happened that day. I was weighted with dread. Guy's death had generated something far worse than grief. What I experienced was not sorrow, but a heavy regret that was wedged in my chest like an undigested lump of hot meat. I didn't sleep well. My eyes seemed to come open every twenty minutes or so. I changed positions and adjusted the covers. First I was too hot, then too cold. I kept thinking the next arrangement of limbs would offer sufficient comfort to lure me to sleep. I lay on my stomach with my arms shoved under my pillow, turned on my back with my shoulders uncovered. I tried my left side, knees pulled up, arms tucked under, switched to my right side with one foot sticking out. I must have set the alarm without thinking about it because the next thing I knew, the damn thing was going off in my ear, bringing me straight up out of the only decent sleep I'd managed all night. I turned off the alarm. I refused to run. There was no way I was budging from the chrysalis of heat-generating quilts. Next thing I knew, it was nine-fifteen and I felt compelled to drag myself out of bed. I had a date with Jonah Robb down at the police station. I checked my reflection in the bathroom mirror. Nice. My color was bad and I had bags under my eyes.

As it turned out, it wasn't Jonah I spoke to but Lieutenant Bower. She kept me waiting for fifteen minutes, sitting on a little two-person bench in what I suppose would be referred to as the lobby at the police station. Under the watchful gaze of the officer at the desk, I shifted in my seat and stared at the rack of crime prevention pamphlets. I also eavesdropped shamelessly while six whining drivers came to complain about their traffic tickets. Finally, Lieutenant Bower peered around the door from the Investigative Division. "Miss Millhone?"

I'd never met Betsy Bower, but I'd been curious about her. The name suggested someone perky and blond, a former varsity cheerleader with terrific thighs and no brains. To my dismay, Lieutenant Bower was the least perky woman I'd had the pleasure to meet. She was the police equivalent of an Amazon: statuesque, eight inches taller than I, and probably fifty pounds heavier. She had dark hair that she wore skinned straight back, and little round, gold-rimmed glasses. She had a flawless complexion. If she wore makeup at all, it was artfully done. When she spoke, I caught sight of endearingly crooked teeth, which I realized later might have explained her reluctance to smile. It was also possible she didn't like me and longed to squash me like a bug.

I followed her into a small cubicle with two wooden chairs and a scratched wooden table that had a tendency to wobble if you tried to rest your arm on it, pretending to be relaxed. She had nothing with her—no pen, no legal pad, no file, no notes. She looked directly at me, offering a few brisk sentences after which it was my turn. Somehow I had the feeling she'd remember every word I said. More likely our conversation was being recorded surreptitiously. I would have done a furtive feel-check for wiring along the underside of the table, but I was worried about the wads of old chewing gum and dried boogers parked there.

She said, "We appreciate your coming in. I understand you were hired by the estate to locate Guy Malek. Can you tell me how you went about that?" Her gaze was watchful, her manner subdued.

The question caught me by surprise. I felt a sudden flash of fear, color rising in my cheeks as if I'd just emerged from a tanning booth. I stalled like a little airplane with a tank full of bad fuel. Too late, I realized I should have prepared for this. Ordinarily, I don't lie to police officers because that would be very naughty, wouldn't it? At heart, I'm a law-and-order type. I believe in my country, the flag, paying taxes and parking tickets, returning library books on time, and crossing the street with the light. Also, I'm inclined to get tears in my eyes every time I hear the National Anthem sung by somebody who really knows how to belt it out. Right then, however, I knew I was going to have to do a little verbal tap dance because how I "went about" finding Guy Malek wasn't exactly legitimate. Neither Darcy Pascoe nor I had any business dipping into CFI's computer system to do a DMV check on a matter completely unrelated to an insurance claim. I'd probably violated some kind of civil ordinance or penal code number something-something. At the very least, the two of us were in serious breach of company policy, department regulations, common decency, and proper etiquette. This might well go down on my permanent record, something my elementary school principal had threatened me with every time I fled school with Jimmy Tait in the fifth and sixth grades. I didn't think what I'd done was a jailable offense, but I was, after all, sitting at the police station and I did have my private investigator's license to protect. Since I'd now hesitated a conspicuous five seconds, I thought it was wise to launch in on *something.*

I said, "Ah. Well. I met with Donovan, Bennet, and Jack Malek last Wednesday. In the course of those conversations, I was given Guy Malek's date of birth and his Social Security number. So late in the day on Thursday, I went over to the DMV offices and asked the clerk if there was any record of a driver's license in Guy Malek's name. The information that came back was that his license had been surrendered in 1968, but that he'd been issued a California identification card. His mailing address was listed in Marcella, California. I reported that to Tasha Howard, the attorney for the estate, and to Donovan Malek, who authorized me to drive up to Marcella to verify the address. Marcella's a small town. I wasn't there ten minutes before I got a line on Guy. Frankly, I didn't think he should come down here."

"Why is that?"

Hey, as long as my butt wasn't on the line, I didn't care who I ratted out here. "His brothers were upset at having to give him a share of their father's estate. They felt he'd been paid all the monies he was entitled to. There was the issue of a second will, which came up missing when the old man died. Bennet was convinced his father had disinherited Guy, but since that will was never found, the prior will was the one being entered into probate." I did a little detour at that point, giving Lieutenant Bower the gist of the business about Max Outhwaite, whose letter to the *Dispatch* had set all the adverse publicity in motion. She didn't leap up with excitement, but it did serve to distract her (I hoped) from the issue of my illegal computer access.

She took me through a series of questions related to the Maleks' attitude toward Guy, which I characterized as hostile. I told her about the outburst I'd witnessed between Donovan and Bennet. She asked me a number of pointed questions about Jack's statements regarding Guy, but I honestly couldn't think of anything he'd said that suggested a homicidal bent. In our initial conversation, he'd expressed bitterness at Guy's defection, but that had been almost eighteen years ago, so I wasn't convinced it was relevant. Though I didn't say so to her, I'd pegged Jack as the family mascot, someone harmless and doglike, trained to distract others with his antics. I didn't feature him as a prime player in any ongoing domestic drama.

"When did you last talk to Guy?" she asked.

"He called Monday night. He needed a break so I drove over to the house and met him near the side gate. I was glad to hear from him. I'd been worried because I knew the media had picked up the story. Peter Antle, the pastor of his church up north, had been trying to get in touch with him. The house was literally under siege and it wasn't possible to get a call through. I'd driven over there once before, hoping to make contact, and I'd just about given up."

"Why were you so interested in talking to him?"

"Largely, because Peter and his wife, Winnie, were concerned."

"Aside from that."

I stared at her, wondering what she had in mind. Did she think I was *romantically* involved? "You never met Guy," I said, stating it as fact and not a question.

"No." Her face was without animation. Her curiosity was professional and had an analytic cast to it. That was her job, of course, but I found myself struggling to articulate his appeal.

"Guy Malek was a beautiful man," I said in a voice suddenly fragile. Inexplicably, I found myself pricked by grief. My eyes stung with tears. I could feel my face get puffy and my nose turn hot. It seemed odd that in Henry's company I'd felt nothing while there, but in the face of Betsy Bowers's cold authority, all my unprocessed sorrow was surfacing. I took a deep breath, trying to cover my emotions. I was avoiding her eyes, but she must have picked up on my distress because she produced a tissue from somewhere that suddenly appeared in my field of vision. I took it with gratitude, feeling vulnerable and exposed.

Within moments, I was fine. I have strong self-control and managed to get my emotions back in the box again. "Sorry. I'm not sure where that came from. I really haven't felt much sorrow since I heard about his death. I should have guessed it was down there. He was a good person and I'm really sorry he's gone."

"I can understand that," she said. "Would you care for some water?"

"I'll be fine," I said. "It's funny—I really only saw him three times. We talked on the phone, but we weren't exactly best friends. He seemed boyish, a young soul. I must have a weakness for guys who never quite manage to grow up. I'd already given Donovan an invoice and I figured my job was done. Then Guy called on Saturday. Donovan had called him, urging him to come down so they could talk about the will. Personally, I didn't think the visit was such a hot idea, but Guy was determined."

"Did he say why?"

"He had emotional accounts to pay. At the time he left home, he was messed up on drugs. He'd been in a lot of trouble and alienated just about everyone. Once he was settled in Marcella, he cleaned up his act, but he'd left a lot of unfinished business. He said he wanted to make his peace."

"When you last spoke to him, did he mention contact with other people from his past?"

"No. I know a letter was delivered—Christie mentioned it last night—but that came on Monday and Guy never said a word about it when I saw him. As far as I know, there was nothing else. Was it significant?"

"We'd rather not discuss the content until we check it out."

"Who wrote it? Or would you rather not discuss that either?"

"Right."

"Was it typed?"

"Why do you ask?"

"Because of the letter to the *Dispatch* that generated all the hype. If the papers hadn't been tipped off, no one would have known he was back in town."

"I see what you're saying. We'll follow up."

"Can I ask about the autopsy?"

"Dr. Yee hasn't finished yet. Lieutenant Robb is there now. We'll know more when he gets back."

"What about the murder weapon?"

Her face went blank again. I was wasting my breath, but I couldn't seem to let go. "You have a suspect?" I asked.

"We're pursuing some possibilities. We're doing backgrounds on a number of people associated with the family. We're also checking everybody's whereabouts to see if all the stories add up."

"In other words, you won't say."

Chilly smile. "That's correct."

"Well. I'll do what I can to help."

"We'd appreciate that."

She made no move to close, which was puzzling. From my perspective, we'd pretty much wound up our chat. She'd asked all her questions and I'd told her what I knew. In the unspoken structure of a police interview, Detective Bower was in charge and I'd have to dance to her tune. In the unexpected pause, I could see that it was suddenly her turn to stall.

She said, "Rumor has it you're involved with Lieutenant Robb."

I squinted at her in disbelief. "*He* told you that?"

"Someone else. I'm afraid this is a small town, even smaller when it comes to law enforcement. So it's not true?"

"Well, I *was* involved, but I'm not now," I said. "What makes you ask?"

The look on her face underwent a remarkable alteration. The careful neutrality fell away and in one split second, she went from blank to blushing.

I sat back in my chair, taking a new look at her. "Are you *smitten* with him?"

"I've been out with him twice," she said cautiously.

"Ohhh, I see. Now I get it," I said. "Listen, I'm fond of Jonah, but it's strictly over between us. I'm the least of your worries. It's the dread Camilla you'd better be concerned about."

Detective Betsy Bower had abandoned any pose of professionalism. "But she's living with some guy and she's *pregnant.*"

I raised a hand. "Trust me. In the continuing saga of Jonah and Camilla, the mere fact of this infant has no bearing on their relationship. He may act like he's cured, but he isn't, believe me. Camilla and Jonah are so enmeshed with each other I don't know what it would take to split up their act. Actually, now that I think about it, you probably have as good a shot at it as any."

"You really think so?"

"Why not? I was always too caught up in my own abandonment issues. I hated being a minor player in their little theater production. We're talking seventh-grade bonding. Junior high school romance. I couldn't compete. I lack the emotional strength. You look like you could tackle it. You have self-esteem issues? Are you a nail biter? Bed wetter? Jealous or insecure?"

She shook her head. "Not a bit."

"What about confrontation?"

"I like a good fight," she said.

"Well, you better get ready then because in my experience, she's indifferent to him until someone else comes along. And for God's sake, don't play fair. Camilla goes for broke."

"Thanks. I'll remember. We'll be in touch."

"I can't wait."

On the street again, I felt as if I was emerging from a darkened tunnel. The sunlight was harsh and all the colors seemed too bright. Nine black-and-white patrol cars were lined up along the curb. Across the street, a row of small California bungalows were painted in discordant pastel shades. Flowering annuals in fuchsia, orange, and magenta stood out in bold relief against the vibrant green of new foliage. I left my car in the public parking lot and walked the remaining blocks to work.

I entered Kingman and Ives by the unmarked side door. I unlocked my office and let myself in, glancing down at the floor. On the carpet, there was a plain white business-size envelope with my name and address typed across the front. The postmark was Santa Teresa, dated Monday P.M. Distracted, I set my bag on the desk, took out Bader's file, and set it on top of the file cabinet. I went back to the letter and picked it up with care. I centered it on my desk, touching only the corners while I lifted the handset and dialed Alison in reception.

"Hi, Alison. This is Kinsey. You know anything about this letter that was slipped under my door?"

"It was delivered yesterday afternoon. I held on to it up here, thinking you'd be back and finally decided it was better to go ahead and stick it under your door. Why, did I do something wrong?"

"You did fine. I was just curious."

I put the phone down and stared at the envelope. I'd picked up a fingerprint kit at a trade show recently and for a moment I debated about dusting for latents. Seemed pointless to tell the truth. Alison had clearly handled it and even if I brought up a set of prints, what was I to do with them? I couldn't picture the cops running them on the basis of my say-so. Still, I decided to be cautious. I took out a letter opener and slit the flap of the envelope, using the tip to slide the note onto my desk. The paper was cheap bond, folded twice, with no date and no signature. I used a pencil eraser to open the paper, anchoring opposite corners with the letter opener and the edge of my appointment book.

Dear Miss Milhone,

I thought I should take a moment to inlighten you on the subject of Guy Malek. I

> wonder if you rilly know who your dealing with. He is a liar and a theif. I find it sickning that he could get a second chance in life threw the acquisition of Sudden Riches. Why should he get the benefitt of five million dollars when he never urned one red cent? I don't think we can count on him making amens for his passed crimes. You better be carefull your not tared with the same brush.

I found a transparent plastic sleeve and slid the letter inside, then opened my desk drawer and took out the copy of the letter Max Outhwaite had written to Jeffrey Katzenbach, placing the two side by side for comparison. On superficial examination, the typefont looked the same. As before, my name was misspelled. Thanks, it's two *l*'s, please. The sender seemed to have a problem distinguishing *your* from *you're* and consistently reversed the two. The use of *threw* for *through* was the same, but there were other oddities of note. My letter was less than half the length of the one to Katzenbach, yet it had more spelling mistakes. To my untutored eye, the two sets of errors were curiously inconsistent. If the writer were relying strictly on phonetics, why would words like *acquisition, aforementioned,* and *besieges* be spelled right? Certainly in my letter, there were far fewer commas, exclamation points, and Capitalizations! It was possible there was a certain level of carelessness at work, but I also had to wonder if the writer weren't simply *pretending* to use language badly. There was something vaguely amusing about the use of the word *amens* instead of *amends,* especially in the context of a born-again.

From another angle, why affix the name *Max Outhwaite* to the first letter, tacking on the embellishment of a phony address, and leave mine unsigned? I had to guess that *Outhwaite* imagined (quite correctly, as it turned out) that an unsigned letter to the *Dispatch* would get thrown in the trash. It was also likely the sender had no idea I'd end up with both. While I understood the reasoning behind the letter to the *Dispatch,* why this one to me? What was Outhwaite's intent?

I took out my magnifying glass and cranked up my three-way bulb to maximum illumination. Under magnification, other similarities became apparent. In both documents, the letter *a* was twisted on its axis, leaning slightly to the left, and on the lowercase *i* a portion of the serif was broken off along the bottom. Additionally, the lowercase *e, o, a,* and *d* were dirty and tended to print as filled dots instead of circles, suggestive of an old-fashioned fabric ribbon. On my portable Smith-Corona, I'd been known to use a straight pin to clean the clogged typewriter keys.

I left the letters on my desk and took a walk around the room. Then I sat down in my swivel chair, opened my pencil drawer, and pulled out a pack of index cards. It took me fifteen minutes to jot down the facts as I remembered them, one piece of information per card until I'd exhausted my store. I laid them out on my desk, rearranging the order, shuffling them into columns, looking for connections I hadn't seen before. It didn't amount to much from my perspective, but there'd soon be more information available. The autopsy was done by now and the medical examiner would have a concrete opinion about the manner and cause of death. We were all assuming Guy died from blunt-force trauma to the head, but there might be some underlying pathology. Maybe he'd died of a heart attack, maybe he'd been poisoned, expiring in his sleep before the first blow was struck. I couldn't help but wonder what difference any of it made. Guy would be laid to rest, his body probably taken back to Marcella for burial up there. The various forensic experts would go on sifting through the evidence until the case was resolved. Eventually, the story would be told in its entirety and maybe I'd understand then how everything fit. In the meantime, I was left with all the unrelated fragments and a sick feeling in my stomach.

I took the letters down the hall, the one still encased in its plastic sleeve. At the Xerox machine, I made a copy of each so that I now had two sets. The copies I placed in my briefcase, along with the notes I'd made on my index cards. The originals I locked away carefully in my bottom drawer. When the phone rang, I let the answering machine pick up. "Kinsey, this is Christie Malek. Listen, the police were just here with a warrant for Jack's arrest—"

I snatched up the receiver. "Christie? It's me. What's going on?"

"Oh, Kinsey. Thank God. I'm sorry to bother you, but I didn't know what else to do. I put a call through to Donovan, but he's out in the field. I don't know where Bennet's gone. He left about nine, without a word to anyone. Do you know the name of a good bail bondsman? Jack told me to get him one, but I've looked in the Yellow Pages and can't tell one from the other."

"Are you sure he's in custody? They didn't just take him to the station for another interview?"

"Kinsey, they put him in *handcuffs.* They read him his rights and took him off in the back of an unmarked car. We were both in shock. I don't have any money—less than a hundred bucks in cash—but if I knew who to call . . ."

"Forget about the bondsman. If Jack's being charged with murder, it's a no-bail warrant. What he needs is a good criminal attorney and the sooner the better."

"I don't know any attorneys, except Tasha!" she shrieked. "What am I supposed to do, pick a name out of a *hat?*"

"Wait a minute, Christie. Just calm down."

"I don't want to calm down. I'm scared. I want help."

"I know that. I know. Just wait a minute," I said. "I have a suggestion. Lonnie Kingman's office is right next door to mine. You want me to go see if he's in? You can't do better than Lonnie. He's a champ."

She was silent for an instant. "All right, yes. I've heard of him. That sounds good."

"Give me a few minutes and we'll see what we can do."

16

I caught Lonnie's secretary, Ida Ruth, on her way back from the kitchen with a coffeepot in hand. I hooked a thumb in the direction of Lonnie's door. "Is he in there?"

"He's eating breakfast. Help yourself."

I tapped on the door and then opened it, peering in. Lonnie was sitting at his desk with an oversized plastic container of some kind of chalky-looking protein drink. I could see bubbles of dried powder floating on the surface and the barest suggestion of a milky mustache on Lonnie's upper lip. From assorted bottles, he'd emptied out a pile of vitamins and nutritional supplements, and he was popping down pills between sips of a shake so thick it might have been melted ice cream. One of the gel caps was the size and the color of a stone in a topaz dinner ring. He swallowed it as though he were doing a magic trick.

Lonnie more nearly resembles a bouncer than an attorney. He's short and stocky—five feet four, two hundred four pounds—bulging with muscles from his twenty years of power lifting. He's got one of those revved-up metabolisms that burns calories like crazy and he radiates high energy along with body heat. His speech is staccato and he's generally amped up on coffee, anxiety, or lack of sleep. I've heard people claim he's on the sauce—shooting anabolic steroids in concert with all the iron he pumps. Personally, I doubt it. He's been manic for the whole nine years of our acquaintance and I've never seen him exhibit any of the rage or aggression allegedly generated by extended steroid use. He's married to a woman with a black belt in karate and she's never once complained about testicles shriveled to the size of raisins, another unhappy side effect of steroid abuse.

His usually shaggy hair had been trimmed and subdued. His dress shirt was pulled tightly across his shoulders and biceps. I don't know his neck size, but he claims a tie makes him feel he's on the brink of being hanged. The one he was wearing was pulled askew, his collar unbuttoned, and his suit jacket off. He'd hung it neatly from a hanger hooked through the handle of a file drawer. His shirt was spanking white, but badly wrinkled, and he had rolled up the sleeves. Sometimes he wears a vest to conceal his rumpled state, but not today. He swallowed the last of a palmful of pills, holding up a hand to indicate that he was aware of me. He chugged off the balance of his protein drink and shook his head with satisfaction. "Whew, that's good."

"Are you tied up at the moment?"

"Not at all. Come on in."

I entered the office and closed the door behind me. "I just got a call from Christie Malek. Have you been following that story?"

"The murder? Who hasn't? Sit, sit, sit. I'm not due in court until two P.M. What's up?"

"Jack Malek's been arrested and needs to talk to an attorney. I told Christie I'd see if you were interested." I took a seat in one of two black leather client chairs.

"When was he picked up?"

"Fifteen or twenty minutes ago, I'd guess."

Lonnie began to screw the lids back on the motley collection of bottles sitting on his desk. "What's the deal? Fill me in."

I brought him up to speed on the case as succinctly as possible. This was our first conversation about the murder and I wanted him to have as thorough an understanding as I could muster on short notice. As I spoke, I could see Lonnie's gears engage and the wheels start to turn. I was saying, "Last I heard—this was from the housekeeper—Guy and Jack quarreled after hours of heavy drinking and Jack went off to a pairings' party at the country club."

"I wonder how the cops are gonna bust that one. You'd think at least half a dozen people would have seen him there." Lonnie shot a glance at his watch and began to roll his sleeves down. "I'll pop on over to the station house and see what's going on. I hope Jack has sense enough to keep his mouth shut until I get there."

He pushed away from his desk and took his suit jacket from the hanger. He shrugged himself into it, secured his collar button, and slid his tie into place. Now he looked more like a lawyer, albeit a short, beefy one. "By the way, where does Jack fit? He the oldest or the youngest?"

"The youngest. Donovan's the oldest. He runs the company. Bennet's in the middle. I wouldn't rule him out if you're looking to divert suspicion. He was the most vocal in his opposition to Guy's claim on the estate. You want me to do anything before you get back?"

"Tell Christie I'll be in touch as soon as I've talked to him. In the meantime, go on over to the house. Let's put together a list of witnesses who can confirm Tuesday night. The cops find the murder weapon?"

"They must have. I know they did a grid search of the property because I saw 'em doing it. And Christie says they carted off all kinds of things."

"Once I finish with Jack, I'll have a chat with the cops and find out why they think he's good for this. It'd be nice to have some idea what we're up against."

"Am I officially on the clock?"

He looked at his watch. "Go."

"The usual rates?"

"Sure. Unless you want to work for free. Of course, it's always possible Jack won't hire me."

"Don't be silly. The man's desperate," I said. I caught Lonnie's look and amended my claim. "Well, you know what I mean. He's not hiring you because he's desperate—"

"Get out of here," Lonnie said, smiling.

Briefcase in hand, I hiked back over to the public parking lot, where I retrieved my car. My attitude toward Jack Malek had already undergone a shift. Whether Jack was guilty or innocent, Lonnie would hustle up every shred of exculpatory evidence and plot, plan, maneuver, and strategize to establish his defense. I was no particular fan of Jack's, but working for Lonnie Kingman I'd be kept in the loop.

As I approached the Maleks', I was relieved to see that the roadway on either side of the estate was virtually deserted. The shoulder was churned with tire prints, the ground strewn with cigarette stubs, empty cups, crumpled paper napkins, and fast-food containers. The area outside the gate had the look of abandonment, as if a traveling circus had packed up and crept away at first light. The press had all but disappeared, following the patrol car taking Jack to County Jail. For Jack, it was the beginning of a process in which he'd be photographed, frisked, booked, fingerprinted, and placed in a holding cell. I'd been through the process myself about a year ago and the sense of contamination was still vivid. The facility itself is clean and freshly painted, but institutional nonetheless; no-frills linoleum and government-issue furniture built to endure hard wear. In my brush with them, the jail officers were civil, pleasant, and businesslike, but I'd felt diminished by every aspect of the procedure, from the surrender of my personal possessions to the subsequent confinement in the drunk tank. I can still remember the musky smell in the air, mixing with the odors of stale mattresses, dirty armpits, and bourbon fumes being exhaled. As far as I knew, Jack had never been arrested and I suspected he'd feel as demoralized as I had.

As I drove the VW up to the gate, a hired security guard stepped forward, blocking my progress until I identified myself. He waved me on and I eased up the driveway into the cobblestone courtyard. The house was bathed in sunlight, the grounds dappled with shade. The old, sprawling oak trees stretched away on all sides, creating a hazy landscape as if done in watercolors. Tones of green and gray seemed to bleed into one another with the occasional spare sapling providing sharp contrast. I could see two gardeners at work; one with a leaf blower, one with a rake. The sounds of machinery suggested that branches were being trimmed somewhere out of sight. The air smelled of mulch and eucalyptus. There was no sign of the search team and no uniformed officer posted at the front door. To all intents and purposes, life had reverted to normal.

Christie must have been watching, perhaps hoping for Donovan. Before I was even out of the car, she'd come onto the porch and down the steps, walking in my direction. She wore a white T-shirt and dark blue wraparound skirt, her arms folded in front of her as though for comfort. The sheen in her dark hair had faded to a dull patina, like cheap floor wax on hardwood. Her face showed little of her emotions except for a thin crease, like a hairline crack, that had appeared between her eyes. "I heard the car on the drive and thought it might be Bennet or Donovan. Lord, I'm glad to see you. I've been going crazy here by myself."

"You still haven't gotten through to Donovan?"

"I left word at the office, saying it was urgent. I didn't want to blab all our business to his secretary. I've been waiting by the phone, but so far I haven't heard a word from him. Who knows where Bennet is. What about Lonnie Kingman? Did you talk to him?"

I filled her in on Lonnie's intentions. "Have the police unsealed the bedroom?"

"Not yet. I meant to ask about that when they showed up this morning. I thought they came to *do* something up there. Take photographs or measure or move the furniture. I never imagined they were here to arrest anyone. I wish you could have seen Jack. He was scared to death."

"I'm not surprised. What about you? How are you holding up?"

"I'm antsy. And feel my fingers. They're as cold as ice. I catch myself pacing, half the time jabbering away. This is all so unreal. We may have problems, but we don't kill one another. It's ridiculous. I don't understand what's going on. Everything was fine and now this." She seemed to shudder, not from cold, but from tension and anxiety. In the wake of Jack's arrest, she'd clearly erased all her earlier complaints.

I followed her around the front and into the house. The foyer felt chilly and again I was struck by the shabbiness. A wall sconce hung awry. In the hanging chandelier, several flame-shaped bulbs were missing and some were tilted like crooked teeth. The tapestries along the wall were genuine, faded and worn, depicting acts of debauchery and cruelty picked out in thread. I felt my gaze pulled irresistibly toward the stairs, but the landing above was empty and there was no unusual sound to set my teeth on edge. The house was curiously quiet, given events of the past few days. These people didn't seem to have friends rushing in with offers of help. I wasn't aware of anyone bringing food or calling to ask if there was anything to be done. Maybe the Maleks were the sort who didn't invite such familiarities. Whatever the reason, it looked like they were coping without the comfort of friends.

Christie was still chatting, processing Jack's arrest. I've noticed that people tend to drone on and on when they're unnerved. "When I saw Detective Robb on the doorstep, I honestly thought they were coming with information and then they asked if Jack was in and I still didn't think anything about it. I don't even know what's supposed to happen next."

We moved into the library, where I sank into a club chair and Christie paced the floor. I said, "I guess it depends on what he's charged with and if bail's been set. Once he's booked in, the DA has twenty-four hours to file his case. Jack has to be arraigned within forty-eight hours, excluding Sundays and holidays, of course. So this is what, Thursday? They'll probably take him before a magistrate today or tomorrow."

"What's arraignment? What does that mean? I don't know the first thing. I've never known anyone who's been arrested, let alone charged with *murder.*"

"Arraignment's the process by which he's formally charged. They'll take him into court and identify him as the person named in the warrant. He'll be told the nature of the charges against him and he'll be asked to plead guilty, not guilty, or no contest."

"And then what?"

"That's up to Lonnie. If he thinks the evidence is weak, he'll demand a preliminary hearing without waiving time. That means within ten court days—two weeks—they'll have to have him in there for a prelim. For that, the prosecuting attorney's present, the defendant and his counsel, the clerk, and the investigating officer, blah, blah, blah. Witnesses are sworn in and testimony's taken. At the end of it, if it appears either that no public offense has been committed or that there's not sufficient cause to believe the defendant's guilty, then he's discharged. On the other hand, if there's sufficient evidence to show the offense has been committed and sufficient cause to believe the defendant's guilty, then he's held to answer. An information's filed—that's a formal, written accusation—in Superior Court, he enters a plea, and the matter's set for trial. There's usually a lot of bullshit thrown in, but that's essentially what happens."

She paused in her pacing and turned to stare at me, aghast. "And Jack's in *jail* all this time?"

"He's not allowed to post bail on a homicide."

"Oh my God."

"Christie, I've been in jail myself. It's not the end of the world. The company's not that great and the food's off the charts when it comes to fat content—hey, no wonder I liked it," I added in an aside.

"It isn't funny."

"Who's being funny? It's the truth," I said. "There are worse things in life. Jack might not like it, but he'll survive."

She reached out and placed a hand on the mantelpiece to steady herself. "Sorry. I'm really sorry. I didn't mean to snap at you."

"You better have a seat."

She did as I suggested, perching on the edge of the chair next to mine. "You must have come for some reason. I never even asked what it was."

"Lonnie was hoping you'd know who was at the club that night. We need someone who can verify Jack's presence at the pairings' party."

"That shouldn't be too hard. I guess the police are already talking to people at the country club. I'm not sure what the deal is on that. I've gotten two calls this morning, one from Paul Trasatti, who says he needs to talk to Jack, like pronto."

"Were they together Tuesday night?"

"Yes. Jack picked him up and took him to the club. I'm sure they sat at the same table. Paul can give you the names of the other eight sitting with them. This is all so crazy. How can they possibly think Jack's guilty of anything? There must have been tons of people there that night."

"What's Paul's number?"

"I don't know. It's got to be in the book. I'll go look it up."

"Don't worry about it. I can check that out in a bit. Once he confirms Jack's alibi, it should go a long way."

Christie made a face. " 'Alibi.' God, I can't stand the word. Alibi implies you're guilty and you've cooked up some story to cover your ass."

"Can I use your phone?"

"I'd prefer it if you'd wait until Donovan or Bennet check in. I want to keep the line free until I hear from them. I hope you don't mind."

"Not at all," I said. "You mentioned the police picking up some items. Do you have any idea what they took?"

She leaned her elbows on her knees and put her hands across her eyes. "They left a copy of the warrant and a list of items seized. I know it's around here somewhere, but I haven't seen it yet. Donovan went down to the pool house as soon as they left. He says they took a lot of sports equipment—golf clubs and baseball bats."

I winced, thinking of the impact of such items on the human skull. Switching the subject, I asked, "What about Bennet? Where was he that night?"

"He went back to the restaurant he's remodeling, to see what the workers had done that day. Construction's been a nightmare and he spends a lot of time down there."

"Did anybody see him?"

"You'd have to ask him," she said. "Donovan and I were here. We'd had quite a lot to drink at dinner and I went straight to bed." There was a marked tremor in the hand Christie was running through her hair.

"Have you had anything to eat?"

"I couldn't touch a bite. I'm too anxious."

"Well, you ought to have *something*. Is Enid here yet?"

"I think so."

"Let me check in the kitchen and have her make you a cup of tea. You should have a cookie or a piece of fruit. You look awful."

"I feel awful," she said.

I left her in the library and headed down the hall. I couldn't believe I'd put myself on tea detail again, but simply being in the house made me tense. Any activity helped. Besides, I didn't want to pass up the chance to talk to Enid if she was on the premises.

"Me again," I said when I entered the kitchen.

She was standing at the island with a cutting board in front of her, smashing garlic with the blade of a Chinese cleaver. She was wrapped in a white apron with a white cotton scarf around her head, looking as round and as squeezable as a roll of toilet paper. While I watched, she laid down assorted sizes of unpeeled cloves, placed the wide blade on top of them, and pounded once with her fist. I could feel myself flinch. If the blade were angled incorrectly, she was going to end up whacking down on it with the outer aspect of her own hand, hacking straight to the bone. I stopped in my tracks. With her eyes pinned on me politely, she repeated the process, fist smashing down. She lifted the blade. Under it, the hapless garlic had been crushed like albino cockroaches, the peel sliding off with the flick of a knife tip.

"I thought I'd fix Christie a cup of tea," I said. "She needs something in her system—do you have a piece of fruit?"

Enid pointed at the refrigerator. "There are grapes in there. Tea bags up in the cabinet. I'd do it myself, but I'm trying to get this sauce under way. If you set up a tray, I'll take it in to her."

"No problem. You go right ahead."

She leaned to her left and slid open a compartment in which the trays were stored, pulling out a teak server with a rim around the edge. She placed it on the marble counter next to six big cans of crushed tomatoes, two cans of tomato paste, a basket of yellow onions, and a can of olive oil. On the stove top, I noticed a stainless steel stockpot.

I moved over to the cabinet and removed a mug, pausing to fill the electric kettle as I'd seen Myrna do. I glanced at Enid casually. "You have paper napkins somewhere?"

"Third drawer on the right."

I found the napkins and placed one, along with a teaspoon, on the tray. "I take it you heard about Jack's arrest."

She nodded assent. "I was coming in the gate just as they were taking him away. I wish you could have seen the look on his face."

I shook my head regretfully, as if I gave a shit. "Poor thing," I said. "It seems so unfair." I hoped I hadn't laid it on too thick, but I needn't have worried.

"The police were asking about his running shoes," she said. "Something about a pattern on the soles—so there must have been bloody footprints in the bedroom where Guy was killed."

"Really," I replied, trying to disguise my startlement. Apparently, she felt no reluctance about discussing the family's business. I'd thought I'd have to be cunning, but she didn't seem to share Myrna's reservations about tattling. "They picked up the shoes yesterday?"

"No. They called me this morning at home. Before I left for work."

"Lieutenant Robb?"

"The other one. The woman. She's a cold fish, I must say. I hope she's not a friend of yours."

"I only met her this morning when I went in to be interviewed."

She flicked me a look as if taking my measure. "Myrna tells me you're a detective. I've seen 'em on the TV, of course, but I never met one in real life."

"Now you have," I said. "In fact, I work in the same firm as Jack's attorney, Lonnie Kingman. He's on his way over to the station house to talk to Jack." I was anxious to press her on the matter of the shoes, but worried she would clam up if I seemed too intent.

She dropped her eyes to her work. She was tapping the Chinese cleaver in a rapid little dance that reduced all the garlic to the size of rice grains. "They searched for the shoes all day yesterday. You've never seen anything like it. Going through all the closets and trash cans, digging in the flowerbeds."

I made a little mouth noise of interest. It was clear Enid had an avid interest in all the trappings of police work.

She said, "They told me I was actually the one who put 'em on the right track. Of course, I had no idea the shoes would turn out to be Jack's. I feel terrible about that. Myrna's beside herself. She feels so guilty about mentioning the quarrel."

"It must have been a shock about the shoes," I prodded.

"Jack's my favorite among the boys. I came to work here twenty-five years ago. This was my first job and I didn't expect to stay long."

"You were hired as a nanny?"

"The boys were too old for that. I was more like a companion for Mrs. Malek," she said. "I never trained as a cook. I simply learned as

I went along. Mrs. Malek—Rona—was beginning to fail and she was in and out of the hospital all the time back then. Mr. Malek needed someone to run the house in her absence. Jack was in junior high school and he was pretty much at loose ends. He used to sit out in the kitchen with me, hardly saying a word. I'd bake a batch of cookies and he'd eat a whole plate just as fast as he could. He was really like a little kid. I knew what he was hungry for was his mother's praise and attention, but she was much too sick. I did what I could, but it nearly broke my heart."

"And Guy was how old?"

She shrugged. "Eighteen, nineteen. He'd already given them years of aggravation and grief. I never saw anything like him for the trouble he made. It was one scrape after another."

"How did he and Jack get along?"

"I think Jack admired and romanticized him. They didn't pal around together, but there was always a certain amount of hero worship. Jack thought Guy was like James Dean, rebellious and tragic, you know, misunderstood. They never had all that much to do with one another, but I can remember how Jack used to look at him. Now, Bennet and Jack, they were close. The two younger boys tended to gravitate to one another. I never had much use for Bennet. Something sneaky about him."

"What about Donovan?"

"He was the smartest of the four. Even then he had a good head for business, always calculating the odds. When I first came to work, he'd already been off to college and was planning to come back and work for his dad full-time. Donovan loves that company more than any man alive. As for Guy, he was the troublemaker. That seemed to be his role."

"You really think Jack might have been involved in Guy's death?"

"I hate to believe it, but I know he felt Guy broke faith with him. Jack's a fanatic about loyalty. He always was."

"Well, that's interesting," I said. "Because the first time I was here, he said much the same thing. He was off at college when Guy left, wasn't he?"

Enid was shaking her head. "That wouldn't have mattered. Not to him. Somehow, in Jack's mind, when Guy went off on his great adventure, he should have taken him along."

"So he saw Guy's departure as betrayal."

"Well, of course he did. Jack's terribly dependent. He's never had a job. He's never even had a girl. He has no self-esteem to speak of and for that, I blame his dad. Bader never took the time to teach them they were worth anything. I mean, look at the reality. None of them has ever left home."

"It couldn't be healthy."

"It's disgraceful. Grown men?" She opened the can of olive oil and poured a short stream in the stockpot while she turned up the flame. She moved the cutting board from the counter and balanced the edge of it on the pot, sliding garlic across the surface. The sound of sizzling arose, followed moments later by a cloud of garlic-scented steam.

"What's the story on the shoes? Where did they turn up?"

She paused to adjust the flame and then returned the board to the counter, where she picked up an onion. The peeling was as fragile as paper, crackling slightly as she worked. "At the bottom of a box. You remember the cartons of Bader's clothing Christie packed away? They were sitting on the front porch. The Thrift Store Industries truck stopped by for an early-morning pickup first thing yesterday."

"Before the body was discovered?"

"Before anyone was even up. I don't know how I connected it. I saw the receipt lying on the counter and didn't think much about it. Later, it occurred to me—if the shoes weren't on the premises, they must be somewhere else."

"How'd you figure out where they were?"

"Well, that's just it. I was loading the dishwasher, you know, humming a little tune, and boom, I just knew."

"I've done the same thing. It's almost like the mind makes an independent leap."

Enid flashed me a look. "Exactly. He must have realized he left a shoe print on the carpeting upstairs."

"Did you see it yourself?"

"No, but Myrna says she saw it when she went in Guy's room." She paused, shaking her head. "I don't want to think he did it."

"It *is* hard to believe," I said. "I mean, in essence, he must have killed Guy, seen the footprint, slipped off his shoes, and shoved them in the box on his way out of the house. He was lucky—or thought he was."

"You don't sound convinced."

"I just have trouble with the notion. Jack doesn't strike me as that decisive or quick. Doesn't that bother you?"

She thought about that briefly and then gave a shrug of dismissal. "A killer would have to depend on luck, I guess. You can't plan for everything. You'd have to ad-lib."

"Well, it backfired in this case."

"If he did it," she said. She picked up a can and tilted it into the electric opener. She pressed a lever and watched as the can went round and round, rotating blades neatly separating the lid from the can. Kitchens are dangerous, I thought idly as I looked on. What an arsenal—knives and fire and all that kitchen twine, skewers, meat pounders, and rolling pins. The average woman must spend a fair portion of her time happily contemplating the tools of her trade: devices that crush, pulverize, grind, and puree; utensils that pierce, slice, dissect, and debone; not to mention the household products that, once ingested, are capable of eradicating human life along with germs.

Her eyes came up to mine. "Do you believe in ghosts?"

"No, of course not. What makes you ask?"

She glanced toward the corner of the kitchen where I noticed, for the first time, a staircase. "Yesterday I went upstairs to put some linens away. There was a Presence in the hall. I wondered if you believed in them."

I shook my head in the negative, remembering the chill in the air and the roaring in my ears.

"This one smells of animal, something damp and unclean. It's very strange," she said.

17

I left the Maleks' shortly after one o'clock. Driving home, I spotted a pay phone at a corner gas station. I pulled in and parked. Outside the service bay, a group of kids from the local alternative high school had organized a car wash. According to the hand-lettered sign, the price was $5.00 and proceeds were being used to pay for a trip to San Francisco. There was not a customer in sight. Buckets of soapy water waited at the ready and the kids milled around in a manner that suggested they were about to spray one another down with hoses. With luck, I wouldn't end up in the line of fire.

I looked up Paul Trasatti in the telephone book. There were two numbers listed; one a residence on Hopper Road, the other—with no address—simply said Paul Trasatti, Rare Books. I found a handful of loose change at the bottom of my handbag and fed coins into the slots. I dialed the business number first, thinking it more likely I'd catch him at his desk. Trasatti answered before the phone on his end had finished ringing the first time.

"Trasatti," he said, tersely. He sounded like a man who'd been waiting for a call regarding drop-off instructions for the ransom money.

"Mr. Trasatti, my name is Kinsey Millhone. I'm a private investigator, working with Jack Malek's attorney. You knew he'd been arrested?"

"I heard about that this morning. I called to talk to Jack and his sister-in-law told me they'd just taken him away. Did she tell you to call?"

"Well, no. Not really. I—"

"How'd you get my number?"

"I looked you up in the telephone book. I need information and I thought maybe you could help."

"What kind of information?"

"I'll be talking to Lonnie Kingman and I know he'll want to hear about Jack's activities that night."

"Why can't he ask Jack?"

"I'm sure he will," I said, "but we're going to need someone who can verify Jack's claims. Christie says he drove you over to the country club Tuesday evening. Is that true?"

There was a fractional hesitation. "That's right. He picked me up after dinner. Truth is, I ended up trading places with him, so I was the one driving. He was too tipsy. This is strictly off the record, right?"

"I'm not a journalist, but sure. We can keep it off the record, at least for now," I said. "Tipsy, meaning drunk?"

"Let's just say I was the designated driver in this case."

I closed my eyes, listening for the subtext, while cars passed back and forth on the street behind me. "Were you seated at the same table?"

"Tables were reserved. We had assigned seats," he said. He was being as cagey as a politician. What was going on here?

"That's not what I asked. I'm wondering if you can verify his presence at the pairings' party."

A brief, most curious silence ensued. "Can I ask you a question?" he said.

"What's that?"

"If you're working for this attorney . . . what'd you say his name was?"

"Lonnie Kingman."

"Okay, this Kingman fellow. I know he can't repeat anything said between him and Jack, but what about you? Does the same thing apply to you?"

"Our conversation isn't privileged, if that's what you want to know. Anything relevant to Jack's defense, I'll be reporting to Lonnie. That's my job. I *can* be trusted with information. Otherwise, I'd be out of business by now," I said. "Were you sitting with Jack?"

"See, that's what the police have been asking me," he said. His mouth must have been dry because I could practically hear him lick his lips before he spoke. "Jack's a good friend and I don't want to get him in any more trouble than he's in. I've done everything I could short of telling lies."

"You don't want to lie to the cops," I said. Maybe the line was tapped and they were checking my attitude.

"Well, no, I wouldn't. And that's just it," he said. "I didn't come right out and say so, but there was a stretch when Jack was, you know, uhm, off somewhere. What I mean is, I couldn't say he was right there in my line of sight."

"Uhn-hun. How long a stretch?"

"Might have been as much as an hour and a half. I didn't think anything of it at the time, but you know, later—like when this other business came up—I did wonder about the time frame. I wouldn't want to be quoted, but just between us."

"Do you know where he was?"

"I know where he *said* he was. Out walking the tenth hole."

"In the *dark?*"

"That's not as odd as it sounds. I've done the same thing myself. Smokers go outside to have a cigarette sometimes. Most club members know the course by heart so it's not as if you're likely to get lost or fall down a hole."

"But why would he do that in the middle of a pairings' party?"

"He was upset—I'd say real upset—when he came to pick me up. That's another reason I insisted on driving. Jack tends to be careless about things like that."

"Did he say what upset him?" I waited. "I can keep it to myself," I said.

"He said him and Guy got into an argument."

"About what?"

"Probably the money. I'd say the money."

"You're talking about the money Guy was due to inherit."

"That's right."

"So Jack was drunk and upset and when the two of you arrived at the club, he disappeared."

"Uhn-hun."

"Did you believe him?"

"About taking a walk? More or less. I mean, it makes sense—you know, if he was trying to sober up and cool off."

"And *did* he seem cooler when he got back?"

For a moment, I thought the line went dead. "Mr. Trasatti?"

"I'm here. See, the thing is, he didn't actually get back in time to give me a ride. I had to find someone else."

"And that's what you told the police?"

"Well, I had to. I felt bad, but they were real persistent and it's like you said, I couldn't *lie*."

"Was his car still there?"

"I think so. I couldn't swear to it. I thought I saw it in the parking lot when I was set to go, but I might have been mistaken."

"But you're sure there was no sign of Jack?"

"That's right. A friend of mine said he saw him take off across the fairway at the first hole. Then this other fellow ended up giving me a ride home."

"Can I have both those names?" I cocked one shoulder, anchoring the handset against my ear while I fumbled in my bag for a pen and a scrap of paper. I made a note of the names, neither of which rang a bell. "And how did you find out where Jack had been?"

"He called first thing the next morning to apologize and that's when he explained."

"He called Wednesday morning?"

"I just said that."

"I wanted to make sure I understood you correctly. Do you remember what time he called?"

"About eight, I guess."

"So this was before anyone knew Guy Malek was dead."

"Must've been. I know Jack never mentioned it. You'd think if he knew he'd have spoken up."

"Is there anything else you remember from your conversation with him?"

"Not that I can think of. I probably got him in enough trouble as it is. I hope you won't tell him I told you all this."

"I doubt I'll have occasion to talk to Jack," I said. "I appreciate your help. You may hear from Lonnie Kingman or me again on this." You're certainly going to end up on the witness stand, I thought.

"I guess it can't be helped," he said glumly, as if reading my mind. He disconnected before I could press him for anything else.

I checked the pile of change I'd laid on the shelf near the coin box. I dropped more coins in the slot and dialed Lonnie's private line. He picked up on his end without identifying himself.

"This is Kinsey," I said. "How'd it go?"

"Don't let me handle any sharps. I might open a vein."

"You heard about the shoes?"

"Did I ever," he said. "Lieutenant Robb delivered the happy news with glee."

"I take it the pattern on the sole matched the print at the scene."

"Oh, sure. And to make things even better, he says the lab found bits and pieces of Guy Malek's brain spattered on the instep. I mean, Jesus, how's Jack going to explain a fleck of brain matter buried in the eyelet of his shoes? This is not like 'Oh gee fellas, Guy-accidentally-cut-himself-and-must-have-bled-on-me.' "

"What'd Jack have to say?"

"I haven't had a chance to ask. Once he invoked, the cops hustled him out to County Jail for booking. I'm going out there later and have a long chat with him. He'll probably tell me the shoes were stolen. Oh yeah, right."

"What about the murder weapon?"

"They found a baseball bat shoved in with a bunch of sports equipment down at the pool house. Somebody'd made a clumsy attempt to wipe it clean, but traces of blood were still on the hitting area. At least there were no prints, so we can thank God for small favors. What about his alibi? I hope you're going to tell me a hundred club members had an eye on him at all times."

"No such luck," I said. I laid out the sequence of events as Paul Trasati had reported them.

I could hear Lonnie sigh. "Too bad Jack wasn't out there screwing somebody's wife. You have a theory, I'm sure."

"He could have left the club on foot. There are half a dozen places near the road where he could've climbed the fence."

"And then what?" Lonnie said. "The country club is miles from the Malek estate. How's he going to get from there to the house again without somebody seeing him?"

"Lonnie, I hate to tell you this, but the man has a Harley-Davidson. He could have hidden his motorcycle earlier. The house might be an hour away on foot, but it's only ten minutes by car."

"But so what? Where was Bennet that night? And what about Donovan. He was right there on the premises when the murder occurred."

"I can talk to Bennet this afternoon."

"Did anybody see Jack climb the fence? I doubt it. Anybody see the Harley during the period we're discussing?"

"I can check it out," I said.

"I know the line the cops are taking. They're saying Jack's room adjoined Guy's. All he had to do was slip from one room to the other, bash his brains out, and slip back again."

"Not that simple," I said. "Don't forget he's got to hide the shoes at the bottom of the thrift box, wipe the blood off the bat, and return it to the pool house before he hightails it back to the country club."

"Good point. Is there a guardhouse at the club? Someone might have noted what time he left."

"I'll pop over there and check. I can also clock the time it takes to get from there to the house and back."

"Hold off on that. We'll get to that eventually. For now, let's focus on finding someone else to blame."

"That shouldn't be too hard. I mean, Jack's not the only one with access to Guy's room. Anybody in the house could have entered the same way. The cops have the murder weapon, but from what you've said, they don't have Jack's fingerprints."

"Yeah, they can't find anybody else's either."

"So how are they going to prove Jack was wielding the damn thing? Maybe he was framed."

Lonnie snorted in my ear. "Somebody'd have to take a pair of forceps and fuckin' *tweeze* up brain material, then tiptoe into Jack's room, find the shoes in the closet, and deposit all the little brainy bits."

"It's always possible, though, isn't it?"

"It's possible Santa Claus came down the chimney and did the deed himself. Stinks. The whole thing stinks."

"I like the idea about eyewitnesses. So far it doesn't sound like there's anyone who can place him at the murder scene."

"Not so far, no, but I'm sure the cops are out scouring the neighborhood."

"Well, then we'll scour some, too."

"You're such an optimist," he said.

I laughed. "Actually, I can't believe I'm standing here defending him. I don't even like Jack."

"We're not paid to like him. We're being paid to get him out of this," Lonnie said.

"I'll do what I can."

"I know you will."

Before I left the service station, I paused long enough to pull up to the pump so I could fill my gas tank. On the hood of my car, the early-morning dew had now combined with the dust from Monday's Santa Ana winds. My former VW was dingy beige and never showed dirt. With this snappy 1974 model, the streaks were more conspicuous, rivulets of pale blue cutting through a speckled patina of soot. A bird had passed its judgment on the hood as well. I paid for the gas and then turned the key in the ignition, peered over my right shoulder, and backed up into the area where the car wash was being held. The kids began to whistle and clap, and I found myself smiling at their enthusiasm.

I stood to one side while one of them crawled inside with a bottle of window cleaner. Another fired up the Shop-Vac and began to suck grit off the floor mats. A crew of three were sudsing down the outside, all of them towering over the vehicle. The kid with the Shop-Vac finished cleaning the interior and I watched him approach from the far side of the car with an envelope in hand. He held it out to me. "Have you been looking for this?"

"Where did that come from?"

"I found it beside the passenger seat in front. Looks like it slipped down in the crevice."

"Thanks." I took the envelope, half expecting to see the now-familiar typeface. Instead, my name was scrawled across the front in ballpoint pen. I waited until the kid had moved away and then I opened the envelope and removed the single sheet of paper. The message was handwritten in black ink; the penmanship distinct, a peculiar blend of cursive and printing. I flicked a glance at the signature. *Guy Malek.* I could feel ice crystals forming between my shoulder blades.

Monday night. Waiting for you to show.

Hey K . . .

Sure hope I have the nerve to pass you this note. I guess I must have if you're reading it. I haven't asked a girl on a date since I was fifteen years old and that didn't work out so hot. I got a big zit on my chin and spent the whole evening trying to think up excuses to keep my face turned the other way.

Anyway, here goes.

Once this family mess is settled, would you like to take off for a day and go to Disneyland with me? We could eat snowcones and do Pirates of the Caribbean and then take the boat ride through Small World singing that song you can't get out of your head for six months afterward. I could use some silliness in my life and so could you.

Think on't and let me know so I can stock up on Clearasil.

Guy Malek

P.S. Just for the record, if anything should happen to me, make sure my share of Dad's estate goes to Jubilee Evangelical Church. I really love those folk.

By the time I finished reading, my eyes had filled with tears. This was like a message from the dead. I stared off across the street, blinking rapidly. I could feel pain in my chest and my facial features were instantly defined by heat as my nasal passages seized up. I wondered if grief had the capacity to suffocate. In conjunction with the sorrow came a rush of pure rage. I sent Guy my thoughts across the Ether. I'm going to find out who killed you and I'm going to find out why. I swear I will do this. I swear it.

"Miss? Your car's ready."

I took a deep breath. "Thanks. It looks great." I gave the kid ten bucks and took off with the radio cranked up full blast.

When I got home, I spotted Robert Dietz's little red Porsche parked out in front of my apartment. I set my briefcase on the pavement while I stood at the curb and studied it, afraid to believe. He'd told me he was going to be gone two weeks. This was just coming up on one. I circled the car and checked the license plate, which read DIETZ. I picked up my briefcase and let myself in the gate. I rounded the corner and unlocked my door. Dietz's suitcase was sitting beside the couch. His garment bag was hooked across the top of the bathroom door.

I said, "Dietz?"

No response.

I left my handbag and the briefcase on the counter and crossed the patio to Henry's, where I peered in the kitchen window. Dietz was sitting in Henry's rocking chair, his pant leg pulled up to expose his injured knee. The swelling had visibly diminished and from various gestures he was making, it seemed safe to guess he'd had the fluid drained out of it. Even his pantomime of a hypodermic needle being stuck into his flesh made my palms start to sweat. At first he didn't see me. It was like watching a silent movie, the two men earnestly engrossed in medical matters. Henry, at eighty-five, was so familiar to me—handsome, good-hearted, lean, intelligent. Dietz was constructed along sturdier lines—solid, tough, stubborn, impulsive, just as smart as Henry, but more streetwise than intellectual. I found myself smiling at the two of them. Where Henry was mild, Dietz was restless and rough, without artifice. I valued his honesty, distrusted his concern, resented his wanderlust, and yearned for definition in our relationship. In the midst of all the heaviness I felt, Dietz was leavening.

He glanced up, spotting me. He raised a hand in greeting without rising from the chair.

Henry crossed to the door and let me in. Dietz lowered his pant leg with a brief aside to me about a walk-in medical clinic up in Santa Cruz. Henry offered coffee, but Dietz declined. I don't even remember now what the three of us talked about. In the course of idle chitchat, Dietz put his hand on my elbow, setting off a surge of heat. Out of the corner of my eye, I caught his quizzical look. Whatever I was feeling must have been transmitted through the wires to him. I must have been buzzing like a power line because even Henry's easy flow of conversation seemed to falter and fade. Dietz glanced at his watch, making a startled sound as if late for an appointment. We made our hasty excuses, moving out of Henry's backdoor and across to my place without exchanging a word.

The door closed behind us. The apartment felt cool. Pale sunlight filtered through the shuttered windows in a series of horizontal lines. The interior had the look and the feel of a sailboat: compact, simple, with royal blue canvas chairs, walls of polished teak and oak. Dietz undid the bed in the window bay, easing out of his shoes. I slipped my clothes off, aware of flickering desire as each garment was removed. Dietz's clothes joined mine in a heap on the floor. We sank together, in a rolling motion. The sheets were chill at first, as blue as the sea, warming at contact with our bare limbs. His skin was luminous, as polished as the surface of an abalone shell. Something about the play of shadows infused the air with a watery element, bathing us both in its transparent glow. It felt as if we were swimming in the shallows, as smooth and graceful as a pair of sea otters tumbling through the surf. Our lovemaking played out in silence, except for a humming in his throat now and then. I don't often think of sex as an antidote to pain, but that's what this was and I fully confess—I used intimacy with the one man to offset the loss of the other. It was the only means I could think of to console myself. Even in the moment, what seemed odd to me was the flicker of confusion about which man I betrayed.

Later, I said to Dietz, "Are you hungry? I'm starving."

"I am, too," he said. Gentleman that he was, he'd padded over to the refrigerator where he stood buck naked in a shaft of hot light, contemplating the interior. "How could we be out of food? Don't you eat when I'm gone?"

"There's food," I said defensively.

"A jar of bread-and-butter pickles."

"I can make sandwiches. There's bread in the freezer and half a jar of peanut butter in the cupboard up there."

He gave me a look like I'd suggested cooking up a mess of garden slugs. He closed the refrigerator door and opened the freezer compartment, poking through some cellophane-wrapped packages of meat products covered in ice crystals and suffering from freezer burn. He closed the freezer, returned to the sofa bed, and got under the sheets. "I'm not going to last long. We have to eat," he said.

"I couldn't believe you came back. I thought you were taking the boys off on a trip."

"Turns out they had plans to go camping with friends in Yosemite and didn't know how to tell me. When I read about the murder in the Santa Cruz papers, I told them I needed to drive back. I felt guilty as hell, but they were thrilled to death. Given the perversity of human nature, it pissed me off somehow. They could hardly get me in the car fast enough. I pull away and I'm looking in the rearview mirror. They don't even stop to wave. They're galloping up the outside stairs to grab their sleeping bags."

"You had a few days together."

"And that was good. I enjoyed them," he said. "So tell me about you and what's been happening down here."

Having been through the drill with Lonnie, I laid out events with remarkable efficiency, faltering only slightly in my account of Guy. Even the sound of his name touched a well of sorrow in me.

"You need a game plan," he said, briskly.

I waggled my hand, maybe-so-maybe-not. "Jack will probably be arraigned tomorrow if he hasn't been already."

"Will Lonnie waive time?"

"I have no idea. Probably not."

"Which means he'll insist on a prelim within ten court days. That doesn't give us much time. What about this business of Max Outhwaite? We could try chasing that down."

I noted the "we," but let it sit there unacknowledged. Was he seriously proposing help? "What's to chase?" I asked. "I tried the hall of records and voter registration. Also the city directories. The name's as phony as the address."

"What about the crisscross?"

"I did that."

"Old telephone books?"

"Yeah, I did that, too."

"How far back?"

"Six years."

"Why six? Why not take it all the way back to the year Guy Malek left? Even before that. Max Outhwaite could be the victim of a rip-off during his teen crime years."

"If the name's a fake, it's not going to matter how far back I go."

"In other words, you were too lazy," he said, mildly.

"Right," I said, without taking offense.

"What about the letters themselves?"

"One's a fax. The other's typed on ordinary white bond. No distinguishing marks. I could have dusted for prints, but there didn't seem to be much point. We've got no way to run them and nothing for comparison even if a latent turned up. I did put the one letter in a plastic sleeve to protect it to some extent. Then I made copies of both letters. I left one set at the office, locked away in my desk. I get paranoid about these things."

"You have the other set here?"

"In my briefcase."

"Let's take a look."

I pushed the sheet back and got up. I retrieved my briefcase from the kitchen counter and sorted through the contents, returning to the sofa bed with my pack of index cards and the two letters. I slid between the sheets again and handed him the paperwork, turning over on my side so I could watch him work. He put his glasses on. "This is really romantic, you know that Dietz?"

"We can't screw around all day. I'm fifty. I'm old. I have to save my strength."

"Yeah, right."

We propped up the pillows and settled in side by side while Dietz read the two letters and thumbed through my index cards. "What do you think?" I asked.

"I think Outhwaite's a good bet. Seems like the object of the exercise is to find another candidate, divert attention from Jack if nothing else."

"Lonnie said the same thing. The evidence looks damning, but it's all circumstantial. Lonnie's hoping we can find someone else to point a finger at. I think he favors Donovan or Bennet."

"The more the merrier. If the cops think Jack's motivation was Guy's share of the inheritance, then the same case could be made for the other two. It would have been just as easy for one of them to slip into Guy's room." He was thumbing through the index cards. He held a card up. "What's this mean? What kind of scam are you referring to?"

I took the card and studied it. The note said: *widow cheated out of nest egg*. "Oh. I'm not sure. I wrote down everything I could remember from my first interview with Donovan. He was talking about the scrapes Guy'd been in over the years. Most sounded petty—acts of vandalism, joyriding, stuff like that—but he was also involved in a swindle of some kind. I didn't ask at the time because I was just starting my search and I was focusing on ways to track him down. I didn't care what he'd done unless it somehow pertained."

"Might be worth it to take a good hard look at his past. People knew he was back. Maybe somebody had a score to settle."

"That crossed my mind, too. I mean, why else would Max Outhwaite notify the paper?" I said. "I've also toyed with the idea that one of Guy's brothers might have written the letters."

"Why?"

"To make it look like he had enemies, someone outside the family who might have wanted him dead. By the way, Bader kept a file of newspaper clippings, detailing Guy's escapades."

Dietz turned and looked at me. "Anything of interest?"

"Well, nothing jumps right out. I've got it at the office, if you want to see for yourself. Christie offered to let me take it when I was at the house."

"Let's do that. It sounds good. It might help us develop another lead." He went back to the two letters, analyzing them closely. "What about the third one? What did Guy's letter say?"

"I have no idea. Lieutenant Bower wouldn't tell me and I couldn't get much out of her. But I'd bet money it's the same person in all three cases."

"Cops probably have their forensic experts doing comparisons."

"Maybe. They may not care about Max Outhwaite now that Jack's in custody. If they're convinced he's good for it, why worry about someone else?"

"You want some help with the grunt work?"

"I'd love it."

18

I dropped Dietz at the public library while I drove out the freeway to Malek Construction. I hadn't expected to be gone long, but as I turned into the parking lot, I spotted Donovan getting into a company truck. I called his name and gave a quick wave, pulling into a visitor's space two spots away from his. He waited while I approached and then leaned over and rolled down the window on the passenger side.

Donovan's face creased with a smile, his dark eyes all but invisible behind dark sunglasses. "How are you?" he asked. He slid his glasses up on top of his head.

"Fine. I can see I caught you on your way out. Will you be gone long? I have some questions."

"I've got some business at the quarry. I'll only be gone about an hour if you want to come along with me."

I thought about it briefly. "Might as well," I said.

He moved his hard hat from the passenger seat to the floor, then opened the truck door for me. I hopped in. He wore blue jeans and a jean vest over a blue plaid sportshirt with the sleeves rolled up. His feet were shod in heavy-duty work boots with soles as waffled as tire treads.

"Where's the quarry?"

"Up the pass." He fired up the pickup and pulled out of the parking lot. "What's the latest word from Jack?"

"I haven't talked to him, but Lonnie Kingman had a meeting with him before they took him off to jail. You talked to Christie?"

"I took a late lunch," he said. "I must have gotten home about ten minutes after you left. I had no idea this stuff was going on. How's it looking at this point?"

"Hard to say. Lonnie's in the process of working out his strategy. I'll probably take a run over to the country club later to start canvassing members who were there on Tuesday. We'd love to find someone who could place Jack at the club between nine-thirty and eleven-thirty."

"Shouldn't be too hard."

"You'd be surprised," I said.

I'm about as perky as an infant when it comes to riding in trucks. Before we'd even reached the narrow highway that snaked up the pass, I could feel the tension seeping out of me. There's something lulling being a passenger in a moving vehicle. In Donovan's pickup, the combination of low grinding sound and gentle bumping nearly put me to sleep. I was tired of thinking about murder, though I'd have to bring the subject around to it eventually. In the meantime, I asked him about the business and took inordinate pleasure in the length of his reply. Donovan steered with one hand, talking over the rattle of the truck.

"We've gotten into recycle crushing where we take broken concrete and asphalt. We have a yard in Colgate where we collect it and we have a portable plant—well, we have two portable plants now—one in Monterey and one in Stockton. I think we were one of the first in this area to do that. We're able to crush the materials into road base that meets the specifications. It costs more to haul the materials here than it does the material itself, so you have a cost advantage in the haul."

He went on in this vein while I wondered idly if it might be worthwhile to verify his claims about the company's solvency. When I tuned back in, he was saying, "Right now, we produce about the same quantity out at the rock quarry as we do out at the sand and gravel mine. By far the majority of the sand and gravel operation goes into the production of asphalt concrete. We're the closest asphalt concrete plant to Santa Teresa. We used to have one in Santa Teresa where we hauled in the sand and the gravel and the liquid asphalt and we made it there, but again, it was more economical to make the product here and haul it into Santa Teresa. I'm probably the only man alive who rhapsodizes about road base and Portland Cement. You want to talk about Jack."

"I'd rather talk about Guy."

"Well, I can tell you Jack didn't kill him because it makes no sense. The first thing the cops are going to look at is the three of us. I'm surprised Bennet and I aren't under scrutiny."

"You probably are, though at the moment, all the evidence seems to point to Jack." I told him about the running shoes and the baseball bat. "You have any idea where the Harley-Davidson was that night?"

"Home in the garage, I'd guess. The Harley's Jack's baby, not mine. I really didn't have occasion to see it that night. I was upstairs watching TV."

We headed up the pass on a winding road bordered by chaparral. The air was still, lying across the mountains in a hush of hot sun. The woody shrubs were as dry as tinder. Farther up the rocky slopes, weeds and ornamental grasses—ripgut and woodland brome, foxtail fescue and ryegrass—had spread across the landscape in a golden haze that softened the stony ridges. Scarcely a breeze stirred outside, but late in the day, the warm descending air would begin to blow down the mountainside. Relative humidity would drop. The wind, squeezing through the canyons, would start picking up speed. Any tiny flame from a campfire, burning cigarette, or the inadvertent spark from weed abatement equipment, might be whipped up in minutes to a major burn. The big fires usually struck in August and September after months under high-pressure areas. However, lately the weather had been moody and unpredictable and there was no way to calculate the course it might take. Below us and at a distance, the Pacific Ocean stretched away to the horizon in a haze of blue. I could see the irregularities of the coastline as it curved to the north.

Donovan was saying, "I didn't see Jack that night once he left for the club so I can't help you there. Aside from his whereabouts, I guess I'm not really sure what you're looking for."

"We can either prove Jack didn't do it or suggest someone else who did. Where was Bennet that night? Can he account for his time?"

"You'd have to ask him. He wasn't home, I know that much. He didn't come in until late."

"The first time we met you told me about some of Guy's bouts with the law. Couldn't someone have a grudge?"

"You want to go back as far as his days in Juvenile Hall?"

"Maybe. And later, too. You mentioned a 'widder' woman he cheated out of money."

Donovan shook his head. "Forget it. That's a dead end."

"How so?"

"Because the whole family's gone."

"They left town?"

"They're all dead."

"Tell me anyway."

"The widow was a Mrs. Maddison. Guy was gone by then and when the old man heard what Guy'd done, he refused to make good. It was one of the few times he got tough. I guess he'd finally gotten sick of cleaning up after him. He told the woman to file charges, but I'm sure she never got around to it. Some people are like that. They don't take action even when they should."

"So what's the story?"

We reached the summit and the road opened out to a view I love, a caramel-colored valley dotted with dark green mounds of live oak. Ranches and campgrounds were woven into the land, but most were invisible from up here. The two-lane highway widened into four and we sped across the span of the Cold Spring Bridge. "Guy got involved with a girl named Patty Maddison. That's two *d*'s in Maddison. She had an older sister named Claire."

I heard a dim clang of recognition, but couldn't place the name. I must have made some kind of sound because Donovan turned and gave me a quick look. "You know her?" he asked.

"The name's familiar. Go on with the story. It'll come to me."

"Their old man never had a dime, but he'd somehow acquired some rare documents—letters of some kind—worth a big chunk of change. He'd been sick and the deal was, when he died the mother was supposed to sell 'em to pay for the girls' educations. The older sister had graduated from a college back East and she was waiting around to go to medical school. Some of the money was earmarked for her and some for Patty's college.

"The Christmas before he took off, Guy knocks on this woman's door. He says he's a friend of Patty's and presents himself as an appraiser of rare documents. He tells her there's some question about the authenticity of the letters. Rumor has it, says he, these are fakes and he's been hired by the father to take a look at them."

"This was while the father was still alive?"

He shook his head. "He'd been dead a month by then. He died at Thanksgiving time. Mom's feeling very nervous because the letters are really all she has. She doesn't know beans about an appraiser being hired, but it all sounds legitimate—like something her husband would have done toward the end—so she hands the letter over to Guy and he takes them away."

"Just like that?" I asked. "She didn't ask for ID or credentials?"

"Apparently not. He had some business cards done up and he handed her one, which she took at face value. You have to understand, this was all pieced together months afterward. What the hell did she know? She needs an appraisal done anyway in preparation for selling."

"I can't believe people are so trusting."

"That's what keeps con artists in business," he said.

"Go on."

"Well, Guy keeps the letters for two weeks. He claims he's subjecting them to a number of scientific tests, but what he's really doing is making copies, elaborate forgeries. Or, not so elaborate as it turns out. At any rate, he's putting together a set of fakes good enough to pass superficial inspection. After two weeks, he takes the copies back and gives her the bad news. 'Golly, gee, Mrs. Maddison, these really *are* fakes,' he says, 'and they're not worth a *dime*.' He tells her to ask any expert and they'll tell her the same. She nearly drops dead from shock. She takes 'em straight to another expert and he confirms what Guy's said. Sure enough, the letters are completely worthless. So here's this lady whose husband's dead and she suddenly has nothing. Next thing you know, she's knocking on Dad's door demanding restitution."

"How'd she figure out it was Guy?"

"He'd been seeing Patty Maddison . . ."

I said, "Ohhh. That Patty. I get it. Guy told me about her the day we walked the property. He said he'd broken up with her. Sorry to interrupt, but I just remembered where I'd heard the name. So how'd they know it was him? Did Patty point a finger?"

Donovan shook his head. "Far from it. Patty tried to protect him, but Guy had just taken off and Mrs. Maddison put two and two together."

"Mrs. Maddison hadn't met him?"

"Only the one time when he showed up for the appraisal. Obviously, he didn't use his own name."

Donovan slowed and turned left off the main highway. We followed a two-lane paved road for a mile until it turned to gravel, small rocks popping as the truck bounced upward. Ahead, I could see white dust, like smoke, drifting across the road as it curved around to the left where it widened to reveal the quarry site. Massive benches of raw soil and rock had been cut into the hillside. There were no trees and no vegetation in the area. The din of heavy machinery filled the still mountain air. Much of the area was a flat, chalky gray contrasting sharply with the surrounding gray-green hills and a sky of pale blue. The mountains beyond were cloaked in dark green vegetation interspersed with the gold of short dry grassy patches. Tiers had been cut into the side of the hill. Everywhere there were steep piles of earth and gravel, shale and sandstone, eroding raw earth and rock. Conveyor belts trundled rock upward toward the crusher, where rocks as big as my head were being shaken down into vibrating jaws that reduced them to rubble. Rugged horizontal and inclined screens and feeders sorted the crushed rock into various sizes.

Donovan pulled up close to a trailer, turned off the ignition, and set the hand brake. "Let me take care of business and I can finish the story on the way back. There's a hard hat in the back if you want to take a walk around."

"You go ahead. I'll be fine."

Donovan left me in the pickup while he conferred with a man in coveralls and a hard hat. The two disappeared into the trailer while I waited. From a distance, the machinery was the size of Matchbox toys. I watched as a conveyor belt moved loose rock in a steady stream that poured off the end into a cascading pile. I lifted my chin, shifting my sights to the countryside stretched out in a pristine canvas of hazy mountain and low-growing dark green. I let my gaze drift across the site, trying to make sense out of what Donovan had said. As nearly as I remembered Guy's passing reference to Patty, he saw his discretion with her as his one decent act. He'd described her as unstable, emotionally fragile, something along those lines. It was hard to believe he'd try to convince me of his honor when he'd gone to such lengths to rip her mother off. In truth, he'd ripped Patty off too since the money from the letters was supposed to go to her.

The sun was beating down on the cab of the pickup. Donovan had left the windows open so I wouldn't cook to death. White dust clouded the air and the growling of heavy equipment battled the quiet. I could hear the clank of metal, the high whine of shifting gears as a wheel loader grumbled across flat ground as barren as a moonscape. I unsnapped my seat belt and slouched down on my spine with my knees propped on the dashboard. I didn't want Guy to be guilty of a crime of this magnitude. What was done was done, but this was bad, bad, bad. I was prepared for pranks, willing to accept minor acts of mischief, but grand larceny was tough to overlook, even at this remove.

I didn't realize I'd been dozing until I heard the crunch of work boots and Donovan opened the truck door on the driver's side. I awoke with a start. He kicked the sides of his boots against the floor frame, knocking gravel loose before he slid in beneath the steering wheel. I sat up and refastened my seat belt.

"Sorry it took so long," he said.

"Don't worry about it. I was just resting my eyes," I said dryly.

He slammed the door, clicked his seat belt into place, and turned the key in the ignition. Within moments, we were bouncing down the road toward the highway again. "Where was I?" he asked.

"Guy switched a set of forged letters for the real ones and then disappeared. You were saying your father refused to make good."

"I'll say. The letters were worth something close to fifty thousand dollars. In those days, Dad didn't have that kind of money and wouldn't have paid anyway."

"What happened to the letters? Did Guy sell them?"

"He must have, because as far as I know, they were never seen again. Paul Trasatti could tell you more. His father was the appraiser brought in once the switch was made."

"So he was the one who confirmed the bad news to Mrs. Madison?"

"Right."

"What happened to her?"

"She was a lush to begin with and she'd been popping pills for years. She didn't last long. Between the alcohol and cigarettes, she was dead in five years."

"And Patty?"

"That was unfortunate. In May of that year—this was two months after Guy left—Patty turned up pregnant. She was seventeen years old and didn't want anyone to know. She'd had a lot of mental problems and I think she was worried they'd put her away, which they probably would have. At any rate, she had an illegal abortion and died of septicemia."

"What?"

"You heard me right. She had what they referred to as a 'backroom' abortion, which was more common than you'd think. Procedure wasn't sterile—just some hack down in San Diego. She developed blood poisoning and she died."

"You're kidding."

"It's the truth," he said. "We weren't down on Guy for nothing. I know you think we're nothing but a bunch of hostile jerks, but this is what we've had to live with and it hasn't been easy."

"Why wasn't something said before now?"

"In what context? The subject never came up. We all knew what happened. We discussed it among ourselves, but we don't run around airing our dirty laundry in front of other people. You think we like owning up to his part in it?"

I brooded about it, staring out at the passing roadside. "I'm really having trouble believing this."

"I'm not surprised. You don't want to think Guy would do a thing like that."

"No, I don't," I said. "Guy told me Patty was hung up on him. He considered it his one decent act that he didn't seduce her when he had the chance. Now why would he say that?"

"He was hoping to impress you. Stands to reason," he said.

"But there wasn't any context. This was passing conversation, something he brought up. He didn't go into any detail. What's to be impressed about?"

"Guy was a liar. He couldn't help himself."

"He might have been a liar back then, but why lie about the girl all these years later? I didn't know her. I wasn't pressing for information. Why bother to lie when he had nothing to gain?"

"Look, I know you liked him. Most women did. You start feeling sorry for him. You feel protective. You don't want to accept the fact he was twisted as they come. This is the kind of shit he pulled."

"It isn't that," I said, offended. "He'd undergone a lot of soul-searching. He'd committed his life to God. There wasn't any point fabricating some tall tale about Patty Maddison."

"He was busy revising history. It's something we all do. You repent your sins and then in memory, you start cleaning up your past. Pretty soon, you're convinced you weren't nearly as bad as everyone said. The other guy was a jerk, but you had good reason for anything you did. It's all bunk, of course, but which of us can stand to take a look at ourselves? We whitewash. It's human nature."

"You're talking about the Guy Malek of the old days. Not the one I met. All I know is, I have a hard time picturing Guy doing this."

"You knew him less than a week and believed everything he said. He was a bad egg."

"But Donovan, look at the nature of his crimes. None of them were like this," I said. "As a kid, he was into vandalism. Later, he stole cars and stereos to pay for drugs. Forgery's too sophisticated a scheme for someone who spent his days getting high. Trust me. I've been high. You think you're profound but you're barely functional."

"Guy was a bright boy. He learned fast."

"I better talk to Paul," I said, unwilling to concede.

"He'll tell you the same thing. In fact, that's probably what put the idea in Guy's head in the first place. You have a good friend whose dad deals in rare documents, it doesn't take any great leap to figure it out when you've got access to something valuable."

"I hear what you're saying, but it isn't sitting right."

"You know anything about liars?" Donovan asked.

"Sure, I think I can say so. What about 'em?"

"A liar—a truly dedicated liar—lies because he can, because he's good at it. He lies for the pure pleasure, because he loves getting away with it. That's how Guy was. If he could tell you some lie—even if it meant nothing, even if there was nothing to be gained—he couldn't resist."

"You're telling me he was a pathological liar," I said, restating his claim in a tone of skepticism.

"I'm saying he enjoyed lying. He couldn't help himself."

"I don't believe that," I said. "I happen to think I'm a pretty good judge of liars."

"You know when some people lie, but not all."

"What makes you such an expert," I said, beginning to take offense. Donovan was just as annoyed with me.

He made a dismissive gesture. I suspected he wasn't used to having women argue with him. "Forget it. Have it your way," he said. "I can tell I'm not going to persuade you of anything."

"Nor I you," I said tartly. "What happened to the older sister?"

Donovan grimaced with exasperation. "Are you going to take my word for it or is this an excuse for another round of arguments?"

"I'm arguing about Guy, not the Maddisons, okay?"

"Okay. Claire—the older one—abandoned her plans for med school. She had no money and her mom was sinking like a stone. For a while she came back to take care of her. That was maybe six months or so. Once mom was gone, she went back to the East Coast—Rhode Island or some place. Might have been Connecticut. She got married to some fellow, but it didn't work out. Then about a year ago, she offed herself. Or so I heard."

"She committed suicide?"

"Why not? Her whole family was gone. She had no one. The family was a bit dicey to begin with—bunch of manic-depressives. I guess something must have finally pushed her over the edge."

"What'd she do, jump off a building?"

"I don't know how she did it. I wasn't being literal. There was a notice in the local paper. It happened back east somewhere."

I was silent again. "So maybe one of the Maddisons killed Guy. Wouldn't that make sense?"

"You're fishing. I just told you, they're all gone."

"But how do you know there isn't someone left? Cousins, for instance? Aunts and uncles? Patty's best friend?"

"Come on. Would you really murder someone who wronged a relative of yours? A sibling, maybe. But a cousin or a niece?"

"Well, no, but I'm not close to my relatives. Suppose something like that happened to your family."

"Something did happen to my family. Guy was killed," he said.

"Don't you want revenge?"

"Enough to kill someone? Absolutely not. Besides, if I cared enough to kill, I wouldn't wait this long. You're talking eighteen years."

"But Guy was missing all that time. You notice, once he came home, he was dead within days."

"True enough," he said.

"Does the name Max or Maximilian Outhwaite figure into this in any way? It could even be Maxine. I can't swear to gender."

Donovan turned and looked at me with surprise. "Where'd you come up with that one?"

"You know the name?"

"Well, sure. Maxwell Outhwaite's the name Guy used on the business cards he made to cheat Mrs. Maddison."

I squinted at him. "Are you sure?"

"That isn't something I'd forget," he said. "How'd you come across it?"

" 'Max Outhwaite' was the one who wrote the letters to the *Dispatch* and the L.A. *Times*. That's how the press knew Guy was home."

19

Once back at Malek Construction, I left Donovan in the parking lot and picked up my car. I was feeling anxious and confused. This Max Outhwaite business made no sense at all. Maybe Dietz had come up with a line on him. Throw the Maddisons into the mix and what did it add up to? I glanced at my watch, wincing when I saw how late it was. The trip up the pass had taken more than an hour and a half.

Dietz was waiting in front of the public library. I pulled over to the curb and he slid into the passenger seat. "Sorry I'm late," I said.

"Don't worry about it. I got news for you. Outhwaite's a myth. I checked the city directories for the last twenty-five years and then went across the street and checked the County Clerk's office. No one by that name was ever listed in the phone book or anywhere else. No marriages, no deaths, no real property, building permits, lawsuits, you name it. Everybody alive leaves a trail of some kind. The name has to be phony unless we're missing a bet."

"There *is* a connection, but it's not what you'd expect," I said. I filled him in on my conversation with Donovan while we headed for home. I'd forgotten how nice it was to have someone to consult. I told him about the Maddisons and Guy's alleged involvement in the family's downfall. "Maxwell Outhwaite was the name used by the fictitious appraiser who stole fifty thousand dollars worth of rare documents. I'm not convinced it was Guy, but Donovan seems to take it for granted. Now, honestly," I said. "If you'd known about the Maddisons, wouldn't you have told someone?"

"Namely you?"

"Well, yes, me," I said. "Donovan could have *mentioned* it. Same with Max Outhwaite. The name pops up again years later—why didn't he tell someone?"

"Maybe Katzenbach never told him there was a letter and that Outhwaite was the name of the sender."

"Oh. I see what you're saying. I guess it's possible," I said. "It still annoys me no end. I wish we could find the typewriter. That would be a coup."

"Forget it. There's no way."

"What makes you say that? It has to be around here somewhere. Someone typed both those letters on the same machine."

"So what? If I were writing poison-pen notes, I'd hardly sit at my desk and use my own IBM. I'm too paranoid for that. I'd use one of the rental typewriters at the public library. Or maybe find a place selling typewriters and use one of theirs."

"This machine isn't new. The typeface has an old-fashioned look to it and a lot of the letters are clogged. It's probably got a fabric ribbon instead of carbon film."

"Those typewriters at the library aren't exactly hot off the assembly line."

"Pick me up some samples and we'll do a comparison. There are a couple of typeface defects that should help us pin it down. I'm sure a document expert could find others. I've only eyeballed it."

"The clogged letters don't mean much. Go after 'em with cleaning fluid and poof, those are gone."

"Sure, but don't you think the majority of people who write anonymous letters assume they're safe from discovery?"

"They might assume they're safe, but they're not," Dietz said. "The FBI maintains extensive files of anonymous letters. Plus, they have samples of type from most known machines. Post Office does, too, and so does the Treasury Department. They can determine the make and model of almost any machine. That's how they nail cranks, especially people who send threatening letters to public officials. The only way to play it safe is to dismantle the machine."

"Yeah, but who's going to trash a typewriter? If you thought you were safe enough to use your own machine, you wouldn't turn around and toss it in the garbage afterward. And in this case, why bother? Those letters were a nuisance, but hardly actionable."

Dietz smiled. "What, you picture it sitting out on someone's desk?"

"Maybe. It's possible."

"Keep an eye out."

"I know you're just saying that to humor me," I said.

"What else did Donovan have to say about the Maddisons?"

"Not much. He claims they're all gone, but I don't think we should take his word for it."

"It's worth pursuing," Dietz said. "As stories go, it's not bad."

"What do you mean, 'it's not bad'? I think it's fabulous. I mean, talk about a motive for murder. It's the best lead we've had—"

"The only lead," he pointed out.

I ignored the obvious. "On top of that, we have Outhwaite, who seems to tie right back to them."

"Shouldn't be too hard to track down the name Maddison with two *d*'s. Even if they're not local, they had to come from somewhere."

"Donovan says the father died around Thanksgiving of 1967 and

Patty followed, probably in May or June of 1968. The mother died five years later, but that's as much as I know. You may not find Claire at all. He says she moved back to the East Coast and married. He does remember reading about her death in the local paper, so there must have been a notice in the *Dispatch.* Maybe she kept her maiden name?"

"I'll get on it first thing."

"You will? I can't believe you're volunteering. I thought you hated doing this stuff."

"Good practice. It's nice to keep a hand in. This way I know I haven't lost my touch," he said. "We might try the newspaper morgue if we can get Katzenbach's cooperation. They might have old clips on the Maddisons along with the obits."

"That's a sexy suggestion."

"I'm a sexy guy," he said.

When we got home, I changed into my sweats in preparation for jogging. I had slept through my usual six A.M. run and I was feeling the effects. I left Dietz in the living room with his leg propped up, icing his bum knee while he flipped from channel to channel, alternately watching CNN, talk shows, and obscure sporting events. I headed out the front door, thankful for the opportunity to spend time alone.

There was scarcely any breeze coming off the ocean. The late-afternoon sun had begun to fade, but the daylong baked beach was still throwing off heat saturated by the smell of kelp and brine. The fronds of the palm trees looked like construction paper cutouts, flat dark shapes against the flat blue sky. I lengthened my stride, running at a pace that felt good. The stiffness and fatigue gradually gave way to ease. My muscles became liquid and sweat trickled down my face. Even the burning in my chest felt good as my body was flooded with oxygen. At the end of the run, I flung myself down on the grass, where I lay panting. My mind was a blank and my bones were washed clean. Finally, my breathing slowed and the run-generated heat in my body seeped out. I did a series of stretches and then roused myself. As I headed for home, I could feel the return of the Santa Ana winds lufting down the mountainside. I showered and changed clothes, throwing on a T-shirt and jeans.

Dietz and I had dinner up at Rosie's. William was working behind the bar again. At the age of eighty-seven, this was like a whole new career for him. Since their marriage, the two of them had settled into a comfortable routine. More and more, Rosie seemed to be turning management over to him. She'd always maintained tight control of the day-to-day operation, but William had persuaded her to pay decent wages and as a consequence, she'd been able to hire better employees. And she'd begun to delegate responsibility, which gave her more time to spend with him. William had given up some of his imaginary illnesses and she'd surrendered some of her authoritarianism. Their affection for each other was obvious and their occasional spats seemed to blow over without incident. Dietz was talking to William about Germany, but I was only half attentive, wondering if the two of us would ever reach an accommodation. I pictured Dietz at eighty-seven, me a comparatively youthful seventy-two; retired from the stresses of private-eye work, riddled with arthritis, bereft of our teeth. What would we do, open a private-detective school?

"What are you thinking? You look odd," he said.

"Nothing. Retirement."

"I'd rather eat my gun."

At bedtime, Dietz offered to hobble up the spiral stairs. "My knee's killing me again so I'm probably not much good except for company," he said.

"You're better off downstairs. My bed's not big enough, especially with that knee of yours. I'd just lie there worrying I'd bump you wrong."

I left him below opening up the sofa bed while I ambled up the stairs, talking to him over the rail.

"Last chance," he said, smiling up at me.

"I'm not sure it's smart getting used to you."

"You should take advantage while you can."

I paused, looking down. "That's the difference between us in a nutshell, Dietz."

"Because I live in the moment?"

"Because for you that's enough."

First thing Friday morning, Dietz took his car and headed over to the *Santa Teresa Dispatch* offices while I drove to Paul Trasatti's house. Hopper Road was located midway between the Maleks' and the country club. The neighborhood was small, the street lined with elm trees and dappled with shade. The house was built in the style of an English country cottage, the sort you'd see pictured on a deck of playing cards; gray stone with a thatched roof that undulated like an ocean wave where the gables appeared. The windows were small-paned, leaded glass, the wood trim and the shutters painted white. Two narrow stone chimneys bracketed the house like a pair of matching bookends. The yard was enclosed with a white picket fence, pink and red hollyhocks planted along the front. The small yard was immaculate, thick grass bordered in dark ivy with small flowerbeds along the brick walk leading to the door. Birds twittered in the young oak growing at the corner of the property.

I'd called the night before, of course, wanting to be certain Trasatti would be home. Even on the porch, I could smell bacon and eggs and the scent of maple syrup. My whimper probably wasn't audible above the sound of the mower two doors down. In response to my ring, Trasatti came to the door with his napkin in hand. He was tall and thin, as bald as a lightbulb. He had a large nose, thick glasses, and a jutting chin. His chest was narrow, slightly sunken, swelling to a thickened waistline. He wore a white dress shirt and a pair of stovepipe pants. He frowned at me, looking at his watch with surprise. "You said nine."

"It is nine."

"This says eight." He held his watch to his ear. "Shit. Come on in.

You caught me at breakfast. Have a seat in here. I'll be back in a second. You want coffee?"

"I'm fine. Take your time," I said.

The living room was small and perfectly appointed, more like a doctor's office than a place to put your feet up. The furniture had a vaguely Victorian air, though to my untutored eye, it didn't appear to be the real thing. The chairs were small and fussy, rimmed with carved wooden fruit. There were three dark wood tables topped with pink-veined marble slabs, an array of Sotheby's catalogs neatly lined up on one. The carpeting was a short-cut wool pile, pale blue with a border of Chinese dragons and chrysanthemums. Two cloisonné vases were filled with artificial pink and blue flowers of some generic sort. A clock on the mantel had a second hand that clicked distinctly as it inched its way around. I leafed through a Sotheby's catalog, but didn't see much of interest except a letter from the Marquis de Sade, which was being offered at two thousand dollars. The passage quoted was in French and seemed petulant. There was also a pretty little greeting from Erik Satie to Mme Ravel with "decorated borders and raised blind relief heading showing in colour two hands held in front of a rose . . ." Lots of talk about "*jolies fleurs*" and "*respecteusements.*" My thoughts exactly. I've often said as much.

I strolled the perimeter, taking in numerous framed letters and autographs. Laurence Sterne, Franz Liszt, William Henry Harrison, Jacob Broom (whoever he was), Juan José Flores (ditto). There was a long, incomprehensible letter bearing the signature S. T. Coleridge, and some kind of receipt or order blank signed by George Washington. There was another letter written in a crabbed hand, dated August 1710, fraught with brown ink and cross-outs and looking crumpled and stained. Who'd had the presence of mind to save all this litter? Were there people with foresight going through the dustbins back then?

Across the hall, I could see what must have been a dining room done up as an office. There were bookshelves on every wall, some extending across the windows, which greatly diminished the incoming light. Every surface was stacked ten deep, including tables, chairs, and floors. No typewriter on the premises as far as I could see. I had no reason to think Trasatti was involved, but it would have been nice to have a piece of the puzzle fall into place. The air smelled of old dust and book mold, glue, aging paper, and dust mites. A large tortoiseshell cat picked its way daintily across a desk piled with books. This creature had only a stump for a tail and looked like it might be searching out a place to pee.

"Making yourself at home?" came the voice behind me.

I started, making ever so slight a leap.

"I was admiring this enormous cat," I said casually.

"Sorry if I startled you. That's Lady Chatterley."

"What happened to her tail?"

"She's a Manx."

"She looks like a character," I said. Animal people seem to love it when you say things like this. Trasatti didn't seem to warm to it. He gestured me into the office, where he took a seat at his desk, pushing aside an irregular stack of hardback books.

"No secretary?" I asked.

"Business isn't big enough for clerical help. Anything I need done, I use the Mac upstairs. Go ahead and make a space for yourself," he said, indicating the only chair in the room.

"Thanks." I placed some books, a briefcase, and a pile of newspapers on the floor, and sat down.

"Now what can I help you with? I really can't add to what I've already given you in regard to Jack," he said.

"This was in regard to something else," I said while the fifteen-pound cat hopped onto my lap and settled between my knees. Up close, Lady Chatterley smelled like a pair of damp two-week-old socks. I scratched that little spot just above the base of its tail which made the back end of the cat rise up until its rosebud was staring me in the face. I pushed the back end down. I peppered my preface with lots of reassuring phrases—"off the record," "just between us," and other felicitous expressions of confidentiality—before getting down to business. "I'm wondering what you can tell me about the Maddisons—Patty and her sister, Claire."

He seemed to take the question in stride. "What would you like to know?"

"Anything you care to tell," I said.

Paul straightened the stack of books in front of him, making sure all the edges were aligned and the top right-hand corners matched. "I didn't know the sister. She was older than we were. She was off at college by the time the family moved into the area and Patty started hanging out with Guy."

"The Maddisons were new in town?"

"Well no, not really. They'd been living out in Colgate and bought a house closer in. They never had the kind of money we did, the rest of us—not that we were wealthy," he added. "Bader Malek did well back in those days, but he wasn't what you'd call rich."

"Tell me about Patty."

"She was pretty. Dark." He put his hand at eye level, indicating bangs. "Hair down to here," he said. "She'd kind of peer out like this. She was strange, lots of phobias and nervous mannerisms. Bad posture, big tits. She chewed her nails to the quick and liked to stick herself with things." Trasatti put his hands in his lap, trying not to touch the items on his desk.

"She stuck herself? With what?"

"Needles. Pencils. Safety pins. I saw her burn herself one time. She put a lighted cigarette on her hand—casually, like it was happening to someone else. She never even flinched, but I could smell cooked flesh."

"Was Guy serious about her?" I pushed the cat's hind end down again and it began to work its claws into the knees of my jeans.

"She was serious about him. I have no idea what he thought of her."

"What about the others? Donovan and Bennet."

"What about them?"

"I just wondered what they were up to during this period."

"Donovan was working for his dad, as I remember. He was always working for his dad, so that's a safe bet. Jack was back at school by then, so he was only home on occasion. Christmas and spring break."

"And his mother's funeral," I said. I extracted the cat's claws from my knee and held its right paw between my fingers. I could feel its claws protrude and retract, but the cat seemed content, probably thinking about mice. "What about Bennet? Where was he?"

"Here in town. He and I were both finishing at UCST."

"Majoring in what?"

"My major was art history. His was economics or business, maybe public finance. He switched around some. I forget."

"Did it surprise you when Patty turned up pregnant?"

Trasatti snorted, shaking his head. "Patty would screw anyone. She was desperate for attention and we were happy to oblige."

"Really," I said. "Donovan never said she was promiscuous."

"She wasn't the only one. There was lots of screwing in those days. Free love, we called it. We were all smoking dope. Bunch of small-town hippies, or as close as we could get. We were always horny and hungry. Half the girls we hung out with were as fat as pigs. Except for Patty, of course, who was gorgeous, but whacked out."

"Nice of you boys to help yourselves to a minor," I said. "Given her loose ways, how'd you know the baby was Guy's?"

"Because she said it was."

"She could have lied. If she was crazy and stoned, she might have made things up. How do you know the baby wasn't yours?"

Trasatti shifted uncomfortably. "I had no money to speak of. Where's the benefit in claiming it's mine. The Maleks had class. She might have been crazy, but she wasn't stupid. It's like the old joke—"

"I know the old joke," I said. "Was there ever any proof? Did anybody run blood tests to establish paternity?"

"I hardly think so. I'm sure they didn't. This was sixty-eight."

"How do you know Guy wasn't blamed because it was convenient? He was gone by then. Who better to accuse than a chronic screwup like him?"

Trasatti picked up a pencil and then put it down. His expression had gone blank. "What does this have to do with Jack? I thought you were working to try to get him off."

"That's what I'm doing."

"Doesn't sound like that to me."

"Donovan told me about Patty yesterday. I thought the story might pertain, so I'm following up. Did you ever see the letters Guy allegedly forged?"

"Why put it that way? It's what he did."

"Did you actually see him do it."

"No, of course not."

"Then it's all supposition. Did you ever see the letters?"

"Why would I?"

"Your father did the appraisal when the forgeries were discovered. I thought he might have showed you the copies, if he was training you to follow in his footsteps."

"Who told you that?"

"He handed the business over to you, didn't he?"

Trasatti smiled at me, blinking. "I don't understand where you intend to go with this. Are you accusing me of something?"

"Not at all," I said.

"Because if you are, you're out of line."

"That wasn't an accusation. I never said you did anything. I'm saying Guy Malek didn't. I'm saying someone else did it all and blamed him. What about 'Max Outhwaite'? How does he fit in?"

"Outhwaite?"

"Come on, Trasatti. That's the name Guy supposedly used on his fake business cards."

"Right, right, right. I remember now. Sure thing. I knew it sounded familiar. What's the link?"

"That's why I'm asking you. I don't know," I said. "I think the story of Patty Maddison ties in somehow. Her death, the forged letters. I'm just fishing around."

"You better try something else. The family's gone."

"What makes you so sure?"

Paul Trasatti was silent. He began to arrange a row of paper clips on the side of a magnetized holder on his desk. Each one had to be exactly the same distance from the one above it and the one below.

"Come on. Just between us," I said.

"I tried to find them once."

"When was this?"

"About ten years ago."

"Really," I said, trying not to seem interested. "What was that about?"

"I was curious. I thought there might be other rare documents. You know, passed down to other members of the family."

"How'd you go about it?"

"I hired a genealogist. I said I was trying to find some long-lost relatives. This gal did a search. She took months. She traced the name back to England, but on this end—the California branch—there weren't any male heirs and the line died out."

"What about aunts, uncles, cousins . . . ?"

"The parents were both the only children of only children. There was no one left."

"What happened to the copies of the documents?"

"The forgeries were destroyed."

"And the originals?"

"No one's ever seen them again. Well, I haven't in any case. They've never come up for sale in all the years I've done business."

"Do you know what they were?"

"I have the itemized list. My dad kept meticulous records. You want to see it?"

"I'd love to."

Trasatti got up and crossed to a closet. I caught a glimpse of a wall safe and four gray metal file cabinets. Above them, on shelves, there was a series of old-fashioned card files. "I'm going to get all this on computer one of these days." He seemed to know right where he was going and I wondered if this was something he'd done recently. He extracted a card, glanced at it briefly, and then closed the drawer again. He left the closet door ajar and returned to his desk, handing me the card as he passed my chair. The cat had gone to sleep, lying across my knees like a fifteen-pound bag of hot sand.

The list detailed six documents: a framed Society of Boston Membership Certificate and a personal letter, both signed by George Washington and valued at $11,500 and $9,500, respectively; a judicial writ signed by Abraham Lincoln, dated December 1847, valued at $6,500; a wartime document signed by John Hancock, valued at $5,500; a ten-page fragment from an original manuscript by Arthur Conan Doyle valued at $7,500; and a letter signed by John Adams, valued at $9,000.

"I'm impressed," I said. "I don't know beans about rare documents, but these seem fabulous."

"They are. Those prices you're looking at are twenty years out of date. They'd be worth more today."

"How did Patty Maddison's father get his hands on items like these?"

"Nobody really knows. He was an amateur collector. He picked some up at auction and the rest, who knows? He might have stolen them for all I know. My father'd heard about 'em, but Francis—Mr. Maddison—would never let him examine them."

"His widow must have been an idiot to hand 'em over the way she did."

Trasatti made no comment.

"How did Guy hear about the letters?" I asked.

"Patty probably told him."

"Why would she do that?"

"How do I know? Showing off. She was nuts. She did all kinds of weird things."

I saw him glance at his watch. "You have an appointment?" I asked.

"As a matter of fact, I'm hoping we can wrap this up. I have work to do."

"Five minutes more and I'll be on my way."

Trasatti shifted restlessly, but motioned me on.

"Let me try out a little theory. None of this came to light until after Guy took off, right?"

Trasatti stared at me, without offering encouragement.

I was forced to go on, feeling like Perry Mason in a courtroom confrontation, only this wasn't going as well as his always did. "So maybe Jack was the one who got Patty knocked up. I heard Jack was the randy one. According to Guy, he screwed anything that moved."

"I told you he was off at college. He wasn't even here," Trasatti said.

"He came back for his mother's funeral and again for spring break. That was March, wasn't it?"

"I really don't remember."

"As I understand it, Guy had hit the road by then. Jack felt betrayed. He was crushed that Guy'd left without him so maybe he turned to Patty for consolation. At that point, she must have needed comfort as much as he did."

Trasatti kept his face expressionless, his fingers laced together on the desk. "You're never going to get me to say anything about this."

"Jack could have forged the letters. You two were buddies. Your father was an appraiser. You could have cooked up the scheme yourself and showed Jack how to do it."

"I'm finding this offensive. It's pure speculation. It doesn't mean a thing."

I let that one slide, though what he said was true. "Everything was cool until Guy came home again."

"What difference would that make?"

"In the old days, Guy took the blame for everybody's sins, so it just stands to reason everyone felt safe until he showed up again."

"I'm not following."

"Maybe the motive for Guy's murder was never money," I said. "Maybe Jack was just trying to protect himself."

"From what? I don't get it. There's really nothing at stake. The theft was eighteen years ago. The statute of limitations has run out. There's no crime on the books. Even if your guess is correct, Jack's the one who ends up with his ass in a sling. You said you were here to help, but it's blowing right back on him."

"You know what? Here's the truth. I don't really give a shit what blows back on him. If he's guilty, so be it. That isn't my concern."

"Well, that's nice. You want me to pick up the phone and call Lonnie Kingman? He's going to love your attitude and so will Jack. As far as I know, he's the one paying your bills."

"You go right ahead. Lonnie can always fire me if he doesn't like what I'm doing."

20

I stopped at a pay phone and put a call through to Lonnie, who had the good grace to laugh when he heard my account of the conversation with Paul Trasatti. "Forget it. The guy's a prick. He was just on the phone to me, whining and complaining about harassment. What a jerk."

"Why's he so worried about Jack?"

"Forget Jack for now. I'll take care of him. You better go talk to Bennet; I couldn't get to him. According to the grapevine, he's talking to an attorney in case the hairy eyeball of the law falls on him next. He's still got no alibi, as far as I've heard."

"Well, that's interesting."

"Yeah, people are getting nervous. That's a good sign," he said. He gave me the address of Bennet's restaurant, which was located downtown on a side street off State. The neighborhood itself was marked by a tire store, a minimart, a video rental shop, and a billiard parlor where fights erupted without much provocation beyond excess beer. Parking didn't seem to be readily available and it was hard to picture where the restaurant trade would be coming from.

Apparently, the place had once been a retail store, part of a chain that had filed for bankruptcy. The old sign was still out, but the interior had been gutted. The space was cavernous and shadowy, the floor bare concrete, the ceiling high. Heating ducts and steel girders were exposed to view, along with all of the electrical conduit. Toward the rear, an office had been roughed in: a desk, file cabinets, and office equipment arranged in a bare-framed cubicle. The back wall was solid and through a narrow doorway, I could see a toilet and a small sink with a medicine cabinet above it. It was going to take a lot of money to complete construction and get the business on its feet. No wonder Bennet had been so eager to get his hands on the second will. If Guy's share was divided among his brothers, each would be richer by more than a million, which he could clearly use.

To the right, a huge rolling metal door had been opened onto a weedy vacant lot. Outside, the sun was harsh, sparkling on the broken bottles while its heat baked a variety of doggy turds. There was not a soul in sight, but the building was wide open and I kept thinking Bennet, or a construction worker, would show up before long. While I waited, I wandered into the office area and took a seat at Bennet's desk. The secretarial chair was rickety and I imagined he made his phone calls upright with his hip resting on the desk, which seemed sturdier. Everything in the office had an air of having been borrowed or picked up on the cheap. The calculator tape showed a long series of numbers that didn't add up to anything. I could have checked in the drawers, but I was too polite. Besides, my recent clash with Paul Trasatti had chastened me some. I didn't want Lonnie getting two complaints in a single day.

There was a manual typewriter sitting on a rolling cart. My gaze slid across it idly and then came back. It was an ancient black Underwood with round yellowed keys that looked like they'd be hard to press. The ribbon was so worn it was thin in the middle. I looked over at the rolling door and then surveyed the whole of the empty restaurant space. Still no one. My bad angel was hovering to my left. It was she who pointed out the open packet of typing paper sitting right there in plain sight.

I pulled out a sheet and rolled it into the machine, settling myself on the wobbly typing chair. I typed my name. I typed that old standby: *The quick brown fox jumps over the lazy dog.* I typed the name *Max Outhwaite.* I typed *Dear Miss Milhone.* I peered closely. The vowels didn't appear to be clogged, which (as Dietz had pointed out) didn't mean that much. This could still be the typewriter used for the notes. Maybe Bennet had simply made a point of cleaning his keys. I pulled the paper out and folded it, then stood up and slipped it in the pocket of my jeans. When I got back to the office, I'd see if the defective *a* and *i* were visible under magnification. I still hadn't seen the anonymous letter Guy had received the Monday before he died, but maybe Betsy Bower would relent and let me pirate a copy.

The telephone rang.

I stared at it briefly and then lifted my head, listening for footsteps heading in my direction. Nothing. The phone rang again. I was tempted to answer, but I really didn't need to because the answering machine kicked in. Bennet's voice message was brief and very businesslike. So was the caller.

"Bennet. Paul here. Give me a call as soon as possible."

The machine clicked off. The message light blinked off and on. My bad angel tapped me on the shoulder and pointed. I reached out and pressed DELETE. A disembodied male voice told me the message had been erased. I headed for the front door, breaking into a trot when I reached the street. Trasatti was a busy boy, calling everyone.

A Harley-Davidson rumbled into view. Shit. Bennet was back just when I thought I'd escaped. I slowed my pace, as if I had all the time in the world. Bennet rolled Jack's motorcycle up to the curb less than ten feet away. He killed the engine and popped the kickstand into place. He peeled off his helmet and cradled it under his arm. I noticed his hair was tightly frizzed and matted with sweat. Despite the heat, he was wearing a black leather jacket, probably protection in case he flipped the bike and skidded. "Working again?"

"I'm always working," I said.

"Did you want to talk to me?" His jacket creaked when he walked. He headed into the restaurant.

I followed. "How goes construction? It's looking pretty good," I said. It looked like a bomb crater, but I was kissing butt. Our footsteps echoed as we crossed the raw concrete floor.

"Construction's slow."

I said, "Ah. What's your target for opening?"

"April, if we're lucky. We have a lot of work to do."

"What kind of restaurant?"

"Cajun and Caribbean. We'll have salads and burgers, too, very reasonably priced. Maybe jazz two nights a week. We're really aiming for the singles' market."

"Like a pickup bar?"

"With class," he said. "This town doesn't have a lot going on at night. Get some dance music in here weekends, I think we're filling a niche. A chef from New Orleans and all the hot local bands. We should pull crowds from as far away as San Luis Obispo."

"That sounds rowdy," I said. We'd reached the office by then and I saw him flick a glance at his answering machine. I was only half listening, trying to think how to keep the conversation afloat. "Any problem with parking?"

"Not at all," he said. "We'll pave the lot next door. We're in negotiations at the moment. There's room for thirty cars there and another ten on the street."

"Sounds good," I said. He had an answer for everything. Mr. Slick, I thought.

"I'll comp you some tickets for the grand opening. You like to dance?"

"No, not really."

"Don't worry about it. We'll get you in and you can cut loose.

Forget your inhibitions and get down," he said. He snapped his fingers, dipping his knees in a move meant to be oh so hip.

My least favorite thing in life is some guy encouraging me to "cut loose" and "get down." The smile I offered him was paper thin. "I hope this business with Jack has been resolved by then."

"Absolutely," he said smoothly, his expression sobering appropriately. "How's it looking so far?"

"He can't account for his time, which doesn't help," I said. "The cops are claiming they found a bloody print from his shoe on the carpet up in Guy's room. I won't bore you with details. Lonnie wanted me to ask where you were."

"The night of the murder? I was club-hopping down in L.A."

"You drove to Los Angeles and back?"

"I do it all the time. It's nothing. Ninety minutes each way," he said. "That night, some of the time I was on the road."

"Did you have a date?"

"This was strictly business. I'm trying to get a feel for what works and what doesn't, sampling menus. You know, listening to some of the L.A. bands."

"I'm assuming you have credit card receipts to back you up."

A fleeting change of expression suggested I'd caught him out on that one. "I might have a few. I'll have to look and see what I've got. I paid cash in the main. It's easier that way."

"What time did you get in?"

"Close to three," he said. "You want to come in the back? I've got some beer in a cooler. We could have a drink."

"Thanks. It's a bit early."

"Where you going?"

"Back to the office. I have a meeting," I said.

On the way back to the office, I stopped off at a deli and picked up some soft drinks and sandwiches. Dietz had said he'd be joining me as soon as he'd finished his research. I stashed the soft drinks in the little refrigerator in my office and dumped my handbag on the floor beside my chair. I put the sack of sandwiches on the file cabinet and grabbed the folder full of clippings, which I tossed on my desk. I sat down in my swivel chair and assembled my index cards, the typewritten letters, and the sample I'd just taken from Bennet's machine, lining everything up in an orderly fashion. In the absence of definitive answers, it's good to look organized.

I turned on the desk lamp and pulled out my magnifying glass. The type was no match. I was disappointed, but I wasn't surprised. I took Guy's last letter from my handbag and read the contents again. Aside from his invitation to Disneyland, which I'd have accepted in a flash, I realized that what I was looking at, in essence, was a holographic will. The letter was written entirely by hand and he'd specified in the postscript what he'd wanted done with his share of his father's estate. I didn't know all the technicalities associated with a holographic will, but I thought this might qualify. The handwriting would have to be verified, but Peter Antle could do that when I saw him next. I knew Guy had received a disturbing letter late that Monday afternoon, and whatever its contents, he must have been sufficiently alarmed to want to make his wishes clear. I got up and left the office, taking his letter with me to the copy room. I ran a Xerox and then locked the originals with the others in my bottom drawer. The copy I slid in the outer pocket of my handbag.

I tried to picture Guy, but his face had already faded in my mind's eye. What remained was his sweetness, the sound of his "Hey," the feeling of his whiskers when he'd brushed my cheek with his lips. If he'd lived, I'm not sure we would have had a very strong relationship. Kinsey Millhone and a born-again was probably not a combination that would have gone anywhere. But we might have been friends. We might have gone to Disneyland once a year to experience some silliness.

I went back to my index cards and began to make notes. Every investigation has a nature of its own, but there are certain shared characteristics, namely the painstaking accumulation of information and the patience required. Here's what you hope for: a chance remark from the former neighbor on a skip-trace, a penciled notation on the corner of a document, an ex-spouse with a grudge, the number on an account, an item overlooked at the scene of a crime. Here's what you expect: the dead ends, bureaucratic bullheadedness, the cul-de-sacs, trails that go nowhere or simply fade into thin air, denials, prevarications, the blank-eyed stares from all the hostile witnesses. Here's what you know: that you've done it before and you have the toughness and determination to pull it off again. Here's what you want: justice. Here's what you'll settle for: something equivalent, the quid pro quo.

I glanced down at my desk, catching sight of the label on the file of clippings. The label had been neatly typed: *Guy Malek, Dispatch Clippings.* The two letters from Outhwaite were lined up with the label itself, which is what made me notice for the first time that the lowercase *a* and the lower case *i* were both defective on all three documents. Was that true? I peered closely, picking up my magnifying glass again and scrutinizing the relevant characters. It would take a document expert to prove it, but to me it looked like the letters had been typed on the same machine.

I reached for the phone and called the Maleks. In the tiny interval between punching in the number and waiting for it to ring, I was scrambling around in my imagination, trying to conjure up a reason for the call I was making. Shit, shit, shit. Christie picked up on her end, greeting me coolly when I identified myself. I figured she'd talked to Paul Trasatti, but I didn't dare ask.

I said, "I was just looking for Bennet. Is he home, by any chance? I stopped by the restaurant, but he was out somewhere."

"He should be here in a bit. I think he said he was coming home for lunch. You want him to call you?"

"I'm not sure he'll be able to reach me. I'm down at the office, but I've got some errands to run. I'll call back later."

"I'll pass the message along." She was using her good-bye tone.

I had to launch in with something to keep the conversation afloat.

"I talked to Paul this morning. What an odd duck he is. Is he still on medication?"

I could hear her focus her attention. "Paul's on medication? Who told you that? I never heard that," she said.

I let a beat pass. "Uhh, sorry. I didn't mean to breach anybody's confidence. Forget I said anything. I just assumed you knew."

"Why bring it up at all? Is there a problem?"

"Well, nothing *huge.* He's just so paranoid about Jack. He actually sat there and accused me of undermining Jack's credibility, which couldn't be further from the truth. Lonnie and I are working our butts off for him."

"Really."

"Then he turned around and called Lonnie. I think he's probably on another phone rampage, hounding everyone he knows with those wild stories of his. Ah, well. It doesn't matter. I'm sure he means well, but he's not doing anybody any favors."

"Is that what you wanted to talk to Bennet about?"

"No, that was something different. Lonnie wanted me to verify Bennet's whereabouts Tuesday night."

"I'm sure he'll be happy to talk to you. I know he's told the police and they seem satisfied. I can leave him a note."

"Perfect. I'd appreciate that. Can I ask you about something? You remember the file I borrowed?"

"With all the clippings?"

"Exactly. I wondered about the label. Did you type that yourself?"

"Not me. I never took typing. My mother warned me about that. Bader probably typed the label or he gave it to his secretary. He thought typing was restful. Shows how much he knew."

"That must have been a while ago. I don't remember seeing a typewriter in his office when I was there."

"He got himself a personal computer a couple of years ago."

"What happened to the typewriter?"

"He passed it on to Bennet, I think."

I closed my eyes and stilled my breathing. Christie's attitude had changed and she was sounding friendly again. I didn't want to alert her to the importance of the information. "What'd Bennet do with it? That's not the one he's using at the restaurant, is it?"

"Nuhn-uhn. I doubt it. It's probably in his room. What's this about?"

"Nothing much. No big deal. Just a little theory of mine, but I'd love to see it sometime. Would it be all right with you if I stopped by to take a look?"

"Well, it's all right with me, but Bennet might object unless he's here, of course. His room is like the inner sanctum. Nobody goes in there except him. We're just on our way out. We have an appointment at eleven. Why don't you ask Bennet when you talk to him?"

"I can do that. No problem. That's a good idea," I said. "And one more quick question. The night of the murder, could you really see Donovan? Or did you just assume he was watching television because the set was turned on in the other room?"

Christie put the phone down without another word.

The minute I hung up, I wrote a hasty note to Dietz, put a couple of pieces of blank paper in the file, and shoved it in my handbag. I headed out the side door and took the stairs down to the street, skipping two at a time. I wasn't sure which "we" had an appointment at eleven, but I was hoping it was Christie and Donovan. If I could get to the Maleks' before Bennet came home, I could probably bullshit my way upstairs and take a look at the machine. It had occurred to me more than once that Jack or Bennet might be behind the letters and the leak to the press. I couldn't pinpoint the motivation, but getting a lock on the typewriter would go a long way toward shoring up the connection. I was also thinking tee-hee on you, Dietz, because I'd told him whoever wrote the letters wouldn't trash the machine. It's the same way with guns. Someone will use a handgun in the commission of a crime and instead of disposing of the weapon, he'll keep it in his closet at home or shove it under the bed. Better to pitch it in the ocean.

I reached the Maleks' in record time, burning up the route I'd driven so many times before. As I approached the estate, I could see the front gates swing open and the nose of a car just appearing around the curve in the drive. I slammed on my brakes and slid into the nearest driveway, fishtailing slightly, my eyes pinned on my rear-view mirror for a moment until the BMW sped past. Donovan was driving, his gaze fixed on the road ahead. I thought I caught sight of Christie, but I couldn't be sure. I heard a car horn toot and looked out through my windshield. The Maleks' neighbor, in a dark blue station wagon, was waiting patiently for me to get out of his driveway. I made lots of sheepish gestures as I put my car in reverse. I backed out of the driveway and pulled over to let him pass. I mouthed the word *Sorry* as he turned to look at me. He smiled and waved, and I waved back at him. Once he was out of sight, I pulled out, crossing the road to the Maleks' entrance gates.

The security guard had been relieved of his duties. I leaned out toward the call box and punched in the gate code Tasha had given me. There was a happy peeping signal. The gates gave a little wiggle and then swung open to admit me. I eased up the driveway and around the curve. Vaguely, it occurred to me that Christie might have stayed home. I'd have to think of a whopper to account for my arrival. Oh, well. Often the best lies are the ones you think up in a pinch.

There were no cars in the courtyard, a good sign I thought. Two of the three garages were standing open and both were empty. I had to leave my vehicle out front, but there didn't seem to be any way around that. If my purpose was legitimate, why would I bother to conceal my car? If the Maleks returned, I'd find a way to fake it. I bypassed the front door and hiked around to the kitchen, pulling the file from my handbag as I rounded the house. Enid was visible through the bay window, standing at the sink. She spotted me and waved, moving toward the backdoor to let me in. She was still drying her hands on a towel when she stepped back, allowing me to precede her into the room.

I said, "Hi, Enid. How are you?"

"Fine," she said. "What are you doing coming to the backdoor?

You just missed Christie and Donovan going out the front." She was wearing a big white apron over jeans and a T-shirt and her hair was neatly tucked under a crocheted cap.

"Really? I didn't see them. I rang the front doorbell twice. I guess you couldn't hear me so I thought I'd come around. I can't believe I missed them. My timing's off," I said.

I could see the ingredients for a baking project laid out on the counter: two sticks of butter with the paper removed, a sixteen-ounce measuring cup filled with granulated sugar, a tin of baking powder, and a quart container of whole milk. The oven was preheating and a large springform pan had already been buttered and floured.

She returned to the counter where she picked up her sifter and began sifting cake flour into a mountain that had a perfect point on top. While I watched, she used a spatula to scoop more flour. I seldom bake anything and when I do, I tend to assemble the items as needed, not realizing I'm missing some essential ingredient until I get to the critical moment in the recipe. "Quickly fold in whipped egg whites and finely minced fresh ginger . . ." Enid was methodical, washing up as she went along. I knew she wouldn't bake anything from mixes and her cakes would never fall.

"Where'd everybody go? I didn't see any cars in the garages," I said.

"Myrna's lying down. I imagine she'll be up in a bit."

"What's wrong with her? Is she ill?"

"I don't know. She seems worried and I don't think she's been sleeping that well."

"Maybe I should talk to her. Where's everyone else?"

"Christie says Bennet's coming home at lunchtime. She and Donovan went over to the funeral home. The coroner's office called. The body's being released this afternoon and they've gone to pick out a casket."

"When's the funeral? Has anybody said?"

"They're talking about Monday, just for family and close friends. It won't be open to the public."

"I should think not. I'm sure they've had their fill of media attention."

"Can I help you with anything?"

"Not really. I talked to Christie a while ago and told her I'd be returning this file. She said to stick it in Bader's office. I can let myself out the front door when I'm done."

"Help yourself," she said. "Take the back stairs if you want. You know how to find the office?"

"Sure. I've been up there before. What are you making?"

"Lemon pound cake."

"Sounds good," I said.

I trotted up the back stairs, folder in hand, slowing my pace when I reached the top landing. The back hall was utilitarian, floors uncarpeted, windows bare. This mansion was built in an era when the wealthy had live-in servants who occupied nooks and crannies squeezed into wings at the rear of the house, or wedged into attic spaces that were broken up into many small rooms. Cautiously, I opened a door on my left. A narrow stairway ascended into the shadows above. I eased the door shut and moved on, checking into a large linen closet and a cubicle with an ancient commode. The corridor took a ninety-degree turn to the right, opening into the main hall through an archway concealed by heavy damask drapes on a wrought-iron rod.

I could see the polished rail of the main stair at the midpoint in the hall. Beyond the stair landing, there was another wing of the house that mirrored the one I was now in. A wide Oriental runner stretched the length of the gloomy hall. At the far end, damask drapes suggested an archway and yet another set of stairs. The wallpaper was subdued, a soft floral pattern repeated endlessly. At intervals, tulip-shaped crystal fixtures were mounted on the walls. They'd probably been installed when the house was built and converted at some point from gas to electricity.

There were three doors on my left, each sealed with an enormous X of crime scene tape. I had to guess that one door led to Guy's bedroom, one to Jack's, and one to the bathroom that connected the two. On the right, there were two more doors. I knew the second was Bader's suite: bedroom, bath, and home office. The door closest to me was closed. I flicked a look behind me, making sure Enid hadn't followed. The whole house was silent. I put my hand on the knob and turned it with care. Locked.

Well, now what? The lock was the simple old-fashioned type requiring a skeleton key that probably fit every door up here. I scanned the hall in both directions. I didn't have time to waste. Bader's suite was closest. I did a racewalk to his bedroom and tried the knob. This room was unlocked. I peered around the door. There was a key protruding neatly from the keyhole on the other side. I extracted it and hurried back to Bennet's room. I jammed the key in the lock and tried turning it. I could feel the key hang, but there was some tolerance to the lock. I applied steady pressure while I jiggled the door gently. It took close to thirty seconds, but the key gave way suddenly and I was in.

21

I scanned the room quickly, taking in as much as I could. Two table lamps had been left on. This had to be Bennet's bedroom. He was still in possession of all the paraphernalia from his boyhood hobbies. Model airplanes, model cars, stacks of vintage comic books, early issues of *MAD* magazine, Little League trophies. He'd framed a paint-by-numbers likeness of Jimmy Durante and a color snapshot of himself at the age of thirteen wearing spiffy black dress pants, a pink dress shirt, and a black bolo tie. His bulletin board was still hanging on the back of his closet door. Tacked to the cork were various newspaper headlines about the assassinations of Martin Luther King, Jr., and Bobby Kennedy. There were photographs of the *Apollo 8* spacecraft the day it was launched from Cape Kennedy. A framed movie poster from *The Odd Couple* still hung above his unmade bed. It wasn't hard to pinpoint the peak year in his life. There was no memorabilia beyond 1968.

I flicked on the overhead light and crossed the room, placing my handbag on the floor near my feet. His desk was built-in and ran along the front wall from one side of the room to the other, punctuated by two windows. Bookshelves had been hung on the wall above the desk. Most of the books looked dated, the titles suggestive of textbooks accumulated over the years. I let my gaze skip across the spines. *Ring of Bright Water,* Maxwell; *No Room in the Ark,* Moorehead; *Stalking the Edible Life,* Gibbons; *The Sea Around Us,* Carson. Little or no fiction. Not surprising somehow. Bennet didn't strike me as intellectual or imaginative. A personal computer occupied his desk at center stage, complete with an oversized printer. The machine had been shut down and the glassy gray screen of the monitor reflected distorted slices of the light from the hall door. Everything was a jumble; bills, loose papers, invoices, and stacks of unopened mail everywhere. I spotted the typewriter to the left, covered with a black plastic typewriter "cozy" complete with dust. A stack of books had been placed on top.

I backed up and stuck my head out into the hallway. I did a quick survey, seeing no one, and then closed myself into Bennet's room. If I were caught, there was no way I was going to explain my presence. I went back to the desk, lifted the stack of books from the typewriter, and removed the cover. The machine was an old black high-shouldered Remington with a manual return. Bader must have hung on to the damn thing for forty years. I reached into my bag and removed a piece of blank paper from the folder. I rolled it into the machine, typing precisely the phrases and sentences I'd typed before. *The quick brown fox jumps over the lazy dog.* The typewriter made a racket that seemed remarkably noisy, but it couldn't be helped. With the door to the hall closed, I thought I was safe. *Dear Miss Milhone. Max Outhwaite.* Even at a glance, I knew I was in business. The *a* and the *i* were both askew. This was the machine I'd been looking for. I rolled the paper from the machine, folded it, and slipped it in my pocket. Out of the corner of my eye, the name Outhwaite suddenly popped into view. Was I seeing things? I checked the line of textbooks again, squinting as I pulled out the two books that caught my attention. *Ring of Bright Water,* Gavin Maxwell, was the first in that row. In the middle, about six books down, was *Atlantic: History of an Ocean.* The author was Leonard Outhwaite. I stared, feeling rooted in place. Gavin Maxwell and Leonard Outhwaite. *Maxwell Outhwaite.*

I slipped the cover over the typewriter and put the stack of books back in place. I heard a low rumble, like thunder. I paused. Empty coat hangers began to ring, tinkling together in the closet like wind chimes. All the joints in the house began to squeak quietly and the window glass gave a sharp rattle where the putty had shrunk away from the panes. Nails and wood screws chirped. I put a hand on the bookshelf to steady myself. Under me, the whole house shifted back and forth, perhaps no more than an inch, but with a movement that felt like a sudden gust of strong wind or a train rocking on a track. I didn't feel any fear, but I was alert, wondering if I'd have time to clear the premises. An old house like this must have survived many a temblor, but you never quite knew what was coming with these things. So far, I pegged it in the three- or four-point range. As long as it didn't go on and on, it shouldn't do much damage. Lights flickered faintly as if wires were loose and touching one another intermittently. The strobe effect sparked a series of jerky pale blue images, in the midst of which a dark shape appeared across the room. I peered, blinking, trying to see clearly as the shadow moved toward one corner and then blended into the wall.

I made a small sound in my throat, paralyzed. The trembling gradually ceased and the lights stabilized. I clung to the bookshelf and leaned my head weakly on my arm, trying to shake off the frosty feeling that was creeping down my spine. Any minute, I expected to hear Enid calling from the kitchen stairs. I pictured Myrna on her feet, the three of us comparing notes about the earthquake. I didn't want either one of them coming up to search for me. I snagged my handbag and crossed the room. I moved out into the hall, looking quickly in both directions. I locked the door behind me, cranking the key in the lock so hard it nearly bent under my hand.

I ran down the hall on tiptoe, making a hasty detour into Bader's room. I put the key back in the door where I'd found it, then crossed swiftly into his home office. I opened a file cabinet and shoved the folder between two unrelated files where I could find it later. I crossed the room again and went out into the corridor. I walked quickly toward the heavy drapes at the end of the hall, pushed my way through the arch, and hurried along the back corridor. I clattered down the stairs and into the kitchen. There was no sign of Myrna. Enid was calmly pouring a thick yellow batter into the springform pan.

I put my hand on my chest to still my breathing. "Jesus. That was something. I thought for a minute there we were really in for it."

She looked up at me blankly. I could tell she didn't have the faintest idea what I was talking about.

I stopped in my tracks. "The temblor," I said.

"I wasn't aware of any temblor. When was this?"

"Enid, you're kidding. Don't do this to me. It must have been at least four points on the Richter scale. Didn't the lights flicker down here?"

"Not that I noticed." I watched her use a rubber spatula to sweep the last of the batter from the bowl into the pan.

"The whole house was shifting. Didn't you feel *anything?*"

She was silent for a moment, her gaze dropping to her bowl. "You hang on to people, don't you?"

"What?"

"You have trouble letting go."

"I do not. That's not a bit true. People tell me I'm too independent for my own good."

She was shaking her head before I reached the end of the sentence. "Independence has nothing to do with hanging on," she said.

"What are you talking about?"

"Ghosts don't haunt us. That's not how it works. They're present among us because we won't let go of *them.*"

"I don't believe in ghosts," I said, faintly.

"Some people can't see the color red. That doesn't mean it isn't there," she replied.

When I reached the office, Dietz was sitting in my swivel chair with his feet up on the desk. One of the sandwich packets had been opened and he was munching on a BLT. I still hadn't eaten lunch so I reached for the other sandwich. I removed a soft drink from the refrigerator and sat down across from him.

"How'd you do at the *Dispatch?*"

He laid the four Maddison obituaries on the desk so I could study them. "I had Jeff Katzenbach dig through the files. Mother's maiden name was Bangham, so I went over to the library and checked the city directory for other Banghams in the area. None. Three of those obits I've verified at the Hall of Records, checking death certificates. Claire's still a question mark."

"How so?" I popped the top on my soda can and began to pick at the cellophane and plastic packet in which my sandwich was sealed.

Dietz was saying, "There's no suggestion how she died. I'd be interested in seeing if we can get the suicide confirmed just to put that one to bed. I got the name of a PI in Bridgeport, Connecticut, and left a lengthy message with her service. I'm hoping someone will return my call."

"What difference does it make how she died?" I tried biting the seal on the cellophane. Was this kiddie-proof, like poison? Dietz held his hand out for the wrapped sandwich and I passed it across the desk to him.

"Suppose she was murdered? Suppose she was the victim of a hit-and-run accident?" He freed the sandwich and gave it back to me.

"You've got a point," I said. I paused to eat while I reread the information. The obits were in date order, starting with the father's death in late November 1967. Dietz had had all four of them copied onto one page.

> MADDISON, Francis M., 53,
> departed suddenly on Tuesday, November 21. Loving, adored husband of 25 years to Caroline B. Maddison; beloved father to daughters, Claire and Patricia. He was a service manager at Colgate Automotive Center and a member of the Community Christian Church. He was much loved and will be missed by family and friends. Funeral: 11:30 A.M. Friday. In lieu of flowers, donations to the American Heart Association would be appreciated.

I glanced up at him and said, "Fifty-three. That's young."

"They were all young," Dietz said.

> MADDISON, Patricia Anne, 17,
> died Thursday, May 9, at Santa Teresa Hospital. She is survived by her loving mother, Caroline B. Maddison, and a devoted sister, Claire Maddison. At the family's request, services will be private.

> MADDISON, Caroline B., 58,
> died Tuesday, August 29, at her home after a lengthy illness. She was born on January 22 to Helen and John Bangham, in Indianapolis, Indiana, graduating from Indiana University with a degree in home economics. Caroline was a devoted wife, mother, a homemaker, and a Christian. Preceded in death by her husband, Francis M. Maddison, and her daughter Patricia Anne Maddison. Survived by loving daughter Claire Maddison of Bridgeport, Connecticut. No services are planned. Contributions may be made to Hospice of Santa Teresa.

MADDISON, Claire, 39,
formerly of Santa Teresa, died Saturday, March 2, in Bridgeport, Connecticut. Daughter of the late Francis M. and Caroline B. Maddison, Claire was preceded in death by her only sister, Patricia. Claire graduated from Santa Teresa High School in 1963 and the University of Connecticut in 1967. She pursued her secondary teaching credential and M.A. in Romance Languages at Boston College. She taught French and Italian at a private girls' academy in Bridgeport, Connecticut. Service, Tuesday in the Memorial Park Chapel.

I read Claire's death notice twice. "This was just last year."

"Thank goodness she'd gone back to her maiden name," he said. "I don't know how we'd have found her if she'd been using her ex-hubby's moniker."

"Whoever he was," I said. "She'd probably been divorced for ages. There wasn't much family to speak of. You watch the names of the survivors diminish until there's no one left. It's depressing, isn't it?"

"I thought the mother might have surviving family members in Indiana, but I can't seem to get a line on them," Dietz said. "I tried directory assistance in Indianapolis. There weren't any Banghams listed, so at least on the face of it, we're not talking about a large close-knit clan. Just to be on the safe side, I checked the CALI Directory and put a call through to an Indianapolis private investigator. I asked him to check Caroline Bangham's birth records to see if that nets us anything. We might not glean much, but he said he'd get back to us."

I made a face. "You know what? I think we're spinning our wheels on this one. I just don't buy the idea that some distraught family member would seek revenge eighteen years later."

"Maybe not," he said. "If it weren't for Bader's death, there wouldn't have been a reason to look for Guy at all. He might have gone on living in Marcella for the rest of his days."

"It wasn't strictly Bader's death. It was the will," I said.

"Which brings us back to the five million."

"I guess it does," I said. "I'll tell you what hurts. I feel like I was part of what happened to Guy."

"Because you found him."

"Exactly. I didn't cause his death, in any strict sense of the word, but if it hadn't been for me, he'd be safe the way I see it."

"Hey, come on. That's not true. Tasha would have hired herself some other detective. Maybe not as good as you . . ."

"Don't suck up."

"Look, someone would have found him. It just happened to be you."

"I suppose," I said. "It still feels like shit."

"I'm sure it does."

The phone rang. Dietz answered and then handed me the handset, mouthing the name *Enid.*

I nodded and took the phone. "Hi, Enid. This is Kinsey. How are you?"

"Not so good," she said, fretfully. "Did Myrna call you?"

"Not as far as I know. Let me check my messages." I put a hand across the mouthpiece. "Did the Maleks' housekeeper call or leave a message for me?"

Dietz shook his head and I went back to Enid. "No, there's nothing here."

"Well, that's odd. She swore she was going to call you. I made her promise she would. I went to the supermarket and I was only gone fifteen or twenty minutes. She said she'd be here when I got back, but she's gone and there's no sign of her. I thought you might have asked her to come in."

"Sorry. I never heard from her. What'd she want to talk to me about?"

"I'm not sure. I know something's been bothering her, but she wouldn't be specific. Her car's still out back. That's what's so strange," she said.

"Could she have gone to the doctor's? If she really wasn't feeling well, she might have called a cab."

"It's always possible, but you'd think she would have waited to have me take her. This is just so unlike her. She told me she'd help me with dinner. I have a meeting at seven and I have to be out of here early. We discussed it in detail."

"Maybe she's out walking somewhere on the property."

"I thought of that," she said. "I went out there myself, calling, but she's disappeared."

"Enid, let's be realistic. I don't think being gone less than an hour constitutes a disappearance."

"I'm worried something's happened."

"Like what?"

"I don't know. That's why I called you. Because I'm scared."

"What's the rest?"

"That's it."

"No, it's not. You're leaving something out. I mean, so far this doesn't make sense. Do you think she's been abducted by aliens, or what?"

I could hear her hesitation. "I got the impression she knew something about the murder."

"Really. She said that?"

"She hinted as much. She was too nervous to say more. I think she saw something she wasn't supposed to see that night."

"She told me she was sleeping."

"Well, she was. She'd taken some pain medication and a sleeping pill. She slept like the dead, but then she remembered later that she woke up at one point to find someone standing at the foot of her bed."

"Wait a minute, Enid. You're not talking about this woo-woo stuff . . ."

"Not at all. I promise. This is what she said. She said she thought she'd been dreaming, but the more she thought about it, the more convinced she was that it was real."

"What was?"

"The person she saw."

"I gathered that, Enid. Who?"

"She wouldn't tell me. She felt guilty she hadn't said anything before now."

"Myrna feels guilty about everything," I said.

"I know," Enid said. "But I think she was also worried about the consequences. She thought she'd be in danger if she opened her mouth. I told her to tell the police, in that case, but she was afraid to do that. She said she'd rather talk to you first and then she'd talk to them. It's not like her to go off without a word."

"You did check her room?"

"That's the first thing I did. And that's the other thing that bothers me. Something doesn't seem right. Myrna's very fussy. Everything has to be just so with her. I don't mean to criticize, but it's the truth."

"Her room is messed up?"

"It's not exactly messed up, but it doesn't look right."

"Who else is there? Is anybody home besides you?"

"Bennet was here, but I think he's gone. He came in for lunch. I fixed him a sandwich and he took it up to his room. He must have left again while I was at the market. Christie and Donovan are due back any minute. I don't mean to be a bother, but I don't feel right about this."

Dietz was giving me an inquisitive look. Having eavesdropped on my end of the conversation with her, he was suitably mystified. "Hang on a second." I put a palm across the mouthpiece. "How long will you be here?"

"At least an hour," he said. "If you'd ever get off the phone, I might get this call from the East Coast that I've been waiting for. What's the problem?"

"It's Myrna. I'll tell you in a minute." I went back to Enid. "Why don't I come over there," I said. "She might have mentioned something to Christie before they left for the funeral home. You're sure she didn't leave a note?"

"Positive."

"I'll be there in fifteen minutes."

"I don't want you to go to any trouble."

"It's no trouble."

I took my sandwich and soda with me, driving with one hand while I finished my lunch. I kept the chilled soda can between my thighs. Shifting gears is a pain in the ass when you're trying to dine in style. At least I knew the route. I could have done it with my eyes shut.

Enid had left the gate open for me. I pulled into the courtyard and left my car in a spot I was beginning to think should be reserved for me. Donovan's pickup truck was parked to one side of the garage. At first, I thought he was back, but then I remembered that he'd been driving the BMW when he left. Both the open garages were still empty. The driveway angled up along the house on the left. For the first time, I noticed a separate parking pad nearby with spaces for three vehicles. Currently, I could see a bright yellow VW convertible and what looked like a Toyota, a pale metallic blue, maybe three or four years old.

Enid had the backdoor ajar and was standing in the opening. She'd taken off her apron to do the marketing and she now wore a jacket as though chilled by circumstance.

I moved into the utility room. "Still no sign of her?" I asked, following Enid through a door that opened into a rear hall.

"Not a peep," she said. "I'm sorry to be a bother. I'm probably being silly."

"Don't worry about it. You've had a murder in the house. Everybody's nerves are on edge. Is one of those cars out there hers?"

"The Toyota," she said. She paused in front of a door at the end of the hall. "This is hers."

"Have you tried knocking on her door since we talked?"

Enid shook her head. "I think I scared myself. I didn't want to do anything until you arrived."

"Geez, Enid. You're scaring me," I said. I knocked on the door, my head tilted against the panel, listening for sounds that might indicate Myrna was back. I was reluctant to barge right in. She might be napping or naked, just out of the shower. I didn't want to catch her with her dentures out or her wooden leg unstrapped. I tapped again with one knuckle. "Myrna?"

Dead silence.

I tried the knob, which turned easily. I opened the door a crack and peered around the frame. The sitting room was empty. Across from me, the door to the bedroom was standing open and the room appeared to be empty. "Myrna, you in here? It's Kinsey Millhone," I said. I waited a moment and then crossed the room. In passing, I put my hand on the television set, but the housing was cold.

"I told you she wasn't here," Enid said.

I looked into the bedroom. I could see why Enid felt something was wrong. On the surface, both rooms seemed tidy and untouched, but there was something amiss. It was the little things, the minutiae. The bed was made, but the coverlet was not quite smooth. A picture on the wall was ever so slightly tilted.

"When was the last time you actually saw her?" I leaned down and peeked under the bed, feeling like an idiot. There was nothing under there except an old pair of bedroom slippers.

"Must have been noon."

"Was Bennet here at that point?"

"I don't remember. He was gone when I got back from the market. That's all I know."

In the sitting room, the shade on the floor lamp was askew and it was clear from the dents in the carpet the base had been moved from its usual place. Had there been a struggle of some kind? I looked in the closet. Enid followed me like a kid, about three steps back, possibly feeling the same eerie sense of intrusion that I felt.

"Can you tell if all her clothes are here? Anything missing? Shoes? Coat?"

Enid studied the rack. "I think everything's here," she said and then pointed. "That's her suitcase and her garment bag."

"What about her handbag?"

"It's in the kitchen. I knew you'd ask so I opened it. Her wallet's in there, driver's license, cash, all that stuff."

I moved into the bathroom. I heard a little pop under my shoe, followed by the kind of scratching sound that makes you think of broken glass on ceramic floor tile. I looked down. There was a touch of dry soil, as from the bottom of a shoe, and two tiny pieces of gravel. "Be careful. I don't want us to disturb that," I said to Enid, who was crowding into the room on my heels.

"Was someone in here?"

"I don't know yet. It could be."

"It looks like someone tried to straighten up and didn't do a very good job of it," she said. "Myrna always left notes if she was going somewhere. She wouldn't just walk out."

"Don't start babbling. I'm trying to concentrate."

I checked the medicine cabinet. All the obvious toiletries were still sitting on the shelf: toothbrush, toothpaste, deodorant, odds and ends of makeup, prescription bottles. The shower curtain was bone-dry, but a dark blue washcloth had been draped over the rim of the basin and it had been recently used. I peered closely at the basin. There was a trace of water around the small brass ring fixture for the outflow valve. Unless my eyes were deceiving me, the water was ever so faintly pink. I lifted the washcloth and squeezed out some of the excess water. There was a splash of bright red against the white of the basin. "You better call 9-1-1. This is blood," I said.

While Enid went off to call the police, I closed the door to Myrna's apartment and I retraced my steps through the utility room to the backdoor. In the kitchen, I could hear Enid on the phone, sounding shaken and slightly shrill. Someone must have been waiting to catch Myrna alone. Outside, I crossed the small back patio and took a right at the driveway. Myrna's car was locked, but I circled the exterior, peering in at the front seats and backseats. Both were empty. Nothing on the dashboard. I was curious if the trunk was locked, but I didn't want to touch it. Let the cops do that. To the right, the driveway formed a dead end with space for three more cars. Beyond that, I saw a long line of drab pink stucco wall and a tangle of woods. Suppose she'd been killed in haste? What would you do with the body?

I headed back toward the garages. Donovan's pickup was parked much closer to the front of the house than the back. There was something about the traces of gravel and dried soil that bothered me. I put a hand out. The hood of the pickup was warm. I walked around the truck, hands behind my back as I scrutinized the exterior. The bed liner was littered with gravel and dead leaves. I peered over the tailgate, looking closely at the liner. There was what looked like a dark smear on one edge. I left that alone. Whatever had happened, they couldn't blame Jack this time.

In the distance, I heard the rumble of a motorcycle and moments later, I looked up to see Bennet roaring down the drive on Jack's Harley-Davidson. I moved away from the truck, watching as he went through his parking ritual. His black leather gloves looked as clumsy as oven mitts. He pulled them off and laid them on the seat, placing his helmet on top. He didn't seem that thrilled to see me. "What are you doing here?"

"Enid called about Myrna. When did you last see her?"

"I saw her at breakfast. I didn't see her at lunch. Enid told me she wasn't feeling well. What's going on?"

"I have no idea. Apparently, she's disappeared. Enid called the police. They'll be here shortly, I'd imagine."

"The police? What for?"

"Why don't you save the bullshit for the cops." I said.

"Wait a minute. 'Bullshit'? What's the matter with you? I'm tired of being treated like a creep," he said.

I started walking away.

"Where are you going?"

"What difference does it make? If I stand here another minute, I'll just end up insulting you."

Bennet walked alongside me. "That wouldn't be a first. I heard about your meeting with Paul. He was pissed as hell."

"So what?" I said.

"I know you think we did something."

"Of course I do!"

He touched my arm. "Look. Hang on a minute and let's talk about this."

"Go ahead and talk, Bennet. I'd love to hear what you have to say."

"All right. Okay. I might as well level with you because the truth isn't nearly as bad as you think."

"How do you know what I think? I think you cheated the Maddisons out of fifty thousand dollars' worth of rare documents."

"Now wait a minute. Now wait. We didn't mean any harm. It was just a prank. We wanted to go to Vegas, but we were broke. We didn't have a dime between us. All we wanted was a few bucks. We were only kids," he said.

"Kids? You weren't kids. You were twenty-three years old. You committed a felony. Is that your rationalization, calling it a prank? You should have gone to prison."

"I know. I'm sorry. It got out of hand. We never thought we could pull it off and by the time we realized how serious it was, we didn't have the courage to admit what we'd done."

"It didn't seem to bother you to blame Guy," I said.

"Listen, he was gone. And he'd done all that other stuff. The family was down on him and Dad just assumed. We were assholes. I know that. We were wrong. I've never felt right about it since."

"Well, that absolves you," I said. "What happened to the letters? Where are they?"

"Paul has them at his place. I told him to destroy them, but he couldn't bear to do it. He's been afraid to put them in circulation."

I could feel my mouth pull down with disgust. "So you didn't even get the money? You are a creep," I said. "Let's talk about Patty."

"The baby wasn't mine. I swear. I never screwed her."

"Paul did, didn't he? And so did Jack."

"A lot of fellas screwed her. She didn't care."

"Not Guy. He never laid a hand on her," I said.

"Not Guy," he repeated. "I guess that's true."

"So whose baby was it?"

"Probably Jack's," Bennet said. "But that doesn't mean he killed Guy. I didn't either. I wouldn't do that," he said.

"Oh, come on. Grow up. You never accepted any responsibility for what happened, the whole lot of you. You let Guy take the blame for everything you did. Even when he came back, you never let him off the hook."

"What was I supposed to say? It was too late by then."

"Not for him, Bennet. Guy was still alive at that point. *Now,* it's too late."

I looked up to see Enid standing by the hedge. I had no idea how much she'd overheard. She said, "Your partner's on the phone. The police are on the way."

I moved past Enid and walked down the short flight of stairs, crossing the patio to the kitchen door. I found the handset on the counter and I picked it up. "It's me. What's going on?"

"Are you all right? You sound bad."

"I can't stop to tell you. It would take too long. I should have fallen on Bennet and beat the man to death."

"Catch this. I just had a chat with the private investigator in Bridgeport, Connecticut. This gal was at the courthouse when she called in to pick up messages. She went right to the clerk and filled out a request for Claire Maddison's death certificate."

"What was the cause of death?"

"There wasn't one," he said. "As long as she was at it, she made a couple more phone calls and got her last known address. According to the utility company, Claire was living in Bridgeport until last March."

"How did the *Dispatch* end up printing her obituary?"

"Because she sent them one. No one ever asked for proof. I called the *Dispatch* myself and verified the whole procedure. They take down the information and they print it as given."

"She made the whole thing up?"

"I'm sure she did," he said.

"So where did she go?"

"I'm just getting to that. This PI in Bridgeport picked up one more little item. Claire never worked as a teacher. She was a private-duty nurse."

"Shit."

"That's what I said. I'm coming over. Don't do anything until I get there," he said.

"What's to do? I can't move."

How long did I stand at the kitchen counter with the phone in my hand? In a flash, I could see how all the pieces fit. I was missing a few answers, but the rest of them finally fell into place. Somehow Claire Maddison heard about Bader's terminal illness. She shipped the *Dispatch* an obituary just to close that door. She turned herself into Myrna Sweetzer, packed her personal belongings, and headed back to Santa Teresa. Bader was difficult. As a patient, he was probably close to impossible. He must have gone through a number of private-duty nurses, so it was only a matter of Myrna's biding her time. Once she was in the house, the family was hers. She had waited a long time, but the chance to wreak havoc must have been something she savored.

I tried to put myself in her place. Where was she now? She'd accomplished much of her mission, so it was time to fade. She'd left her car, her handbag, and all her clothes. What would I do if I were Claire Maddison? The whole psychodrama of the missing Myrna was just a cover for her escape. She must have pictured the cops digging up the property, looking for a body that was never there. To have the disappearance play out properly, she had to make an exit without being seen, which ruled out a taxicab. She might steal a car, but that was risky on the face of it. And how would she leave town? Would she hitchhike? A motorist passing through might never be aware that anyone was missing or presumed dead. Plane, train, or bus?

She might have a confederate, but much of what she'd done to date required a solitary cunning. She'd been gone more than an hour—plenty of time to walk through the back of the property to the road. I lifted my head. I could hear voices in the foyer. The cops had probably arrived. I didn't want to go through this whole rigmarole. Enid was saying, "It was just so unlike her so I called . . ."

I slipped out the backdoor, racewalking across the patio and out to the driveway. I got in my car and turned the key in the ignition. My brain was clicking along, trying to make sense of circumstances. Claire Maddison was alive and had been living in Santa Teresa since last spring. I wasn't really sure how she'd managed the setup, but I was relatively certain she was responsible for Guy's death. She'd also gone to some lengths to implicate the others, setting it up so that Jack looked guilty, with Bennet as the backup in case the evidence of Jack's culpability failed to persuade police.

The gate swung open in front of me. I reached the road and turned left, trying to picture the way the property was laid out in relation to the surrounding terrain. I didn't imagine she'd head into the Los Padres National Forest. The mountain was too steep and too inhospitable. It was possible, of course, that in the last eighteen years, Claire Maddison had become an expert at living in the wild. Maybe she planned to make a new home for herself among the scrub oaks and chaparral, feasting on wild berries, sucking moisture from cactus pads. More likely, she'd simply crossed the few acres of undeveloped land that lay between the Maleks' and the road. Bader had purchased everything within range, so it was possible she was still trudging across acreage he owned.

I tried to think what she'd do once she hit the main artery. She could choose left or right, setting out in either direction on foot. She could have hidden a bicycle somewhere in the brush. She might depend on her ability to thumb a ride. Maybe she'd called a taxicab and had it waiting when she emerged on the road. Again, I dismissed that option because I didn't really think she'd take the risk. She wouldn't want to have anyone who could identify or describe her later. She might have purchased another vehicle and parked on a side street, gassed up and ready to be driven away. I tried to remember what I knew of her and realized just how little it was. She was approaching forty. She was overweight. She made no effort to enhance her personal appearance. Given cultural standards, she'd made herself invisible. Ours is a society in which slimness and beauty are equated with status, where youth and charm are rewarded and remembered with admiration. Let a woman be drab or slightly overweight and the collective eye slides right by, forgetting afterward. Claire Maddison had achieved the ultimate disguise because, aside from the physical, she'd adopted the persona of the servant class. Who knows what conversations she'd been privy to straightening the bed pillows, changing the sheets. She'd run the household, served canapés, and freshened the drinks while the lords and ladies of the house had talked on and on, oblivious to her presence because she wasn't one of them. For Claire, it had been perfect. Their dismissal of her would have fueled her bitterness and hardened her determination to take revenge. Why should this family, largely made up of fakes, enjoy the privileges of money while she had nothing? Because of them, she'd been cheated of her family, her medical career. She'd been robbed, violated, and abused, and for this she blamed Guy.

I was now on the two-lane road that I was guessing defined the Malek property along its southernmost boundary. I found a city map in my glove compartment and flapped it open as I drove. I made a clumsy fold and propped it up against the steering wheel, searching for routes while I tried not to ram into telephone poles. I started with the obvious, turning off at the first street, driving in a grid. I should have waited for Dietz. One of us could have been watching for pedestrians while the other drove. How far could she get?

I returned to the main road and drove on for maybe half a mile. I spotted her tramping along a hundred yards ahead of me. She was wearing jeans and good walking shoes, toting a backpack, no hat. I rolled down the window on the passenger side. As soon as she heard the rattle of my VW, she glanced once in my direction and then stared doggedly at the pavement in front of her.

"Myrna, I want to talk to you."

"Well, I don't want to talk to you."

I idled alongside her while cars coming up behind me honked impatiently. I motioned them around, keeping an eye fixed on Myrna who trudged on, tears running down her face. I gunned the engine, speeding off, pulling into the berm well ahead of her. I turned the engine off and got out, walking back to meet her.

"Come on, Myrna. Slow down. It's finally over," I said.

"No, it's not. It's never over until they pay up."

"Yeah, but how much? Listen, I understand how you feel. They took everything you had."

"The bastards," she said.

"Myrna . . ."

"My name is Claire."

"All right, Claire then. Here's the truth. You killed the wrong man. Guy never did anything to you or to your family. He's the only one who ever treated Patty well."

"Liar. You're lying. You made that up."

I shook my head. "Patty slept around. You know she had problems. Those were wild times. Dope and free love. We were all goofy with goodwill, with the notion of world peace. Remember? She was a flower child, an innocent—"

"She was schizophrenic," Claire spat.

"Okay. I'll take your word for it. She probably did LSD. She ate mushrooms. She stuck herself with things. And all the fellows took advantage of her, except Guy. I promise. He really cared about her. He told me about her and he was wistful and loving. He'd tried to get in touch. He wrote to her once, but she was dead by then. He had no idea. All he knew was he never heard from her and he felt bad about that."

"He was a turd."

"All right. He was a turd. He did a lot of shitty things back then, but at heart, he was a good man. Better than his brothers. They took advantage of him. Patty probably wished the baby was his, but it wasn't."

"Whose then?"

"Jack's. Paul Trasatti's. I'm not really sure how many men she slept with. Guy didn't forge the letters, either. That was Bennet and Paul, a little scheme they cooked up to earn some money that spring."

"They took everything away from me. Everything."

"I know. And now you've taken something away from them."

"What?" she said, her eyes blazing with disdain.

"You took the only decent man who ever bore the Malek name."

"Bader was decent."

"But he never made good. Your mother asked him for the money and he refused to pay."

"I didn't blame him for that."

"Too bad. You blamed Guy instead and he was innocent."

"Fuck off," she said.

"What else? What's the rest? I know there's more to this," I said. "You wrote the anonymous letter to Guy, the one the cops have, right?"

"Of course. Don't be dumb. I wrote all the letters up on Bennet's machine. For Guy's letter, I used the Bible. I thought he'd like that . . . a message from Deuteronomy . . . 'And thy life shall hang in doubt before thee; and thou shalt fear day and night, and shalt have none assurance of thy life.' You like that?"

"Very apt. A good choice," I said.

"That's not all, doll. You missed the best part . . . the obvious . . . you and that fancy-pants probate attorney. I found both wills months ago when I first started working here. I searched through Bader's files every chance I had. I tore up the second will so someone would have to go out looking for Guy. You did all the work for me. I appreciate that."

"What about the blood in your bathroom? Where did that come from?"

She held her thumb up. "I used a lancet. I left a couple drops on the patio and another in the truck. There's a shovel behind the toolshed. That's got blood on it, too."

"What about the dirt and gravel on the bathroom floor?"

"I thought Donovan should have a turn in the barrel. Didn't you think of him when you saw it?"

"Actually he did cross my mind. I'd have gone after him if I hadn't figured out what was going on. But what now? None of this is going to work. The whole plan's caving in. Trying to hike out was dumb. You weren't that hard to find."

"So what? I'm out of here. I'm tired. Get away from me," she said.

"Myrna . . ." I said, patiently.

"It's Claire," she snapped. "What do you *want?*"

"I want the killing to stop. I want the dying to end. I want Guy Malek to rest easy wherever he is."

"I don't care about Guy," she said. Her voice quaked with emotion and her face looked drawn and tense.

"What about Patty? Don't you think she'd care?"

"I don't know. I've lost track. I thought I'd feel better, but I don't." She walked on down the road with me trotting after her. "There aren't any happy endings. You have to take what you get."

"There may not be a happy ending, but there are some that satisfy."

"Name one."

"Come back. Own up to what you did. Turn and face your demons before they eat you alive."

She was weeping freely, and in some curious way, she seemed very beautiful, touched with grace. She turned and started walking backward, her arm out, hand turned up, as though thumbing a ride. I was walking at the same pace, the two of us face-to-face. She caught my eye and smiled, shot a look over her shoulder to check for traffic coming the other way.

We had reached an intersection. There was a wide curve in the road ahead. The stoplight had changed and cars had surged forward, picking up speed. Even now, I'm not certain what she meant to do. For a moment, she looked at me fully and then she made a dash for it, flinging herself into the line of traffic like a diver plunging off a board. I thought she might escape destruction because the first vehicle missed her and a second car seemed to bump her without injury or harm. The drivers in both lanes were slamming on their brakes, swerving to avoid her. She ran on, stumbling as she entered the far lane. An oncoming car caught her and she sailed overhead, as limp as a rag doll, as joyous as a bird.

Epilogue

Peter and Winnie Antle came down for Guy's funeral service, which Peter conducted Monday afternoon. I thought the Maleks might object, but they seemed to think better of it. Tasha agreed to submit Guy's holographic will for probate and eventually his portion of the estate will be passed on to Jubilee Evangelical Church. I said nothing of Claire's destruction of the second will. Guy deserved his fair share and I don't think the family will make a fuss about his final wishes.

Last night, Guy Malek came to me in a dream. I don't remember now what the dream was about. It was a dream like any other, set in a landscape only half familiar, filled with events that didn't quite make sense. I remember feeling such relief. He was alive and whole and so very like himself. Somehow in the dream, I knew he'd come to say good-bye. I'd never had a chance to tell him how much he'd meant to me. I hadn't known him long, but some people simply affect us that way. Their sojourn is brief, but their influence is profound.

I clung to him. He didn't speak. He never said a word, but I knew he wanted me to let him go. He was far too polite to chide me for my reluctance. He didn't hurry me along, but he let me know what he needed. In the dream, I remember weeping. I thought if I refused, he would be mine to keep. I thought he could be with me forever, but it doesn't work that way. His time on earth was done. He had other places to go.

In the end, I set him free, not in sorrow, but in love. It wasn't for me. It was something I did for him. When I woke, I knew that he was truly gone. The tears I wept for him then were the same tears I'd wept for everyone I'd ever loved. My parents, my aunt. I had never said good-bye to them, either, but it was time to take care of it. I said a prayer for the dead, opening the door so all the ghosts could move on. I gathered them up like the petals of a flower and released them to the wind. What's done is done. What is written is written. Their work is finished. Ours is yet to do.

N
IS FOR NOOSE

For Steven,

who makes my life possible

The author wishes to acknowledge the invaluable assistance of the following people: Steven Humphrey; Eric S. H. Ching; Shelly Dumas and Sergeant Dick Wood, Inyo County Sheriff's Department; Leon Brune, Inyo County Coroner; Donna Milovich, Spellbinder Books; Robert Failing, M.D.; Dennis Prescott, Supervisor (retired), and Larry Gillespie, Senior Investigator, Santa Barbara County Coroner's Office; Deputy Eric Raney, Commander Bill Crook, and Commander Terry Bunn, Santa Barbara County Sheriff's Department; Captain Ed Aasted, Santa Barbara Police Department; Bruce Bennet; Sheila Millington, Automobile Club of Southern California; Sylvia Stallings; Joe Peus, M.D.; B. J. Seebol; and John Hunt, CompuVision, for saving chapter 22.

N

IS FOR NOOSE

1

Sometimes I think about how odd it would be to catch a glimpse of the future, a quick view of events lying in store for us at some undisclosed date. Suppose we could peer through a tiny peephole in Time and chance upon a flash of what was coming up in the years ahead? Some moments we saw would make no sense at all and some, I suspect, would frighten us beyond endurance. If we knew what was looming, we'd avoid certain choices, select option B instead of A at the fork in the road: the job, the marriage, the move to a new state, childbirth, the first drink, the elective medical procedure, that long-anticipated ski trip that seemed like such fun until the dark rumble of the avalanche. If we understood the consequences of any given action, we could exercise discretion, thus restructuring our fate. Time, of course, only runs in one direction, and it seems to do so in an orderly progression. Here in the blank and stony present, we're shielded from the knowledge of the dangers that await us, protected from future horrors through blind innocence.

Take the case in point. I was winding my way through the mountains in a cut-rate rental car, heading south on 395 toward the town of Nota Lake, California, where I was going to interview a potential client. The roadway was dry and the view was unobstructed, weather conditions clear. The client's business was unremarkable, at least as far as I could see. I had no idea there was any jeopardy waiting or I'd have done something else.

I'd left Dietz in Carson City, where I'd spent the last two weeks playing nurse/companion while he recovered from surgery. He'd been scheduled for a knee replacement and I'd volunteered to drive him back to Nevada in his snazzy little red Porsche. I make no claims to nurturing, but I'm a practical person and the nine-hour journey seemed the obvious solution to the problem of how to get his car back to his home state. I'm a no-nonsense driver and he knew he could count on me to get us to Carson City without any unnecessary side trips and no irrelevant conversation. He'd been staying in my apartment for the two previous months and since our separation was approaching, we tended to avoid discussing anything personal.

For the record, my last name is Millhone, first name Kinsey. I'm female, twice divorced, seven weeks shy of thirty-six, and reasonably fit. I'm a licensed private detective, currently residing in Santa Teresa, California, to which I'm attached like a tetherball on a very short cord. Occasionally, business will swing me out to other parts of the country, but I'm basically a small-town shamus and likely to remain so for life.

Dietz's surgery, which was scheduled for the first Monday in March, proceeded uneventfully, so we can skip that part. Afterward, I returned to his condominium and toured the premises with interest. I'd been startled by the place when I first laid eyes on it, as it was more lavish and much better appointed than my poor digs back in Santa Teresa. Dietz was a nomad and I'd never pictured his having much in the way of material possessions. While I was closeted in a converted single-car garage (recently remodeled to accommodate a sleeping loft and a second bathroom upstairs), Dietz maintained a three-bedroom penthouse that probably encompassed three thousand square feet of living space, including a roof patio and garden with an honest-to-god greenhouse. Granted, the seven-story building was located in a commercial district, but the views were astounding and the privacy profound.

I'd been too polite to pry while he was standing right there beside me, but once he was safely ensconced in the orthopedic ward at Carson/Tahoe Hospital, I felt comfortable scrutinizing everything in my immediate range, which necessitated dragging a chair around and standing on it in some cases. I checked closets and files and boxes and papers and drawers, pockets and suitcases, feeling equal parts relief and disappointment that he had nothing in particular to hide. I mean, what's the point of snooping if you can't uncover something good? I did have the chance to study a photograph of his ex-wife, Naomi, who was certainly a lot prettier than he'd ever indicated. Aside from that, his finances appeared to be in order, his medicine cabinet contained no sinister pharmaceutical revelations, and his private correspondence consisted almost entirely of assorted misspelled letters from his two college-age sons. Lest you think I'm intrusive, I can assure you Dietz had searched my apartment just as thoroughly during the time he was in residence. I know this because I'd left a few booby traps, one of which he'd missed when he was picking open my locked desk drawers. His license might have lapsed, but (most of) his operating skills were still current. Neither of us had ever mentioned his invasion of my privacy, but I vowed I'd do likewise when the opportunity arose. Between working detectives, this is known as professional courtesy. You toss my place and I'll toss yours.

He was out of the hospital by Friday morning of that week. The ensuing recovery involved a lot of sitting around with his knee wrapped in bandages as thick as a bolster. We watched trash television, played gin rummy, and worked a jigsaw puzzle with a picture depicting a roiling nest of earthworms so lifelike I nearly went off my feed. The first three days I did all the cooking, which is to say I made sandwiches, alternating between my famous peanut-butter-and-pickle extravaganza and my much beloved sliced hot-hard-boiled-egg confection, with tons of Hellmann's mayonnaise and salt. After that, Dietz seemed eager to get back into the kitchen and our menus expanded to include pizza, take-out Chinese, and Campbell's soup—tomato or asparagus, depending on our mood.

By the end of two weeks Dietz could pretty well fend for himself. His stitches were out and he was hobbling around with a cane between bouts of physical therapy. He had a long way to go, but he could drive to his sessions and otherwise seemed able to tend to his own needs. By then, I thought it entirely possible I'd go mad from trailing after him. It was time to hit the road before our togetherness began to chafe. I enjoyed being with him, but I knew my limitations. I kept my farewells perfunctory; lots of airy okay-fine-thanks-a-lot-I'll-see-you-laters. It was my way of minimizing the painful lump in my throat, staving off the embarrassing boo-hoos I thought were best left unexpressed. Don't ask me to reconcile the misery I felt with the nearly giddy sense of relief. Nobody ever said emotions made any sense.

So there I was, barreling down the highway in search of employment and not at all fussy about what kind of work I'd take. I wanted distraction. I wanted money, escape, anything to keep my mind off the subject of Robert Dietz. I'm not good at good-byes. I've suffered way too many in my day and I don't like the sensation. On the other hand, I'm not that good at relationships. Get close to someone and next thing you know, you've given them the power to wound, betray, irritate, abandon, or bore you senseless. My general policy is to keep my distance, thus avoiding a lot of unruly emotion. In psychiatric circles, there are names for people like me.

I flipped on the car radio, picking up a scratchy station from Los Angeles, three hundred miles to the south. Gradually, I began to tune in to the surrounding landscape. Highway 395 cuts south out of Carson City, through Minden and Gardnerville. Just north of Topaz, I had crossed the state line into eastern California. The backbone of the state is the towering Sierra Nevada Range, the uptilted edge of a huge fault block, gouged out later by a series of glaciers. To my left was Mono Lake, shrinking at the rate of two feet a year, increasingly saline, supporting little in the way of marine life beyond brine shrimp and the attendant feasting of the birds. Somewhere to my right, through a dark green forest of Jeffrey pines, was Yosemite National Park, with its towering peaks and rugged canyons, lakes, and thundering waterfalls. Meadows, powdered now in light snow, were once the bottom of a Pleistocene lake. Later in the spring, these same meadows would be dense with wildflowers. In the higher ranges, the winter snowpack hadn't yet melted, but the passes were open. It was the kind of scenery described as "breathtaking" by those who are easily winded. I'm not a big fan of the outdoors, but even I was sufficiently impressed to murmur "wow" speeding past a scenic vista point at seventy miles an hour.

The prospective client I was traveling to meet was a woman named Selma Newquist, whose husband, I was told, had died sometime within the last few weeks. Dietz had done work for this woman in the past, helping her extricate herself from an unsavory first marriage. I didn't get all the details, but he alluded to the fact that the financial "goods" he'd gotten on the husband had given Selma enough leverage to free herself from the relationship. There'd been a subsequent marriage and it was this second husband whose death had apparently generated questions his wife wanted answered. She'd called to hire Dietz, but since he was temporarily out of commission, he suggested me. Under ordinary circumstances, I doubted Mrs. Newquist would have considered a P.I. from the far side of the state, but my trip home was imminent and I was heading in her direction. As it turned out, my connection to Santa Teresa was more pertinent than it first appeared. Dietz had vouched for my integrity and, by the same token, he'd assured me that she'd be conscientious about payment for services rendered. It made sense to stop long enough to hear what the woman had to say. If she didn't want to hire me, all I'd be out was a thirty-minute break in the journey.

I reached Nota Lake (population 2,356, elevation 4,312) in slightly more than three hours. The town didn't look like much, though the setting was spectacular. Mountains towered on three sides, snow still painting the peaks in thick white against a sky heaped with clouds. On the shady side of the road, I could see leftover patches of snow, ice boulders wedged up against the leafless trees. The air smelled of pine, with an underlying scent that was faintly sweet. The chill vapor I breathed was like sticking my face down in a half-empty gallon of vanilla ice cream, drinking in the sugary perfume. The lake itself was no more than two miles long and a mile across. The surface was glassy, reflecting granite spires and the smattering of white firs and incense cedars that grew on the slopes. I stopped at a service station and picked up a one-page map of the town, which was shaped like a smudge on the eastern edge of Nota Lake.

The prime businesses seemed to be clustered along the main street in a five-block radius. I did a cursory driving tour, counting ten gas stations and twenty-two motels. Nota Lake offered low-end accommodations for the ski crowd at Mammoth Lakes. The town also boasted an equal number of fast-food restaurants, including Burger King, Carl's Jr., Jack in the Box, Kentucky Fried Chicken, Pizza Hut, a Waffle House, an International House of Pancakes, a House of Donuts, a Sizzler, a Subway, a Taco Bell, and my personal favorite, McDonald's. Additional restaurants of the sit-down variety were divided equally between Mexican, Bar-B-Que, and "Family" dining, which meant lots of screaming toddlers and no hard liquor on the premises.

The address I'd been given was on the outskirts of town, two blocks off the main highway in a cluster of houses that looked like they'd been built by the same developer. The streets in the area were named for various Indian tribes; Shawnee, Iroquois, Cherokee, Modoc, Crow, Chippewa. Selma Newquist lived on a cul-de-sac called Pawnee Way, the house a replica of its neighbors: frame siding, a shake roof, with a screened-in porch on one end and a two-car garage on the other. I parked in the driveway beside a dark Ford sedan. I locked the car from habit, climbed the two porch steps, and rang the bell—*ding dong*—like the local Avon representative. I waited several minutes and then tried again.

The woman who came to the door was in her late forties, with a small compact body, brown eyes, and short dark tousled hair. She was wearing a red-blue-and-yellow plaid blouse over a yellow pleated skirt.

"Hi, I'm Kinsey Millhone. Are you Selma?"

"No, I'm not. I'm her sister-in-law, Phyllis. My husband, Macon, was Tom's younger brother. We live two doors down. Can I help you?"

"I'm supposed to meet with Selma. I should have called first. Is she here?"

"Oh, sorry. I remember now. She's lying down at the moment, but she told me she thought you'd be stopping by. You're that friend of the detective she called in Carson City."

"Exactly," I said. "How's she doing?"

"Selma has her bad days and I'm afraid this is one. Tom passed away six weeks ago today and she called me in tears. I came over as quick as I could. She was shaking and upset. Poor thing looks like she hasn't slept in days. I gave her a Valium."

"I can come back later if you think that's best."

"No, no. I'm sure she's awake and I know she wants to see you. Why don't you come on in?"

"Thanks."

I followed Phyllis across the entrance and down a carpeted hallway to the master bedroom. In passing, I allowed myself a quick glance into doorways on either side of the hall, garnering an impression of wildly overdecorated rooms. In the living room, the drapes and upholstery fabrics were coordinated to match a pink-and-green wallpaper that depicted floral bouquets, connected by loops of pink ribbon. On the coffee table, there was a lavish arrangement of pink silk flowers. The cut-pile wall-to-wall carpeting was pale green and had the strong chemical scent that suggested it had been only recently laid. In the dining room, the furniture was formal, lots of dark glossy wood with what looked like one too many pieces for the available space. There were storm windows in place everywhere and a white film of condensation had gathered between the panes. The smell of cigarette smoke and coffee formed a musky domestic incense.

Phyllis knocked on the door. "Selma, hon? It's Phyllis."

I heard a muffled response and Phyllis opened the door a crack, peering around the frame. "You've got company. Are you decent? It's this lady detective from Carson City."

I started to correct her and then thought better of it. I wasn't from Carson City and I certainly wasn't a lady, but then what difference did it make? Through the opening I caught a brief impression of the woman in the bed; a pile of platinum blond hair framed by the uprights on a four-poster.

Apparently, I'd been invited in, because Phyllis stepped back, murmuring to me as I passed. "I have to get on home, but you're welcome to call me if you need anything."

I nodded my thanks as I moved into the bedroom and closed the door behind me. The curtains were closed and the light was subdued. Throw pillows, like boulders, had tumbled onto the carpet. There was a surplus of ruffles, bold multicolored prints covering walls, windows, and puffy custom bedding. The motif seemed to be roses exploding on impact.

I said, "Sorry to disturb you, but Phyllis said it would be okay. I'm Kinsey Millhone."

Selma Newquist, in a faded flannel nightie, pulled herself into a sitting position and straightened the covers, reminding me of an invalid ready to accept a bedtray. I estimated her age on the high side of fifty, judging by the backs of her hands, which were freckled with liver spots and ropy with veins. Her skin tones suggested dark coloring, but her hair was a confection of white-blond curls, like a cloud of cotton candy. At the moment, the entire cone was listing sideways and looked sticky with hair spray. She'd drawn in her eyebrows with a red-brown pencil, but any eyeliner or eye shadow had long since vanished. Through the streaks in her pancake makeup, I could see the blotchy complexion that suggested too much sun exposure. She reached for her cigarettes, groping on the bed table until she had both the cigarette pack and lighter. Her hand trembled slightly as she lit her cigarette. "Why don't you come over here," she said. She gestured toward a chair. "Push that off of there and sit down where I can see you better."

I moved her quilted robe from the chair and placed it on the bed, pulling the chair in close before I took a seat.

She stared at me, puffy-eyed, a thin stream of smoke escaping as she spoke. "I'm sorry you had to see me this way. Ordinarily I'm up and about at this hour, but this has been a hard day."

"I understand," I said. Smoke began to settle over me like the fine spray from someone's sneeze.

"Did Phyllis offer you coffee?"

"Please don't trouble. She's on her way back to her place and I'm fine anyway. I don't want to take any more time than I have to."

She stared at me vaguely. "Doesn't matter," she said. "I don't know if you've ever lost anyone close, but there are days when you feel like you're coming down with the flu. Your whole body aches and your head feels so stuffy you can't think properly. I'm glad to have company. You learn to appreciate any distraction. You can't avoid your feelings, but it helps to have momentary relief." She tended, in speaking, to keep a hand up against her mouth, apparently self-conscious about the discoloration on her two front teeth, which I could now see were markedly gray. Perhaps she'd fallen as a child or taken medication as an infant that tinted the surface with dark. "How do you know Robert Dietz?" she asked.

"I hired him myself a couple of years ago to handle my personal security. Someone threatened my life and Dietz ended up working for me as a bodyguard."

"How's his knee doing? I was sorry to hear he was laid up."

"He'll be fine. He's tough. He's already up and around."

"Did he tell you about Tom?"

"Only that you were recently widowed. That's as much as I know."

"I'll fill you in then, though I'm really not sure where to start. You may think I'm crazy, but I assure you I'm not." She took a puff of her cigarette and sighed a mouthful of smoke. I expected tears in the telling, but the story emerged in a Valium-induced calm. "Tom had a heart attack. He was out on the road . . . about seven miles out of town. This was ten o'clock at night. He must have had sufficient warning to pull over to the side. A CHP officer—a friend of ours, James Tennyson—recognized Tom's truck with the hazard lights on and stopped to see if he needed help. Tom was slumped at the wheel. I'd been to a meeting at church and came home to find two patrol cars sitting in my drive. You knew Tom was a detective with the county sheriff's?"

"I wasn't aware of that."

"I used to worry he'd be killed in the line of duty. I never imagined he'd go like he did." She paused, drawing on her cigarette, using smoke as a form of punctuation.

"It must have been difficult."

"It was awful," she said. Up went the hand again, resting against her mouth as the tears began to well in her eyes. "I still can't think about it. I mean, as far as I know, he never had any symptoms. Or let's put it this way: If he did, he never told me. He did have high blood pressure and the doctor'd been on him to quit smoking and start exercising. You know how men are. He waved it all aside and went right on doing as he pleased." She set the cigarette aside so she could blow her nose. Why do people always peek in their hankies to see what the honking noseblow has just netted them?

"How old was he?"

"Close to retirement. Sixty-three," she said. "But he never took good care of himself. I guess the only time he was ever in shape was in the army and right after, when he went through the academy and was hired on as a deputy. After that, it was all caffeine and junk food during work hours, bourbon when he got home. He wasn't an alcoholic—don't get me wrong—but he did like to have a cocktail at the end of the day. Lately, he wasn't sleeping well. He'd prowl around the house. I'd hear him up at two, three, five in the morning, doing god knows what. His weight had begun to drop in the last few months. The man hardly ate, just smoked and drank coffee and stared out the window at the snow. There were times when I thought he was going to snap, but that might have been my imagination. He really never said a word."

"Sounds like he was under some kind of strain."

"Exactly. That was my thought. Tom was clearly stressed, but I don't know why and it's driving me nuts." She picked up her cigarette and took a deep drag and then tapped the ash off in a ceramic ashtray shaped like a hand. "Anyway, that's why I called Dietz. I feel I'm entitled to know."

"I don't want to sound rude, but does it really make any difference? Whatever it was, it's too late to change, isn't it?"

She glanced away from me briefly. "I've thought of that myself. Sometimes I think I never really knew him at all. We got along well enough and he always provided, but he wasn't the kind of man who felt he should account for himself. His last couple of weeks, he'd be gone sometimes for hours and come back without a word. I didn't ask where he went. I could have, I guess, but there was something about him . . . he would bristle if I pressed him, so I learned to back off. I don't think I should have to wonder for the rest of my life. I don't even know where he was going that night. He told me he was staying home, but something must have come up."

"He didn't leave you a note?"

"Nothing." She placed her cigarette on the ashtray and reached for a compact concealed under her pillow. She opened the lid and checked her face in the mirror. She touched at her front teeth as though to remove a fleck. "I look dreadful," she said.

"Don't worry about it. You look fine."

Her smile was tentative. "I guess there's no point in being vain. With Tom gone, nobody cares, including me if you want to know the truth."

"Can I ask you a question?"

"Please."

"I don't mean to pry, but were you happily married?"

A little burble of embarrassed laughter escaped as she closed the compact and tucked it back in its hiding place. "I certainly was. I don't know about him. He wasn't one to complain. He more or less took life as it came. I was married before . . . to someone physically abusive. I have a boy from that marriage. His name is Brant."

"Ah. And how old is he?"

"Twenty-five. Brant was ten when I met Tom, so essentially Tom raised him."

"And where is he?"

"Here in Nota Lake. He works for the fire department as a paramedic. He's been staying with me since the funeral though he has a place of his own in town," she said. "I told him I was thinking about hiring someone. It's pointless in his opinion, but I'm sure he'll do whatever he can to help." Her nose reddened briefly, but she seemed to gain control of herself.

"You and Tom were married for what, fourteen years?"

"Coming up on twelve. After my divorce, I didn't want to rush into anything. We were fine for most of it, but recently things began to change for the worse. I mean, he did what he was supposed to, but his heart wasn't in it. Lately, I felt he was secretive. I don't know, so . . . tight-lipped or something. Why was he out on the highway that night? I mean, what was he doing? What was so precious that he couldn't tell me?"

"Could it have been a case he was working on?"

"It could have been, I suppose." She thought about the possibility while she stubbed out her cigarette. "I mean, it might have been job-related. Tom seldom said a word about work. Other men—some of the deputies—would swap stories in social situations, but not him. He took his job very seriously, almost to a fault."

"Someone in the department must have taken over his workload. Have you talked to them?"

"You say 'department' like it was some kind of big-city place. Nota Lake's the county seat, but that still isn't saying much. There were only two investigators, Tom and his partner, Rafer. I did talk to him—not that I got anything to speak of. He was nice. Rafer's always nice enough on the surface," she said, "but for all of the chit-chat, he managed to say very little."

I studied her for a moment, running the conversation through my bullshit meter to see what would register. Nothing struck me as off but I was having trouble understanding what she wanted. "Do you think there's something suspicious about Tom's death?"

She seemed startled by the question. "Not at all," she said, "but he was brooding about something and I want to know what it was. I know it sounds vague, but it upsets me to think he was withholding something when it clearly bothered him so much. I was a good wife to him and I won't be kept in the dark now he's gone."

"What about his personal effects? Have you been through his things?"

"The coroner returned the items he had on him when he died, but they were just what you'd expect. His watch, his wallet, the change in his pocket, and his wedding ring."

"What about his desk? Did he have an office here at the house?"

"Well, yes, but I wouldn't even know where to begin with that. His desk is a mess. Papers piled up everywhere. It could be staring me in the face, whatever it is. I can't bring myself to look and I can't bear to let go. That's what I'd like you to do . . . see if you can find out what was troubling him."

I hesitated. "I could certainly try. It would help if you could be more specific. You haven't given me much."

Selma's eyes filled with tears. "I've been racking my brain and I have no idea. Please just do *something*. I can't even walk in his den without falling apart."

Oh boy, just what I needed—a job that was not only vague, but felt hopeless as well. I should have bagged it right then, but I didn't, of course. More's the pity, as it turned out.

2

Toward the end of my visit with her, the Valium seemed to kick in and she rallied. Somehow she managed to pull herself together in a remarkably short period of time. I waited in the living room while she showered and dressed. When she emerged thirty minutes later, she said she was feeling almost like her old self again. I was amazed at the transformation. With her makeup in place, she seemed more confident, though she still tended to speak with a hand lifted to conceal her mouth.

For the next twenty minutes, we discussed business, finally reaching an agreement about how to proceed. It was clear by then that Selma Newquist was capable of holding her own. She reached for the phone and in the space of one call not only booked my accommodation but insisted on a ten-percent discount on what was already the off-season rate.

I left Selma's at two o'clock, stopping off in town long enough to flesh out my standard junk food diet with some Capt'n Jack's fish and chips and a large Coke. After that, it was time to check in to the motel. Obviously, I wouldn't be leaving Nota Lake for another day yet, at the very least. The motel she'd booked was the Nota Lake Cabins, which consisted of ten rustic cottages set in a wooded area just off the main highway about six miles out of town. Tom's widowed sister, Cecilia Boden, owned and managed the place. When I pulled into the parking lot, I could see that the area was a bit too remote for my taste. I'm a city girl at heart and generally happiest close to restaurants, banks, liquor stores, and movie theaters, preferably bug free. Since Selma was paying, I didn't think I should argue the point, and in truth the rough-hewn log exteriors did look more interesting than the motels in town. Silly me.

Cecilia was on the telephone when I stepped into the office. I pegged her at sixty, as small and shapeless as a girl of ten. She wore a red plaid flannel shirt tucked into dark stiff blue jeans. She had no butt to speak of, just a flat plain in the rear. I was already wishing she'd quit perming the life out of her short cropped hair. I also wondered what would happen if she allowed the natural gray to emerge from under the uniform brown dye with which she'd doused it.

The reception area was compact, a pine-paneled cubbyhole hardly large enough for one small upholstered chair and the rack of pamphlets touting the countless recreational diversions available. A side door marked MANAGER probably led to her private apartment. The reception desk was formed by a twelve-inch writing surface mounted on the lower half of the Dutch door that separated the miniature lobby from the office, where I could see the usual equipment: desk, file cabinets, typewriter, cash register, Rolodex, receipt ledger, and the big reservations book she was consulting in response to her caller's inquiry. She seemed ever so faintly annoyed with the questions she was being asked. "I got rooms on the twenty-fourth, but nothing the day after. . . . You want fish cleaning and freezing, try the Elms or the Mountain View. . . . Uh-huh. . . . I see. . . .

Well, that's the best I can do. . . ." She smiled to herself, enjoying some kind of private joke. "Nope. . . . No room service, no weight room, and the sauna's broke. . . ."

While I waited for her to finish, I pulled out several pamphlets at random, reading about midweek ski lift and lodging packages closer to Mammoth Lakes and Mammoth Summit. I checked the local calendar of events. I'd missed the big annual trout derby, which had taken place the week before. I was also too late to attend February's big fishing show. Well, dang. I noticed the festivities in April included another fishing show, the trout opener press reception, the official trout opener, and a fish club display, with a Mule Days Celebration and a 30K run coming up in May. It did look like it might be possible to hike, backpack, or mulepack my way into the Eastern Sierras, where I imagined a roving assortment of hungry wildlife lunging and snapping at us as we picked our way down perilously narrow trails with rocks rattling off the mountainside into the yawning abyss.

I looked up to find Cecilia Boden staring at me with a flinty expression. "Yes, ma'am," she said. She kept her hands braced on the Dutch door as if defying me to enter.

I told her who I was and she waved aside my offer of a credit card. Mouth pursed, she said, "Selma said to send her the bill direct. I got two cottages available. You can take your pick." She took a bunch of keys from a hook and opened the lower half of the Dutch door, leaving me to follow as she headed through the front door and down a path packed with cedar chips. The air outside was damp and smelled of loam and pine resin. I could hear the wind moving in the trees and the chattering of squirrels. I left my car where I'd parked it and we proceeded on foot. The narrow lane leading to the cabins was barred by a chain strung between two posts. "I won't have cars back in this part of the camp. The ground gets too tore up when the weather's bad," she said, as if in answer to my question.

"Really," I murmured, for lack of anything better.

"We're close to full up," she remarked. "Unusual for March."

This was small talk in her book and I made appropriate mouth noises in response. Ahead of us, the cabins were spaced about seventy-five feet apart, separated by bare maples and dogwoods, and sufficient Douglas firs to resemble a cut-your-own Christmas tree farm. "Why do they call it Nota Lake? Is that Indian?"

Cecilia shook her head. "Nope. Ancient times, nota was a mark burned into a criminal's skin to brand him a lawbreaker. That way you always knew who the evildoers were. Bunch of desperadoes ended up over in this area; scoundrels deported to this country from England back in the mid–seventeen hundreds. Some reason all of them were branded; killers and thieves, pickpockets, fornicators—the worst of the worst. Once their indenture'd been served, they became free men and disappeared into the west, landing hereabouts. Their descendants went to work for the railroad, doing manual labor along with assorted coolies and coloreds. Half the people in this town are related to those convicts. Must have been a randy bunch, though where they found women no one seems to know. Ordered 'em by mail, if my guess is correct."

We'd reached the first of the cabins and she continued in much the same tone, her delivery flat and without much inflection. "This is Willow. I give 'em names instead of numbers. It's nicer in my opinion." She inserted her key. "Each one is different. Up to you."

Willow was spacious, a pine-paneled room maybe twenty feet by twenty with a fireplace made up of big knobby boulders. The inner hearth was black with soot, with wood neatly stacked in the grate. The room was pungent with the scent of countless hardwood fires. Against one wall was a brass bedstead with a mattress shaped like a hillock. The quilt was a crazy patch and looked as if it smelled of mildew. There was a bed table lamp and a digital alarm clock. The rug was an oval of braided rags, bleached of all color, thoroughly flattened by age.

Cecilia opened a door on the left. "This here's the bath and your hanging closet. We got all the amenities. Unless you fish," she added, in a small aside to herself. "Iron, ironing board, coffeemaker, soap."

"Very nice," I said.

"The other cabin's Hemlock. Located over near the pine grove by the creek. Got a kitchenette, but no fireplace. I can take you back there if you like." For the most part, she spoke without making eye contact, addressing remarks to a spot about six feet to my left.

"This is fine. I'll take this one."

"Suit yourself," she said, handing me a key. "Cars stay in the lot. There's more wood around the side. Watch for black widder spiders if you fetch more logs. Pay phone outside the office. Saves me the hassle of settling up for calls. We got a cafe down the road about fifty yards in that direction. You can't miss it. Breakfast, lunch, and dinner. Open six o'clock in the morning until nine-thirty at night."

"Thanks."

After she left, I waited a suitable interval, allowing her time to reach the office ahead of me. I returned to the parking lot and retrieved my duffel, along with the portable typewriter I'd stashed in the rental car. I'd spent my off-hours at Dietz's catching up on my paperwork. My wardrobe, in the main, consists of blue jeans and turtlenecks, which makes packing a breeze once you toss in the fistful of underpants.

In the cabin again, I set the typewriter by the bed and put my few articles of clothing in a crudely made chest of drawers. I unloaded my shampoo and placed my toothbrush and toothpaste on the edge of the sink, looking around me with satisfaction. Home sweet home, barring the black widders. I tried the toilet, which worked, and then inspected the shower, artfully concealed behind a length of white monk's cloth hanging from a metal rod. The shower pan looked clean, but was constructed of the sort of material that made me want to walk on tiptoe. Outings at the community pool in my youth had taught me to be cautious, bare feet still recoiling instinctively from the clots of soggy tissues and rusted bobby pins. There were none here in evidence, but I sensed the ghostly presence of some old-fashioned crud. I could smell the same chlorine tinged with someone else's shampoo. I checked the coffeemaker, but the plug seemed to be missing one prong and there were no complimentary packets of coffee grounds, sugar, or nondairy coffee whitener. So much for the amenities. I was grateful for the soap.

I returned to the main room and did a quick survey. Under the side window, a wooden table and two chairs had been arranged with an eye to a view of the woods. I hauled out the typewriter and set it up on the tabletop. I'd have to run into town and find a ream of bond and a copy shop. These days, most P.I.s use computers, but I can't seem to get the hang of 'em. With my sturdy Smith-Corona, I don't require an electrical outlet and I don't have to worry about head crashes or lost data. I pulled a chair up to the table and stared out the window at the spindly stand of trees. Even the evergreens had a threadbare look. Through a lacework of pine needles, I could see a line of fencing that separated Cecilia's property from the one behind. This part of town seemed to be ranchland, mixed with large undeveloped tracts that might have been farmed at one point. I pulled out a tatty legal pad and made myself some notes, mostly doodles if you really want to know.

Essentially, Selma Newquist had hired me to reconstruct the last four to six weeks of her late husband's life on the theory that whatever had troubled him probably took place within that time frame. I don't generally favor spouses spying on one another—especially when one of the parties is dead—but she seemed convinced the answers would give her closure. I had my doubts. Maybe Tom Newquist was simply worried about finances, or brooding about how to occupy his time during his retirement.

I'd agreed to give her a verbal report every two to three days, supplemented by a written account. Selma had demurred at first, saying verbal reports would be perfectly adequate, but I told her I preferred the written, in part to detail whatever information I collected. Productive or not, I wanted her to see what ground I was covering. It was just as important for her to be aware of the information I *couldn't* verify as it was for her to have a record of the facts I picked up along the way. With verbal reports, much of the data gets lost in translation. Most people aren't trained to listen. Given the complexity of our mental processes, the recipient tunes out, blocks, forgets, or misinterprets eighty percent of what's been said. Take any fifteen minutes' worth of conversation and try to reconstruct it later and you'll see what I mean. If the communication has any emotional content whatever, the quality of the information retained degrades even further. A written report was for my benefit, too. Let a week pass and I can hardly remember the difference between Monday and Tuesday, let alone what stops I made and in what order I made them. I've noticed that clients are confident about your abilities until payment comes due and then, suddenly, the total seems outrageous and they stand there wondering exactly what you've done to earn it. It's better to submit an invoice with a chronology attached. I like to cite chapter and verse with all the proper punctuation laid in. If nothing else, it's a demonstration of both your IQ and your writing skills. How can you trust someone who doesn't bother to spell correctly or can't manage to lay out a simple declarative sentence?

The other issue we'd discussed was the nature of my fees. As a lone operator, I really didn't have any hard-and-fast rules about billing, particularly in a case like this where I was working out of town. Sometimes I charge a flat fee that includes all my expenses. Sometimes I charge an hourly rate and add expenses on top of that. Selma had assured me she had money to burn, but frankly, I felt guilty about eating into Tom's estate. On the other hand, she'd survived him and I thought she had a point. Why should she live the rest of her life wondering if her husband was hiding something from her? Grief is enough of an affront without additional regrets about unfinished business. Selma was already struggling to come to terms with Tom's death. She needed to know the truth and wanted me to supply it. Fair enough. I hoped I could provide her with an answer that would satisfy.

Until I got a sense of how long the job would take, we'd agreed on four hundred bucks a day. From Dietz, I'd borrowed a boilerplate contract. I'd penned in the date and details of what I'd been hired to do and she'd written me a check for fifteen hundred dollars. I'd run that by the bank to make sure it cleared before I got down to business. I'm sorry to confess that while I sympathize with all the widows, orphans, and underdogs in the world, I think it's wise to make sure sufficient funds are in place before you rush to someone's rescue.

I closed the cabin and locked it, hiked back to my rental car, and drove the six miles into town. The highway was sparsely strung with assorted businesses: tractor sales, a car lot, trailer park, country store, and a service station. The fields in between were gold with dried grass and tufted with weeds. The wide sweep of sky had turned from strong blue to gray, a thick haze of white obscuring the mountain tops. Away to the west, a torn pattern of clouds lay without motion. All the near hills were a scruffy red brown, polka-dotted with white. Wind rattled in the trees. I adjusted the heater in the car, flipping on the fan until tropical breezes blew against my legs.

For my stay in Carson City, I'd packed my tweed blazer for dress-up and a blue denim jacket for casual wear. Both were too light and insubstantial for this area. I cruised the streets downtown until I spotted a thrift store. I nosed the rental car into a diagonal parking space out front. The window was crowded with kitchenware and minor items of furniture: a bookcase, a footstool, stacks of mismatched dishes, five lamps, a tricycle, a meat grinder, an old Philco radio, and some red Burma-Shave signs bound together with wire. The top one in the pile read DOES YOUR HUSBAND. What, I thought. Does your husband what? Burma-Shave signs had first appeared in the 1920s and many persisted even into my childhood, always with variations of that tricky, bumping lilt. *Does your husband . . . have a beard? . . . Is he really very weird? . . . If he's living in a cave . . . Offer him some . . . Burma-Shave.* Or words to that effect.

The interior of the store smelled like discarded shoes. I made my way down aisles densely crowded with hanging clothes. I could see rack after rack of items that must have been purchased with an eye to function and festivity. Prom gowns, cocktail dresses, women's suits, acrylic sweaters, blouses, and Hawaiian shirts. The woolens seemed dispirited and the cottons were tired, the colors subdued from too many rounds in the wash. Toward the rear, there was a rod sagging under the burden of winter jackets and coats.

I shrugged into a bulky brown leather bomber jacket. The weight of it felt like one of those lead aprons the technician places across your body while taking dental X rays from the safety of another room. The jacket lining was fleece, minimally matted, and the pockets sported diagonal zippers, one of which was broken. I checked the inside of the collar. The size was a medium, big enough to accommodate a heavy sweater if I needed one. The price tag was pinned to the brown knit ribbing on the cuff. Forty bucks. What a deal. *Does your husband belch and rut? Does he scratch his hairy butt? If you want to see him bathe . . . tame the beast with Burma-Shave.* I tucked the jacket over my arm while I moved up and down the aisles. I found a faded blue flannel shirt and a pair of hiking boots. On my way out, I stopped and untwisted the wire connecting the Burma-Shave signs, reading them one by one.

DOES YOUR HUSBAND

MISBEHAVE?

GRUNT AND GRUMBLE

RANT AND RAVE?

SHOOT THE BRUTE SOME

BURMA-SHAVE.

I smiled to myself. I wasn't half-bad at that stuff. I went out to the street again with my purchases in hand. Let's hear it for the good old days. Lately, Americans have been losing their sense of humor.

I spotted an office supply store across the street. I crossed, stocked up on paper supplies, including a couple of packs of blank index cards. Two doors down, I found a branch of Selma's bank, made sure her check cleared, and came out with a wad of twenties in my shoulder bag. I retrieved my car and pulled out, circling the block until I was headed in the right direction. The town already felt familiar, neatly laid out and clean. Main Street was four lanes wide. The buildings on either side were generally one to two stories high, sharing no particular style. The atmosphere was vaguely Western. At each intersection, I caught sight of a wedge of mountains, the snow-capped peaks forming a scrim that ran the length of the town. Traffic was light and I noticed most of the vehicles were practical: pickups and utility vans with ski racks across the tops.

When I arrived back at Selma's, the garage door was open. The parking space on the left was empty. On the right, I spotted a late-model blue pickup truck. As I got out of my car, I noticed a uniformed deputy emerging from a house two doors down. He crossed the two lawns between us, walking in my direction. I waited, assuming this was Tom's younger brother, Macon. At first glance, I couldn't tell how much younger he was. I placed him in his late forties, but his looks might have been deceptive. He had dark hair, dark brows, and a pleasant, unremarkable face. He was close to six feet tall, compactly built. He wore a heavy jacket, cropped at the waist to allow ready access to the leather holster on his right hip. The wide belt and the weapon gave him a look of heft and bulk that I'm not sure would have been evident if he'd been stripped of his gear.

"Are you Macon?" I asked.

He offered me his hand and we shook. "That's right. I saw you pull up and thought I'd come on over and introduce myself. You met my wife, Phyllis, a little earlier."

"I'm sorry about your brother."

"Thank you. It's been a rough one, I can tell you," he said. He hooked a thumb toward the house. "Selma's not home. I believe she went off to the market a little while ago. You need in? Door's open most times, but you're welcome to come to our place. It sure beats setting out in the cold."

"I should be fine. I expect she'll be home in a bit and if not, I can find ways to amuse myself. I would like to talk to you sometime in the next day or two."

"Absolutely. No problem. I'll tell you anything you want, though I admit we're baffled as to Selma's purpose. What in the world is she worried about? Phyllis and I can't understand what she wants with a private detective, of all things. With all due respect, it seems ridiculous."

"Maybe you should talk to her about that," I said.

"I can tell you right now what you're going to learn about Tom. He's as decent a fellow as you'd ever hope to meet. Everybody in town looked up to him, including me."

"This may turn out to be a short stay, in that case."

"Where'd Selma put you? Someplace nice, I hope."

"Nota Lake Cabins. Cecilia Boden's your sister, as I understand it. You have other siblings?"

Macon shook his head. "Just three of us," he said. "I'm the baby in the family. Tom's three years older than Cecilia and close to fifteen years my senior. I've been trailing after them two ever since I can remember. I ended up in the sheriff's department years after Tom hired on. Like that in school, too. Always following in somebody else's footsteps." His eyes strayed to the street as Selma's car approached and slowed, pulling into the driveway. "Here she is now so I'll leave you two be. You let me know what I can do to help. You can give us a call or come knocking on our door. It's that green house with white trim."

Selma had pulled into the garage by then. She got out of the car. She and Macon greeted each other with an almost imperceptible coolness. While she opened the trunk of her sedan, Macon and I parted company, exchanging the kind of chitchat that signals the end of a conversation. Selma lifted out a brown paper sack of groceries and two cleaner's bags and slammed the trunk lid down. Under her fur coat, she wore smartly pressed charcoal slacks and a long-sleeved shirt of cherry-colored silk.

As Macon walked back to his house, I moved into the garage. "Let me give you a hand with that," I said, reaching for the bag of groceries, which she relinquished to me.

"I hope you haven't been out here long," she said. "I decided I'd spent enough time feeling sorry for myself. Best to keep busy."

"Whose pickup truck? Was that Tom's?" I asked.

Selma nodded as she unlocked the door leading from the garage into the house. "I had a fellow from the garage tow it the day after he died. The officer who found him took the keys out and left it locked up where it was. I can't bring myself to drive it. I guess eventually I'll sell it or pass it along to Brant." She pressed a button and the garage door descended with a rumble.

"You met Macon, I see."

"He came over to introduce himself," I said as I followed her into the house. "One thing I ought to mention. I'm going to be talking to a lot of people around town and I really don't know yet what approach I'll take. Whatever you hear, just go along with it."

She put her keys back in her purse, moving into the utility room with me close behind. She closed the door after us. "Why not tell the truth?"

"I will where I can, but I gather Tom was a highly respected member of the community. If I start asking about his personal business, nobody's going to say a word. I may try another tack. It won't be far off, but I may bend the facts a bit."

"What about Cecilia? What will you say to her?"

"I don't know yet. I'll think of something."

"She'll fill your ear. She's never really liked me. Whatever Tom's problems, she'll blame me if she can. Same with his brother. Macon was always coming after Tom for something—a loan, advice, good word in the department, you name it. If I hadn't stepped in, he'd have sucked Tom dry. You can do me a favor: Take anything they say with a grain of salt."

The disgruntled are good. They'll tell you anything, I thought.

Once in the kitchen, Selma hung her fur coat on the back of a chair. I watched while she unloaded the groceries and put items away. I would have helped, but she waved aside the offer, saying it was quicker if she did it herself. The kitchen walls were painted bright yellow, the floor a spatter of seamless white-and-yellow linoleum. A chrome-and-yellow-plastic upholstered dinette set filled an alcove with a bump-out window crowded with . . . I peered closer . . . artificial plants. She indicated a seat across the table from hers as she folded the bag neatly and put it in a rack bulging with other grocery bags.

She moved to the refrigerator and opened the door. "What do you take in your coffee? I've got hazelnut coffee creamer or a little half-and-half." She took out a small carton and gave the pouring spout an experimental sniff. She made a face to herself and set the carton in the sink.

"Black's fine."

"You sure?"

"Really. It's no problem. I'm not particular," I said. I took off my jacket and hung it on the back of my chair while Selma rounded up two coffee mugs, the sugar bowl, and a spoon for herself.

She poured coffee and replaced the glass carafe on the heating element of the coffee machine, heels *tap-tap-tapping* on the floor as she crossed and recrossed the room. Her energy was ever so faintly tinged with nervousness. She sat down again and immediately flicked a small gold Dunhill to light a fresh cigarette. She inhaled deeply. "Where will you begin?"

"I thought I'd start in Tom's den. Maybe the answer's easy, sitting right up on the surface."

3

I spent the rest of the afternoon working my way through Tom Newquist's insufferably disorganized home office. I'm going to bypass the tedious list of documents I inspected, the files I sorted, the drawers I emptied, the receipts I scrutinized in search of *some* evidence of his angst. In reporting to Selma, I did (slightly) exaggerate the extent of my efforts so she'd appreciate what fifty bucks an hour was buying in the current marketplace. In the space of three hours, I managed to go through about half the mess. Up to that point, whatever Tom was fretting about, he'd left precious little in the way of clues.

He was apparently compulsive about saving every scrap of paper, but whatever organizational principle he employed, the accumulation he left behind was chaotic at best. His desk was a jumble of folders, correspondence, bills paid and unpaid, income tax forms, newspaper articles, and case files he was working. The layers were twelve to fifteen inches deep, some stacks toppling sideways into the adjacent piles. My guess was he knew how to put his hands on just about anything he needed, but the task I faced was daunting. Maybe he imagined that any minute he'd have the clutter sorted and subdued. Like most disorganized people, he probably thought the confusion was temporary, that he was just on the verge of having all his papers tidied up. Unfortunately, death had taken him by surprise and now the cleanup was mine. I made a mental note to myself to straighten out my underwear the minute I got home. In the bottom drawer of his desk, I found some of his equipment—handcuffs, nightstick, the flashlight he must have carried. Maybe his brother, Macon, would like them. I'd have to remember to ask Selma later.

I went through two big leaf bags of junk, taking it upon myself to throw away paid utility stubs from ten years back. I kept a random sampling in case Selma wanted to sell the house and needed to average her household expenses for prospective buyers. I kept the office door open, conducting an ongoing conversation with Selma in the kitchen while I winnowed and pitched. "I'd like to have a picture of Tom."

"What for?"

"Not sure yet. It just seems like a good idea."

"Take one of those from the wall by the window."

I glanced over my shoulder, spotting several black-and-white photographs of him in various settings. "Right," I said. I set aside the lapful of papers I was sorting and crossed to the closest grouping. In the largest frame, an unsmiling Tom Newquist and the sheriff, Bob Staffer, were pictured together at what looked to be a banquet. There were several couples seated at a table, which was decorated with a handsome centerpiece and the number *2* on a placard in the middle. Staffer had signed the photograph in the lower right-hand corner: "To the best damn detective in the business! As Ever, Bob Staffer." The date was April of the preceding year. I lifted the framed photo from the hook and held it up to the fading light coming in the window.

Tom Newquist was a youthful sixty-three years old with small eyes, a round bland face, and dark thinning hair trimmed close to his head. His expression was one I'd seen on cops ever since time began—neutral, watchful, intelligent. It was a face that gave away nothing of the man within. If you were being interrogated as a suspect, make no mistake about it, this man would ask tough questions and there would be no hint from him about which replies might relieve you of his attention. Make a joke and his smile in response would be thin. Presume on his goodwill and his temper would flash in a surprising display of heat. If you were questioned as a witness, you might see another side of him—careful, compassionate, patient, conscientious. If he was like the other law enforcement officers of my acquaintance, he was capable of being implacable, sarcastic, and relentless, all in the interest of getting at the truth. Regardless of the context, the words *impulsive* and *passionate* would scarcely spring to mind. On a personal level, he might be very different, and part of my job here was determining just what those differences might consist of. I wondered what he'd seen in Selma. She seemed too brassy and emotional for a man skilled at camouflage.

I glanced up to find her standing in the doorway, watching me. Despite the fact that her clothes looked expensive, there was something indescribably cheap about her appearance. Her hair had been bleached to the texture of a doll's wig, and I wondered if up close I could see individual clumps like the plugs of a hair transplant. I held up the picture. "Is this one okay? I'd like to have it cropped and copies made. If I'm backtracking his activities for the past couple of months, the face could trigger something where a name might not."

"All right. I might like to have one myself. That's nice of him."

"He didn't smile much?"

"Not often. Especially in social situations. Around his buddies, he relaxed . . . the other deputies. How's it coming?"

I shrugged. "So far there's nothing but junk." I went back to the masses of paper in front of me. "Too bad you weren't in charge of the bills," I remarked.

"I'm not good with numbers. I hated high school math," she said. And then after a moment, "I'm beginning to feel guilty having you snoop through his things."

"Don't worry about it. I do this for a living. I'm a diagnostician, like a gynecologist when you have your feet in the stirrups and your fanny in the air. My interest isn't personal. I simply look to see what's there."

"He was a good man. I know that."

"I'm sure he was," I said. "This may net us nothing and if so, you'll feel better. You're entitled to peace."

"Do you need help?"

"Not really. At this point, I'm still picking my way through. Anyway, I'm about to wrap it up for this afternoon. I'll come back tomorrow and take another run at it." I jammed a fistful of catalogs and advertising fliers in the trash bag. I glanced up again, aware that she was still standing in the door.

"Could you join me for supper? Brant's going to be working, so it would just be the two of us."

"I better not, but thanks. Maybe tomorrow. I have some phone calls to make and then I thought I'd grab a quick bite and make an early night of it. I should finish this in the morning. At some point, we'll have telephone records to go through. That's a big undertaking and I'm saving it for last. We'll sit side by side and see how many phone numbers you can recognize."

"Well," she said, reluctantly. "I'll let you get back to work."

When I had finished for the day, Selma gave me a house key, though she assured me she generally left the doors unlocked. She told me she was often gone, but she wanted me to have the run of the place in her absence. I told her I'd want to look through Tom's personal effects and she had no objections. I didn't want her walking in one day to find me poking through his clothes.

It was fully dark when I left and the streetlights did little to dispel the sense of isolation. The traffic through town was lively. People were going home to dinner, businesses were shutting down. Restaurants were getting busy, the bar doors standing open to release the excess noise and cigarette smoke. A few hardy joggers had hit the sidewalks along with assorted dog owners whose charges were seeking relief against the shrubs.

Once I was out on the highway, I became aware of the vast tracts of land that bore no evidence of human habitation. By day, the fences and the odd outbuildings created the impression the countryside had been civilized. At night, the mountain ranges were as black as jet and the pale slice of moon scarcely brushed the snowy peaks with silver. The temperature had dropped and I could smell the inky damp of the lake. I felt a flicker of longing to see Santa Teresa with its red-tile roofs, palm trees, and the thundering Pacific.

I slowed when I saw the sign for Nota Lake Cabins. Maybe a crackling fire and a hot shower would cheer me up. I parked my car in the small lot near the motel office. Cecilia Boden had provided a few low-voltage lights along the path to the cabins, small mushroom shapes that cast a circle of dim yellow on the cedar chips. There was a small lighted lamp mounted by the cabin door. I hadn't left any lights on for myself, sensing (perhaps) that the management would frown on such extravagance. I unlocked the door and let myself in, feeling for the light switch. The overhead bulb came on with its flat forty-watt wash of light. I crossed to the bed and clicked on the table lamp, which offered forty watts more. The digital alarm was flashing 12:00 repeatedly, which suggested a minor power outage earlier. I checked my watch and corrected the time to its current state: 6:22.

The room felt drab and chilly. There was a strong smell of old wood fires and moisture seeping through the floorboards from underneath the cabin. I checked the wood in the grate. There was a stack of newspapers close by meant for kindling. Of course, there was no gas starter and I suspected the fire would take more time to light than I had time to enjoy. I went around the room, closing cotton curtains across the windowpanes. Then I peeled off my clothes and stepped into the shower. I'm not one to waste water, but even so, the hot began to diminish before my four minutes were up. I rinsed the last of the shampoo from my hair a split second before the cold water descended full force. This was beginning to feel like a wilderness experience.

Dressed again, I locked the cabin and headed back toward the road, walking briskly along the berm until I reached the restaurant. The Rainbow Cafe was about the size of a double-wide trailer, with a Formica counter with eight stools running down its length and eight red Naugahyde booths arranged along two walls. There was one waitperson (female), one short-order cook (also female), and a boy busperson in evidence. I ordered breakfast for dinner. There's nothing so comforting as scrambled eggs at night; soft cheery yellow, bright with butter, flecked with pepper. I had three strips of crisp bacon, a pile of hash browns sautéed with onion, and two pieces of rye toast, drenched in butter and dripping with jam. I nearly crooned aloud as the flavors blended in my mouth.

On the way back to my cabin, I paused to use the pay phone outside the office. This consisted of an old-fashioned glass-and-metal booth missing the original bifold door. I used my credit card to call Dietz. "Hey, babe. How's the patient?" I said when he answered.

"Dandy. How are you?"

"Not bad. Now on retainer."

"In Nota Lake?"

"Where else? Standing in a phone booth in the piney woods," I said.

"How's it going?"

"I'm just getting started so it's hard to tell. I'm assuming Selma talked to you about Tom."

"Only that she thought he had something on his mind. Sounds vague."

"Extremely. Did you ever meet him yourself?"

"Nope. In fact, I haven't even seen her for over fifteen years. How's she holding up?"

"She's in good shape. Upset, as who wouldn't be in her shoes."

"What's the game plan?" he asked.

"The usual. I spent time today going through his desk. Tomorrow I'll start talking to his friends and acquaintances and we'll see what develops. I'll give it until Thursday and then see where we stand. I'd love to be home by the weekend if this job doesn't pan out. How's the knee?"

"Much better. The PT's a bitch, but I'm getting used to it. I miss your sandwiches."

"Liar."

"No, I'm serious. As soon as you finish there, I think you ought to head back in this direction."

"Uh-unh. No thanks. I want to sleep in my own bed. I haven't seen Henry for a month." Henry Pitts was my landlord, eighty-six years old. His would be the cover photo if the AARP ever did a calendar of octogenarian hunks.

"Well, think on it," Dietz said.

"Oh, right. Listen, my Florence Nightingale days are over. I have a business to run. Anyway, I better go. It's friggin' cold out here."

"I'll let you go then. Take care."

"Same to you," I said.

I put a call through to Henry and caught him on his way out the door. "Where you off to?" I asked.

"I'm on my way to Rosie's. She and William need help with the dinner crowd tonight," he said. Rosie ran the tavern half a block from my apartment. She and Henry's older brother William had been married the previous Thanksgiving and now William was rapidly becoming a restaurateur.

"What about you? Where're you calling from?"

I repeated my tale, filling him in on my current situation. I gave him both Selma's home number and that of the office at the Nota Lake Cabins in case he had to reach me. We continued to chat briefly before he had to go. Once he rang off, I placed a call to Lonnie's office and left a message for Ida Ruth, again giving her my location and Selma's number if she should have to reach me for some reason. I couldn't think of any other way to feel connected. After I hung up, I stuck my hands in my jacket pockets, vainly hoping for shelter from the wind. The notion of spending the evening in the cabin seemed depressing. With only two forty-watt lightbulbs for illumination, even reading would be a chore. I pictured myself huddled, squinting, under that damp-looking quilt, spiders creeping from the woodpile the minute I relaxed my vigilance. It was a sorry prospect, given that all I had with me was a book on identifying tire tracks and tread marks.

I crossed to the motel office and peered in through the glass door. A light was on, but there was no sign of Cecilia. A hand-lettered sign said RING FOR MGR. I let myself in. I bypassed the desk bell and knocked on the door marked MANAGER. After a moment, Cecilia appeared in a pink chenille bathrobe and fluffy pink slippers. "Yes?"

"Hi, Cecilia. Could I have a word with you?"

"Something wrong with the room?"

"Not at all. Everything's fine. More or less. I was wondering if you could spare a few minutes to talk about your brother."

"What about him?"

"Has Selma said anything about why I'm here in Nota Lake?"

"Said she hired you is all. I don't even know what you do for a living."

"Ah. Well, actually, I'm a field investigator with California Fidelity Insurance. Selma's concerned about the liability in Tom's death."

"Liability for what?"

"Good question. Of course, I'm not at liberty to discuss this in any detail. You know, *officially* he wasn't working, but she thinks he might have been pursuing departmental business the night he died. If so, it's always possible she can file a claim." I didn't mention that Tom Newquist wasn't represented by CFI or that the company had fired me approximately eighteen months before. I was prepared to flash the laminated picture ID I still had in my possession. The CFI logo was emblazoned on the front, along with a photograph of me that looked like something the border patrol might keep posted for ready reference.

She stared at me blankly and for one heart-stopping moment I wondered if she was recently retired from some obscure branch of county government. She appeared to be mulling over all the rules and regulations, trying to decide which were in effect on the night in question. I was tempted to embellish, but decided I might be getting in too deep. With lies, it's best to skip across the surface like a dragonfly. The more said at the outset, the more there is to retract later if it turns out you really put your foot in it. She held the door open to admit me. "You better come on in. I don't mind telling you the subject's painful."

"I can imagine it is and I'm sorry to intrude. I met Macon earlier."

"He's useless," she remarked. "No love lost between us. Of course, I never thought of Selma as family either and I'm sure it's ditto from her perspective."

Cecilia Boden's apartment was on a par with my cabin, which is to say, drab, poorly lighted, and faintly shabby. The prime difference was that my place was icy cold where she seemed to keep her room temperature somewhere around "pre-heat." The floor cover was linoleum made to look like wood parquet. She had pine-paneled walls, overstuffed furniture covered with violent-colored crocheted throws. A large television set dominated one corner, with all the furniture oriented in that direction. Cecilia's reading glasses were perched on the arm of the sofa nearest the set. I could see that she was in the process of filling out the crossword puzzle in the local paper. She did this in ballpoint pen without any visible corrections. I revised my estimate of her upward. I couldn't perform such a feat with a gun to my head.

We took a few minutes to get settled in the living room. While my story sounded plausible, it didn't give me much room to inquire into Tom's character. In any event, why would I imagine Cecilia would have information about what he was doing the night he died? As it turned out, she didn't question my purpose and the longer we chatted, the clearer it became that she was perfectly comfortable discussing Tom and his wife, their marriage, and anything else I cared to ask about.

"Selma says Tom was preoccupied with something in the past few weeks. Do you have any idea what it might have been?"

Cecilia narrowed her eyes at the section of floor she was studying. "What makes her think there was anything wrong with him?"

"Well, I'm not sure. She said he seemed tense, smoking more than usual, and she thought he was losing weight. She said he slept poorly and disappeared without explanation. I take it this wasn't typical. Did he say anything to you?"

"He didn't confide anything specific," she said cautiously. "You'll have to talk to Macon about that. They were a lot closer to each other than either one of them was to me."

"But what was your impression? Did you feel he was under some kind of strain?"

"Possibly."

Too bad I wasn't taking notes, what with the wealth of data pouring out. "Did you ever ask him about it?"

"I didn't feel it was my place. That wasn't the nature of our relationship. He went about his business and I went about mine."

"Any *hunches* about what was going on?"

She hesitated for a moment. "I think Tom was unhappy. He never said as much to me, but that's my belief."

I made a sort of *mmm* sound, verbal filler accompanied by what I hoped was a sympathetic look.

She took this for encouragement and launched into her analysis. "Far be it from me to criticize Selma. *He* married her. I didn't. It's possible there was more to her than meets the eye. We'd certainly have to hope so. If you want my opinion, my brother could have done a lot better for himself. Selma's a snob, if you want to know the truth."

This time I murmured, "Really."

Her gaze brushed my face and then drifted off again. "You look like a good judge of character, so I don't feel I'm telling tales out of school when I say this. She has no spiritual foundation, even if she does go to church. She's a mite materialistic. She seems to think she can use acquisitions to fill the void in her life, but it won't do."

"For example," I said.

"You saw the new carpet in the living room?"

"Yes, I saw that."

Cecilia shot me a glance filled with satisfaction. "She had that installed about ten days ago. I thought it was in poor taste, doing it so soon, but Selma never asked me. Selma's also confided she's considering having those two front teeth capped, which is not only vain, but completely trivial. Talk about a waste of money. I guess now she's a widder, she can do anything she likes."

What I thought was, what's wrong with vanity? Given the range of human failings, self-absorption is harmless compared to some I could name. Why not do whatever you deem relevant to feeling better about yourself—within reason, of course. If Selma wanted to get her teeth capped, why should Cecilia give a shit? What I said was, "I got the impression she was devoted to Tom."

"As well she should have been. And he to her, I might add. Tom spent his life trying to satisfy the woman. If it wasn't one thing, it was another. First, she had to have a house. Then she wanted something bigger in a better neighborhood. Then they had to join the country club. And on and on it went. Anytime she didn't get what she wanted? Well, she pouted and sulked until he broke down and got it for her. It was pitiful in my opinion. Tom did everything he could, but there wasn't any way to make her happy."

I said, "My goodness." This is the way I talk in situations like this. I could not, for the life of me, think where to go from here. "He was a nice-looking man. I saw a picture of him at the house," I said, vamping.

"He was downright handsome. Why he married Selma was a mystery to me. And that son of hers?" Cecilia pulled her lips together like a drawstring purse. "Brant was a pain in the grits from the first time I ever laid eyes on the boy. He had a mouth on him like a trucker and he was bratty to boot. Back talk and sass? You never heard the like. Did poorly in school, too. Problems with his temper and what they call his impulse control. Of course, Selma thought he was a saint. She wouldn't tolerate a word of criticism regardless of what he did. Poor Tom nearly tore his hair out. I guess he finally managed to get the boy squared away, but it was no thanks to her."

"She mentioned Brant worked as a paramedic. That's a responsible job."

"Well, that's true enough," she conceded grudgingly. "About time he took hold. You can credit Tom for that."

"Do you happen to know where Tom was going that night? I understand he was found somewhere on the outskirts of town."

"A mile north of here."

"He didn't drop in to see you?"

"I wish he had," she said. "I was visiting a friend down in Independence and didn't get back here until shortly after ten fifteen or so. I saw the ambulance pass, but I had no idea it was meant for him."

4

Tuesday morning at nine, I stopped by the offices of the Nota County Coroner. I hadn't slept well the night before. The cabin was poorly insulated and the night air was frigid. I'd moved the thermostat up to 70, but all it did was click off and on ineffectually. I'd crawled into bed wearing my sweats, a turtleneck, and a pair of heavy socks. The mattress was as turgid as a trough of mud. I curled up under a comforter, a quilt, and a wool blanket, with my heavy leather jacket piled on top for the weight. Just about the time I got warm, my bladder announced that it was filled to capacity and required my immediate attention or a bout of bed-wetting would ensue. I tried to ignore the discomfort and then realized I'd never sleep a wink until I'd heeded the message. By the time I got back under the covers, all the ambient heat had been dispelled and I was forced to suffer through the cold again until I drifted off to sleep.

When I woke up at seven, my nose felt like a Popsicle and my breath was visible in puffs against the wan morning light. I showered in tepid water, dried myself, shivering, and dressed in haste. Then I dog trotted down the road to the Rainbow Cafe where I stoked up on another breakfast, sucking down orange juice, coffee, sausages, and pancakes saturated with butter and syrup. I told myself I needed all the sugar and fat to refuel my depleted reserves, but the truth was I felt sorry for myself and the food was the simplest form of consolation.

The coroner's office was located on a side street in the heart of downtown. In Nota County, the coroner is a four-year elected official, who in this case doubled as the funeral director for the county's only mortuary. Nota County is small, less than two thousand square miles, tucked like an afterthought between Inyo and Mono Counties. The coroner, Wilton Kirchner III, generally referred to as Trey, had occupied the position for the past ten years. Since there was no requirement for formal training in forensic medicine, all coroner's cases were autopsied by a forensic pathologist under contract to the county.

In the event of a homicide in the county, the Nota County Coroner handles the on-scene investigation, in conjunction with the sheriff's department's investigator and an investigator from the Nota County District Attorney's office. The forensic autopsy is then conducted in the "big city" by a pathologist who does several homicide autopsies per month and is called to court numerous times during the year to testify. Since Nota County only has one homicide every two years or so, the coroner prefers that an outside agency provide its expertise, in both autopsy services and testimony.

Kirchner & Sons Mortuary appeared to have been a private residence at one time, probably built in the early twenties with the town growing up around it. The architectural style was Tudor with a facade of pale red brick trimmed in dark-painted timbers. Thin cold sunlight glittered against the leaded glass windows. The surrounding lawns were dormant, the grass as drab and brittle as brown plastic. Only the holly bushes lent any color to the landscape. I could imagine a time when the house might have sat on a sizeable piece of land, but now the property had shrunk and the lots on either side sported commercial establishments: a real estate office and a modest medical complex.

Trey Kirchner came out to the reception area when he heard I was there, extending a hand in greeting as he introduced himself. "Trey Kirchner," he said. "Selma called and said you'd be in here today. Nice to meet you, Miss Millhone. Come on back to my office and let's find out what you need."

Kirchner was in his mid-fifties, tall, broad-shouldered, with a waistline only slightly softer than it might have been ten years before. His hair was a clean gray, parted on the side and trimmed short around his ears. His smile was pleasant, creating concentric creases on either side of his mouth. He wore glasses with large lenses and thin metal frames. The corners of his eyes drooped slightly, somehow creating an expression of immense sympathy. His suit was close-fitting, well pressed, and the dress shirt he wore looked freshly starched. His tie was conservative, but not somber. Altogether, he presented an air of comforting competence. There was something solid about him; a man who, by nature, looked like he could absorb all the sorrow, confusion, and rage generated by death.

I followed him down a long corridor and into his office, which had served as the dining room when the house was first built. The carpet was pale, the wood floors pickled to the color of milk-washed pine. The drapes were beige, silk or shantung, some fabric with a touch of sheen. The mortuary decor leaned to wainscoting, topped with wallpaper murals showing soft mountain landscapes, forests of evergreens with paths meandering through the woods. This was a watercolor world; pastel skies piled with clouds, the faintest suggestion of a breeze touching the tips of the wallpaper trees. On either side of the corridor at intervals, wide sliding doors had been pushed back to reveal the slumber rooms, empty of inhabitants, bare except for the ranks of gray metal folding chairs and a few potted ferns. The air was cool, underheated, spiced with the scent of carnations though none were in view. Perhaps it was some weird form of mortuary air freshener wafting through the vents. The entire environment seemed geared to somnambulistic calm.

The office we entered seemed designed for the public, not a book, a file, or a piece of paper in sight. I suspected somewhere in the building Trey Kirchner had an office where the real work was done. Somewhere out of sight, too, was the autopsy paraphernalia: cameras, X-ray equipment, stainless steel table, Stryker saw, scalpels, hanging scale. The room where we sat was as bland as a pudding—no smell of formalin, no murky Mason jars filled with snippets of organs—giving no indication of the mechanics of the body's preparation for cremation or burial.

"Have a seat," he said, indicating two matching upholstered chairs arranged on either side of a small side table. His manner was relaxed, pleasant, friendly, curiously impersonal. "I take it you're here about Tom's death." He reached over and opened the drawer, pulling out a flat manila folder containing a five-page report. "I ran a copy of the autopsy report in case you're interested."

I took the folder. "Thanks. I thought I might have to talk you into this."

He smiled. "It's public record. I could have popped it in the mail and saved you a trip if Selma'd asked for it sooner."

"Tom's death was classified as a coroner's case?"

"Of necessity," he said. "You know he died out Highway 395 with no witnesses and probably not much warning. He hadn't seen his doctor in close to a year. We figured it was his heart, but you never really know about these things until the post. Could have been an aneurysm. Anyway, Calvin Burkey did the autopsy. He's the forensic pathologist for Nota and Mono Counties. Couple of us in attendance. Nothing remarkable showed up. No surprises, nothing unexpected. Tom died of a massive acute myocardial infarction due to severe arteriosclerosis. You'll see it. It's all there. Sections of the coronary artery confirmed ninety-five percent to one hundred percent occlusion. Sixty-three years old. Really, it's amazing he lasted as long as he did."

"Nothing else came to light?"

"In the way of abnormalities? Nope. Liver, gallbladder, spleen, kidneys were all unremarkable. Lungs looked bad. He'd been smoking all his life, but there was no indication of invasive disease. He'd eaten recently. According to our report, he'd stopped off at a cafe for a bite of supper. No pills or capsules in his digestive system and the toxi report was clear. What makes you ask?"

"Selma said he'd been losing weight. I wondered if he knew something he wasn't telling her."

"No ma'am. No cancer, if that's what you mean. No tumors, no blood clots, and no hemorrhaging, aside from the myocardium," he said. "Doc said there were signs of a minor heart attack sometime in the past."

I thought about it. "So maybe he knew his days were numbered. That would give him reason to brood."

"Could be," he said. "Tom wasn't in the peak of health, I can assure you of that. The absence of pathology doesn't necessarily mean you feel all that good. I knew him for years and never heard him complain, but he was sixty pounds overweight. Smoked like a chimney, drank like a fish, just to cover both clichés. He was a hell of an investigator, I can tell you that. What's Selma's worry?"

"It's hard to say. I think she feels he was holding out on her, keeping secrets of some kind. She didn't press him for answers so now it's unfinished business and it bothers her a lot."

"And she has no idea what it was?"

"It might not be anything, which is where I come in. Do you have any theories?"

"I don't think you'll turn up anything scandalous. Tom was churchgoing, a good soul. Well liked, well-thought-of in the community, generous with his time. If he had any faults, I'd have to say he was straitlaced, too rigid. He saw the world in terms of all black or all white with not a lot in between. I guess he could see the gray, but he never knew what to do with it. He didn't believe in bending the rules, though I've seen him do it from time to time. He was a real straight-ahead guy, but that's good in my opinion. We could use a few more like him. We're going to miss him around here."

"Did you spend any time with him in the past few weeks?"

"Nothing to speak of. Mostly, I saw him in the context of his job. Not surprisingly, the county sheriff's department and the coroner's office are just like that," he said, crossing his fingers. "I'd run into him around town. Played pool with him once. Sucked back a few beers. Bunch of us did a weekend fishing trip last fall, but it's not like we laid around at night baring our souls. Fellow you ought to talk to is his partner, Rafe."

"Selma mentioned him. What's his last name?"

"LaMott."

I sat in the rental car in the Kirchner & Sons parking lot, leafing through Tom Newquist's autopsy report, his death certificate spelling out the particulars of his passing. Age, date of birth, Social Security number, and his usual address; the place and cause of his death and the disposition of his remains. He'd arrived at Nota County Hospital ER as a DOA, autopsied a day later, buried the day after that. On paper, his progression to the grave seemed all too swift, but in truth, once death occurs, the human body is just a big piece of meat quickly going sour. There was something flat and abrupt in the details. . . . Tom Newquist deceased . . . his life neatly packaged; beginning, middle, and end. Under the death certificate was a copy of a hand-scrawled note that I gathered had been written by the CHP officer who found him in his truck.

> At appx 21 50 2/3 Ambulance call to roadside 7.2 mi. out Hiway 395. Subj in pick-up, removed to side of road. CPR started @ 22 00. EMT from Nota Lake taking

over @ appx. 22 15. Subj DOA on arrival at Nota Lake ER. Coroner notified.

The notation was signed "J. Tennyson." The autopsy report followed; three typewritten pages detailing the facts as Trey Kirchner had indicated.

I'd been hoping the explanation was obvious, that Tom Newquist was caught in the grip of some terminal disease, his preoccupation as simple as an intimation of his mortality. This was not the case. If Selma's perceptions were correct and he was brooding about something, the subject wasn't an immediate threat to his health or well-being. It was always possible he'd been experiencing heart problems—angina pain, arrhythmia, shortness of breath on exertion. If so, he might have been weighing the severity of his symptoms against the consequences of consulting his physician. Tom Newquist might have seen enough death to view the process philosophically. He might have been more fearful of medical intervention than the possibility of dying.

I set the folder on the seat beside me and started the car. I wasn't sure where to go next, but I suspected the logical move would be to talk to Tom's partner, Rafer LaMott. I checked my map of Nota Lake and spotted the sheriff's substation, which was part of the Civic Center on Benoit about six blocks west. The sun had been climbing through a thin layer of clouds. The air was chilly, but there was something lovely about the light. Along the main thoroughfare, the buildings were constructed of stucco and wood with corrugated metal roofs: gas stations, a drugstore, a sporting goods shop, and hair salon. Rimming the town was the untouched beauty of distant mountains. The digital thermometer on the bank sign showed that it was forty-two degrees.

I parked across the street from the Nota Lake Civic Center, which also included the police station, the county courthouse, and assorted community services. The complex of administrative offices was housed in a building that had once been an elementary school. I know this because the words "Nota Lake Grammar School" were carved in block letters on the architrave. I could have sworn I could still see the faint imprint of construction paper witches and pumpkins where they'd been affixed to the windows with cellophane tape, the ghosts of Halloweens Past. Personally, I hated grade school, having been cursed with a curious combination of timidity and rebellion. School was a minefield of unwritten rules that everyone but me seemed to sense and accept. My parents had died in a car crash when I was five, so school felt like a continuation of the same villainy and betrayal. I was inclined to upchuck without provocation, which didn't endear me to the janitor or classmates sitting in my vicinity. I can still remember the sensation of recently erupted hot juices collecting in my lap while students on either side of me flocked away in distaste. Far from experiencing shame, I felt a sly satisfaction, the power of the victim wreaking digestive revenge. I'd be sent down to the school nurse where I could lie on a cot until my aunt Gin came to fetch me. Often at lunchtime (before I learned to barf at will) I'd beg to go home, swearing to look both ways when I was crossing the street, promising not to talk to strangers even if they offered sweets. My teachers rebuffed every plaintive request, so I was doomed to remain; fearful and anxious, undersized, fighting back tears. By the time I was eight, I learned to quit asking. I simply left when it suited me and suffered the consequences later. What were they going to do, shoot me down in cold blood?

The entrance to the Civic Center opened into a wide corridor that served as a lobby, currently undergoing renovations. File cabinets and storage units had been moved into the uncarpeted space. The walls were lined with panels of some unidentified wood. The ceiling was a low gridwork of acoustical tiles. Portions of the hallway were marked off with traffic cones strung together with tape, hand-lettered signs pointing to the current locations of several displaced departments.

I found the sheriff's substation, which was small and consisted of several interconnecting offices that looked like the "Before" photos in a magazine spread. Fluorescent lighting did little to improve the ambience, which was made up of a hodgepodge of technical manuals, wall plaques, glossy paneling, office machines, wire baskets, and notices taped to all the flat surfaces. The civilian clerk was a woman in her thirties who wore running shoes, jeans, and an M.I.T. sweatshirt over a white turtleneck. Her name tag identified her as Margaret Brine. She had chopped-off black hair, oval glasses with black frames, and a dusting of freckles under her powder and blush. Her teeth were big and square, with visible spaces between.

I took out a business card and placed it on the counter. "I wonder if I might talk to Rafer LaMott."

She picked up my card, giving it a cursory look. "Will he know what this is about?"

"The coroner suggested I talk to him about Tom Newquist."

Her gaze lifted to mine. "Just a minute," she said. She disappeared through a door in the rear that I assumed led into other offices. I could hear a murmur, and moments later Rafer LaMott appeared, shrugging himself into a charcoal brown sportscoat. He was an African American in his forties, probably six feet tall, with a caramel complexion, closely cropped black hair, and startling hazel eyes. His mustache was sparse, and he was otherwise clean-shaven. The lines in his forehead resembled parallel seams in a fine-grained leather. The sportscoat he wore over black gabardine pants looked like cashmere. His shirt was pale beige, his tie a mild brown with a pattern of black paperclips arranged in diagonal lines up and down the length.

He had my card in his hand, reading out the information in a slightly cocky tone. "Kinsey Millhone, P.I. from Santa Teresa, California. What can I help you with?"

I could feel a prickly sensation at the back of my neck. His expression was noncommital. Technically, he wasn't rude, but he certainly wasn't friendly and I sensed from his manner he was not going to be much help. I tried a public smile, nothing with any sincerity or warmth. "Selma Newquist hired me. She has some questions about Tom."

He regarded me briefly and then moved through the gate at one end of the counter. "I have to be someplace, but you can follow me out. What questions?"

I had no choice but to trot along beside him as he headed down the hall toward a rear entrance. "She says he was upset about something. She wants to know what it was."

He pushed the door open and passed through, picking up his pace in a manner that suggested mounting agitation. I caught the door as it swung shut and passed through right after him. I had to two-step to keep up. He pulled his car keys from his pocket as he descended the steps. He walked briskly across the parking lot and slowed when he reached a nondescript, white compact car, which he proceeded to unlock. As he opened the car door, he turned to look at me. "Listen, here's the truth and no disrespect intended. Selma was always trying to pry into Tom's business, always pressing him for something just in case the poor guy had a fleeting thought of his own. The woman comes equipped with emotional radar, forever scanning her environment, trying to pick up matters of no concern to her. Repeat that and I'll deny it, so you can save your breath."

"I have no intention of repeating it. I appreciate your candor—"

"Then you can appreciate this," he said. "Tom never said a word against her, but I can tell you from experience, she's exhausting to be around. Tom was a good guy, but now that he's gone, it's a relief not to have to see her. My wife and I never really wanted to spend time with Selma. We socialized when we had to out of our affection for him. If that sounds spiteful, I'm sorry, but that's the bottom line. My best advice to you is leave the man in peace. He's barely cold in his grave and she's trying to dig him up again."

"Could he have been worried about a case?"

He glanced away from me then with a quick smile of disbelief that I'd pursued the point. I could see him rein himself in, struggling to be patient in hopes of getting rid of me. "He had as many as ten, fifteen files on his desk when he died. And no, you can't see them so don't even ask."

"But nothing particularly distressing?"

"I'm afraid I can't tell you what distressed Tom and what didn't."

"Who's taken over his workload?"

"I took some files. A new guy just hired on and he's taking the rest. None of that information is for public consumption. I don't intend to compromise any ongoing investigation to satisfy Selma's morbid curiosity, so you can bag that idea."

"Do you think Tom had personal problems he didn't want her to know?"

"Ask somebody else. I don't want to say anything more about Tom."

"What's the big deal? If you'd give me some help, I'd be out of here," I said.

By way of an answer, he got into the car and pulled the door shut. He turned the key in the ignition, pressing a button in the console. The car window slid down with a mild whir. When he spoke again, his tone was more pleasant. "Hey, this may sound rude, but do yourself a favor and let it drop, okay? Selma's a narcissist. She thinks everything's about her."

"And this isn't?"

He pressed the button again and the window slid back into place. End of subject. End of Q&A. He put the car in reverse and backed out of the space, taking off with a little chirp as he threw the gear into first. I could only stare after him. Belatedly, I sensed a stinging heat rise in my face. I raised a hand to my cheek as though I'd been slapped.

5

I got in my car and headed back to Selma's, still completely unenlightened. I couldn't tell if Rafer knew something or if he was simply annoyed at Selma's hiring a private detective. Oddly enough, I found his rudeness more inspirational than daunting. Tom had died without much warning, out on the highway, with no opportunity to clean up his business. For the moment, I was operating on the assumption that Selma's intuition was correct.

I left my car out in front and crossed the lawn to the porch. Selma'd left a note taped to the door saying she'd be over at the church until noon. I tried the door, which was unlocked, so I didn't need the key she'd given me the night before. I let myself in, calling a hello as I entered in case Brant was on the premises. There was no call in response, though several lights in the house were on. I took a few minutes to move through the empty rooms. The house was one story and most of the living space was laid out on one floor.

Just off the kitchen, I found a set of stairs leading down to the basement.

I flipped on the light and descended halfway, peering over the rail. I could see woodworking equipment, a washer and dryer, a hot-water heater, and various odds and ends of furniture, including a portable barbecue and lawn chairs. A half-open door on the far wall led to the furnace room. There appeared to be ample storage. I'd nose around later, going through the cardboard boxes and built-in cabinets.

I returned to Tom's office and sat down at his desk, wondering what secrets he might have kept from view. What I was looking for—if, indeed, there was anything—didn't have to be related to Tom's work. It could have been anything: drink, drugs, pornography, gambling, an affair, an affinity for young boys, a tendency to cross-dress. Most of us have something we'd prefer to keep to ourselves. Or maybe there was nothing. I didn't like to admit it, but Rafer's attitude toward Selma was already having an effect. I'd resisted his view, but a small touch of doubt was beginning to stir.

I abandoned Tom's desk, feeling restless and bored. So far, I hadn't turned up one significant scrap of paper. Maybe Selma was nuts and I was wasting my time. I went out to the kitchen and poured myself a glass of water. I opened the refrigerator and stared at the contents while I pretended to quench my thirst. I closed the refrigerator door and checked the pantry. All the stuff she'd brought back from the store looked alarming; artificial and imitation products of the Miracle Whip variety. There was a plate of what looked like raisin-oatmeal cookies on the counter, with a note that said "Help yourself." I ate several. I left the glass in the drainboard and wandered into the hall. The phone seemed to ring every fifteen minutes, but I let the machine pick up messages. Selma was much in demand, but it was all charity-related work—the church bazaar, a fund-raising auction for the new Sunday school wing.

I turned my attention to the master bedroom. Tom's clothes were still hanging in his half of the closet. I began to go through his pockets.

I checked the top shelf, his shoe boxes, dresser drawers, his change caddy. I found a loaded Colt .357 Magnum in one bed table drawer, but there was nothing else of importance. The remaining contents of the drawer was that embarrassing assortment of junk everyone seems to keep somewhere: ticket stubs, matchbooks, expired credit cards, shoelaces. No dirty magazines, no sex toys. I looked under the bed, slid a hand along under the mattress, peeked behind picture frames, tapped with a knuckle across the walls in the closet, pulled up a corner of the rug, looking for hidden panels in the floor.

In the master bath, I checked the medicine cabinet, the linen closet, and the hamper. Nothing leaped out at me. Nothing seemed out of place. For a while, in despair, I stretched out on the master bedroom floor, breathing in carpet fumes and wondering how soon I could decently quit.

I went back into the den, where I finished going through the remaining junk on his shelves. Aside from feeling virtuous for cleaning out his desk drawers, I'd acquired absolutely no insights about Tom Newquist's life. I checked his credit card receipts for the past twelve months, but neither his Visa nor his MasterCard showed anything unusual. Most activity on the card could easily be matched to his desk calendar. For instance, a series of hotel and restaurant charges the previous February were related to a seminar he'd attended in Redding, California. The man was systematic. I gave him points for that. Any work-related charges to his telephone bill were later invoiced to his work and reimbursed accordingly. He didn't pad his account by so much as a penny. There was no pattern of outlandish expenses and nothing to suggest any significant or unexplained outlay of cash.

I heard a car pull into the drive. If this was Selma coming in, I'd tell her I was quitting so she wouldn't waste any more of Tom's hard-earned money. The front door opened and closed. I called a "Hello" and waited for a response. "Selma, is that you?" I waited again. "The Booger Man?"

This time I got a manly "Yo!" in response, and Selma's son, Brant, appeared in the doorway. He was wearing a red knit cap, a red sweatsuit, and pristine white leather Reeboks, with a white towel wrapped around his neck. Brant, at twenty-five, was the kind of kid matronly housewives in the supermarket turned around and checked out in passing. He had dark hair and fierce brows over serious brown eyes. His complexion was flawless. His jaw was boxy, his cheeks as honed as if his face had been molded and shaped in clay first and then carved out of flesh. His mouth was fleshy and his color was good; a strong winter tan overlaid with the ruddy burn of snow glare and wind. His posture was impeccable; square shoulders, flat stomach, skinny through the hips. If I were younger, I might have whimpered at the sight of him. As it is, I tend to disqualify any guy that much younger than me, especially in the course of work. I've had to learn the hard way (as it were) not to mix pleasure with business.

"My mom's not here yet?" he asked, pulling the towel from around his neck. He removed his knit cap at the same time and I could see that his hair was curling slightly with the sweaty dampness of his workout. His smile showed straight white teeth.

"Should be any minute. I'm Kinsey. Are you Brant?"

"Yes ma'am. I'm sorry. I should have introduced myself." I shook hands with him across the littered expanse of his father's desk. His palm was an odd gray. When he saw that I noticed, he smiled sheepishly. "That's from weightlifting gloves. I just came from the gym," he said. "I saw the car out front and figured you were here. How's it going so far?"

"Well enough, I guess."

"I better let you get back to it. Mom comes, tell her I'm in the shower."

"Sure thing."

"See you in a bit," he said.

Selma got home at 12:15. I heard the garage door grumble up and then down. Within minutes, she'd let herself in the door that led from the garage into the kitchen. Soon afterward, I could hear the clattering of dishes, the refrigerator door opening and shutting, then the chink of flatware. She appeared in the den doorway, wearing a cotton pinafore-style apron over slacks and a matching sweater. "I'm making chicken salad sandwiches if you'd like to join us. You met Brant?"

"I did. Chicken salad sounds great. You need help?"

"No, no, but come on out and we can talk while I finish up."

I followed her to the kitchen where I washed my hands. "You know what I haven't come across yet is Tom's notebook. Didn't he take field notes when he was working an investigation?"

Surprised, Selma turned from the counter where she was putting together sandwiches. "Absolutely. It was a little loose-leaf notebook with a black leather cover, about the size of an index card, maybe a little bigger, but not much more than that. It must be around here someplace. He always had it with him." She began to cut sandwiches in half, placing them on a platter with sprigs of parsley around the edge. Every time I buy parsley, it turns to slime. "Are you sure it's not there?" she asked.

"I haven't come across it. I checked his desk drawers and his coat pockets."

"What about his truck? Sometimes he left it in the glove compartment or the side pocket."

"Good suggestion. I should have thought of that myself."

I opened the connecting door and moved into the garage. I skirted Selma's car and opened the door to the pickup on the driver's side. The interior smelled heavily of cigarette smoke. The ashtray bulged with cigarette butts buried in a shallow bed of ash. The glove compartment was tidy, bearing only a batch of road maps, the owner's manual, registration, proof of insurance, and gasoline receipts. I looked in the side pockets in both doors, looked behind the visors, leaned over and scanned the space under the bucket seats. I checked the area behind the seats, but there was only a small tool kit for emergencies. Aside from that, the interior revealed nothing. I slammed the driver's side door shut, glancing idly along the garage shelves in passing. I don't know what I thought I'd see, but there was no little black notebook within range.

I returned to the kitchen. "Scratch that," I said. "Any other ideas?"

"I'll have a look myself later on today. He could have left the notebook at work, though he seldom did that. I'll call Rafer and ask him."

"Won't he claim the notes are department property?"

"Oh, I'm sure not," she said. "He told me he'd do anything he could to help. He was Tom's best friend, you know."

But not yours, I thought. "One thing I'm curious about," I said tentatively. "The night he died . . . if he'd had any warning . . . he could have called for help if he'd had a radio. Why no CB in his truck? Why no pager? I know a lot of guys in law enforcement who have radios installed in their personal vehicles."

"Oh, I know. He meant to do that, but hadn't gotten around to it. He was always busy. I couldn't get him to take the time to drop it off and get it done. That's the sort of thing you tend to remember when there's no way to deal with it."

Brant reappeared, wearing the blue uniform that identified him as an emergency medical technician for the local ambulance service. B. NEWQUIST was embroidered on the left. His skin radiated the scent of soap and his hair was now shower-damp and smelled of Ivory shampoo. I allowed myself one small inaudible whine of the sort only heard by dogs; neither Brant nor his mother seemed to pick up on it. I sat at the kitchen table, just across from him, politely eating my sandwich while I listened to them chat. Midway through lunch, the telephone rang again. Selma got up. "You two go ahead. I'll pick that up in Tom's den."

Brant finished his sandwich without saying much and I realized it was going to be my job to initiate conversation.

"I take it Tom adopted you."

"When I was thirteen," Brant said. "My . . . I guess you'd call him a birth father . . . hadn't been in touch for years, since my mom and him divorced. When she married Tom, he petitioned the court. I'd consider him my real dad whether he adopted me or not."

"You must have had a good relationship."

He reached for the plate of cookies on the counter and we took turns eating them while we continued our conversation. "The last couple of years we did. Before that, we didn't get along all that great. Mom's always been easygoing, but Tom was strict. He'd been in the army and he came down real hard on the side of obeying rules. He encouraged me to get involved with Boy Scouts—which I hated—karate, and track, stuff like that. I wasn't used to having restrictions laid on me so I fought back at first. I guess I did just about anything I could think of to challenge his authority. Eventually he shaped up," he said, smiling slightly.

"How long have you been a paramedic?"

"Three years. Before that, I didn't do much of anything. Went to school for a while, though I wasn't any great shakes as a student back then."

"Did Tom talk to you about his cases?"

"Sometimes. Not lately."

"Any idea why?"

Brant shrugged. "Maybe what he was working on wasn't that interesting."

"What about the last six weeks or so?"

"He didn't mention anything in particular."

"What about his field notes? Have you seen those?"

A frown crossed his face. "His field notes?"

"The notes he kept—"

Brant interrupted. "I know what field notes are, but I don't understand the question. His are missing?"

"I think so. Or put it this way, I haven't been able to lay hands on his notebook."

"That's weird. When it wasn't in his pocket, he kept it in his desk drawer or his truck. All his old notes he bound up in rubber bands and stored in boxes in the basement. Have you asked his partner? Might be at the office."

"I talked to Rafer once but I didn't ask about the notebook because at that point, I hadn't even thought to look."

"Can't help you on that one. I'll keep an eye out around here."

After lunch, both Selma and Brant took off. Brant had errands to run before he reported for work and Selma was involved in her endless series of volunteer positions. She'd posted a calendar on the refrigerator and the squares were filled with scribbles for most days of the week. A silence settled on the house and I felt a mild ripple of anxiety climb my frame. I was running out of things to do. I went back to the den and pulled the phone book out of Tom's top drawer. Given the size of the town, the directory was no bigger than a magazine. I looked up James Tennyson, the CHP officer who'd found Tom that night. There was only one Tennyson, a James W., listed on Iroquois Drive in this same development. I checked my city map, grabbed my jacket and my handbag, and headed out to the car.

Iroquois Drive was a winding roadway lined with two-story houses and an abundance of evergreens. Residents were apparently encouraged to keep their garage doors closed. Backyards in this section were fully fenced or surrounded by hedges and I could see swing sets and jungle gyms as well as above-ground swimming pools, still covered for the winter. The Tennysons lived at the end of the street in a yellow stucco house with dark green shutters and a dark green roof. I parked out in front, snagging the morning paper from the lawn as I passed. I pushed the doorbell, but heard no reassuring *ding dong* inside. I waited a few minutes and then tried a modest knock.

The door was opened by a young woman in jeans with a sleeping baby propped against her shoulder. The child might have been six months old; sparse golden curls, flushed cheeks, flannel sleepers with feet, and a big diapered butt.

"Mrs. Tennyson?"

"That's right."

"My name is Kinsey Millhone. I was hoping to have a word with your husband. I take it, he's the one who works for the CHP."

"That's right."

"Is he at work?"

"No, he's here. He works nights and sleeps late. That's why the doorbell's turned off. You want to come in and wait? I just heard him banging around so it shouldn't be long."

"If you don't mind." I held up the newspaper. "I brought this in. I trust it's yours."

"Oh, thanks. I don't even bother until he's up. The baby gets into it and tears the whole thing to pieces if I'm not looking. Cat does the same thing. Sits there and bites on it just daring me to get mad."

She moved aside to admit me and I stepped into the entrance. Like Selma's, this house seemed overheated, but I may have been reacting to the contrast with the outside cold. She closed the door behind me. "By the way, I'm Jo. Your name's Kimmy?"

"Kinsey," I corrected. "It was my mother's maiden name."

"That's cute," she said, flashing me a smile. "This is Brittainy. Poor baby. We call her Bugsy for some reason. Don't know how that got started, but she'll never live it down." Jo Tennyson was trim, with a ponytail and bangs, her hair a slightly darker version of her daughter's. She couldn't have been much more than twenty-one and may have become a mother before she could legally drink. The baby never stirred as we proceeded to the kitchen. Jo put the newspaper on the kitchen table, indicating a seat. She moved around the room, setting up her husband's breakfast one-handed while the baby slept on. I watched with fascination as she opened a fresh cereal box, shook some of the contents in a bowl, and fetched a spoon from the drawer, which she closed with one hip. She retrieved the milk carton from the refrigerator, poured coffee into three mugs, and pushed one in my direction. "You're not in sales, I hope."

I shook my head and then murmured a thank you for the coffee, which smelled great. "I'm a private investigator. I have some questions for your husband about Tom Newquist's death."

"Oh, sorry. I didn't realize it was business or I could have called him first thing. He's just fooling around. He likes to take his time in the morning because the rest of his day's so hectic. Let me see where he's at. If you want any more coffee, help yourself. I'll be right back."

During her absence, I took the opportunity to engage in a little sit-down observation. The house was untidy—I'd seen that in passing—but the kitchen was particularly disorganized. Counters were cluttered, the cabinet doors hung open, the sink piled with dishes from the last several meals. I thought the vinyl floor tile was gray with a dark mottled pattern, but on closer inspection it turned out to be white overlaid with an assortment of sooty footprints. I straightened up as she returned.

"He'll be right here. I didn't peg you for a detective. Are you local?"

"I'm from Santa Teresa."

"I didn't think you looked familiar. You should talk to Tom's wife. She lives in this subdivision, over in that direction about six blocks, on Pawnee. The snooty street we call it."

"She's the one who hired me. You know her?"

"Uh-hun. We go to the same church. She's in charge of the altar flowers and I help when I can. She's really good-hearted. She's the one who gave Bugsy her little christening dress. Here's James. I'll leave the two of you alone so you can talk."

I got to my feet as he entered the kitchen. James Tennyson was fair-haired, clean-cut, and slender, the kind of earnest young man you want assisting you on the highway when your fan belt goes funny or your rear tire's blown. He was dressed in civilian clothes: jeans, a sweatshirt, and a pair of sheepskin slippers. "James Tennyson. Nice to meet you."

"Kinsey Millhone," I said as the two of us shook hands. "I'm sorry to bother you at home, but I was over at the Newquists and it seemed so close. I saw your name on a report I picked up from the coroner and looked you up in the book."

"Not a problem. Sit down."

"Thanks. Go ahead with your breakfast. I didn't mean to intrude."

He smiled. "I guess I will if you don't mind. What can I do for you?"

While James ate his cereal, I laid out Selma's concerns. "I take it you knew him personally?"

"Yeah, I knew Tom. Mean, we weren't real good friends . . . him and Selma were older and ran with a different crowd . . . but everybody in Nota Lake knew Tom. I tell you, his death shook me. I know he's kind of old, but he was like a fixture around here."

"Can you tell me how you found him? I know he had a heart attack. I'm just trying to get a feel for what happened."

"Well, this was . . . what . . . five, six weeks ago . . . and really nothing unusual. I was cruising 395 when I spotted this vehicle off to the side of the road. Hazard lights were on and the engine was running so I pulled in behind. I recognized Tom's pickup. You know he lives here in the neighborhood so I see the truck all the time. At first I thought he might be having engine problems or something like that. Both the doors were locked, but once I got close I could see him slumped over. I tapped on the window, thinking he'd pulled over and fell asleep at the wheel. I figured the heater was running because the windshield was covered with condensation, windows all cloudy."

"How'd you get in?"

"Well, the window on the driver's side was open a crack. I had a wire in my car and popped the lock up with that. I could see he's in trouble. He looked awful, his eyes open, muck in the corners of his mouth."

"Was he still alive at that point?"

"I'm pretty sure he was gone, but I did what I could. I tell you my hands were shaking so bad, I couldn't make 'em do right. I nearly busted the window and would have if I hadn't managed to snag the lock when I did. I hauled him down out of the truck onto the side of the road and did CPR right there. I couldn't pick up a heartbeat. His skin was cool to the touch, or at least it seemed like that to me. It was freezing outside and even with the heater turned on, temperature inside the truck had dropped. You know how it does. I radioed for help . . . got an ambulance out there as fast as I could, but there was nothing for it. Doc in ER declared him dead on arrival."

"You think he knew what was happening and pulled over to the side?"

"That'd be my guess. He must have had some kind of chest pain, maybe shortness of breath."

"Did you happen to see Tom's notebook? Black leather, about this big?"

He thought back for a moment, shaking his head slowly. "No ma'am. I don't believe so. Of course, I wasn't looking for it. It was in his truck for sure?"

"Well, no, but Selma says he kept it with him and it hasn't turned up yet. I thought maybe you spotted it and turned it in to the department."

"I'da probably done that if I'd seen it. I wouldn't want my notes circulating. A lot of it looks like gibberish, but you need 'em when you type up your reports and if you're called on to testify in court. Wasn't among his personal items? The coroner's office would've returned all his clothes and anything he had on him. You know, his watch, contents of his pockets, and like that."

"I asked Selma the same thing and she hasn't seen it. Anyway, we'll keep looking. I appreciate your time. If anything comes to mind, you can reach me through her."

"I can't imagine there's anything to investigate about him. You couldn't meet a nicer fellow. He's the best. A good man and a good cop."

"So I gather."

• • •

I went back to the motel. I couldn't face another minute of sitting in Tom's den. For all we knew, Tom might have been suffering from a chemical depression. We'd been assuming his problem was situational, but it might not have been. *My* problem was situational. I was homesick and wanted out.

I let myself into the cabin, noting with approval that the room had been done up. The bed was made and the bathroom had been scrubbed, the toilet paper left with a point folded in the first sheet. I sat down at the table and rolled a piece of paper in my Smith-Corona. I began to type out an account of the last day's activities. Selma Newquist was just going to have to make her peace with Tom's passing. Death always leaves unfinished business in its wake, mysteries beyond fathoming, countless unanswered questions amid the detritus of life. All the stories are forgotten, the memories lost. Hire anyone you want and you're still never going to find out what a human being is made of. I could sit here and type 'til I was blue in the face. Tom Newquist was gone and I suspected no one would ever know what his final moments had been.

6

I found myself that night in a place called Tiny's Tavern, one of those shit-kicking bars so many small towns seem to spawn. Cecilia had indicated this was a popular hangout for off-duty law enforcement and I was there trolling as much as anything. I was also avoiding the cabin, with its frigid inside temperatures and depressive lighting. Tiny's had rough plank walls, sawdust on the floor, and a bar with a brass footrail that stretched the length of the room. As in an old Western saloon, there was a long mirror behind the bar with a glittering double image of all the liquor bottles on display. The place was gray with cigarette smoke. The air was overheated and smelled of spilled beer, faulty plumbing, failed deodorant, and cheap cologne. The jukebox was gaudy green and yellow with tubes of bubbles running up the sides and stocked with a strange mix of gospel tunes interspersed with country music, the latter dominant. Occasionally, a couple would clomp around mechanically on the ten-by-ten dance floor while the other patrons looked on, calling out encouragement in terms I thought rude.

I wasn't sure about the unspoken assumptions in a place like this. A woman alone might look like an easy mark for any guy on the loose. For a weeknight, there seemed to be a fair number of unattached fellows in the place, but after an hour on the premises no one seemed to take any particular notice of me. So much for my fantasy of being accosted by cads. I perched on a barstool, sipping bad beer and shelling peanuts from a brass bowl that might have enjoyed a previous life as a spittoon. There was something satisfactory about tossing shells on the floor, though sometimes I ate the shells too, figuring the fiber was healthy in a diet like mine, burdened as it is with all that cholesterol and fat.

The bartender was a guy in his twenties with a shaved head, a dark mustache and beard, and a tattoo of a scorpion on the back of his right hand. I flirted with him mildly just to occupy my time. He seemed to understand there was no serious chance of a wild sexual encounter in his immediate future. I put some quarters in the jukebox. I chatted with the waitress named Alice, who had bright orange hair. I made trips to the ladies' room. I practiced a little balancing trick with a fork and a burnt match. If there were any off-duty cops on the premises, I realized I wouldn't recognize them in their off-duty clothes.

At ten, Macon Newquist came in. He was in uniform, moving through the bar at a leisurely pace, checking the crowd for drunks, minors, and any other form of trouble in the making. He spoke to me in passing, but didn't seem inclined to make small talk. Shortly after he left, my idleness paid off when I spotted the civilian clerk from the sheriff's substation. I couldn't for the life of me remember her name. She came in as a part of a foursome with a fellow I assumed to be her husband and another couple, all of them roughly the same age. The four were dressed in a combination of cowboy and ski attire: boots, jeans, Western-cut shirts, down parkas, ski mittens, and knit caps. They found an empty table on the far side of the room. I stared at the clerk with her dark hair cropped short above her ears, dark brown eyes glinting behind her small oval glasses. The other woman was auburn-haired, top-heavy, and pretty, probably plagued with unwanted suggestions about breast-reduction surgery. The clerk's hubby held a consultation and then headed in my direction, pausing at the far end of the bar where he ordered a pitcher of beer and four oversized mugs. In the meantime, the women shed their jackets, took up their purses, and left the table, heading toward the ladies' room. I signaled for another beer just to hold my place and then made a beeline for the facilities myself. My path intersected theirs and the three of us reached the door at just about the same time. I slowed my pace and allowed the two of them to enter first.

The clerk was saying, "Oh, honey. Billie's taken up with that trashy fellow from the video store. You know the one with the attitude? I don't know what she sees in him unless it's you-know-what. I told her she ought to think a little more of herself. . . ."

The two continued to talk as they passed through the door and into the first two out of three toilet stalls. I entered the third and eavesdropped my tiny heart out while the three of us peed in a merry chorus. What the hell was her name? She and her companion discussed Billie's son, Seb, who suffered from genital warts so persistent his penis looked like a pink fleshy pickle according to someone named Candy who'd dumped him forthwith. Three toilets were flushed in succession and we reassembled at the sinks so we could wash our hands. The other woman skipped her personal cleanliness and moved on to the ritual of combing her hair and adjusting her makeup. I was tempted to point out the sign on the wall, urging us to curb the spread of disease, but I realized the warning was intended for tavern employees. Apparently, the rest of us were at liberty to contaminate anyone we touched. I tried to set a good example, lathering like a surgeon on the brink of an operation, but the woman didn't follow suit.

Miraculously, just then, my brain supplied the clerk's name in a satisfying mental burp. I caught her eye in the mirror and flashed her a smile as she was pulling out a paper towel so she could dry her hands. "Aren't you Margaret?"

She looked at me blankly and then said "Oh hi" without warmth. I couldn't tell if she'd forgotten me, or remembered and simply didn't want to be engaged in conversation. Probably the latter. She crumpled the paper towel and pushed it down in the wastebasket.

"Kinsey Millhone," I prompted, as if she'd recently inquired. "We met this morning at the office when I was talking to Detective LaMott." I held out my hand and she was too polite to decline a handshake.

She said, "Nice seeing you again."

"I thought I recognized you the minute you came in, but I couldn't remember where I knew you from." I turned and gave a little wave to the other woman. "Hi. How are you? Kinsey Millhone," I said. "And you're . . . ?"

She seemed to hesitate, glancing at Margaret. "Earlene." She held her hand out and I had no choice but to take it, germs and all.

"My best friend," Margaret interjected.

"Well, isn't that nice," I said. Earlene's handshake consisted of laying her fingers passively across mine. It was like having a half pound of cooked linguini placed in your palm for safekeeping. She had a round pretty face with a button nose and plump lips, a mutant body that was all breasts, with diminishing hips and legs that petered out into tiny feet. She darted another look at Margaret, clearly picking up on her lack of enthusiasm. I was acting like a salesperson, forcing chitchat to gain a foothold in the conversation. Telemarketers use this device all the time, as if the rest of us don't know what their phony friendliness is all about.

Margaret wasn't fooled. She tucked her bag up against her body and gripped it closely with her arm. "I don't know what you said to Rafer, but he was ticked off all day and I was the one had to take the flak."

"Really? I'm sorry to hear that. I didn't mean to set him off."

"Everything sets him off since Tom passed away. They worked together for years, long before I hired on."

"I can see where he'd be upset." I was making myself sick with all this conciliatory bullshit, though it seemed to be having the desired effect.

Margaret rolled her eyes. "He'll get over it, I guess, but I wouldn't advise you to cross paths with him if you can help it."

"I'll avoid him if possible, but I'm only in town for another couple of days and I'm not sure where else to get information."

I was hoping this would prompt an offer of assistance, but Margaret didn't seem to care. She stood there without a word, forcing me to blunder on. "Why don't I just tell you what I need and maybe you can help. Honestly, I'm not looking for any dirt on Tom Newquist. That's not my intention. I've heard he's a great guy and everybody seems real sorry that he's gone."

"Well, that's true," she said, grudgingly.

"I wasn't sure what to make of your boss. I mean, I could tell he was aggravated, but I couldn't figure out what I'd done."

"It's not you in particular. Rafer says Selma's the one stirring up trouble. Says he's sick and tired of her meddling in Tom's affairs."

"It's hardly meddling," I said. "She was married to the man and has a legitimate concern."

"About what?"

"She told me Tom was worried about something. He slept badly. He brooded. She kept hoping he'd confide in her, but he never said a word. She wanted to ask him, but she couldn't bring herself to do it. You know how it is. You've got a subject you want to talk about and you keep trying to find the perfect time to do it. I guess he was prickly and she was reluctant to irritate him. At any rate, before she could broach the subject, he dropped dead, so now she's stuck."

"That still doesn't entitle her to mess around in Tom's business."

"Of course not, but she's troubled by the possibility he died with some burden. She's heartsick she didn't barge in when she had the chance. That's why she's hired me."

"Good luck," Margaret said in a tone that really meant she hoped I'd fall in a hole.

"I don't think my chances are good, but I don't blame her for trying. She's hoping to make amends. What's wrong with that? In her place, you'd do the same thing, wouldn't you?"

Margaret said, "Well." I could see she was having trouble marshaling an argument. She was good at put-downs; not so good when it came to defending her position. I was feeling damp from the effort at telling the truth. Lies are always easier because the only thing you risk is getting caught. Once you stoop to the truth, you're screwed because if the other person isn't buying, you've got nothing left to sell.

Earlene was watching us like a spectator at a tennis match. Her bright blue eyes darted with interest between my face and Margaret's. I really couldn't tell whose side she was on, but I decided to pull her in. "What do you think, Earlene? What would you do in Selma's place?"

"Same thing, I guess. I can see your point." She flicked a look at Margaret. "You said yourself Tom was a bear the last few weeks before he passed." She looked back at me, hooking a thumb in Margaret's direction. "She thought he was going through the change. You know, moody and short-tempered . . ."

"*Earlene.*"

"Well, it's the truth."

"Of course it's true, but that doesn't mean it bears repeating in the ladies' room." This from the woman discussing someone's genital warts.

"Do you have any idea what was bothering him?" I asked.

Margaret was indignant. "I most certainly do not. And I have to tell you I think she'd be better off letting sleeping dogs lie. If he'd wanted her to know, he'd have told her, so it's really none of her concern. Even if he was crabby and hard to get along with, that's hardly a crime."

"But who'd know? Who should I be talking to if not Rafer?"

Earlene raised her hand. "Wouldn't hurt to ask Hatch."

"Would you butt out?" Margaret snapped.

"Who's Hatch?" I asked Earlene.

"Hatch's her husband. He's sitting right out there," she said, pointing toward the bar.

Margaret snorted. "He won't help and I give you odds Wayne won't either. Wayne hasn't worked for Tom in years so what's he know about anything?"

"Hatch worked for Tom?" I said to Margaret.

"Uh-hun. Both him and Wayne are sheriff's deputies, only Wayne covers Whirly Township and Hatch is working days down here."

"It couldn't do any harm," I said.

Margaret thought about it and then frowned. "I don't guess I can stop you, but it's a waste of time if you ask me."

The three of us left the ladies' room together.

"I'll grab my beer and be right back," I said.

I hustled my butt over to the bar to get my things. I figured in my absence Margaret could go to work on her husband, thus advancing my case. I grabbed my beer mug and jacket and moved over to their table, watching as Hatch dutifully scrounged up an extra chair from a table nearby. I went through another round of introductions, trying to seem winsome as I shook hands with both men. "Winsome" is not a quality I normally project. "Did Margaret tell you what I was up to?"

Hatch said, "Yes ma'am." He was a big rangy man with a thatch of blond hair shorn close along the sides. His face was bony, all jaw and cheekbones, with a big bumpy nose. His ears stuck out like handles on a vase.

Earlene's husband, Wayne, took a swig of beer and put the mug down with a tap. He was dark-haired with a receding hairline, the hair itself cut short and combed forward. He had the pretty-boy handsomeness of a small-time thug. He didn't seem to like me. He avoided my eyes, his attention diverting to other parts of the room. Once in a while he tuned in to the conversation, but he made it plain he didn't like the idea of discussing Tom with anyone.

Hatch at least *seemed* friendly, so I focused on him. "I understand you knew Tom."

"Everybody knew Tom," he said.

"Can you tell me a little bit about him?"

Hatch regarded me uneasily, shaking his head. "You're not going to get me to say anything bad about the man."

"Absolutely not. I'm hoping to get a sense of who he was. I never met him myself so I'm operating in the dark. How long did you know him?"

"Little over fifteen years, since way before I joined the sheriff's department. I'd moved up here from Barstow and first thing you know, someone broke into my apartment and took my stereo. Tom was the one showed up when I dialed 9-1-1."

"What was he like?"

"With regard to what?"

"Anything. Was he smart? Was he funny? Was he a hang-loose kind of guy?"

Hatch tilted his head, allowing one shoulder to creep up toward his ear. "I'd say Tom was a good cop, first, last, and always. You just about couldn't separate the man from the job. He was smart, for sure, and he played by the book."

"Someone who didn't bend the rules," I said, repeating the coroner's comment.

"Yeah, right. You know, little things, he might try to give a guy a break, but high-ticket crime, he was a strictly law-and-order type. All this victim stuff you see nowadays cut no ice with him. He believed you're accountable and there's no two ways about it. He took a hard line on that and I think he was right. Small town like this, somebody breaks the law, you might have dated their sister or they lived down the street from you way back when. In Tom's mind, it wasn't personal. He wasn't mean or anything like that. Business was just business and you had to respect him for his attitude."

"Can you give me an example?"

"I can't think of one offhand. What about you, Wayne? You know what I'm saying. What's the kind of thing Tom did?"

Wayne shook his head. "Hey, Hatch. This is your party. By me."

Hatch scratched at his chin, pulling at the flesh underneath. "Well now, here's one I remember and this is pretty typical I'd say. We had this good ol' boy named Sonny Gelson. Remember him, hon? This was maybe five, six years ago, I guess. He used to live over by Winona in a big old falling-down house." He didn't wait for a response, but I could see Margaret nod as her husband went on. "His wife shot 'im one night by mistake. She thought he was an intruder and pumped a big hole in his chest. About six months before, she'd reported a prowler and Sonny got her a Smith & Wesson. So one night he's out of town and she's home by herself. She hears someone in the downstairs hall, pulls the gun out of a drawer, and pops the guy as he comes in. Problem was the gun misfired and blew up in her hand. Sonny'd packed the reload himself and I guess he'd done it wrong, or that's what it looked like at any rate. Bullet still exited the gun and hit him smack in the chest. I think he died before Judy could even dial 9-1-1. Meantime, Judy's got a hand full of fragments and she's bleeding all over everywhere. See, but now here's the point. Tom got it in his head that this's premeditated murder. He's convinced the whole thing's a setup. So here's Judy Gelson crying her heart out for her terrible mistake. She swears she didn't know it was him. The whole town's up in arms. Everybody out there protesting. DA was going to let her plead out and let it go at that. I doubt she'd have served time because her record was clean. Save the county a ton of money, plus a lot of bad press. Tom just kept digging and pretty soon he comes up with this hefty insurance policy. Turns out Judy had a lover and the two of 'em concocted this plan to get rid of her husband, take the money, and run. She's the one jimmied the cartridge with an overload of fast powder so she'd look like an innocent victim of circumstance herself. Tom's the one nailed her and he'd went *steady* with her once upon a time. She's homecoming queen in high school and they nearly run off together the night of the senior prom. Cut no ice with him and that's the point I'm trying to make."

"What happened to Judy Gelson?"

"She's doing twenty-five to life somewhere. Lover dropped out of sight. In fact, nobody ever figured out who he was. Maybe somebody local with a lot to lose. Tom was always workin' that one, trying to get a line on the guy. It bugged him to see a fellow get away with anything."

"He liked to work old cases?"

"Everybody does. Always the chance you'll crack one and make a name for yourself. Anyway, it's more than that; it's putting paid to an account. 'Closure' they call it nowadays, but it amounts to the same thing."

I glanced at Margaret, saying, "That's all Selma wants."

Hatch shook his head at the mention of her name. "Well, now Selma. She's something else. I wouldn't want to say anything bad about her. Tom was crazy about her, worshiped the ground she walked on, and that's no lie."

Margaret chimed in. "The rest of us find Selma pretty hard to take."

"How so?"

"Oh, you know, she's easily offended, imagines slights where there's none intended. Tom tried his best to reassure her, but it was never enough. You'd run into the two of 'em out in public and he'd always make sure she was included in the conversation, didn't he?" she said, turning to Earlene for confirmation. "I think he knew people didn't like her and he wanted her to look good."

"That's right. He'd sit there and draw her out . . . get her to talking like anybody gave a shit. Everybody liked him and hadn't any use for her."

"So in a way, her insecurity was justified," I said.

Earlene laughed. "Sure, but if she wasn't so self-centered, people might like her better. Selma's convinced the sun rises and sets in her own hineybumper and she had Tom convinced of it, too. He used to jump every time she snapped her fingers. On top of that she's a social climber, acting like she's so much better than the rest of us. In a town this size, we all tend to socialize. You know, go to the same church, join the same country club. Selma has to be there, right out in front. The woman's tireless, I'll give her that. Ask her to do anything and she's got it done just like that."

Earlene's husband, Wayne, had caught my eye more than once in the course of her recital. I thought he was irritated that she was talking to me. Given the fact that Wayne had worked with Tom, I suspected he didn't like his wife being so free with her opinions. He seemed guarded, remote, his eyes pinned on the table while the other three exchanged anecdotes. I couldn't get a fix on the source of his disaffinity. Maybe Rafer'd had a chat with him and made it clear he didn't want any of his deputies to cooperate with me. Or maybe his attitude reflected the habitual reluctance of a cop to share information, even at the level of gossip and personal opinion.

I caught his attention. "What about you, Wayne? Anything you'd care to add?"

He smiled, but more to himself than at me. "Ask me, them three are doing pretty good."

"You agree with their assessment?"

"Basically, I don't see Tom's marriage as any of our business. What him and Selma worked out is between them."

Earlene tossed a crumpled paper napkin in his direction. "You old sourpuss," she said.

"You're not going to get me to respond," he replied airily.

"Oh, loosen up. Honest to Pete. You never liked Selma any better than the rest of us so why not admit it?"

"Say what you want. You're not going to draw me into this."

"Let him be," I said. I was suddenly feeling tired. The combination of tension and smoke-filled air was giving me a headache. I'd asked for general information and that's what I'd received. It was clear no one was going to offer up much more than that. "I think I'll head on back to the motel," I said.

"Don't go away mad. Just go away," Wayne said, smiling.

"Very funny. Ha ha," Earlene said to him.

"We'd best be off, too," Margaret said, glancing at her watch. "Oh, geez. I have to be at work at eight and look what time it is. Eleven forty-five."

Earlene reached for her jacket. "I didn't realize it was that late, and we still have to drop you off at your place."

"We can walk. It's not far," Margaret said.

"Don't be silly. It's no trouble. It's right on our way."

The four of them began to gather their belongings, shrugging into their parkas, scraping chairs back as they rose.

"Catch you later," I said.

Various good-bye remarks were made, the yada-yada-yada of superficial social exchange. I watched them depart, and then returned to the bar where I settled my tab. Alice, the orange-haired waitress, was just taking a break. She pulled up a stool beside me and lit a cigarette. Her eyes were rimmed in black eyeliner and she had a fringe of thick dark lashes that had to be false; bright coral lipstick, a swathe of blusher on each cheek. "You a cop?"

"I'm a private investigator."

"Well, that explains," she said, blowing smoke to one side. "I heard you're asking around about Tom Newquist."

"Word travels fast."

"Oh, sure. Town this small there's not much to talk about," she said. "You're barking up the wrong tree with that bunch you were talking to. They're all law enforcement, loyal to their own. You're not going to get anyone to say a bad word about Tom."

"So I discover. You have something to add?"

"Well, I don't know what's been said. I knew him from in here.

I knew her somewhat better. I used to run into the two of them at church on occasion."

"I gather she wasn't popular. At least from what I've heard."

"I try not to judge others, but it's hard not to have *some* opinion. Everybody's down on Selma and it seems unfair. I just wish she'd quit worrying about those silly teeth of hers." Alice put a hand to her mouth. "Have you noticed her doing this? Half the time I can hardly hear what's she saying because she's so busy trying to cover up her mouth. Anyway, Tom was great. Don't get me wrong . . . I grant you Selma's abrasive . . . but you know what? He got to look good by comparison. He wasn't confrontational. Tom'd never dream of getting in your face about anything. And why should he? He had Selma to do that. She'd take on anyone. Know what I mean? Let her be the bitch. She's the one takes all the heat. She does the work of the relationship while he gets to be Mr. Good-Guy, Mr. Nice-As-Pie. You see what I'm saying?"

"Absolutely."

"It might have suited them fine, but it doesn't seem right to hold her entirely accountable. I know her type; she's a pussycat at heart. He could have pinned her ears back. He could have raised a big stink and she'd have backed right off. He didn't have the gumption so why's that her fault? Seems like the blame should attach equally."

"Interesting," I said.

"Well, you know, it's just my reaction. I get sick and tired of hearing everyone trash Selma. Maybe I'm just like her and it cuts too close. Couples come to these agreements about who does what. I'm not saying they set down and discuss it, but you can see my point. One might be quiet, the other talkative. Or maybe one's outgoing where the other one's shy. Tom was passive—pure and simple—so why blame her for taking over? You'd have done it yourself."

"Selma says he was very preoccupied in the last few weeks. Any idea what it was?"

She paused to consider, drawing on her cigarette. "I never thought much about it, but now you mention it, he didn't seem like himself. Tell you what I'll do. Let me ask around and see if anybody knows anything. It's not like people around here are dishonest or even secretive, but they protect their own."

"You're telling me," I said. I took out a business card and jotted down my home number in Santa Teresa and the motel where I was staying.

Alice smiled. "Cecilia Boden. Now there's a piece of work. If that motel gets to you, you can always come to my place. I got plenty of room."

I smiled in return. "Thanks for your help."

I headed out into the night air. The temperature had dropped and I could see my breath. After the clouds of smoke in the bar, I wondered if I was simply exhaling the accumulation. The parking lot was only half full and the lighting just dim enough to generate uneasiness. I took a moment to scan the area. There was no one in sight, though the line of pine trees on the perimeter could have hidden anyone. I shifted my car keys to my right hand and hunched my handbag over my left shoulder as I moved to the rental car and let myself in.

I slid under the wheel, slammed the car door, and locked it as quickly as possible, listening to the locks flip down with a feeling of satisfaction. The windshield was milky with condensation and I wiped myself a clear patch with my bare hand. I turned the key in the ignition, suddenly alerted by the sullen grinding that indicated a low charge on the battery. I tried again and the engine turned over reluctantly. There was a series of misses and then the engine died. I sat there, projecting a mental movie in which I'd be forced to return to the bar, whistle up assistance, and finally crawl into bed at some absurd hour after god knows what inconvenience.

I caught a flash of headlights in the lane behind me and checked the source in my rearview mirror. A dark panel truck was passing at a slow rate of speed. The driver, in a black ski mask, turned to stare at me. The eyeholes in the knit mask were rimmed with white and the opening for the mouth was thickly bordered with red. The driver and I locked eyes, our gazes meeting in the oblong reflection of the rearview mirror. I could feel my skin prickle, the pores puckering with fear. I thought *male.* I thought *white.* But I could have been wrong on both counts.

7

I could hear the crunch of gravel, a dull popping like distant gunfire. The truck slowed and finally came to a halt. I could hear the engine idling against the still night air. I realized I was holding my breath. I wasn't sure what I'd do if the driver got out and approached my car. After an interminable thirty seconds, the truck moved on while I followed its reflection in my rearview mirror. There was no lettering on the side so I didn't think the vehicle was used for commercial purposes. I turned my head, watching as the panel truck reached the end of the aisle and took a left. There was something unpleasant about being the subject of such scrutiny.

I tried starting my car again. "Come *on*," I said. The engine seemed, if anything, a little less energetic. The panel truck was now passing from right to left along the lane in front of me, the two of us separated by the intervening cars, parked nose to nose with mine. I could see the driver lean forward, the masked face now tilted in my direction. It was the blankness that unnerved me, the shapeless headgear wiping out all features except the eyes and mouth, which stood out in startling relief. Terrorists and bank robbers wore masks like this, not ordinary citizens concerned about frostbite. The panel truck stopped. The black ski mask was fully turned in my direction, the prolonged look intense. I could see that both the eyeholes and the mouth hole had been narrowed by big white yarn stitches, with no attempt to disguise the modification. The driver extended a gloved right hand, index finger pointing at me like the barrel of a gun. Two imaginary bullets were fired at me, complete with recoil. I flipped him the bird in return. This brief digital exchange was charged with aggression on his part and defiance on mine. The driver seemed to stiffen and I wondered if I should have kept my snappy metacarpal retort to myself. In Los Angeles, freeway shootings have been motivated by less. For the first time, I worried he might have a real weapon somewhere down by his feet.

I pumped the gas with my foot and turned the key again, uttering a low urgent sound. Miraculously, the engine coughed to life. I put the car in neutral and applied pressure on the accelerator, flipping on the headlights while I gunned the engine. The arrow on the voltage indicator leaned repeatedly to the right. I flicked my attention to the panel truck, which was just turning out of the lot at the far end. I released the emergency brake and put the car in reverse.

I backed out of the slot, shifted gears, and swung the car into the lane heading in the opposite direction, peering through the dark to see what had happened to the panel truck. I could hear my heart thudding in my head, as if fear had forced the hapless organ up between my ears. I reached the marked exit and eased forward, searching the streets beyond for signs that the panel truck was rounding the block. The street was empty as far as I could see. I patted myself on the chest, a calming gesture designed to comfort and reassure. Nothing had actually happened. Maybe the driver was mistaken, thinking I was an acquaintance and then realizing his error. Someone passing in a panel truck had turned and looked at me, firing symbolically with a pointed index finger and a wiggle of his thumb. I didn't think the incident would make the national news.

It wasn't until I was midway through town that I caught a glimpse of the truck falling into line half a block back. I could see now that one headlight was sitting slightly askew, the beam directed downward, like someone with one crossed eye. I checked in all directions, but I could see no other traffic and no pedestrians. At this late hour, the town of Nota Lake was deserted, stores locked for the night with only an occasional cold interior light aglow. Even the gas station was shut down and cloaked in darkness. The streetlights washed the empty sidewalks with the chilliest of illumination. Stoplights winked silently from green to red and then to green again.

Was this a problem or was it not? I considered my options. My gas gauge showed half a tank. I had plenty of gas to get back to the motel, but I didn't like the idea of someone following me and I didn't want to try to outrun my pursuer if it came to that. Highway 395, leading out to the Nota Lake Cabins, represented one long continuous stretch of darkened road. The few businesses along the highway would be closed for the night, which meant my vulnerability would increase as the countryside around me became less populated. I glanced in the rearview mirror. The panel truck still hung half a block back, matching my speed, a sedate twenty miles an hour. I could feel myself shuddering from some internal chill. I turned on the heater. I was desperate to get warm, desperate for the sight of another human being. Didn't people walk their dogs? Didn't parents dash out for a quart of milk or a croupy child's cough medicine? How about a jogger I could flag down on sight? I wanted the driver of the panel truck to see that I had help.

I turned left at the next street and drove on for three blocks, eyes pinned to the rearview mirror. Within seconds, the panel truck came around the corner behind me and took up its surveillance. I continued west for six blocks and then turned left again. This street paralleled Main, though it was narrower and darker, a quiet residential neighborhood with no house lights showing. Ordinarily, I keep a gun in my briefcase, which is tucked into the well behind the VW's backseat. But this car was a rental and when I'd left Santa Teresa, I was with Dietz. Why did I need a weapon? The only jeopardy I imagined was living in close quarters with an invalid. Given my nature, what scared me was the possibility of emotional claustrophobia, not physical danger.

I was checking the rearview mirror compulsively every couple of seconds. The panel truck was still there, with one headlight focused on the street and one on me. I've taken enough self-defense classes to know that women, by nature, have trouble assessing personal peril. If followed on a darkened street, many of us don't know when to take evasive action. We keep waiting for a sign that our instincts are correct. We're reluctant to make a fuss, just in case we're mistaken about the trouble we're in. We're more concerned about the possibility of embarrassing the guy behind us, preferring to do nothing until we're sure he really means to attack. Ask a woman to scream for help and what you get is a pathetic squeak with no force behind it and no power to dissuade. Oddly, I found myself suffering the same mind-set. Maybe the guy in the panel truck was simply on his way home and I happened to be taking the very path he intended to take all along. Uh-hun, uh-hun. On the other hand, if the driver in the truck was trying to psych me out, I didn't want to give him the satisfaction of any overt reaction.

I refused to speed up. I refused to play tag. I turned left again, driving at a measured rate as the blocks rolled by. Ahead of me, close to the intersection, was the Nota Lake Civic Center, with the sheriff's headquarters. Next door was the fire department and next door to that was the police station. I could see the outside lights, though I wasn't sure the place was even open this close to midnight. I coasted to a stop and idled the engine with my headlights on. The panel truck rolled up even with my car and the driver turned, as before, to stare. I could have sworn there was a smile showing through the red-rimmed knit mouth. The driver made no other move and, after a tense moment, he drove on. I checked the rear license plate, but it was covered with tape and no identifying numbers showed. The truck began to speed up, turned left at the intersection, and disappeared from sight. I felt my insides turning luminous as adrenaline poured through me.

I waited a full five minutes, though it felt like forever. I studied the street on all sides, craning my head to scan the area behind, lest someone approach on foot. I was afraid to shut down my engine, worried I wouldn't be able to get the car started again. I squeezed my hands between my knees, trying to warm my icy fingers. The feeling of apprehension was as palpable as a fever, racking my frame. I caught a glimpse of headlights behind me again and when I checked the rearview mirror, I saw a vehicle come slowly around the corner. I made a sound in my throat and leaned on the horn. A howling blare filled the night. The second vehicle eased up beside me and I could see now that it was James Tennyson, the CHP officer, in his patrol car. He recognized my face and rolled down the window on the driver's side. "You okay?" he mouthed.

I pressed a button on the console and opened the window on the passenger side of my car.

"Something I can help you with?" he asked.

"Someone's been following me. I didn't know what else to do but come here and honk."

"Hang on," he said. He spotted a parking place across the street and pulled his patrol car over to the stretch of empty curb. He left his vehicle running while he crossed the street. He walked around to my side of the car and hunkered so we could talk face-to-face. "What's the story?"

I explained the situation, trying not to distort or exaggerate. I wasn't sure how to convince him of the alarm I'd felt, but he seemed to accept my account without any attempt to dismiss my panic as foolish or unwarranted. He was in his twenties by my guess and I suspected I'd seen more in the way of personal combat than he had.

Still, he was a cop in uniform and the sight of him was reassuring. He was earnest, polite, with that fair unlined face and all the innocence of youth.

"Well, I can see where that'd worry you. It seems creepy to me, too," he said. "Might have been a guy sitting in the bar. Sometimes the fellows around here get kind of weird when they drink. Sounds like he was waiting for you to come out to the parking lot."

"I thought so, too."

"You didn't notice anybody in Tiny's staring at you?"

"Not at all," I said.

"Well, he probably didn't mean any harm, even if he scared you some."

"What about the truck? There couldn't be that many black panel trucks in a town this size."

"I haven't seen it, but I've been cruising the highway south of town. I was passing the intersection when I caught a glimpse of your headlights so I doubled back. Thought you might be having car trouble, but I wasn't sure." He tilted his head in the direction of the police station. "They're locked up for the night. You want me to see you home? I'd be happy to."

"Please," I said.

He escorted me the six miles to the motel, driving ahead of me so I could keep my gaze fixed on the sight of his patrol car. There was no sign of the panel truck. Once at the Nota Lake Cabins, we parked side by side and he walked me to the cabin, waiting while I unlocked the door and flipped on the light inside. I intended to check the premises, but he held out an arm like the captain of the grade school safety patrol. "Let me do this."

"Great. It's all yours," I said.

I make no big deal about these things. I'm a strong, independent woman, not an idiot. I know when it's time to turn the task over to a cop; someone with a gun, a nightstick, a pair of handcuffs, and a paycheck. He did a cursory inspection while I followed close on his heels, feeling like a cartoon character, with slightly quaking knees. If a mouse had jumped out, I'd have shrieked like a fool.

He glanced in the closet, behind the bathroom door. He moved the shower curtain aside, got down on his hands and knees, and looked under the bed. He didn't seem any more impressed with the place than I'd been. "Never been inside one of these before. I believe I'd take a pass if it came right down to it. Doesn't Ms. Boden believe in heat?"

"I guess not."

He got to his feet and brushed the soot from his knees. "What kind of money does she get for this?"

"Thirty bucks a night."

"That much?" He shook his head with amazement. He made sure the windows were secured. While I waited in the cabin, he made a circuit of the place outside, using his flashlight beam to cut through the dark. He came back to the door. "Looks clear to me."

"Let's hope."

He let his gaze settle on my face. "I can take you somewhere else if you'd prefer. We got motels in the heart of town if you think you'd feel safer. You'd be warmer, too."

I considered it briefly. I was both keyed up and exhausted. Moving at this hour would be a pain in the ass. "This is fine," I said. "I didn't see any sign of the truck on the way out. Maybe it was just a practical joke."

"I wouldn't count on that. World's full of freaks. You don't want to take something like this lightly. You might want to talk to the police in the morning and file a report. Wouldn't hurt to lay the groundwork in case something comes up again."

"Good point. I'll do that."

"You have a flashlight? Why don't you take this tonight and you can return it to me in the morning. I got another in the car. You'll feel better if you have a weapon."

I took the flashlight, hefting the substantial weight of it in my hand. You could really hurt somebody if you whacked 'em up the side of the head. I'd seen scalps laid wide open when the edge hit just right. I felt like asking for his nightstick and his radio, but I didn't want to leave him denuded of equipment.

I held up the flashlight. "Thanks. I'll drop it off to you first thing."

"No hurry."

Once he was gone, I locked the door and then went through the cabin carefully, doing just as he'd done. I made sure the windows were locked, looked under every piece of furniture, in closets, behind curtains. I turned the lights out and let my eyes adjust to the dark, then moved from window to window, eyeing the exterior. The black wasn't absolute. There was a moon up there somewhere, bathing the surrounding woods in a silvery glow. The trunks of the birches and the sycamores shone as pale as ice. The evergreens were dense, shapeless, and compelling against the night landscape. I should have gone to another motel. I regretted the isolation, wishing that I could find myself safely ensconced in one of the big chains—a Hyatt or a Marriott, one with hundreds of identical rooms and numerous in-house security. In my current situation, I had no phone and no immediate neighbors. The rental car was parked at least a hundred yards away, not readily available if I should have to make a hasty exit.

I leaned my forehead against the glass. From out the highway, I could catch flashes of light as an occasional car sped by, but none seemed to slow and none turned into the motel parking area. Times like this, I longed for a husband or a dog, but I never could decide which would be more trouble in the long run. At least husbands don't bark and tend to start off paper trained.

I remained fully dressed and brushed my teeth in the dark, barely letting the water run as I washed my face. Frequently, I paused, listening to the silence. I took my shoes off, but kept them by the side of the bed within easy reach. I crawled under the covers and propped myself against the pillows, flashlight in hand. Twice, I got up and looked out the windows, but there was nothing to see and eventually I felt calm return.

I didn't sleep well, but in early morning light, I felt better.

I was blessed with a full three minutes of hot water before the pipes began to clank. I walked out to the highway into a morning filled with icy sunlight and air clear as glass. I could smell loam and pine needles. There was no sign of the panel truck. Nobody in a ski mask paused to stare at me. I had breakfast at the Rainbow, taking a certain comfort at the mundane nature of the place. I watched the short-order cook, a young black girl working with remarkable efficiency and concentration.

Afterward, I returned to Selma's.

Her sister-in-law, Phyllis, was in the kitchen. The two of them were working at the breakfast table, which was covered with paperwork. File folders were spread out, lists of names on legal pads with removable tags attached. I gathered they were determining the seating for some country club event, arguing about who to seat by whom for maximum entertainment and minimum conflict.

"Nawp. I wouldn't do that," Phyllis said. "The fellows like each other, but the women don't speak. Don't you remember that business between Ann Carol and Joanna?"

"They're not still mad about that, are they?"

"Sure are."

"Unbelievable."

"Well, trust me. You seat them together, you got a war on your hands. I've seen Joanna throw one of those hard dinner rolls at Ann Carol. She bonked her right in the eye and raised a welt this big."

Selma paused to light a cigarette while she studied the chart. "How about put her at Table thirteen?"

Phyllis made a rueful face. "I guess that'd do. I mean, it's dull, but not bad. At least Ann Carol wouldn't be subject to an attack by flying yeast bread."

Selma looked up at me. "Morning, Kinsey. What's on your plate today? Are you about finished in there?"

"Almost," I said. I glanced at Phyllis, wondering if this was a subject to be discussed in front of her.

Selma caught my hesitation. "That's fine. Go ahead. You don't have to worry about her. She knows all this."

"I'm drawing a blank. I don't doubt your story. I'm sure Tom was worried about something. Other people have told me he didn't seem like himself. I just can't find any indication of what was troubling him. Really, I'm no better informed now than when I started. It's frustrating."

I could see the disappointment settle across Selma's face.

"It's only been two days," she murmured. Phyllis was frowning slightly, straightening a pile of papers on the table in front of her. I hoped she had something to offer, but she said nothing so I went on.

"Well, that's true," I said. "And there's always the chance something will pop up unexpectedly, but so far there's nothing. I just thought you should know. I can give you a rundown when you have a minute."

"I guess you can only do your best," Selma said. "Coffee's hot if you want some. I left you a mug alongside that little pitcher of milk over there."

I crossed to the coffeemaker and poured myself a cup, taking a quick whiff of the milk before adding it to my coffee. I debated whether to mention the business with the panel truck, but I couldn't see the point. The two of them were already back at work and I didn't want to have to deal with their concern or their speculation. I might net myself a little sympathy, but to what end?

"See you in a bit," I said. The two didn't lift their heads. I shrugged to myself and moved into the den.

I stood in the doorway while I sipped my coffee, staring at the disarray that still littered the room. I'd been working my way through the mess in an orderly fashion, but the result seemed fragmented. Many jobs were half done and those I'd completed hadn't gotten me anything in the way of hard data. I'd simply proceeded on the assumption that if Tom Newquist was up to something he had to have left a trace of it somewhere. There were numerous odd lots of paperwork I wasn't sure how to classify. I'd piled much of it on the desk in an arrangement invisible to the naked eye. I was down to the dregs and it was hard to know just where to go from here. I'd lost all enthusiasm for the project, which felt dirty and pointless. I did have six banker's boxes stacked along one wall. Those contained the files that I'd labeled and grouped: previous income tax forms, warranties, insurance policies, property valuations, various utility stubs, telephone bills, and credit card receipts. Still no sign of his field notes, but he might have left them at the station. I made a mental note to check with Rafer on that.

I set my mug on an empty bookshelf, folded together a fresh banker's box, and began to clear Tom's desk. I placed papers in the box with no particular intention except to tidy the space. I was here as an investigator, not as char in residence. Once I cleared the desk, I felt better. For one thing, I could see now that his blotter was covered with scribbles: doodles, telephone numbers, what looked like case numbers, cartoon dogs and cats in various poses, appointments, names and addresses, drawings of cars with flames shooting from the tailpipes. Some of the numerals had been cast in three dimensions, a technique I employed sometimes while I was talking on the phone. Some items of information were boxed in pen; some were outlined and shaded in strokes of different thicknesses. I pored over the whole of it as though it were hieroglyphic, then panned across the surface item by item. The drawings were much like the ones sixth-grade boys seemed to favor in my elementary days—daggers and blood and guns firing fat bullets at somebody's cartoon head. The only repeat item was a length of thick rope fashioned into a hangman's noose. He'd drawn two of those; one with an X'd out phone number in the center, the second with a series of numbers followed by a question mark. In one corner of the blotter was a hand-drawn calendar for the month of February, the numbers neatly filled in. I did a quick check of the calendar and realized the numbers didn't correspond to February of this year. The first fell on a Sunday, and the last two Saturdays of the month had been X'd out. I paused long enough to make a detailed list of all the telephone and case numbers.

Intrigued, I retrieved the file of telephone records from the past six months, hoping for a match. I was temporarily sidetracked when I spotted seven calls to the 805 area code, which covers Santa Teresa County, as well as Perdido County to the south and San Luis Obispo County to the north of us. One number I recognized as the Perdido County Sheriff's Department. There were six calls to another number spaced roughly two weeks apart. The most recent of these was late January, a few days before his death. On impulse, I picked up the phone and dialed the number. After three rings, a machine clicked on, a woman's voice giving the standard "Sorry I'm not here right now to receive your call, but if you'll leave your name, number, and a message, I'll be happy to get back to you as soon as I can. Take as long as you need and remember, wait for the beep." Her voice was throaty and mature, but that was the extent of the information I gleaned. I waited for the beep and then thought better of a message, quietly replacing the handset without saying a word. Maybe she was a friend of Selma's. I'd have to ask when I had the chance.

I made a note of the number and went back to work. I tried comparing the numbers on the phone bills with the numbers on the blotter and that netted me a hit. It looked as if someone—I assumed Tom—had completed a call to the number I'd seen X'd out in the center of one noose, though that number had been noted without the 805 area code attached. I tried the number myself and the call was picked up by a live human being. "Gramercy. How may I direct your call?"

"Gramercy?"

"Yes ma'am."

"This is the Gramercy Hotel in downtown Santa Teresa?"

"That's correct."

"Sorry. Wrong number."

I depressed the plunger and disconnected. Well, that was odd. The Gramercy Hotel was a fleabag establishment down on lower State Street. Why would the Newquists call them? I circled the number in my notes, adding a question mark, and then I went back to my survey of telephone bills. I could find no other number that seemed significant on the face of it. I placed another banker's box on the desk top and continued packing.

At ten, I paused to stretch my legs and did a few squats. I still had the lower cabinets to unload, two of which were enclosed by wide doors spanning the width of the bookshelves. I decided to get the worst of it over with. I got down on my hands and knees and began to pull boxes out of the lefthand side. The storage space was so commodious I had to insert my head and shoulders to reach the far corners. I heaved two boxes into view and then sat there on the floor, going through the contents.

At the top of the second box, I came across two blue big-ring loose-leaf binders that looked promising. Apparently, Tom had photocopies of the bulk of the reports in the sheriff's department case books. This was the log of unsolved crimes kept on active status, though many were years old, copies yellowing. These were the cases detectives reworked any time new information came to light or additional leads came in. I leafed through with interest. This was Nota County crime from the year 1935 to the present. Even reading between the lines, there wasn't much attention paid to the rights of the defendant in the early cases. The notion of "victim's rights" would have seemed a curious concept in 1942. In those days, the victim had the right to redress in a court of law. These days, a trial isn't about guilt or innocence. It's a battle of wits in which competing attorneys, like intellectual gladiators, test their use of rhetoric. The mark of a good defense attorney is his ability to take any given set of facts and recast them in such a light that, *presto change-o,* as if by magic, what appeared to be absolute is turned into a frame-up or some elaborate conspiracy on the part of the police or government. Suddenly, the perpetrator becomes the victim and the deceased is all but forgotten in the process.

"Kinsey?"

I jumped.

Phyllis was standing in the doorway.

"Shit, you scared me," I said. "I didn't hear you come in."

"I'm sorry. I'm just on my way home. Can I talk to you for a minute?"

"Sure. Come on in."

"In private," she added, and then turned on her heel.

8

I scrambled to my feet and followed her down the hall. Behind us, I could hear Selma chatting with someone on the phone. When we reached the front door, Phyllis opened it and moved out onto the porch. I hesitated and then joined her, stepping to one side as she pulled the door shut behind us. The cold hit like a blast. The sky had turned hazy, with heavy gray clouds sliding down the mountains in the distance. I crossed my arms and kept my feet close together, trying to preserve body heat against the onslaught of nippy weather.

The outfit Phyllis sported was thin cotton and looked more appropriate for a summer barbecue. She wore abbreviated tennis socks, little pom-poms resting on the backs of her walking shoes. No coat or jacket. She spoke in a low tone, as if Selma might be hovering on the far side of the door. "There's something I thought I better mention while I had the chance."

"Aren't you cold?" I asked. There she stood with her bare arms in a skimpy cotton blouse, her skirt blowing against her bare legs. I was wearing a long-sleeved turtleneck and jeans and I was still on the verge of lockjaw trying to keep my teeth from chattering.

She made a careless gesture, brushing aside the bitter chill. "I'm used to it. Doesn't bother me. This will only take a minute. I should have said something sooner, but I haven't had the chance."

For mid-March, her face seemed remarkably tanned. I had to guess it was from skiing, given that the rest of her was pale. Her face was nicely creased, lines radiating from the corners of her eyes, lines bracketing her mouth. Her nose was long and straight, her teeth very white and even. She looked like the perfect person to have with you when you were down; pleasant and capable without being too earnest.

Out in the yard, a stiff breeze ruffled through the dead grass. I clamped my mouth shut, trying to keep from whining like a dog. I could feel my eyes water from the cold. Soon my nose would start running, and me with no hankie. I sniffed, trying to postpone the moment I'd have to use my shirtsleeve. I focused on Phyllis, already chatting away.

"You know Macon joined the sheriff's department because of Tom. The two fellows were always close—despite the difference in their ages—and of course when Tom married Selma, we wished him all the best."

"Aren't there any other jobs in this town? Everyone I've met is in law enforcement."

Phyllis smiled. "We all know each other. We tend to hang out together, like a social club."

"I guess so," I said, mentally begging her to hurry since I was freezing my ass off.

"Tom was a wonderful man. I think you'll find that out when you start asking around."

"So everybody says. In fact, most people seem to prefer him to her," I said.

"Oh, Selma has her good points. Not everybody likes her, but she's all right. I wouldn't say we're friends . . . in fact, we're not even that close, which may seem surprising given the fact we live two doors away . . . but you can see somebody's weaknesses and still like them for their better qualities."

"Absolutely," I said. This was hardly an endorsement, but I understood what she was saying. I felt like making that rolling hand gesture that says *Come on, come on.*

"Selma'd been complaining to me for months about Tom. I guess it's the same thing she told you. Well, in September . . . this was about six months ago . . . Tom and Macon went to a gun show in Los Angeles and I tagged along. Selma wasn't really interested—she had some big event that weekend—so she didn't come with us. Anyway, I happened to see Tom with this *woman* and I remember thinking, uh oh. Know what I mean? Just something about the way they had their heads bent together didn't look right to me. Let's put it this way. This gal was interested. I could tell by the way she looked at him."

I felt a flash of irritation. I couldn't believe she was telling me this. "Phyllis, I wish you'd mentioned this before *now.* I've been in there slogging through that bullshit and what I hear you saying is that Tom's 'problem' didn't have anything to do with paperwork."

"Well, that's just it. I don't really know. I asked Macon about the woman and he said she was a sheriff's investigator over on the coast. Perdido, I believe, though I could be wrong about that. Anyway, Macon said he'd seen her with Tom on a couple of occasions. He told me to keep my mouth shut and that's what I did, but I felt awful. Selma was planning this big anniversary party at the country club and I kept thinking if Tom was . . . well, you know . . . if he was *involved* with someone, Selma was going to end up looking like a fool. Honestly, what's humiliating when your husband's having an affair is realizing everybody in the whole town knows about it but you. I don't know if you've ever had the experience yourself—"

"So you told her," I suggested, trying to jump her like a game of checkers. I did conclude from her comments that Macon had subjected her to the very humiliations she was so worried about for Selma.

Phyllis made a face. "Well, no, I didn't. I never worked up my nerve. I hate to defy Macon because he turns into such a bear, but I was debating with myself. I adored Tom and I couldn't decide how much I owed Selma as a sister-in-law. I mean, sometimes friendship takes precedence irregardless. On the other hand, you don't always do someone a favor telling something like that. In some ways, it's hostile. That's just the way I see it. At any rate, the next thing I knew, Tom had passed away and Selma was beside herself. I've felt terrible ever since. If I'd told her what I suspected, she could have confronted him right then and put a stop to it."

"You know for a fact he was having an affair?"

"Well, no. That's the point. I thought Selma should be warned, but I didn't have any *proof.* That's why I was so reluctant to speak up. Macon felt like it was none of our business, and with him breathing down my neck I was caught between a rock and a hard place."

"Why tell me now?"

"This was the first opportunity I had. When I was listening to you in there, I realized how frustrating this must be from your perspective. I mean, you might turn up evidence if you knew where to look. If he was scr—misbehaving, so to speak—he had to leave *some* trace, unless he's smarter than most men."

The front door burst open and Selma popped her head out. "*There* you are. I thought the two of you'd gone off and left me. What's this all about?"

"We were just jawing," Phyllis said, without missing a beat. "I was on my way home and she was nice enough to walk me out."

"Would you look at her? She's frozen. Let the poor thing come in here and get thawed out, for Pete's sake!"

Gratefully, I scurried into the house while the two of them discussed another work session the next morning. I headed for the kitchen where I washed my hands. I should have considered another woman in the mix. It might explain why Tom's buddies were being so protective of him. It might also explain the six 805 calls to the unidentified woman whose message I'd picked up from her answering machine.

A few minutes later, Selma came in, agitated. "Well, if that doesn't take the cake. I cannot believe it. She was just telling me about a dinner party coming up in the neighborhood, but have I been invited? Of course not," she was saying. "Now I'm a widow, I've been dropped like a hot potato. I know Tom's friends . . . the fellows . . . would include me, but you know how women are; they feel threatened at the thought of a single woman on the loose. When Tom was alive, we were part of a crowd that went everywhere. Cocktail parties, dinners, dances at the club. We were always included in the social scene, but in the weeks since he died I haven't left the house. The first couple of days, of course, everybody pitched in. Casseroles and promises. That's how I think of it. Now, I sit here night after night and the phone hardly rings except for things like this. Scut work, I call it. Good old Selma's always up for a committee. I do and I do. I really knock myself out and what's the point? The women are all too happy to pass off responsibility. Saves them the effort, if you know what I mean."

"But Selma, it's only been six weeks. Maybe people are trying to show their respects, giving you time to grieve."

"I'm sure that's their version," she said tartly.

I made some reply, hoping to get her off the subject. Her view was distorted, and I wondered what would happen if she could see herself as others saw her. It was her very grandiosity that offended, not her insecurities. Selma seemed to be unaware of how transparent she was, oblivious to the disdain with which she was regarded for her snobbery.

She seemed to shake off her mood. "Enough of this pity party. It won't change anything. Can I fix you a bite of lunch? I'm heating some soup and I can make us some grilled cheese sandwiches."

"Sounds great," I said. Already I felt guilty accepting her hospitality when I'd sat around listening to other people's withering assessments. I'd told myself it was part of the information I was gathering, but I could have protested the venom with which such opinions had been delivered. By now familiar with the kitchen, I opened the cupboard door and took down soup bowls and plates. "Will Brant be joining us?"

"I doubt it. He's still in his room, probably dead to the world. He goes to the gym three days a week, so he likes to sleep in on the mornings between. Let me go check." She disappeared briefly and returned shaking her head. "He'll be right out," she said. "Why don't you tell me what you've found out so far."

I took out an extra plate and bowl, then opened the silverware drawer and took out soup spoons. While she heated the soup and grilled sandwiches, I filled her in on activities to date, giving her a verbal report of where I'd been and who I'd talked to. My efforts sounded feeble in the telling. Because of what Phyllis had told me, I now had a new avenue to explore, but I was unwilling to mention it when I was only dealing with suspicions. Selma had never even *suggested* the possibility of another woman, and I wasn't going to introduce the subject unless I found some reason to do so.

Brant appeared just as we were sitting down to eat. He was wearing jeans and cowboy boots, his snug white T-shirt emphasizing the effectiveness of his workouts. Selma ladled soup into bowls and cut the sandwiches in half, putting one on each plate.

We began to eat in the kind of silence I found mildly unsettling. "What made you decide to become a paramedic?" I asked.

I had caught Brant with his mouth full. He smiled, embarrassed, signaling the delay while he tucked half the food in his cheek. "I had a couple of friends in the fire department so I took a six-month course. Bandages and driving. I think Tom was hoping I'd join the sheriff's department, but I couldn't see myself doing that. I enjoy what I do. You know, it's always something."

I nodded, still eating. "Is the job what you expected?"

"Sure. Only more fun," he said.

I might have asked him more, but I could see him glance at his watch. He wolfed down the last of his sandwich and crumpled his paper napkin. He pushed back from the table, picking up his half-empty bowl and his plate. He stood at the sink and drank a few mouthfuls of soup before he rinsed his bowl and set it in the dishwasher.

Selma gestured. "I'll get that."

"I got it," he said as he added his sandwich plate. I heard his spoon *chink* in the silverware container just before he snapped the dishwasher shut. He gave his mother's cheek a quick buss. "Will you be here a while?"

"I've got a meeting at the church. What about you?"

"I think I'll drive on down to Independence and see Sherry."

"Will you be back tonight?"

"I wouldn't count on it," he said.

"You drive carefully."

"Twenty-five whole miles. I think I can handle it." He snagged the four remaining cookies from the plate, placing one in his mouth with a grin. "Better make more cookies. This was a short batch," he said. "See you later."

Selma left the house after lunch, so I didn't have the chance to broach the subject that was beginning to tug at me—a quick trip to Santa Teresa to pick up my car. I'd had the rental for over three weeks and the cost was mounting daily. I'd never imagined an extended stay in Nota Lake so my current wardrobe was limited. I longed to sleep in my own bed even for one night. The issue of the female sheriff's investigator I could dig into once I got home. Anything else of interest here could wait 'til I got back to Nota Lake.

Meanwhile, it was time to have a chat with the Nota Lake Police Department. Given the new lead, I couldn't see how last night's incident could be tied to my investigation, but I thought I should do the smart thing and report it anyway. I left a note for Selma, shrugged on my leather jacket, took my shoulder bag, and headed off.

The Nota Lake Police Department was housed in a plain one-story building with a stucco exterior, a granite entryway, and two wide granite steps. The windows and the plate glass door were framed in aluminum. An arrow under a stick figure in a wheelchair indicated an accessible entrance somewhere to the left. The bushes along the front had been trimmed to window height and from the flagpole both the American and the State of California flags were snapping in the breeze. Six radio antennae had been erected on the roof like a series of upright fishing poles. As with the Nota Lake Fire Department, located next door, this was generic architecture, a strictly functional facility. No tax dollars had been heedlessly squandered here.

The interior was consistent with its no-frills decor, strongly reminiscent of the sheriff's headquarters two doors down: a lowered ceiling of fluorescent panels and acoustical tile, metal file cabinets, wood-grained laminate counters. On the desks, I could see the backs of the two computer monitors and attendant CPU's from which countless electrical cords sprouted like airborne roots.

The desk officer was M. Corbet, a fellow in his forties with a smooth round face, thinning hair, and a tendency to wheeze. "Thiss-iss asthma in case you're thinking I'm contagious," he said. "Cold air gets to me and this dry heat doesn't help. Excuse me a second." He had a small inhaler that he placed in his lips, sucking deeply of the mist that would open up his bronchi. He set the inhaler aside with a shake of his head. "Thiss-iss the damndest thing. Never had a problem in my life until a couple years back. Turns out I'm allergic to house dust, animal hair, pollen, and mold. What's a fella supposed to do? Quit breathing altogether is the only cure I know."

"That's a tough one," I said.

"Doctor tells me it's more and more people developing allergies. Says he has this one patient reacts to inside air. Synthetics, chemicals, microbes coming through the heating vents. Poor woman has to tote around a oxygen trolley everywhere she goes. Passes out and falls down the minute she encounters any alien pathogens. Thankfully, I'm not yet as bad off as her, though the chief had to take me off active duty and put me on desk. Anyway, that's my story. Now what can I help you with?"

I gave him my business card, hoping to establish my credibility before I launched into a description of the events involving the driver of the panel truck. Officer Corbet was polite, but I could tell just by looking at him that the issue of someone in a ski mask staring at me real hard wasn't going to qualify as a major case for the Crimes Against Persons unit, which probably consisted solely of him. Lungs awhistle, he took my report, printing the particulars in block letters on the proper form. He placed his hands on the counter, tapping with his fingers as if he was playing a little tune. "I do know someone with a truck like that."

"You do?" I said, surprised.

"Yes ma'am. Sounds like Ercell Riccardi. He lives right around the corner about three doors down. Keeps his truck parked in the drive. I'm surprised you didn't see it on your way over here."

"I didn't come from that direction. I turned right off of Main."

"Well, you might want to have a look. Ercell leaves it sit out any time it's not in use."

"With keys in the ignition?"

"Yes ma'am. It's not like Nota Lake is the auto-theft capital of the world. I think he started doing it maybe five, six years back. We had us a rash of break-ins, bunch of kids busting into cars, smashing windows, taking tape decks, going joyriding. Ercell got tired of replacing the stereo so he 'give up and give in' is how he puts it. Last time his truck was broke into he didn't even bother to file a claim. Said it was driving his rates up and to hell with the whole thing. Now he leaves the truck open, keys in the ignition, and a note on the dash saying, 'Please put back in the drive when you're done.' "

"So people take his truck any time they like?"

"Doesn't happen that often. Occasionally, somebody borrys it, but they always put it back. It's a point of honor with folks and Ercell's a lot happier."

The telephone began to ring and Officer Corbet straightened up.

"Anyway, if you think the truck was Ercell's, just give us a call and we'll talk to him. It's not something he'd do, but anybody could have hopped in his vehicle and followed you."

"I'll take a look."

Out on the street again, I shoved my hands in my jacket pockets and headed for the corner. As soon as I turned onto Lone Star, I saw the black panel truck. I approached it with caution, wondering if there were any way I could link this truck to the one I'd seen. I circled the vehicle, leaning close to the headlights. Impossible in daylight to see if the beams were askew. I moved around to the rear and ran a finger across the license plate, scrutinizing the surface where I could see faint traces of adhesive. I stood up and turned to study the house itself. A man was stationed at the window, looking out at me. He stared, scowling. I reversed my steps and returned to my parking spot.

When I reached the rental car, Macon Newquist was waiting, his black-and-white vehicle parked behind mine at the curb. He glanced up at me, catching my eye with a smile. "Hi. How are you? I figured this was your car. How's it going?"

I smiled. "Fine. For a minute, I thought you were giving me a ticket."

"Don't worry about that. In this town, we tend to reserve tickets for people passing through." He crossed his arms and leaned a hip against the side of the rental. "I hope this doesn't seem out of line, but Phyllis mentioned that business about the gun show. I guess she passed along her opinion about the gal Tom was talking to."

I felt my reaction time slow and I calculated my response. Phyllis must have felt guilty about telling me and blabbed the minute she got home. I thought I better cover so I shrugged it aside. "She said something in passing. I really didn't pay that much attention."

"I didn't want you to get the wrong impression."

"No problem."

"Because she attached more to it than was warranted."

"Ah."

"Don't get me wrong. You don't know the ladies in this town. Nothing escapes their notice and when it turns out to be nothing, they make it into something else. The woman Tom was talking to, that was strictly professional."

"Not surprising. Everybody tells me he was good at his job. You know her name?"

"I don't. I never heard it myself. She's a sheriff's investigator. I do know that much because I asked him about it later."

"You happen to know what county?"

He scratched at his chin. "Not offhand. Could be Kern, San Benito, I forget what he said. I could see Phyllis put the hairy eyeball on the two of them and I didn't want you to be misled. Last thing Selma needs is some kind of gossip about him. All she has is her memories and once those are tainted, what's she got left?"

"I couldn't agree more. Trust me, I'd never be irresponsible about something like that."

"That's good. I'm glad to hear that. People don't like the notion you're using up Tom's money on a wild-goose chase. So what's your timetable on this?"

"That remains to be seen. If you have any ideas, I hope you'll let me know."

Macon shook his head. "I wish I could help, but I realize I'm the wrong one to ask. I know I offered, but this is one of those circumstances where I'm not going to be objective. People admired Tom and I'm not just saying that because I admired him myself. If there was something tacky in his life . . . well, people aren't going to want to know that about him. You take somebody like Margaret's husband. I believe you talked to him at Tiny's. Hatch was a protégé of Tom's, and the other fellow, Wayne, was somebody Tom rescued from a bad foster care situation. See what I mean? You can't run around asking those fellows what Tom was *like.* They don't take to it that well. They'll be polite, but it's not going to sit right."

"I appreciate the warning."

"I wouldn't call it a warning. I don't want to give you the wrong impression. It's just human nature to want to protect the people we care about. All I'm saying is, let's not be hasty and cause trouble for no reason."

"I wouldn't dream of it."

9

I went back to the motel, making a brief detour into the Rainbow Cafe, where I picked up a pack of chips and a can of Pepsi. I was eating for comfort, but I couldn't help myself. I hadn't jogged for three weeks and I could feel my ass getting larger with every bite I ate. The young black woman who handled the griddle had paused to follow the weather channel on a small color television at the end of the counter. She was trim and attractive, with loopy corkscrew curls jutting out around her head. I saw a frown cross her face when she saw what was coming up. "Hey now. I'm sick of this. Whatever happened to spring?" she asked of no one in particular.

Out in the Pacific, the radar showed the same clustered pattern of color as a CAT scan of the brain, areas of storm activity represented in shades of blue, green, and red. I was hoping to hit the road for home before the bad weather reached the area. March was unpredictable, and a heavy snowstorm could force the mountain passes to close. Nota Lake was technically located out of the reach of such blockades, but the rental car had no chains and I had scant experience driving in hazardous conditions.

Back in the cabin, I finished typing up my notes, translating all the pointless activity into the officious-sounding language of a written report. What ended up on paper didn't add up to anything because I'd neatly omitted the as-yet-unidentified female sheriff's investigator, who may or may not have been interested in Tom Newquist and he in her. San Benito or Kern County, yeah, right, Macon.

At two, I decided to make a trip to the copy shop in town. I locked the cabin behind me and headed for my car. Cecilia must have been peering out the office window because the minute I walked by, she rapped on the glass and made a beckoning motion. She came to the door, holding a piece of paper aloft. Cecilia was so small she must have been forced to buy her clothes in the children's department. Today's outfit consisted of a long red sweatshirt with a teddy bear appliquéd on the front worn over white leggings, with a pair of enormous jogging shoes. Her legs looked as spindly as a colt's, complete with knobby knees. "You had a telephone call. Alice wants you to get in touch. I took the number this time, but in future, she ought to try reaching you at Selma's. I run a motel here, not an answering service."

Her aggrieved tone was irritating and inspired a matching complaint. "Oh, hey, now that I've got you, do you think I could get some heat? The cabin's almost unliveable, close to freezing," I said.

An expression of annoyance flashed across her face. "March first is the cutoff date for heating oil out here. I can't just whistle up delivery because a couple of short-term visitors to the area make a minor fuss." Her tone suggested she'd been beleaguered with grumbles the better part of the day.

"Well, do what you can. I'd hate to have to complain to Selma when she's footing the bill."

Cecilia gave the door a little bang as she withdrew. Good luck to me, getting any other messages. I crossed to the pay phone and stood there, searching for change in the bottom of my handbag. I found a little cache of coins tucked in one corner along with assorted hairs and a ratty tissue. I dropped some money in the slot and dialed. Alice picked up on the fourth ring just about the time I expected her machine to kick in. "Hello?"

"Hello, Alice? Kinsey Millhone. I got your message. Are you at work or home?"

"Home. I'm not due at Tiny's until four. I was in the process of setting my hair. Hang on a sec while I get the curlers out on this side. Ah, better. Nothing like a set of bristles sticking in your ear. Listen, this might not be helpful, but I thought I'd pass it along. The waitress who works counter over at the Rainbow is a good friend of mine. Her name's Nancy. I mentioned Tom and told her what you were up to. She says he came in that night about eight-thirty and left just before closing. You can talk to her yourself if you want."

"Is she the black girl?"

"Nuhn-uhn. That's Barrett, Rafer LaMott's daughter. Nancy doubles as a cashier. Brown hair, forties. I'm sure you've seen her in there because she's seen you."

"What else did she say? Was he alone or with someone?"

"I asked that myself and she says he was alone, at least as far as she could see. Said he had a cheeseburger and fries, drank some coffee, played some tunes on the jukebox, paid his ticket, and left about nine-thirty, just as she was closing out the register. Like I said, it might not mean anything, but she said she'd never known him to come in at that hour. You know the night he was found, he was out on 395, but he was heading toward the mountains instead of home to his place."

"I remember that," I said. "The coroner mentioned his having eaten a meal. According to Selma, he was in for the night. He didn't even leave a note. By the time she got back from church, he was DOA at the local emergency room. Maybe he got a phone call and went to meet someone."

"Or maybe he just got hungry, hon. Selma's the type who'd make him eat veggies and brown rice. He could have sneaked out for something decent." She laughed at herself. "I always said the food out there would kill you. I'll bet his arteries seized up from all the fat he took in."

"At least we know where he was in the hour just before he died."

"Well, that's hardly news. Nancy says the coroner covered the same ground. Anyways, I told you it wouldn't count for much. I guess that about says it for my detective career."

"You never know. Oh, one more thing as long as I have you on the line. You ever hear rumors about Tom and any other woman?"

She barked out a laugh. "Tom? You gotta be kidding. He was stuffy about sex. Lot of guys, you can tell just by looking they got a problem around dominance. Ass-grabbers and pinchers, fellows telling dirty jokes and gawking at your boobs. They wouldn't mind a quick bounce on the front seat of their pickups, but believe me, romance is the fartherest thing from their minds. Tom was always pleasant. I've never known him to flirt and I never heard him make any kind of off-color remark. What makes you ask?"

"I thought he might have been at the Rainbow for a rendezvous."

"Oh, a *rahndez-vous.* That's rich. Listen, if you're fooling around in this town, you'd best meet somewhere else unless you want everyone to know. Why take the risk? If his sister'd showed up, she'd have spotted him first thing. Cecilia's not that fond of Selma, but she'd have told on him anyway. That's how people around here operate. Anything you find out is fair game."

"I take it word's gone out about me."

"You bet."

"What's the consensus? Anybody seem upset?"

"Oh, grumbles here and there. You're picking up notice, but nothing serious that I've heard. Town this size, everybody has an opinion about something—especially fresh blood like yours. Some of the guys were wondering if you're married. I guess they noticed no wedding ring."

"Actually, I took my ring off to have the diamond reset."

"Bullshit."

"No, really. My husband's *huge.* He's always pumped up on steroids so he's touchy as all get out. He'd tear the head off anyone who ever laid a hand on me."

She laughed. "I bet you've never been married a day in your life."

"Alice, you would be surprised."

As predicted, the weather was turning nasty as the front moved in. The morning had been clear, the temperatures in the fifties, but by early afternoon, a thick mass of clouds had accumulated to the north. The sky changed from blue to a uniform white, then to a misty-looking dark gray, which made the day seem as gloomy as a solar eclipse. All the mountain peaks had been erased and the air became dense with a fine, biting spray.

Here's what I did with my afternoon. I drove into town and went to the copy shop, where I made copies of my typewritten report and several cropped five-by-seven photocopy enlargements of the head shot of Tom Newquist. I dropped the original photograph and the original of my report in Selma's mailbox, drove six blocks over, and left the flashlight inside the storm door on James Tennyson's front porch. And I still had hours to kill before I could decently retire.

In the meantime, I was bored and I wanted to get warm. Nota Lake didn't have a movie theater. Nota Lake didn't have a public library or a bowling alley that I could spot. I went to the lone bookstore and wandered up and down the aisles. The place was small but attractive, and the stock was more than adequate. I picked up two paperbacks, returned to the cabin, crawled under a pile of blankets, and read to my heart's content.

At six, I hunched into my jacket and walked over to the Rainbow through an odd mix of blowing sleet and buffeting rain. I ate a BLT on wheat toast and then chatted idly with Nancy while she rang up my bill. I already knew what she had to say, but I quizzed her nonetheless, making sure Alice had reported accurately. At 6:35, I went back to the cabin, finished the first book, tossed that aside, and reached for the next. At ten o'clock, exhausted from a hard day's work, I got up, brushed my teeth, washed my face, and climbed back in bed, where I fell promptly asleep.

A sound filtered into the tarry dream I was having. I labored upward, slow swimming, my body weighted with dark images and all the leaden drama of sleep. I felt glued to the bed. My eyes opened and I listened, not even sure where I was. Nota Lake crept back into my consciousness, the cabin so cold I might as well have slept outside. What had I heard? I turned my head with great effort. According to the clock, it was 4:14, still pitch black. The tiny scrape of metal on metal . . . not the sound of a key . . . possibly a pick being worked into the door lock. Fear shot through me like a bottle rocket, lighting my insides with a shower of adrenaline. I flung the covers aside. I was still fully dressed, but the chill in the cabin was numbing to both my face and my hands. I swung my legs over the side of the bed, felt for my shoes, and shoved my feet in without bothering to tie the laces.

I stood where I was, tuned now to the silence. Even in the depths of the country with minimal light pollution, I realized the dark wasn't absolute. I could see the blocks of six lighter gray squares that were the windows on three sides. I glanced back at the bed, empty white sheets advertising my departure. Hastily, I arranged the pillows to form a plump body shape, which I covered with my blankets. This always fooled the bad guys. I eased over to the door, trying to pick up the scratchings of my intruder over the pounding of my heart. I felt along the door jamb. There was no security chain so once the lock was jimmied, there was nothing else between me and my night visitor. The cabin, though dark, was beginning to define itself. I surveyed the details in memory, looking for a weapon somewhere among the homely furnishings. Bed, chair, soap, table, shower curtain. On my side of the door, I kept my fingers on the thumb lock to prevent its turning. Maybe the guy would assume his skills were rusty or the lock was stiff. On the other side of the door, I could hear a faint chunking across wood chips as my visitor retreated in search of some other means of ingress. I tiptoed to the table and picked up a wooden chair. I returned to the door and eased the top rail under the knob, jamming the legs against the floor. It wouldn't hold for long, but it might slow him down. I took a brief moment to bend down and tie my shoes, unwilling to risk the sound of my laces clicking across the expanse of bare wooden floor. I could hear faint sounds outside as the intruder patiently circled the cabin.

Were the windows locked? I couldn't recall. I moved from window to window, feeling for the shape of the latches. All of them seemed to be secured. A slight parting of the curtains allowed me a thin slice of the exterior. I could see dense Christmas tree shapes, a series of evergreens that dotted the landscape. No traffic on the highway. No lights in neighboring cabins. To the left, I caught movement as someone disappeared around the side of the cabin toward the rear.

I crossed the room in silence, entering the darker confines of the bathroom. I felt for the shower curtain, hanging by a series of rings from a round metal rod. I let my fingers explore the brackets, which were screwed into the wall on either side of the shower stall. Carefully, I lifted the rod from the slots, sliding the curtain off, ring by ring. Once in hand, I realized the rod was useless, too light, too easily bent. I needed a weapon, but what did I have? I glanced at the frosted glass of the bathroom window, which appeared infinitesimally paler than the dark of the wall surrounding it. Framed in the center was the intruder's head and shoulders. He cupped his hands to the glass to afford himself a better look. It must have been frustrating to discover the dark was too dense to penetrate. I stood without moving though I could see his movements outside. A snippet of sound, perhaps the faint scrape of a clawhammer being eased into the crack between the frame and the glass.

Feverishly, I reviewed the items in the cabin, hoping to remember something I could use as a weapon. Toilet paper, rug, clothes hangers, ironing board. Iron. I set the curtain rod aside, taking care not to make a sound. I moved to the closet, feeling through the dark until my fingers encountered the ironing board. I raised up on tiptoe and lifted the iron from the shelf above, shielding the contours with my hand so as to avoid banging into anything. I searched for the end of the plug, holding the prongs while I unwrapped the cord. Blindly, I felt for the outlet near the sink, inserted the prongs, and slid the heat lever on the iron as far to the right as it would go. I set the iron upright on the counter. I glanced back at the window. The head-and-shoulders silhouette was no longer visible.

I eased my way across the room to the door, where I leaned closer and pressed my ear to the lock, trying not to disturb the chair. I could hear the key pick slide in again. I could hear the tiny torque wrench join its mate as the two rods of metal crept across the tumblers. Behind me, I could hear a ticking from the bathroom as the iron picked up heat. I'd rammed the setting up to LINEN, a fabric known to wrinkle more easily than human flesh. I longed to feel the weight of the iron in my hand, but I didn't dare yank the plug from the socket just yet. I could feel pain in my chest where the rubbery muscle of my heart slapped the wooden pales of my rib cage. I'd picked many a lock myself and I was well acquainted with the patience required for the task. I'd never known anyone who could use a lock pick wearing gloves, so the chances were he was using his bare hands. From the depths of the lock, I fancied I could hear the pick ease across the tumblers and lift them one by one.

I placed my right hand lightly on the knob. I could feel it turn under my fingers. With the chair still in place, I did a quick tiptoe dance across the room to the bath. I could feel heat radiating from the iron as I pulled the plug from the socket. I wrapped my fingers around the handle and returned to the door, taking up my vigil. My night visitor was now in the process of easing the door open, probably fearful of creaks that might alert me to his presence. I stared at the doorframe, willing him to appear. He pushed. The chair began to inch forward. As stealthily as a spider, his fingers crept around the frame. I lunged, iron extended. I thought my timing was good, but he was quicker than I expected. I made contact, but not before he'd kicked the door in. The chair catapulted past me. I could smell the harsh chemical scent of scorched wool. I pressed the iron into him again and sensed burning flesh this time. He uttered a harsh expletive—not a word but a yelp.

At the same time, he swung and his fist caught me in the face. I staggered backward, off balance. The iron flew out of my hand and clattered heavily across the floor. He was fast. Before I knew what was happening, he'd kicked my feet out from under me. I went down. He had my arm racked up behind me, his knee planted squarely in the middle of my back. His weight made breathing problematic and I knew within minutes I'd black out if he didn't ease up. I couldn't fill my lungs with sufficient air to make a sound. Any movement was excruciating. I could smell stress sweat, but I wasn't sure if it was his or mine.

Now you see? This is precisely the kind of moment I was talking about. There I was, face down on Cecilia Boden's bad braided rug, immobilized by a fellow threatening serious bodily harm. Had I foreseen this sorry development the day I left Carson City, I'd have done something else . . . dumped the rental car and flown home, bypassing the notion of employment in Nota Lake. But how was I to know?

Meanwhile, the thug and I were at a temporary impasse while he decided what kind of punishment to inflict. This guy was going to hurt me, there was no doubt of that. He hadn't expected resistance and he was pissed off that I'd put up even so puny a fight as I had. He was supercharged, juiced up on rage, his breathing labored and hoarse. I tried to relax and, at the same time, steel myself for the inevitable. I waited for a bash on the back of the head. I prayed that a pocketknife or semiautomatic didn't appear on his list of preferred weapons. If he yanked my head back, he could slit my throat with one quick swipe of a blade. Time hung suspended in a manner that was almost liberating.

I'm not a big fan of torture. I've always understood that in situations of extreme duress—offered the choice between, say, a hot poker in the eyeball or betraying a friend—I'd rat out my pal. This is one more reason to keep others at a distance, since I clearly can't be trusted to keep a confidence. Under the current circumstances, I surely would have begged for mercy if I'd been capable of speech.

Hostility energizes. Once unleashed, anger is addicting and the high, while bitter, is irresistible. He half-lifted himself away from me and slammed his knee into my rib cage, knocking the breath out of me. He grabbed the index finger of my right hand and in one swift motion snapped it sideways, dislocating the finger at what I later learned was the proximal interphalangeal joint. The sound was like the hollow pop of a raw carrot being snapped in two. I heard myself emit a note of anguish, high pitched and ragged as he reached for the next finger and popped the knuckle sideways in its socket. I could sense that both fingers protruded now in an unnatural relationship to the rest of my hand. He delivered a kick and then I heard his heavy breathing as he stood staring down at me. I closed my eyes, fearful of provoking further attack.

I kept my face down against the rug, sucking in the odor of damp cotton fiber saturated with soot, feeling absurdly grateful when he didn't kick me again. He crossed the cabin in haste. I heard the door bang shut behind him and then the sound of his muffled footsteps as they faded away. In due course, at a distance, I heard a car engine start. I was alive. I was hurt. Time to move, I thought.

I rolled over on my back, cradling my right arm. I could feel my hands tremble and I was making noises in my throat. I'd broken out in a sweat, so much heat coursing through my body that I thought I'd throw up. At the same time, I began to shake. A stress-induced personality had separated herself from the rest of me and hovered in the air so that she could comment on the situation without having to participate in my pain and humiliation.

You really should get help, she suggested. *The injuries won't kill you, but the shock well could. Remember the symptoms? Pulse and breathing become faster. Blood pressure drops. Weakness, lethargy, a little clamminess? Does that ring a bell here?*

I was laboring to breathe, struggling to keep my wits about me while my vision brightened and narrowed. It had been a long time since I'd been hurt and I'd nearly forgotten how it felt to be consumed by suffering. I knew he could have killed me, so I should have been happy this was the worst he'd conjured up. What exhilaration he must have felt. I had been brought low and my attempts at self-defense seemed pathetic in retrospect.

I held my hand against my chest protectively while I eased onto my side and from there to my knees. I pushed upward with my left elbow, supporting myself clumsily as I struggled to my feet. I was mewing like a kitten. Tears stung my eyes. I felt abased by the ease with which I'd been felled. I was nothing, a worm he could have crushed underfoot. My cockiness had left me and now belonged to him. I pictured him grinning, even laughing aloud as he sped down the highway. He would shake his fist in the air with joy, reliving my subjugation in much the same way I would in the days to come.

I turned on the overhead light and looked down at my hand. Both my index finger and my insult finger jutted out at thirty-degree angles. I really couldn't feel much, but the sight of it was sickening. I found my bag near the bed. I picked up my jacket and laid it across my shoulders like a shawl. Oddly, the cabin wasn't that disordered. The iron had been flung into the far corner of the room. The wooden chair had been knocked over and the braided rug was askew. Tidy little bun that I am, I righted the chair and flopped the rug back into place, picked the iron up and returned it to the top closet shelf, cord dangling. Now I had only myself to accommodate.

I locked the cabin with effort, using the unaccustomed left hand. I headed toward the motel office. The night was cold and a soft whirl of snow whispered against my face. I drank deeply of the cold, refreshed by the dampness in the air. Out near the road, I could see the glow of the motel vacancy sign, a red neon beacon issuing its invitation to passing motorists. There was no traffic on the highway. None of the other cabins showed any signs of life. Through the office window, I could see a table lamp aglow. I went in. I leaned against the doorframe while I knocked on Cecilia's door. Long minutes passed. Finally, the door opened a crack and Cecilia peered out.

I could hear the mounting roar of a fainting spell rising around my ears. I longed to sit down and put my head between my knees. I took a deep breath, shaking my head in hopes of clearing it.

Still squinting, she tied the sash of her pink chenille robe as she emerged. "What's this about?" she said, crossly. "What's the matter with you?"

I held up my hand. "I need help."

10

Cecilia dialed 9-1-1 and reported the break-in and the subsequent attack. The dispatcher said he'd send an ambulance, but Cecilia assured him she could get me to the hospital in the time it would take the paramedics to arrive. She threw on her sweats, a coat, and running shoes, and put me in her boat-sized Oldsmobile. To give her credit, she seemed properly concerned about my injury, patting me occasionally and saying things like, "You hang on now. You'll be fine. We're almost there. It's just down the road." She drove with exaggerated care, both hands on the steering wheel, chin lifted so she could see over the rim. Her speed never exceeded forty miles an hour and she solved the problem of which lane to drive in by keeping half the car in each.

I no longer felt pain. Some natural anesthesia had flooded through my system and I was woozy with its effect. I leaned my head back against the seat. She studied me anxiously, no doubt worried I'd barf on the hard-to-clean upholstery fabric.

"You're dead white," she said. She depressed the window control, opening the window halfway so that a wide stream of icy air whipped against my face. The highway was glossy with moisture, snow blowing across the road in diagonal lines. At this hour of the night, there was a comforting silence across the landscape. So far, the snow wasn't sticking, but I could see a powdering of white on tree trunks, an airy accumulation in the dead and weedy fields.

The hospital was long and low, a one-story structure that stretched in a straight line like some endless medical motel. The exterior was a mix of brick and stucco, with a roof of three-tab asphalt shingle. The parking area near the ambulance entrance was virtually deserted. The emergency room was empty, though the few brave souls on duty roused themselves and appeared in due course, one of them a clerk whose name tag read L. LIPPINCOTT. I was guessing *Lucille, Louise, Lillian, Lula.*

Ms. Lippincott's gaze flicked away from my bristling bouquet of digits. "How did you fall?"

"I didn't. I was assaulted," I said and then proceeded to give her an abbreviated account of the attack.

Her facial expression shifted from distaste to skepticism, as though there must be portions of the story I'd neglected to tell. Perhaps she fantasized some bizarre form of self-abuse or S&M practices too nasty to relate.

I sat in a small upholstered chair, reciting my personal data—name, home address, insurance carrier—while she entered the information into her computer. She was in her sixties, a heavy-boned woman with graying hair arranged in perfect wavelets. Her face looked like half the air had leaked out, leaving soft pouches and seams. She wore a nursy-looking pantsuit of waffle-patterned white polyester with large shoulder pads and big white buttons down the front. "Where'd Cecilia disappear to? Wasn't she the one brought you in?"

"I think she's gone off to find a rest room. She was sitting right out there," I said, indicating the waiting area. A newfound talent allowed me to point in two directions simultaneously—index and insult fingers going northwest, ring finger and pinkie steering east-northeast. I tried to avoid the sight, but it was hard to resist.

She made a photocopy of my insurance card, which she set to one side. She entered a print command and documents were generated, none of which I was able to sign with my bunged-up right hand. She made a note to that effect, indicating my acceptance of financial responsibility. She assembled a plastic bracelet bearing my name and hospital ID number and affixed that to my wrist with a device resembling a hole punch.

Chart in hand, she accompanied me through a doorway and showed me a seat in an examining room about the size of a jail cell. She stuck my chart in a slot mounted on the door before she left. "Someone'll be right with you."

The place looked like every other emergency room I'd ever been exposed to: beige speckled floor glossy with wax, making it easy to remove blood and other body fluids; acoustical tile on the ceiling, the better to dampen all the anguished cries and screams. The prevailing smell of rubbing alcohol made me think about needles and I desperately needed to lie down that instant. I set my jacket aside and crawled up on the examining table, where I lay on the crackling paper and stared at the ceiling. I wasn't doing well. I was shivering. The lights seemed unnaturally bright and the room oscillated. I laid my left arm across my eyes and tried to think about something nice, like sex.

I could hear a low conversation in the corridor and someone came in, picking up my chart from the door. "Miss Millhone?" I heard the click of a ballpoint pen and I opened my eyes.

The ER nurse was black, her name tag identifying her as V. LaMott. She had to be Rafer LaMott's wife, mother to the young woman working as a short-order cook over at the Rainbow Cafe. Was theirs the only African American family in Nota Lake? Like her daughter, V. LaMott was trim, her skin the color of tobacco. Her hair was cropped close, her face devoid of makeup. "I'm Mrs. LaMott. You've met my husband, I believe."

"We spoke briefly."

"Let's see the hand."

I held it up. Something about her mention of Rafer made me think he'd confessed to her fully about his rudeness to me. She looked like the kind of woman who'd have given him a hard time about that. I hoped.

I kept my face averted while she completed her inspection. I could feel myself tense up, but she was careful to make only gingerly contact. There was apparently no nurse's aide on duty so she checked my vital signs herself. She took my temperature with an electronic thermometer that gave nearly instant results and then she held my left arm against her body as she pumped up the blood pressure cuff and took a reading. Her hands were warm while mine felt bloodless. She made notes on my chart.

"What's the *V* stand for?" I asked.

"Victoria. You can call me Vicky if you like. We're not formal around here. Are you on any medication?"

"Birth control pills."

"Any allergies?"

"Not that I know of."

"Have you had a tetanus shot in the last ten years?"

My mind went blank. "I can't remember."

"Let's get that over with," she said.

I could feel the panic mount. "I mean, it's really not necessary. It's not a problem. I have two dislocated fingers, but the skin wasn't broken. See? No cuts, no puncture wounds. I didn't step on a nail."

"I'll be right back."

I felt my heart sink. In my weakened condition, I hadn't thought to lie. I could have told her anything about my medical history. She'd never know the difference and it was my lookout. Lockjaw, big deal. This was all too much. I'm phobic about needles, which is to say I sometimes faint at the very idea of injections and become giddy at the sight of an *S-Y-R-I-N-G-E.* I've been known to pass out when *other* people get shots. In traveling, I would never go to a country that required immunizations. Who wants to spend time in an area where smallpox and cholera still run rampant among the citizens?

What I hate most in the world are those obscene newscasts where there's sudden minicam coverage of wailing children being stabbed with hypodermics in their sweet, plump little arms. Their expressions of betrayal are enough to make you sick. I could feel the sweat breaking out on my palms. Even lying down I was worried I'd lose consciousness.

She came back in a flash, holding the you-know-what on a little plastic tray like a snack. In my only hope of control, I persuaded her to stick me in the hip instead of my upper arm, though lowering my blue jeans was a trick with one hand.

"I don't like it either," she said. "Shots scare me silly. Here we go."

Stoically, I bore the discomfort, which truly wasn't as bad as I remembered it. Maybe I was maturing. Ha ha ha, she said.

"Shit."

"Sorry. I know it stings."

"It's not that. I just remembered. My last tetanus shot was three years ago. I took a bullet in the arm and they gave me one then."

"Oh, well," she said. She inserted the syringe into a device labeled "sharps" and neatly snapped off the needle, like I might snatch it away and stick myself with it six more times for fun. Ever the professional, I took advantage of the opportunity to quiz her about the Newquists while we waited for the doctor. "I gather Rafer and Tom were good friends," I said, for openers.

"That's right."

"Did the four of you spend much time together?" The answer seemed slow in coming so I offered a prompt. "You might as well be honest. I've heard it all by now. Nobody likes Selma."

Vicky smiled. "We spent time together when we had to. There

were occasions when we couldn't avoid her so we made the best of it. Rafer didn't want to make a scene, nor did I for that matter. I swear to god, she once said to me—these are her exact words—'I'd have invited you over, but I thought you'd be more comfortable with your own kind.' I had to bite my tongue. What I wanted to say is 'I sure wouldn't want to hang out with a bunch of white trash like you.' And just to complicate matters, our daughter, Barrett, was going out with her son."

"She must have loved that."

"She could hardly object. She was always so busy acting like she wasn't prejudiced. What a joke. If it wasn't so pitiful it'd have cracked me up. The woman has no education and no intelligence to speak of. Rafer and I both graduated from U.C.L.A. He's got a degree in criminology . . . this was before he applied for the position with the sheriff's department. I've got a B.S. in nursing and an R.N. on top of that."

"Selma knew the kids were dating?"

"Oh, sure. They went steady for years. Tom was crazy about Barrett. I know he felt she was a good influence on Brant."

"Does Brant have a problem?"

"Basically, he's a good person. He was just screwed up back then, like a lot of kids that age. I don't think he ever did drugs, but he drank quite a bit and rebelled every chance he had."

"Why'd they break up?"

"You'd have to ask Barrett. I try not to mess in her business. You want my assessment, I think Brant was too needy and dependent for someone like her. He tended to be all mopey and clinging. This was years ago, of course. He was twenty, at that point. She was just out of high school and didn't seem that interested in getting serious."

Her comments were cut short when the doctor came in. Dr. Price was in his late twenties, thin and boyish, with bright blue eyes, big ears, dark auburn hair, and a pale freckled complexion. I could still see the indentation on his cheek where he'd bunched up his pillow to sleep. I pictured the entire ER staff napping on little cots somewhere. He wore surgical greens and a white lab coat, stethoscope coiled in his pocket like a pet snake. I wondered how he'd ended up at a hospital as small as this. I hoped it wasn't because he was at the bottom of his med school class. He took one look at my fingers and said, "Oh wow! Keen!" I liked his enthusiasm.

We had a chat about my assailant and the job he'd done. He studied my jaw. "He must have clipped you good," he said.

"That's right. I'd forgotten about that. How's it look?"

"Like you put eye shadow in the wrong place. Any other abrasions or contusions? That's doctor talk," he said. "Means little hurt places on your body."

"He kicked me twice in the ribs."

"Let's take a look," he said, pulling up my shirt.

My rib cage on the right side was swiftly turning purple. He listened to my lungs to make sure a rib hadn't been thrust into them on impact. He palpated my right arm, wrist, hand, and fingers, and then proceeded to deliver a quick course on joints, ligaments, tendons, and exactly what happens when someone wrenches them asunder. We trooped into the other room where a rumpled-looking technician took X rays of both my chest and my hand. I returned to the table and lay down again, feeling thoroughly air-conditioned as the room spun.

When the film had been developed, he invited me into the corridor, where he tucked the various views onto the lighted screen. Vicky joined us. We stood there, the three of us, and studied the results. I felt like a colleague called in for consultation on a troublesome case. My ribs were bruised, but not cracked, likely to be sore for days, but requiring no further medical attention. Roentgenographically speaking, the two pesky fingers were completely screwed. I could see that no bones were broken, though Dr. Price did point out two small chips he said my body would reabsorb.

I went back to the table where I reclined again with relief. My butt was still smarting from the sting of the tetanus, so I hardly noticed when the doctor, with a merry whistle, stuck me repeatedly in the joints of both fingers. I'd ceased to care by then. Whatever they did, I was too grossed out to notice. While I stared at the wall, the doctor maneuvered my digits back into their original upright position. He left the room briefly. When I finally dared to look at my hand, I saw that the injured fingers were now fat and reddened. While the fingers would now bend, the knuckles were swollen as though with sudden rheumatoid arthritis. I placed my mouth against the hot, numb flesh like a mother gauging a baby's fever with her lips.

Dr. Price returned with (1) a roll of adhesive tape, (2) a packet of gauze, and (3) a metal splint that looked like a bent Popsicle stick, for which my insurance company would ultimately be charged somewhere in the neighborhood of five hundred dollars. He taped the two fingers together and then affixed them to the ring finger with another wrapping of tape, all supported by the splint. I could sense my premiums going up. Medical insurance is only valid if the benefits are never used. Otherwise, you're rewarded with a cancellation notice or a hefty increase in rates.

I could hear another conference in the hallway and a deputy appeared outside the examining room door. He chatted with Dr. Price and then the doctor departed, leaving me alone with him. This was a fellow I hadn't seen before; a tall skinny kid with a long face, dark hair, dark ragged eyebrows that met in the middle, and shiny metal braces on his teeth. Well, I was filled with confidence.

"Ms. Millhone, I'm Deputy Carey Badger. I understand you had a problem. Can you tell me what happened?"

I said, "Sure," and went through my sad tale of woe again.

With his left hand, he jotted the information in a small spiral-bound notebook, his eyes never leaving my face. His pencil was the size you'd use on a bridge tally, small and thin, the point looking blunt. He might have been a waiter making a little memo to himself . . . tuna on wheat toast, hold the mayo. "Any idea who this fellow was?" he asked.

"Not a clue."

"What about height and weight? Can you give me an estimate?"

"I'd say close to six feet and he must have outweighed me by a good sixty pounds. I'm one eighteen, which would put him at a hundred and seventy-five or one eighty minimum."

"Anything else? Scars, moles, tattoos?"

"It was pitch black. He wore a ski mask and heavy clothing so I didn't see much of anything. Night before, the same guy followed me out of Tiny's parking lot. I couldn't swear on a stack of Bibles, but I can't believe two different fellows would come after me like that. The first time, he drove a black panel truck with no plate numbers visible. I reported it this morning to the Nota Lake Police."

"Can you tell me anything else about him?"

"He smelled strongly of sweat."

He turned the page, still writing, and then frowned at his notes. "What'd he do the first encounter? Did he accost you on that occasion?"

"He stared and did this," I said, making a little shooting gesture with my left hand. "It doesn't sound like much, but it was meant to intimidate me and it did."

"He didn't talk to you either time?"

"Not a word."

"What about the vehicle he was driving? Was it the same one last night?"

"I didn't see. He must have parked out by the road and walked back to the cabin where I was staying."

"So he must have known which one it was, unless this was random breaking and entering."

I looked at him with interest. "That's true. I hadn't thought of that. I wonder how he found out which cabin I was in. I woke while he was picking the lock. When that didn't work, he tried the window in the bathroom. After that, he went to work on the door again."

"And after he dislocated your fingers, he took off?"

"Correct. I could hear a car start in the distance, but I have no idea what kind it was. At that point I was focused on pulling myself together to get help."

Deputy Badger made an additional note for himself and then tucked his little book in his pocket with the pencil in the coil of wire. "I guess that's it then. I'll pass this information on to the deputy works days."

There was conversation outside the door and Rafer LaMott appeared. He shook hands with the deputy, who soon excused himself and disappeared down the hall. I could see Rafer's wife out at the nurse's station, her body language suggesting that she was well aware of his presence. I wondered if she'd called him herself. He looked freshly showered and shaved, natty in a pair of tan corduroy trousers and a soft red cashmere vest with a dress shirt under it. His expression was neutral. He put his hands in his pockets, leaning casually against the wall. He looked like an ad in a menswear catalog. "Cecilia was tired so I told her to go on home. As soon as you're finished here, I'll take you anywhere you want."

11

It was six A.M. by the time Rafer finally put me in the front seat of his car. The offer of a ride was as close to an apology as I was likely to get. No doubt his true motivation was to quiz me about the current state of my investigation, but I really didn't care. The sun was not officially up and the early-morning air was curiously gloomy. I was at a loss where to have him deliver me. I couldn't bear the idea of being in the cabin by myself. I didn't think Selma would be up at this hour and I couldn't believe Cecilia would welcome my further company. As if reading my mind, Rafer said, "Where to?"

"I guess you better drop me at the Rainbow. I can hang out there until I figure out what to do next."

"I'd like to check the cabin. I've got a print tech from Independence coming up at seven, as soon as he gets in. Maybe we'll get lucky and find out your intruder left his prints."

"Perform an exorcism while you're at it. I don't expect a good night's sleep until I'm out of there."

He glanced over at me. "You thinking about going home?"

"I've been thinking about that ever since I arrived."

He was silent for a while, turning his attention to the road. The town was beginning to come to life. Cars passed us, headlights almost unnecessary as the sky began to alter in gradients from steel gray to dove. At one of the intersections, a restaurant called Elmo's was ablaze with light, patrons visible through the windows. I could see heads bent over breakfast plates. A waitress moved from table to table with a coffeepot in each hand, offering refills. Out on the sidewalk, two women in sweatsuits were absorbed in conversation as they jogged. They arrived at the corner as the light turned red and began to run in place. We moved forward again.

Rafer finally spoke up. "Last time I had anything to do with a P.I.? Guy claimed to be working a missing-persons case. I went to quite a bit of trouble to follow up, taking two days of my time to track his fellow down in another state. Turns out the P.I. lied to me. He was trying to collect on a bad debt. I was pissed."

"I don't blame you," I said. I began to rack my brain, trying to remember if I'd lied to him myself.

"You have a theory about last night's attack?"

"I'm assuming this was the same guy who followed me from Tiny's," I said.

His gaze returned to the road. "I heard about that. Corbet made sure we got a copy of the report. I passed it on to the CHP so they could keep an eye out as well. Anything missing?"

"I didn't even bother to look. I was too busy taking care of this," I said, lifting my hand. "Anyway, I doubt the motive was theft. I think the point was to discourage my investigation."

"Why?"

"You tell me. I guess he feels protective of Tom Newquist. That's the best I can do."

"I'm not convinced this has anything to do with Tom."

"And I can't prove it does so where does that leave us?"

"You could be mistaken, you know. You're single and you're attractive. That makes you a natural target—"

"For what? This wasn't sexually motivated. It was plain old assault and battery. The guy wanted to cause me great bodily harm."

"What else?"

"What else, what? There's nothing else," I said. "Here's a question for you: Where's Tom's notebook? It's missing. No one's seen it since he died."

He shot me a look and then shook his head blankly. I could see him casting back in his mind. "I'm trying to remember when I last saw it. He usually kept it somewhere close, but I know it's not in his desk drawers because we cleaned those out."

"The CHP officer doesn't remember seeing it in the truck. It didn't occur to him to look for it, but it does seem odd. I know it must irritate you that I'm pursuing the point—"

"Look. I was out of line on that. I get huffy about Selma. It has nothing to do with you."

I could feel the distance between us easing. There's nothing as disarming as a concession of that sort. "It may not be relevant in any event," I said. "What's the procedure on reports? Wouldn't most of his notes have already been written up and submitted?"

"Possibly. He kept his own copies of every report in the particular file he was working. The originals are sent to the records section down in Independence. Reports are submitted at regular intervals. Newer officers seem to be better organized about this stuff. Old timers like me and Tom tend to do things when we get around to it."

"Would there be any way to work backward by checking to see what reports were missing?"

"I don't know how you'd do that and it wouldn't tell you much. You'd have no way of knowing where he'd been and who he'd talked to, let alone the content of conversations. It's not uncommon to have a file with a couple of reports missing . . . especially if he was working a case and hadn't typed up his notes yet. Besides, all notes wouldn't be incorporated, just the information he judged relevant. You might scribble down a lot of stuff that wouldn't amount to a hill of beans when you get right down to it."

"Suppose he was developing information on a case of his?"

"He probably was. It also might have been a case someone else had worked that he was reworking for some reason."

"Such as?"

Rafer shrugged. "He might have picked up a new lead. Occasionally, there's a case in the works where the information is sensitive . . . might be an informant in another state, or something to do with Internal Affairs."

"My point exactly. I mean, what if Tom was privy to something he didn't know how to handle."

"He'd have told me. We talked about everything."

"Suppose it concerned you?"

He made a little move that indicated agitation. "Let's get off this, okay? I'm not saying we can't talk about this further, but let me think about it some."

"One more thing. And don't get all testy on me. Just tell me what you think. Is there any possibility Tom might have been involved with another woman."

"No."

I laughed. "Try to keep your answer to twenty-five words or less," I said. "Why not?"

"He was a deeply moral man."

"Well, couldn't that explain his brooding? A man with no conscience wouldn't be at war with himself."

"Objection, your honor. Purely speculative."

"But Rafer, something was troubling him. Selma's not the only one who saw that. I don't know if it was personal or professional, but from what I gather, he was truly distressed."

We pulled into the parking area between the Rainbow Cafe and the Nota Lake Cabins. Rafer put the car in park and then opened his door. "Come on. I'll buy you breakfast. I got a daughter works here."

I struggled with the handle and then gave up. I sat while he walked around the car and opened the door on my side. He even offered a helping hand as I emerged. "Thanks. I can see this is going to be a pain."

"It'll be good for you," he said. "Force you to deal with your dependency issues."

"I don't have dependency issues," I said stoutly.

Rafer smiled in response.

He held the cafe door open and I entered ahead of him. The place was bustling, all men, clearly the stopping-off place of early risers, ranchers, cops, and laborers on their way to work. The interior was, as usual, overheated, and smelled of coffee, bacon, sausages, maple syrup, and cigarettes. The brown-haired waitress, Nancy, was taking an order from a table full of fellows in overalls while Barrett, behind the counter, was focused on a griddle spread with pancakes and omelettes in the making. Rafer took the lead and found us an empty booth. As we passed the intervening tables, I could see we were attracting any number of stares. I was guessing the jungle drums had already spread the news about my assailant.

"How'd you end up in Nota Lake?" I asked, as we slid into the seats.

"I started out as a dispatcher for the L.A.P.D., working on my degree at night. Once I graduated, I applied to the academy. I was hired on at San Bernardino, eventually assigned to robbery detail, but when Barrett was born, Vicky started bugging me to leave L.A. She was working as an ER nurse at Queen of Angels, and hated the commute. Even on two salaries, we couldn't afford to buy a house in any of the areas we liked. I heard about an opening in the sheriff's department up here. Vick and I drove up one weekend and fell in love with the place. That's been twenty-three years. Tom was already here. He grew up in Bakersfield."

Two tables over, I caught sight of Macon with his gaze fixed on me. He leaned forward, making some comment. The man with him made one of those casual turns, pretending to glance idly around the room when he was really taking aim at me. I picked up a menu, pretending I didn't notice him pretending not to notice me. Margaret's husband, Hatch.

"You know what you want?" Rafer asked. "I do the works myself. I keep trying to reform, but I can't resist."

"I'm with you," I said. "Your daughter's name is Barrett?"

"That was Vick's idea. I'm not sure where she got it, but it seems to fit. The job is temporary, by the way. She's applied to med school. She wants to be a shrink. This allows her to live at home and save her money 'til she goes."

"Where'd she do her undergraduate work? U.C.L.A.?"

"Where else?" he said, smiling. "What about you?"

"I hated school," I said. "I made it through high school by the hair of my chinny-chin-chin, but that's as far as I went. Well, I guess I did three semesters of junior college, but I hated that, too."

"How so? You seem smart."

"I'm too rebellious," I said. "I graduated from police academy, but that was more like boot camp than academia."

"You're a cop?"

"I was. I was rebellious about that, too."

Nancy appeared with a coffeepot in hand. She was in her forties, hair pulled back in a smooth chignon over which she wore a net. She had large brown eyes, a beauty mark high on her right cheek, and the sort of body men seem to have trouble keeping their hands off. She wore a T-shirt, generously cut slacks, and brown oxfords with an inch-thick crepe sole. "You're out early," she remarked to Rafer. We both pushed our mugs in her direction and she filled them.

"You met Kinsey?"

"Not formally, but I know who she is. I'm Nancy. You talked to Alice about me."

"How are you," I said. "I'd shake hands if I could."

"Yeah, I heard about that. Cecilia stopped by when we were opening the place. She says you took quite a hit. I can see your jaw turning blue."

I put a hand to the place. "I keep forgetting about that. It must look terrific."

"Gives you character," she said. She glanced at Rafer. "What's for breakfast?"

He looked back at the menu. "Well, let's see. I'm trying to keep my cholesterol up so I think I'll have the blueberry pancakes, sausage, couple of scrambled eggs, and coffee."

"Make that two," I said.

"You want orange juice?"

"Oh sure. What the heck?" he said.

"Back in a flash," she said.

I saw Rafer's gaze flicker to the window. "Excuse me. I see Alex. I'll take him on back to the cabin and get him started."

I had to use two hands to hold my coffee mug, given that three fingers on my right hand were taped together like an oven mitt. The doctor had told me I could remove the tape after a day or two, as long as it felt comfortable. He'd given me four painkillers, neatly sealed in a small white envelope. I remembered a similar envelope from my childhood churchgoing days, when my nickel or dime offering was placed in the collection plate. The plate itself was wood, passed from hand to hand until it reached an usher at the end of the pew. I'd been kicked out of any number of Sunday school classes for reasons I've repressed, but my aunt Gin, feeling huffy in my behalf, decided I was entitled to go to proper church services. I suppose her intention was to expose me to spiritual admonition. Mostly what I learned was how hard it is to do an accurate visual count of organ pipes.

I glanced out the window, watching Rafer cross the parking pad, heading toward the cabin in the company of a young man carrying a black case, like a doctor's bag. I took a physical inventory, noting the sore ribs on my right side. I didn't think my jaw was swollen, but it was clearly bruised. No teeth missing or loose. I could feel a knot on my butt the size of a silver dollar and I knew from experience it would itch like a son of a bitch for weeks on end.

"Miss Millhone, can I talk to you?"

I looked up. James Tennyson was standing at the table in his tan CHP uniform, complete with all its creaking paraphernalia: nightstick, flashlight, keys, holster, gun, bullets.

"Sure. Have a seat."

He put a hand against his holster, securing his gun as he slid into the booth. I thought he was ill at ease, but I didn't know him well enough to be certain. "I saw Rafer step away from the table and figured you might have a few minutes."

"This is fine. Nice to see you. You got your flashlight back?"

"Yes ma'am. I appreciate your returning it. Jo found it inside the storm door when she went out to get the paper." He pointed at my hand. "I just heard about the fellow coming after you last night. You all right?"

"More or less."

"He meant business."

"I'll survive," I said.

"The reason I came over . . . I didn't even think about this until yesterday. The night Tom died? I was cruising along 395 when I spotted his truck . . . you know, with the hazard lights on. At first, I didn't realize it was him because he was still some distance away, but I intended to stop and see if there was anything I could do. Anyway, there was a woman walking along the road, heading toward town."

"A woman?"

"Yes ma'am. I'm almost sure."

"And she was facing you?"

"That's right, but she veered off about then. This was shortly before I passed so I didn't get a good look at her, just a fleeting impression. She was bundled up pretty good. If it hadn't been for Tom and trying to get help for him, I'd have cruised back in her direction in case she needed help."

"Is it unusual to see someone walking out there?"

"Yes ma'am. At least, I thought it was at the time. This was miles from anywhere and there's very little in the way of houses out there, except for one subdivision. She could have been out for a jog, but she didn't seem dressed for that, and in the dark? I doubt it. Anyway, it struck me as odd. I guess in my mind I was thinking she might have got mad at her boyfriend and taken off on foot. I didn't see another vehicle so I don't think it was a flat tire or anything like that."

"And this was no one you knew?"

"I really couldn't say. It was nobody I recognized under the circumstances. Like I said, I didn't think much about it and later it slipped my mind entirely. I don't even know what made me think of it. Just the fact that you asked."

I thought about it for a moment. "How far away was she from the truck when you saw her?"

"It couldn't have been a quarter of a mile because I could see Tom's hazard lights blinking in the distance."

"Do you think she was *with* him?"

"I suppose it's possible," he said. "If he was having chest pains, she might have been on her way to find help."

"Why not flag you down?"

"Beats me. I don't know what to make of it," he said.

"I'd like to see the spot where Tom's truck was parked," I said. "Could you maybe take me out there later?"

"Sure, I'd be happy to, but the place isn't hard to find. It's maybe a mile in that direction. You look for a couple big boulders near a pine with the top sheared off. Thing was struck by lightning in a big storm last year. Just keep an eye out. You can't miss it. It's on the right-hand side."

"Thanks."

He glanced toward one of the tables near the front of the cafe. "My breakfast is here. You have any more questions, give me a call."

I watched him move away. Hatch and Macon stood together near the cash register, waiting for Nancy to take their money. My conversation with James hadn't gone unnoticed, though both men made a big display of their disinterest. Rafer returned, entering the cafe without the technician, whom I assumed was busy at the cabin with his little brushes and powders. Rafer eased into the seat, saying, "Sorry about that. I told him we'd join him as soon as we finished here."

When we reached the cabin after breakfast, the door was standing open. I could see smudges of powder along the outside edges of the sills. Rafer introduced me to the fingerprint technician, who rolled a set of my prints for elimination purposes. Later, he'd ink a set of Cecilia's prints, along with the prints of any cleaning or maintenance workers. He could have saved himself the trouble. The cabin yielded nothing in the way of evidence: no useful prints on the window glass, nothing on the hardware, no footprints in the damp earth leading to or from the cabin.

The interior seemed dank, the bed still lumpy with the pillows I'd tucked under the pile of blankets. The place was drab. It was cold. The digital clock was blinking, which meant there'd been another power failure. The adrenaline had seeped slowly out of me like gray water down a clogged drain. I felt like crap. A rivulet of revulsion trickled over me and I was embarrassed anew at the inadequacies of my attempt to defend myself. Anxiety whispered at the base of my spine, a feathery reminder of how vulnerable I was. A memory burbled up. I was five years old again, bruised and bloodied after the wreck that killed my parents. I'd forgotten the physical pain because the wrenching emotional loss had always taken precedence.

While Rafer and the tech conferred outside, talking in low tones, I hauled out my duffel and began to pack my things. I went into the bathroom, gathered up my toiletries, and tossed them in the bottom of the bag. I didn't hear Rafer come in, but I was suddenly aware of him standing in the doorway. "You're taking off?" he asked.

"I'd be crazy to stay here."

"I agree with you on that, but I didn't think you were finished with your investigation."

"That remains to be seen."

His gaze rested on me with concern. "You want to talk?"

I looked up at him. "About what? This is a simple job to me, not some moral imperative. I'm getting paid for a piece of work. I guess I have my limits on that score."

"You're going to quit?"

"I didn't say that. I'll talk to Selma first and then we'll see where we go from here."

"Look, I can see you're upset. I'd offer you protection, but I don't have a deputy to spare. We operate on a shoestring—"

"I appreciate the sentiment. I'll let you know what I decide."

"It wouldn't hurt to have help. You know anybody who could pitch in on personal security?"

"Oh, please. Absolutely not. I wouldn't do that. This is strictly my problem and I'll handle it," I said. "Trust me, I'm not being pigheaded or proud. I hired a bodyguard once before, but this is different."

"How so?"

"If that guy meant to kill me, he'd have done it last night."

"Listen, I've been beat up in my day and I know what it can do to you. Screws your head up. You lose your confidence. It's like riding a horse—"

"No, it's not! I've been beaten up before—" I raised a hand, stopping myself with a shake of my head. "Sorry. I didn't mean to snap at you. I know you mean well, but this is mine to deal with. I'm fine. I just don't want to spend another minute in this godforsaken place."

"Well," he said, infusing the single syllable with skepticism. He paused, silent, hands in his pockets, rocking back on his heels. I zipped the duffel, picked up my jacket and my handbag, looking around the cabin. The table was still littered with my papers and I'd forgotten about the Smith-Corona, still sitting in its place with the lid half closed. I snapped the cover into place and stuffed papers in a manila envelope that I shoved into an outer pocket of the duffel.

Using my left hand, I lifted the typewriter case. "Thanks for the ride and thanks for breakfast."

"I have to get on in to work, but you let me know if there's anything I can do to help."

"You can carry this," I said, passing him the typewriter. He did me one better, carrying both the duffel and the Smith-Corona as he escorted me to the car. I waited until he'd pulled away and then I headed for the office and stuck my head in the door. There was no sign of Cecilia. The usual table lamp was still on, but her door was shut and I imagined her catching up on the sleep she'd lost taking me to the emergency room. I got into my car and pulled out of the parking lot, turning left onto 395.

I kept an eye on the odometer, clocking off a mile, and then began to look for the spot where Tom's truck had been parked the night he died. As Tennyson indicated, it wasn't hard to find. Two massive boulders and a towering pine tree with the top missing. I could see the raw white inner wood where the lightning had slashed away at the trunk.

I eased over onto the berm and parked. I got out of the car, draping my heavy leather jacket across my shoulders. There was no traffic at this hour and the morning air was silent. The sky was massed with dark gray, the mountains obscured by mist. Snow had begun to fall; big lacy flakes that settled on my face like a series of kisses. For a moment, I leaned my head back and let the snow touch my tongue.

There was, of course, no remaining trace of vehicles having been parked here six weeks before. If the truck, Tennyson's patrol car, and the ambulance had chewed up the soil and gravel along the shoulder, nature had come afterward and smoothed away any suggestion of events. I did a grid search, my gaze fixed on the barren ground as I walked a linear pattern. I imagined Tom in his pickup, the pain like a knife wedged between his shoulder blades. Nausea, clamminess, the chill sweat of Death forcing him to concentrate. For the time being, I set aside the image of the woman walking down the road. For all I knew, she was a figment of James Tennyson's imagination, some piece of misdirection designed to throw me off. In any investigation, you have to be careful about accepting information without a touch of skepticism. I wasn't sure of his motivation. Maybe, as implied, he was just a genuinely helpful guy who took his job seriously and wanted to apprise me of his recollection. What interested me here was the possibility that Tom had dropped his notebook out the window, or that he'd somehow destroyed the contents in the final moments of his life.

I covered every inch of ground within a radius of a hundred feet. There was no notebook, no pages fluttering in the breeze, no confetti of torn paper, no nook or cranny into which folded notes might have been secreted. I kicked over rocks and dead leaves, set aside fallen branches, and dug into crusty patches of snow. It was hard to believe Tom had dragged himself out here to take care of such business. I was operating on the assumption that his field notes were sensitive and that he'd made some effort to secure the confidentiality of the contents. Then again, perhaps not. The notes might not have been relevant.

I returned to my car and turned the key in the ignition, not without struggle. The tape on my right hand made everything slightly awkward and I suspected that the compensatory effort over the next couple of days was going to wear me down. While the injury wasn't major, it was annoying and inconvenient, a constant reminder that I'd suffered at someone's hands. I did a U-turn onto the highway and headed back to Selma's. By ten A.M., I was on the road for home.

12

Shortly after leaving Nota Lake, I'd thought I caught a glimpse of a county sheriff's cruiser keeping me company from half a mile back. The car was too far away to identify the driver, but the effect was to make me feel I was being ushered across the county line. I kept my eye on the rearview mirror, but the black-and-white maintained a discreet distance. When we reached the junction of 395 and 168, a road sign indicated that it was five miles to Whirly Township, seven miles to Rudd. The patrol car turned off. Whether the escort was deliberate or coincidental, I couldn't be sure. Nor could I determine whether the intention was benign or belligerent. Earlene's husband, Wayne, was the deputy who worked in Whirly Township, so maybe it was only him on his way to work.

After that, the desert landscape sped by in a monotonous repetition of scrub-covered low hills, and I spent the rest of the journey in a haze of road-induced hypnosis. The intervening towns were few—

Big Pine, Independence, Lone Pine, Cartago, Olancha—unexpected small enclaves that consisted primarily of gas stations, wooden cottages, coffee shops, perhaps a pizza restaurant or a Frosty Freeze, sometimes still boarded over for the winter. In most towns, there seemed to be more buildings abandoned than were currently in use. The structures were low wood fronts with a Western or Victorian feel to them. In some areas, the commercial businesses seemed to be devoted almost entirely to propane sales and service. An occasional feed store would be tucked in among the cottonwoods and pines. I passed one of those plain motel-style brown-and-yellow churches that made you suspect it would be depressing to believe whatever they believed.

Between townships, the empty stretches of wilderness picked up. The air felt clear, warming as the road descended from the higher elevations. The snow had disappeared, soft flakes turning into an even softer rain. What should have been a clear, unobstructed view was subdivided by the march of power lines, telephone poles, and oil derricks—the cost of doing business in an otherwise pristine countryside. Out of the raw hills to my left I could see the occasional cinder cone and the dark craggy outcroppings of lava from ancient volcanic activity. Rocks dotted the landscape: green, red, brown, and cream. The area was undercut by two major fault lines—the San Andreas and the Garlock—that in 1872 had generated one of the largest earthquakes in California history.

Gradually, I let my thoughts drift back to events I'd left behind. I'd spent an hour at Selma's before I'd departed Nota Lake. So far, given my four days' work, I'd earned a thousand dollars of the fifteen hundred she'd paid me in advance. That meant that I would owe *her* money if I decided to quit . . . which I confess had crossed my mind. My medical insurance would cover the expenses incurred in behalf of my bunged-up hand. She'd been properly upset by what had happened and we'd gone through the predictable litany of horror and remorse. "I feel sick. This is my fault. I got you into this," she'd said.

"Don't be silly, Selma. It isn't *your* fault. If nothing else it gives credence to your hunch about Tom's 'secret,' if you want to call it that."

"But I never dreamed it'd be dangerous."

"Life is dangerous," I said. I was feeling oddly impatient, ready to move on to the job at hand. "Look, we can sit here and commiserate, but I'd much prefer to use the time constructively. I've got a big pile of phone bills. Let's sit down together and see how many numbers you recognize. Any that seem unfamiliar, I can check from Santa Teresa."

Which is what we'd done, eliminating slightly more than three-quarters of the calls listed for the past ten months. Many were Selma's, related to her church work, charity events, and assorted friendships outside the 619 area code. Some of the remaining numbers she'd recognized as business calls, a fact confirmed by judicious use of Tom's Rolodex. I'd placed the entire file of last year's phone bills in my duffel and then I'd gone down to the basement to take a look at the storage boxes I'd seen previously. There, in the dry, overheated space that smelled of ticking furnace and hot paper, a curious order prevailed.

Despite the fact that both Tom's desk and his den upstairs were an ungodly mess, Tom Newquist was systematic, at least where work was concerned. On a shelf to my left were a series of cardboard boxes where he'd placed bundles of field notes going back twenty-five years, including his days at the academy. Once a notebook had been filled, his method was to remove the six-hole lined pages, apply a wrapper showing the inclusive dates, and then secure them with a rubber band. Many times several bundles of notes pertained to the same case and those tended to be packed in separate manila envelopes, again labeled and dated. I could walk my fingers back through his investigations, year after year, without gaps or interruptions. Occasionally, on the outside of an envelope he'd penned a note indicating that a call or teletype had come through regarding the particulars of a case. He would then type an update and include a copy with his notes, indicating the agency making the call, the nature of the inquiry, and the details of his response. He was clearly prepared to substantiate his findings with court testimony where required, on every investigation he'd done since he'd been in Nota Lake. The last of the bundled notes were dated the previous April. Missing were notes from May and June of last year until the time of his death. I had to assume the missing notebook covered the previous ten months. There was no other gap in his records of that magnitude.

I went back upstairs, through the kitchen, and into the garage, where I searched the truck again—more thoroughly than I had the first time around. I even eased onto one shoulder so I could shine a flashlight up under the seats, thinking Tom might have secured his notebook in the springs. There was no sign of it, so essentially I was back to square one. My only consolation was knowing I'd left no stone unturned—as far as I could tell. Clearly, I'd overlooked *something* or I'd have his notes in hand.

The rain increased as I drove south. At Rosamond, I found a McDonald's and stopped to use the rest room. I picked up a big cola, a large order of fries, and a QP with cheese. I downed a painkiller while I was at it. Twelve minutes later, I was on the road again. The closer I came to Los Angeles, the more my spirits lifted. I hadn't even realized how depressed I was until my mood began to improve. The rain became my companion, the windshield wipers keeping a steady rhythm as the highway sizzled under my tires. I turned on the radio and let the drone of bad music fill the car.

When I reached Highway 5, I turned north as far as the junction with Highway 126, where I cut west again through Fillmore and Santa Paula. Here the landscape was made up of citrus and avocado groves, the roadway populated with produce stands, beyond which tracts of houses stretched out as far as the eye could see. Route 126 spilled into 101 and I nearly whimpered aloud at the sight of the Pacific. I rolled the window down and tilted my head sideways, letting raindrops blow on my face. The scent of the ocean was dense and sweet. The surf made its relentless approach and retreat, soft pounding at the shoreline, where occasional sea birds race-walked along the hard-packed sand. The water was silken, endless reams of gray taffeta–churning lace at the edge. I'm not fond of mountains, in part because I have so little interest in winter sports, especially those requiring costly equipment. I avoid activities associated with speed, cold, and heights, and any that involve the danger of falling down and breaking significant body parts. As fun as it all sounds, it's never appealed to me. The ocean is another matter, and while I can spend brief periods in land-locked locations, I'm never as happy as I am when close to deep water. Please understand, I don't go *in* the water, because there are all manner of biting, stinging, tentacled, pincered, slimy things down there, but I like to *look* at the water and spend time in its immense, ever-changing presence. For one thing, I find it therapeutic to consider all the creatures not devouring me at any given moment.

Thus cheered, I powered through the final few miles into Santa Teresa. I took the Cabana off-ramp and turned left, passing the bird refuge on my right and shortly thereafter, the volleyball courts on the sand at East Beach. By that time, I'd been on the road for five hours, so focused on home that my foot felt as if it was welded to the accelerator. I was exhausted. My neck was stiff. My mouth tasted like hot metal. My bruised fingers were deadened by drugs yet somehow managed to throb with pain. Also, my butt hurt along with everything else.

My neighborhood looked the same, a short residential street a block from the beach: palms, tall pines, wire fences, crooked sidewalks where tree roots had buckled the concrete. Most houses were stucco with aging red-tile roofs. An occasional condominium appeared between single-family dwellings. I found a parking spot across the street from my apartment, once a single-car garage, now a two-story hideaway attached by a sunporch to the house where my landlord lives. This month marked the fifth anniversary of my tenancy and I treasure the space I've come to think of as mine.

It took me two trips to unload the rental car, passing in and out of

Henry's squeaking gate. I made a pile on the small covered porch, unlocked the front door, left the typewriter by the desk, went back for my duffel, and hauled it up the spiral stairs. I stripped off my clothes, removed the bandages from my hand, and treated myself to a long hot shower wherein I washed my hair, did a left-handed leg shave, and sang a medley of show tunes with half the lyrics consisting of *dah-dah-dah.* The luxury of being clean and warm was almost more than I could bear. I skipped my flossing for once, did a left-handed toothbrushing, and anointed myself with an inexpensive drugstore cologne that smelled like lilies of the valley. I put on a fresh turtleneck, a fresh pair of jeans, clean socks, Reeboks, and a touch of lipstick. I checked my reflection in the bathroom mirror. Nah, that looked dumb. I rubbed off the lipstick on a piece of toilet paper and pronounced myself whole. After that, all I had to do was spend approximately twenty minutes trying to get my fingers splinted and retaped. This was going to be ob-*noxious.*

I ducked out my door and splashed across the patio in the rain. Henry's garden was just coming to life again. The weather in Santa Teresa is moderate all year long, but we do enjoy a nearly indiscernible spring in which green shoots nudge through the hard ground as they do every place else. Henry had begun to clear the flower beds where his annuals and a few tomato plants would eventually go. I could smell the wet walkways, bark mulch, and the few narcissus that must have opened in the rain. It was quarter to five and the day was gloomy with approaching twilight, the light a mild gray from the rain clouds overhead.

I peered through the window in Henry's backdoor while I rapped on the glass. Lights were on and there was evidence he was in the midst of a cooking project. For many years, Henry Pitts earned his living as a commercial baker and now that he's retired, he still loves to cook. He's lean-faced, tanned, and long-legged, a gent with snowy white hair, blue eyes, a beaky nose, and all of his own teeth. At eighty-six, he's blessed with intelligence, high spirits, and prodigious energy. He came into the kitchen from the hallway carrying a stack of the small white terry cloth towels he uses when he cooks. He usually has one tucked in his belt, another resting on his shoulder, and a third that occasionally serves as an oven mitt. He was wearing a navy T-shirt and white shorts, covered by a big baker's apron that extended past his knees. He set the towels on the counter and hurried to unlock the door, his face wreathed in smiles.

"Well, Kinsey. I didn't expect you back today. Come on in. What happened to your hand?"

"Long story. In a minute, I'll give you the abbreviated version."

He stepped aside and I entered, giving him a hug as I passed. On the counter I could see a tall Mason jar of flour, a shorter jar of sugar, two sticks of butter, a tin of baking powder, a carton of eggs, and a bowl of Granny Smith apples; pie tin, rolling pin, grater.

"Something smells wonderful. What's cooking?"

Henry smiled. "A surprise for Rosie's birthday. I've got a noodle pudding in the oven. This is a Hungarian dish I hope you won't ask me to pronounce. I'm also making her a Hungarian apple pie."

"Which birthday?"

"She won't say. Last I heard, she was claiming sixty-six, but I think she's been shaving points for years. She has to be seventy. You'll be joining us, I hope."

"I wouldn't miss it," I said. "I'll have to sneak out and find a gift. What time?"

"I'm not going over 'til six. Sit, sit, sit and I'll fix a pot of tea."

He settled me in his rocking chair and put the kettle on for tea while we filled each other in on events during the weeks I'd been gone. In no particular order, we went through the usual exchange of information: the trip, Dietz's surgery, news from the home front. I laid out the job as succinctly as I could, including the nature of the investigation, the players, and the attack the night before, a process that allowed me to listen to myself. "I have a couple of leads to check. Apparently, Tom was in touch with a local sheriff's investigator, though, at this point, I'm not sure if the contact was personal or professional. The way I heard it, they had their heads bent together and the woman's manner was noticeably flirtatious. Strictly rumor, of course, but it's worth looking into."

"And if that doesn't pan out?"

"Then I'm stumped."

While I finished my tea, Henry put together the pie crust and began to peel and grate apples for the filling. I washed my cup and saucer and set them in his dish rack. "I better whiz out and find a present. Are you dressing for the party?"

"I'm wearing long pants," he said. "I may rustle up a sportscoat. You look fine as you are."

As it turned out, Rosie's entire restaurant had been given over to her birthday party. This tacky neighborhood tavern has always been my favorite. In the olden days (five years ago), it was often empty except for a couple of local drunks who showed up daily when it opened and generally had to be carried home. In the past few years, for reasons unknown, the place has become a hangout for various sports teams whose trophies now grace every available surface. Rosie, never famous for her good humor, has nonetheless tolerated this band of testosterone-intoxicated rowdies with unusual restraint. That night, the ruffians were out in full force and in the spirit of the occasion had decorated the restaurant with crepe paper streamers, helium balloons, and hand-lettered banners that read WAY TO GO ROSIE! There was a huge bouquet of flowers, a keg of bad beer, a stack of pizza boxes, and an enormous birthday cake. Cigarette smoke filled the air, lending the room the soft, hazy glow of an old tintype. The sportsers had seeded the jukebox with high-decibel hits from the 1960s and they'd pushed all the tables back so they could do the twist and the Watusi. Rosie looked on with an indulgent smile. Someone had given her a cone-shaped hat covered with glitter, a strand of elastic under her chin, and a feather sticking out the top. She wore the usual muumuu, this one hot pink with a three-inch ruffle around the low-cut neck. William looked dapper in a dark three-piece suit, white dress shirt, and a navy tie with red polka dots, but there was no sign of anyone else from the neighborhood.

Henry and I sat to one side—he in jeans and a denim sportscoat, I in jeans and my good tweed blazer—like spectators at a dance contest. I'd spent the better part of an hour at a department store downtown, finally selecting a red silk chemise I thought would tickle her fancy.

We ducked out at ten and scurried home through the rain.

I locked the door behind me and moved through the apartment, marveling at the whole of it: the porthole window in the front door, walls of polished teak and oak, cubbyholes of storage tucked into all the nooks and crannies. I had a sofa bed built into the bay window for guests, two canvas director's chairs, bookshelves, my desk. Up the spiral stairs, in addition to the closet built into one wall, I had pegs for hanging clothes, a double-bed mattress laid on a platform with drawers built into it, and a second bathroom with a sunken tub and a window looking out toward the ocean. I felt as if I were living on a houseboat, adrift on some river, snug and efficient, warm, blessed with light. I was so thrilled to be home I could hardly bear to go to bed. I crawled, naked, under a pile of quilts and listened to the rain tapping on the Plexiglas skylight. I felt absurdly possessive—my pillow, my blanket, my secret hideaway, my home.

The next thing I knew, it was six A.M. I hadn't set my alarm, but I woke automatically, reverting to habit. I tuned in to the sound of rain, bypassed the thought of jogging, and went back to sleep again. I roused myself at eight and went through my usual morning ablutions. I had breakfast, read the paper, and then set the typewriter case on the desk top. I paused, making a quick trip upstairs where I retrieved my notes from the duffel. My first chore of the morning would be to return the rental car. That done, I'd take a cab to the office, where I'd put in an appearance and catch up with the latest lawyerly gossip. I still hadn't decided whether to work from the office or home. I'd either stay where I was or bum a ride home from someone at Kingman and Ives.

In the meantime, I thought I'd get my typewriter set up and begin the painful hunt-and-peck addition to my progress report. It wasn't until I opened the typewriter case that I saw what I'd missed in the process of packing to leave Nota Lake. Someone had taken the middle two rows of typewriter keys and twisted the metal into a hopeless clot. Some of the keys had been broken off and some were simply bent sideways like my fingers. I sat down and stared with a sense of bafflement. What was going on?

13

I decided to skip the office and concentrate on running down the one or two leads I had. In my heart of hearts, I knew perfectly well the trashing of my typewriter had taken place in Nota Lake before I'd left. Nonetheless, the discovery was disconcerting and tainted my sense of security and well-being. Annoyed, I opened my bottom desk drawer and took out the Yellow Pages, flicked through to TYPEWRITERS-REPAIRING, and made calls until I found someone equipped to handle my vintage Smith-Corona. I made a note of the address and told the shop owner I'd be there within the hour.

I took out my notes and found the local numbers I'd cribbed from the surface of Tom Newquist's blotter. When I'd dialed the one number from Tom's den, the call had been picked up by an answering machine. I was operating on the assumption that the woman I'd heard was the same female sheriff's investigator Phyllis claimed she'd seen flirting with Tom. If I could have a talk with her, it might go a long way toward cleaning up my questions. I punched in the number. Once again a machine picked up and the same throaty-voiced woman told me what I could do with myself at the sound of the beep. I left my name, my home and office numbers, and a brief message indicating that I'd like to talk to her about Tom Newquist. Next, I called the Perdido Sheriff's Department, saying: "I wonder if you could help me. I'm trying to get in touch with a sheriff's investigator, a woman. I believe she's in her forties or fifties. I don't have her name, but I think she's employed by the Perdido County Sheriff's Department. Does any of this ring a bell?"

"What division?"

"That's the point. I'm not sure."

The fellow on the phone laughed. "Lady, we've got maybe half a dozen female officers fit that description. You're going to have to be more specific."

"Ah. I was afraid of that," I said. "Well, I guess I'll have to do my homework. Thanks anyway."

"You're entirely welcome."

I sat there, mentally chewing on my pencil. What to do, what to do. I dialed Phyllis Newquist's number in Nota Lake and naturally got an answering machine, into which I entrusted the following. "Hi, Phyllis. This is Kinsey. I wonder if you could give me the name of the female sheriff's investigator Tom was in touch with down here. I've got a home telephone number, but it would help if you could find out what her name is. That way, I can try her at work and maybe speed things along. Otherwise, I'm stuck waiting for this woman to call back." Again, I left both my home and office numbers and moved down my mental list.

The second number I'd picked up from Tom's blotter was for the Gramercy Hotel. I thought that one deserved my personal attention. I tucked Tom's photograph in my handbag, grabbed my jacket and an umbrella, and headed out into the rain. My fingers, though bruised and swollen, were not throbbing with pain and for that I was grateful. I used my left hand where I could, fumbling with car keys, transferring items from one hand to the other. The simplest transactions were consequently slowed since the splint on my right hand forced me to proceed by awkward degrees. I made a second trip for the typewriter, which I placed on the front seat.

I dropped off the typewriter, extracting a promise from the repair guy to get it back to me as soon as possible. I returned the rental to the agency's downtown office, completed the financial transactions, and then took a cab back to my apartment. I picked up my car, which—after a series of groans and stutters—finally coughed to life. Progress at last.

I drove into downtown Santa Teresa and left my car in a nearby public parking garage. Umbrella tilted against the rain, I walked one block over and one block down. The Gramercy Hotel was a chunky three-story structure on lower State Street, a residential establishment favored by the homeless when their monthly checks came in. The stucco building was painted the sweet green of a crème de menthe frappé and featured a covered entrance large enough to accommodate six huddled smokers seeking shelter from the rain. A marquee across the front spelled out the hotel rates.

SGL RMS $9.95 DBL RMS. $13.95 DAILY*WEEKLY*MONTHLY
RATES ALSO AVAILABLE ON REQUEST

A fellow using a plastic garbage bag as a rain cloak greeted me rheumy-eyed as he moved his feet to allow me passage into the lobby. I lowered my umbrella, trying not to stab any of those assembled for their morning libations. It seemed early for package liquor, but maybe that was fruit juice being passed in the brown paper bag.

The hotel must have been considered elegant once upon a time. The floor was green marble with a crooked path of newspapers laid end to end to soak up all the rainy footsteps that criss-crossed the lobby. In places, where the soggy papers had been picked up, I could see that the newsprint had left reverse images of the headlines and text. Six ornate pilasters divided the gloomy space into sections, each of which sported a blocky green plastic couch. To all appearances, the clientele was discouraged from spending time lounging about on the furniture as a hand-printed sign offered the following admonishments:

NO SMOKING
NO SPITTING
NO LOITERING
NO SOLICITING
NO DRINKING ON THE PREMISES
NO FIGHTING
NO PEEING IN THE PLANTERS

Which just about summed up my personal code. I approached the long front desk, located beneath an archway decorated with white plaster scrolls and ornamental vegetation. The fellow behind the marble counter was leaning forward on his elbows, clearly interested in my intentions. This felt like one more fool's errand, but it was truly the only thing I could think to do at this point.

"I'd like to talk to the manager. Is he here?"

"I guess that's me. I'm Dave Estes. And your name?"

"Kinsey Millhone." I took out my business card and passed it across to him.

He read it with serious attention to each word. He was in his thirties, a cheerful-looking fellow with an open countenance, glasses, a crooked smile, slight overbite, and a hairline that had receded to reveal a long sloping forehead like an expanse of empty seashore when the tide is out. What hair he had was a medium brown and cropped close to his head. He wore a brown jumpsuit with many zippered pockets, like an auto mechanic's. The sleeves were rolled up to reveal muscular forearms.

"What can I help you with?"

I placed the photograph of Tom Newquist on the counter in front of him. "I'm wondering if you happen to have seen this man. He's an investigator for the Nota County Sheriff's Department. His name is Tom—"

"Hold on, hold on," he cut in. He held a hand up to silence me, motioning me to wait a moment, during which time he made the kind of face that precedes a sneeze. He closed his eyes, screwed up his nose, and opened his mouth, panting. His expression cleared and he pointed at me. "Newquist. Tom Newquist."

I was astonished. "That's right. You know him?"

"Well, no, I don't know him, but he was in here."

"When was this?"

"Oh, I'd say June of last year. Probably the first week. I'd say the fifth if forced to guess."

I was so unprepared for the verification, I couldn't think what to ask next.

Estes was looking at me. "Did something happen to him?"

"He died of a heart attack a few weeks back."

"Hey, too bad. Sorry to hear that. He didn't seem that old."

"He wasn't, but I don't think he took very good care of himself. Can you tell me what brought him in here?"

"Oh, sure. He was looking for some guy who'd just been released from jail. We seem to get a lot of fellows here in that situation. Don't ask me why. Classy place like this. Word must go out that we got good rates, clean rooms, and won't tolerate a lot of nonsense."

"Do you remember the name of the man he was looking for?"

"That's an easy one to remember for other reasons, but I like to test myself anyway. Hang on." He went through the same procedure, face screwed up to show how hard he was working. He paused in his efforts. "You're probably wondering how I do this. I took a course in mnemonics, the art of improving the memory. I spend a lot of time by myself, especially at night when I'm on desk duty. Trick is you come up with these devices, you know—aids and associations—that help fix an item in the mind."

"That's great. I'm impressed."

"Reason I remember the time frame for your Newquist's visit is I started my study just about the time he came in. He was my first practice case. So the name Newquist? No problem. *New* because the fellow was new to me, right? *Quist* as in question or query. New fellow came in with a question, hence *Newquist.*"

"That's good," I said. "What about his first name?"

Estes smiled. "You told me that. I'd forgotten it myself."

"And the other guy? The one he was inquiring about?"

"What did I come up with for that? Let's see. It had something to do with dentists. Oh, yes. His last name was Toth. That's *tooth* with an *O* missing. That was a good one because the fellow had a tooth missing so it all tied together. His first name was Alfie. Dentists connect to doctors. And like at the doctor's, you say 'Ahh' when they stick that tongue depressor in your mouth? First name began with *A.* So mentally, I go through all the *A* names I can think of. Allen, Arnold, Avery, Alfie. And there you have it."

"So Tom Newquist was here on business."

"That's correct. Trouble is, he missed him. Toth'd been here two weeks, but he moved out June one, shortly before this detective of yours came in."

"Do you have any idea why he was looking for Toth?"

"Said he was developing a lead on a case he was working. I remember that because it was just like the movies. You know, Clint Eastwood comes in, flashing a badge and real serious. All I know is Newquist never had the chance to talk to him because Toth was gone by then."

"Did he leave a forwarding address?"

"Well, no, but I have his ex-wife's address, under 'nearest relative not living with you.' That's so we got someone to call if a guy trashes the room or drops dead. It's a hassle trying to figure out what to do with a dead body."

"I can imagine," I said. "Is there any way I could get the ex-wife's name and address?"

"Sure. No problem. This's not confidential information as far as I'm concerned. People check in, I tell 'em the hotel files are open to the authorities. Cops come in asking to see records. I don't insist on a subpoena. That'd be obstruction of justice, in my opinion."

"I'm sure the police appreciate your attitude, but don't the hotel guests object?"

Dave Estes shrugged. "I guess the day I get sued, we'll change the policy. You know, another fellow came in, too. Plainclothes detective. This was earlier, maybe June one. I wasn't working that day or I'd have have filed it away in the old noggin," he said with a tap to his temple. "I told Peck he better take the same course I did, but so far I haven't managed to talk him into it."

"Too bad," I said. "So who was this other detective who came in?"

"Can't help you there and that's my point. If Peck took this course, he could recall in detail. Since he didn't? No dice. The slate's blank. End of episode."

"Could I talk to Peck myself?"

"You could, but I can tell you exactly what's he going to say. He remembers this investigator came in—had a warrant and all, but Toth wasn't on the premises. In fact, he checked out later that day so maybe he was worried about the law catching up with him. Detective called back the next morning and Peck gave him the address and telephone number of Toth's ex-wife, same as I would."

"Did you tell Tom Newquist about the other detective?"

"Same way I'm telling you. I figured it must have been a cop he knew."

"What about Toth's ex? Did you tell him how to get in touch with her?"

"Sure did. The woman had a regular parade coming through the door."

"Hasn't anybody suggested you shouldn't be quite so free passing out information?"

"Lady, I'm not the guardian of public safety. Some cop comes in looking for information, I don't want to get in his way."

"What about the warrant? Was that local?"

"Can't answer that. Peck doesn't pay attention to these items the same way I do. He's got the right idea—we're here to cooperate. Place like this, you want the cops on your team. Fight breaks out, you want action when you hit 9-1-1."

"Not to mention help with all the bodies afterward."

"Now you're getting it."

"Could we just back up a minute and see if I got this straight? Alfie Toth was here two weeks, from sometime in the middle of May."

"Right."

"Then a plainclothes detective came in with a warrant for his arrest. Alfie heard about it and, not surprisingly, checked out later that day. The detective called back and Peck told him how to get in touch with Alfie Toth's ex-wife."

"Sure. Peck figured that's where Toth went," Estes said.

"Then around June fifth, Tom Newquist came in and you passed the same information along to him."

"Hey, I don't show favorites, is my motto. That's why I'm giving it to you. Why say yes to one and no to someone else is the way I look at it."

"You haven't given me anything yet," I said.

He reached for a piece of scratch paper and jotted down a woman's name, address, and telephone number, apparently off the top of his head. He passed it across the counter.

I took the paper, noting at a glance the Perdido address. "Sounds like Alfie Toth was suddenly very popular."

"Yep."

"And you have no idea why?"

"Nope."

"What's Peck's first name?"

"Leland."

"Is he in the phone book if I need to talk to him?"

Estes shook his head. "Number's unlisted. Now *that* I wouldn't give out without getting his permission."

I thought about it for a moment, but couldn't think what other ground I should cover. I could always check with him later if something else occurred to me. "Well. Thanks for the help. You've been very generous and I appreciate that." I reached for my umbrella, shifting my handbag from my right shoulder to my left so I could manage both.

"Don't you want to hear the rest of it?"

I hesitated. "What rest?"

"The guy's dead. Murdered. Some backpacker found his body up near Ten Pines couple months ago. January thirteen. Reason I remember is it's my great-aunt's birthday. Death. Birth. Doesn't take a wizard to make that connection. I got it locked right in here."

I stared at him, remembering a brief mention of it in the paper. "*That* was Alfie Toth?"

"Yep. Coroner figured he'd been dead six, seven months—since right about the time everybody came looking for him, including the fellow with the warrant and your Tom Newquist. Somebody must have caught up with him. Too bad Peck's never bothered to develop his skills. He might've been the state's star witness."

"To what?"

"Whatever comes up."

I sat in my car, trying to figure out what this meant. Everybody had wanted to talk to Alfie Toth until he turned up dead. I'd have to search back issues of the local newspaper, but as nearly as I remembered, there was precious little information. Decomposed remains had been found in a remote area of the Los Padres National Forest, but I hadn't registered the name. There was no mention of cause of death, but the presumption was of foul play. The police had been stingy with the details, but perhaps they'd told the papers everything they knew. I hadn't been aware of any other reference to the matter and I'd thought no more of it. The Angeles and Los Padres National Forests are both dumping grounds for homicide victims, whose corpses one imagines littering the hiking trails like bags of garbage.

I dutifully fired up the VW and drove the eight blocks to the public library, where I turned up the relevant paragraph in a copy of the *Santa Teresa Dispatch* for January 15.

BODY FOUND IN LOS PADRES
THAT OF TRANSIENT

The decomposed remains discovered by a hiker in the Los Padres National Forest January 13 have been identified as a transient, Alfred Toth, 45, according to the Santa Teresa County Sheriff's Department. The body was found Monday in the rugged countryside five miles east of Manzanita Mountain. Detectives identified Toth through dental work after linking the body to a missing-persons report filed by his ex-wife, Perdido resident Olga Toth. The case is being investigated as a homicide. Anyone with information is asked to call Detective Clay Boyd at the Sheriff's Department.

I found a pay phone outside the building, scrounged a couple of coins from the bottom of my handbag, dialed the Santa Teresa County Sheriff's Department, and asked for Detective Boyd.

"Boyd." The tone was flat, professional, all business. All he'd done so far was give me his name and already I knew he wasn't going to be my best friend.

"Hi, my name is Kinsey Millhone," I said, trying not to sound too chirpy. "I'm a local private investigator working on a case that may connect to the death of Alfie Toth."

Pause. "In what way?"

"Well, I'm not sure yet. I'm not asking for confidential information, but could you give me an update? The last mention in the paper was back in January."

Pause. This was like talking to someone on a time delay. I could have sworn he was taking notes. "What's the nature of your interest?"

"Ah. Well, that's tricky to explain. I'm working for the wife—I guess I should make that the widow—of a sheriff's investigator up in Nota Lake. Tom Newquist. Did you know him by any chance?"

"Name doesn't sound familiar."

"He drove down last June to talk to Alfie Toth, but by the time he reached the Gramercy, Toth had moved out. They might have connected later—I'm not sure about that yet—but I'm assuming this was part of an ongoing investigation."

"Uh-hun."

"Do you have any record of Newquist's contacting your department?"

"Hang on." He sounded resigned, a man who couldn't be accused later of thwarting the public's right to know.

He put me on hold. I listened to the mild hissing that signals one's entrance into telephone hyperspace. I sent up a little prayer of thanks that I wasn't being subjected to polka music or John Philip Sousa. Some companies patch you in to news broadcasts with the volume pitched too low and you sit there wondering if you're flunking some bizarre hearing test.

Detective Boyd clicked back in. He apparently had the file open on the desk in front of him, as I could hear him flipping pages. "You still there?" he asked idly.

"I'm here."

"Tom Newquist didn't get in touch with us when he was here, but I do show we've been in communication with Nota Lake."

I said, "Really. I wonder why he didn't let you know he was coming down."

"Gosh, I don't know. That's a stumper," he said blandly.

"If he'd gotten in touch, would there be a note of it?"

"Yes ma'am."

I could see how this was going to go. I was on a fishing expedition and Detective Boyd was responding only to direct questions. Anything I didn't ask, he wasn't going to volunteer. Somehow I had to snag his interest and inspire his cooperation. "Why don't I tell you my problem," I said conversationally. "His widow's convinced her husband was deeply troubled about something."

"Uh-hun."

I could feel my frustration mount. How could this man be so

pleasant and so completely obtuse at the same time? I switched gears. "Was Alfie Toth wanted for some crime at the time of his death?"

"Not that I'm aware of. He'd just finished serving time on a conviction for petty theft."

"The desk clerk at the Gramercy says a plainclothes detective came in with a warrant for his arrest."

"Wasn't one of ours."

"You don't show any outstanding warrants?"

"No ma'am, I don't."

"But there must have been *some* connection or Tom Newquist wouldn't have bothered to drive all the way down here."

"I'll tell you what. If this is just a question of satisfying Mrs. Newquist's curiosity, I can't see any reason to share information. Why don't you talk to Nota Lake and see what they have to say. That'd be your best bet."

"Are you telling me you *have* information?"

"I'm telling you I'm not going to reveal the substance of an ongoing investigation to any yahoo who asks. You have knowledge of the facts—something new to contribute—we'd be happy to have you come in."

"Has there been a resolution to the case?"

"Not so far."

"The newspapers indicated that this was being investigated as a homicide."

"That's correct."

"Do you have a suspect?"

"Not at this time. I wouldn't say that, no."

"Any leads?"

"None that I'm willing to tell you about," he said. "You want to make a trip out here, I could maybe have you talk to the watch commander, but as far as giving out information by phone, it ain't gonna fly. I don't mean to cast aspersions, but you could be anyone . . . a journalist."

"God forbid," I said. "Surely you don't think I'm anyone that low."

I could hear him smile. At least he was enjoying himself. He seemed to think about it briefly and then he said, "Let's try this. Why don't you give me your number and if anything comes up I'm at liberty to pass along, I'll be in touch."

"You're entirely too kind."

Detective Boyd laughed. "Have a good day."

14

Olga Toth opened the door to her Perdido condominium wearing a bright yellow outfit that consisted of form-fitting tights and a stretchy cotton tunic, cinched at the waist with a wide white bejeweled plastic belt. The fabric clung to her body like a bandage that couldn't quite conceal the damage time had inflicted on her sixty-year-old flesh. Her knee-high boots looked to be size elevens, white vinyl alligator with a fancy pattern of stitchwork across the instep. She'd had some work done on her face, probably collagen injections, given the plumpness of her lips and the slightly lumpy appearance of her cheeks. Her hair was a dry-looking platinum blond, her brown eyes heavily lined, with a startling set of eyebrows drawn in above. I could smell the vermouth on her breath before she said a word.

I'd driven the thirty miles to Perdido in the midst of a drizzling rain, that sort of fine spray that required the constant flip-flop of windshield wipers and the fiercest concentration. The roadway was slick, the blacktop glistening with a deceptive sheen of water that made driving hazardous. Under ordinary circumstances, I might have delayed the trip for another hour or two, but I was worried the cops would somehow manage to warn Alfie's ex-wife of my interest, urging her to keep her mouth shut if I knocked on her door.

The address I'd been given was just off the beach, a ten-unit complex of two-story frame townhouses within view of the Pacific. Olga's was on the second floor with an exterior stairway and a small sheltered entrance lined with potted plants. The woman who answered the doorbell was older than I'd expected and her smile revealed a dazzling array of caps.

"Mrs. Toth?"

She said, "Yes?" Her tone conveyed a natural optimism, as though, having sent in all the forms, having held on to the matching numbers that established her eligibility, she might open the door to someone bearing the keys to her new car or, better yet, that oversized check for several million bucks.

I showed her my card. "Could I talk to you about your ex-husband?"

"Which one?"

"Alfie Toth."

Her smile faded with disappointment, as though there were better ex-husbands to inquire about among her many. "Honey, I'm sorry to be the one to tell you, but he's deceased so if you're here about his unpaid bills, the line forms at the rear."

"This is something else. May I come in?"

"You're not here to serve process?" she asked, cautiously.

"Not at all. Honest."

"Because I'm warning you, I put a notice in the paper the day we separated saying I'm not responsible for debts other than my own."

"Your record's clean as far as I'm concerned."

She studied me, considering, and then stepped back. "No funny business," she warned.

"I'm never funny," I said.

I followed her through the small foyer, watching as she retrieved a martini glass from a small console table. "I was just having a drink in case you're interested."

"I'm fine for now, but thanks."

We entered a living room done entirely in white; trampled-looking, white nylon cut-pile carpeting, white nylon sheers, white leatherette couches, and a white vinyl chair. There was only one lamp turned on and the light coming through the curtains had been subdued by the rain. The room felt damp to me. The glass-and-chrome coffee table bore a large arrangement of white lilies, a pitcher of martinis, several issues of *Architectural Digest,* and a recent issue of *Modern Maturity*. Her eye fell on the latter about the same time mine did. She leaned forward impatiently. "That belongs to a friend. I really hate those things. The minute you turn fifty, the AARP starts hounding you for membership. Not that I'm anywhere close to retirement age," she assured me. She poured herself another drink, adding olives she plucked from a small bowl nearby. She licked her fingertips with enthusiasm. "Olives are the best part," she remarked. Her nails, I noticed, were very long and pink, thick enough to suggest acrylics or poorly done silk overlays.

"What sort of work do you do?" I asked.

She motioned me into a seat at one end of the couch while she settled at the other end, her arm stretched out along the back. "I'm a cosmetologist and if you don't mind my saying so—"

I held up a hand. "Don't give me beauty tips. I can't handle 'em."

She laughed, an earthy guttural sound that set her breasts ajiggle. "Never hurts to try. You ever get interested in a makeover, you can give me a buzz. I could do wonders with that mop of yours. Now what's this about Alfie? I thought all his problems were over and done with, the poor guy."

I filled her in on the nature of the job I'd been hired to do, thinking that as a widow, she might appreciate Selma Newquist's concern about her husband's mental state in the weeks before he died.

"I remember the name Newquist. He was the one called me a couple weeks after Alfie took off. Said it was important, but it really wasn't urgent, as far as I could tell. I told him Alfie was still around someplace and I'd be happy to go looking for him if he'd give me a day or two."

"How long was Alfie here?"

"Two days, maybe three. I don't let any ex of mine stay longer than that. Otherwise, you have fellows camping on your doorstep every time you turn around. They all want the same thing." She lifted her right hand, ticking off the items as she mentioned them. "They want sex, want their laundry done, and a few bucks in their pocket before you send 'em on their way."

"What made Alfie leave the Gramercy?"

"I got the impression he was nervous. I noticed he was jumpy, but he never said why. Alfie was always restless, but I'd say he was looking for a place to hole up. I think he was hoping for the chance to set up permanent residence here, but I wasn't having any. I tried to discourage any long-range plans of his. He was a sweet man, the sweetest. He was twenty years younger than me though you never would have guessed. We were married for eight years. Of course, he was in and out of jail for most of it which is why we lasted as long as we did."

"What was he in jail for?"

She waved the question away. "It was never anything big—bad checks, or petty thievery, or public drunkenness. Sometimes he did worse, which is how he ended up in prison. Nothing violent. No crimes against persons. His problem was he couldn't figure out how to outsmart the system. It wasn't in his nature, so what could you do? You couldn't fault him for being dumb. He was just born that way. He tended to fall into bad company, always taking up with some loser with a harebrained scheme. He was easily dominated. Anybody could lead poor Alfie around by the nose. It all sounded good to him. That's how innocent he was. Most of it ended in disaster, but he never seemed to learn. You had to love that about him. He was good-looking, too, in a goofy sort of way. What he did, he did well, and the rest you might as well write off as a dead loss."

"What was it he did well?"

"He was great in the sack. The man was hung like a donkey and he could fuck all day."

"Ah. And how did you two meet?"

"We met in a bar. This was when I was still doing the singles scene, though I've about given that up. I don't know about you, but these days, I stick to the personal ads. It's a lot more fun. Are you single? You look single."

"Well, I am, but it seems to suit me."

"Oh, I know what you mean. I don't mind living on my own. I have no problem with that. I prefer it, to tell the truth. I just don't know how else to get *laid.*"

"You run ads for sex?"

"Well, you don't come right out and say so. That'd be dumb," she remarked. "There's a hundred cute ways to put it. 'Party-Hearty,' 'Girls Just Want to Have Fun,' 'Passionate at Heart Seeks Same.' Use the right terminology and guys get the point."

"But doesn't that make you nervous?"

"What?" she said, her big eyes fixed on me blankly.

"You know, picking up a bed partner through a newspaper ad."

"How else are you going to get 'em? I'm not promiscuous by any stretch, but I've got your normal appetite for these things. Three, four times a week, I get the itch to go lookin' for love." She shimmied in her seat, snapping her fingers to indicate the joys of the bump-and-grind single life, something I'd obviously missed. "Anyway, at the time I met Alfie, I was still cruising the clubs which, believe me, in Perdido really limits your range, not to mention your choices. Looking at Alf, I never guessed his talents would be so impressive. The man never got tired—just kept banging away. I mean, in some ways, it was fortunate he spent so much time in jail." She paused to sip her martini, lifting her eyebrows appreciatively.

I made some bland comment, wondering what might constitute a proper response to these revelations. "So he was here less than a week last June," I said, trying to steer her back onto neutral ground.

She set the glass on the table. "Something like that. Couldn't have been long, because I met the fellow I'm currently balling at the end of May. Lester didn't take kindly to the idea of Alfie's sleeping on my couch. Men get territorial, especially once they start jumping your bones."

"Where'd he go when he left?"

"Your guess is as good as mine. Last time I saw him he was gathering up his things. Next thing I know, they're asking about his bridgework, trying to identify his body from the crowns on his molars. This was the middle of January so he'd been gone six months."

"Do you think something frightened him into leaving when he did?"

"I didn't think so at the time, but that could have been the case. The cops seemed to think he'd been killed shortly after he took off."

"How'd they pinpoint the time?"

"I asked the same thing, but they wouldn't give me any details."

"Did you identify his body?"

"What was left of it. I'd reported him missing, oh I'd say early September. His parole officer had somehow tracked down my address and telephone number and he was in a tiff because Alfie hadn't been reporting. There he was chewing me out. I told him what he could do with it."

"Why'd you wait so long to call the cops?"

"Don't be silly. Somebody spends as much time as Alfie did on the wrong side of the law, you don't call the cops just because he hasn't showed his face in two months. He was usually missing, as far as I was concerned. In jail or out of town, on the road . . . who the hell knows? I finally filed a report, but the cops didn't take it seriously until the body showed up at Ten Pines."

"Did the police have a theory about what happened to him?"

She shook her head. "I'll tell you this. He wasn't killed for his money because the man was stone broke."

"You never told me why Newquist was looking for Alfie in the first place."

"That was in regard to a homicide in Nota County. He'd heard Alfie was friends with a fellow whose body was found back in March of last year. I guess they had reason to believe the two were traveling together around the time of this man's death."

"Alfie was a suspect?"

"Oh, honey, the cops will never say that. They think you'll be more cooperative if they tell you they're looking for a potential witness to a crime. In this case, probably true. Alfie was a sissy. He was scared to death of violence. He'd never kill anyone and I'd swear to that on a stack of condoms."

"How did Tom Newquist find out Alfie was here?"

"The fellow at the hotel told him."

"I mean, in Santa Teresa."

"Oh. I don't know. He never said a word about that. He might have run the name through the computer. Alfie'd just done a little jail time so he'd have popped right up."

"What about the victim? Did Newquist give you the name of the other man?"

"He didn't have to. I knew him through Alfie. Fellow by the name of Ritter. He and Alfie met in prison. This was six years ago at Chino. I forget what Alfie was doing time for at that point, something stupid. Ritter was vicious, a real son of a bitch, but he protected Alfie's backside and they hung around together after they got out. Alfie wanted Ritter to stay here as well, but I said absolutely not. Ritter was a convicted rapist."

" 'Ritter' was the first name or last?"

"Last. His first name was something fruity, maybe Percival. Everybody called him Pinkie."

"What was Alfie's reaction when he heard about Ritter's death?"

"I never had the chance to tell him. I looked all over town for him, but by then he was gone and I figured he took off. As it turns out, he was probably dead within days, at least according to the cops."

"I take it he was good about keeping in touch?"

"The man never went a week without calling to borrow money. He referred to it as his stud fee, but that was just a joke between us. Alfie was proud."

"I'm sure he was," I said.

"I really miss the guy. I mean, Lester's okay, but he can be prissy about certain sexual practices. He's opposed to anything south of the border, if you know what I mean."

"You don't think Lester had anything to do with Alfie's death? He might have been jealous."

"I'm sure he would have been if he'd known, but I never said a word. I told him Alfie was camping out on my couch, but he had no idea we were screwing like bunny rabbits every chance we got. Bend over to tie your shoe, Alfie'd be right on you, the big dumb lug."

"And no one else called or came around looking for him?"

"I was off at work most days so I don't really know what Alfie did with himself, except drink, play the ponies, and watch the soaps on TV. He liked to shop. He dressed sharp so that's where a lot of his money went. Why the credit card companies kept sending him plastic is beyond my comprehension. He filed bankruptcy twice. Anyway, he might have had friends. He usually did. Like I said, he was a sweet guy. You know, horny, but kind."

"He sounds like a nice man," I murmured, hoping God wouldn't strike me dead.

"Well, he was. He wasn't quarrelsome or hard to get along with. He never got in bar fights or said a cross word to anyone. He was just a big dumb Joe with a hard-on," she said, voice wavering. "Seems like, anymore, people don't get killed for a reason. It's just something that happens. Alfie was a bumpkin and he didn't always show good sense. Someone could have killed him for the fun of it."

I drove back to Santa Teresa, trying not to think much about the information I'd gleaned. I let thoughts wash over me without trying to put them in order or make any sense of them. I was getting closer to something. I just wasn't sure what it was. One thing seemed certain: Tom Newquist was on the same track and maybe what he'd found caused him untold distress.

I reached my apartment shortly after three o'clock. The rain had passed for the moment, but the sky was darkly overcast and the streets were still wet. I bypassed the puddles, my furled umbrella tucked under my arm, moving through the gate with a sense of relief at being home. I unlocked my door and flipped on the lights. By then, my hand was beginning to ache mildly and I was tired of coping with the splint. I shed my jacket, went into the kitchenette for water, and took some pain medication. I perched on a stool and removed the gauze wrap from my fingers. I tossed the splint but left the tape in place. The gesture was symbolic, but it cheered me up.

I checked the answering machine, which showed one message. I pressed Replay and heard Tom's contact at the sheriff's department, who'd left me one sentence. "Colleen Sellers here, home until five if you're still interested."

I tried her number. She picked up quickly, almost as though she'd been waiting for the call. Her "Hello" was careful. No infusion of warmth or friendliness.

"This is Kinsey Millhone, returning your call," I said. "Is this Colleen?"

"Yes. Your message said you wanted to get in touch with me regarding Tom Newquist."

"That's right. I appreciate your getting back to me. Actually, this is awkward. I'm assuming you've heard that he passed away." I hate the phrase *passed away* when what you really mean is *died,* but I thought I should practice a little delicacy.

"So I heard."

That was as much as she gave me so I was forced to plunge right on. "Well, the reason I called . . . I'm a private investigator here in town—"

"I know who you are. I checked it out."

"Well, good. That saves me an explanation. Anyway, for reasons too complicated to go into, I've been hired by his widow to see if I can find out what was going on the last two months of his life."

"Why?"

"Why?"

"Why is it too complicated to go into?"

"Is there any way we can do this in person?" I asked.

There was a momentary pause, during which I heard an intake of breath that led me to believe she was smoking. "We could meet someplace," she said.

"That would be good. You live in Perdido? I'd be happy to drive down, if you like, or . . ."

"I live in Santa Teresa, not that far from you."

"That's great. Much better. You just let me know when and where."

Again, the pause while she processed. "How about the kiddy park across from Emile's in five minutes."

"See you there," I said, but she was gone by then.

I spotted her from a distance, sitting on one of the swings in a yellow slicker with the hood up. She had swiveled the seat sideways, the chains forming a twisted *X* at chest height. When she lifted her feet, the chains came unwound, swiveling her feet first in one direction and then another. She tipped back, holding herself in position with her toes. She pushed off. I watched her straighten her legs in a pumping motion that boosted her higher and higher. I thought my approach would interrupt her play, but she continued swinging, her expression somber, her gaze fixed on me.

"Watch this!" she said and at the height of her forward arc she let herself fly out of the swing. She sailed briefly and then landed in the sand, feet together, her arms raised above her head as though at the end of a dismount.

"Bravo."

"Can you do that?"

"Sure."

"Let's see."

Geez, the things I'll do in the line of duty, I thought. I'm a shameless suck-up when it comes to information. I took her place on the swing, backing up as she had until I was standing on tiptoe. I pushed off, holding on to the chains. I leaned back as I straightened my legs and then pumped back, leaning forward, continuing in a rocking motion as the trajectory of the swing increased. I went higher and higher. At the top of the swing, I released myself and flew forward as she had. I couldn't quite stick the landing and was forced to take a tiny side step for balance.

"Not bad. It takes practice," she said charitably. "Why don't we walk? You got your bumbershoot?"

"It's not raining."

She pushed her hood back and looked up. "It will before long. Here. You can share mine."

She put up her umbrella, a wide black canopy above our heads as we walked. The two of us held the shank, forced to walk shoulder to shoulder. Up close, she smelled of cigarettes, but she didn't ever light one in my presence. I placed her in her late forties, with a square face, oversized glasses set in square red frames, and shoulder-length blond hair. Her eyes were a warm brown, her wide mouth pushing into a series of creases when she smiled. She was large-boned and tall with a shoe size that probably compelled her to shop out of catalogs.

"You don't work today?" I asked.

"I'm taking a leave of absence."

"Mind if I ask why?"

"You can ask anything you want. Believe me, I'm experienced at avoiding answers when the questions don't suit. I turn fifty this coming June. I'm not worried about aging, but it does make you take a long hard look at your life. Suddenly, things don't make sense. I don't know what I'm doing or why I'm doing it."

"You have family in town?"

"Not anymore. I grew up in Indiana, right outside Evansville. My parents are both gone . . . my dad since 1976, my mom just last year. I had two brothers and a sister. One of my brothers, the one who lived here, was diagnosed with a rare form of leukemia and he was dead in six months. My other brother was killed in a boating accident when he was twelve. My sister died in her early twenties of a botched abortion. It's a very strange sensation to be out on the front lines alone."

"You have any kids?"

She shook her head. "Nope, and that's another thing I question. I mean, it's way too late now, but I wonder about that. Not that I ever wanted children. I know myself well enough to know I'd be a lousy mom, but at this stage of my life, I wonder if I should have done it differently. What about you? You have kids?"

"No. I've been married and divorced twice, both times in my twenties. At that point, I wasn't ready to have children. I wasn't even ready for marriage, but how did I know? My current lifestyle seems to preclude domesticity so it's just as well."

"Know what I regret? I wish now I'd listened more closely to family stories. Or maybe I wish I had someone to pass 'em on to. All that verbal history out the window. I worry about what's going to happen to the family photograph albums once I'm gone. They'll be thrown in the garbage . . . all those aunts and uncles down the tubes. Junk stores, you can sometimes buy them, old black-and-white snapshots with the crinkly edges. The white frame house, the vegetable garden with the sagging wire fence, the family dog, looking solemn," she said. Her voice dropped away and then she changed the subject briskly. "What'd you do to your hand?"

"A fellow dislocated my fingers. You should have seen them . . . pointing sideways. Made me sick," I said.

We strolled on for a bit. To the right of us, a low wall separated the sidewalk from the sand on the far side. There must have been two hundred yards of beach before the surf kicked in; all of this looking drab in current weather conditions. "How are we doing so far?" I asked.

"In what respect?"

"I assume you're sizing me up, trying to figure out how much you want to tell."

"Yes, I am," she said. "Tom confided in me and I take that seriously. I mean, even if he's dead, why would I betray his trust?"

"That's up to you. Maybe this is unfinished business and you have an opportunity to see it through for him."

"This is not about Tom. This is about his wife," she said.

"You could look at it that way."

"Why should I help her?"

"Simple compassion. She's entitled to peace of mind."

"Aren't we all?" she said. "I never met the woman and probably wouldn't like her even if I did, so I don't give a shit about her peace of mind."

"What about your own?"

"That's my concern."

That was as much as I got out of her. By the time we'd walked as far as the wharf, the rain was beginning to pick up again. "I think I'll peel off here. I'm a block down in that direction. If you decide you have more to tell me, why don't you get in touch."

"I'll think about that."

"I could use the help," I said.

I trotted toward home under a steadily increasing drizzle that matted my hair. What was it with these people? What a bunch of anal-retentives. I decided it was time to quit horsing around. I ducked into the apartment long enough to run a towel through my hair, grab my handbag and umbrella, and lock up again. I retrieved my car and drove the ten blocks to Santa Teresa Hospital.

15

I caught Dr. Yee on his way to the parking lot. I'd left the VW in a ninety-minute spot at the curb across from the hospital emergency room and I was circling the building, intending to enter by way of the main lobby. Dr. Yee had emerged from a side door and was preparing to cross the street to the parking garage. I called his name and he turned. I waved and he waited until I'd reached his side.

Santa Teresa County still utilizes a sheriff-coroner system, in which the sheriff, as an elected official, is also in charge of the coroner's office. The actual autopsy work is done by various forensic pathologists under contract to the county, working in conjunction with the coroner's investigators. Steven Yee was in his forties, a third-generation Chinese American, with a passion for French cooking.

"You looking for me?" He was easily six feet tall, slender and handsome, with a smooth round face. His hair was a straight glossy black, streaked with exotic bands of white, that he wore combed straight back.

"I'm glad I caught you. Are you on your way home? I need about fifteen minutes of your time, if you can spare it."

He glanced at his watch. "I'm not due at the restaurant for another hour," he said.

"I heard about that. You have a second career."

He smiled with pleasure, shrugging modestly. "Well, the money's not great, but I make enough here. It's restful to chop leeks instead of . . . other things."

"At least you're skilled with a boning knife," I said.

He laughed. "Believe me, nobody trims meat as meticulously as I do. You ought to come in some night. I'll treat you to a meal that'll make you weep for the pure pleasure."

"I could use that," I said. "You know me and Quarter Pounders with cheese."

"So what's up? Is this work?"

"I'm looking for information about a man named Alfie Toth. Are you familiar with the case?"

"Should be. I did the post," he said. He hooked a thumb in the direction of the building. "Come on back to my office. I'll show you what we have."

"This is great," I said happily, as I followed him. "I understand Toth's death may be related to a suspected homicide in Nota Lake . . . a fellow named Ritter. One of the sheriff's investigators there was working on the case when he died of a heart attack a few weeks back. His name was Tom Newquist. Did he get in touch with you?"

"I know the name, but he didn't contact me directly. I spoke to the Nota Lake coroner by phone and he mentioned him. What's your connection? Is this an insurance claim?"

"I don't work for CF these days. I've got an office in Lonnie Kingman's law firm on Capillo."

"What happened to CF?"

"They fired my sorry butt, which is fine with me," I said. "It was time for a change, so now I'm doing mostly freelance work. Newquist's widow hired me. She says her husband was stressed out and she wants me to find out why. Nota Lake law enforcement's been very tight-lipped on the subject and the cops here aren't much better."

"I'll bet."

When we reached the elevator, he punched the Down button and we chatted idly of other matters as we descended into the bowels of the building.

Dr. Yee's office was a small bare box down the hall from the morgue. The anteroom was lined with beige filing cabinets, the office itself barely large enough for his big rolltop desk, his swivel chair, and a plain wooden chair for guests. His medical books had been moved to the shelves of a freestanding bookcase and the top of his desk was now reserved for a neat row of French cookbooks, trussed on either side by a large jar of murky formalin in which floated something I didn't care to inspect. He was using a gel breast implant as a paperweight, securing a pile of loose notes. "Hang on a second and I'll pull the file," he said. "Have a seat."

The chair was stacked with medical journals so I perched on the edge, grateful Dr. Yee was willing to trust me. Dr. Yee was never careless with information, but he wasn't as paranoid as the police detectives. He returned with a file folder and a manila envelope and took his seat in the swivel chair, tossing both on the desk beside me.

"Are those the photographs? Can I see?"

"Sure, but they won't tell you much." He reached for the envelope and extracted a set of color photographs, eight-by-ten prints showing various views of the scene where Alfie Toth had been found. The terrain was clearly rugged: boulders, chaparral, an ancient live oak. "Toth was identified through his skeletal remains, largely dental work. Percy Ritter's body in Nota Lake was found in much the same circumstances; same MO and a similar remote locale. In both cases, it took a while before anyone stumbled across the remains."

I paused, staring at one close-up view with perplexity, not quite sure what I was looking at; probably the lower half of Alfie Toth's body crumpled on the ground. The pelvic bones appeared to be still joined, but the femur, tibia, and fibulas were tangled together in a heap, like bleached kindling. The haphazard skeletal assortment looked like a Halloween decoration badly in need of assembly.

Dr. Yee was saying, "Ritter's mummified body was found fully clothed with various personal items in his pockets . . . expired California driver's license, credit cards. Identification was confirmed by his fingerprints, which had to be reconstituted. Must have been dry out there because bacterial growth and putrefaction are halted when the body moisture diminishes below fifty percent. Ritter's flesh was as stiff as leather, but Kirchner managed to retrieve all but the right-hand thumb and ring finger. Ritter'd had his prints in the system since 1972. What a bad ass. Real scum."

"I didn't know you could salvage prints like that."

He shrugged. "You sometimes have to sever the fingers first. To rehydrate, you can soak 'em in a three-percent lye solution or a one-percent solution of Eastman Kodak Photo-Flo 200 for a day or two. Another method is to use successive alcohol solutions, starting at ninety percent and gradually decreasing. With Ritter, the first presumption was of suicide, though Kirchner said he had big doubts and the county sheriff did, too. Keep in mind, there wasn't any suicide note at the scene, but there was also no environmental disorder and no signs of trauma on the body. No fractured hyoid to suggest cervical compression, no evidence of knife wounds, skull fractures, gunshot—"

"In other words, no signs of foul play."

"Right. Which is not to say he couldn't have been subdued in some way. Same thing with Toth, except there was no personal ID. Sheriff's department went back through months' worth of missing-persons reports, contacting relatives. They made the initial match that way."

"So what are we looking at?" I asked, turning the photograph so he could see.

"To all appearances, both guys tied a rope around a boulder, put a noose around their necks, pushed the rock through the *Y* of a tree limb, and hung themselves. It wasn't until later that the similarities came to light."

I stared at him. "That's odd." I glanced down at a photograph, in which I could now see the crisscross of rope circling the circumference of a rock about the size of a large watermelon. Toth's torso and extremities had separated, falling in a tumble on one side of the tree while the upper half of his body, pulled by the weight of the boulder, had fallen on the other still attached by the length of rope.

"Nothing remarkable about the rope, in case you're wondering. Garden variety clothesline available at any supermarket or hardware store," he said. Dr. Yee watched my face. "Not to be racist about it, but the method's more compatible with an Asian sensibility. Some dude out in Nota County, how'd it even occur to him? And then a second one here? I mean, it's possible Toth heard about his pal's alleged suicide and imitated his methodology, but even so, it seems off. As far as I know, the Nota Lake cops kept the specifics to themselves. That was information only shared between agencies."

"Really. If Alfie Toth wanted to kill himself, you'd think he'd blow his brains out; something simple and straightforward, more in keeping with his lifestyle."

Dr. Yee shifted back in his chair with a squeak. "A more plausible explanation is that both victims were killed by the same party. The reason the cops are so paranoid is to avoid all the kooks and the copycats. Someone ups and confesses, you don't want anyone other than the killer in possession of the details. So far the papers haven't gotten wind of it. They know a body was found here, but that's about the extent of it. I'm not sure reporters have put two and two together with the deceased in Nota Lake. That didn't get any play here."

"What's the estimated time of death for Ritter?"

"Oh, he'd been there five years, from Kirchner's estimate. A gasoline receipt among his effects was dated April 1981. Gas station attendant remembers the two of them."

"Quite a gap between deaths," I said. "Have you ever run across a methodology like this?"

"Only in a textbook. That's what makes it curious. Take a look at this." He reached backward and pulled a thin oversized volume from the bottom shelf. "Tomio Watanabe's *Atlas of Legal Medicine.* This was first published in 'sixty-eight, printed in Japan, so it's hard to find these days." He flipped the pages open to a section on hangings and turned the book so I could see. The photographs were of Japanese suicide victims, apparently supplied by various police headquarters and medical examiner's offices in Japan. One young woman had wedged her neck in the *V* of a tree, which effectively compressed her carotid artery. Another woman had made a double loop of long rope, which she wound around her neck and then put her feet through, achieving strangulation by ligature. In the method Dr. Yee'd referred to, a man tied a rope around a stone, which he placed on a chair. He'd wrapped the same rope around his neck, sat with his back to the chair back, and then tilted the chair forward so the stone rolled off the seat and strangled him. I studied the photographs on adjoining pages, which depicted in graphic detail the ingenuity employed by human beings in extinguishing their lives. In every case, I was looking at the face of despair. I stared at the floor for a moment, running the scenario through my head like a piece of film. "There's no way two men on opposite sides of California would have independently devised the same method."

"Probably not," he said. "Though, given the fact they were friends, it's possible they overheard someone describe the technique. If you're intent on suicide, the beauty of it is once you topple the boulder through the fork in the tree, there's no way back. Also, death is reasonably quick; not instantaneous, but you'd lose consciousness within a minute or less."

"And these are the only two deaths of this kind that you know of?"

"That's right. I don't think this is serial, but the two have to be connected."

"How'd you hear about Ritter's death?"

"Through Newquist. He'd known about Ritter since his body was discovered back in March of this past year. When a backpacker came across Toth, he reported it to the local sheriff's department and they contacted Nota Lake because of the similar MO."

"Isn't there a chance Toth killed his friend Ritter, hoping to make it look like suicide instead of murder, and then ended up killing himself the same way? There'd be a certain irony in that."

"It's possible," he said dubiously, "but what's your picture? Toth commits a murder and five years pass before he finds himself overwhelmed with guilt?"

"Doesn't make much sense, does it?" I said, in response to his tone. "I talked to his ex-wife and from what she said, he wasn't behaving like a man who was terminally depressed." I checked my watch. It was close to 4:45. "Anyway, I better let you go. I appreciate the information. This has been a big help."

"My pleasure."

When I got home at five o'clock, Henry's kitchen lights were on and I found him sitting at his kitchen table with a file box in front of him. I tapped on the glass and he motioned me in. "Help yourself to a cup of tea. I just made a pot."

"Thanks." I took a clean mug from the dish rack and poured myself a cup of tea, then sat at the kitchen table watching Henry work.

"These are rebate coupons. A new passion of mine in case you're wondering," he said. Henry had always been enthusiastic about saving money, sitting down daily with the local paper to clip and sort coupons in preparation for his shopping trips.

"Can I help?"

"You can file while I cut," he said. He passed me a pile of proof of purchase seals, which I could see were separated according to the company offering to refund a portion of the price. He was saying, "Short's Drugs has started a Receipt Savers Rebate Club, which allows you to collect your rebates and send them in all at once. There's no point in trying to get fifty cents back when it costs you nearly thirty-five cents for stamps."

"I can't believe the time you put in on this," I remarked as I filed. Over-the-counter diet remedies, detergent, soap, mouthwash.

"Some are products I use anyway so who can resist? Look at this one. Free toothpaste. Makes your smile extra white it says."

"Your smile's already white."

"Suppose I end up preferring the taste of this one. There's no harm in trying something new," he said. "Here's one for shampoo. You get one free if you buy before April first. Only one per customer and I've got mine already, so I kept this for you if you're interested."

"Thanks. You do this in addition to the store coupons?"

"Well, yes, but this takes a lot more patience. Sometimes it takes as long as two to three months, but then you get a nice big check. Fifteen bucks once. Like found money. You'd be surprised how quickly it adds up."

"I'll bet." I took a sip of my tea.

Henry passed me another ragged pile of clippings. "When you finish that batch, you can start on these."

"I don't mean to sound petty," I said, bringing the conversation around to my concerns, "but honestly, Rosie paid more attention to those rowdies than she did to us last night. It didn't hurt my feelings so much as piss me off."

Henry seemed to smile to himself. "Aren't you overstating your case?"

"Well, it may be too strong a term, but you get my point. Henry, how much children's aspirin do you take these days? I counted fifteen of these."

"I donate the extras to charity. Speaking of pain relievers, how's your hand?"

"Good. Much better. It hardly hurts," I said. "I take it, Rosie's attitude doesn't bother you."

"Rosie's Rosie. She's never going to change. If it bugs you, tell her. Don't complain to me."

"Oh right. I see. You want me to take the point."

"Battle of the Titans. I'd like to see that," he remarked.

At six, I left Henry's, stopping by my apartment to pick up my umbrella and a jacket. Once again, the rain had eased off, but the cold saturated the air, making me grateful to step into the tavern. Rosie's was quiet, the air scented with the pungent smell of cauliflower, onions, garlic, bacon, and simmering beef. There were two patrons sitting in a booth, but I could see they'd been served. The occasional clink of flatware on china was the only sound I heard.

Rosie was sitting at the bar by herself, absorbed in the evening paper, which was open in front of her. A small television set was turned on at the far end of the bar, the sound muted. There was no sign of William and I realized if I was going to catch her, this would be my only chance. I could feel my heart thump. My bravery seldom extends to interactions of this kind. I pulled out the stool next to hers and perched. "Something smells good."

"Lot of somethings," she said. "I got William fixing deep-fried cauliflower with sour cream sauce. Also hot pickled beef, and beef tongue with tomato sauce."

"My favorite," I said dryly.

Behind us, the door opened and a foursome came in, admitting a rush of cold air before the door banged shut again. Rosie eased down off her stool and moved across the room to greet them, playing hostess for once. The door opened again and Colleen Sellers was suddenly standing in the entrance. What was *she* doing here? So much for my confrontation with Rosie. Maybe Colleen had decided to give me some help.

• • •

"I don't even know what I'm doing here," she said, glumly. Her blond hair drooped with the damp and her glasses had fogged over from the heat in the place.

"Talking about Tom."

"I guess."

"You want to tell me the rest of it?"

"There's nothing much to tell."

We were seated in the back booth I usually claim as my own. I'd poured her a glass of wine, which was now sitting in front of her untouched. She removed her glasses, holding them by the frames while she pulled a paper napkin from the dispenser and cleaned the lenses in a way that made me worry she was scratching them. Without the glasses, she looked vulnerable, the misery palpable in the air between us.

"When did you first meet him?"

"At a conference up in Redding a year ago. He was there by himself. I never did meet his wife. She didn't like to come with him, or at least that's what I heard. I gathered she was a bit of a pain in the ass. Not that he ever admitted it, but other people said as much. I don't know what her gig was. He always spoke of her like she was some kind of goddess." She pushed her hair back from her face and tucked it behind her ears in a style that wasn't flattering. She put on her glasses again and I could see smears on the lenses.

"Did you meet by chance or by design?"

Colleen rolled her eyes and a weary smile played around her mouth. "I can see where you're headed, but okay . . . I'll bite. I knew he was going to be there and I looked him up. How's that?"

I smiled back at her. "You want to tell it your way?"

"I'd appreciate that," she said dryly. "Until the conference in Redding, I only dealt with him by phone. He sounded terrific, so naturally, I wanted to meet him in person. We hit it off right away, chatting about various cases we'd worked, at least the interesting ones. You know how it is, trading professional tales. We got talking department politics, his experiences versus mine, the usual stuff."

"I don't mean to sound accusatory, but someone seemed to think the two of you were very chummy."

"Chummy?"

"That you were flirtatious. I'm just telling you what I heard."

"There's no law against flirting. Tom was a doll. I never knew a man yet who couldn't use a little boost to his ego, especially at our age. My god. Who the hell's telling you this stuff? Someone trying to make trouble, I can tell you that."

"How well did you know him?"

"I only saw him twice. No, correction. I saw him three times. It was all work at first, starting with the case he was on."

"What case was that?"

"County sheriff up in Nota Lake found an apparent suicide in the desert, an ex-con named Ritter, who'd hung himself from a branch of a California white oak. Identification was confirmed through his fingerprints and Tom tracked him back as far as his release from Chino in the spring of 'eighty-one. Ritter had family in this area; Perdido to be precise. He talked to them by phone and they told him Ritter'd been traveling with a pal."

"Alfie Toth," I supplied. I was curious to hear her version, but I didn't want her to think I was completely ignorant of the facts.

"How'd you hear about him?" she asked.

"Hey, I have my sources just like you have yours. I know Tom drove down here in June to look for him."

"That's right. I was the one got a line on the guy. Toth had been arrested here on a minor charge. I called Tom and he said he'd be down within a day. This was mid-April. I told him I'd be happy to make the contact, but he preferred doing it himself. I guess he got caught up in work and it was June by the time he made it down here. By then, Toth was out of jail and gone."

"So Tom never talked to him?"

"Not that I know of. As it turned out, Toth's body was the one found in January of this year. The minute the ID was made, I called Tom. The MO was the same for both Ritter and Toth and that was worrisome. The two deaths had to be related, but it was tough to determine what the motivation might have been."

"From what I hear, the murders were separated by a five-year time gap. You have a theory about that?"

I could see her mouth pull down and she wagged her head to convey her ambivalence. "This was one time when Tom and I didn't agree on anything. It could have been a double-cross . . . you know, a bank heist or burglary with Ritter and his sidekick betraying an accomplice. Fellow catches up with them and kills Ritter on the spot. Then it takes another five years to hunt down his pal Toth."

"What was Tom's idea?"

"Well, he thought Toth might have been a witness to Ritter's murder. Something happens in the mountains and Pinkie Ritter dies. Toth manages to get away and eventually the killer catches up with him."

I said, "Or maybe Alvin Toth killed Ritter and someone else came along and avenged Ritter's death."

She smiled briefly. "As a matter of fact, I suggested that myself, but Tom was convinced the perpetrator was the same in both cases."

I thought about Dr. Yee's assessment, which was the same as Tom's. "It would help if I knew how to get in touch with Ritter's family."

"I can give you the phone number. I don't have it with me, but I could call you later if you like."

"That'd be great. One other thing. I know this is none of my business, but were you in love with Tom? Because that's what I'm picking up, reading between the lines," I said.

Her body language altered and I could see her debate with herself about how much to reveal. "Tom was loyal as a dog, completely devoted to his wife, which he let me know right off the bat. Ain't that always the way? All the good men are married."

"So they say."

"But I'll tell you something. We had real chemistry between us. It's the first time I ever understood the term *soul mate*. You know what I mean? We were soul mates. No kidding. It was like finding myself in this other guise . . . my spiritual counterpart . . . and that was heady stuff. We'd be in a room together with five or six hundred other people and I always knew where he was. It was like tentacles stretching all the way across the auditorium. I wouldn't even have to look for him. The bond was that strong. There wasn't anything I couldn't say to him. And laugh? God, we laughed."

"You go to bed with him?" I asked, casually.

A blush began to saturate Colleen's cheeks. "No, but I would have. Hell, I was so crazy about him I broached the subject myself. I was shameless. I was wanton. I'd have taken him on any basis . . . just to be with him once." She shook her head. "He wouldn't do it, and you know why? He was honorable. Decent. Can you imagine the gall of it in this day and age? Tom was an honorable man. He made a promise to be faithful and he meant it. That's one of the things I admired most about him."

"Maybe it's just as well. He wouldn't have been good at deceit even if he'd been willing to try."

"So I've told myself."

"You miss him," I said.

"I've cried every day since I heard about his death. I never even had the chance to say good-bye to him."

"It must be tough."

"Awful. It's just awful. I miss him more than I missed my own mother when she died. So maybe if I'd slept with him, I'd have had to kill myself or something. Maybe the loss and the pain would have been impossible to bear."

"You might have had less respect for him if he'd given in."

"That's a risk I'd have taken, given half a chance."

"At any rate, I'm sorry for your pain."

"No sorrier than I am. I'm never going to find another guy like him. So what can you do? You soldier on. At least his wife has the luxury to mourn in public. Is she taking it hard?"

"That's why she hired me, trying to find relief."

Colleen looked away from me casually, trying to conceal her interest. "What's she like?"

I thought for a moment, trying to be fair. "Generous with her time. Terribly insecure. Efficient. She smokes. Sort of hard-looking, platinum blond hair teased out to here. She has slightly gaudy taste and she's crazy about her son, Brant. This was Tom's stepson."

"Do you like her? Is she nice?"

"People claim she's neurotic, but I do like the woman. A few don't, but that's true of all of us. There's always someone who thinks we're dogshit."

"Did she love him?"

"Very much, I'd say. It was probably a good marriage . . . maybe not perfect, but it worked. She doesn't like the idea of his dying with unfinished business."

"Back to that," she said.

"I'd do the same for you if you hired me to find answers."

Colleen's gaze came back to mine. "You thought it was me. That we were having an affair."

"It crossed my mind."

"If I'd had an affair with him, would you have told his wife the truth?"

"No. What purpose would it serve?"

"Right." She was silent for a moment.

"Do you know why Tom was so distressed?" I asked.

"I might."

"Why so protective?"

"It's not up to me to ease her mind," she said. "Who's easing mine?"

I held my hands up in surrender. "I'm just asking the question. You have to do as you see fit."

"I have to go," she said abruptly, gathering up her coat. "I'll call you later with the phone number for Ritter's daughter."

I held a finger up. "Hang on. I just remembered. I have something for you if you're interested." I reached into the outer zippered compartment of my shoulder bag and pulled out one of the black-and-white photographs of Tom at the April banquet. "I had these done up in case I needed 'em. You might like to have something to remember him by."

She took the picture without comment, a slight smile playing across her mouth as she studied it.

I said, "I never met him myself, but I thought it captured him."

She looked up at me with tears rimming her eyes. "Thank you."

16

When I returned from my run the next morning, there was a message from Colleen Sellers on my answering machine, giving me the name and Perdido address of a woman named Dolores Ruggles, one of Pinkie Ritter's daughters. As this represented the only lead I had, I gassed up the VW and headed south on 101 as soon as I was showered and dressed.

On my left, I could see fields under cultivation, the newly planted rows secured by layers of plastic sheeting as slick and gray as ice. Steep hills, rough with low-growing vegetation, began to crowd up against the highway. On my right, the bleak Pacific Ocean thundered against the shore. Surfers in black wet suits waited on rocking boards like a scattered flock of sea birds. The rains had moved on, but the sky was still white with a ceiling of sluggish clouds and the air was thick with the mingled scents of brine and recent precipitation. Snow would be falling in the high Sierras near Nota Lake.

I took the Leeward off-ramp and made two left turns, crossing over the freeway again in search of the street where Dolores Ruggles lived. The neighborhood was a warren of low stucco structures, narrow streets intersecting one another repeatedly. The house was a plain box, sitting in a plain treeless yard with scarcely a bush or a tuft of grass to break up the monotonous flat look of the place. The porch consisted of a slab of concrete with one step leading up to the front door and a small cap of roofing to protect you as you rang the bell, which I did. The door was veneer with long sharp splinters of wood missing from the bottom edge. It looked like a dog had been chewing on the threshold.

The man who opened the door was drying his hands on a towel tucked into the waist of his trousers. He was easily in his sixties, maybe five-foot-eight, with a coarsely lined face and a thinning head of gray-white hair the color of wood ash. His eyes were hazel, his brows a tangle of wiry black and gray. "Keep your shirt on," he said, irritably.

"Sorry. I thought the bell was broken. I wasn't even sure anyone was home. I'm looking for Dolores Ruggles."

"Who the hell are you?"

I handed him my card, watching his lips move while he read my name. "I'm a private investigator," I said.

"I can see that. It says right here. Now we got that established, what do you want with Dolores? She's busy at the moment and doesn't want to be disturbed."

"I need some information. Maybe you can help me and we can spare her the imposition. I'm here about her father."

"The little shithead was murdered."

"I'm aware of that."

"Then what's it to you?"

"I'm trying to find out what happened."

"What difference does it make? The man is *D-E-A-D* dead and not soon enough to suit my taste. I've spent years coping with all the damage he did."

"Could I come in?"

He stared at me. "Help yourself," he said abruptly and turned on his heel, leaving me to follow. I scurried after him, taking a quick mental photograph as we passed through the living room. Not to sound sexist, but the room looked as if it had been designed by a man. The floors were bare hardwood, stained dark. I noted a tired couch and a sagging upholstered chair, both shrouded by heavy woven Indian-print rugs. I thought the coffee table was antiqued, but I could see as I passed the only patina was dust. The walls were lined with books: upright, sideways, slanting, stacked, packed two deep on some shelves, three deep on others. The accumulation of magazines, newspapers, junk mail, and catalogs suggested a suffocating indifference to tidiness.

"I'm doing dishes out here," he said, as he moved into the kitchen. "Grab a towel and you can pitch in. You might as well be useful as long as you're picking my brain. By the way, I'm Homer, Dolores's husband. Mr. Ruggles to you."

His tone had shifted from outright rudeness to something gruff, but not unpleasant. I could see he'd been rather good-looking in his day; not wildly handsome, but something better—a man with a certain amount of character and an appealing air. His skin was darkly tanned and heavily speckled with sun damage, as if he'd spent all his life toiling in the fields. His shirt was an earth brown with an elaborately embroidered yoke done in threads of gold and black. He wore cowboy boots that I suspected were intended to add a couple of inches to his height.

By the time I reached the kitchen, he'd turned on the water again and he was already back at work, washing plates and glassware. "Towel's in there," he said, nodding at the drawer to his immediate left. I took out a clean dish towel and reached for a plate still hot from the rinse water. "You can stack those on the kitchen table. I'll put 'em up when we're done."

I glanced at the table. "Uhm, Mr. Ruggles, the table needs to be wiped. Do you have a sponge?"

Homer turned and gave me a look. "This is a telling trait of yours, isn't it?"

"Oh, sure," I said.

"Skip the Mr. Ruggles bit. It sounds absurd."

"Yes, sir."

That netted me half a smile. He wrung out the cloth and tossed it in my direction with a shake of his head. I wiped off the tabletop, setting several items aside: newspaper; salt-and-pepper shakers shaped like the Wolf and Little Red Riding Hood; a clutch of pill bottles with Dolores's name plastered on them, along with various warning labels. Whatever she was taking, she was supposed to avoid alcohol, excessive exposure to sunlight, and the operation of heavy machinery. I wondered if this referred to cars, tractors, or Amtrak locomotives. When I'd finished, I handed him the rag and then picked up the dish towel and resumed wiping the plate.

"So what's the deal?" he said belatedly. "What's your interest in Pinkie Ritter? Nice girl like you should be ashamed."

"I didn't know anything about him until yesterday. I've been tracking down a friend of his, who may have been . . . Could we just skip this part? It's almost too tricky to explain."

"You're talking Alfie Toth."

"Thank you. That's right. Everybody seems to know about him."

"Yeah, well, Alfie was a birdbrain. Women thought he was attractive, but I couldn't see it myself. How can you think some guy's handsome when you know he's dim? To my way of thinking, it spoils the whole effect. I think he hung out with my father-in-law for protection, which just goes to show you how dumb he was."

"You knew Alfie was dead."

"You bet. The police told us about it when his body turned up. They came around asking the same question you probably want answered, which is what's the connection and who did what to whom? I'll give you the same answer I gave them. I don't know."

"What's the story on Pinkie? I take it you didn't think much of him."

"That's a gross understatement. I really hated his guts. Whoever killed Pinkie saved me life in prison. Pinkie had six kids—three sons and three daughters—and mistreated every one of them from the day they were born 'til they got big enough to fight back. Nowadays there's all this talk of abuse, but Pinkie did the real thing. He punched them, burned them, made 'em drink vinegar and hot sauce for talking back to him. He locked them in closets, set them out in the cold. He screwed 'em, starved 'em, threatened them. He hit 'em with belts, boards, metal pipes, sticks, hairbrushes, fists. Pinkie was the meanest son of a bitch I ever met and that's goin' some."

"Didn't anybody intervene?"

"People tried. Lot of people blew the whistle on him. Trick was trying to prove it. Teachers, guidance counselors, next-door neighbors. Sometimes Children's Services managed to take the kids away from him and foster them out. Judge always gave 'em back." He shook his head. "Pinkie knew how the game was played. He kept a clean house—the kids saw to that—and he did like to cook—that was his specialty. It's what he did for a living when he wasn't breaking their heads or breaking the law. Social workers came around and everything looked fine. Kids knew better than to open their mouths. Dolores says she can remember the six of them lined up in the living room, answering questions just as nice as you please. Pinkie wouldn't be in the room, but he was always somewhere close. Kids knew better than to rat on him or they'd be dead by dark. They'd stand there and lie. Said social workers knew, but couldn't get anything on him without their assistance. Only thing saved 'em was his getting thrown in jail."

"What about his wife? Where was she all this time?"

"Dolores thinks he killed her, though it couldn't be proved. He claims she ran off with some barfly and was never heard from again. Dolores says she remembers as a kid waking up in the dead of night. Pinkie was out in the woods behind the house with a power saw. Lantern on the ground throwing these big shadows up against the trees. Moths fluttering around the light. She still has nightmares about that. She was the baby in the family, six years old at the time. I think the oldest was fifteen. She went out there next day. The ground was all turned, probably to hide the blood. She still remembers the smell—like a package of chicken when it's gone funny and has to be thrown out. Mom was never seen or heard from again."

"Pinkie sounds like a very nasty piece of work."

"The worst."

"So anybody could have killed him, including one of his kids. Is that what you're saying?"

"That would cover it," he said. "Of course, by the time he died, they were out from under his control. The rest of the kids had scattered to hell and gone. Couple of 'em still in California, though we don't see 'em all that much." Homer finished the last dish and turned the water off. I continued drying silverware while he put away the clean plates.

"When did you see him last?"

"Five years ago in March. The minute he got out of Chino, he headed straight up here, arrived on the twenty-fifth, and stayed a week."

"Good memory," I remarked.

"The cops asked me about that so I looked it up. How I pinpointed the date is I withdrew five hundred bucks from a bank account the day Pinkie left. I counted backward from that and the date stuck in my mind. Anything else you want to quiz me about?"

"I didn't mean to interrupt. Go on."

"Dolores was the only kid of his still living in the area, so naturally, he felt she owed him room and board for as long as he liked."

"She agreed to that?"

"Of course."

"Didn't you object?"

"I did, but that was an argument I couldn't win. She felt guilty. She's a hell of a gal and what she's endured, believe me, you don't want to know—but the upshot is, she's anxious to please, easily manipulated—especially when it came to him. She wanted that man's love. Don't ask me to explain, given what she suffered. He was still Daddy to her and she couldn't turn him away. He was just like he always was; demanding, critical. He refused to lift a finger, expecting her to wait on him hand and foot. I finally got fed up and told him to clear out. Pinkie says, 'Fine, no problem. I won't stay where I'm not wanted. To hell with you,' he says. He was sore as a boil and feeling much put upon, but I was damned if I'd back down."

"Toth was with him at the time?"

"Off and on. I think Alfie's ex-wife lived in town somewhere. He mooched off her when he wasn't here mooching off us."

"And the two left together?"

"As far as I know. At least, that was the plan."

"And where were they headed?"

"Los Angeles. You piece it together later and it turns out they stole a car in Los Angeles and drove up to Lake Tahoe."

"What about Pinkie's parole officer? Wasn't he supposed to report in?"

"Hey, you're talking a career criminal. Following the rules wasn't exactly his strong suit. Who the hell knows how he got away with it? Same with Toth."

"You think someone could have been after them?"

"I wouldn't know," he said. "Pinkie didn't act like he was worried. Why? You think someone might have been trailing them?"

"It's possible," I said.

"Yeah, well it's also possible Pinkie overstepped his bounds for once. He was one of those little guys, chip on his shoulder and feisty as all get out. I can't say that about Alfie. He seemed harmless. Pinkie's another matter. Whoever killed Pinkie should get a medal, in my opinion. And don't quote me. Dolores gets upset if she hears me talkin' like that. I notice I'm doing all the talking."

"I appreciate that."

"This is good. I appreciate your appreciation. Now it's your turn. What's a private investigator doing in the middle of a homicide investigation? Last I heard they didn't have a suspect so you can't be working for the public defender's office."

Given his cooperation, I thought he was entitled to an explanation. I filled him in on the situation, beginning with Selma Newquist and ending with Colleen Sellers. The only thing I omitted were details of the two killings. He didn't seem curious about specifics and I wouldn't have revealed the information for all the money in the world. In the meantime, on an almost subliminal level, I could hear an odd series of voices from another room. At first, I thought the sound was coming from a radio, or television set, but the phrases were repeated, the tone lifeless and mechanical. Homer heard it, too, and his eye caught mine. He tilted his head in the direction of the short hallway that seemed to lead into a back bedroom. "Dolores's back there. You want to talk to her?"

"If you think it's okay."

"She can handle it," he said. "Give me a second and I'll tell her what's going on. She might have something to add."

He moved down the hall to the door, tapping once before he entered. As he eased through the opening, I felt a moment's unease. Here I was in a strange house in the company of a man I'd never laid eyes on before. I had taken him at face value, trusting him on instinct though I wasn't sure why. Really, I only had his word for it that Dolores was in the other room. I had one of those flash fantasies of him emerging from the bedroom with a butcher knife in hand. Fortunately, life, even for a private eye, is seldom this interesting. The door opened again and Homer motioned me in.

At first sight, I thought Dolores Ruggles couldn't have been a day over twenty-one. Later, I found out that she was twenty-eight, which still seemed too young to be married to a man Homer's age. Slim, petite, she sat at a workbench in a room filled with Barbie dolls. Floor to ceiling, wall to wall, dressed in an astonishing array of styles, these bland plastic women were decked out in miniature sundresses, evening clothes, suits, furs, shorts, capes, pedal pushers, bathing suits, baby doll pajamas, sheaths—each outfit complete with appropriate accessories. There was a whole row of Barbie brides, though I'd never thought of her as married. The row below showed twenty Barbies uniformed as flight attendants and nurses, which must have represented the entire gambit of career options available to her. Some of the dolls were still in their boxes and some were freestanding, affixed to round plastic mounts. There was a row of seated Barbies—black, Hispanic, blond, brunette—their long perfect legs extended like a chorus line, all shoeless, their unblemished limbs ending in nearly pointed toes. Their arms were long and impossibly smooth. Their necks must have contained extra vertebrae to support the weight of their tousled manes of hair. I confess I found myself at a loss for words. Homer leaned against the open door, watching for my reaction.

I could tell something was expected of me so I said, "Amazing," in what I hoped was a properly respectful tone.

Homer laughed. "I thought you'd like that. I don't know a woman alive who can resist a room full of dolls."

I said, "Ah."

Dolores glanced at me shyly. She had a doll in her lap, not a Barbie to all appearances, but some other type. With a little hammer and an X-acto knife, she was cutting open its stomach. There was a box of identical little plastic girls, sexless, unmarred, standing close together with their chests pierced in a pattern of holes like those old-fashioned radio speakers. Beside them, there was a box of little girls' heads, eyes demurely closed, a smile turning up the corners of each set of perfect lips. "Chatty Cathys," she said. "It's a new hobby. I fix their voices so they can talk again."

"That's great."

Homer said, "I'll leave you girls to your own devices. You have a lot you want to talk about."

He closed me into the room with her, as pleased with himself as a parent introducing two new best friends to each other. Clearly, he hadn't guessed my unfortunate history with surrogate children. My first, a Betsy Wetsy, if she'd survived, would have had to enter therapy at some point in her life. At age six, I thought it was a bore to be constantly feeding her those tiny bottles of water and it annoyed me no end every time she peed in my lap. Once I figured out it was the water, I quit feeding her altogether and then I used her as the pedestrian I ran over with my trike. This was my definition of motherly love and probably explains why I'm not a parent today.

"How many Barbies do you have?" I asked, feigning enthusiasm for the little proto-women.

"A little over two thousand. That's the star of my collection, a number one Barbie still in her original package. The seal's been broken, but she's in near-mint condition. I'm afraid to tell you what I paid," she said. Her speech was uninflected, her manner without affect. She made little eye contact, addressing most of her comments to the doll as she worked. "Homer's always been very supportive."

"I can see that," I said.

"I'm a bit of a purist. A lot of collectors are interested in others in the line—you know, Francie, Tutti and Todd, Jamie, Skipper, Christie, Cara, Casey, Buffy. I never cared for them myself. And certainly not Ken. Did you have a Barbie as a kid?"

"I can't say I did," I said. I picked one up and examined her. "She looks like she's suffering from some sort of eating disorder, doesn't she? What prompted you to get into Chatty Cathys? That seems far afield for a Barbie purist."

"Most of the Chatties aren't mine. I'm repairing them for a friend who runs a business doing this. It's not as far-fetched as it seems. Chatty Cathy was introduced in 1960, the year after Barbie. Chatty Cathy was more realistic—freckles, buck teeth, little pot belly—this in addition to her ability to speak. Even with Barbie, 1967 to 1973 is known as the Talking Era, which includes the Twist 'n' Turn dolls. Few people realize that."

"I know I didn't," I said. "What's that thing?"

"That's the little three-inch vinyl record of Cathy's sayings. When you pull the string, it activates a spring that makes that little rubber belt drive the turntable. The early versions of the doll had eleven sayings, but that was increased to eighteen. Odd thing about Chatties is that no two look alike. Of course, they were mass-produced, but they all seem to be different. It's almost creepy in some ways. Anyway, I'm sure you didn't drive all the way down here to talk about dolls. You're interested in my father."

"Homer filled me in, but I'd like to hear your version. I understand he and Alfie Toth spent some time with you just after they were released from Chino."

"That's right. Pops was feeling sorry for himself because none of the other kids wanted anything to do with him. He tried to spend a night with my brother Clint—he lives down in Inglewood by the L.A. airport. Clint's still bitter about Pops. He refused to let him in, but he told him he could sleep in the toolshed if he wanted to. Pops was furious, of course, so he left in a huff, but not before he broke into Clint's house. Him and Alfie waited 'til Clint was gone, stole his cash, and busted up all his furniture."

"That must have been a big hit. Did Clint report it to the police?"

Dolores seemed startled, the first real reaction I'd seen. "Why would he do that?"

"I've heard there was a plainclothes detective trying to serve a warrant against Toth around the time of his death. I'm wondering if it dated back to that same incident."

Dolores shook her head. "I'm sure not. Clint would never do a thing like that. He might not want Pops in his house, but he'd never snitch on him. It's odd, but when my sister Mame called—this was just about a year ago—to say they'd found his body, I started laughing so hard I peed my pants. Homer had to call the doctor when it turned out I couldn't quit. Doctor gave me a shot to calm me down. He said it was hysteria, but it was actually relief. We hadn't heard from him for five years by then so I guess I was waiting for the other shoe to drop."

"Why do you think he went from Clint's to Lake Tahoe?"

"My sister lives up there. Or one of them, at any rate. Not in Lake Tahoe exactly, but that vicinity."

"Really? I've been curious what prompted him to travel in that direction."

"I don't think Mame's husband was any happier to see him than Homer was."

"How long was he with her?"

"A week or so. Mame told me later him and Alfie went off to go fishing and that's the last anyone ever saw Pops as far as I know."

"Do you think I could talk to her? I'm sure the police have covered this ground, but it would be helpful to me."

"Oh, sure. She isn't hard to find. She works as a clerk in the sheriff's department up there."

"Up there where?"

"Nota Lake. Her name is Margaret, but everybody in the family calls her Mame."

17

When I got home, Henry was in the backyard, kneeling in the flower bed. I crossed the lawn, pausing to watch him at work. He was aware of my presence, but seemed content with the quiet. He wore a white T-shirt and farmer's pants with padded knees. His feet were bare, long, and bony, the high arches very white against the faded grass. The air was sweet and mild. Even with the noon sun directly overhead, the temperature was moderate. I could already see crocuses and hyacinths coming up in clusters beside the garage. I sat down on a wooden lawn chair while he turned the soil with a hand trowel. The earth was soft and damp, worms recoiling from the intrusion when his efforts disturbed them. His rose bushes were barren sticks, bristling with thorns, the occasional leaf bud suggesting that spring was on its way. The lawn, which had been dormant much of the winter, was beginning to waken with the encouragement of recent rains. I could see a haze of green where the new blades were beginning to push up through the brown. "People tend to associate autumn with death, but spring always seems a lot closer to me," he remarked.

"Why's that?"

"There's no deep philosophical significance. Somehow in my history, a lot of people I love have ended up dying this time of year. Maybe they yearn to look out the window and see new leaves on the trees. It's a time of hope and that might be enough if you're on your way out; allows you to let go, knowing the world is moving on as it always has."

"I have to go back to Nota Lake," I said.

"When?"

"Sometime next week. I'd like to hang out here long enough to get my hand back in working order."

"Why go at all?"

"I have to talk to someone."

"Can't you do that by phone?"

"It's too easy for people to tell lies on the phone. I like to see faces," I said. I was silent, listening to the homely chucking of his trowel in the dirt. I pulled my legs up and wrapped my arms around my knees. "Remember in the old days when we talked about vibes?"

I could see Henry smile. "You have bad vibes?"

"The worst." I held up my right hand and tried flexing the fingers, which were still so swollen and stiff I could barely make a fist.

"Don't go. You don't have anything to prove."

"Of course I do, Henry. I'm a girl. We're always having to prove something."

"Like what?"

"That we're tough. That we're as good as the guys, which I'm happy to report is not that hard."

"If it's true, why do you have to prove it?"

"Comes with the turf. Just because we believe it, doesn't mean guys do."

"Who cares about men? Don't be macha."

"I can't help it. Anyway, this isn't about pride. This is about mental health. I can't afford to let some guy intimidate me like that. Trust me, somewhere up in Nota Lake he's laughing his ass off, thinking he's run me out of town."

"The Code of the West. A girl's gotta do what a girl's gotta do."

"It feels bad. The whole thing. I don't remember feeling this much dread. That son of a bitch *hurt* me. I hate giving him the opportunity to do it again."

"At least your tetanus shot's up to date."

"Yeah, and my butt still hurts. I got a knot on my hip the size of a hard-boiled egg."

"So what worries you?"

"What worries me is I got my fingers dislocated before I knew jack-shit. Now that I'm getting closer, what's the guy going to do? You think he'll go down without trying to take me with him?"

"Phone's ringing," he remarked.

"God, Henry. How can you hear that? You're eighty-six years old."

"Three rings."

I was off the chair and halfway across the yard by then. I left my door open and caught the phone on the fly, just as the machine kicked in. I pressed Stop, effectively cutting off the message. "Hello, hello, hello."

"Kinsey, is that you? I thought this was your machine."

"Hi, Selma. You lucked out. I was out in the yard."

"I'm sorry to have to bother you."

"Not a problem. What's up?"

"Someone's been searching Tom's study. I know this sounds odd, but I'm sure someone came in here and moved the items on his desk. It's not like the room was trashed, but something's off. I can't see that anything's missing and I don't know how I'd prove it even if there was."

"How'd they get in?"

She hesitated. "I was only gone for an hour, maybe slightly more. I hardly ever lock the door for short periods like that."

"What makes you so sure someone was there?"

"I can't explain. I'd been sitting in Tom's den earlier, before I went out. I was feeling depressed and it seemed like a comfort just to sit in his chair. You know how it is when you think about things. You're aware of your surroundings because your gaze tends to wander while your mind is elsewhere. I guess I was realizing how much work you'd done. Anyway, when I got home, I set my handbag on the kitchen table and went back to the car. I'd picked up some boxes to finish packing Tom's books. The minute I walked into his den I could see the difference."

"You haven't had any visitors?"

"Oh, please. You know how people have been treating me. I might as well hang out a sign . . . 'Town siren. Straying husbands apply here.' "

"What about Brant? How do you know he wasn't in there looking for something on Tom's desk?"

"I asked him, but he was at Sherry's until a few minutes ago. I had him check the perimeter, but there's no sign of forced entry."

"Who'd bother to force entrance with all the doors unlocked?" I said. "Can Brant tell if anything's missing?"

"He's in the same boat I'm in. It's certainly nothing obvious, if it's anything at all. Whoever it was seemed to work with great care. It was only coincidental that I'd been in there this morning or I don't think I'd have noticed. Do you think I should call the sheriff's office?"

"Yeah, you better do that," I said. "Later, if it turns out something's been stolen, you can follow up."

"That's what Brant said." There was a tiny pause while she changed tacks, her voice assuming a faintly injured tone. "I must say, I've been upset about your lack of communication. I've been waiting to hear from you."

"Sorry, but I haven't had the chance. I was going to call you in a bit," I said. I noticed how defensive I sounded in response to her reproof.

"Now that I have you on the line, could you tell me what's happening? I assume you're still working even if you haven't kept in touch."

"Of course." I controlled my desire to bristle and I filled her in on my activities the past day and a half, sidestepping the personal aspects of Tom's relationship with Colleen Sellers. Telling a partial truth is much harder than an outright lie. Here I was, trying to protect her, while she was chiding me for neglect. Talk about ungrateful. I was tempted to tell all, but I repressed the urge. I kept my tone of voice professional, while my inner kid hollered *Up yours.* "Tom came down here in June as part of an investigation. Do you remember the occasion? He was probably gone overnight."

"Yes," she said, slowly. "It was two days. What's the relevance?"

"There was a homicide down here Tom felt was connected to some skeletal remains found in Nota County last spring."

"I know the case you're referring to. He didn't say much about it, but I know it bothered him. What about it?"

"Well, if we're talking about an active homicide investigation, I don't have the authority. I'm a private investigator, which is the equivalent of doing freelance research. I can't, even on your say-so, stick my nose into police business."

"I don't see why not. Surely there's no law against asking questions."

"I *have* asked questions and I'm telling you what I found. Tom was stressed out about matters that had nothing to do with you."

"Why didn't he tell me what it was, if that's true?"

"You were the one who said he played things close to his chest, especially when it came to work."

"Well yes, but if this is strictly professional, then why would someone go to all the trouble to search the house?"

"Maybe the department needed his notes or his files or a telephone number or a missing report. It could be anything," I said, rattling off the possibilities as quickly as they occurred to me.

"Why didn't they call and ask?"

"How do I know? Maybe they were in a hurry and you weren't home," I said, exasperated. It all sounded lame, but she was backing me into corners and it was annoying me no end.

"Kinsey, I am paying you to get to the bottom of this. If I'd known you weren't going to help, I could have used that fifteen hundred dollars to get my teeth capped."

"I'm doing what I can! What do you want from me?" I said.

"Well, you needn't take *that* attitude. A week ago, you were cooperative. Now all I'm hearing are excuses."

I had to bite my tongue. I had to talk in very distinct, clipped syllables to keep from screaming at her. I took a deep breath. "Look, I have one lead left. As soon as I get up there, I'll be happy to check it out, but if this is sheriff's department business, then it's out of my hands."

There was one of those silences that sounded like it contained an exclamation point. "If you don't want to finish the job, why don't you come right out and say so?"

"I'm not saying that."

"Then when are you coming back?"

"I'm not sure yet. Next week. Maybe Tuesday."

"Next *week*?" she said. "What's wrong with today? If you got in your car now, you could be here in six hours."

"What's the big hurry? This has been going on for weeks."

"Well, for one thing, you still owe me five hundred dollars' worth of work. For that kind of money, I would think you'd want to get here as soon as possible."

"Selma, I'm not going to sit here and argue about this. I'll do what I can."

"Wonderful. What time shall I expect you?"

"I have no idea."

"Surely, you can give me *some* idea when you might arrive. I have other obligations. I'll be gone all day tomorrow. I go to ten o'clock services and then spend some time with my cousin down in Big Pine. I can't sit around waiting for you to show up any time it suits. Besides, if you're coming, I'll need to make arrangements."

"I'll call when I get there, but I'm not going to stay at the Nota Lake Cabins. I hate that place and I won't be put in that position. It's too remote and it's dangerous."

"Fine," she said, promptly. "You can stay here at the house with me."

"I wouldn't dream of imposing. I'll find another motel so there won't be any inconvenience for either one of us."

"It's no inconvenience. I could use the company. Brant thinks it's high time he moved back to his place. He's already in the process of packing up. The guest room is always ready. I insist. I'll have supper waiting and no arguments about that, please."

"We'll talk about it when I get there," I said, trying to conceal my irritation. I was rapidly reassessing my opinion of the woman, ready to cast my vote with her legions of detractors. This was a side of her I hadn't seen before and I was churning with indignation. Of course, I noticed I'd already started revising my mental timetable, preparing to hit the road as soon as possible. Having consented, in effect, I now found myself wanting to get it over with. I shortened the fare-thee-wells, trying to get her off the phone while I could.

The minute I replaced the receiver, I picked it up again and placed a call to Colleen Sellers. While the interminable ringing of her line went on, I could feel my impatience mount. "Come on, come on. Be there . . ."

"Hello?"

"Colleen, it's Kinsey here."

"What can I do for you?"

She didn't sound that thrilled to hear from me, but I was through pussyfooting around. "I just spent thirty minutes with Pinkie Ritter's daughter Dolores and her husband. Turns out Pinkie has another daughter in Nota Lake, which is why he and Alfie went up there in the first place."

"And?"

"This is someone I've met, a woman named Margaret who works for the sheriff's department as a clerk. I'm going to have to go back up there and talk to her again, but I can't go without knowing what I'm up against."

"Why call me? I can't help."

"Yes, you can—"

"Kinsey, I don't know anything about this and frankly, I'm annoyed you keep pressing the point."

"Well, *frankly*, I guess I'll just have to risk your irritation. What's the matter with you, Colleen?"

"Does it ever occur to you that I might find this painful? I mean, I'm sorry as hell for Selma, but she's not the only one who's suffered a loss. I was in love with him, too, and I don't appreciate your constantly picking at the wound."

"Oh, really. Well, it's interesting that you should say so because you want to know what I think is going on? I think it pisses you off that you never had any power or any control in that relationship. Tom may have taken the moral high ground, acting from his lofty-sounding principles, but the fact is he left you with nothing and this is your payback."

"That's not true."

"Try again," I said.

"What's to pay back? He never did anything to me."

"Tom was a tease. He was willing to flirt, but he was quick to draw lines you couldn't cross. He could afford to enjoy your attention because it didn't cost him a thing. He accepted the tribute without taking any risks, which meant he got to feel virtuous while you were left like a kid with your nose pressed to the glass. You could see what you wanted, but you weren't allowed to touch. And now you're thinking that's the best you'll ever have, which is *really* bullshit because you didn't have anything. All this talk about pain is an attempt to sanctify a big, fat, emotional zero." I knew I was only ragging on her because Selma had ragged on me, but it felt good nonetheless. Later, I'd feel guilty for being such a bitch, but for now it seemed like the only way to get what I wanted.

She was silent for a moment. I could hear the intake of cigarette smoke, followed by the exhale of her breath. "Maybe."

"Maybe, my ass. It's the truth," I said. "Everybody sees him as noble, but I think he was supremely egotistical. How honorable was he when he never had the courage to tell his wife?"

"Tell her what?"

"That he was tempted to be unfaithful because of his attraction to you. He didn't act on his feelings, but it's no bloody wonder she ended up feeling insecure. And what did it net you? You're still hung up on him and you may never get yourself off the hook."

"Look, you really don't know what you're talking about so let's skip all the homegrown psychology. Tell me what you want and get it over with."

"You have to level with me."

"Why?"

"Because my life may depend on it," I snapped. "Come on, Colleen. You're a professional. You know better. You sit there doling out little tidbits of information, hanging on to the crumbs because it's all you have. This is serious damn shit. If Tom were in your position, do you think he'd withhold information in a situation like this?"

She inhaled again. "Probably not." Grudgingly.

"Then let's get on with it. If you know what's going on, for god's sake, let's have it."

She seemed to hesitate. "Tom was facing a moral crisis. I was the easy part, but I wasn't all of it."

"What do you mean, you were the easy part?"

"I'm not sure how to explain. I think he could do the right thing with me and it was a comfort to him. That situation made sense while the other problem he was facing was more complicated."

"You're just guessing at this or do you know for a fact?"

"Well, Tom never came out and said so, but he did allude to the issue. Something about not knowing how to reconcile his head and his gut."

"In regard to what?"

"He felt responsible for Toth's murder."

"He felt *responsible*? How come?"

"A breach of confidentiality."

"As in what? I don't get it."

"Toth's whereabouts," she said. "I gave him the address and phone number of the Gramercy. Tom thought someone used the information to track Toth down and kill him. It was driving him crazy to think the man might have died because of his carelessness."

I felt myself blinking at the phone, trying to make sense of what she'd said. "But Selma tells me Tom was always tight-lipped. That was one of her complaints. He never talked about anything, especially when it came to his work."

"It wasn't *talk* at all. He thought someone took an unauthorized look at his notes."

"But his notebook is missing."

"Well, it wasn't back then."

"Who did he suspect? Did he ever mention a name?"

"Someone he worked with. And that's my guess, by the way, not something he said to me directly. Why else would it bother him if it wasn't someone betraying the department?"

I felt myself grow still. I flashed on the officers I'd met in Nota Lake: Rafer LaMott; Tom's brother, Macon; Hatch Brine; James Tennyson; Earlene's husband, Wayne. Even Deputy Carey Badger, who'd taken my report on the night of the assault. The list seemed to go on and on and all of them were connected with the Nota Lake Sheriff's Department or the CHP. At the back of my mind, I'd been flirting with a possibility I'd scarcely dared to admit. What I'd been harboring was the suspicion that my attacker had been trained at a police academy. I'd been resisting the notion, but I could feel it begin to take root in my imagination. He'd taken me down with an efficiency I'd been taught once upon a time myself. Whether he was currently employed in some branch of law enforcement, I couldn't be sure, but the very idea left me feeling cold. "Are you telling me one of Tom's colleagues was involved in a double homicide?"

"I think that was his suspicion and it was tearing him apart. Again, this wasn't something he said. This is my best guess."

This time I was silent for a moment. "I should have seen that. How stupid of me. Shit."

"What will you do now?"

"Beats the hell out of me. What would you suggest?"

"Why not talk to someone in Internal Affairs?"

"And say what? I'm certainly willing to give them anything I have, but at this point, it's all speculation, isn't it?"

"Well, yes. I guess that's one reason I didn't call myself. I've got nothing concrete. Maybe if you talk to Pinkie's daughter up there, it will clarify the situation."

"Meanwhile alerting the guy that I'm breathing down his neck," I said.

"But you can't do this on your own."

"Who'm I gonna call? The Nota Lake Sheriff's Department?"

"I'm not sure I'd do that," she said, laughing for once.

"Yeah, well if I figure it out, I'll let you know," I said. "Any other comments or advice while we're on the subject?"

She thought about it briefly. "Well, one thing . . . though you may have already thought about this. It must have been general knowledge Tom was working on this case, so once he dropped dead, the guy must have thought he was home free."

"And now I come along. Bad break," I said. "Of course, the guy can't be sure how much information Tom passed to his superiors."

"Exactly. If it's not in his reports, it might still be in circulation somewhere, especially with his notes gone. You'd better hope you get to 'em before someone else does."

"Maybe the guy already has them in his possession."

"Then why's he afraid of you? You're only dangerous if you have the notes," she said.

I thought about the search of Tom's den. "You're right."

"I'd proceed with care."

"Trust me," I said. "One more question while I have you on the line. Were you ever in Nota Lake yourself?"

"Are you kidding? Tom was too nervous to see me there."

I replaced the receiver, distracted. My anxiety level was rising ominously, like a toilet on the verge of overflowing. The fear was like something damp and heavy sinking into my bones. I have a thing about authority figures, specifically police officers in uniform, probably dating from that first encounter while I was trapped in the wreckage of my parents' car at the age of five. I can still remember the horror and the relief of being rescued by those big guys with their guns and nightsticks. Still, the sense of jeopardy and pain also attached to that image. At five, I wasn't capable of separating the two. In terms of confusion and loss, what I'd experienced was irrevocably bound up with the sight of men in uniform. As a child, I'd been taught the police were my pals, people to turn to if you were lost or afraid. At the same time, I knew police had the power to put you in jail, which made them fearful to contemplate if you were sometimes as "bad" as I was. In retrospect, I can see that I'd applied to the police academy, in part, to ally myself with the very folks I feared. Being on the side of the law was, no doubt, my attempt to cope with that old anxiety. Most of the officers I'd known since had been decent, caring people, which made it all the more alarming to think that one might have crossed the line. I couldn't think when anything had frightened me quite as much as the idea of going up against this guy, but what could I do? If I quit this one, then what? The next time I got scared, was I going to quit that job, too?

I went up the spiral stairs and dutifully started shoving items in my duffel.

18

The ocean was white with fog, the horizon fading into milk a hundred yards offshore. The sun behind clouds created a harsh, nearly blinding light. Colors seemed flattened by the haze, which lent a chill to the air. A quick check of the weather channel before I'd departed showed heavy precipitation in the area of California where I was headed, and within the first twenty-five miles, I could already sense the shift.

I took Highway 126 through Santa Paula and Fillmore until I ran into Highway 5, where I doglegged over to Highway 14. I drove through canyon country—balding, brown hills, tufted with chaparral, as wrinkled and hairy as elephants. Power lines marched across the folds of the earth while the highway spun six lanes of concrete through the cuts and crevices. Residential developments had sprung up everywhere, the ridges dotted with tract houses so that the natural rock formations looked strangely out of place. There was evidence of construction still in progress—earth movers, concrete mixers, temporary equipment yards enclosed in wire fencing in which heavy machinery was being housed for the duration. An occasional Porta-Potty occupied the wide aisle between lanes of the freeway. The land was the color of dry dirt and dried grass. Trees were few and didn't seem to assert much of a presence out here.

By the time I'd passed Edwards Air Force Base, driving in a straight line north, the sky was gray. The clouds collected in ascending layers that blocked out the fading sun overhead. The drizzle that began to fall looked more like a fine vapor sheeting through the air. Misty-looking communities appeared in the distance, flat and small, laid out in a grid, like an outpost on the moon. Closer to the road, there would be an occasional outbuilding, left over from god knows what decade. The desert, while unforgiving, nevertheless tolerates man-made structures, which remain—lopsided, with broken windows, roofs collapsing—long after the inhabitants have died or moved on. I could see the entire expanse of rain-swept plains to the rim of hushed buff-colored mountains. The telephone poles, extending into the horizon ahead of me, could have served as a lesson in perspective. Behind the barren, pointed hills, rugged granite outcroppings grew darker as the rain increased. Gradually, the road moved into the foothills. The mountains beyond them were imposing. Nothing marred the featureless, pale surface—no trees, no grass, no mark of human passage. At higher elevations, I could see vegetation where low-hanging clouds provided sufficient moisture to support growth.

I'd tucked my semiautomatic in the duffel. The gun experts, Dietz among them, were quick to scoff at the little Davis, but it was a handgun I knew and it felt far more familiar to me than the Heckler and Koch, a more recent acquisition. Given the state of my bunged-up fingers, I doubted I'd be capable of pulling the trigger in any event, but the gun was a comfort in my current apprehensive state.

Little by little, I was giving up my initial irritation with Selma. As with anything else, once a process is under way, there's no point in railing against the Fates. I regretted that I hadn't had time to contact Leland Peck, the clerk at the Gramercy Hotel. I'd taken his co-worker's word that he had nothing to report. Any good investigator knows better. I should have taken the trouble to look him up so I could quiz him about his recollections of the plainclothes detective with the warrant for Toth's arrest.

In the meantime, secure in my ignorance of events to come, I thought idly of the night ahead. I truly hate being a guest in someone's home. The bed seldom suits me. The blankets are usually skimpy. The pillows are flat or made out of hard rubber that smells of half-deflated basketballs. The toilet refuses to flush fully or the handle gets stuck or the paper runs out so that you're forced to search all the cabinets looking for the ever so cunningly hidden supply. Worst of all, you have to "make nice" at all hours. I don't want someone across the table from me while I'm eating my breakfast. I don't want to share the newspaper and I don't want to talk to anyone at the end of the day. If I were interested in that shit, I'd be married again by now and put a permanent end to all the peace and quiet.

By the time I arrived in Nota Lake at 6:45, night had settled on the landscape and the weather was truly nasty. The drizzle had intensified into a stinging sleet. My windshield wipers labored, collecting slush in an arc that nearly filled my windshield. My guess was the people of Nota Lake, like others in perpetually cold climates, had strategies for coping with the shifting character of snow. From my limited experience, the freezing rain seemed extremely hazardous, making the roadway as slick as a skating rink. In moments, I could feel the vehicle slide sideways and I slowed to a snail's pace. At the road's edge, the dead grass had stiffened, collecting feathery drifts of whirling snow. Selma had bullied me into having supper with her. I'm easily influenced in food matters, having been conditioned these past years by Rosie's culinary imperiousness. When ordered about by any woman with a certain autocratic tone, I do as I'm told, largely helpless to resist.

I parked out in front of Selma's, snagged my duffel, and hurried to the front porch, head bent, shoulders hunched as though to avoid the combination of blowing rain and biting snow. I knocked politely, shifting impatiently from foot to foot until she opened the door. We exchanged the customary chitchat as I stepped into the foyer and dried my feet on a rag rug. I shrugged off my leather jacket and eased out of my shoes, conscious of the pristine carpet. The house was toasty warm, hazy from the cigarette smoke sealed into the winterproofed rooms. I shivered with belated relief at being out of the cold. I padded after Selma, who showed me to the guest room. "Take whatever time you need to freshen up and get settled. I cleared some space in the closet and emptied a drawer for your things. I'll be out in the kitchen putting the finishing touches on supper. You know your way around, but don't hesitate to holler if you need anything."

"Thanks."

Once the door closed behind me, I surveyed the room with dismay. The carpet here was hot pink, a cut-pile cotton shag. There was a four-poster bed with a canopy and a puffy, quilted spread of pink-and-white checked gingham. The same fabric continued in the dust ruffle and ruffled pillow shams, stacked three deep. A collection of six quilted teddy bears were grouped together in a window seat. The wallpaper was pink-and-white stripes with a floral border across the top. There was an old-fashioned vanity table with a padded seat and a pink-and-white ruffled skirt. Everything was trimmed in oversized white rickrack. The guest bath was an extension of this jaunty decorative theme, complete with a crocheted cozy for the extra roll of toilet paper. The room smelled as though it had been closed up for some time and the heat here seemed more intense than in the rest of the house. I could feel myself start to hyperventilate with the craving for fresh air.

I crossed to the window, like a hot prowl thief trying to escape. I managed to inch up the sash, only to be faced with a seriously constructed double-glazed storm window. I worked at the latches until I loosened all of them. I gave the storm window a push and it fell promptly out of the frame and dropped into the bushes below. *Oops.* I stuck my head through the gap and let the blessed sleet blow across my face. The storm window had landed just beyond my grasp so I left it where it was, resting in the junipers. I lowered the sash again and adjusted the ruffled curtains so the missing storm window wasn't evident. At least, at bedtime, I could sleep in a properly refrigerated atmosphere.

Selma had urged me to freshen up and I used her advice to stall my return to the kitchen. I peed, washed my hands, and brushed my teeth, happy to occupy my time with these homely ablutions. I stood in the bathroom and stared at myself in the mirror, wondering if I'd ever develop an interest in the painful process of plucking my eyebrows. Not likely. My jaw was still bruised and I paused to admire the ever-changing hue. Then I stood in the bedroom and did a quick visual scan. I removed my handgun from the duffel and hid it between the mattress and the box springs near the head of the bed. This would fool no one, but it would allow me to keep the gun close. I didn't think it would be wise to pack a rod in this town, especially without the proper permit. Finally, there was nothing for it but to take a deep breath and present myself at the supper table.

Selma seemed subdued. Her attitude surprised me, given the fact that she'd gotten her way. I was back in Nota Lake, staying at her house, which was the last thing I wanted. "I kept everything simple. I hope you don't mind," she said.

"This is fine," I said.

She took a moment to stub out her cigarette, blowing the final stream of smoke to one side. This, for a smoker, constitutes etiquette. We pulled out our chairs and took seats at the kitchen table.

Given my usual diet, a home-cooked meal of any kind is an extraordinary treat. Or so I thought before I was faced with the one she'd prepared. This was the menu: iced tea with Sweet 'N Low already mixed in, a green Jell-O square with fruit cocktail and an internal ribbon of Miracle Whip, iceberg lettuce with bottled dressing the color of a sunset. For the main course, instant mashed potatoes with margarine and a stout slice of meatloaf, swimming in diluted cream of mushroom soup. As I ate, my fork exposed a couple of pockets of dried mashed potato flakes. The meatloaf was strongly reminiscent of something served at the Perdido County Jail, where there was an entire (much-dreaded) punishment referred to as being "on meatloaf." On meatloaf means an inmate is placed on a diet of meatloaf and two slices of squishy white bread twice a day, with only drinking water from the faucet. The meatloaf, a six-inch patty made of turkey, kidney beans, and other protein-rich filler, is served on something nominally known as gravy. Every third day the law mandates that the inmate has to be served three square meals for one day, then back to meatloaf. By comparison to Selma's version, a simple QP with cheese came off looking like a gourmet feast. Especially since I knew for a fact she didn't feed Brant this way.

Selma was quiet throughout the meal and I didn't have much to contribute. I felt like one of those married couples you see out in restaurants—not looking at each other, not bothering to say a word. The minute we'd finished eating, she lit up another cigarette so I wouldn't miss a minute of the tars and noxious gases wafting across the table. "Would you like coffee or dessert? I have a nice coconut cream pie in the freezer. It won't take a minute to thaw. I can pop it in the microwave."

"Golly, I'm full. This was great."

"Are you cold? I saw you shiver. I can turn the heat up if you like."

"No, no. Really. I'm toasty warm. This was wonderful."

She tapped her cigarette ash on the edge of her plate. "I didn't ask you about your fingers."

I held up my right hand. "They're a little stiff yet, but better."

"Well, that's good. Now that you're back, what's the plan?"

"I was just thinking about that," I said. "I'm not sure what to make of this and I don't want it going any further, but I think I have a line on what was bothering Tom."

"Really."

"After we spoke this morning, I made another phone call. Without going into any detail . . ." I paused. "I'm not even sure how to tell you this. It seems awkward."

"For heaven's sake. Just say it."

"It looks like Tom suspected a fellow officer in that double homicide he was investigating."

Selma looked at me, blinking, while she absorbed the information. She took a deep drag of her cigarette and blew out a sharp stream of smoke. "I don't believe it."

"I know it sounds incredible, but stop and think about it for a minute. Tom was trying to establish the link between the two victims, right?"

"Yes."

"Well, apparently he believed one of his colleagues lifted Alfie Toth's address from his field notes. Toth was murdered shortly afterward. Toth was always on the move, but he'd just gotten out of jail and he was living temporarily in a fleabag hotel. This was the first time anyone had managed to pin him down to one location. No one else in Nota Lake knew where Alfie Toth was hanging out except him."

"What makes you so sure? He might have mentioned it to someone. Or someone else might have come up with the information independently," she said.

"You're right about that. The point is, Tom must have gone crazy thinking he played a role in Alfie's death. Worse yet, suspecting someone in the department had a hand in it."

"But you don't really *know*," she said. "This is just a guess on your part."

"How are we ever going to *know* anything unless someone 'fesses up? And that seems unlikely. I mean, so far this 'someone' has gotten away with it."

"Who told you this?"

"Don't worry about that. It was someone with the sheriff's department. A confidential source."

"Confidential, my foot. You're making a serious allegation."

"You think I don't know that? Of course I am," I said. "Look, I don't like the idea any better than you do. That's why I came back, to pin it down."

"And if you can't?"

"Then, frankly, I'm out of ideas. There is one possibility. Pinkie Ritter's daughter, Margaret . . ."

Selma frowned. "That's right. I'd forgotten their relationship. The connection seems odd, what with her working for Tom."

"Nota Lake's a small town. The woman has to work somewhere, so why not the sheriff's department? Everybody else seems to work there," I pointed out.

"Why didn't she speak up when you were here before?"

"I didn't know about Ritter until yesterday."

"I think you better talk to Rafer."

"I think it's best to keep him out of this for now." I caught the odd look that crossed her face. "What?"

She hesitated. "I ran into him this afternoon and told him you'd be back this evening."

I felt my eyes roll in despair and I longed to bang my head on the tabletop just one time for emphasis. "I wish you'd kept quiet. It's hard enough as it is. Everybody here knows everybody else's business."

She waved aside my objection like a pesky horsefly sailing through the smoke-filled air. "Don't be silly. He was Tom's best friend. What will you do?"

"I'll talk to Margaret tonight and see what she knows," I said. "After that, my only option is to go back to Santa Teresa and confer with the sheriff's department there."

"And tell them what? You don't have much."

"I don't have *anything*," I said. "Unless something develops, I'm at a dead loss."

"I see. Then I suppose that's it." Selma stubbed out her cigarette and got up without another word. She began to clear the dinner dishes, moving from the table to the sink.

"Let me help you with that," I said, getting up to assist.

"Don't trouble." Her tone of voice was frosty, her manner withdrawn.

I began to gather up plates and silverware, moving to the sink where she was already scraping leftover Jell-O into the garbage disposal. She ran water across a plate, opened the door to the dishwasher, and placed it in the lower rack. The silence was uncomfortable and the clattering of plates contained a note of agitation.

"Is something on your mind?" I asked.

"I hope I didn't make a mistake in hiring you."

I glanced at her sharply. "I never offered you a guarantee. No responsible P.I. could make a promise like that. Sometimes the information simply isn't there," I said.

"That's not what I meant."

"Then what were you referring to?"

"I never even asked you for references."

"A little late at this point. You want to talk to some of my past employers, I'll make up a list."

She was silent again. I was having trouble tracking the change in her demeanor. Maybe she thought I was giving up. "I'm not saying I'll quit," I said.

"I understand. You're saying you're out of your league."

"You want to go up against the cops? Personally, I've got more sense."

She banged a plate down so hard it broke down the middle into two equal pieces. "My husband *died.*"

"I know that. I'm sorry."

"No, you're not. Nobody gives a shit what I've gone through."

"Selma, you hired me to do this and I'm doing it. Yes, I'm out of my league. So was Tom, for that matter. Look what happened to him. It broke his heart."

She stood at the sink, letting the hot water run while her shoulders shook. Tears coursed along her cheeks. I stood there for a moment, wondering what to do. It seemed clear she'd go on weeping until I acted sincerely moved. I patted her awkwardly, making little murmurings. I pictured Tom doing much the same thing in his life, probably in this very spot. Water gurgled down the drain while the tears poured down her face. Finally, I couldn't stand it. I reached over and turned off the water. Live through enough droughts, you hate to see the waste. Where originally her grief had seemed genuine, I now suspected the emotion was being hauled out for effect. At long last, with much blowing and peeking at her nose products, she pulled herself together. We finished up the dishes and Selma retreated to her room, emerging shortly afterward in her nightie and robe, intending to make herself a glass of hot milk and get in bed. I fled the house as soon as it was decently possible. Nothing like being around a self-appointed invalid to make you feel hard-hearted.

Margaret and Hatch lived close to the center of town on Second Street. I'd called from Selma's before I left the house. I'd scarcely identified myself when she cut in, saying, "Dolores said you came to see her. What's this about?"

In light of her father's murder, the answer seemed obvious. "I'm trying to figure out what happened to your father," I said. "I wondered if it'd be possible to talk to you tonight. Is this a bad time for you?"

She'd seemed nonplussed at my request, conceding with reluctance. I couldn't understand her attitude, but I wrote it off to my imagination. After all, the subject had to be upsetting, especially in light of his past abusiveness. Twice she put a palm across the mouthpiece and conferred with someone in the background. My assumption was that it was Hatch, but she made no specific reference to him.

The drive over was uneventful, despite the treacherous roads and the continuous sleet. There was no accumulation of snow so far, but the pavement was glistening and my tires tended to sing every time I hit a slippery patch. I had to use the brakes judiciously, pumping gently from half a block back when I saw the stoplights ahead of me change. Paranoid as I was at that point, I did note the close proximity of the Brines' house to the parking lot at Tiny's Tavern where I'd been accosted. Once Wayne and Earlene dropped the Brines off at home, Hatch could easily have doubled back. I found myself scouring the streets for sight of a black panel truck, but of course saw nothing.

I entered a tract of brick ranch houses maybe fifteen years old, judging from the maturity of the landscaping. Tree trunks were now sturdy, maybe eight inches in diameter, and the foundation plantings had long ago crept over the windowsills. I slowed when I spotted the house number. The Brines had two cars and a pickup truck parked in or near the drive. I found a parking spot two doors down and sat at the curb wondering if there was a party in progress. I turned in my seat and studied the house. There were dim lights in front, brighter lights around the side and toward the portion of the rear that I could see from my vantage point. This was Saturday night. She hadn't mentioned a Tupperware party or Bible study, nor had she suggested I come at some other time. Maybe they were having friends in to watch a little network television. I debated with myself. I didn't like the idea of walking into a social gathering, especially since I could always talk to her tomorrow. On the other hand, she'd said I could come and meeting with her tonight would delay my return to Selma's. I still had a key to her place and the plan was for me to let myself in the front door whenever I got back that night. The car became noticeably colder the longer I sat. The neighborhood was quiet, with little traffic and no one visible on foot. Someone peeking out the windows would think I'd come to case the joint.

I got out of the car and locked the doors. The sidewalks must have been warmer than the streets. Snowflakes melted instantly, leaving shallow pools in lieu of icy patches. The trees in the yard were some deciduous variety, caught by surprise with tiny green buds in sight. March in this area must have been a constant series of nature pranks. I knocked on the door, hoping I wasn't walking in on a naughty lingerie party. Maybe that's why she'd invited me, in hopes I'd purchase a drawerful of underpants to replace all my tatty ones.

Margaret opened the door wearing blue jeans and a thick, red sweater with a Nordic design across the front; snowflakes and reindeer. She wore clunky calf-high suede boots with a sheepskin lining that must have felt warm on a night like this. With her black hair and oval glasses, she looked like a teenager hired to babysit. "Hi. Come on in."

"Thanks. I hope I'm not interrupting. I saw cars in the drive."

"Hatch's poker night. The boys are in the den," she said, hooking a thumb toward the rear. "I'm on kitchen detail. We can talk out there."

Like Selma's house, this one smelled as if it had been sealed for the winter, the rubber gaskets on the storm windows insuring the accumulation of smoke and cooking smells. The wall-to-wall carpet was a burnt orange high-low, the walls in the living room painted a shade of café au lait. The eight-foot sofa was a chocolate brown, and two black canvas butterfly chairs were arranged on either side of the coffee table. "You didn't have any trouble finding the place?" she asked.

"Not at all," I said. "You prefer Margaret or Mame? I know Dolores refers to you as Mame."

"Either one is fine. Suit yourself."

I followed her to the kitchen at the end of the hall. She was in the process of preparing food, platters of cold cuts on the long wood-grained Formica counter. There were bowls of chips, two containers of some kind of dip made with sour cream, and a mixture of nuts and Chex cereals tossed with butter and garlic powder. I know this because all the ingredients were still in plain view. "If you'll help me move these snacks to the dining room, we can get 'em out of the way and we can talk."

"Sure thing."

She picked up two bowls and shoved the swinging door open with a hip, holding it for me while I moved through with the tray of sliced cheeses and processed meats. Of course, it was all so unwholesome I was immediately hungry, but my appetite didn't last long. Through an archway to my left, I saw Hatch and his five buddies sitting on metal folding chairs at the poker table in the den. There were countless beer bottles and beer mugs in evidence, cigarettes, ashtrays, poker chips, dollar bills, coins, bowls of peanuts. To a man, the entire gathering turned to look at me. I recognized Wayne, James Tennyson, and Brant; the other two fellows I'd never seen before. Hatch made a comment and James laughed. Brant raised his hand in greeting. Margaret paid little attention to the lot of them, but the chill from the room was unmistakable.

I placed bowls on the table and moved back to the kitchen, trying to behave as though unaffected by their presence. Here's the truth about my life. Just about any jeopardy I encounter in adulthood I experienced first in elementary school. Guys making private jokes have struck me as sinister since I was forced to pass the sixth-grade boys every morning on my way to "kinney garden." Even then, I knew no good could come of such assemblages and I avoid them where possible.

I picked up a platter from the kitchen counter and intercepted Margaret as she reached the swinging door. "Why don't I pass these to you and you can put them on the table," I said, feigning helpfulness. In truth, I couldn't bear subjecting myself to that collective stare.

She took the platter without comment, holding the door open with her hip. "You might want to open a couple more beers. There's some on the bottom shelf of the refrigerator out on the utility porch."

I found six bottles of beer and the beer flip and made myself useful removing caps. Once we'd assembled the eats, Margaret pulled the swinging door shut and sighed with relief. "Lucky they don't play more than once a month," she said. "I told Hatch they should rotate, but he likes to have 'em here. Usually Earlene tags along with Wayne and helps me set up, but she's coming down with a cold and I told her to stay home. Shit—excuse my language—I forgot to put out the paper plates. I'll be right back." She snatched up a giant package of flimsy paper plates and moved toward the dining room. "You want anything to eat, you can help yourself," she said. As I was still burping meatloaf, I thought it wise to decline.

She came back to the kitchen and tossed the cellophane packaging in the trash, then turned and leaned against the counter, crossing her arms in front. "What can I help you with?" The question suggested cooperation, but her manner was all business.

"I'm just wondering what you can tell me about your father's last visit. I'm assuming he and Alfie Toth came to the area to see you that spring."

"That's right," she said. As though to distract herself, she began to screw lids on the pickle jars, stowing mustard and mayonnaise back in the refrigerator. "I hope you don't think this is disrespectful, but my father was a loser and we all knew that. Truthfully, I was happiest when he was in jail. He always seemed to cause trouble."

"Was he a problem on this visit?"

"Of course. Mostly chasing women. Like any woman here was that hard up," she said.

"From what little I know, I never pictured him as a ladies' man."

"He wasn't, but he'd just gotten out of jail and he was itching to get laid. He'd be at Tiny's at four, the minute the doors opened. Once he started drinking, he'd hit on anyone who crossed his path. He thought he was irresistible and he'd be angry and combative when his ham-handed flirtations didn't get him what he wanted."

"Anybody in particular?"

Margaret shrugged. "A waitress at the Rainbow and one at Tiny's. Alice, the one with red hair."

"I know her," I said.

"That's all he talked about, how horny he was. *Poontang,* he called it. I was embarrassed. I mean, what kind of talk is that coming from your dad? He couldn't have been more obnoxious. He got in fights. He borrowed money. He dinged the truck. People around here won't tolerate behavior like that. It drove Hatch insane so, of course, the two of us were fighting. Hatch wanted them out of here and I can't say I blamed him. What are you going to do though, your own dad? I could hardly ask him to leave. He'd been here less than a week."

"So what finally happened?"

"We sent him and Alfie off on a fishing trip. Anything to get them out from underfoot for a couple of days. Hatch lent 'em a couple of fishing rods he never did get back. He was p.o.'d about that. Anyway, I don't know what happened, but something must have gone wrong. Next morning, Alfie showed up and said they'd decided to take off and he'd come for their things."

"Where was your father?"

"Alfie told us Daddy was waiting for him and he had to get a move on or Pinkie'd be furious with him. I didn't think anything about it. I mean, it did sound like him. He was always trying to get Alfie to fetch and carry for him."

"Did Tom know all this?"

"I told him in March when Daddy's remains turned up. Once the body was identified, Tom notified me and I passed the news on to the rest of the family. Before that, as far as I knew, Dad was fine."

"Didn't it strike you as odd that no one in the family ever heard from him once he supposedly left here?"

"Why should it? Bad news travels fast. We always figured if something happened to him, someone would be in touch. Police or a hospital. He always carried ID. Besides, we heard from Alfie now and then. I guess the two of them split up, or that's the impression he gave."

"Why did he call?"

Margaret shrugged. "Beats me. Just to see how we were doing is what he said."

"Did he ever ask about your dad?"

"Well, yes, but it wasn't like he really wanted to get in touch. You know how it is. How's your dad? . . . What do you hear from him? . . . And that sort of thing."

"So he was wondering if Pinkie ever showed up again. Is that it?"

"I guess. Finally, he stopped calling and we lost touch with him."

"Maybe he realized Pinkie wasn't ever going to put in an appearance."

"That's what Tom said. He thought Daddy might have been murdered the very day Alfie left, though there was never any way to prove it. One thing they found was a gas receipt he'd tucked in his pocket. That was dated the day before. Him and Alfie filled up the tank on their way to the lake. You think Alfie knew something?"

"Almost certainly," I said.

"Maybe the two of them quarreled."

"It's always possible," I said. "Judging from his behavior, he was either trying to create the impression that Pinkie was alive, or he really wasn't sure himself. The last time you saw him . . . when he stopped by to pick up their belongings . . . did he seem okay to you?"

"Like what?"

"He wasn't nervous or in a hurry?"

"He was in a hurry for sure, but no more than he'd be with Daddy waiting."

"Any signs he'd been in a scuffle?"

"Nothing that I noticed. There wasn't any dirt or scratches."

"How did they plan to travel? Bus, train, plane? Hitchhiking?"

"They must have gone by bus. I mean, that was my assumption because the truck was left over at the Greyhound station. Hatch spotted it in the parking lot later that same day," she said.

19

By the time I left Margaret's, it was close to nine-thirty. I unlocked the VW and slid under the wheel, sticking the key in the ignition. A car approached and as it pulled up alongside, I could see that it was Macon, driving a black-and-white. Even through the car window I could tell he was better dressed for the cold than I was. I was wearing my brown leather bomber jacket, but was short the gloves, scarf, and cap. I rolled down my window. His car idled, static from the radio filling the air. The temperature had dropped. I blew on my fingers briefly and then turned the key in the ignition, firing up the VW just to get the engine warm. I adjusted the heat, which in a VW consists of moving one lever from OFF to ON. "What's up?" I asked.

"I'm on tonight anyway so I thought I might as well follow you home. I talked to Selma a little while ago and she told me what was going on. I'm glad you came back. She was worried you'd abandon ship."

"Believe me, I was tempted. I'd rather be at home," I said.

"I remember this Pinkie Ritter business. Ornery son of a gun. Was Margaret any help?"

"About what you'd expect," I said, evading the issue. "I'm heading over to Tiny's. She says he hustled one of the waitresses, so I'll see what she says. It might not mean anything, but I could pick up additional information. Maybe a jealous husband or a boyfriend was dealing out paybacks. You have any other suggestions?"

"Not offhand. You seem to be doing pretty good," Macon said, but he didn't sound convinced. "Why don't you let me ask around and see what I can find out. Seems like the fewer people who know what you're after the better."

"My sentiments exactly. Anyway, I better get a move on before I freeze."

Macon glanced at his watch. "How long will this take?"

"Not that long. Thirty minutes at best. I'm not even sure Alice works Saturdays. I'm assuming she does."

"Why don't I follow you as far as the parking lot? I can swing back in half an hour and follow you to Selma's. If the woman isn't working, have a Coke or something until I show up."

"I'd appreciate that. Thanks."

I rolled up the window and put the car in gear. Macon pulled out first, waiting for me to do a U-turn so I could follow him. With the boys entrenched in their poker game inside, I was feeling safer than I had all day.

The parking lot at Tiny's was packed with cars, RVs, and pickup trucks with camper shells. I tucked the VW into a small gap at the end of the last row. Macon waited, watching me cross two aisles, passing through the shadowy spaces between vehicles. Once I was at the rear entrance, I turned and waved to him and he took off with a little toot of his horn. I checked my watch. 10:05. I had until 10:30, which should give me plenty of time.

Saturday night at Tiny's was a rowdy affair; two alternating live bands, line dancing, contests, whooping, hollering, and much thumping of cowboy boots on the wooden dance floor. There were six waitresses working in a steady progression from the bar to the crowded tables. I spotted Alice with her gaudy orange hair half a room away and I pushed my way through the jostling three-deep bystanders ringing the room. I had to yell to make myself heard. She got the message and pointed toward the ladies' room. I watched her deliver a sloshing pitcher of beer and six tequila shooters, then collect a fistful of bills that she folded and pushed down the front of her shirt. She angled in my direction, taking orders as she came. The two of us burst into the empty ladies' room and pushed the door shut. The quiet was remarkable, the noise in the tavern reduced by more than half.

"Sorry to drag you away," I said.

"Are you kidding? I'm thrilled. This is hell on earth. It's like this most weekends and the tips are shit." She opened the first stall door and stepped just inside. She took a pack of cigarettes out of her apron pocket. "Keep an eye out for me, would you? I'm not supposed to stop for a smoke, but I can't help myself." She shook a cigarette free and fired it up in no time. She inhaled deeply, with a moan of pleasure and relief. "Lord, that's good. What are you doing here? I thought you went home to wherever it is."

"I left. Now I'm back."

"That was quick."

"Yeah, well I know a lot more now than I did two days ago."

"That's good. More power to you. I hear you're investigating a murder. Margaret Brine's father, or that's the word."

"It's slightly more complicated, but that's about it. As a matter of fact, I was just at her place, asking about his last visit."

Alice snorted. "What a horse's ass he was. He hustled my butt off, the randy little shit. I pinned his ears back, but he was hard to shake."

"Who else did he hustle? Anyone in particular? Margaret tells me he was horny as all get out—"

Alice held up a hand. "Mind if I interrupt for a sec? Something I should mention before you go on."

I hesitated, alerted by something in her tone. "Sure."

Alice studied the tip of her lighted cigarette. "I don't know how to say this, but people around here seem to be concerned about you."

"Why? What'd I do?"

"That's what everybody's asking. Grapevine has it you're into drugs."

"I am not! How ridiculous. That's ludicrous," I said.

"Also, you shot a couple of fellows in cold blood a while back."

"*I* did?" I said, laughing in startlement. "Where'd you hear *that*?"

"You never killed anyone?"

I felt my smile start to fade. "Well, yes, but that was self-defense. Both were killers, coming after me—"

Alice cut in. "Look, I didn't get the details and I don't really give a shit. I'm willing to believe you, but folks around here take a dim view of it. We don't like the idea of somebody coming in here starting trouble. We take care of our own."

"Alice, I promise. I've never shot anyone without provocation. The idea's repugnant. I swear. Where did this come from?"

"Who knows? This is something I picked up earlier. I overheard the fellows talking."

"This was tonight?"

"And yesterday some, too. This was shortly after you left. I guess someone did some digging and came up with the facts."

"Facts?"

"Yeah. One guy you killed was hiding in a garbage can—"

"That's bullshit. He wasn't hiding, *I* was."

"Well, maybe *that's* what I heard. You were lying in wait, which somebody pointed out was pretty cowardly. Word is, the most recent incident was three years back. It was in the Santa Teresa papers. Someone saw a copy of the article."

"I don't believe this. What article?"

Alice drew on her cigarette, regarding me with skepticism. "You weren't involved in a shoot-out in some lawyer's office?"

"The guy was trying to *kill* me. I just told you that. Talk to the cops if you don't want to take my word for it."

"Don't get so defensive. I'm telling you for your own good. I might've done the same thing if I'd been in your place, but this is redneck country. Folks here close ranks. You better watch your step is all I'm saying."

"Somebody's trying to discredit me. That's what this is about," I said, hotly.

"Hey, it's not up to me. I don't give a damn. You can whack anyone you want. There's times *I'd* do it myself, given half a chance," she said. "The point is, people are getting pissed. I thought I should warn you before it went too far."

"I appreciate that. I wish you could tell me where it's coming from."

Alice shrugged. "That's the way it is in small towns."

"If you remember where the story originated, will you let me know?"

"Sure thing. In the meantime, I'd avoid crossing paths with the cops if I were you."

I felt a pang of anxiety, like an icicle puncturing my chest wall. "What makes you say that?"

"Obviously, Tom was a cop. They're mad as hell."

Alice dropped the lighted cigarette in the toilet with a *spat* and then she flushed the butt away, waving at the air as if she could clear the smoke with a swishing hand. "You want anything else?"

I shook my head, not trusting myself to speak.

I waited at the side exit, my hands in my pockets though the chill I felt was internally generated. I kept my mind on other things, defending against a mounting surge of uneasiness. Maybe this was why Macon was suddenly being so protective.

The night sky was overcast, and where the air should have been crystalline, a ground fog began to drift across the darkened parking lot. Two couples left together. One of the women was blind-drunk, laughing boisterously as she staggered across the icy tarmac. Her date had his arm across her shoulders and she leaned against him for support. She stopped in her tracks, held her hand up like a traffic cop, and then turned away to be sick. The other woman leaped backward, shrieking in protest. The ill woman lingered, holding on to a parked car 'til she was done and could move on.

The foursome reached their vehicle and piled in, though the sick woman sat sideways with her head hanging out the door for a good five minutes before they were finally able to pull away. I searched the empty rows of cars, checking the dark. The music from the bar behind me was reduced to a series of dull, repetitive thumps. I caught a flash of light and saw a car pull in. I stepped back into the shadows until I was assured it was Macon in his black-and-white. He pulled up beside me and sat there with his engine running. I moved forward, walking around the front of the patrol car to the window on the driver's side. He rolled it down as I approached.

"How'd it go?" he asked. I could hear the rachet of his car radio, dispatcher talking to someone else. He turned the volume down.

I put a hand on the door. "Alice tells me there's a rumor going around that I'm some sort of dope-crazed vigilante."

He looked off to one side. He stirred restlessly, tapping the steering wheel with his gloved hand. "Don't worry about gossip. Everybody talks in this town."

"Then you heard it, too?"

"Nobody pays any attention to that stuff."

"Not true. Someone went to the trouble to do a background check."

"And got what? It's all bullshit. I don't believe a word of it." Which meant he'd heard the same stories everyone else had been treated to. "I better see you home. I got a call to check out."

I got in my car and he followed me as far as Selma's driveway, his engine idling while I crossed the front lawn.

Selma had left the porch light on and my key turned easily in the lock. I waved from the doorway and he took off. I slipped out of my wet shoes and carried them down the hall to the guest room. The house was quiet, not even the murmur of a television set to suggest Selma was awake.

I slipped into the guest room and closed the door behind me. She'd turned on a bed table lamp and the room was washed in cheery pink. On the nightstand, she'd left me a plate of homemade chocolate chip cookies secured in plastic wrap. I ate two, savoring the flavors of butter and vanilla. I ate two more to be polite before I stripped off my jacket. Apparently, Selma was not in the habit of turning down the furnace at night and the room felt close with heat. I crossed to the window, pushed the curtains aside, and raised the sash. Frigid air poured through the gap left by the storm window, still resting against the bushes three feet down.

I stared out at the portion of the street that I could see. A car passed at a slow speed and I pulled back out of sight, wondering if the occupants had spotted me. I hated being in Nota Lake. I hated being an outsider, the target of local gossip that misrepresented my actions. I hated my suspicions. The thought of a uniform was beginning to make me salivate like a dog subjected to some odd form of Pavlovian conditioning. Where once the badge and the nightstick had been symbols of personal safety, I now found myself picturing them with trepidation, as if stung by electric shocks. If I was right about the guy's connection to law enforcement, then his was the badge of authority and what was I? Some little pipsqueak P.I. with a prissy sense of justice. Talk about a mismatch.

Why couldn't I just hop in my car and barrel home tonight? I needed to be in a place where people cared for me. For a moment, the pull was overpowering. If I left within the hour, I could be in Santa Teresa by four A.M. I pictured my snug platform bed with its blue-and-white quilt, stars visible through the Plexiglas dome overhead. Surely, the sky there would be clear and the air would smell like the Pacific thundering close by. I visualized the morning. Henry would bake cinnamon rolls and we'd have breakfast together. Later I could help him in the yard, where he'd kneel at his flower beds, the pale soles of his feet like something cast in plaster of Paris. I stepped away from the window, effectively breaking the spell. The only road home is through the forest, I thought.

Within minutes, I'd peeled off my clothes and pulled on the oversized T-shirt I was using as a gown. Usually I sleep nude, but in someone else's house, it pays to be prepared in case of fire. I washed my face and brushed my teeth with the usual difficulty. I returned to the bedroom and circled restlessly. The bookshelves were filled with knickknacks. There was not so much as a magazine in view and I'd forgotten to bring a book this time. I was too wired for sleep. I took the file from the duffel and got into bed, adjusting the reading lamp so I could review the notes I'd typed. The only item that leapt out at me was James Tennyson's report of the woman walking down the road the night Tom died. According to his account, she was approaching from the direction of Tom's truck and she veered off into the woods when she caught sight of his patrol car. Was he lying about that? Had he invented the woman in an attempt to throw me off? He hadn't struck me as devious, but the touch would have been nice since it suggested Tom had been in the woman's company when he was stricken with his fatal heart attack. I wondered what kind of woman would have walked off and left him in the throes of death. Perhaps someone who couldn't afford to be seen with him. Knowing what I knew of him, I didn't believe he was having an affair, so if the woman existed, why conceal her presence? I knew he'd been at the Rainbow Cafe at some unaccustomed hour.

What was interesting was that James had told me about this alleged female as an addendum to his original comments. I tend to be suspicious of elaborations. Eyewitness reports are notoriously unreliable. The story changes each time it's told, modified for every passing audience; amplified, embellished, until the final version is a twisted variation of the truth. Certainly, the memory is capable of playing tricks. Images can be camouflaged by emotion, popping into view later when the mental film is rewound. Conversely, people sometimes swear to have seen things that were never there at all. For the second time, I wondered if Tom had gone to the Rainbow Cafe to meet someone. I'd asked Nancy about it once, but it might be time to press.

I set my notes aside and doused the lights. The mattress was soft and seemed to list to one side. The sheets had a satin finish that felt slick to the touch and generated little traction to offset my tendency to slide. The quilted spread was puffy, filled with down. I lay there and basted in my own body heat. In testimony to my constitution, I fell asleep at once.

I woke to the distant sound of the phone ringing in the kitchen. I thought the answering machine would pick up, but on the eighth persistent *ding-a-ling,* I flung off the covers and trotted down the hall in my T-shirt and underpants. There was no sign of Selma and the machine had been turned off. I lifted the receiver. "Newquists' residence."

Someone breathed in my ear and then hung up.

I replaced the receiver and stood there for a moment. Often, someone calling a wrong number will dial the same number twice, convinced the error is yours for not being who they wanted. The silence extended. I reactivated the answering machine, and then checked Selma's appointment calendar, posted on the refrigerator door. There was nothing marked, but this was Sunday and I remembered her mentioning a visit to a cousin down in Big Pine after church. The dish rack was empty. I opened the dishwasher. I could see that she'd eaten breakfast, rinsed her plate and coffee cup, and left them in the machine, which was otherwise empty. The interior walls of the dishwasher exuded a residual heat and I assumed she'd done a load of dishes first thing this morning before she'd left. The coffee machine was on. The glass carafe held four cups of coffee that smelled as if it had sat too long. I poured myself a mug, adding sufficient milk to offset the scorched flavor.

I padded back to the guest room, where I brushed my teeth, showered, and dressed, sipping coffee while I girded my loins. I didn't look forward to another day in this town, but there was nothing for it except to get the job done. Like a dutiful guest, I made my bed, ate the remaining three cookies to fortify myself, and returned the empty coffee mug and plate to the kitchen, where I tucked both in the dishwasher, following Selma's good example. I grabbed my leather jacket and my shoulder bag, locked the house behind me, and went out to the car. Phyllis was pulling into her driveway two doors down. I waved, convinced she'd spotted me, but she kept her eyes averted and I was left, feeling foolish, with the smile on my lips. I got in the car, forcing myself to focus on the job at hand. The gas gauge was close to E and since I was heading toward the Rainbow, I stopped for gas on my way out of town.

I pulled up to the full-serve pump and turned the engine off, reaching into my bag to find my wallet and gasoline credit card. I glanced over at the office windows, where I could see two attendants in coveralls chatting together by the cash register. Both turned to look at my VW and then resumed their conversation. There were no other cars at the pumps. I waited, but neither came forward to assist me. I turned on the engine and gave the car horn a sharp toot. I waited two minutes more. No action at all. This was annoying. I had places to go and didn't want to sit here all day, waiting for a lousy tank of gas. I opened the car door and stepped out, peering across the top of the car to the open bay. The two attendants were no longer visible. Irritated, I slammed the car door and moved toward the office, which had been deserted.

"Hello?"

Nothing.

"Could I get some service out here?"

No one.

I went back to the car, where I waited another minute. Maybe the two lads had inexplicably quit work or had been devoured by extraterrestrials hiding in the gents'. I started the engine and honked sharply, a display of impatience that netted nothing in the way of help. Finally, I pulled out with a little chirp of my tires to demonstrate my agitation. I slid into the flow of traffic on the main street and drove six blocks before I spotted another station. Ha ha ha, thought I. So much for the competition. I had no credit card for this rival brand, but I could afford to pay cash. Filling a VW never amounts to that much. I pulled into the second station, doing much as I had before. I turned the engine off, checked my wallet for cash. There was a car at the adjacent pump and the attendant was in the process of removing the nozzle from the tank. He glanced at me briefly and then I saw the alteration in his gaze.

I said, "Hi. How're you?"

He took the other woman's credit card and disappeared into the office, returning moments later with her receipt on a tray. She signed and took her copy. The two chatted for a moment and then she pulled out. The attendant went back to the office and that was the last I saw of him. What was going on? I checked myself with care, wondering if I'd been rendered invisible in my sleep.

I stared at the office window and then checked for another service station within range. I could see an off-brand station three doors down. Even with my gauge showing empty, I knew my trusty VW could soldier on for many miles yet, given the mileage I got. Still, I was reluctant to squander the last of a tank of gas looking for a place to buy the next tank of gas. I started my engine, put the car in gear, drove out of that gas station, and into the one two hundred yards away.

This time I saw an attendant in the service bay and I pulled in there first. Let's get this out in the open, whatever it was. I leaned over and rolled down the window on the passenger side. Pleasantly, I said, "Hi. Are you open for business?"

His blank stare sparked a moment of uneasiness. What was wrong with him?

I tried a smile that didn't feel right, but was the best I could manage. "Do you speak English? *Habla Inglés?*" Or something to that effect.

His return smile was slow and malevolent. "Yeah, lady, I do. Now why don't you get the fuck out of here? You want service in this town, you're out of luck."

"Sorry," I said. I shifted my eyes, keeping my expression neutral as I drove out of the station and turned right at the first street. Under my jacket, the sweat was soaking through the back of my shirt.

20

Once out of sight, I pulled over and parked on a side street to assess my situation. The word had clearly gone out, but I wasn't sure whether these guys were cueing off my car or my personal description. I removed my leather bomber jacket and tossed it in the backseat, then rooted through the assorted garments I keep for just such emergencies. I donned a plain red sweatshirt, a pair of sunglasses, and a Dodgers baseball cap. I got out, opened the trunk, and took out the five-gallon gasoline can I keep in there. I locked the car and hiked over to the main street, where I headed for a service station I hadn't tried so far.

I bypassed the office and went straight to the service bay, where a cursing mechanic was struggling to loosen a stubborn lug nut on a flat tire. I checked the sign posted by the door that said MECHANIC ON DUTY with the guy's name, ED BOONE, on a plastic plaque inserted in the slot. I moved out of the bay and sidled up to the office where I poked my head in the door. The attendant was maybe nineteen, with a bleached-blond crew cut and green-painted fingernails, his attentions focused on the glossy pages of a pornographic magazine.

"Uncle Eddy told me I could fill this. My pickup ran out of gas about a block from here. This is mine, by the way," I said, holding up the can. I didn't want the fellow claiming later that I'd stolen it. Given my current reputation as a stone-cold killer, the theft of a gasoline can would have been right in character. I fancied I saw a flicker of uncertainty cross his face, but I went about my business like I owned the place.

I walked to the self-serve pump, giving him a sidelong glance to see if he was on the telephone. He stared through the plate glass window, watching me without expression as I filled the container. The total was $7.45. I returned to the office and handed him a ten, which he tucked in his pocket without offering change. His gaze dropped to his magazine again as I walked off. Nice to know that regardless of how low you sink, someone's always willing to make a profit at your expense. I returned to my car, where I emptied the five gallons of gasoline into my tank. I returned the can to the trunk and took off with the gauge now almost at the halfway mark.

My heart was beating as though I'd run a race and perhaps I had. Apparently, my actions would be observed and curtailed wherever possible from here on. Never had I felt quite so alienated from my surroundings. I was already on unfamiliar turf and in subtle and not-so-subtle ways, I depended on the ordinary day-to-day pleasantries for my sense of well-being. Now I was being shunned and the process was frightening me. Scouring the moving traffic, I realized my pale blue VW was highly visible among all the pickups, campers, utility vehicles, horse vans, and 4×4s.

Six miles out of town, I pulled onto the gravel apron of the Rainbow Cafe, angling around to the left where I backed into a parking spot on the far side of the big garbage bins. I sat for a moment, trying to get "centered," as Californians say. I've no idea what the term means, but in my present circumstance, it seemed applicable.

If I was being banished from the tribe, I better make sure I had a grip on my "self" before I went any further. I took a couple of deep breaths and got out. The morning was overcast, the mountains looming in the distance like an accumulation of thunderclouds. Down here, where large tracts of land stretched out empty and desolate, the wind whistled along the surface, chilling everything in its path. Snow flurries, like dust motes, hung in the icy air.

Crossing the gravel parking area, I felt extraordinarily conspicuous. I glanced at the cafe windows and could have sworn I saw two customers stare at me and then avert their eyes. A chill went through me, all the ancient power of ostracism by the clan. I imagined church services in progress, the Catholics and the Baptists and the Lutherans all singing hymns and giving thanks, attentive to their respective sermons. Afterward, the Nota Lake devout would crowd into the local restaurants, still dressed in their Sunday best and eager for lunch. I said a little prayer of my own as I pushed through the door.

The cafe was sparsely occupied. I did a quick visual sweep. James Tennyson was sitting at the counter with a cup of coffee. He wore jeans, the newspaper open in front of him. Close at hand were an empty water glass and a crumpled blue-and-black Alka-Seltzer packet. There was no sign of his wife, Jo, or his baby, whose name escaped me. Rafer's daughter, Barrett, with her back to me, was working the grill. She wore a big white apron over jeans and a T-shirt. A white chef's toque concealed her springy, flyaway hair. Deftly, she wielded her spatula, rolling sausage links, flipping a quartet of pancakes. While I watched, she moved the steaming food to a pair of waiting plates. Nancy picked up the order and delivered it to the couple sitting by the window. Rafer and Vicky LaMott sat in the booth midway down the line of empty tables. They'd finished eating and I could see that Vicky was in the process of collecting her handbag and overcoat. James looked baggy-eyed and drawn. He caught sight of me and nodded, his manner a perfect blend of good manners and restraint. His fair-skinned good looks were only slightly marred by what I imagined was a hangover. I headed for a booth in the far corner, murmuring a greeting to Rafer and Vicky as I breezed by. I was afraid to wait for a response lest they cut me dead. I sat down and positioned myself so I could keep an eye on the door.

Nancy caught my attention. She seemed distracted, but not unfriendly, crossing toward the counter to pick up a side of oatmeal. "I'll be with you in just a minute. You want coffee?"

"I'd love some." Apparently, she wasn't a party to the social boycott. Alice, the night before, had been friendly as well . . . at least to the point of warning me about the freeze coming up. Maybe it was just the guys who were shutting me out; not a comforting thought. It was a man, after all, who'd dislocated my fingers only three days earlier. I found myself rubbing the joints, noticing for the first time that the swelling and the bruises gave them the appearance of exotic, barely ripe bananas. I turned my crockery mug upright in anticipation of the coffee, noting that the fingers still refused to bend properly. It felt like the skin had stiffened, preventing flexion.

While I waited for service, I studied James in profile, wondering about his contact with Pinkie Ritter and Alfie Toth. As a CHP officer, he would have been removed from any sheriff's department action, but he might have exploited his friendships with the deputies to glean information about the homicide investigation. He was certainly first at the scene the night Tom died, giving him the perfect opportunity to lift Tom's notes. I was still toying with the possibility that he invented the walking woman, though his motive remained opaque. It wasn't Colleen. She'd assured me she'd never visited the area, a claim I tended to believe. Tom had had too much to lose if he'd been seen with her. Besides, if she'd been in the truck, she wouldn't have deserted him.

The LaMotts emerged from their booth, hunching into overcoats in preparation for their departure. Vicky crossed to the counter to chat with Barrett while Rafer moved to the register and paid the check. As usual, Nancy did double duty, setting her coffeepot aside to take his twenty and make change. James rose at the same time, leaving his money on the counter beside his plate. He and Rafer exchanged a few words and I saw Rafer glance my way. James pulled on his jacket and left the restaurant without a backward look. Vicky joined her husband, who must have told her to go out and wait for him in the car. She nodded and then busied herself with her gloves and knit cap. I wasn't sure if she was ignoring me or not.

Once she was gone, Rafer ambled in my direction, his hands in his coat pockets, a red cashmere scarf wrapped around his neck. The coat was beautifully cut, a dark chocolate brown setting off the color of his skin. The man did dress well.

"Hello, Detective LaMott," I said.

"Rafer," he corrected. "How's the hand?"

"Still attached to my arm." I held my fingers up, wiggling them as though the gesture didn't hurt.

"Mind if I sit down?"

I indicated the place across from me and he slid into the booth. He seemed ill-at-ease, but his expression was sympathetic and his hazel eyes showed disquiet, not the coldness or hostility I'd half-expected. "I had a long talk with some Santa Teresa fellows about you."

I felt my heart start to thump. "Really. Who?"

"Coroner, couple cops. Homicide detective named Jonah Robb," he said. He put one elbow on the table, tapping with his index finger while he stared out across the room.

"Ah. Tracking down the stories going around about me."

His gaze slid back to mine. "That's right. I might as well tell you, from the perspective of the sheriff's department, you're okay, but I've heard rumbles I don't like and I'm concerned."

"I'm not all that comfortable myself, but I don't see any way around it. Responding to rumors only makes you look guilty and defensive. I know because I tried it and got nowhere."

He stirred restlessly. He turned in the seat until he was facing me squarely, his hands laced in front of him. His voice dropped a notch.

"Listen, I know about your suspicions. Why don't you tell me what you have and I'll do what I can to help."

I said, "Great," wondering why I didn't sound more sincere and enthusiatic. I thought about it briefly, experiencing a frisson of uneasiness. "I'll tell you what concerns me at the moment. A plainclothes detective—or someone posing as one—showed up at a fleabag hotel in Santa Teresa with a warrant for Toth's arrest. The Santa Teresa Sheriff's Department has no record of an outstanding warrant anywhere in the system, so the paper was probably bogus, but I don't have a way to check that because I don't have access to the computer."

"I can run that," he said smoothly. "What else?"

I found myself choosing my words with care. "I think the guy was a phony, too. He might have been a cop, but I think he misrepresented himself."

"What name did he give?"

"I asked about that, but the clerk I talked to wasn't on the desk that day and he claims the other fellow didn't get a name."

"You think it was someone in our department," he said, making it a statement, not a question.

"Possibly."

"Based on what?"

"Well, doesn't the timing seem a tiny bit coincidental?"

"How so?"

"Tom wanted to talk to Toth in connection with Pinkie Ritter's death. The other guy got there first and that was the end of poor old Alfie. Tom was a basket case starting in mid-January when Toth's body turned up, right?"

"That's Selma's claim." Rafer's manner was now guarded and he started tapping, the tip of his index finger drumming a rapid series of beats. Maybe he was sending me a message in Morse code.

"So isn't it possible this is what Tom was brooding about? I mean, what else could it be?"

"Tom was a consummate professional for thirty-five years. He was the investigating officer in a homicide matter that I would say, yes, captured his interest, but no, did not in any way cause him to lie awake at night and bite his nails. Of course he thought about his work, but it didn't cause his heart attack. The idea's absurd."

"If he was under a great deal of stress, couldn't that have been a contributing factor?"

"Why would Toth's death cause him any stress at all? This was his *job*. He never even met the man, as far as I know."

"He felt responsible."

"For what?"

"Toth's murder. Tom believed someone gained access to his notebook, where he'd jotted down Toth's temporary address and the phone number at the Gramercy."

"How do you know what Tom *believed*?"

"Because that's what he confided to another sheriff's investigator."

"Colleen Sellers."

"That's right."

"And Tom told her this?"

"Well, not explicity. But that's how the killer could have found Toth and murdered him," I said.

"You still haven't said why you suspect someone from our department."

"I'll broaden the claim. Let's say, someone in law enforcement."

"You're fishing."

"Who else had access to his notes?"

"Everyone," he said. "His wife, his son, Brant. Half the time, the house was unlocked. Add his cleaning lady, the yard man, his next-door neighbor, the guy across the street. None of them are involved in law enforcement, but any one of them could have opened his front door and walked right in. And what makes you so sure it wasn't someone in Santa Teresa? The leak didn't necessarily come from this end."

I stared at him. "You're right," I said. He had a point.

The tapping stopped and his manner softened. "Why don't you back off and let us handle this?"

"Handle what?"

"We haven't been entirely idle. We're developing a lead."

"I'm glad to hear that. About bloody time. I hate to think I'm the only one out here with my ass on the line."

"Cut the sarcasm and don't push. Not your job."

"Are you saying you have a line on Alfie's killer?"

"I'm saying you'd be smart to go home and let us take it from here."

"What about Selma?"

"She knows better than to interfere with an official investigation. So do you."

I tried Selma's line. "There's no law against asking questions."

"That depends on who you ask." He glanced at his watch. "I got Vick in the car and we're late for church," he said. He got up and adjusted his coat, taking his leather gloves from one pocket. I watched him smooth them into place and thought, inexplicably, of his early-morning arrival at the emergency room; freshly showered and shaven, nattily dressed, wide awake. He looked down at me. "Did anyone ever fill you in on local history?"

"Cecilia did."

He went on talking as if I hadn't spoken. "Bunch of convicts were shipped to the colonies from England. These were hardened criminals, literally branded for the heinousness of their behavior."

"The 'nota' of Nota Lake," I supplied dutifully.

"That's right. The worst of 'em came west and settled in these mountains. What you're dealing with now are their descendants. You want to watch your step."

I laughed uneasily. "What, this is like a Western? I'm being warned off? I have to be out of town by sundown?"

"Not a warning, a suggestion. For your own good," he said.

I watched him leave the restaurant and realized how dry my

mouth had become. I had that feeling I used to get before the first day of school, a low-level dread that acted as an appetite suppressant. Breakfast didn't sound like such a hot idea. The place had cleared out. The couple by the window was getting up to leave. I saw them pay their check, Barrett taking over the cash register while Nancy hurried in my direction with a coffeepot and menu, all apologies. She handed me the menu. "Sorry it took me so long, but I was brewing a new pot and I could see you and Rafer had your heads together," she said. She filled my mug with hot coffee. "You have any idea what you want to eat? I don't mean to rush you. Take your time. I just don't want to hold you up, you've been so patient."

"I'm not hungry," I said. "Why don't I move to the counter so we can talk?"

"Sure thing."

I picked up my mug and reached for the silverware.

"I'll get that," she said. She took the menu and the flatware, moving to the counter where she set a place for me between the griddle and the cash register. Barrett was in the process of cleaning the grill with a flat-edged spatula. Bacon fat and browned particles of pancake and sausage were being pushed into the well. Nancy rinsed a rag and twisted out the excess water, wiping the counter clean. "Alice says you've been asking about Pinkie Ritter."

"You remember him?"

"Every woman in Nota Lake remembers him," she said tartly.

"Did he ever bother you?"

"Meaning what, unwanted sexual advances? He attacked me one night when I got off work. He waited in the parking lot and grabbed me by the neck as I was getting in my car. I kicked his ass up between his shoulder blades and that was the last of that. He was convicted of rape twice and that's just the times he was caught."

"Did you report it?"

"What for? I took care of it myself. What's the law going to do, come along afterwards and smack his hand?"

Barrett had now come over to the small sink just below the

counter in front of us and she was in the process of rinsing plates and arranging them in the rack for the industrial dishwasher I assumed was in the rear. She had her father's light eyes and she made no secret of the fact that she was listening to Nancy's tale and enjoying her attitude.

I caught her attention. "Did he ever come on to you?"

"Uhn-uhn. No way," she said, a blush creeping up her cheeks. "I was close to jailbait at that point, barely eighteen years old. He knew better than to mess with me."

I turned to Nancy. "What about other women? Anyone in particular? Earlene or Phyllis?"

Nancy shook her head. "Not that I heard, but that doesn't mean he didn't try. Guy like that goes after anyone who seems weak."

"Could I ask you about something else?"

"Sure."

"The night Tom Newquist died, he was in here earlier, wasn't he?"

"That's right. He came in about nine o'clock. Ordered a cheeseburger and fries, sat around and smoked cigarettes, like he was killing time. Occasionally he'd look at his watch. I couldn't figure it out. He never came in at that hour. I figured he was meeting someone, but she never showed up."

"Why do you say 'she'? Couldn't it have been a man?"

Nancy seemed surprised at the idea. "I never thought about that. I just assumed."

"Did he mention anyone by name?"

"No."

"Did he use the telephone?"

She shook her head with some uncertainty and then turned to Barrett with a quizzical look. "You remember if Tom Newquist used the phone that night?"

"Not that I saw."

Again, I directed a question to Barrett. "Did you get the impression he was here to meet someone?"

Barrett shrugged. "I guess."

Nancy spoke up again. "You know what I think it was? He was freshly shaved. I remember remarking about his cologne or his after-shave. He looked sharp, like he'd gussied himself up. He wouldn't do that if he were here to meet some guy."

"You agree with that?" I asked Barrett.

"He did look nice, now you mention it," she said. "I noticed that myself."

"Did he seem annoyed or upset, like he'd been stood up?"

"Not a bit of it," Nancy said. "Nine-thirty, got up, paid his check, and went out to his truck. I never saw him afterwards. I did closing that night so I was stuck in here. Did you see him out there?"

"In the parking lot? Not me."

"You must have. You took off shortly before he did."

Barrett thought about it, frowning slightly before she shook her head. "Maybe he was parked around back."

"Where were you parked that night?" I asked.

"Nowhere. I didn't have a car. My dad was picking me up."

"She just lives over there on the other side of that subdivision, but her folks don't like her walking home at night. They're real protective, especially her dad."

Barrett smiled, her dark skin underlined with the pink of her embarrassment. "I could be a preacher's daughter. That'd be worse."

We chatted on for a while. The place began to fill with the after-church crowd and I was clearly in the way. I was also hoping to avoid further confrontation with any irate citizens. I hunched into my jacket and went out to the car. Since the parking spot I'd found was around to the rear, I didn't think I was visible to passing vehicles. I didn't have the nerve to drive into town just yet. I couldn't bear the idea of wandering around on my own, risking rudeness and rejection on the basis of floating rumors. People in the cafe had been fine, so maybe it was just the service station attendants who'd passed a vote of no confidence.

I saw Macon Newquist pull off the highway and into the parking lot in a pickup truck. He was dressed in a suit that looked as unnatural on him as a bunny costume. I knew if he saw me, he'd start pumping me for information. I torqued myself around, reaching for my briefcase as though otherwise occupied. Along with my case notes, I'd tucked in the packets of index cards. I waited until he disappeared into the cafe before I got out of the car and locked it. I took my briefcase with me as I crunched along the berm to the Nota Lake Cabins.

Out front, the red Vacancy sign was lighted. The office lobby was unlocked and there was a flat plastic clock face hanging on the doorknob with the hands pointing to 11:30. The sign said BACK IN A JIFFY. I went in, crossing to the half door that opened onto the empty office. "Cecilia? Are you here?"

There was no answer.

I was tempted, as usual, by the sight of all those seductive-looking desk drawers. The Rolodex and the file cabinets fairly begged to be searched, but I couldn't for the life of me think what purpose it would serve. I sat down in the upholstered chair and opened a pack of index cards. I began to read through my notes, transferring one piece of information to each card with a borrowed ballpoint pen. In some ways, this was busywork. I could feel productive and efficient while sheltered from public scrutiny. Transcribing my notes had the further advantage of diverting my attention from the state of discomfort in which I found myself. Whereas last night I longed for home, I couldn't picture turning tail and running on the basis of Rafe's veiled "suggestion" about my personal safety. So what was I doing? Trying to satisfy myself that I'd done what I could. The deal I made with myself was to keep following leads until the trail ran out. If I came up against a blank wall, then I could return home with a clear conscience. In the meantime, I had a job and I was intent on doing it. Yeah, right, you chickenshit, I thought.

I went through a pack and a half of index cards without any startling revelations. I shuffled them twice and laid them out like a hand of solitaire, scanning row after row for telling details. For instance, I'd made a note that Cecilia'd told me she got home around ten o'clock the night Tom died. She said she'd seen the ambulance, but had no idea it had been summoned for her brother. Could she have seen the woman walking down the road? It occurred to me the woman might have been staying at the Nota Lake Cabins, in which case her stroll might not have had anything to do with Tom. Worth asking, at any rate, just to eliminate the issue.

21

Cecilia was late getting back. Instead of returning at 11:30, it was closer to 12:15 when she finally walked in the door. She was dressed for church in a baggy blue tweed suit with bumblebee scatter pins on the lapel. The white blouse underneath featured a frothy burst of lace at the neck. She expressed no surprise when she saw me, and in my paranoid state, I imagined my presence had been reported in advance. She opened the half door to the office, closed it behind her, put her handbag on the desk, and turned to look at me. "Now. What can I do for you? I hear you're staying at Selma's, so it can't be a cabin you've come to ask about."

"I'm still working on this business of Tom's death."

"Seven weeks ago tomorrow. Hard to take it in," she said.

"Do you happen to remember who was staying here that weekend?"

"At the motel? That's easy." She reached for the registration ledger, licked her index finger, and began to page back through the weeks. March became February as she reversed the days. The week of February 1 appeared. She ran a finger down the list of names. "A party of skiers, maybe six of 'em in two cabins. I gave 'em Hemlock and Spruce, as far away from the office as I could make it because I knew they'd get to partying. That type always do. I remember them toting in more cases of beer than they had luggage. Complained a lot, too. Water pressure, heat. Nothing suited them," she said, shooting me a look.

"Anyone else? Any single women?"

"Meaning what?"

"Not meaning anything, Cecilia," I said patiently. "I'm following up on the CHP report. Tennyson says he saw a woman walking down the road. She may have been a figment of his imagination. It's possible she had nothing to do with Tom. It would be helpful to find her so I'm hoping against hope she was staying here that night. That way you could tell me how to get in touch with her."

She checked the register again. "Nope. Married couple from Los Angeles. Or so they claimed. Only saw that pair when they crawled out of bed to take meals. And one other family with a couple of kids. Wife was in a wheelchair so I doubt he saw her."

"What about you? When you came back from the movies, was there anyone on the road? This would have been between ten and ten-thirty."

Cecilia seemed to give it some thought and then shook her head. "The only thing I remember is someone using the phone out there. I try to discourage strangers stopping off to make calls; tromping up and down the porch stairs, ripping pages from the telephone book. Handset's been stolen twice. This is private property."

"I thought the pay phone was public."

"Not as far as I'm concerned. That's strictly for motel customers. One of the amenities," she said. "Anyway, I could see the Rainbow was closed and the outside lights were off. I poked my head out, but it was only Barrett calling her dad to pick her up. I offered her a lift, but she said he was already on his way."

"You have any idea if Rafer had picked up on the 9-1-1 dispatch?"

"You mean, the ambulance for Tom? Probably," she said. "Or James might have called him, knowing they were such good friends." She closed the ledger. "Now, I hope you'll excuse me. I have someone joining me for Sunday lunch."

"Sure. No problem. I appreciate your help."

I tucked my papers in the briefcase, gathered up the index cards, put a rubber band around them, and dropped them in there, too. I shrugged into my jacket, grabbed my handbag and the briefcase, and returned to my car at the Rainbow. So here's the question I asked myself: If Barrett left work at nine-thirty, why did it take her forty-five minutes to call her dad? I sat in the car, watching the clouds gather in a dark gray sky, watching the light dim down to a twilight state. It was only one o'clock in the afternoon, but the dark was so pervasive that the photosensor on Cecilia's exterior lights popped to life. Snow began to fall, big airy flakes settling on the windshield like a layer of soapsuds. I waited, watching the rear of the Rainbow Cafe.

By two-thirty, the lunch crowd was all but gone. I sat with the inborn patience of the cat watching for a lizard to reappear from the crevice between two rocks. At 2:44, the backdoor opened and Barrett came out, wearing her apron and her chef's toque and carrying a large plastic garbage bag intended for the trash bin to my left. I rolled down the window. "Hi, Barrett. You have a minute?"

She dumped the garbage bag and moved closer. I leaned over and unlocked the passenger door, pushing it open a crack. "Hop in. You'll freeze to death out there."

She made no move. "I thought you were gone."

"I was visiting Cecilia. What time do you get off work?"

"Not for hours."

"Why don't you take a break? I'd like to talk to you."

She hesitated, looking toward the Rainbow. "I'm really not supposed to, but it's okay for just a minute." She got in the car, slammed the door, and crossed her bare arms against the cold. I'd have run the engine for the heat, but I didn't want to waste the gas and I was hoping her discomfort would motivate her to tell me what I wanted to know.

"Your dad says you're on your way to med school."

"I haven't been accepted yet," she said.

"Where're you thinking to go?"

"Did you want something in particular? Because Nancy doesn't know I'm out here and I really don't have a coffee break until closer to three."

"I should get to the point, now you mention it," I said. I could feel a fib start to form. For me, it's the same sensation as a sneeze in the making, that wonderful reaction of the autonomic nervous system when something tickles my nose. "I was curious about something." Please note, she didn't ask what. "Wasn't it you Tom Newquist was here to meet that night?"

"Why would he do that?"

"I have no idea. That's why I'm asking you," I said.

She must have done some acting at one point; maybe high school, the senior play, not the lead. She made a show of frowning, then shook her head in bafflement. "I don't think so," she said, as though racking her brain.

"I have to tell you, he made a note on his desk calendar. He wrote *Barrett* plain as day."

"He did?"

"I ran across it today, which is why I was asking earlier who he was here to meet. I was hoping you'd be honest, but you dropped the ball," I said. "I would have let it pass, but then the story was confirmed, so here I am. You want to tell me how it went?"

"Confirmed?"

"As in verified," I said.

"Who confirmed it?"

"Cecilia."

"It wasn't anything," she said.

"Well, great. Cough it up, in that case. I'd like to hear."

"We just talked a few minutes and then he started feeling bad."

"What'd you talk about?"

"Just stuff. We were chatting about my dad. I mean, it was nothing in particular. Just idle conversation. Me and Brant used to go steady and he was asking about the breakup. He always felt bad that we didn't hang in together. I knew he was leading up to something, but I didn't know what. Then he started feeling sick. I could see the color drain from his face and he started sweating. I was scared."

"Did he say he was in pain?"

She nodded, her voice wavering when she spoke. "He was clutching his chest and his breathing was all raspy. I said I'd go back to the motel and get some help and he said, fine, do that. He told me to lock the truck door and not mention our meeting to anyone. He was real emphatic about that, made me *promise.* Otherwise, I might have told you when you asked the first time." She fumbled in her uniform pocket and found a tissue. She swiped at her eyes and blew her nose.

I waited until she was calmer before I went on. "Did he say anything else?"

She took a deep breath. "Stay off the road if any cars came along. He didn't want anyone to know I'd been talking to him."

"Why?"

"He didn't want to put me in any danger, was what he said."

"He didn't say from whom?"

"He didn't mention anyone by name," she said.

"What else?"

"That's everything."

"He didn't give you his notebook for safekeeping?"

She shook her head mutely.

"Are you sure?"

"Positive."

"I thought he gave you the little black book where he kept his field notes."

"Well, he didn't."

"Barrett, tell the truth. Please, please, please? Pretty please with sugar on it? Trust me, I won't say a word to anyone about your having it."

"I'm telling you the truth."

I shook my head. "I hate to contradict you, but Tom always kept it with him and yet nobody's seen it since he died."

"So?"

"So everybody's been assuming he was by himself that night. Now it turns out you were in his truck. Where else could it be? He was anxious to protect the notebook so he must have given it to you. That's the only way it adds up. If you can think of another explanation, I'd love to hear it."

The silence was exquisite. I let it drag on a bit without breathing another word.

"I went for help."

"I'm sure you did," I said. "The CHP officer saw you on the road. What about the notebook?"

Barrett looked out the window. "You don't have any proof," she said, faintly.

"Well, yeah, I know. I mean, except for the fact that Cecilia saw you on the motel porch that night," I said. "She says your dad came and picked you up, which is what you said yourself. You just fudged a tiny bit about the sequence of events. I can't *prove* you have the notebook, but it stands to reason."

Nancy poked her head out of the Rainbow's backdoor. Barrett opened the door and leaned out, calling, "I'll be right there!" Nancy nodded and waved.

"So where's the notebook?"

"In my purse," she said glumly.

"Could you give it to me?"

"What's so important about the notes?"

"He was investigating two murders so I'm assuming his notes are somehow relevant. Did you read them yourself?"

"Well, yeah, but it's just a bunch of interviews and stuff. Lots of dates and abbreviations. It's no big deal."

"Then why does it matter if you pass it on to me?"

"He told me to hide it 'til he could decide what to do with it."

"He didn't know he would die."

"What a bummer," she said.

"Look, if you'll give it to me now, I'll make a copy first thing tomorrow and give it back to you."

After an agonizing moment, she said, "All right."

She got out of the car on her side and I got out on mine, locking the doors quickly before I followed her in. She kept her handbag in the storage room to the left of the kitchen door. Barrett took the notebook out of her bag and passed it to me. She seemed irritated that I'd managed to outmaneuver her somehow. "The other thing he said was the key's on his desk," she said.

"The key's in his desk?"

"That's what he told me. He said it twice."

"In or on?"

"On, I think. I have to go."

"Thanks. You're a doll." I put my finger to my lips. "Top secret. Not a word to anyone."

"Shit. Then why did I tell you?"

Nancy stuck her head in the kitchen door. "Oh, Kinsey. You're here. Brant's on the phone," she said.

I went out into the cafe proper, which was virtually deserted. The receiver was face down on the counter by the register. "Brant, is that you?"

He said, "Hi, Kinsey."

"Where are you? How'd you know I was here?"

"I'm at Mom's. I drove past the Rainbow a while ago and saw your car parked out back. I just wanted to check and make sure you're okay."

"I'm fine. Is your mother home yet?"

"She won't get back 'til close to nine," he said. "You need anything?"

"Not really. If you have a way to call her, would you let her know I got it?"

"Got what?"

I curled my fingers around the mouthpiece, feeling like a character in a spy movie. "The notebook."

"How'd you manage that?"

"I'll explain later. I'll be home in a few minutes. Can you wait?"

"Not really. I just stopped by for some stuff I'll be taking to Sherry's later."

"You work weekends?"

"Not usually," he said. "I'm filling in for someone and hoping to run some errands first. We'll talk tomorrow."

"Right. I'll see you then," I said.

I let myself into Selma's house and headed out to the kitchen. The house was dim, silent, insufferably warm. Everything was much as I'd left it, except for a plastic-wrapped plate of brownies with chocolate frosting sitting on the counter with a note attached: HELP YOURSELF. The condensation on the wrap suggested it had been refrigerated or frozen until recently. Brant must have assumed the note was meant for him because a plate and fork, showing telltale traces of chocolate, were sitting on the table at the place he occupied. I was sorry I'd missed him. We could have put our heads together.

I went into Tom's study and sat down in his swivel chair. I turned on his desk light and started going through the notebook. The cover was a pebbly black leather, soft with wear, the corners bent. I took the obvious route, starting at the first page—dated June 1—and working through to the last, which was dated February 1, two days before he died. Here, at last, were the eight months' worth of missing notes. The scribbles, on thin-lined paper, covered all the miscellaneous cases he'd been working on during that period. Each was identified by a case number in the margin to the left, and included complaints, crime scene investigations, names, addresses, and phone numbers of witnesses. In a series of nearly indecipherable abbreviations, I could trace the course of successive interviews on any given matter; Tom's notes to himself, his case references, the comments and questions that cropped up as he proceeded. There, in something close to hieroglyphics, I read about the discovery of Pinkie's body, the findings of the coroner, Trey Kirchner . . . whom Tom referred to as III. Any recurring name Tom generally reduced to its first letter. I found references to *R* and *B,* which I assumed were Rafer and Tom's boss, Sheriff Bob Staffer. By copious squints and leaps of imagination, I could see that he'd worked backward from Pinkie's death to his incarceration in Chino and his friendship with Alfie Toth, a fact confirmed by *MB,* Margaret Brine at *NLSD,* Nota Lake Sheriff's Department. *CS* I took to refer to Colleen Sellers, sometimes referred to as *C,* who'd called to report Alfie Toth's jail time in ST. I found the summary of his trip to Santa Teresa in June, including dates, times, mileage, and expenditures for food and lodging. As I'd learned earlier, he'd talked to Dave Estes at the Grammercy on 6-5. Later, he'd talked to Olga Toth, her address and phone number neatly noted. By the time *CS* called again to report the discovery of Toth's remains, Tom's notes had become cursory. Where previously he'd been meticulous about detailing the contents of conversations, he was suddenly circumspect, reverting I suspected to a code of some kind. The last page of notes contained only some numbers—8, 12, 1, 11, and 26—writ large and underlined with an exclamation point and question mark. Even the punctuation suggested a disbelief most emphatic. I sat and stared at the numbers until they danced on the page.

I got up and went to the kitchen, where I paced the floor. I poured myself some water from the tap and I drank it, making the most satisfactory gulping sounds. I burped. I put the glass in the dishwasher and then in a fit of tidiness added Brant's fork and his plate. I let my brain off the hook, tending to idle occupations while I picked at the riddle. What the hell did the numbers 8, 12, 1, 11, and 26 signify? A date? The combination to a safe? I thought about Tom's telling Barrett about the "key" in or on his desk. I'd been working at his desk for a week and hadn't seen any key that I remembered. What kind of key? The key to what? It's not as though his notebook had a tiny lock like a teenager's diary.

I went back to the den and sat down at his desk, immediately searching through his drawers again. Maybe he had a lockbox. Maybe he had a home safe. Maybe he had a storage cupboard secured by a small combination lock. How many bags full of garbage had I thrown out this past week? How could I be sure I hadn't tossed the key he was referring to? I felt a wave of panic at the idea that I'd thrown out something crucial to his purposes and critical to mine.

One by one, I emptied the contents of each drawer, then removed the drawer itself, checking the back panel and the bottom. I got down on my hands and knees and peered at the underside of the desk, feeling along the sides in case a key had been taped in place. In the drawer with his handcuffs and nightstick, I came across his flashlight and used that as I felt along the drawer rails, tilted his swivel chair back to check the underside of the seat. Did he mean the key, as "a thing that explains or solves something else," or a literal key, as an instrument or device to open a lock? I put the drawers back together and moved everything off the top. I ran a finger across his blotter, looking for a repetition of the numbers among the notes he'd scribbled. The numbers were there—8, 12, 1, 11, 26—appearing in the center of a noose. They were written twice more, once with a pen line encircling them and once in a box with a shaded border done in pencil. What if I'd discarded the critical information? Had the trash been picked up? I was working hard to suppress the nagging worry I felt. I was in a white hot sweat. The house, as usual, felt like an oven. I crossed to the window and lifted the sash. I loosened the catches on the storm window and pushed the glass out unceremoniously, watching with satisfaction as the window dropped to the ground below. I swallowed mouthfuls of fresh air, hoping to quell my anxiety.

I sat down at the desk again and shook my head. I cleared my mind of emotion, thinking back through the work I'd done earlier in the week. I didn't remember a key, but if I'd seen one I knew I would never have discarded it. If I hadn't found the key yet, there was still the chance that I'd uncover it somewhere. So. The point was to keep searching, as calmly and thoroughly as possible. Again, I went through each drawer, looking carefully at the contents. I checked each item in Tom's file folders, looked in envelopes, opened boxes of paper clips and staples, peered at pens, rulers, labels, tape. Maybe the key was a saying or a phrase that would make everything else clear. At the back of my mind, I kept returning to the notion that the numbers were a code of some kind. I'd never heard any mention of Tom's having worked in Intelligence so if I was right, the code was probably something simple and easily accessible.

On or in his desk.

I found a piece of paper and wrote out the alphabet in sequence, attaching the numbers 1 through 26 underneath. If the numbers 8, 12, 1, 11, and 26 were simple letter substitutions, then the name or initials would be *HLAKZ*. Which meant what? Nothing on the face of it. *Something-Los Angeles-Something-Something?* Didn't suggest anything to me. I tried the same sequence backward, letting *A* correspond with the number 26, *B* correspond with 25, and so forth until I reached the number 1, which I assumed represented *Z*. If this were the case, then the numbers 8, 12, 1, 11, 26 would spell out *SOZPA*. Another puzzlement. What the hell was this? A name? My frustration level mounted at a pace with my confusion.

8, 12, 1, 11, 26. Months of the year? August, December, January, November? Then what did the 26 denote? And why out of order? Was I supposed to add? Subtract? Sound out the words phonetically like a vanity license plate? I repeated them aloud. "Eight. Twelve. One. Eleven. Twenty-six." This meant nothing. If the numbers represented letters and this was a word, then all I knew for sure was that the five letters were different . . . with no repetitions. Someone's name? I thought about Nota Lake and how many people I'd met here who had five-letter first names. Brant, Macon, Hatch, Wayne. James Tennyson. Rafer. I looked at the exclamation point and the question mark. *!?* Which said what? Consternation? Dismay?

I realized I was famished . . . a manifestation of my anxiety no doubt. Waiting for Barrett in the cafe parking lot, I'd skipped lunch altogether and this was the price I paid. It was now four-fifteen. I went back to the kitchen in search of sustenance. I was so hungry and so befuddled, my brain cells felt like they'd quit holding hands. I looked in Selma's refrigerator, greeted by plastic-wrapped leftovers from last night's dinner. Not memorable to begin with and certainly not worth re-eating. I checked the bread drawer. No crackers. I checked the cupboards. No peanut butter. What kind of household did she run? I glanced at her note and in the absence of wholesome foodstuffs, I allowed myself to lift a corner of the plastic wrap and help myself to several brownies. The texture was off—a bit dry for my taste—but the icing was nice and gooey, only a faint chemical taste suggesting she'd used a boxed mix. Anyone who'd eat Miracle Whip would eat that shit, I thought. This was not Selma's best effort by a long stretch, but I figured my days consuming her cooking were just about over. I drank some milk from the carton, figuring to save a glass.

Thus fortified, I was prepared to tackle the problem. I went back to Tom's swivel chair and swiveled. What if 8, 12, 1, 11, and 26 were page numbers, referring to the notes themselves? I tried that approach, but the contents of the pages seemed in no way related, sharing no visible common elements and no designated page numbers. The afternoon was stretching toward evening and I was getting nowhere. I went back to the original premise. Selma had hired me to find out why Tom was distressed. I slouched down on my spine and leaned my head on the back of the chair. Why was Tom brooding, Kinsey asked herself? I rocked, allowing myself to ruminate at my leisure. If someone he knew had violated his privacy, reading his notes and using the information to get to Alfie Toth to kill him, that would certainly do the trick. But why would Hatch's involvement . . . or James's or Wayne's . . . have generated a moment's uneasiness or hesitation. Tom played by the rules. I'd been told over and over, he was strictly a law-and-order type. If he'd suspected any one of them, he'd have acted at once. Wouldn't he? Why would he not? It wouldn't have meant anything to him if Wayne had violated the sanctity of his field notes. My gaze dropped to the blotter. I pushed a stack of files aside. Down in the right-hand corner, Tom had drawn a grid, penning in the days of the month of February, the year unspecified. The first fell on a Sunday, the twenty-eighth on a Saturday. The last two Saturdays of the month—the twenty-first and the twenty-eighth—were crossed out. Was the year 1908? 1912, 1901, 1911, or 1926? I got up and went to the bookshelf, where I took down a copy of his almanac. I thumbed to the index and found the page numbers for a perpetual calendar. In a table to the left the years between 1800 and 2063 were listed in order. Beside each year was a number corresponding to a numbered template, representing all the variations in the way the months could be laid out. Calendar number one was a year in which January 1 fell on a Sunday; February 1 fell on a Wednesday; and each month thereafter was depicted. Calendar number two represented any and all years in which January 1 fell on a Monday; February 1 fell on Thursday; and so forth. If you wanted to know the day of the month for a particular date—say, March 5, 1966—you simply checked the master list for the year 1966, beside which appeared the number seven. Moving to Calendar number seven, you could see that March 5 fell on a Saturday.

I flipped on the desk light and studied the series of calendar pages, looking at the Februaries laid out like the one he'd drawn. Calendar number five was like that. February 1 fell on a Sunday and the twenty-eighth fell on the last Saturday of the month. Calendar number twelve was similar except there were twenty-nine days instead of twenty-eight. I checked the years that corresponded, starting with 1900. 1903 was such a year, but not 1908 and not 1912. In 1914, the first fell on a Sunday and the twenty-eighth on the last Saturday, but the same wasn't true of 1926. 1925, 1931, 1942, 1953, 1959, 1970, 1981, 1987, 1998. Why were these particular Februaries important? The year couldn't be relevant, could it? And why had he crossed out the last two Saturdays of that month? I thought about it for a minute. Eliminating those two Saturdays cut the number of days from twenty-eight to twenty-six—the number of letters in the alphabet. I tried that approach, lining up the letters with the days of the month. The answer was still *HLAKZ*.

Still rocking in his desk chair, I swiveled toward the window. It was nearly five-thirty, fully dark outside. Cold air still spilled through the gap where I'd raised the window. I could almost discern the waves of household heat pouring out in exchange. The room was decidedly chilly. I leaned forward and closed the window, staring at my reflection in the smoke-clouded glass. What the hell did those numbers mean? I could feel a draft from somewhere. Was there a draft coming down the chimney? Curious, I got up and moved out of the den. I walked along the front hall to the living room, where I turned on the table lamps. The drapes were wavering as though pushed by an unseen hand. I peered up the chimney and flipped the flue to the shut position. I checked the perimeter doors. The front door was closed and locked, as was the backdoor, and the door to the garage. That wasn't it. I poked my head into Selma's bedroom. All was undisturbed yet the draft was such that the curtains rippled in the windows. I proceeded down the hall. All the windows in Brant's old bedroom were closed.

I stopped where I was. The door to my room was ajar. Had I left it that way? I pushed it open with apprehension. Curtains flapped and fluttered. The room was a shambles. There were jagged shards of glass on the carpet. The window, which I'd oh-so-carefully locked, had been shattered by a hammer that someone had left on the floor. Pebbles of glass the size of rock salt were spread out across the sill like discarded diamonds. The sash had been pushed up, probably from the outside. Someone had clearly entered. I moved to the bed and slid my hand between the box spring and mattress. My gun was missing.

22

I glanced at my watch. 5:36. I walked back to the kitchen prepared to dial 9-1-1. I hesitated, my hand on the receiver. Who was I going to call? Rafer? Brant? Tom's brother, Macon? I wasn't sure I trusted any one of them. I stood there, trying to determine whom I could confide in at this point. A chill went through me. Surely, there wasn't anybody in the house *with* me. I hadn't gone to the guest room since I'd returned to the house early in the afternoon, so the intruder had probably been here and departed long before I showed up. Ordinarily, I'd have gone to my room to drop my jacket. After the day I'd had, I might have showered or napped—anything to perk myself up and restore my confidence—but I'd been intent on Tom's notes and I'd gone directly to his den. I felt disembodied, my mind having been separated from my flesh by the harrowing sensation of fear.

The phone shrilled with extraordinary loudness, setting off a surge of nausea. I jumped, nerves raw, my reflexes responding sharply, almost to the point of pain. I snatched up the receiver before it had ceased to ring. "Hello?"

"Hey, Kinsey. Brant here. Is my mom home yet?" He sounded young and carefree, relaxed, unconcerned.

My stomach churned in response. "You need to come home," I said. My voice seemed to be coming from a curious distance.

He must have been alerted by my tone because his shifted. "Why? What's going on?"

"Someone's broken in. There's glass on the bedroom floor and my gun is gone."

"Where's Mom?"

"I don't know. Yes. Wait. At your cousin's in Big Pine. I'm here alone," I said.

"Stay where you are. I'll be right there."

He hung up.

I replaced the receiver. I turned and leaned my back up against the wall, making little mewling sounds. A town full of cowboys and someone was coming after me. I held my hands out in front of me. I could see my fingers tremble, the recently dislocated digits looking all puffy and useless. My gun had been stolen. I had to have a weapon, some way to defend myself against the coming onslaught. I started opening the kitchen drawers, one after the other, in search of a knife. One drawer flew off its rails and banged against my thigh, spilling out its contents. Utensils jangled together, tumbling to the floor at my feet. I could feel the tears stinging my lids. I gathered a fistful of items and tossed them back in the drawer, but I couldn't seem to get it mounted on its track again. I banged it on the countertop so hard a metal spatula bounced and flew out. I left the drawer where it was. I found a steak knife, some generic brand that looked like a giveaway in a box of detergent. The overhead light glinted off its surface. I could see the bevel on the blade. What good would a serrated steak knife do against a speeding bullet?

Hours seemed to go by.

I could hear the second hand on the kitchen clock tick each passing second in turn.

Outside, I heard the squeal of brakes, and then a car door slammed shut. I turned and stared at the front door. What if it was someone else? What if it was them? The door flew open and I could see Brant in his civilian clothes. He moved toward me with all the comforting bulk of a battleship. I put a hand out and he took it.

"Jesus, you look awful. How'd the guy get in?"

I pointed to my room and then found myself following as he moved purposefully down the hall in that direction. His assessment was brief, the most cursory of glances. He turned away from the guest room and toured the rest of the house methodically, looking in every closet, every nook and cranny. He went down to the basement. I waited at the top of the stairs, one hand plucking at the other. My injured fingers held a particular fascination for me—clumsy and swollen. Where was my gun? How could I defend myself when I'd left the knife on the counter?

Brant returned to the kitchen. I followed him like a duckling. I could tell by his tone he was trying to control himself. Something in his manner conveyed the seriousness of the situation. "Did he get the notebook?"

I found myself grinding my teeth. "Who?"

"The guy who broke in," he said sharply.

"It was in my bag," I said. "Is that what he was after?"

"Of course," Brant said. "I can't think why else he'd risk it. Tell me exactly what you did today. What time did you leave and how long were you gone?"

I felt burbling and incoherent, spilling out the story of my rebuff, the refusal of the gas station attendants to do business with me, my subsequent stop at the Rainbow to talk to Nancy. I told him I'd run into Rafer and Vick, that I'd talked to Cecilia and Barrett. My brain was moving at twice the speed of my lips, making me feel sluggish and stupid. Brant, god bless him, seemed to follow the staccato pace of the narrative, filling in the blanks when an occasional word came up missing. What was wrong with me? I knew I'd felt like this before—this scared—this powerless—this out of it . . .

Brant was staring at me. "You actually talked to him?"

What was he talking about? "Who?" I sounded like an owl.

"Rafer."

What had I asked? What had he said before this? What did Rafer have to do with anything? "What?"

"Rafer. At the Rainbow."

"Yes. I ran into him at the Rainbow."

"I know that. You told me. I'm asking you if you talked to him," he said, with exaggerated patience.

"Sure."

"You *talked* to him?!" His voice had risen with alarm. I could see the question mark and the exclamation point hurling through the air at me. "I brought him up to date," I said. My voice was delayed, like something in an echo chamber. Words in balloons bumped together above my head, images like projectiles flying off in all directions.

"I told you to wait 'til I could check it out. Who do you think started all the rumors?"

"Who?"

Brant took me by the shoulders and gave me a little shake. He seemed angry, his fingers biting into my shoulders. "Kinsey, wake up and pay attention. This is serious," he said.

"You're not saying it was him?"

"Of *course*, it was him. Who else could it be? Think about it, dummy."

"Think about what?" I asked, confused. The immediacy of his discomposure was contagious. I was relying on him for help, but his anxiety was pushing mine into the danger zone.

His voice pounded on, pleading and cajoling, wheedling. "You told Mom it was someone in law enforcement. Do you honestly think my father would have lost even one night's sleep if it was anyone but Rafer? Rafer was his best friend. The two of them had worked together for years and years. Dad thought Rafer was one of the finest cops who ever lived. Now he finds out he killed two guys? Geez. He must have shit himself when he understood what was going on. Didn't he write this down? Isn't this in his notes?"

His words were like streamers, blowing above his head.

I heard snapping, like flags. "The notes are in code. I can't read them."

"Where? Can you show me? Maybe I can crack it."

"In there. You think he was on the verge of talking to Internal Affairs."

"Of course! The decision couldn't have been easy, but even as loyal as he was to Rafer, the department came first. He must have been praying for a way out, hoping he was wrong."

My brain worked lickety-cut. It was my mouth that fumbled, thoughts crashing against my teeth like rocks. I had to clamp my jaw shut, barely moving my lips. "I talked to Barrett. She was with Tom in the truck just before he died," I said.

"What did they talk about? Why did he do that?"

"Something. I can't remember."

"Didn't you press her for answers? You had the girl right there in the palm of your hand," he said. His words appeared in the air, written in big capital letters.

"Quit yelling."

"I'm not yelling. What's the matter with you?"

"Barrett never said a word about Rafer." I remembered then. She did say Tom had asked about her father.

"Why would she? She doesn't know you from Adam. She's not going to confide. She wouldn't tell you something like that. Her own father? For god's sake, she'd have to be nuts," he shrilled.

"But why give me the notes? Wouldn't she assume they'd be incriminating?"

"Barrett doesn't have a clue. She has no idea."

"How do you know what he did?"

"Because I can add," he said, exasperated. "I put two and two together. Listen, Tom met with Barrett. He was probably trying to find out about Rafer's whereabouts when Pinkie was murdered. Same with Alfie Toth. He saw the connection. He worried someone in the department would get wind of his suspicions, didn't you say that? Someone had already ripped him off for the information about Toth. Who do you think it was? *Rafer.*"

"Rafer," I said. I was nodding. I could see what he was saying. I'd been thinking the same thing. Tom's friendship with Rafer was such that he'd think long and hard before he turned him in to the authorities, betraying their friendship. A conflict of that magnitude would have caused him extreme distress. My brain was clicking and buzzing. *Click, click, click.* Rafer. It was like a pinball game. Thoughts ricocheted around, setting off bells, bouncing against the rails. I thought about the clerk at the Gramercy. Why didn't he tell me the phony plainclothes detective was black? You'd think he'd remember something so obvious. My mind kept veering. I couldn't hold a thought in one place and follow it to its conclusion. *Click, click.* Like pool balls. The cue ball would break and all the other balls on the table would fly off in separate directions. I wished I'd talked to Leland Peck before I left Santa Teresa. I was feeling very weird. So anxious. Sound fading in and out. I could see it undulate through space, sentences like surfers cresting on the waves of air.

Brant was still talking. He seemed to be speaking gibberish, but it all made a peculiar sense. "Pinkie went after Barrett. She was hiking in the mountains and stumbled across their fishing camp."

On and on he went, creating word pictures so vivid I thought it was happening to me.

"Barrett was assaulted. He put a gun to her head. She was raped. She was attacked and sexually abused. Pinkie sodomized and hurt her. He forced her to perform unspeakable acts. Alfie did nothing—offered her no assistance—ran off, leaving her to Pinkie's mercy. Barrett came back hysterical, in a state of shock. Rafer went after Pinkie and took him down. He strung him up, hung him from the limb of a tree and let him die slowly for what he had done to her. He would have killed Alfie, too, but Alfie escaped and blew town. Rafer thought he was safe all these years and then Pinkie's body turned up and Dad found the link between the two men. He drove all the way to Santa Teresa to talk to him, but Rafer got there first. He hung Toth the same way he hung Pinkie." Brant was looking at me earnestly. "What's wrong with your eyes?"

"My eyes?" Once he mentioned it, I realized my field of vision had begun to oscillate, images sliding side to side, like bad camera work. I felt giddy, as if I was on the verge of fainting. I sat down. I put my head between my knees, a roaring in my ears.

"Are you okay?"

"Fine." Lights seemed to pulsate and sounds came and went. I couldn't keep it straight. I knew what he was saying, but I couldn't make the words stand still. I saw Rafer with the noose. I saw him tighten it on Pinkie's neck. I saw him hang Alfie in the wilderness. I felt his rage and his pain for what they'd done to his only daughter. I said, "How do you know all this?"

"Because Barrett told me when it happened. Jesus, Kinsey. That's why I broke up with her. I was twenty years old. I couldn't handle it," he said, anguished.

"I'm sorry. I'm sorry," I said, but immediately forgot who was more deserving of my pity—Barrett for being raped, Brant for not having the maturity to deal with it.

Brant's tone became accusatory. "You're loaded. I don't believe it. What the hell are you high on?"

"I'm high?" Of course. Daniel playing the piano. My ex-husband. So beautiful. Eyes like an angel, a halo of golden curls and how I'd loved him. He'd given me acid once without telling me and I watched the floor recede into the mouth of hell.

Brant's head came up. "What's that?" he hissed.

"What?"

"I heard something." His agitation washed over me. His fear was infectious, as swift as an airborne virus. I could smell corruption and death. I'd been in situations like this before.

"Hang on." Brant strode down the hall. I saw him look out of the small ornamental window in the front door. He pulled back abruptly and then gestured urgently in my direction. "A car cruised by with its lights doused. He's parked across the street about six doors down. You have a gun?"

"I told you someone stole it. Whoever broke in. I don't have a gun. What's happening?"

"Rafer," he said grimly. He crossed to the drawer in his mother's kitchen desk where she did her menu planning. He pulled out a gun and thrust it in my hand. "Here. Take this."

I stood and stared at it with bewilderment. "Thanks," I whispered. The gun was a basic police revolver, Smith & Wesson. I'd nearly bought one like it once, .357 Magnum, four-inch barrel, checkered walnut stocks. I studied the grooves in the stock. Some of them were so deep, I couldn't see to the bottom.

"Rafer will come in with guns blazing," Brant was saying. "No deals. He's told everyone that you're a killer, that you do drugs, and here you are stoned on something."

"I didn't do anything," I said, mouth dry. The brownies. I was higher than he knew. I racked back through my memory, classes at the police academy, my years in uniform on the street, trying to remember symptoms; phencyclidines, stimulants, hallucinogens, sedative-hypnotics, narcotics. What had I ingested? Confusion, paranoia, slurred speech, nystagmus. I could see the columns marching across the pages of the text. PCP vocabulary. Rocket Fuel, DOA, KJ, Super Joint, Mint Weed, Gorilla Biscuits. I was out of my brain on speed.

"You found him out. He'll have to kill you. We'll have to shoot it out," Brant said.

"Don't leave me. You talk to him. I can get away," I burbled.

"He's thought of that. He'll have help. Probably Macon and Hatch. They both hate you. We better get down to business."

When Brant peeled off his outer jacket, I smelled stress sweat, the scent as acrid and piercing as ammonia. I glanced at his hands.

Given any visual field, the eye tends to stray to the one different item in a ground of like items. Even bombed, I caught sight of a blemish on his right wrist, a dark patch . . . a tattoo or a birthmark . . . shaped like the prow of a ship. The blot stood out like a brand on the clean white surface of his skin. Sizzling, my brain zapped through the possibilities: scar, hickey, smudge, scab. I was slow on the uptake. I looked back and then I saw it for what it was. The mark was a burn. The healing discoloration was a match for the tip of the ticking hot iron I'd pressed on him. Adrenaline rushed through me. Something close to euphoria filled my flesh and bones. My mind made an odd leap to something else altogether. I'd been struggling to break the code with logic and analysis when the answer was really one of spatial relationships. Vertical, not horizontal. That's how the numbers worked. Up and down instead of back and forth across the lines.

I put the gun on the kitchen table. "I'll be right back," I said. With extraordinary effort, I propelled myself into Tom's den, hand to the wall to steady my yawing gait. 8, 12, 1, 11, and 26. I sat down at his desk and looked at the calendar Tom had drawn. I could see the month of February, twenty-eight days penned in with the first falling on a Sunday and the last two Saturdays, the twenty-first and the twenty-eighth, crossed out, leaving twenty-six numbers. I'd suspected the code was simple. If Tom encrypted his notes, he had to have an uncomplicated means by which to convert letters to numbers.

I found a pencil. I turned to the calendar grid that he'd drawn on the corner of his blotter. I wrote the letters of the alphabet, inserting one letter per day, using vertical rows this time. If my theory was correct, then the code would confirm what I already knew: 8 would represent the letter *B.* The number 12 would stand in for the letter *R.* The number 1 would be *A,* and 11 would represent *N,* and the 26 would be *T.*

B-R-A-N-T.

Brant.

I could feel a laugh billow up. I was stuck in the house with him. He would have had easy access to his father's notes. The search of the den—the broken window—both had been a cover, suggesting to the rest of us that someone from the outside had entered the house in hopes of finding the notes. It wasn't Barrett at all. Pinkie hadn't raped and sodomized Barrett. It was Brant he'd humiliated and degraded.

"What are you doing?"

I jumped. Brant was standing in the doorway. I was standing in horseshit up to my underpants. The sight of him wavered, shimmering, image moving side to side. I couldn't think of a way to answer. Nystagmus. Something in the brownies, possibly PCP. Aggression, paranoia. I was smarter than him. Oh, much smarter. I was smarter than anyone that day.

"What are you looking at?"

"Tom's notes."

"Why?"

"I can't make heads or tails of them. The code."

He stared at me. I could tell he was trying to determine if what I'd said was true. I kept my mind empty. I don't think I'd ever seen him looking so lean and young and handsome. Death is like that, a lover whose embrace you sink into without warning. Instead of flight or resistance, voluptuous surrender. He held out his hand. "I'll take the notes."

I passed the notebook across to him, picturing the Smith & Wesson. Where had I heard about a gun like that before? I could feel my brain crackling, thoughts popping like kernels banging against the lid of a popcorn pan. There was no way in the world he would give me a gun unless he intended to see that I was killed with it. Rafer LaMott wasn't outside and neither was anybody else. This was a charade, setting me up in some way. I envisioned the scene—the two of us skulking through the house, ostensibly waiting for an attack that would never come. Brant could shoot me anytime he chose, claiming later he'd mistaken me for an intruder, claiming self-defense, claiming I was stoned out of my gourd, which I was. Even as the thought formed, I felt the drugs kick up a notch. I could feel myself expanding. I could outsmart him. He was strong, but I had more experience than he did. I knew more about him than he knew about me. I'd been a cop once. I knew everything he knew, plus some.

"Is the car still out there?" I asked.

Brant dropped back into his fantasy. He moved to the window and put his face close the the glass, peering off to the right. "Down half a block. You can barely see it from here."

"I think we should turn the lights out. I don't like standing here in plain view."

He studied me for a second, picturing the house black as pitch. "You're right. Hit the switch. I'll take care of all the other lights in the house."

"Good." I turned the den light out. I waited until I heard him moving down the hall toward the front. Then I eased to the window, flipped the lock, and pushed the sash up about six inches. I dropped down to the floor, felt my way across the room to the cabinet, and slid myself feet-first into the space beneath the bookshelves. Birth in reverse. I was hidden from view. Moments went by, the house becoming darker by the minute as lamps were being switched off in every room Brant entered.

"Kinsey?" Brant was back.

Silence.

I heard him come to the den. He must have stood in the doorway, allowing his eyes to adjust to the black. He crossed to the window, bumping into cardboard boxes. I heard him force the window open and look out. I was gone. There was no sign of me running across the grass. "Shit!" He slammed the window shut and said, "Shit, shit, *shit*!" He must have had a gun because I heard him rack one into the chamber.

He left the den, hollering my name as he went. Now he was mad. Now he didn't care if I knew he was coming. I pulled myself out of the cabinet, hanging on to the shelf as I staggered to my feet. I crossed to the desk and opened the bottom drawer as quietly as possible. I took out Tom's handcuffs and tucked them in my back pocket. I could feel myself swell with power. I was suddenly larger than life, far beyond fear, luminous with fury. As I turned right out of the den into the darkness of the hallway, I could see him moving ahead of me, his body mass blacker than the charcoal light surrounding him. I began to run, picking up speed, my Reeboks making no sound on the carpet. Brant sensed my presence, turning as I lifted myself into the air. I snapped a hard front kick to his solar plexis, taking him down with one pop. I heard his gun thump dully against the wall, banging against wood as it flew out of his hand. I kicked him again, catching him squarely on the side of the head. I scrambled to my feet and stood over him. I could have crushed his skull, but as a *courtesy*, I refrained from doing so. I pulled the handcuffs from my pocket. I grabbed the fingers of his right hand and bent them backward, encouraging compliance. I lay the cuff on his right wrist and snapped downward, smiling grimly to myself as the swinging arm of the cuff locked in place. I put my left foot on the back of his neck while I yanked his right arm behind him and grabbed for his left. I would have stomped down on his face, pulverizing his nose if he'd so much as whimpered. He was out cold. I double-locked both handcuffs in place. All of this without hesitation. All of this in the dark.

The light in the kitchen was snapped on. Selma appeared in the doorway, still wearing her fur coat. She stood as still as a soldier and took in the sight before her. Brant was now moaning. Blood was pouring from his nose and he was struggling for breath. "Mom, watch out. She's stoned," he croaked.

Selma backed into the kitchen. I was moving away from her down the corridor, looking for Brant's gun when she showed up again, this time with the Smith & Wesson in her right hand. I had no idea where Brant's gun had gone. I remembered the telltale thump at the end of its airborne journey.

"Stop right there," she said. She was now holding the gun with two hands, arms extended stiffly at shoulder height. I went about my business, ignoring her little drama. She had no way of knowing I'd been sanctified by Angel Dust. I was higher than a kite on PCP, methamphetamines, whatever it was—some amazing mix of excitation and immortality. The unpleasant side effects were now gone and I was detached from all feeling, secure in the sense that I would prevail over this bitch and anyone else who came after me.

"You're not going to take my son away from me."

As much as anything, I was annoyed with her. "I told you to forget it. You should have left well enough alone. Now you've not only lost Tom, you've lost Brant as well," I said, conversationally. I got down on my hands and knees and felt under the chair. Where the hell was Brant's gun?

"You are completely mistaken. I haven't lost Brant at all," she said. "Now get up right this minute! Do as I say!"

"Blow it out your ass, Selma. Do you see Brant's gun? I heard it bang against the wall. It's gotta be here somewhere."

"I'm warning you. I'll count to three and then I'm going to shoot you."

"You do that," I said. I moved into the dining room, convinced the gun had somehow become wedged under the hutch, the centerpiece in Selma's entire set of handsome, formal, glossy dark wood furniture. I placed my shoulder against the floor, reaching under the hutch as far as the length of my arm. It was in this awkward position—me spread-eagled on my stomach, Brant handcuffed and moaning in the hall, Selma angling herself into position to blow my head off if she could manage it—that I chanced to look up at her, watching in slow-motion amazement as she screwed up her face, closed her eyes, turned her head, and squeezed the trigger. There was a bright flash and a large bang. The bullet exited the barrel at a lethal velocity. The normal football-shaped muzzle flash out the front of the gun and the vertical fan-shaped flashes at the cylinder gap seemed to be enhanced, a dazzling yellow. Brant had apparently packed the first cartridge with an overload of fast powder. I thought I knew now who Judy Gelson's lover was the night she blew a hole in her husband's chest. The chamber and the top strap ruptured. The blast unlatched the cylinder and drove it out to the left side of the gun. The brass cartridge case shredded and tiny bits of brass peppered Selma's hands, flakes of unburned powder peppering her face as well. Simultaneously, as though by magic, all the glass in the cabinet doors, including the crystal goblets and the bone china plates, exploded like fireworks and formed a glittering starburst of falling glass and debris.

"Fuck. That was great. You should try that again," I said.

Selma was weeping as I walked to the phone and dialed 9-1-1.

Epilogue

Later, the Nota County Sheriff gave me permission to read the file on the Ritter/Toth murders. Rafer and I sat down together and by comparing Tom's notes with other reports submitted in the case, we managed to piece together the course of Tom's investigation. The irony, of course, was that the evidence he'd collected was not only spotty, but entirely circumstantial. None of it was sufficient to result in an arrest, let alone a conviction. Tom realized Brant had committed double murder and he knew it was something he couldn't keep to himself for long. Revealing the truth would destroy his marriage. Concealing the truth would destroy everything else he valued. Tom had died in silence, and if Selma had been content to leave it there, the case might have died, too.

Brant is currently out on bail on a charge of attempted murder for what he did to me. Selma's hired a fancy-pants attorney who (naturally) advised him to plead not guilty. I suspect if we get to court this same attorney will find a way to blame the whole thing on me. That's the way justice seems to work these days.

In the meantime, Selma's house is on the market and she's leaving Nota Lake. The town is unforgiving and the people there never liked her anyway. I guess what it all boils down to is a lesson in personal insecurity and low self-esteem. If I'd been clairvoyant—if I'd been capable of seeing all of these events in advance—I'd have told her to have her teeth capped instead of hiring me. She'd have been better off that way.

Respectfully submitted,
Kinsey Millhone

O

IS FOR OUTLAW

The author wishes to acknowledge the invaluable assistance of the following people: Steven Humphrey; Detective Peggy Moseley, Los Angeles Police Department; Captain Ed Aasted and Sergeant Brian Abbott, Santa Barbara Police Department; Pat Zuberer, Library Clerk, Barbara Alexander and Betsey Daniels, Librarians, Ronetta Coates, student, Louisville Male High School; Beverly Herrlinger, Curriculum Coordinator, Jefferson County High School Admissions Office; Ray Connors; Kathy Humphrey, Communications Director, California State Senate; Marshall Morgan, M.D., Medical Director, Emergency Room, UCLA Medical Center; H. Ric Harnsberger, M.D., Professor of ENT/Neuroradiology and Director, Neuroradiology Section, University of Utah Medical Center; Barry and Bernice Ewing, Eagle Sportschairs; Lee Stone; Harriet Miller, Mayor, City of Santa Barbara; Danny Nash, Jefferson County Clerk's Office, Louisville, Kentucky; Erik Raney, Deputy, Santa Barbara County Sheriff's Department; Kevin Rudan, Resident Agent, Secret Service; Don and Marilyn Gevirtz; Julianna Flynn; Ralph Hickey; Lucy Thomas and Nadine Greenup, Librarians, Reeves Medical Center, Cottage Hospital; Denise Huff, R.N., Cottage Hospital Emergency; Gail Abarbanel, Director, Rape Treatment Center, Santa Monica/UCLA Medical Center; Jay Schmidt; Jamie Clark; and Mary Lawrence Young.

To the reader,

Just a brief note to clarify the time frame for these "alphabet" novels. For those of you confused about what appear to be errors in my calculation of ages and dates, please be aware that *"A" Is for Alibi* takes place in May of 1982, *"B" Is for Burglar* in June of 1982, *"C" Is for Corpse* in August of 1982, and so forth. Since the books are sequential, Ms. Millhone is caught up in a time warp and is currently living and working in the year 1986, without access to cell phones, the Internet, or other high-tech equipment used by modern-day private investigators. She relies instead on persistence, imagination, and ingenuity: the stock-in-trade of the traditional gumshoe throughout hard-boiled history. As her biographer, I generally avoid mention of topical issues and date-related events. You'll find few, if any, references to current movies, fads, fashions, or politics. This book is an exception in that events connect back to the Vietnam War, which ended in 1975, eleven years before the incidents described herein. Given narrative requirements, I populate historical actions with fictional characters and project wholly invented persons into academic institutions and political arenas, in which their "real-life" counterparts will doubtless dispute their presence. In my view, the delight of fiction is its enhancement of the facts and its embellishment of reality. Aside from that—as my father used to say—"I know it's true because I made it up myself."

Respectfully submitted,
Sue Grafton

FOR MY GRANDDAUGHTER, KINSEY,

with a heart full of love

O

IS FOR OUTLAW

1

The Latin term *pro bono,* as most attorneys will attest, roughly translated means *for boneheads* and applies to work done without charge. Not that I practice law, but I am usually smart enough to avoid having to donate my services. In this case, my client was in a coma, which made billing a trick. Of course, you might look at the situation from another point of view. Once in a while a piece of old business surfaces, some item on life's agenda you thought you'd dealt with years ago. Suddenly, it's there again at the top of the page, competing for your attention despite the fact that you're completely unprepared for it.

First there was a phone call from a stranger; then a letter showed up fourteen years after it was sent. That's how I learned I'd made a serious error in judgment and ended up risking my life in my attempt to correct for it.

I'd just finished a big job, and I was not only exhausted but my bank account was fat and I wasn't in the mood to take on additional work. I'd pictured a bit of time off, maybe a trip someplace cheap, where I could lounge in the sun and read the latest Elmore Leonard novel while sipping on a rum drink with a paper umbrella stuck in a piece of fruit. This is about the range and complexity of my fantasies these days.

The call came at 8 A.M. Monday, May 19, while I was off at the gym. I'd started lifting weights again: Monday, Wednesday, and Friday mornings after my 6 A.M. run. I'm not sure where the motivation came from after a two-year layoff, but it was probably related to thoughts of mortality, primarily my own. In the spring, I'd sustained damage to my right hand when a fellow dislocated two fingers trying to persuade me to his point of view. I'd been hurt once before when a bullet nicked my right arm, and my impulse in both instances had been to hit the weight machines. Lest you imagine I'm a masochist or accident-prone, I should state that I make a living as a private investigator. Truth be told, the average P.I. seldom carries a gun, isn't often pursued, and rarely sustains an injury more substantial than a paper cut. My own professional life tends to be as dull anyone else's. I simply report the exceptions in the interest of spiritual enlightenment. Processing events helps me keep my head on straight.

Those of you acquainted with my personal data can skip this paragraph. For the uninitiated, I'm female, thirty-six years old, twice divorced, and living in Santa Teresa, California, which is ninety-five miles north of Los Angeles. Currently, I occupy one small office in the larger suite of offices of Kingman and Ives, attorneys at law. Lonnie Kingman is my attorney when the occasion arises, so my association with his firm seemed to make sense when I was looking for space. I'd been rendered a migrant after I was unceremoniously shit-canned from the last job I had: investigating arson and wrongful death claims for California Fidelity Insurance. I've been with Lonnie now for over two years, but I'm not above harboring a petty desire for revenge on CFI.

During the months I'd been lifting weights, my muscle tone had improved and my strength had increased. That particular morning, I'd worked my way through the customary body parts: two sets, fifteen reps each, of leg extensions, leg curls, ab crunches, lower back, lat rows, the chest press and pec deck, along with the shoulder press, and various exercises for the biceps and triceps. Thus pumped up and euphoric, I let myself into my apartment with the usual glance at my answering machine. The message light was blinking. I dropped my gym bag on the floor, tossed my keys on the desk, and pressed the PLAY button, reaching for a pen and a pad of paper in case I needed to take notes. Before I leave the office each day, I have Lonnie's service shunt calls over to my apartment. That way, in a pinch, I can lie abed all day, dealing with the public without putting on my clothes.

The voice was male, somewhat gravelly, and the message sounded like this: "Miss Millhone, this is Teddy Rich. I'm calling from Olvidado about something might innerest you. This is eight A.M. Monday. Hope it's not too early. Gimme a call when you can. Thanks." He recited a telephone number in the 805 area code, and I dutifully jotted it down. It was only 8:23 so I hadn't missed him by much. Olvidado is a town of 157,000, thirty miles south of Santa Teresa on Highway 101. Always one to be interested in something that might "innerest" me, I dialed the number he'd left. The ringing went on so long I thought his machine would kick in, but the line was finally picked up by Mr. Rich, whose distinctive voice I recognized.

"Hi, Mr. Rich. This is Kinsey Millhone up in Santa Teresa. I'm returning your call."

"Hey, Miss Millhone. Nice to hear from you. How are you today?"

"Fine. How are you?"

"I'm fine. Thanks for asking, and thanks for being so prompt. I appreciate that."

"Sure, no problem. What can I do for you?"

"Well, I'm hoping this is something I can do for you," he said. "I'm a storage space scavenger. Are you familiar with the term?"

"I'm afraid not." I pulled the chair out and sat down, realizing Ted Rich was going to take his sweet time about this. I'd already pegged him as a salesman or a huckster, someone thoroughly enamored of whatever minor charms he possessed. I didn't want what he was selling, but I decided I might as well hear him out. This business of storage space scavenging was a new one on me, and I gave him points for novelty.

He said, "I won't bore you with details. Basically, I bid on the contents of self-storage lockers when the monthly payment's in arrears."

"I didn't know they did that on delinquent accounts. Sounds reasonable, I suppose." I took the towel from my gym bag and ruffed it across my head. My hair was still damp from the workout and I was getting chillier by the minute, longing to hit the shower before my muscles stiffened up.

"Oh, sure. Storage unit's been abandoned by its owner for more'n sixty days, the contents go up for auction. How else can the company recoup its losses? Guys like me show up and blind-bid on the contents, paying anywheres from two hundred to fifteen hundred bucks, hoping for a hit."

"As in what?" I reached down, untied my Sauconys, and slipped them off my feet. My gym socks smelled atrocious, and I'd only worn them a week.

"Well, most times you get junk, but once in a while you get lucky and come across something good. Tools, furniture—stuff you can convert to hard cash. I'm sure you're pro'bly curious what this has to do with you."

"It crossed my mind," I said mildly, anticipating his pitch. For mere pennies a day, you too can acquire abandoned bric-a-brac with which to clutter up your premises.

"Yeah, right. Anyways, this past Saturday, I bid on a couple storage bins. Neither of 'em netted much, but in the process I picked up a bunch of cardboard boxes. I was sorting through the contents and came across your name on some personal documents. I'm wondering what it's worth to you to get 'em back."

"What kind of documents?"

"Lemme see here. Hold on. Frankly, I didn't expect to hear so soon or I'd have had 'em on the desk in front of me." I could hear him rattling papers in the background. "Okay now. We got a pink-bead baby bracelet and there's quite a collection of school-type memorabilia: drawings, class pictures, report cards from Woodrow Wilson Elementary. This ringin' any bells with you?"

"*My* name's on these papers?"

"Kinsey Millhone, right? Millhone with two *l*'s. Here's a history report entitled 'San Juan Capistrano Mission,' with a model of the mission made of egg cartons. Mrs. Rosen's class, fourth grade. She gave you a D plus. 'Report is not bad, but project is poorly presented,' she says. I had a teacher like her once. What a bitch," he said idly. "Oh, and here's something else. Diploma says you graduated Santa Teresa High School on June tenth, 1967? How'm I doin' so far?"

"Not bad."

"Well, there you go," he said.

"Not that it matters, but how'd you track me down?"

"Piece of cake. All I did was call Directory Assistance. The name Millhone's unusual, so I figure it's like the old saying goes: apples don't fall far from the tree and so forth. I proceeded on the assumption you were somewheres close. You could've got married and changed your name, of course. I took a flier on that score. Anyways, the point is, how d'you feel about gettin' these things back?"

"I don't understand how the stuff ended up in Olvidado. I've never rented storage space down there."

I could hear him begin to hedge. "I never said Olvidado. Did I say that? I go to these auctions all over the state. Lookit, I don't mean to sound crass, but if you're willing to pony up a few bucks, we can maybe make arrangements for you to get this box back."

I hesitated, annoyed by the clumsiness of his maneuvering. I remembered my struggle in Mrs. Rosen's class, how crushed I'd been with the grade after I'd worked so hard. The fact was, I had so little in the way of personal keepsakes that any addition would be treasured. I didn't want to pay much, but neither was I willing to relinquish the items sight unseen.

I said, "The papers can't be worth much since I wasn't aware they were missing." Already, I didn't like him and I hadn't even met him yet.

"Hey, I'm not here to argue. I don't intend to hose you or nothin' like that. You want to talk value, we talk value. Up to you," he said.

"Why don't I think about it and call you back?"

"Well, that's just it. If we could find time to get together, you could take a look at these items and then come to a decision. How else you going to know if it's worth anything to you? It'd mean a drive down here, but I'm assuming you got wheels."

"I could do that, I suppose."

"Excellent," he said. "So what's your schedule like today?"

"Today?"

"No time like the present is my attitude."

"What's the big hurry?"

"No hurry in particular except I got appointments set up for the rest of the week. I make money turnin' stuff over, and my garage is already packed. You have time today or not?"

"I could probably manage it."

"Good, then let's meet as soon as possible and see if we can work somethin' out. There's a coffee shop down the street from me. I'm on my way over now and I'll be there for about an hour. Let's say nine-thirty. You don't show? I gotta make a run to the dump anyways so it's no skin off my nose."

"What'd you have in mind?"

"Moneywise? Let's say thirty bucks. How's that sound?"

"Exorbitant," I said. I asked him for directions. What a hairball.

I showered and flung on the usual blue jeans and T-shirt, then gassed up my VW and headed south on 101. The drive to Olvidado took twenty-five minutes. Following Ted Rich's instructions, I took the Olvidado Avenue exit and turned right at the bottom of the off-ramp. Half a black from the freeway, there was large shopping mall. The surrounding land, originally given over to agricultural use, was gradually being converted to a crop of new and used cars. Lines of snapping plastic flags defined tent shapes above the asphalt lot where rows of vehicles glinted in the mild May sun. I could see a shark-shaped mini-blimp tethered and hovering thirty feet in the air. The significance escaped me, but what do I know about these things?

Across from the mall, the business establishments seemed to be equally divided among fast food joints, liquor stores, and instant-copy shops that offered passport photos. There was even a facility devoted to walk-in legal services; litigate while you wait. BANKRUPTCY $99. DIVORCE $99. DIVORCE W/KIDS $99 + FILING FEE. *Se habla español.* The coffee shop he'd specified appeared to be the only mom-and-pop operation in the area.

I parked my car in the lot and pushed into the place, scanning the few patrons for someone who fit his description. He'd indicated he was six foot two and movie-star handsome, but then he'd snorted with laughter, which led me to believe otherwise. He'd said he'd watch the door for my arrival. I spotted a guy who raised a hand in greeting and beckoned me to his booth. His face was a big ruddy square, his sunburn extending into the V of his open-collared denim work shirt. He wore his dark hair combed straight back, and I could see the indentation at his temples where he'd removed the baseball cap now sitting on the table next to him. He had a wide nose, drooping upper lids, and bags under his eyes. I could see the scattering of whiskers he'd missed during his morning shave. His shoulders were beefy and his forearms looked thick where he had his sleeves rolled up. He'd removed a dark brown windbreaker, which now lay neatly folded over the back of the booth.

"Mr. Rich? Kinsey Millhone. How are you?" We shook hands across the table, and I could tell he was sizing me up with the same attention to detail I'd just lavished on him.

"Make it Teddy. Not bad. I appreciate your coming." He glanced at his watch as I slid in across from him. "Unfortunately I only got maybe fifteen, twenty minutes before I have to take off. I apologize for the squeeze, but right after we spoke, I hadda call from some guy down in Thousand Oaks needs an estimate on his roof."

"You're a roofer?"

"By trade." He reached in his pants pocket. "Lemme pass you my card in case you need somethin' done." He took out a slim Naugahyde case and removed a stack of business cards. "My speciality is new roofs and repairs."

"What else is there?"

"Hey, I can do anything you need. Hot mops, tear-offs, torch-downs, all types of shake, composition, slate, clay tile, you name it. Corrective and preventative is my area of expertise. I could give you a deal . . . let's say ten percent off if you call this month. What kind of house you in?"

"Rented."

"So maybe you got a landlord needs some roof work done. Go ahead and keep that. Take as many as you want." He offered me a handful of cards, fanned out face down like he was about to do a magic trick.

I took one and examined it. The card bore his name, telephone number, and a post office box. His company was called Overhead Roofing, the letters forming a wide inverted V like the ridgeline of a roof. His company motto was *We do all types of roofing.*

"Catchy," I remarked.

He'd been watching for my reaction, his expression serious. "I just had those made. Came up with the name myself. Used to be Ted's Roofs. You know, simple, basic, something of a personal touch. I could have said 'Rich Roofs,' but that might have gave the wrong impression. I was in business ten years, but then the drought came along and the market dried up—"

"So to speak," I put in.

He smiled, showing a small gap between his two front lower teeth. "Hey, that's good. I like your sense of humor. You'll appreciate this one. Couple years without rain and people start to take a roof for granite. Get it? Granite . . . like the rock?"

I said, "That's funny."

"Anyways, I've had a hell of a time. I hadda shut down altogether and file bankruptcy. My wife up and left me, the dog died, and then my truck got sideswiped. I was screwed big time. Now we got some bad weather coming in, I figured I'd start fresh. Overhead Roofing is a kind of play on words."

"Really," I said. "What about the storage space business? Where did that come from?"

"I figured I hadda do something when the roofing trade fell in. 'As it were,' " he added, with a wink at me. "I decided to try salvage. I had some cash tucked away the wife and the creditors didn't know about, so I used that to get started. Takes five or six thousand if you want to do it right. I got hosed once or twice, but otherwise I been doing pretty good, even if I do say so myself." He caught the waitress's attention and held his coffee cup in the air with a glance back at me. "Can I buy you a cup of coffee?"

"That sounds good. How long have you been at it?"

"About a year," he said. "We're called 'pickers' or storage room gamblers, sometimes resellers, treasure hunters. How it works is I check the papers for auction listings. I also subscribe to a couple newsletters. You never know what you'll find. Couple of weeks ago, I paid two-fifty and found a painting worth more than fifteen hundred bucks. I was jazzed."

"I can imagine."

"Of course, there's rules to the practice, like anything else in life. You can't touch the rooms' contents, can't go inside before the bidding starts, and there's no refunds. You pay six hundred dollars and all you come up with is a stack of old magazines, then it's too bad for you. Such is life and all that."

"Can you make a living at it?"

He shifted in his seat. "Not so's you'd notice. This is strictly a hobby in between roofing engagements. Nice thing about it is it doesn't look good on paper so the wife can't hit me up for alimony. She was the one who walked out, so up hers is what I say."

The waitress appeared at the table with a coffeepot in hand, refilling his cup and pouring one for me. Teddy and the waitress exchanged pleasantries. I took the moment to add milk to my coffee and then tore the corner off a pack of sugar, which I don't ordinarily take. Anything to fill time till they finished their conversation. Frankly, I thought he had the hots for her.

Once she departed, Teddy turned his attention to me. I could see the box on the seat beside him. He noticed my glance. "I can see you're curious. Wanna peek?"

I said, "Sure."

I made a move toward the box and Teddy put a hand out, saying, "Gimme five bucks first." Then he laughed. "You shoulda seen the look on your face. Come on. I'm teasing. Help yourself." He hefted the box and passed it across the table. It was maybe three feet square, awkward but not heavy, the cardboard powdery with dust. The top had been sealed, but I could see where the packing tape had been cut and the flaps folded back together. I set the box on the seat beside me and pulled the flaps apart. The contents seemed hastily thrown together with no particular thought paid to the organization. It was rather like the last of the cartons packed in the moving process: stuff you don't dare throw out but don't really know what else to do with. A box like this could probably sit unopened in your basement for the next ten years, and nothing would ever stimulate a search for even one of the items. On the other hand, if you felt the need to inventory the contents, you'd still feel too attached to the items to toss the assortment in the trash. The next time you moved, you'd end up adding the box to the other boxes on the van, gradually accumulating sufficient junk to fill a . . . well, a storage bin.

I could tell at a glance these were articles I wanted. In addition to the grade school souvenirs, I spotted the high school diploma he'd mentioned, my yearbook, some textbooks, and, more important, file after file of mimeographed pages from my classes at the police academy. Thirty bucks was nothing for this treasury of remembrances.

Teddy was watching my face, trying to gauge the dollar signs in my reaction. I found myself avoiding eye contact lest he sense the extent of my interest. Stalling, I said, "Whose storage space was it? I don't believe you mentioned that."

"Guy named John Russell. He a friend of yours?"

"I wouldn't call him a friend, but I know him," I said. "Actually, that's an in-joke, like an alias. 'John Russell' is a character in an Elmore Leonard novel called *Hombre.*"

"Well, I tried to get ahold of him, but I didn't have much luck. Way too many Russells in this part of the state. Couple of dozen Jonathans, fifteen or twenty Johns, but none were him because I checked it out."

"You put some time in."

"You bet. Took me couple hours before I gave it up and said nuts. I tried this whole area: Perdido, LA County, Orange, San Bernardino, Santa Teresa County, as far up as San Luis. There's no sign of the guy, so I figure he's dead or moved out of state."

I took a sip of my coffee, avoiding comment. The addition of milk and sugar made the coffee taste like a piece of hard candy.

Teddy tilted his head at me with an air of bemusement. "So you're a private detective? I notice you're listed as Millhone Investigations."

"That's right. I was a cop for two years, which is how I knew John."

"The guy's a cop?"

"Not now, but he was in those days."

"I wouldn't have guessed that . . . I mean, judging from the crap he had jammed in that space. I'da said some kind of bum. That's the impression I got."

"Some people would agree."

"But you're not one of 'em, I take it."

I shrugged, saying nothing.

Teddy studied me shrewdly. "Who's this guy to you?"

"What makes you ask?"

"Come on. What's his real name? Maybe I can track him down for you, like a missing persons case."

"Why bother? We haven't spoken in years, so he's nothing to me."

"But now you got me curious. Why the alias?"

"He was a vice cop in the late sixties and early seventies. Big dope busts back then. John worked undercover, so he was always paranoid about his real name."

"Sounds like a nut."

"Maybe so," I said. "What else was in the bin?"

He waved a hand dismissively. "Most of it was useless. Lawnmower, broken-down vacuum cleaner. There was a big box of kitchen stuff: wooden rolling pin, big wooden salad bowl, must have been three feet across the top, set of crockery bowls—what do you call it? That Fiesta Ware shit. I picked up a fair chunk of change for that. Ski equipment, tennis racquets, none of it in prime condition. There was an old bicycle, motorcycle engine, wheel cover, and some car parts. I figure Russell was a pack rat, couldn't let go of stuff. I sold most of it at the local swap meet; this was yesterday."

I felt my heart sink. The big wooden bowl had belonged to my Aunt Gin. I didn't care about the Fiesta Ware, though that was hers as well. I was wishing I'd had the option to buy the wooden rolling pin. Aunt Gin had used it to make sticky buns—one of her few domestic skills—rolling out the dough before she sprinkled on the cinnamon and sugar. I had to let that one go; no point in longing for what had already been disposed of. Odd to think an item would suddenly have such appeal when I hadn't thought of it in years.

He nodded at the box. "Thirty bucks and it's yours."

"Twenty bucks. It's barely worth that. It's all junk."

"Twenty-five. Come on. For the trip down memory lane. Things like that you're never going to see again. Sentimental journey and so forth. Might as well snap it up while you have the chance."

I removed a twenty from my handbag and laid it on the table. "Nobody else is going to pay you a dime."

Teddy shrugged. "So I toss it. Who cares? Twenty-five and that's firm."

"Teddy, a dump run would cost you fifteen, so this puts you five bucks ahead."

He stared at the money, flicked a look to my face, and then took the bill with an exaggerated sigh of disgust with himself. "Lucky I like you or I'd be pissed as hell." He folded the twenty lengthwise and tucked it in his pocket. "You never answered my question."

"Which one?"

"Who's this guy to you?"

"No one in particular. A friend once upon a time . . . not that it's any of your business."

"Oh, I see. I get it. Now, he's 'a friend.' Inneresting development. You musta been close to the guy if he ended up with your things."

"What makes you say that?"

He tapped his temple. "I got a logical mind. Analytical, right? I bet I could be a peeper just like you."

"Gee, Teddy, sure. I don't see why not. The truth is I stored some boxes at John's while I was in the middle of a move. My stuff must have gotten mixed up with his when he left Santa Teresa. By the way, which storage company?"

His expression turned crafty. "What makes you ask?" he said, in a slightly mocking tone.

"Because I'm wondering if he's still in the area somewhere."

Teddy shook his head, way ahead of me. "No go. Forget it. You'd be wasting your time. I mean, look at it this way. If the guy used a phony name, he prob'bly also faked his phone number and his home address. Why contact the company? They won't tell you nothin'."

"I'll bet I could get the information. That's what I do for a living these days."

"You and Dick Tracy."

"All I'm asking is the name."

Teddy smiled. "How much's it worth?"

"How much is it *worth*?"

"Yeah, let's do a little business. Twenty bucks."

"Don't be silly. I'm not going to *pay* you. That's ridiculous."

"So make me an offer. I'm a reasonable guy."

"Bullshit."

"All I'm saying is you scratch my back and I'll scratch yours."

"There can't be that many storage companies in the area."

"Fifteen hundred and eleven, if you take in the neighboring counties. For ten bucks, I'll tell you which little town it's in."

"No way."

"Come on. How else you going to find out?"

"I'm sure I can think of something."

"Wanna bet? Five says you can't."

I glanced at my watch and slid out of the seat. "I wish I could chat, Teddy, but you have that appointment and I have to get to work."

"Whyn't you call me if you change your mind? We could find him together. We could form us a partnership. I bet you could use a guy with my connections."

"No doubt."

I picked up the cardboard box, made a few more polite mouth noises, and returned to my car. I placed the box in the passenger seat and then slid in on the driver's side. I locked both doors instinctively and blew out a big breath. My heart was thumping, and I could feel the damp of perspiration in the small of my back. "John Russell" was the alias for a former Santa Teresa vice detective named Mickey Magruder, my first ex-husband. What the hell was going on?

2

I slouched down in my car, scanning the parking lot from my position at half mast. I could see a white pickup parked at the rear of the lot, the truck bed filled with the sort of buckets and tarps I pictured essential to a roofing magnate. An oversized toolbox rested near the back of the cab, and an aluminum extension ladder seemed to be mounted on the far side with its two metal antislip shoes protruding about a foot. I adjusted the rearview mirror, watching until Ted Rich came out of the coffee shop wearing his baseball cap and brown windbreaker. He had his hands in his pants pockets and he whistled to himself as he walked to the pickup and fished out his keys. When I heard the truck rumble to life, I took a moment to lean sideways out of his line of sight. As soon as he passed, I sat up again, watching as he turned left and entered the line of traffic heading toward the southbound freeway on-ramp.

I waited till he was gone, then got out of the VW and trotted to the public phone booth near the entrance to the parking lot. I placed his business card on the narrow metal shelf provided, hauled up the phone book, and checked under the listings for United States Government. I found the number I was looking for and dug some loose change from the bottom of my shoulder bag. I inserted coins in the slot and dialed the number for the local post office branch printed on Rich's business card. The phone rang twice and a recorded message was activated, subjecting me to the usual reassurances. All the lines were busy at the moment, but my call would be answered in the order it was received. According to the recording, the post office really appreciated my patience, which shows you just how little they know about yours truly.

When a live female clerk finally came on the line, I gave her the box number for Overhead Roofing, possibly known as Ted's Roofs. Within minutes, she'd checked the rental agreement for his post office box and had given me the corresponding street address. I said thanks and depressed the plunger. I put another coin in the slot and punched in the phone number listed on the business card. As I suspected, no one answered, though Rich's machine did pick up promptly. I was happy to hear that Ted Rich was Olvidado's Number 1 certified master installer of fire-free roofing materials. The message also indicated that May was weatherproofing month, which I hadn't realized. More important, Teddy wasn't home and neither, apparently, was anyone else.

I returned to the car, fished an Olvidado city map from the glove compartment, and found the street listed on the ledger. By tracing the number and the letter coordinates, I pinpointed the location, not far from where I sat. Oh, happiness. I turned the key in the ignition, put the car in reverse, and in less than five minutes I was idling in front of Teddy's house, whence he operated his roofing business.

I found a parking spot six doors down and then sat in the car while my good angel and my bad angel jousted for possession of my soul. My good angel reminded me I'd vowed to reform. She recited the occasions when my usual vile behavior had brought me *naught but grief and pain,* as she put it. Which was all well and good, but as my bad angel asserted, this was really the only chance I was going to have to get the information I wanted. If Rich had "shared" the name of the storage company, I wouldn't have to do this, so it was really all his fault. He was currently on his way to Thousand Oaks to give an estimate on some guy's roof. The round-trip drive would take approximately thirty minutes, with another thirty minutes thrown in for schmoozing, which is how men do business. The two of us had parted company at ten. It was now ten-fifteen, so (with luck) he wouldn't be back for another forty-five minutes.

I removed my key picks from my shoulder bag, which I'd left on the backseat under the pile of assorted clothes I keep there. Often in the course of surveillance work, I use camouflage garments, like a quick-change artist, to vary my appearance. Now I pulled out a pair of navy coveralls that looked suitably professional. The patch on the sleeve, which I'd had stitched to my specifications, read SANTA TERESA CITY SERVICES and suggested I was employed by the public works department. I figured from a distance the Olvidado citizens would never know the difference. Wriggling around in the driver's seat, I pulled the coveralls over my usual jeans and T-shirt. I tugged up the front zipper and tucked my key picks in one pocket. I reached for the matching clipboard with its stack of generic paperwork, then locked the car behind me and walked as far as Ted Rich's gravel drive. There were no vehicles parked anywhere near the house.

I climbed the front steps and rang the doorbell. I waited, leafing through the papers on the clipboard, making an official-looking note with the pen attached by a chain. I rang again, but there was no reply. *Quelle surprise.* I moved to the front window, shading my eyes as I peered through the glass. Aside from the fact that there was no sign of the occupant, the place had the look of a man accustomed to living by himself, an aura epitomized by the presence of a Harley-Davidson motorcycle in the middle of the dining room.

Casually, I glanced around. There was no one on the sidewalk and no hint of neighbors watching from across the way. Nonetheless,

I frowned, making a big display of my puzzlement. I checked my watch to show that I, at least, was on time for our imaginary appointment. I trotted down the front steps and headed back along the driveway to the rear of the house. The backyard was fenced, and the shrubbery had grown up tall enough to touch the utility wires strung along the property line. The yard was deserted. Both sectional doors of the two-car garage were closed and showed hefty padlocks.

I climbed the back porch steps and then checked to see if any neighbors were busy dialing 9-1-1. Once assured of my privacy, I peeped in the kitchen window. The lights were off in the rooms within view. I tried the door handle. Locked. I stared at the Schlage, wondering how long it would take before it yielded to my key picks. Glancing down at knee height, I noticed that the bottom half of the door panel boasted a sizable homemade pet entrance. Well, what have we here? I reached down, gave the flap a push, and found myself staring at a section of kitchen linoleum. I thought back to Ted Rich's reference to his divorce and the death of his beloved pooch. The opening to the doggie door appeared to be large enough to accomodate me.

I set the clipboard on the porch rail and got down on my hands and knees. At five feet six inches and 118 pounds, I had only minor difficulties in my quest for admittance. Arms above my head, my body tilted to the diagonal, I began to ease myself through the opening. Once I'd succeeded in squeezing my head and shoulders through the door, I paused for a quick appraisal to assure myself there was no one else in residence. My one-sided view was restricted to the chrome-and-Formica dinette set, littered with dirty dishes, and the big plastic clock on the wall above. I inched forward, rotating my body so I could see the rest of the room. Now that I was halfway through the doggie door, it dawned on me that maybe I should have asked Rich if he'd acquired a new mutt. To my left, at eye level, I could see a two-quart water bowl and a large plastic dish filled with dry dog food. Nearby, a rawhide bone sported teeth marks that appeared to have been inflicted by a creature with a surly disposition.

Half a second later, the object of my speculation appeared on the scene. He'd probably been alerted by the noise and came skidding around the corner to see what was up. I'm not dog oriented by nature and I hardly know one breed from the next, with the exception of Chihuahuas, cocker spaniels, and other obvious types. This dog was big, maybe eighty pounds of lean weight on a heavily boned frame. What the hell was he doing while I was ringing the bell? The least he could have done was barked properly to warn me off. The dog was a medium brown with a big face, thick head, and a short, sleek coat. He was heavy through the chest and he had a dick the size of a hairy six-inch Gloria Cubana. A ruff of coarse hair was standing up along his spine, as though from permanent outrage. He stopped in his tracks and stood there, his expression a perfect blend of confusion and incredulity. I could almost see the question mark forming above his head. Apparently, in his experience, few human beings had tried to slither through his private entrance. I ceased struggling, to allow him time to assess the situation. I must not have represented any immediate threat because he neither lunged nor barked nor bit me cruelly about the head and shoulders. On the contrary, he seemed to feel that something was required of him in the way of polite behavior, though I could tell he was having trouble deciding what would be appropriate. He made a whining sound, dropped to his belly, and crept across the floor to me. I stayed where I was. For a while, we lay face-to-face while I suffered his meaty breath and he thought about life. Me and dogs always seem to end up in relationships like this.

"Hi, how're you," I said finally, in what I hoped was a pleasant tone (from the dog's perspective).

He put his head down on his paws and shot me a worried look.

I said, "Listen, I hope you don't mind if I slide on in, because any minute your neighbor's going to look out the window and catch sight of my hineybumper hanging out the doggie door. If you have any objections, speak now or forever hold your peace."

I waited, but the dog never even bared his gums. Using my elbows for leverage, I completed ingress, saying, "Nice dog," "What a good pooch," and similar kiss-ass phrases. His tail began to thump with hope. Maybe I was the little friend his dad had promised would come and play with him.

Once inside the kitchen, I began to rise to my feet. This, in the dog's mind, converted me into a beast that might require savaging. He leapt up, head down, ears back, beginning an experimental growl, his entire chest wall vibrating like a swarm of bees on the move. I sank down to my original submissive position. "Good boy," I murmured, humbly lowering my gaze.

I waited while the dog tested the parameters of his responsibility. The growling faded in due course. I tried again. Lifting onto my hands and knees seemed acceptable, but the minute I attempted to stand, the growling started up again. Make no mistake about it, this dog meant business.

"You're very strict," I said.

I waited a few moments and tried yet again. This time the effort netted me a furious bark. "Okay, okay." The big guy was beginning to get on my nerves. In theory, I was close enough to the doggie door to effect an escape, but I was fearful of going head first, thus exposing my rear end. I was also worried about going out feet first lest the dog attack my upper body while I was wedged in the opening. Meanwhile, the kitchen clock was ticking like a time bomb, forcing a decision. The curtain or the box? I could visualize Ted Rich barreling down the highway in my direction. I had to do *something*. Still on my hands and knees, I crawled forward a step. The dog watched with vigilance but made no menacing gesture. Slowly, I headed across the kitchen floor toward the front of the house. The dog tagged along beside me, his toenails clicking on the grimy linoleum, his full attention focused on my plodding journey. Already, I realized I hadn't really thought this thing through, but I'd been so intent on my ends, I hadn't fully formulated the means.

Babylike, in my romper, I traversed the dining room, bypassed the motorcycle, and entered the living room. This room was carpeted but otherwise contained little in the way of interest. I crawled down the hallway with the dog keeping pace, his head hanging down till his gaze was level with mine. I suppose I should state right here that what I was doing isn't routine behavior for a private eye. My conduct was more typical of someone intent on petty theft, too mulish and impetuous to use legitimate means (provided she could think of any). In the law enforcement sector, my actions would be classified as trespass, burglary, and (given the key picks in my pocket) possession of burglary tools—California Penal Code sections 602, 459, and 466 respectively. I hadn't stolen anything (yet) and the item I was after was purely intellectual, but it was nonetheless illegal to squirm through a doggie door and start crawling down a hall. Caught in the act, I'd be subject to arrest and conviction, perhaps forfeiting my license and my livelihood. Well, dang. All this for a man I'd left after less than nine months of marriage.

The house wasn't large: a bath and two bedrooms, plus the living room, dining room, kitchen, and laundry room. I must say the world is very boring at an altitude of eighteen inches. All I could see were chair legs, carpet snags, and endless stretches of dusty baseboard. No wonder house pets, when left alone, take to peeing on the rugs and gnawing on the furniture. I passed a door on the left that led back into the kitchen, with the laundry room to one side. When I reached the next door on the left, I crawled in and surveyed the premises, mentally wagging my tail. Unmade double bed, night table, chest of drawers, doggie bed, and dirty clothes on the floor. I did a U-turn and crawled into the room across the hall. Rich was using this one as a combination den and home office. Along the wall to my right, he had a row of banged-up file cabinets and a scarred oak desk. He also had a Barcalounger and a television set. The dog climbed on the recliner with a guilty look, watching to see if I was going to swat his hairy butt. I smiled my encouragement. As far as I was concerned, the dog could do anything he wanted.

I made my way over to the desk. "I'm getting up to take a peek, so don't get your knickers in a twist, okay?" By now, the dog was bored, and he yawned so hard I heard a little squeak at the back of his throat. Carefully, I eased into a kneeling position and searched the surface of the desk. There on a stack of papers lay the answer to my prayers: a sheaf of documents, among them the receipt for Rich's payment to the San Felipe Self-Storage Company, dated Saturday, May 17. I tucked the paper in my mouth, sank down on all fours, and crawled to the door. Since the dog had lost interest, I was able to make quick work of the corridor in front of me. Crawling rapidly, I rounded the corner and thumped across the kitchen floor. When I reached the back door, I grabbed the knob and pulled myself to my feet. Exploits like this aren't as easy as they used to be. The knees of my coveralls were covered with dust, and I brushed off some woofies with a frown of disgust. I took the receipt out of my mouth, folded it, and stuck it in the pocket of my coveralls.

When I glanced through the back door to make sure the coast was clear, I spotted my clipboard still sitting on the porch rail where I'd left it. I was just chiding myself for not tucking it someplace less conspicuous when I heard the sound of gravel popping and the front of Rich's pickup appeared in my field of vision. He pulled to a stop, cranked on the hand brake, and opened the truck door. By the time he got out, I'd taken six giant steps backward, practically levitating as I fled through the kitchen to the laundry room, where I slid behind the open door. Rich had slammed his door and was apparently now making his way to the back porch. I heard him clump up the back steps. There was a pause wherein he seemed to make some remark to himself. He'd probably found my clipboard and was puzzling at its import.

The dog had heard him, of course, and was up like a shot, hurtling for the back door as fast as he could. My heart was thumping so loud it sounded like a clothes dryer spinning a pair of wet tennis shoes. I could see my left breast vibrating against the front of my coveralls. I couldn't swear to this, but I think I may have wee-weed ever so slightly in my underpants. Also, I noticed the cuff of my pant leg was now protruding through the crack in the door. I'd barely managed to conceal myself when Rich clattered in the back door and tossed the clipboard on the counter. He and the dog exchanged a ritual greeting.

On the part of the dog, much joyous barking and leaps; on Rich's part, a series of exhortations and commands, none of which seemed to have any particular effect. The dog had forgotten my intrusion, sidetracked by the merriment of having his master home.

I heard Rich move through the living room and proceed down the hall, where he entered his office and flipped on the television set. Meanwhile, the dog must have been tickled by a tiny whisper of recollection because he set off in search of me, his nose close to the floor. Hide and seek—what fun—and guess who was It? He rousted me in no time, spying my coveralls. Just to show how smart he was, he actually seemed to press one eye to the crack before he gave my pant leg a tug. He shook his head back and forth, growling with enthusiasm while he yanked on my cuff. Without even thinking, I poked my head around the door and raised a finger to my lips. He barked with enthusiasm, thus releasing me, and then he pranced back and forth hoping I would play. I have to say, it was pathetic to see an eighty-pound mutt having so much fun at my expense. Rich, unaware of the cause, bellowed orders to the pooch, who stood there torn between obedience to his master and the thrill of discovery. Rich called him again, and he bounded away with a series of exuberant yelps. Back in the den, Rich told him to sit and, apparently, he sat. I heard him bark once to alert his master there was game afoot.

I didn't dare delay. Moving with a silence I hoped was absolute, I slipped to the back door and opened it a crack. I was on the brink of escape when I remembered my clipboard, which was resting on the counter where Rich had tossed it. I paused long enough to grab it and then I eased out the back door and closed it carefully behind me. I crept down the porch steps and veered left along the drive, tapping the clipboard casually against my thigh. My impulse was to bolt as soon as I reached the street, but I forced myself to walk, not wanting to call attention to my exodus. There's nothing so conspicuous as someone in civilian clothes, running down the street as though pursued by beasts.

3

The drive back to Santa Teresa was uneventful, though I was so juiced up on adrenaline I had to make a conscious effort not to speed. I seemed to see cops everywhere: two at an intersection directing traffic where a stoplight was on the fritz; one lurking near the on-ramp, concealed by a clump of bushes; another parked on the berm behind a motorist, who waited in resignation for the ticket to come. Having escaped from the danger zone, I was not only being meticulous about obeying the law but struggling to regain a sense of normalcy, whatever *that* is. The risk I'd taken at Teddy's house had fractured my perception. I'd become, at the same time, disassociated from reality and more keenly connected to it so that "real life" now seemed flat and strangely lusterless. Cops, rock stars, soldiers, and career criminals all experience the same shift, the plunge from soaring indomitability to unconquerable lassitude, which is why they tend to hang out with others of their ilk. Who else can understand the high? You get amped, wired, blasted out of your tiny mind on situational stimulants. Afterward, you have to talk yourself down, reliving your experience until the charge is off and events collapse back to their ordinary size. I was still awash with the rush, my vision shimmering. The Pacific pulsated on my left. The sea air felt as brittle as a sheet of glass. Like flint on stone, the late morning sun struck the waves in a series of sparks until I half expected the entire ocean to burst into flames. I turned on the radio, tuning the station to one with booming music. I rolled down the car windows and let the wind buffet my hair.

As soon as I got home, I set the cardboard box on the desk, pulled the storage company receipt from my pocket, and tossed the coveralls in the wash. I never should have broken into Teddy's house that way. What was I thinking? I was nuts, temporarily deranged, but the man had irritated me beyond reason. All I'd wanted was a piece of information, which I now possessed. Of course, I had no idea what to do with it. The last thing I needed was to reconnect with my ex.

We'd parted on bad terms, and I'd made a point of abolishing my memories of him. Mentally, I'd excised all reference to the relationship, so that now I scarcely allowed myself to remember his name. Friends were aware that I'd been married at the age of twenty-one, but they knew nothing of who he was and had no clue about the split. I'd put the man in a box and dropped him to the bottom of my emotional ocean, where he'd languished ever since. Oddly enough, while my second husband, Daniel, had betrayed me, gravely injuring my pride, he hadn't violated my sense of honor as Mickey Magruder had. While I may be careless about the penal code, I'm never casual about the law. Mickey had crossed the line, and he'd tried dragging me along with him. I'd moved on short notice, willing to abandon most of my belongings when I walked out the door.

The overload of chemicals began to drain from my system, letting anxiety in. I went into my kitchenette and tranquilized myself with the ritual of a sandwich, smoothing Jif Extra Crunchy peanut butter on two slices of hearty seven-grain bread. I arranged six bread-and-butter pickles like big green polka dots on the thick layer of caramel-colored goo. I cut the finished sandwich on the diagonal and laid it on a paper napkin while I licked the knife clean. One virtue of being single is not having to explain the peculiarities of one's appetites in moments of stress. I popped open a can of Diet Coke and ate at the kitchen counter, perched on a stool with a copy of *Time* magazine, which I read back to middle. Nothing in the front ever seems to interest me.

When I finished, I crumpled the paper napkin, tossed it in the trash, and returned to my desk. I was ready to go through the box of memorabilia, though I half dreaded what I would find. So much of the past is encapsulated in the odds and ends. Most of us discard more information about ourselves than we ever care to preserve. Our recollection of the past is not simply distorted by our faulty perception of events remembered but skewed by those forgotten. The memory is like orbiting twin stars, one visible, one dark, the trajectory of what's evident forever affected by the gravity of what's concealed.

I sat down in my swivel chair and tilted back on its axis. I propped my feet on my desk, the box open on the floor beside me. A hasty visual survey suggested that the minute I'd walked out, Mickey'd packed everything of mine he could lay hands on. I pictured him carting the box through the apartment, snatching up my belongings, tossing them together in a heap. I could see dried-out toiletries, a belt, junk mail and old magazines rubber-banded in a bundle, five paperback novels, and a couple of pairs of shoes. Any other clothes I'd left were long gone. He'd probably shoved those in a trash bag and called the Salvation Army, taking satisfaction in the idea that many much-loved articles would end up on a sale table for a buck or two. He must have drawn the line at memorabilia. Some of it was here, at any rate, spared from the purge.

I reached in and fumbled among the contents, letting my fingers make the selection among the unfamiliar clusters, a grab bag of the misplaced, the bygone, and the abandoned. The first item I retrieved was a packet of old report cards, bound together with thin white satin ribbon. These, my Aunt Gin had saved for reasons that escaped me. She wasn't sentimental by nature, and the quality of my academic performance was hardly worth preserving. I was a quite average student showing no particular affinity for reading, writing, or arithmetic. I could spell like a champ and I was good at memory games. I liked geography and music and the smell of LePage's paste on black and orange construction paper. Most other aspects of school were terrifying. I hated reciting *anything* in front of classmates, or being called on perversely when my hand wasn't even raised. The other kids seemed to enjoy the process, while I quaked in my shoes. I threw up almost daily, and when I wasn't sick at school I would try to manufacture some excuse to stay home or go to work with Aunt Gin. Faced with aggression on the part of my classmates, I quickly learned that my most effective defense was to bite the shit out of my opponent. There was nothing quite as satisfying as the sight of my teeth marks in the tender flesh of someone's arm. There are probably individuals today who still bear the wrathful half moon of dental scars.

I sorted through the report cards, all of which were similar and shared a depressingly common theme. Scanning the written comments, I could see that my teachers were given to much hand wringing and dire warnings about my ultimate fate. Though cursed with "potential," I was apparently a child with little to recommend her. According to their notes, I daydreamed, wandered the classroom at will, failed to finish lessons, seldom volunteered an answer, and usually got it wrong when I did.

"Kinsey's bright enough, but she seems absentminded and she has a tendency to focus only on subjects of interest to her. Her copious curiosity is offset by an inclination to mind everybody else's business. . . ."

"Kinsey seems to have difficulty telling the truth. She should be evaluated by the school psychologist to determine . . ."

"Kinsey shows excellent comprehension and mastery of topics that appeal to her, but lacks discipline. . . ."

"Doesn't seem to enjoy team sports. Doesn't cooperate with others on class projects. . . ."

"Able to work well on her own."

"Undisciplined. Unruly."

"Timid. Easily upset when reprimanded."

"Given to sudden disappearances when things don't go her way. Leaves classroom without permission."

I studied my young self as though reading about a stranger. My parents had been killed in a car wreck on Memorial Day weekend. I'd turned five on May 5 that year, and they died at the end of that month. In September, I started school, armed with a lunch box, my tablet paper, a fat, red Big Bear pencil, and a lot of gritty determination. From my current vantage point, I can see the pain and confusion I hadn't dared experience back then. Though physically undersized and fearful from day one, I was autonomous, defiant, and as hard as a nut. There was much I admired about the child I had been: the ability to adapt, the resilience, the refusal to conform. These were qualities I still harbored, though perhaps to my detriment. Society values cooperation over independence, obedience over individuality, and niceness above all else.

The next packet contained photos from that same period. In class pictures, I was usually half a head shorter than anyone else in my class. My countenance was dark, my expression solemn and wistful, as if I longed to be gone, which of course I did. While others in the class stared directly at the camera, my attention was inevitably diverted by something taking place on the sidelines. In one photograph, my face was a blur because I'd turned my head to look at someone in the row behind me. Even then, life must have seemed more interesting slightly off-center. What I found unsettling was the fact I hadn't changed much in the years between.

I probably should have been out somewhere looking for new clients instead of allowing myself to be distracted by the past. What could have happened that would result in Mickey's belongings being sold at public auction? Not that it was any of my business, but then again, that's exactly what gave the question its appeal.

I went back to the cardboard box and pulled out an old tape recorder as big as a hardback book. I'd forgotten that old thing, accustomed by now to machines the size of a deck of cards. I could see a tape cassette inside. I pushed the PLAY button. No go. The batteries were probably already dead the day Mickey tossed it in the box with everything else. I opened my desk drawer and took out a fresh pack of C batteries, shoving four, end to end, into the back of the machine. I pushed PLAY again. This time the spindles began to turn and I heard my own voice, some rambling account of the case I was working at the time. This was like historical data sealed in a cornerstone, meant to be discovered later after everyone was gone.

I turned it off and set the tape machine aside. I reached into the box again. Tucked down along the side, I found ammo for the 9mm Smith & Wesson Mickey'd given me for a wedding present. There was no sign of the gun, but I could remember how thrilled I'd been with the gift. The finish on the barrel had been S & W blue, and the stock was checked walnut with S & W monograms. We'd met in November and married the following August. By then, he'd been a cop for almost sixteen years, while I'd joined the department in May, a mere three months before. I took the gift of a firearm as an indication that he saw me as a colleague, a status he accorded few women in those days. Now I could see there were larger implications. I mean, what kind of guy gives his young bride a semiautomatic on their wedding night? Impulsively, I pulled open my bottom drawer, searching for the old address book where I'd tucked the only forwarding information I'd ever had for him. The phone number had probably been relinquished and reassigned half a dozen times, the address just as long out of date.

I was interrupted by a knock. I hauled my feet off the desk and crossed to the door, peering through the porthole to find my landlord standing on the porch. Henry was wearing long pants for a change, and his expression was distracted as he stared out across the yard. He'd turned eighty-six on Valentine's Day: tall and lean, a man who never actually seemed to age. He and his siblings, who were respectively eighty-eight, eighty-nine, ninety-five, and ninety-six, came from such vigorous genetic stock that I'm inclined to believe they'll never actually "pass." Henry's handsome in the manner of a fine antique, handcrafted and well constructed, exhibiting a polish that suggests close to nine decades of loving use. Henry has always been loyal, outspoken, kind, and generous. He's protective of me in ways that feel strange but are welcome, nonetheless.

I opened the door. "Hi, Henry. What are you up to? I haven't seen you for days."

"Thank goodness you're home. I have a dental appointment in"—he paused to glance at his watch—"approximately sixteen and three-quarter minutes, and both my cars are out of commission. My Chevy's still in the shop after that paint can fell on it, and now I discover the station wagon's dead. Can you give me a lift? Better yet, if you lend me your car, I can save you the trip. This is going to take awhile and I hate to tie you up." Henry's five-window butter-yellow 1932 Chevy coupe had suffered some minor damage when several paint cans shuddered off the garage shelf during a cluster of baby earthquakes late in March. Henry's meticulous about the car, keeping it in pristine condition. His second vehicle, the station wagon, he used whenever his Michigan-based sibs came to town.

"I'll give you a ride. I don't mind a bit," I said. "Let me grab my keys." I left the door ajar while I snagged my handbag from the counter and fished out the keys from the outer compartment. I picked up my jacket while I was at it and then pulled the door shut behind me and locked it.

We rounded the corner of the building and passed through the gate. I opened the passenger side door and moved around the front of the car. He leaned across the seat and unlocked the door on my side. I slid under the wheel, fired up the ignition, and we were under way.

"Great. This is great. I really appreciate this," Henry said, his tone completely false.

I glanced over at him, making note of the tension that had tightened his face. "What are you having done?"

"A crown 'ack 'ere," he said, talking with his finger stuck at the back of his mouth.

"At least it's not a root canal."

"I'd have to kill myself first. I was hoping you'd be gone so I could cancel the appointment."

"No such luck," I said.

Henry and I share an apprehension about dentists that borders on the comical. While we're both dutiful about checkups, we agonize over any work that actually has to be done. Both of us are subject to dry mouth, squirmy stomachs, clammy hands, and lots of whining. I reached over and felt his fingers, which were icy and faintly damp.

Henry frowned to himself. "I don't see why he has to do this. The filling's fine, really not a problem. It doesn't even hurt. It's a little sensitive to heat, and I've had to give up anything with ice—"

"The filling's old?"

"Well, 1942—but there's nothing *wrong* with it."

"Talk about make-work."

"My point exactly. In those days, dentists knew how to fill a tooth. Now a filling has a limited shelf life, like a carton of milk. It's planned obsolescence. You're lucky if it lasts you long enough to pay the bill." He stuck his finger in his mouth again, turning his face in my direction. "See this? Only fifteen years old and the guy's already talking about replacing it."

"You're kidding! What a scam!"

"Remember when they put fluoride in the city water and everybody thought it was a Communist plot? Dentists spread that rumor."

"Of course they did," I said, chiming in on cue. "They saw the handwriting on the wall. No more cavities, no more business." We went through the same duet every time either one of us had to have something done.

"Now they've cooked up that surgery where they cut half your gums away. If they can't talk you into that, they claim you need braces."

"What a *crock*," I said.

"I don't know why I can't have my teeth pulled and get it over with," he said, his mood becoming morose.

I made the usual skeptical response. "I wouldn't go that far, Henry. You have beautiful teeth."

"I'd rather keep 'em in a glass. I can't stand the drilling. The noise drives me crazy. And the scraping when they scale? I nearly rip the arms off the chair. Sounds like a shovel on a sidewalk, a pickax on concrete—"

"All right! Cut it out. You're making my hands sweat."

By the time I pulled into the parking lot, we'd worked ourselves into such a state of indignation, I was surprised he was willing to keep the appointment. I sat in the dentist's waiting room after Henry's name was called. Except for the receptionist, I had the place to myself, which I thought was faintly worrisome. How come the dentist only had one patient? I pictured Medicaid fraud: phantom clients, double-billing, charges for work that would never be done. Just a typical day in the life of Dr. Dentifrice, federal con artist and cheater with a large sadistic streak. I did give the guy points for having recent issues of all the best magazines.

From the other room, over the burbling of the fish tank, which is meant to mask the shrieks, I could hear the sounds of a high-speed drill piercing through tooth enamel straight to the pulsing nerve below. My fingers began to stick to the pages of *People* magazine, leaving a series of moist, round prints. Once in a while, I caught Henry's muffled protest, a sound suggestive of flinching and lots of blood gushing out. Just the thought of his suffering made me hyperventilate. I finally got so light-headed I had to step outside, where I sat on the mini-porch with my head between my knees.

Henry eventually emerged, looking stricken and relieved, feeling at his numbed lip to see if he was drooling on himself. To distract him on the ride home, I filled him in on the cardboard box, the circumstances under which it originated, Mickey's paranoia, the John Russell alias, and my own B&E adventure at Ted Rich's place. He liked the part about the dog, having urged me repeatedly to get one of my own. We had the usual brief argument about me and household pets.

Then he said, "So, tell me about your ex. You said he was a cop, but what's the rest of it?"

"Don't ask."

"But what do you think it means, his being delinquent with his storage fees?"

"How do I know? I haven't talked to him in years."

"Don't be like that, Kinsey. I hate it when you're stingy with information. I want the story on him."

"It's too complicated to get into. Maybe I'll tell you later, when I've figured it out."

"Are you going to follow up?"

"No."

"Maybe he got lazy about paying his bills," he said, trying to draw me in.

"I doubt it. He was always good about that stuff."

"People change."

"No, they don't. Not in my experience."

"Nor in mine, now you mention it."

The two of us were silent for a block, and then Henry spoke up. "Suppose he's in trouble?"

"Serves him right if he is."

"You wouldn't help?"

"What for?"

"Well, it wouldn't hurt to check."

"I'm not going to *do* that."

"Why not? All it'd take is a couple of calls. What's it going to cost?"

"How do you know what it'd cost? You don't even know the man."

"I'm just saying, you're not busy . . . at least, as far as I've heard. . . ."

"Did I ask for advice?"

"I thought you did," he said. "I'm nearly certain you were fishing for encouragement."

"I was *not.*"

"I see."

"Well, I wasn't. I have absolutely no interest in the man."

"Sorry. My mistake."

"You're the only person in my life who gets away with this shit."

When I got back to my desk, the first thing my eye fell on was my address book lying open to the M's. I flipped the book shut and shoved it in a drawer, which I closed with a bang.

4

I sat down in my swivel chair and gave the carton a shove with my foot. I was tempted to chuck the damn thing, salvage the personal papers and dump the rest in the trash. However, having paid the twenty bucks, I couldn't bring myself to do it. It wasn't so much that I was cheap, though that was certainly a factor. The truth is, I was curious. I reasoned that just because I looked through the box didn't make me responsible for anything else. It certainly wouldn't *obligate* me to try to locate my ex. Sorting through the items would in no way compel me to take action on his behalf. If Mickey'd fallen on hard times, if he was in a jam of some kind, then so be it. *C'est la vie* and so what? It had nothing to do with me.

I pulled the wastebasket closer to the box, pushed the flaps back, and peered in. In the time I'd been gone, the elves and fairies still hadn't managed to tidy up the mess. I started tossing out loose toiletries: a flattened tube of toothpaste and a shampoo bottle with a thin layer of sludge pooled along its length. Something had leaked out and oozed down through the box, welding articles together like an insidious glue. I threw out a hodgepodge of over-the-counter medications, an ancient diaphragm, a safety razor, and a toothbrush with bristles splayed out in all directions. It looked like I'd used it to clean the bathroom grout.

From under the toiletries, I excavated a bundle of junk mail. When I picked up the stack, the rubber band disintegrated, and I plunked the bulk of it in the wastebasket. A few stray envelopes surfaced, and I pulled those from the among discarded magazines and dog-eared catalogs—bullshit from the look of them: a bank statement for an account I'd closed many years before, a department store circular, and a notice from Publisher's Clearing House telling me I'd been short-listed for a million bucks. The third envelope I picked up was a credit card bill that I *sincerely* hoped I paid. What a disgrace that would be, a blot on my credit rating. Maybe that's why American Express wasn't sending me any preapproved cards these days. And here I'd been feeling so superior. Mickey's payments might be delinquent, but not mine, she said.

I turned the bill over to open it. Stuck to the back was another envelope, this one a letter that must have arrived in the same post. I pulled the second envelope free, tearing the paper in the process. The envelope itself bore no return address, and I didn't recognize the writing. The script was tight and angular, letters slanting heavily to the left, as if on the verge of collapsing. The postmark read SANTA TERESA, APRIL 2, 1972. I'd left Mickey the day before, April Fool's Day, as it turned out. I removed the single sheet of lined paper, which was covered with the same inky cursive, as flattened as bent grass.

> Kinsey,
>
> Mickey made me promise not to do this, but I think you should know. He was with me that night, sure, he pushed the guy, but it was no big deal. I know because I saw it and so did a lot of other people whoer on his side. Benny was

fine when he took off. Him and Mickey couldn't have connect after because we went back to my place and he was their till midnight. I told him I'd testify, but he says no because of Eric and his situation. He's completly innocent and desperetly needs your help. What difference does it make where he was as long as he didn't do it? If you love him, you should take his part insted of being such a bitch. Being a cop is his whole life, please don't take that away from him. Otherwise I hope you find a way to live with yourself because your runing everything for him.

D.

I read the note twice, my mind blank except for a clinical and bemused response to all the misspellings and run-on sentences. I'm a snob about grammar and I have trouble taking anyone seriously who gets "there" possessives confused with "there" demonstratives. I didn't "rune" Mickey's life. It hadn't been up to me to save him from anything. He'd asked me to lie for him and I'd flatly refused. Failing that, he'd probably concocted this cover story with "D"—whoever she was. From the sound of it, she knew me, but I couldn't for the life of me remember her. D. That could be Dee. Dee Dee. Donna. Dawn. Diane. Doreen. . . .

Oh, shit. Of course.

There was a bartender named Dixie who worked in a place out in Colgate where Mickey and some of his cop buddies hung out after work. It wasn't uncommon for the guys to band together to do their after-hours drinking. In the early seventies, there were frequent watch parties at the end of a shift, revelries that sometimes went on until the wee hours of the morning. Both public and private drunkenness are considered violations of police discipline, as are extramarital affairs, failure to pay debts, and other scurrilous behavior. Such violations are punishable by the department, because a police officer is considered "on duty" at all times as a matter of public image and because tolerating such conduct might lead to similar infractions while the officer is formally at work. When complaints came in about the shift parties, the officers moved the drink fests from the city to the county, effectively removing them from departmental scrutiny. The Honky-Tonk, where Dixie worked, became their favorite haunt.

At the time I met Dixie, she must have been in her mid-twenties, older than I was by four or five years. Mickey and I had been married for six weeks. I was still a rookie, working traffic, while he'd been promoted to detective, assigned first to vice and then to burglary and theft under Lieutenant Dolan, who later moved on to homicide. Dixie was the one who organized the celebration for any transfer or promotion, and we all understood it was just one more excuse to party. I remembered sitting at the bar chatting with her while Mickey sucked back draft beers, playing pool with his cronies or trading war stories with the veterans coming back from Vietnam. At eighteen, he'd served a fourteen-month combat tour in Korea, and he was always interested in the contrast between the Korean War and the action in Vietnam.

Dixie's husband, Eric Hightower, had been wounded in Laos in April 1971, returning to the world with both legs missing. In his absence, she'd put herself through bartending school and she'd worked at the Tonk since the day Eric shipped out. After he came home, he'd sit there in his wheelchair, his behavior moody or manic, depending on his medications and his alcohol levels. Dixie kept him sedated on a steady regimen of Bloody Marys, which seemed to pacify his rage. To me, she seemed like a busy mother, forced to bring her kid to work with her. The rest of us were polite, but Eric certainly didn't do much to endear himself. At twenty-six, he was a bitter old man.

I used to watch in fascination while she assembled Mai Tais, gin and tonics, Manhattans, martinis, and revolting concoctions like pink squirrels and crème de menthe frappés. She talked incessantly, hardly looking at what she did, eyeballing the pour, spritzing soda or water from the bar hose. Sometimes she constructed four and five drinks at the same time without missing a beat. Her laugh was husky and low-pitched. She exchanged endless ribald comments with the guys, all of whom she knew by name and circumstance. I was impressed with her bawdy self-assurance. I also pitied her her husband, with his sour disposition and his obvious limitations, which I assumed extended into sex. Even so, it never occurred to me that she would screw around on him, especially with *my* husband. I must have been brain-dead not to notice—unless, of course, she was inventing this stuff to provide Mickey with the alibi that I'd declined to supply.

Dixie was my height, rail thin, with a long narrow face and an untidy tangle of auburn hair halfway down her back. Her brows were plucked, a wispy pair of arches that fanned out like wings from the bridge of her nose. Her eyes were darkly charcoaled, and she wore a fringe of fake lashes that made her eyes jump from her face. She was usually braless under her T-shirt, and she wore miniskirts so short she could hardly sit down. Sometimes she veered off in the opposite direction, donning long granny dresses or India-print tunics over wide-legged pantlets.

I read her note again, but sure enough, the content was the same. She and Mickey had been having an affair. That seemed to be the subtext of her communication, though I found it hard to believe. He'd never given any indication he was even *interested* in her, or maybe he had and I'd been too dumb to pick up on it. How could she have stood there and chatted with me if the two of them were making it behind my back? On the other hand, the idea was not entirely inconsistent with Mickey's history.

Before we'd connected, he'd been involved in numerous affairs, but he was, after all, single and savvy enough to avoid emotional entanglements. In the late sixties, early seventies, sex was casual, recreational, indiscriminate, and uncommitted. Women had been liberated by the advent of the birth control pill, and dope had erased any further prohibitions. This was the era of love-ins, psychedelics, dropouts, war protests, body paint, assassinations, LSD, and rumors of kids so stoned their eyeballs got fried because they stared at the sun too long.

It was also the era in which law enforcement began to change. In 1964, the Supreme Court had ruled, in the matter of Escobedo *v.* Illinois, that the refusal by the police to honor Escobedo's request to consult his lawyer during the course of an interrogation constituted a violation of the Sixth Amendment. Two years later, 1966, in Miranda *v.* Arizona, the Supreme Court came down again on the side of the plaintiff, citing a breach of Sixth Amendment rights. From that point on, the climate in law enforcement underwent a shift, and the image of Dirty Harry was replaced by at least the *appearance* of restraint.

Mickey chafed at the limitations set by policy and, on a broader level, at legal restrictions he felt interfered with his effectiveness. He was an old-fashioned cop. He identified with the crime victim. In his mind, theirs were the only claims that counted. Let the perpetrator fend for himself. He hated having to protect the guilty, and he had no patience for the so-called rights of those arrested. I sometimes suspected he'd formed his attitudes from the reams of pulp fiction he'd read growing up. Please understand that none of this was evident to me when we first met. I was not only infatuated with his attitude but wide-eyed with admiration at what I mistook for worldliness. I suspect in Mickey's view certain rules and regulations simply didn't apply to him. He operated outside the standards most other cops finally came to accept. Mickey was accustomed to getting his way, experienced in what he called "certain time-honored methods for persuading a suspect to make himself agreeable in the matter of inculpatory statements." Mickey usually said this in a tone that made everybody laugh.

Mickey was revered by his fellow officers and, until that March, his departmental run-ins were focused on a series of minor infractions. He was late with his reports and occasionally insubordinate, though he seemed to have an instinct for how far he could push. He'd been the subject of two citizen's complaints: once for offensive language and once for excessive use of force. In both incidents the department investigated and found in his favor. Still, it didn't look good. His was an odd mix of the offbeat and the conventional. In his personal life, he was scrupulously honest—about his taxes, his bills, his personal debts. He was loyal to his friends and discreet with regard to others. He also honored his commitments, except (apparently) to me. He would never violate a confidence, never rat out a pal or a fellow officer.

Among men, he was esteemed. With women, he was regarded with an admiration bordering on hero worship. I know because I did this myself, elevating his nonconformity to something praiseworthy instead of faintly dangerous.

Looking back on it, I can see that I didn't want to know the truth about him. I had graduated from the police academy in April of 1971 and was hired by the Santa Teresa Police Department as soon as I turned twenty-one in May. I'd met Mickey the previous November, and I was dazzled by the image he projected: seasoned, gruff, cynical, wise. Within months we fell in love, and by August we were married—all of this before either of us understood what the other was about. Once committed, I was determined to see him as the man I wanted him to be. I needed to believe. I saw him as an idol, so I accepted his version of events even when common sense suggested he was slanting the facts.

In the fall of 1971, after Mickey was reassigned to burglary and theft, he developed what was euphemistically referred to as a "personality conflict" with Con Dolan, who headed crimes against property. Lieutenant Dolan was an autocrat and a stickler for regulations, which caused the two of them to clash time and time again. Their differences put an end to Mickey's hopes for advancement.

Six months later, in the spring of 1972, Mickey resigned from the department to avoid yet another tangle with Internal Affairs. He was, at that time, under investigation for voluntary manslaughter after he'd been involved in a bar dispute. His altercation with a transient named Benny Quintero resulted in the man's death. This was March 17, St. Patrick's Day, and Mickey was off duty, drinking at the Honky-Tonk with a bunch of buddies, who supported his account. He claimed the man was drunk and abusive and exhibited threatening behavior. Mickey removed him bodily to the parking lot, where the two engaged in a brief shoving match. To hear Mickey tell it, he'd pushed the guy around some, but only in response to the drunk's attack. Witnesses swore he hadn't landed any blows. Benny Quintero left the scene, and that was the last anyone reported seeing him until his body was discovered the next day, beaten and bloody, dumped by the side of Highway 154. Internal Affairs launched an investigation, and Mickey's attorney, Mark Bethel, advised him to keep his mouth shut. Since Mickey was the prime suspect, facing the possibility of criminal charges, Bethel was doing what he could to cover his backside. IA can coerce testimony but is forbidden to share findings with the DA's office. There could be serious consequences all the same. Given the overarching need for honest officers, the department was determined to pursue the matter. Mickey resigned in order to avoid questioning. If he hadn't left when he did, he'd have been fired anyway for his refusal to respond.

The day Mickey turned in his badge, his weapon, and his radio, his fellow officers were incensed. Department regulations prohibited his superiors from making any public statement, and Mickey downplayed his departure, which made him look all the more heroic in the eyes of his comrades. The impression he gave was that, despite their treatment of him, his loyalty to the department overrode his right to defend himself against accusations completely contrived and unfair. So convincing was he that I believed him myself right up to the moment when he asked me to lie for him. A criminal investigation was initiated, which is where I came in. Apparently, there were four hours unaccounted for in Mickey's alibi for that night. He refused to say where he'd been or what he'd done between the time he left the Honky-Tonk and the time he arrived home. He was suspected of following the guy and finishing the job elsewhere, but Mickey denied the whole thing. He asked me to cover for him, and that's when I walked.

I left him April 1 and filed for divorce on the tenth of that month. Some weeks later, the findings from the coroner's exam revealed that Quintero, a Vietnam veteran, had suffered a service-related head injury. In combat, he'd been hit by sniper fire, and a stainless steel plate now served where a portion of his skull had been blown away. The official cause of death was a slow hemorrhage in the depths of his brain. Any minor blow could have generated the fatal seepage. In addition, the toxicology report showed a blood alcohol level of .15

with traces of amphetamine, marijuana, and cocaine. There was no actual evidence that Mickey had encountered Benny after their initial scuffle in the parking lot. The DA declined to file charges, so Mickey was off the hook. By then, of course, the damage had been done. He'd been separated from the city and he was, soon afterward, permanently separated from me. In the intervening years, my disenchantment had begun to fade. While I didn't want to see him, I didn't wish him ill. The last I'd heard he was doing personal security, a once-dedicated cop demoted to working night shift in an imitation cop's uniform.

I read the letter again, wondering what I would have done if I'd received it back then. I felt a ripple of anxiety coursing through my frame. If this was true, I had indeed contributed to his ruin.

I opened the drawer and took out my address book, which opened as if by magic to the page where he was listed. I picked up the handset and punched in the number. The line rang twice, and then I was greeted with a big two-tone whistling and the usual canned message telling me the number in the 213 area code was no longer in service. If I felt I'd reached the recording in error, I could recheck the number and then dial it again. Just to be certain, I redialed the number and heard the same message. I hung up, trying to decide if there were any other possibilities I should pursue.

5

I hadn't visited the house on Chapel Street for a good fifteen years. I parked out in front and let myself into the yard through a small wrought-iron gate. The house was white frame, a homely story-and-a-half, with an angular bay window and a narrow side porch. Two second-story windows seemed to perch on the bay, and a simple wood filigree embellished the peaked roof. Built in 1875, the house was plain, lacking sufficient charm and period detail to warrant protection by the local historical preservationists. Out front, a stream of one-way traffic was a constant reminder of downtown Santa Teresa, only two blocks away. In another few years, the property would probably be sold and the house would finish its days as a secondhand furniture store or a little mom-and-pop business. Eventually, the building would be razed and the lot would be offered up as prime commercial real estate. I suppose not every vintage single-family dwelling can be spared the wrecker's ball, but a day will soon come when the history of the common folk will be entirely erased. The mansions of the wealthy will remain where they stand, the more ponderous among them converted for use by museums, art academies, and charitable foundations. A middle-class home like this would scarcely survive to the turn of another century. For the moment, it was safe. The front yard was well tended and the exterior paint looked fresh. I knew from past occasions the backyard was spacious, complete with a hand-laid brick patio, a built-in barbecue pit, and an orchard of fruit trees.

I pressed the front doorbell. A shrill note echoed harshly through the house. Peter Shackelford, "Shack," and his wife, Bundy, had been close friends of Mickey's long before we met. Theirs was a second marriage for both—Shack was divorced, Bundy widowed. Shack had adopted Bundy's four kids and raised them as his own. In those days, the couple entertained often and easily: pizza, potluck suppers, and backyard barbecues, paper plates, plastic ware, and bring-your-own-bottle, with everyone pitching in on cleanup. There were usually babies in diapers, toddlers taking off on cross-lawn forays. The older kids played Frisbee or raced around the yard like a bunch of hooligans. With all the parents on the scene, discipline was casual and democratic. Anyone close to the miscreant was authorized to act. In those days, I wasn't quite so self-congratulatory about my childless state, and I would occasionally keep an eye on the little ones while their parents cut loose.

Mickey and Shack had joined the Santa Teresa Police Department at just about the same time and had worked in close proximity. They were never partners, per se, but the two of them, along with a third cop named Roy "Lit" Littenberg, were known as the Three Musketeers. Lit and Shack were part of the crowd at the Honky-Tonk the year Mickey went down. I was hoping one or the other would know his whereabouts and his current status. I also needed confirmation of the letter's contents. I'd been convinced Mickey was guilty of the beating that resulted in Benny's death. I wasn't sure what I'd do if it turned out he'd had a legitimate alibi for that night. The idea made my stomach roil with anxiety.

Shack answered the door half a minute later, though it took him another ten seconds to figure out who I was. The delay gave me a chance to register the changes in him. In the period when I'd known him, he must have been in his late thirties. He was now in his early fifties and a good twenty-five pounds heavier. Gravity had tugged at all the planes in his face, now defined by a series of downward-turning lines: dense brows over drooping eyelids, sagging cheeks, a bushy mustache and heavy mouth curving down toward his double chin. His thick salt-and-pepper hair was clipped close to his head as though he were still subject to departmental regulations. He was wearing shorts, flip-flops, and a loose white T-shirt, the sagging neckline revealing a froth of white chest hair. Like Mickey, Shack had lifted weights three days a week, and there was still the suggestion of power in the way he carried himself.

"Hello, Shack. How are you?" I said, when I could see that my identity had been noted. I didn't bother to smile. This was not a social visit, and I guessed his feelings for me were neither friendly nor warm.

His tone when he spoke was surprisingly mild. "I always figured you'd show up."

"Here I am," I said. "Mind if I come in?"

"Why not?"

He stepped aside, allowing me to enter the front hall ahead of him. Given the echoes of the past, the quiet seemed unnatural. "Might as well follow me out back. I don't spend a lot of time in this part of the house." Shack closed the door and moved down the hall toward the kitchen.

Even the most cursory glance showed half the furniture was gone. In the living room, I spotted a coffee table, miscellaneous side tables, and a straight-back wooden chair. The silver-dollar-sized circles of matted carpeting indicated where the couch and easy chairs had once been. The built-in bookcases, flanking the fireplace, were now bereft of books. In their place, twenty-five to thirty framed photographs showed a myriad of smiling faces: babies, children, and adults. Most were studio portraits, but there were several enlargements of snapshots from family gatherings.

"Are you moving?"

He shook his head. "Bundy died six months ago," he said. "Most of the furniture was hers anyway. I let the kids take what they wanted. There's plenty left for my purposes."

"Is that them in the photographs?"

"Them and their kids. We got thirteen grandchildren among the four of them."

"Congratulations."

"Thanks. The youngest, Jessie . . . you remember her?"

"Dark curly hair?"

"That's her. The wild one in the bunch. She hasn't married to date, but she adopted two Vietnamese children."

"What's she do for a living?"

"Attorney in New York. She does corporate law."

"Do any of the others live close?"

"Scott's down in Sherman Oaks. They're spread out all over, but they visit when they can. Every six–eight months, I fire up the Harley and do a big round trip. Good kids, all of them. Bun did a hell of a job. I'm a sorry substitute, but I do what I can."

"What are you up to these days? I heard you left the department."

"A year ago this May. I don't do much of anything, to tell you the truth."

"You still lifting weights?"

"Can't. I got hurt. Had an accident on duty. Some drunk ran a red light and broadsided my patrol car. Killed him outright and knocked me all to hell and gone. I got a fractured fifth vertebra so I ended up taking an industrial retirement. A worker's comp claim."

"Too bad."

"No point complaining about things you can't change. The money pays the bills and gives me time to myself. What about you? I hear you're a P.I."

"I've been doing that for years."

He led me through the kitchen to the glassed-in porch that ran along the rear of the house. He seemed to live the way I did, confined to one area like a pet left alone while its owners are off at work. The kitchen was completely tidy. I could see a single plate, a cereal bowl, a spoon, and a coffee mug in the dish rack. He probably used the same few utensils, carefully washing up between meals. Why put anything away when you're only going to take it out and use it again? There was something homely about the presence of the dishes in the rack. From the look of it, he lived almost exclusively in the kitchen and enclosed porch. A futon, doubling as a couch, was set up at one end, blankets neatly folded with the pillows stacked on top. There was a TV on the floor. The rest of the porch was taken up with woodworking equipment: a lathe, a drill press, a router, a couple of C clamps, a vise, wood chisel, a table saw, and an assortment of planes. He was in the process of refinishing two pieces. A chest of drawers had been stripped, pending further attention. A wooden kitchen chair had been laid on its back, its legs sticking out as stiffly as a dead possum's. Shack must sleep every night with the heady scent of turpentine, glue, tung oil, and wood shavings. He caught my look and said, "Virtue of being single. You can do anything you want."

I said, "Amen to that."

Once upon a time, Bundy had sewn the café curtains, hanging them on rods across the middle of the row of windows. The green and white checked cotton, probably permanent press, still looked fresh: crisp, carefully laundered, with little clip-on curtain rings. I found my eyes filling inexplicably with tears and had to feign attention to the backyard, which I could see through the glass. Many of the trees remained, as bent as old spines, curving toward the ground from a once-proud height. A saddle of purple morning glories was cinched to the fence, the chicken wire now swaybacked from the weight of the vines. The barbecue grill top had turned red-brown with rust, replaced by a portable kettle grill parked closer to the back steps.

Shack leaned against the wall with his arms folded across his chest. "So what's the reason for the call?"

"I'm looking for Mickey. The only number I have is a disconnect."

"You have business with him?"

"I may. I'm not sure. Do I need your approval before I telephone the man?"

Shack seemed amused. Bundy had always given him a hard time. Maybe he missed the rough and tumble of conversation. Live alone long enough and you forget what it's like. His smile faded slightly. "No offense, kiddo, but why not leave him alone?"

"I want to know he's okay. I don't intend to bother him. When's the last time you spoke?"

"I don't remember."

"I see. Do you have any idea what's going on with him?"

"I'm sure he's fine. Mickey's a big boy. He doesn't need anyone hovering."

"Fair enough," I said, "but I'd like the reassurance. That's all this is. Do you have his current phone or address?"

Shack shook his head and his mouth pulled down. "Nope. He initiates contact when it suits. In between calls, I make a point of leaving him alone. That's the deal we made."

"What about Lit?"

"Roy Littenberg died. The Big C took him out in less than six weeks. This was three years ago."

"I'm sorry to hear that. I liked him."

"Me too. I see his boy now and then: Tim. You'll never guess what he does."

"I give up."

"He bought the Honky-Tonk. Him and Bundy's boy, Scottie, pal around together whenever Scottie's in town."

I said, "Really. I don't remember meeting either one. I think both were off in Vietnam when Mickey and I were hanging out here." In Santa Teresa, all paths were destined to cross and recross eventually.

Now the next generation was being folded into the mix. "Can you think of anyone else who might know what Mickey's up to?"

Shack studied me. "What's my motive in this?"

"You could be helping him."

"And what's yours?"

"I want the answer to some questions I should have asked back then."

"About Benny?"

"That's right."

His smile was shrewd. He cupped a hand to his ear. "Do I hear guilt?"

"If you like."

"A little late, don't you think?"

"Probably. I'm not sure. The point is, I don't need your permission. Now, will you help me or not?"

He thought about it briefly. "What about the lawyer who represented him?"

"Bethel? I can try. I should have thought of him. That's a good idea."

"I'm full of good ideas."

"You think Mickey was innocent?"

"Of course. I was there and I saw. The guy was fine when he left."

"Shack, he had a *plate* in his head."

"Mickey didn't hit him. He never landed a blow."

"How do you know he didn't go after him again? The two might have gotten into it somewhere else. Mickey wasn't exactly famous for his self-control. That was one of my complaints."

Shack wagged his head. The gesture turned into a neck roll, complete with cracking sound. "Sorry about that. I'm going to see the chiropractor later on account of this effing neck of mine. Yeah, it's possible. Why not? Maybe there was more to it than Mickey let on. I'm telling you what I saw, and it was no big deal."

"Fair enough."

"Incidentally—not that it's any of my business—but you should've stood by him. That's the least you could do. This isn't just me. A lot of the guys resented what you did."

"Well, I resented Mickey's asking me to lie for him. He wanted me to tell the DA he was in at nine o'clock that night instead of midnight or one A.M., whatever the hell time it was when he finally rolled in."

"Oh, that's right," he said snidely. "You never tell lies yourself."

"Not about murder. Absolutely not," I snapped.

"Bullshit. You really think Magruder beat a guy to death?"

"How do I know? That's what I'm trying to find out. Mickey was off course. He was intent on the Might and the Right of the law, and he didn't give a damn what he had to do to get the job done."

"Yeah, and you ask my opinion there should have been more like him. Besides, what I hear, you're not exactly one to be casting stones."

"I'll grant you that one. That's why I'm not in uniform today. But my butt wasn't on the line back then, *his* was. If Mickey had an alibi, he should have said so up front instead of asking me to lie."

Shack's expression shifted and he broke off eye contact.

I said, "Come on, Shack. You know perfectly well where he was. Why don't you fill me in and we can put an end to this?"

"Is that why you're here?"

"In the main," I said.

"I can tell you this much: He wasn't on Highway 154 hassling a vet. He wasn't anywhere within miles."

"That's good. I believe you. Now could we try this? Mickey had a girlfriend. You remember Dixie Hightower? According to her, they were together that night 'getting it on,' to use the time-honored phrase."

"So he was sticking it to Dixie. Whoopee-do. So what? Everybody screwed around in those days."

"I didn't."

"Maybe not when you were married, but you were the same as everyone else . . . only maybe not as open or as honest."

I bypassed the judgment and went back to the subject under discussion. "Someone could have warned me."

"We assumed you knew. Neither of 'em went to any great lengths to cover up. Think of all the times you left the Honky-Tonk before him. What'd you think he was doing, going to night school? He was nailing her. Big deal. She was a bimbo tended bar. She wasn't any threat to you."

I swallowed my outrage, dismissing it as unproductive. I needed information, not an argument. Betrayal is betrayal, no matter when the truth of it sinks in. Whether Dixie was a threat to that marriage was beside the point. Even fourteen years later, I felt humiliated and incensed. I closed my eyes, detaching myself emotionally as though at the scene of a homicide. "Do you know for a fact he was with her that night?"

"Let's put it this way. I saw 'em leave the Tonk together. She was in her car. He was behind her in his. Nights her hubby was home, they checked into that dinky little motel out on Airport Road."

"Wonderful. How considerate of them. They were there that night?"

"Probably. I couldn't say for sure, but I'd be willing to bet."

"Why didn't *you* speak up for him?"

"I would have, for sure. I'd've gone to the wall, but I never had the chance. Mickey turned in his badge and that was the end of it. If you can't reach him, you can always ask her."

"Dixie?"

"Sure. She's around."

"Where?"

"You're the detective. Try the telephone book. She's still married to whosie-face . . . cripple guy. . . ."

"His name was Eric."

"That's right. Him and Dixie made a fortune and bought a mansion. Sixteen thousand square feet, something like that. Big."

"You're kidding."

"I'm not. It's the honest-to-God truth. They're living in Montebello on a regular estate."

"How'd he do that? The last I saw he was a hopeless drunk."

"He got into AA and straightened up his act. Once he sobered up, he figured out a way to build designer wheelchairs. Custom jobs with all the bells and whistles, depending on the disability. Now he's added sports chairs and prostheses. He has a plant in Taiwan, too, making parts for other companies. Donates a ton of stuff to children's hospitals across the country."

"Good for him. I'm glad to hear that. What about her? What's she doing with herself?"

"She's living the life of Riley, turned into Mrs. Gotrocks. Country club membership and everything. You look 'em up, tell 'em I said hi."

"Maybe I'll do that."

After I left Shack's, I went in to the office, where I opened the mail. There was nothing of interest and no pressing business. Most of my other cases were in limbo, pending callbacks or responses to written inquiries of various sorts. I tidied my desk and washed the coffeepot. I dusted the leaves on the fake ficus. I had no reason to stay, but I couldn't go home yet. I was restless, brooding about Mickey in a series of thought loops that went around and around. Had I erred? Had I acted in haste, jumping to conclusions because it suited me? By the time Quintero died, I was disenchanted with Mickey anyway. I wanted out of the marriage, so his involvement in Quintero's death provided the perfect excuse. But maybe that's all it was. Could he have resigned from the department to spare my pride and, at the same time, to avoid exposing Dixie? If Mickey was innocent, if I'd known where he was that night, the case might have gone differently and he might still be a cop. I didn't want to believe it, but I couldn't escape the thought.

I lay down on the carpet and flung an arm across my eyes. Was there really any point in obsessing about this? It was over and done with. Fourteen years had gone by. Whatever the truth, Mickey'd elected to resign. That was a fact. I'd left him, and our lives were irreparably changed. Why pursue the matter when there wasn't any way to alter what had happened?

What was at stake was my integrity, whatever sense of honor I possessed. I know my limitations. I know the occasional lapses I'm capable of, but a transgression of this magnitude was impossible to ignore. Mickey had lost what he'd loved best, and maybe that was simply his inevitable fate. Then again, if I'd been an unwitting accomplice to his downfall, I needed to own up to it and get square with him.

6

Forbes Run was a meandering lane-and-a-half, a ribbon of pavement that snaked back and forth as it angled upward into the foothills. Massive branches of live oak hung out over the road. There were no houses visible, as far as I could see, but a series of markers suggested that large properties branched off at intervals. I watched the numbers progress, the signs leapfrogging from one side of the road to the other, alternating even and odd: 317, 320, 323, 326. The Hightowers' estate, at 329, was surrounded by a low fieldstone wall, accessible through wooden gates that opened electronically as soon as I pressed the button. Either the Hightowers were expecting someone or they didn't much care who appeared at their door.

The driveway extended perhaps a quarter of a mile and conjured up visions of a proper English manor house at the far end, a three-story Tudor with a steeply pitched slate roof. What I spotted, at long last, was nothing of the kind. The house was contemporary: long and low, hugging the ground, with an oversized roofline rising to a center peak. I could see four wide fieldstone chimneys, clusters of fan palms, and colossal black boulders the size of my car that must have erupted from Vesuvius and been transported to the grounds for effect. To the right, I could see a line of four garage doors.

I parked in the large circular parking area in front and made my way up the wide, sloping concrete walk. A woman, perhaps thirty, in tennis shoes, jeans, and a white T-shirt, was already standing in the open doorway, awaiting my arrival. This definitely wasn't Dixie, and I wondered for a fleeting moment if I'd come to the wrong house.

"Ms. Yablonsky?" she said.

"Actually, I'm not. I'm looking for Eric and Dixie Hightower. Am I in the right place?"

"Sorry. Of course. I thought you were someone else. We've been interviewing for staff positions, and the woman's half an hour late. Is Mrs. Hightower expecting you?" The woman herself remained nameless and without title: parlor maid, factotum, personal assistant. I guess she felt she was under no obligation to introduce herself.

"I'm an old friend," I said. I took out a business card and handed it to her.

She read the face of it, frowning. "A private detective? What's this about?"

"I'm hoping they can put me in touch with a mutual acquaintance. A guy named Mickey Magruder. My ex-husband."

"Oh. Why don't you come in and I'll tell Mrs. Hightower you're here."

"Is Eric home?"

"Mr. Hightower's out of town, but he should be home soon."

I stepped into the foyer, waiting uneasily while she disappeared from sight. I'm sometimes puzzled by wealth, which seems to have a set of rules of its own. Was I free to amble about or should I wait where I was? There was an angular stone bench positioned against one wall. The woman hadn't suggested I sit and I was loath to presume. Suppose it turned out to be a sculpture that collapsed under my weight? I did a one-eighty turn so I could scrutinize the place like a burglar-in-training, a little game I play. I noted entrances and exits, wondering about the possibility of a wall safe. If I were bugging the place, where would I tuck the surveillance equipment?

The floors were polished limestone, as pale as beach sand. I could see ancient marine creatures pressed into the surface, a tiny fossil museum at my feet. A wide corridor stretched off to the right. The ceiling was twelve feet high with floor-to-ceiling windows on one side. The facing walls were painted a snowy white and hung with a series of bright abstracts, oil paintings six feet tall, probably expensive and done by someone dead.

Before me, a pair of double doors stood open and I could see into the living room, easily thirty feet long. Again, the walls on the far side were floor-to-ceiling glass, this time with a panoramic view of pines, live oaks, giant ferns, eucalyptus, and the mountains beyond. I listened and, hearing nothing, tiptoed into the room to have a better look. The wood-beamed ceiling slanted upward to near-cathedral height. On the left, there was a marble-faced fireplace with a hearth twenty-six feet long. On the other end of the room, glass-enclosed shelves showcased a variety of art objects. To the left, I could see a built-in wet bar. The furniture was simple: large armless black leather couches and chairs, chrome-and-glass tables, a grand piano, recessed lighting.

I heard footsteps tap-tap-tapping down the hallway in my direction. I'd just managed to giant-step my way across the foyer to my original position when Dixie came into view. She wore skintight blue jeans, boots with spike heels, and a buff-colored blazer over a snowy white silk tank top. Her jewelry was Bakelite, two chunky bracelets that clattered on her narrow wrist. Now forty years old, she was still extremely thin: small hips, flat stomach, scarcely any butt to speak of. The shoulder pads in her jacket made it look like she was wearing protective gear. Her hair was pulled back away from her face, an oh-so-chic mess in a shade that suggested copious chemical assistance, a red somewhere between claret and burnt ocher. Gone were the false lashes and all the heavy black eyeliner. Curiously, the absence of makeup made her eyes seem much larger and her features more delicate. Her skin was sallow and there were dark circles under her eyes, lines in her forehead, cords showing in her neck. Hard to believe she hadn't yet availed herself of a little surgical refreshment. Even so, she looked glamorous. There was something brisk and brittle in the way she carried herself. She seemed to know who I was, using my name with an artificial warmth as she held out her hand. "Kinsey. How nice. What an incredible surprise. Stephie said you were here. It's been years."

"Hello, Dixie. You look great. I wasn't sure you'd remember me."

"How could I forget?" she said. "I'm sorry you missed Eric." Her gaze took me in without so much as a flicker of interest. Like her, I wore jeans, though mine were cut without style, the kind worn to wash cars or clean hair clots from the bathroom standpipe. In the years since I'd seen her, she'd risen in social stature, acquiring an almost indescribable air of elegance. No need to wear diamonds when plastic would do. Her jacket was wrinkled in the manner of expensive fabrics . . . linens and silks . . . you know how it is with that shit.

She glanced at her watch, which she wore on the inner aspect of her wrist. The watch was forties vintage, stingy-sized crystal surrounded by little bitty diamonds on a band of black cording. I'd seen nicer versions at the swap meet, which just goes to show what I know about these things. Hers was probably rare, recognizable on sight by those who shopped in the tony places she did. "Would you like a drink?" she asked. "It's nearly cocktail time."

My watch said 4:10. I said, "Sure, why not?" I almost made a joke about crème de menthe frappés, but a black guy in a white jacket had materialized, a silver tray in hand. A bartender of her own? This was getting good.

She said, "What would you like?"

"Chardonnay sounds fine."

"We'll be out on the patio," she remarked, without directly addressing her faithful attendant. My, my, my. Another cipher accounted for in the nameless servant class. I noticed Dixie didn't need to specify what she'd be drinking.

I followed her through the stone-floored dining room. The table was a rhomboid of cherry, with sufficient chairs assembled for a party of twelve. Something odd was at work, and it took me a moment to figure out what it was. There were no steps, no changes in elevation, no area rugs, and no signs of wall-to-wall carpet within view. I thought of Eric in his wheelchair, wondering if the floors were left bare for his benefit.

It struck me as peculiar that Dixie hadn't yet questioned the reason for my unannounced arrival at her door. Maybe she'd been waiting for me all these years, rehearsing responses to numerous imaginary conversations. She'd always known she'd been screwing around with Mickey, whereas I'd just found out, which put me at a disadvantage. I don't often go up against other women in verbal combat. Such clashes are strange, but not without a certain prurient attraction. I thought of all the male-fantasy movies where women fight like alley cats, pulling at each other's hair while they roll around on the floor. I'd never had much occasion, but maybe that would change. I could feel myself getting in touch with my "inner" mean streak.

Dixie opened a sliding glass door and we passed out onto a spacious screened-in patio. The floor here was smooth stone, and the area was rimmed with a series of twenty-foot trees in enormous terra cotta pots. The branches were filled with goldfinches, all twittering as they hopped from limb to limb. There was a grouping of upholstered patio furniture nearby, in addition to a glass-topped table and four thickly cushioned chairs. Everything looked spotless. I wondered where the little birdies dropped their tiny green and white turds.

"This is actually a combination greenhouse and aviary. These are specimen plants, proteas and bromeliads. South American," she said.

I murmured "gorgeous" for lack of anything better. I thought a bromeliad was a remedy for acid indigestion. She gestured toward the conversational grouping of chairs. From somewhere, I could already smell dinner in the making. The scent of sautéed garlic and onion, like a sumptuous perfume, floated in the air. Maybe one of those no-name indentured servants would appear with a tray of eats, little tidbits of something I could fall on and snarf down without using my hands.

As soon as we sat down, the man reappeared with drinks on his tray. He gave us each a tiny cloth napkin in case we urped something up. Dixie's beverage of choice was a martini straight up in a forties-style glass. Four green olives were lined up on a toothpick like beads on an abacus. We each took a sip of our respective libations. My Chardonnay was delicate, with a long, slow, vanilla finish, probably nothing from a screw-top bottle at the neighborhood Stop 'n' Shop. I watched her hold the gin on her tongue like a communion ritual. She set the glass down with a faint tap and reached into her blazer pocket to extract a pack of cigarettes and a small gold lighter. She lit the cigarette, inhaling with a reverence that suggested smoking was another sacrament. When she caught me observing her, she opened her mouth to emit a thick tongue of smoke that she then sucked up her nose. "You don't smoke these days?"

I shook my head. "I quit."

"Good for you. I'll never give it up myself. All this talk about health is fairly tedious. You probably exercise, too." She cocked her head in reflection, striking a bemused pose. "Let's see. What's in fashion at the moment? You lift weights," she said, and pointed a finger in my direction.

"I jog five days a week, too. Don't forget that," I said, and pointed back at her.

She took another sip of her drink. "Stephie tells me you're looking for Mickey. Has he disappeared?"

"Not as far as I know, but I'd like to get in touch with him. The only number I have turns out to be a disconnect. Have you heard from him lately?"

"Not for years," she said. A smiled formed on her lips, and she checked her fingernails. "That's a curious question. I can't believe you'd ask me. I'm sure there are other folks much more likely to know."

"Such as?"

"Shack, for one. And who's the other cop? Lit something. They were always thick as thieves."

"I just talked to Shack, which is how I got to you. Roy Littenberg died. I didn't realize you and Eric were still in town."

She studied me for a moment through her cigarette smoke. Miss Dixie wasn't dumb, and I could see her analyze the situation. "Where's all this coming from?"

"All what?"

"You have something else in mind."

I reached down for my shoulder bag and removed the letter from the outside pocket. "Got your letter," I said.

"My letter," she repeated blankly, her gaze fixed on the envelope.

"The one you sent me in 1972," I said. "Mickey tossed it in a box with some other mail that must have come the same day. He failed to deliver it, so I never read the letter until today." For once, I seemed to have captured her full attention.

"You're not serious."

"I am." I held up the letter like a paddle in a silent auction: my bid. "I had no idea you were balling my beloved husband. You want to talk about that?"

She laughed and then caught herself. Her teeth were now as perfect as white horseshoes hinged together at the rear of her mouth. "Sorry. I'm sorry. I hope you won't take offense, but you're such a boob when it comes to men."

"Thanks. You know how I value your opinion."

"Nothing to be ashamed of. Most women don't have the first clue about men."

"And you do?"

"Of course." Dixie studied me over the ribbon of cigarette smoke, taking my measure with her eyes. She paused and leaned forward to tap off a cylinder of ash into a cut glass dish on the coffee table in front of her.

"What's your theory, Miss Dixie, if I may be so bold as to inquare?" I said, affecting a Southern accent.

"Take advantage of *them* before they take advantage of you," she said, her smile as thin as glass.

"Nice. Romantic. I better write that down." I pretended to make a note on the palm of my hand.

"Well, it's not *nice* but it's practical. In case you haven't noticed, most men don't give a shit about romance. They want to get in your panties and let it go at that. What else can I say?"

"That about covers it," I said. "May I ask, why him? There were dozens of cops at the Honky-Tonk back then."

She hesitated, apparently considering what posture to affect. "He was very good," she said, with a trace of a smile.

"I didn't ask for an evaluation. I'd like to know what went on."

"Why the attitude? You seem so . . . belligerent. In the end, you'd have left him anyway, so what do you care?"

"Indulge me," I said. "For the sake of argument."

She lifted one thin shoulder in a delicate shrug. "He and I were an item long before the two of you met. He broke it off for a while and then he came back. Why attach anything to it? We were not in love by any stretch. I might have *admired* him, but I can't say I liked him much. He had a rough kind of charm, but then again, you know that. I wouldn't even call it an affair in any true sense of the word. More like sexual addiction, a mutual service we performed. Or I should say, that's what it was for me. I don't know about him. It's a question of pathology. He probably couldn't help himself any more than I."

"Oh, please. Don't give me that horseshit about sexual addiction. What crap," I said. "Did it ever occur to you that wedding vows mean something?"

"Yours didn't seem to mean much. Until death do us part? At least I'm still married, which is more than you can say. Or am I wrong about that? Rude of me. You might have married someone else and had a whole passel of kids. I would have asked before now, but I didn't see a ring."

"Were you with him the night Benny Quintero died?"

Her smiled faded. "Yes." Flat. No hesitation, no emotion, and no elaboration.

"Why didn't he tell me?"

"Did you really want to know?"

"It would have helped. I'm not sure what I'd have done, but it might have made a difference."

"I doubt that. You were such a cocky little thing. Really, quite obnoxious. You knew it all back then. Mickey wanted you spared."

"And why is that?"

"He was crazy about you. I'm surprised you'd have to ask."

"Given the fact he was screwing you," I said.

"You knew his history the day you married him. Did you seriously imagine he'd be monogamous?"

"Why'd you take it on yourself to tattle when Mickey asked you not to?"

"I was afraid he'd get a raw deal—which he did, as it turns out."

"Did Eric know about Mickey?"

There was the tiniest flicker of hesitation. "We've come to an accommodation—"

"I'm not talking about now. Did he know back then?"

She took a long, deliberate drag on her cigarette while she formed her reply. "Life was difficult for Eric. He had a hard time adjusting after he got back."

"In other words, no."

"There was no emotional content between Mickey and me. Why inflict unnecessary pain?"

"How about so your respective spouses knew the truth about you? As long as there's no love—as long as it's simply sexual servicing, as you claim—why couldn't you tell us?"

She was silent, giving me a wide-eyed stare.

"The question isn't hypothetical. I really want to know," I said. "Why not be honest with us if your relationship meant so little?" I waited. "Okay, I'll help. You want the answer? Try this. Because we'd have kicked your respective butts and put an end to it. I don't know about Eric, but I have no tolerance for infidelity."

"Perhaps there are things about loyalty you never grasped," she said.

I closed my eyes briefly. I wanted to lift her front chair legs and flip her backward, just for the satisfaction of hearing her head thud against the stone floor. Instead, I silently recited what I remembered of the penal code: *An assault is an unlawful attempt, coupled with a present ability, to commit a violent injury on the person of another. . . . A battery is any willful and unlawful use of force or violence upon the person of another.*

I smiled. "You think it was okay to make fools of us? To gratify your whims at our expense? If you think *that's* loyalty, you're *really* fucked."

"You don't have to be crude."

Someone spoke from the far side of the patio. "Excuse me. Dixie?"

Both of us looked over. Stephie stood in the doorway.

For once, Dixie seemed embarrassed, and the color rose in her cheeks. "Yes, Stephie. What is it?"

"Ms. Yablonsky's here. Did you want to talk to her now or should I reschedule?"

Dixie exhaled with impatience, stubbing out her cigarette. "Have her wait in my office. I'll be there in a minute."

"Sure. No problem." Stephie closed the sliding glass door, watching for a moment before she moved away.

"This has gone far enough," Dixie said to me. "I can see you enjoy getting up on your high horse. You always liked claiming the moral high ground—"

"I do. That's correct. It's mine to claim in this case."

"When you've finished your drink, you can let yourself out."

"Thanks. This was fun. You haven't changed at all."

"Nor have you," she said.

7

I was halfway down the driveway, heading toward the road, when I saw a vehicle coming my way. It was a custom van of a sort I hadn't seen before, sleek, black, and boxy, with Eric Hightower at the wheel. I'm not sure I would have recognized him if I hadn't been half expecting to see him anyway. I slowed the VW to a crawl and gave a tap to the horn as I rolled down my window. He drew alongside me and pulled to a stop, rolling his window down in response. Underneath the tank top he wore, his bulging shoulders and biceps looked smooth and tanned. In the old Honky-Tonk days, his gaze was perpetually glassy and his skin had the pallor of a man who'd made a science of mixing his medications with alcohol, LSD, and grass. Then, his beard had been sparse and he'd worn his straight black hair loose across his shoulders or pulled back in a ponytail and tied with a rag.

The man who studied me quizzically from the driver's side of the van had been restored to good health. His head was now shaved, his skull as neat as a newborn's. Gone were the beard and the bleary-eyed stare. I'd seen pictures of Eric in uniform before he left for Vietnam: young and handsome, twenty-one years old, largely untouched by life. After two tours of duty, he'd come back to the world looking gaunt and abused, ill-humored and withdrawn. He'd seemed to have a lot on his mind, but nothing he was capable of explaining to the rest of us. And none of us dared ask. One look at his face was sufficient to convince us that what he'd seen was hellish and wouldn't bear close scrutiny. In retrospect, I suspect he imagined us judgmental and disapproving when in truth we were frightened of what we saw in his eyes. Better to look away than suffer that torment.

"Can I help you?" he asked.

"Hi, Eric. Kinsey Millhone. We hung around together years ago at the Tonk out in Colgate."

I watched his features clear and then brighten when he figured out who I was. "Hey. Of course. No fooling. How're you doing?" He leaned his left arm out the window and we touched fingertips briefly, as close to a handshake as we could manage from separate vehicles. His dark eyes were clear. In his drinking days, he'd been scrawny, but the process of aging had added the requisite fifteen pounds. Success sat well on him. He seemed substantial and self-possessed.

I said, "You look great. What happened to your hair?"

He glanced at himself in his rearview mirror, running a hand across his smooth-shaven skull. "You like it? It feels weird. I did that a month ago and can't quite decide."

"I do. It's better than the ponytail."

"Well, ain't that the truth. What brings you here?"

"I'm looking for my ex-husband and thought you might have a line on him." The possibility seemed far-fetched and I wondered if he'd press me on the subject, but he let it pass.

"Magruder? I haven't seen him in years."

"That's what Dixie said. I talked to Mickey's buddy, Shack, a little while ago and your names came up. You remember Pete Shackelford?"

"Vaguely."

"He thought you might know, but I guess not, huh."

Eric said, "Sorry I can't help. What's the deal?"

"I'm not really sure. It looks like I have a debt to settle with him and I'd like to clear it."

"I can ask around, if you want. I still see some of those guys at the gym. One of them might know."

"Thanks, but I can probably manage on my own. I'll call his lawyer, and if that fails I've got some other little ways. I know how his mind works. Mickey's devious."

Eric's gaze held mine, and I felt an unspoken communication scuttle between us like the shadow of a cloud passing overhead. His mood seemed to shift and he let the sweep of his arm encompass the tree-strewn property surrounding us on all sides. "So what do you think? Nine point nine acres and it's paid off—all mine. Well, half mine, given California's community property laws."

"It's beautiful. You've done well."

"Thanks. I had help."

"Dixie or AA?"

"I'd have to say both."

A plumber's truck appeared in the driveway, pulling up behind Eric's van. He glanced back and waved to let the driver know he was aware of him and wouldn't take all day. He turned back to me. "Why don't you turn the car around and come back to the house? We can all have dinner together and spend time catching up."

"I'd love to, but I'd better not. Dixie's got interviews and I have some things to take care of myself. Maybe another time. I'll give you a call and we can set something up." I put my car in gear.

"Great. Do that. You promise?"

"Scout's honor."

The driver of the truck behind him gave an impatient beep on his horn. Eric glanced back at him and waved again. "Anyway, nice to see you. Behave yourself."

"You too."

He rolled his window up, and I could see him accelerate with the help of a device on his steering wheel. It was the only reminder I'd had that he was a double amputee. He tapped his horn as he departed and I continued down the driveway, the two of us moving in opposite directions.

I headed into town, pondering the nature of the divine comedy. Two of my pet beliefs had been reversed in the past few hours. Given the brevity of my marriage to Mickey, I'd always assumed he'd been faithful. That notion turned out to be false so it was stricken from the record, along with any lingering confidence I felt. I'd also suspected—well, let's be honest about this—I'd been *convinced* Mickey'd played a part in Benny Quintero's death. It turned out he hadn't, so we could strike that one, too. Guilty of infidelity, innocent of manslaughter. Someone with talent could convert that to lyrics for a country-western tune. In some ways Dixie'd nailed it. Did I really want to know about this shit? I guess I didn't have a choice. The question was what to do with it?

The minute I hit the office, I hauled out the telephone book and leafed through the yellow pages to the section listing attorneys. I ran a finger down the column until I found Mark Bethel's name in a little box of its own. The ad read CRIMINAL DEFENSE and, under that heading, specified the following: Drugs, Molest, Weapons, White Collar, DUI, Theft/Fraud, Assault, Spousal Abuse, and Sex Crimes, which I thought just about covered it—except for murder, of course. Mark Bethel had been Mickey's attorney when he resigned from the department, a move Mickey'd made on Mark's advice. I'd never been crazy about Mark, and after Mickey's unceremonious departure there was little reason for our paths to cross. On the odd occasion when I ran into him around town, we tended to be cordial, feigning a warmth neither of us felt. We were bound by old business, one of those uneasy alliances that survived more on form than content. Despite my lukewarm attitude, I had to admit he was an excellent attorney, though in the past few years he'd set his practice aside in his bid for public office—one Republican among many hoping for a shot at Alan Cranston's senate seat in the coming November elections. In the past ten years, his political ambitions had begun to emerge. He'd allied himself with the local party machine, ingratiating himself with Republicans by working tirelessly on Deukmejian's 1982 gubernatorial campaign. He'd opened his Montebello home for countless glitzy fund-raisers. He'd run for and won a place on the county board of supervisors; then he'd run for state assembly. Logically, his next step should have been a try for Congress, but he'd skipped that and entered the primary for a U.S. Senate seat. He must have felt his political profile was sufficient to net him the kind of votes he'd need to outstrip Ed Zschau. Fat chance, in my opinion, but then what did I know? I hate politicians; they lie more flagrantly than I do and with a lot less imagination. It helped that Bethel was married to a woman who had a fortune of her own.

I'd heard through the grapevine Laddie Bethel was bankrolling the major portion of his campaign. She'd made a name for herself locally as a fund-raiser of some persuasion for numerous charitable organizations. Whatever worthy cause she adopted, she certainly wasn't shy about sending me donation requests with a return envelope enclosed. Inevitably, there was a series of amounts to be circled: $2,500, $1,000, $500, $250. If the charitable event was an evening affair—"black tie optional" (in case your green one was at the cleaners)—I'd also be offered the opportunity to buy a "table" for my cronies at a thousand dollars a plate. Little did she know I was, by nature, so cheap that I'd sit there and pick the stamp off the prestamped envelope. In the meantime, Mark maintained an office and a secretary with his old law firm.

I dialed Mark Bethel's office, and his secretary answered, followed by an immediate "May I put you on hold?"

By the time I said sure, she was already gone. I was treated to a jazz rendition of "Scarborough Fair."

Mark's secretary clicked back on the line. "Thanks for holding. This is Judy. May I help you?"

"Yes, hi, Judy. This is Kinsey Millhone. I'm an old friend of Mark's. I think I met you at the Bethels' Christmas party a couple of years back. Is he there by any chance?"

"Oh, hi, Kinsey. I remember you," she said. "No, he's off at a committee meeting, probably gone for the day. You want him to call in the morning, or is there something I can do?"

"Maybe," I said. "I'm trying to get in touch with my ex-husband. Mickey Magruder was a client of his."

"Oh, I know Mickey," she said, and right away I wondered if she *knew* him in the biblical sense.

"Do you know if Mark has a current address and phone number?"

"Hold on and I'll check. I know we have something, because he called here a couple months ago and I spoke to him myself." I could hear pages rattling as she leafed through her book.

"Ah, here we go." She recited an address on Sepulveda, but the house number differed from the one I had. The digits were the same but the order was changed, which was typical of Mickey. In his semi-paranoid state, he'd give the correct information but with the numbers transposed so you couldn't pin him down. He thought your address was your own damn business and phones were meant for *your* convenience, not anyone else's. If other people couldn't call him, what did he care? I don't know how he managed to receive his mail or have pizza delivered. Those were not issues he found interesting when his privacy was at stake. Judy chimed back in, and the phone number she recited was a match for the one I had in my book.

I said, "You can scratch that one out. I tried it a while ago, and it's a disconnect. I thought maybe Mickey moved or had the number changed."

I could hear her hesitate. "I probably shouldn't say this. Mark hates when I discuss a client, so please don't tell him I said this—"

"Of course not."

"When Mickey called—this would have been mid-March—he did ask to borrow money. I mean, he didn't ask *me*. This is just what I heard later, after Mark talked to him. Mark said Mickey'd had to sell his car because he couldn't afford the upkeep and insurance, let alone the gas. He's got financial problems even Mark couldn't bail him out of."

"That doesn't sound good. Did Mark lend him any money?"

"I'm not really sure. He might have. Mickey was always one of Mark's favorites."

"Could you check your message carbons and see if Mickey left a number where Mark could reach him?"

"I'll check if you like, but I remember asking at the time, and he said Mark would know."

"So Mark might have another number?"

"It's possible, I guess. I can ask and have him call you."

"I'd appreciate that. He can buzz me tomorrow and we'll take it from there." I left her my number and we clicked off.

My evening was unremarkable—dinner with Henry at Rosie's Tavern half a block away—after which I curled up with a book and read until I fell asleep, probably ten whole minutes later.

I turned off the alarm moments before it was set to ring. I brushed my teeth, pulled on my sweats, and went out for a three-mile jog. The bike path along the beach was cloaked in the usual spring fog, the sky a uniform gray, the ocean blended at the horizon as though a scrim of translucent plastic had been stretched taut between the two. The air temperature was perfect, faintly chill, faintly damp. I was feeling light and strong, and I ran with a rare sense of happiness.

Home again, I showered, dressed, and ate breakfast, then hopped in my car and hit the road for San Felipe with the receipt from the storage company tucked in my pocket. I'd dressed up to some extent, which in my case doesn't amount to much. I only own one dress: black, collarless, with long sleeves and a tucked bodice (which is a fancy word for front). This entirely synthetic garment, guaranteed wrinkle-free (but probably flammable), is as versatile as anything I've owned. In it, I can accept invitations to all but the snootiest of cocktail parties, pose as a mourner at any funeral, make court appearances, conduct surveillance, hustle clients, interview hostile witnesses, traffic with known felons, or pass myself off as a gainfully employed person instead of a freelance busybody accustomed to blue jeans, turtlenecks, and tennis shoes.

Before I departed, I'd taken a few minutes to complete a generic claim form that I'd dummied up from my days of working at California Fidelity Insurance. As I headed south on 101, I practiced the prissy, bureaucratic attitude I affect when I'm masquerading as someone else. Being a private investigator is made up of equal parts ingenuity, determination, and persistence, with a sizable dose of acting skills thrown in.

The drive to San Felipe took forty-five minutes. The scenery en route consisted largely of citrus and avocado groves, stretches of farmland, and occasional roadside markets selling—what else?—oranges, lemons, and avocados. I spotted the storage company from half a mile away. It was just off the main road, countless rows of two-story buildings, occupying two square blocks. The architectural style suggested a newly constructed California prison, complete with floodlights and tall chain-link fences.

I turned in at the gate. The buildings were identical: cinder block and blank doors, with wide freight elevators and a loading ramp at each end. The units were marked alphabetically and numerically in a system I couldn't quite decipher. The doors in each section appeared to be color-coded, but maybe that was simply an architectural flourish. It couldn't be much fun designing a facility that looked like cracker boxes arranged end to end. I passed a number of broad alleyways. Arrows directed me to the main office, where I parked and got out.

I pushed through the glass door to a serviceable space, maybe twenty feet by twenty with a counter running across the center. The area on the far side of the counter was taken up by rental-quality file cabinets and a plain wooden desk. This was not a multilayered company with the administration assuming any lofty position. The sole individual on duty apparently functioned as receptionist, secretary, and plant manager, sitting at a typewriter with a pencil in his mouth while he hunt-and-pecked his way through a memorandum of some sort. I guessed he was in his late seventies, round-faced and balding, with a pair of reading glasses worn low on his nose. I could see his belly bulging out like an infant monkey clinging closely to its mother's chest. "Be with you in just a second," he said, typing on.

"Take your time."

"How do you spell 'mischeevious'?"

"M-i-s-c-h-i-e-v-o-u-s."

"You sure? Doesn't look right."

"Pretty sure," I said.

When he'd finished, he stood up, separated the carbons, and tucked both the original and the copies in matching blue folders. He came over to the counter, hitching up his pants. "Didn't mean to keep you waiting, but I was on a tear," he said. "When business is slow, I write stories for my great-grandson. Kid's barely two and reads like a champ. Loves his pappaw's little booklets written just for him. This one's about a worm name of Wiggles and his escapades. Lot of fun for me, and you should see Dickie's little face light up. I figure one day I'll get 'em published and have 'em done up proper. I have a lady friend offered to do the illustrations, but somebody told me that's a bad idea. I guess these New York types like to hire their own artists."

"News to me," I said.

His cheeks tinted faintly and his tone of voice became shy. "I don't suppose you know an agent might take a look at this."

"I don't, but if I hear of one, I'll let you know."

"That'd be good. Meantime, what can I do for you?"

I showed him my California Fidelity Insurance identification, which bore an old photograph of me and the company seal of approval.

His gaze shifted from the photo to my face. "You oughta get you a new photo. This doesn't do you justice. You're a lot better looking."

"You really think so? Thanks. By the way, I'm Kinsey Millhone. And you're . . . ?"

"George Wedding."

"Nice to meet you."

"I hope you're not selling policies. I'd hate to disappoint, but I'm insured to the hilt."

"I'm not selling anything, but I could use some help." I hesitated. I had a story all ready. I intended to show him a homeowner's claim listing several items lost to flooding when some water pipes broke. Of course, this was all completely false, but I was hoping he'd react with sufficient moral indignation to set the record straight. What I wanted was the address and phone number Mickey'd used when he'd rented the space. I could then compare the information to facts already in my possession and thus (perhaps) figure out where the hell Mickey was. In my mind, on the way down, I'd spun the story out to a convincing degree, but now that I was here I couldn't bring myself to tell it. This is the truth about lying: You're putting one over on some poor gullible dunce, which makes him appear stupid for not spotting the deception. Lying contains the same hostile elements as a practical joke in that the "victim" ends up looking foolish in his own eyes and laughable in everyone else's. I'm willing to lie to pompous bureaucrats, when thwarted by knaves, or when all else fails, but I was having trouble lying to a man who wrote worm adventure stories for his great-grandson. George was patiently waiting for me to go on. I folded the bogus claim in half until the bottom of the page rested a couple of inches from the top and the only lines showing were those containing the name, address, and telephone number of "John Russell." "You want to know the truth?"

"That'd be nice," he said blandly.

"Ah. Well, the truth is I was fired by CFI about three years ago. I'm actually a private investigator, looking for a man I was once married to." I pointed to John Russell's name. "That's not his real name, but I suspect the address may be roughly correct. My ex scrambles numbers as a way of protecting himself."

"Is this police business? Because my records are confidential, unless you have a court order. If you think this fellow was using his storage unit for illegal purposes . . . manufacturing drugs, for instance . . . you might talk me into it. Otherwise, no deal."

I could almost have sworn George was inviting me to fib, given that he'd laid out the conditions under which he might be persuaded to open his files to me. However, having started with the truth, I thought I might as well stick to my guns. "You're making this tough. I wish I could tell you otherwise, but this isn't related to any criminal activity—at least, as far as I know. Uhm . . . wow . . . this is hard. I'm not used to this," I said. "He and I parted enemies and it's just come to my attention I misjudged him badly. I can't live with my conscience until I square things with him. I know it sounds corny, but it's true."

"What'd you do?" George asked.

"It's not what I did. It's what I didn't do," I said. "He was implicated in a murder—well, not a murder, really, manslaughter is more like it. The point is I didn't wait to hear his side of it. I just assumed he was guilty and walked out on him. I feel bad about that. I promised 'for better or for worse' and gave him 'worse.' "

"So now what?"

"So now I'm trying to track him down so I can apologize. Maybe I can make amends . . . if it's not too late."

George's face was a study in caution. "I'm not entirely clear what you want from me."

I passed him the form, tilting my head to read the header along with him. I pointed to the relevant lines. "I think this is partly right. I've got two versions of this address. If yours matches this one or if you have another variation yet, I can probably determine which is correct."

He studied the name and address. "I remember this fellow. Went delinquent on his payments. We emptied his unit and auctioned everything off."

"That's what worries me. I think he's in trouble. Do you think you can help?"

I could see him vacillate. I left the clipboard up on the counter, angled in his direction. I could see his gaze retracing the lines of print. He moved to a file cabinet, scanned the labels on the drawer fronts, and opened the third one down. He pulled out a fat binder and laid it across the open drawer. He wet his thumb and began to leaf through. He found the relevant page, popped open the rings, removed a sheet of paper, and copied it, handing me the information without another word.

8

I returned to the office, where I spent the rest of the day paying bills, returning phone calls, and taking care of correspondence. There was no message from Mark Bethel. I'd try him again if I didn't hear from him soon. I locked my office at four-thirty, shoving my Los Angeles street map in the outer pouch of my bag. I left my car for the time being and walked over to the public library, where I checked the crisscross for the area encompassed by the three differing Sepulveda street numbers Mickey'd listed as his home address. It was impossible to determine the best candidate from looking at a map. I was going to have to make a run down there. It was time to satisfy myself as to his current situation, maybe even time for the two of us to talk. I had a big whack of money in my savings account. I was willing to offer my help if Mickey wasn't too proud to accept. I walked back to the office, where I picked up my car and made the short drive home. I didn't even have the details and I was already sick about the part I'd played in his slide from grace.

I arrived at my apartment to find two gentlemen standing on my doorstep. I knew in a flash they were plainclothes detectives: neatly dressed, clean-shaven, their expressions bland and attentive, the perfect law enforcement presence on this May afternoon. I felt a spritz of electricity coursing through my frame. My hands were left tingling and the skin on my back suddenly felt luminous, like a neon sign flashing GUILT—GUILT—GUILT. My first thought was Teddy Rich had reported an intruder, that an officer had been dispatched, that he'd called for a tech who'd subsequently dusted for prints. Mine would have shown up on the inner and outer aspects of the pet door, on the edge of the desk, on the back doorknob, in other places so numerous I could hardly recall. I'd been a cop for two years and a P.I. since then. (I'd also been arrested once, but I don't want to talk about that now, thanks.)

The point is, my prints were in the system, and the computer was going to put me inside Teddy Rich's house. The cops would ask what I was doing there and what could I say? Was there an innocent explanation? I couldn't think of one to save me. The dog, of course, would pick me out of a police lineup, tugging at my pant leg, joyously barking, jumping, and slobbering on my shoes as they cuffed me and took me away. I could try to plea-bargain right up front or wait until sentencing and throw myself on the mercy of the court.

I hesitated on the walkway, my house keys in hand. Surely, the cops had more pressing cases to pursue these days. Why would they even bother with a crime scene tech? The notion was absurd. These fellows might not be cops at all. Maybe Teddy figured out what I'd done and had sent these two goons to crush my elbows, my knees, and other relevant joints. Somewhat chirpily, I said, "Hi. Are you looking for me?"

The two of them seemed to be approximately the same age: late thirties, trim, fit, one dark, the other fair. The blond carried a briefcase in his left hand like he was doing door-to-door sales. He spoke first. "Miss Millhone?" He wore a red plaid shirt under a tweed sport coat, his Adam's apple compressed by the knot in his solid red tie. His slacks were dark cotton, wrinkled across the crotch from sitting in the car too long.

"That's right."

He held out his right hand. "My name's Felix Claas. This is my partner, John Aldo. We're detectives with the Los Angeles Police Department. Could we talk to you?"

Aldo held out two business cards and a wallet he flipped open to expose his badge. Detective Aldo was a big guy with a muscular body, probably six-three, 240 pounds. He wore his dark hair slightly shaggy, and his dark eyes receded under wide dark eyebrows that came together at the bridge of his nose. His slacks were polyester, and he had a sport coat neatly folded and laid across one arm. His short-sleeved cotton shirt exposed a matting of silky hair on his forearms. He looked like a man who preferred wearing sweats. I'd heard his first name as "John," but I noticed on his business card the spelling was the Italian, Gian, and I made the mental correction. In the flush of apprehension, I'd already forgotten the first detective's name. I glanced down at the cards again. Felix Claas was the blond, Gian Aldo, the darker one.

Claas spoke up again, smiling pleasantly. His blond hair looked wet, parted on the side and combed straight back behind his ears. His eyebrows and lashes were an almost invisible pale gold, so that his blue eyes seemed stark. His lips were full and unusually pink. He had a cleft in his chin. "Great town you have here. The minute we crossed the county line, I could feel my blood pressure drop about fifteen points."

"Thanks. We're lucky. It's like this all year long. We get a marine layer sometimes in the summer months, but it burns off by noon so it's hard to complain." Maybe this pertained to an old case of mine.

Detective Aldo eased into the conversation. "We had a chat with Lieutenant Robb. I hope we haven't caught you at a bad time."

"Not at all. This is fine. You're friends of his?"

"Well, no, ma'am, we aren't. We've talked to him by phone, but we only met today. Seems like a nice guy."

"He's great. I've known Jonah for years," I said. "What's this about?"

"A case we've been working. We'd like to talk to you inside, if you don't object."

Detective Claas chimed in. "This shouldn't take long. Fifteen–twenty minutes. We'll be as quick as we can."

"Sure. Come on in." I turned and unlocked the front door, talking over my shoulder. "When'd you get up here?"

"About an hour ago. We tried calling your office, but they told us you'd left. We must have just missed you."

"I had some errands to run," I said, wondering why I felt I owed them an explanation. I stepped across the threshold and they followed me in. In the past few years, a number of investigations had taken me to Los Angeles. One of the cases I'd handled for California Fidelity had exposed me to a bunch of bad-asses. This was probably related. The criminal element form a special subset, the same names surfacing over and over again. It's always interesting to find out what the cruds are up to.

I took a mental photograph of my apartment, idly aware of how it must appear to strangers. Small, immaculate, as compact as a ship's interior complete with cubbyholes and built-ins. Kitchenette to the right; desk and seating arrangement to the left. Royal-blue shag carpet, a small spiral staircase leading to a loft above. I set my shoulder bag on one of the stools at the kitchen counter and moved the six steps into the living room.

The two detectives waited in the doorway deferentially.

"Have a seat," I said.

Aldo said, "Thanks. Nice place. You live alone?"

"As a matter of fact, I do."

"Lucky you. My girlfriend's a slob. There's no way I can keep my place looking this clean."

Claas sat down on the small sofa tucked into the bay window, setting his briefcase on the floor beside him. While Claas and Aldo seemed equally chatty, Claas was more reserved, nearly prim in his verbal manner, while Aldo seemed relaxed. Detective Aldo took one of the two matching director's chairs, which left me with the other. I sat down, feeling subtly maneuvered, though I wasn't sure why. Aldo slouched in the chair with his legs spread, his hands hanging between his knees. The canvas on the director's chair sagged and creaked beneath his shifting weight. His thighs were enormous, and his posture seemed both indolent and intimidating. Claas flicked him a look and he altered his posture, sitting up straight.

Claas turned his attention back to me. "We understand you were married to a former vice detective named Magruder."

I was completely taken aback. "Mickey? That's right. Is this about him?" I felt a tingle of fear. Connections tumbled together in a pattern I couldn't quite discern. Whatever was going on, it had to be associated with his current financial straits. Maybe he'd robbed a bank, scammed someone, or pulled a disappearing act. Maybe there was a warrant outstanding, and these guys had been assigned the job of tracking him down. I covered my discomfort with a laugh. "What's he up to?"

Claas's expression remained remote. "Unfortunately, Mr. Magruder was the victim of a shooting. He survived . . . he's alive, but he's not doing well. Yesterday we finally got a line on him. At the time of the assault, he didn't have identification in his possession, so he was listed as a John Doe until we ran his prints."

"He was *shot?*" I could feel myself move the needle back to the beginning of the cut. Had I heard him correctly?

"Yes, ma'am."

"He's all right, though, isn't he?"

Claas's tone ranged somewhere between neutrality and regret. "Tell you the truth, it's not looking so good. Doctors say he's stable, but he's on life support. He's never regained consciousness, and the longer this goes on, the less likely he is to make a full recovery."

Or any at all was what I heard. I could feel myself blink. Mickey dying or dead? The detective was still talking, but I felt I was suffering a temporary hearing loss. I held a hand up. "Hang on. I'm sorry, but I can't seem to comprehend."

"There's no hurry. Take your time," Aldo said.

I took a couple of deep breaths. "This is weird. Where is he?"

"UCLA. He's currently in ICU, but he may be transferred to County, depending on his condition."

"He always had good insurance coverage, if it's a question of funds." The notion of Mickey at County didn't sit well with me. I was taking deep breaths, risking hyperventilation in my attempt to compose myself. "Can I see him?"

There was a momentary pause, and then Claas said, "Not just yet, but we can probably work something out." He seemed singularly unenthusiastic, and I didn't press the point.

Aldo watched me with concern. "Are you okay?"

"I'm fine. I'm just surprised," I said. "I don't know what I thought you were doing here, but it wasn't this. I can't believe anything bad could ever happen to him. He was always a brawler, but he seemed invincible . . . at least to me. What happened?"

"That's what we're trying to piece together," Claas said. "He'd been shot twice, once in the head and once in the chest. A patrolman spotted him lying on the sidewalk little after three A.M. The weapon, a semiautomatic, was found in the gutter about ten feet away. This was a commercial district, a lot of bars in the area, so it's possible Mr. Magruder got into a dispute. We have a couple of guys out now canvassing the neighborhood. So far no witnesses. For now, we're working backward, trying to get a line on his activities prior to the shooting."

"When *was* this?"

"Early morning hours of May fourteenth. Wednesday of last week."

Claas said, "Do you mind if we ask you a couple of questions?"

"Not at all. Please do."

I expected one of them to take out a notebook, but none emerged. I glanced at the briefcase and wondered if I was being recorded.

Meanwhile, Claas was talking on. "We're in the process of eliminating some possibilities. This is mostly filling in the blanks, if you can help us out."

"Sure, I'll try. I'm not sure how, but fire away," I said. Inwardly, I flinched at my choice of words.

Claas cleared his throat. His voice was lighter, reedier. "When you last spoke to your ex-husband, did he mention any problems? Threats, disputes, anything like that?"

I leaned forward, relieved. "I haven't spoken to Mickey in fourteen years."

Something flickered between them, one of those wordless conversations married couples learn to conduct with their eyes. Detective Aldo took over. "You're the owner of a nine-millimeter Smith and Wesson?"

"I was at one time." I was on the verge of saying more but decided to rein myself in until I figured out where they were going. The empty box that had originally housed the gun was still sitting in the carton beside my desk, less than six feet away.

Claas said, "Can you tell us when you purchased it?"

"I didn't. Mickey bought that gun and gave it to me as a wedding gift. That was August of 1971."

"Strange wedding present," Aldo remarked.

"He's a strange guy," I said.

"Where's the gun at this time?"

"Beats me. I haven't laid eyes on it for years. I assumed Mickey took it with him when he moved to L.A."

"So you haven't seen the gun since approximately . . ."

I looked from Claas to Aldo as the obvious implications began to sink in. I'd been slow on the uptake. "Wait a minute. *That* was the gun used?"

"Let's put it this way: Yours was the gun that was found at the scene. We're still waiting for ballistics."

"You can't think I had anything to do with it."

"Your name popped up in the computer as the registered owner. We're looking for a starting point, and this made sense. If

Mr. Magruder carried the gun, it's possible someone took it away from him and shot him with it."

"That puts *me* in the clear," I said facetiously. I felt like biting my tongue. Sarcasm is the wrong tack to take with cops. Better to play humble and cooperative.

A silence settled between the two. They'd seemed friendly and confiding, but I knew from experience there'd be a sizable gap between the version they'd given me and the one they'd withheld. Aldo took a stick of gum from his coat pocket and tore it in half. He tucked half in his pocket and slipped the paper wrapper and the foil from the other half. He slid the chewing gum in his mouth. He seemed disinterested for the moment, but I knew they'd spend the return trip comparing notes, matching their reactions and intuitions against the information I'd given them.

Claas shifted on the couch. "Can you tell us when you last spoke to Mr. Magruder?"

"It's Mickey. Please use his first name. This is hard enough as it is. He left Santa Teresa in 1972. I don't remember talking to him after we divorced."

"Can you tell us what contact you've had since then?"

"You just asked that. I've had none."

Claas's gaze fixed on mine, rather pointedly, I thought. "You haven't spoken to him in the past few months," he said—not a question, but a statement infused with skepticism.

"No. Absolutely not. I haven't talked to him."

While Detective Claas tried to hold my attention, I could see that Aldo was making a discreet visual tour of the living room. His gaze moved from item to item, methodically assessing everything within range. Desk, files, box, answering machine, bookshelves. I could almost hear him thinking to himself: *Which of these objects doesn't belong?* I saw his focus shift back to the cardboard box. So far, I hadn't said a word about the delinquent payments on Mickey's storage bin. On the face of it, I couldn't see how withholding the information represented any criminal behavior on my part. What justice was I obstructing? Who was I aiding and abetting? I didn't shoot my ex. I wasn't in custody and wasn't under oath. If it seemed advisable, I could always contact the detectives later when I "remembered" something relevant. All this went through my mind in the split second while I was busy covering my butt. If the two picked up on my uneasiness, neither said a word. Not that I expected them to gasp and exchange significant looks.

Detective Claas cleared his throat again. "What about him? Has he been in touch with you?"

I confess a little irritability was creeping into my response. "That's the same thing, isn't it, whether I talk to him or he talks to me? We divorced years ago. We don't have any reason to stay in touch. If he called, I'd hang up. I don't want to talk to him."

Aldo's tone was light, nearly bantering. "What are you so mad about? The poor guy's down for the count."

I felt myself flush. "Sorry. That's just how it is. We're not one of those couples that turned all lovey-dovey once the papers were signed. I have nothing against him, but I've never been interested in being his best friend . . . nor he mine, I might add."

"Same with my ex," he said. "Still, sometimes there's a piece of business—you know, a stock certificate or news of an old pal. You might forward the mail, even if you hate their guts. It's not unusual for one ex to drop the other a note if something relevant comes up."

"Mickey doesn't write notes."

Claas shifted in seat. "What's he do then, call?"

I could feel myself grow still. Why was he so determined to pursue the point? "Look. For the fourth or fifth time now, Mickey and I don't talk. Honest. Cross my heart. Scout's honor and all that. We're not enemies. We're not antagonistic. We just don't have that kind of relationship."

"Really. How would you characterize it? Friendly? Distant? Cordial?"

"What *is* this?" I said. "What's the relevance? I mean, come on, guys. You can't be serious. Why would I shoot my ex-husband with my own gun and leave it at the scene? I'd have to be nuts."

Aldo smiled to himself. "People get rattled. You never know what they'll do. We're just looking for information. Anything you can give us, we'd appreciate."

"Tell me your theory," I said.

"We don't have a theory," Claas said. "We're hoping to eliminate some angles. You could save us a lot of time if you'd cooperate."

"I'm *doing* that. This is what cooperation looks like, in case you're not accustomed to it. You're barking up the wrong tree. I don't even know where Mickey lives these days."

The two detectives stared at me.

"I'm telling you the truth."

Detective Claas asked the next question without reference to his notes. "Can you tell us where you were on March twenty-seventh?"

My mind went blank. "I haven't the faintest idea. Where were you?" I said. I could tell my hands were going to start shaking. My fingers were cold, and without even thinking about it, I crossed my arms and tucked my hands against my sides. I knew I looked stubborn and defensive, but I was suddenly unnerved.

"Do you have an appointment book you might check?"

"You know what? I think we should stop this conversation right now. If you're here because you think I was somehow involved in a shooting, you'll have to talk to my attorney because I'm done with this bullshit."

Detective Aldo seemed surprised. "Hey, come on. There's no call for that. We're not accusing you of anything. This is an exchange of information."

"What was exchanged? I tell you things, but what do you tell me? Or did I miss that part?"

Aldo smiled, undismayed by my prickliness. "We told you he was injured and you told us you never talked to him. See? We tell you and then you tell us. It's like a dialogue. We're trading."

"Why did you ask where I was March twenty-seventh? What's that about?"

Claas spoke up. "We checked his telephone bills. There was a call to this number that lasted thirty minutes. We assumed the two of you talked. Unless someone else lives here, which you've denied."

"Show me," I said. I held out my hand.

He leaned down and reached into the partially opened briefcase, sliding out a sheaf of phone bills, which he passed to me without comment. On top of the stack was Mickey's bill for April, itemizing his March service. I glanced at the header, noting that the phone number on the account was the same one I had. At that point, his February bill was already in arrears. The past-due notice warned that if his payment wasn't received within ten days, his service would be terminated. I let my eye drift down the column of toll calls and long-distance charges for March. Only two calls had been made, both to Santa Teresa. The first was March 13, made to Mark Bethel's office. I'd heard about that from Judy. The second was to my number. Sure enough, that call was made on March 27 at 1:27 P.M. and lasted, as specified, for a full thirty minutes.

9

I'm not sure how I got through the remainder of the conversation. Eventually the detectives left, with phony thanks on their part for all the help I'd given them, and phony assurances on mine that I'd contact them directly if I had anything more to contribute to their investigation. As soon as the door closed, I scurried into the bathroom, where I stepped into the empty bathtub and discreetly spied on them through the window. I kept just out of sight while Detectives Claas and Aldo, chatting in low tones, got into what looked like a county-issued car and drove away. I'd have given anything to know what they were saying—assuming the discussion was about Mickey or me. Maybe they were talking sports, which I don't give a rat's ass about.

As soon as they were gone, I returned to my desk and flipped back through my desk calendar to the page for March 27. That Thursday was entirely empty, as were the days on either side: no appointments, no meetings, no notation of events, professional or social. Typically,

I'd have spent the day at the office, doing God knows what. I was hoping my desk calendar would jump-start my recollection. For the moment, I was stumped. All I knew was I hadn't talked to Mickey on March 27 or any other day in recent years. Had someone broken into my apartment? That was a creepy prospect, but what other explanation was there? Mickey could have dialed my number and spoken to someone else. It was also possible someone other than Mickey made the call from his place, establishing a connection that didn't actually exist. Who would go to such lengths? A person or persons who intended to shoot my ex-husband and have the finger point at me.

It rained during the night, one of those rare tropical storms that sometimes blow in from Hawaii without warning. I woke at 2:36 A.M. to the sound of heavy raindrops drumming on my skylight. The air gusting through the open window smelled of ocean brine and gardenias. May in California tends to be cool and dry. During the summer months following, vegetation languishes without moisture, a process of dehydration that renders the chaparral as fragile as ancient parchment. The rolling hills turn gold while the roadsides glow hazy yellow with the clouds of wild mustard growing along the berm. By August, the temperatures climb into the 80s and the relative humidity drops. Winds tear down the mountains and squeeze through canyons. Between the sundowners, Santa Anas, and the desiccated landscape, the stage is set for the arsonist's match. Rains might offer temporary relief, delaying the inevitable by a week or two. The irony is that rain does little more than encourage growth, which in turn provides nature with additional combustible fuel.

By the time I woke again at 5:59, the storm had passed. I pulled on my sweats and went out for my run, returning to the apartment only long enough to toss a canvas duffel in the car and head over to the gym. I lifted weights for an hour, working my way through my usual routine. Though I'd only been back at the process for two months, I was seeing results, shoulders and biceps taking form again.

I was home at nine. I showered, ate breakfast, tossed some items in my fanny pack, grabbed my shoulder bag, left a note on Henry's door, and hit the road for L.A. Traffic was fast-moving, southbound cars barreling down the 101. At this time of day, the road was heavily populated with commercial vehicles: pickups and panel trucks, semis and moving vans, empty school buses, and trailers hauling new cars to the showrooms in Westlake and Thousand Oaks. As I crested the hill and eased down into the San Fernando Valley, I could see the gauzy veil of the smog that had already begun to accumulate. The San Gabriel Mountains, often obscured from view, were at least visible today. Every time I passed this way, new construction was under way. What looked like entire villages would appear on the crest of a hill, or a neighborhood of identical condominiums would emerge from behind a stand of trees. Billboards announced the availability of new communities previously unheard of.

Overhead, two bright yellow aircraft circled, one following the other in an aerial surveillance focused on those of us down below. The berm was littered with trash, and at one point I passed one of those perplexing curls of tire tread that defy explanation. Once I reached Sherman Oaks, I turned right on the San Diego Freeway. The foliage along the berm was whipped by the perpetual wind of passing vehicles. Several towering office buildings obstructed the view, like sightseers on a parade route with no consideration for others. I took the off-ramp at Sunset and drove east until the UCLA campus began to appear on my right. I turned right onto Hilgard, right again on Le Conte, and right onto Tiverton, where I paid for a parking voucher. There were no parking spots available in the aboveground lot. I began my descent into the underground levels, circling down and down until I finally found a spot on C-1. I locked my car and took the elevator up. The extensive grass and concrete plaza served both the Jules Stein Eye Clinic and the UCLA Hospital and Medical Center. I crossed to the main entrance and entered the lobby, with its polished granite walls and two-tone gray carpet with a smoky pink stripe along the edge. The reception area on the right was filled with people awaiting word of friends and family members currently undergoing surgery. Two teenage girls in shorts and T-shirts were playing cards on the floor. There were babies in infant seats and a toddler in a stroller, flushed and sweating in sleep. Others were reading newspapers or chatting quietly while a steady foot traffic of visitors crossed and recrossed the lounge. The lobby chairs and adjoining planters were boxy gray modules. On the left, the gift shop was faced in a curious hue somewhere between mauve and orchid. A large glass case contained sample floral arrangements in case you arrived to see someone without a posy in hand.

Dead ahead, above the information desk, the word INFORMATION was writ large. I waited my turn and then asked a Mrs. Lewis, the patient information volunteer, for Mickey Magruder's room. She was probably in her seventies, her eyelids crepey as a turtle's. Age had cut knife pleats in the fragile skin on her cheeks, and her lips were pulled together in a pucker, like a drawstring purse. She did a quick check of her files and began to shake her head with regret. "I don't show anybody by that name. When was he admitted, dear?"

"On the fourteenth. I guess he could be registered as Michael. That's how the name reads on his birth certificate."

She made a note of the name and consulted another source. Her knuckles were knotted with arthritis, but her cursive was delicate. "Well, I don't know what to tell you. Is it possible he's been discharged?"

"I doubt it. I heard he was in a coma in ICU."

"You know, he might have been taken to the Santa Monica facility on Sixteenth Street. Shall I put in a call to them?"

"I'd appreciate that. I drove all the way down from Santa Teresa, and I'd hate to go home without finding him."

I watched her idly as she dialed and spoke to someone on the other end. Within moments, she hung up, apparently without success. "They have no record of him there. You might try Saint John's Hospital or Cedars-Sinai."

"I'm almost certain he was brought here. I talked to police detectives yesterday, and that's what they said. He was admitted early Wednesday morning of last week. He'd been shot twice, so he must have been brought in through emergency."

"I'm afraid that doesn't help. All I'm given is the patient's name, room number, and medical status. I don't have information about admissions."

"Suppose he was transferred? Wouldn't you receive notice?"

"Ordinarily," she said.

"Look, is there anyone else I could talk to about this?"

"I can't think who unless you'd want to speak to someone in administration."

"Can't you check with Intensive Care? Maybe if you describe his injuries, they'll know where he is."

"Well," she said hesitantly, "there *is* a trauma social worker. She'd certainly have been alerted if the patient were the victim of a violent crime. Would you like me to call her?"

"Perfect. Please do. I'd appreciate your help."

By now, other people were lining up behind me, anxious for information and restless at the delay. Mrs. Lewis seemed reluctant, but she did pick up the phone again and make an in-house call. After the first couple of sentences, her voice dropped out of hearing range and she angled her face slightly so I couldn't read her lips. When she replaced the receiver, she wouldn't quite look at me. "If you'd care to wait, they said they'd send someone."

"Is something wrong?"

"Not that I know, dear. At the moment, the social worker's out of her office . . . probably on the floor somewhere. The ICU charge nurse is going to try paging her and get back to me."

"Then you're telling me he's here?"

The man behind me said, "Hey, come on, lady. Give us a break."

Mrs. Lewis seemed flustered. "I didn't say that. All I know is the social worker might help if you want to wait and talk to her. If you could just have a seat. . . ."

"Thanks. You won't forget?"

The man said, "Hell, I'll tell you myself."

I was too distracted to engage in a barking fest, so I let that one pass. I made my way over to an empty chair. Driving down to L.A., I hadn't pictured things turning out this way. I'd fancied a moment by Mickey's bed, some feeling of redemption, the chance to make amends. Now his latent paranoia was rubbing off on me. Had something happened to him? Had Detectives Claas and Aldo been holding out? It was always possible he'd been admitted under an assumed name. Crime victims, like celebrities, are often afforded the added measure of protection. If that were the case, I wasn't sure how I was going to sweet-talk my way into his alias. All I knew was I wouldn't budge until I got a lead on him.

Someone had left behind a tattered issue of *Sunset Magazine.* I began to leaf through, desperate for a diversion from my anxiety about him. I needed to get "centered." I needed serenity, a moment of calm, while I figured out whose butt I was going to kick and how hard. I settled on an article about building a brick patio, complete with layouts. Every ten or fifteen seconds I looked up, checking the clock, watching visitors, patients, and hospital personnel entering the lobby, emerging from the cafeteria, passing through the seeing-eye doors. It was important to dig out the area to a depth of six inches, adding back a layer of gravel and then a layer of sand before beginning to lay brick. I chose the herringbone pattern for my imaginary outdoor living space. Thirty minutes went by. I finished all the articles on horticulture and went on to check out the low-fat recipes utilizing phyllo and fresh fruit. I didn't want to eat anything that had to be kept under a moist towel before I baked it.

Someone sat down in the chair next to mine. I glanced over to find Gian Aldo, and he was pissed. The woman at the desk had clearly ratted me out. Aldo said, "I figured it was you. What the hell's going on? I get a call saying some woman's over here making a stink, trying to get Mickey's room number from a poor unsuspecting volunteer."

I felt the color rise in my cheeks. "I didn't 'make a stink.' I never even raised my voice. I came to see how he was. What's the big deal?"

"We asked to be notified if anyone came in asking for Magruder's room."

"How was I supposed to know? I'm concerned, worried sick. Is that against the law?"

"Depends on your purpose. You could've been the shooter . . . or had you thought about that?"

"Of course I thought about that, but I didn't shoot the man," I said. "I was anxious about him and thought I'd feel better if I could see him."

Aldo's dark brows knit together and I could tell he was struggling to moderate his attitude. "You should have given us warning. We could have met you on arrival and saved you the time and aggravation."

"Your overriding purpose in life."

"Look, I was in the middle of a meeting when the call came through. I didn't have to rush right out. I could have let you sit and stew. It would have served you right." He stared off across the lobby. "Actually, my overriding purpose is protecting Magruder. I'm sure you can appreciate the risk, since we don't have the faintest idea who plugged him."

"I get that." I could see the situation from his perspective. This was an active investigation, and I'd gummed up the works by ignoring protocol. Since Mick was my ex and since mine was the gun that was found at the scene, my sudden appearance at the hospital didn't look that good. "I'm sorry. I get antsy for information and tend to cut to the chase. I should have called you. The fault was mine."

"Let's don't worry about that now." He glanced at his watch. "I have to get back to work, but if you want, I can take you up to ICU for a couple minutes first."

"I can't have time alone with him?"

"That's correct," he said. "For one thing, he's still unconscious. For another, it's my responsibility to keep him safe. I answer to the department, no ifs, ands, or buts. I don't mean to sound harsh, but that's the way it is."

"Let's get on with it then," I said, suppressing the surge of rebelliousness. Clearly, I'd have to yield to him in everything. This man was officially the keeper of the gate. Seeing Mickey was more important than bucking authority or winning arguments.

I got up when he did and followed him through the lobby, feeling like a dog trained to heel. We took a right down the corridor, saying nothing to each other. He pressed for the elevator. While we waited, he pulled out a package of gum and offered me a piece. I declined. He removed a stick for himself, tore it in half, peeled off the paper, and popped the gum in his mouth. The elevator doors slid open. I entered behind him, and we turned and faced front while we ascended. For once I didn't bother to memorize the route. There was no point in scheming to find Mickey on my own. If I pulled any shenanigans, Detective Aldo was going to nail my ass to the wall.

We entered the 7-E Intensive Care Unit, where the detective was apparently known by sight. While he had a brief conversation with the nurses at the desk, I had a chance to get my bearings. The atmosphere was curious: the lights slightly dimmed, the noise level reduced by the teal-and-gray patterned carpeting. I guessed at ten or twelve beds, each in a cubicle within visual range of the nurses' station. The beds were separated by lightweight green-and-white curtains, most of which were drawn shut. These were the patients who teetered on the edge, tethered to life by the slimmest of lines. Blood and bile, urine, spinal fluid, all the rivers in the body were being mapped and charted while the soul journeyed on. Sometimes, between breaths, a patient slipped away, easing into the greater stream from which all of us emerge and to which all must return.

Aldo rejoined me and steered me around the desk to the bed where Mickey lay. I didn't recognize the man, though a quick glance at Aldo assured me this was him. He wasn't breathing on his own. There was a wide band of tape across the lower portion of his face. His mouth was open, attached to a ventilator by a translucent blue tube about the same diameter as a vacuum cleaner hose. The top half of the bed was elevated as if he were on permanent display. He lay close to one side, almost touching the side rails, which had been raised to contain him like the sides of a crib. He wore a watch cap of gauze. The bullet wound had left him with two blackened eyes, puffy and bruised as though he'd been in a fistfight. His complexion was gray. There was a tube in the back of one hand, delivering solutions from numerous bags hanging on an IV pole. I could count the drips one by one, a Chinese water torture designed to save life. A second tube snaked out from under the covers and into a gallon jug of urine accumulating under the bed. What hair I could see looked sparse and oily. His skin had a fine sheen of moisture. Years of sun damage were now surfacing like an image on film bathed in developing fluid. I could see soft down on the edges of his ears. His eyes weren't fully closed. Through the narrow slits I could watch him track an unseen movie or perhaps lines of print. Where was his mind while his body lay so still? I disconnected my emotions by focusing on equipment that surrounded his bed: a cart, a sink, a stainless steel trash can with a pop-up lid, a rolling chair, a glove dispenser, and a paper towel rack—utilitarian articles that hardly spoke of death.

The presence of Detective Aldo lent a strange air of unreality to our reunion. Mickey's chest rose and fell in a regular rhythm, a bellow's effect forcing his lungs to inflate. Under his hospital gown, I could see a tube top of white gauze bandages. When I'd met him, he was thirty-six. He was now almost fifty-three, the same age as Robert Dietz. For the first time I wondered if my involvement with Dietz had been an unwitting attempt to mend the breach with Mickey. Were my internal processes that obvious?

I stared at Mickey's face, watching him breathe, glancing at the blood pressure cuff that was attached to one arm. At intervals, the cuff would inflate and deflate itself, with a whining and a wheeze. The digital readout would then appear on the monitor above his head. His blood pressure seemed stable at 125 over 80, his pulse 74. It's embarrassing to remember love once the feeling's died, all the passion and romanticism, the sentimentality and sexual excess. Later, you have to wonder what the hell you were thinking of. Mickey had seemed solid and safe, someone whose expertise I admired, whose opinions I valued, whose confidence I envied. I'd idealized him without even realizing what I was doing, which was taking my projection as the stone cold truth. I didn't understand that I sought in him the qualities I lacked or hadn't yet developed. I'd have denied to the last breath that I was looking for a father figure, but of course I was.

I became conscious of Gian Aldo, who stared at Mickey with a silence similar to mine. What could either of us say beyond the trite and the obvious? I finally spoke up. "I should let you get back to work. I appreciate this."

"Any time," he said.

He walked me down through the hospital and across the plaza. I punched the elevator button and he waited with me dutifully. "I'm fine," I said, meaning he could leave.

"I don't mind," he said, meaning not-on-your-sweet-life.

When the elevator arrived, I got on and turned, giving him a little wave as the doors slid shut. I found my car, unlocked it, turned the key in the ignition, and put the gears in reverse. By the time I made the three circles upward to ground level, he was waiting in his car by the exit, his engine idling. I pulled out of the lot onto Tiverton, and when I reached Le Conte I turned left. Detective Aldo did likewise, keeping pace with me as I headed toward the freeway. He was still asserting his control, as I was keenly aware. I could understand his desire to see me off, though I felt like the villain in a Western movie being escorted out of town. I kept track of his car in my rearview mirror—not that he made any effort to disguise his intent. West on Sunset, north on the 405, driving toward the 101, we formed a two-car motorcade at sixty miles an hour. I began to wonder if he was going to follow me all the way home.

I watched the cross streets go by: Balboa, White Oak, Reseda . . . did the man have no faith? What'd he think I was going to do, circle back to UCLA? At Tampa, I saw him lean forward and pick up his radio mike, apparently responding to a call. The subject must have been urgent because he suddenly veered off, crossing two lanes of traffic before he headed down the exit ramp. I kept my acceleration constant, my gaze fixed on the mirror to see if he'd reappear. Detective Aldo was a sneak, and I wouldn't put it past him to try a little misdirection. Winnetka, DeSoto, Topanga Canyon passed. It looked like he was gone. For once my angels were in agreement. One said, Nobody's perfect, and the other said, Amen.

I took the next off-ramp.

10

Mickey had been shrewd in listing an address on Sepulveda. According to the *Thomas Guide,* there are endless variations. Sepulveda Boulevard seems to spring forth in the north end of the San Fernando Valley. The street then traces a line south, often hugging the San Diego Freeway, all the way to Long Beach. The North and South Sepulveda designations seem to jump back and forth, claiming ever-shifting sections of the street as it winds from township to township. There are East and West Sepulveda Boulevards, a Sepulveda Lane, Sepulveda Place, Sepulveda Street, Sepulveda Eastway, East Sepulveda Fire Road, Sepulveda Westway. By juggling the numbers, Mickey could just about ensure that no one was ever going to pinpoint his exact location. As it happened, I'd collected three variations of the same four digits: 2805, 2085, and 2580.

I placed the addresses in numerical order, beginning with 2085, moving on to 2580, and then to 2805. I reasoned that even if finances had forced him to sell his car, he still had to get around. He might use a bike or public transportation traveling to and from his place of employment—unless, of course, he'd also lost his job. He probably did his shopping close to home, frequenting the local restaurants when he felt too lazy to prepare a meal, which (if the past was any indication) was most of the time. The detectives had mentioned the shooting had occurred in a commercial district with lots of bars close by. Already in my mind, a mental picture was forming. Mickey'd never owned a house, so I was looking for a rental, and nothing lavish, if I knew him.

I cruised the endless blocks of Sepulveda I'd selected. While this wasn't L.A. at its worst, the route was hardly scenic. There were billboards everywhere. Countless telephone poles intersected the skyline, dense strands of wire stretching in all directions. I passed gas stations, a print and copy shop, three animal hospitals, a 7-Eleven, a discount tire establishment. I watched the numbers climb, from a car wash to a sign company, from a construction site to a quick lube to an auto body shop. In this area, if you weren't in the market for lumber or fast food, you could always buy discount leather or stock up at the Party Smarty for your entertaining needs.

It wasn't until I reached the 2800 block in Culver City that I sensed this was Mickey's turf. The H-shaped three-story apartment building at 2805 had a rough plaster exterior, painted drab gray, with sagging galleries and aluminum sliding-glass doors that looked like they'd be difficult to open. Stains, shaped like stalactites, streaked the stucco along the roofline. Weeds grew up through cracks in the concrete. A dry gully ran along the south side, choked with boulders and refuse. The wire fence marking the property line now leaned against the side of the apartment complex in a tangle of dead shrubs.

I drove past, scanning the nearest intersection, where I saw an electronics shop, a photo lab, a paint store, a mini-mart, a pool hall, a twenty-four-hour coffee shop, two bars, and a Chinese restaurant, Mickey's favorite. I spotted a driveway, and at the first break in traffic I did a turn-around, coming up on the right side of the street in front of 2805. I found a parking place two doors away, turned off the engine, and sat in my car, checking out the ambience, if the concept isn't too grand. The building itself was similar to one Mickey occupied when the two of us first met. I'd been appalled then, as I was now, by his indifference to his environment. The sign out front specified *studios and 1 & 2 bedroom apartments* NOW RENTING, as if this were late-breaking news.

The landscaping consisted of a cluster of banana palms with dark green battered leaves that looked like they'd been slashed by a machete. Traffic in the area was heavy, and I found myself watching the cars passing in both directions, wondering if Detective Aldo was going to drive by and catch me at the scene. The very thought made me squirm. It's not as though he'd forbidden me to make an appearance, but he wasn't going to be happy if he figured it out.

I started the car and pulled away from the curb. I drove down half a block and turned right at the first corner and then right again, into the alley that ran behind the row of buildings and dead-ended at the gully. Someone had compressed the buckling wire fence so that one could cross the boundary and ease down into the ditch. I pulled in beside the garbage bins and made another U-turn, so that I now faced the alley entrance. I took a minute to grab my fanny pack from the backseat and transfer my key picks, a penlight, my mini-tool kit, and a pair of rubber gloves. I clipped the fanny pack around my waist, locked the car, and got out.

I padded down the walkway between Mickey's building and the apartment complex next door. At night this area would be dark, since the exterior light fixtures were either dangling or missing altogether. A line of gray-painted water meters was planted along the side, real shin-bangers. By straining only slightly—which is to say, jumping up and down like a Zulu—I was able to peek in the windows through the wrought-iron burglar bars. Most of what I saw were bedrooms barely large enough for a king-sized bed. The occupants seemed to use the windowsills to display an assortment of homely items: cracker boxes, framed snapshots, mayonnaise jars filled to capacity with foil-wrapped condoms. In one unit, someone was nurturing a handsome marijuana plant.

Mickey's apartment building didn't have a lobby, but an alcove in the front stairwell housed a series of metal mailboxes with names neatly embossed on short lengths of red, blue, and yellow plastic. Even Mickey couldn't buck post office regulations. By counting boxes, I knew there were twenty apartments distributed on three floors, but I had no way to guess how many flats were the one- and two-bedroom units and how many were studios. His was unit 2-H. The manager was on the ground floor in 1-A to my immediate right. The name on the mailbox read HATFIELD, B & C. I decided to postpone contact until after I'd reconnoitered Mickey's place.

I went up the front stairs to the second floor, following the progression of front doors and picture windows that graced each flat. There were no burglar bars up here. Mickey's was the corner unit at the rear of the building on the right-hand side. There was a neat yellow X of crime-scene tape across his door. An official caution had been affixed advising of the countless hideous repercussions if crime-scene sanctity was breached. The gallery continued around the corner and ran along the back of the building, so that Mickey's rear windows overlooked the alleyway below and the gully to the right. A second set of stairs had been tacked on back here, probably to bring the building into compliance with fire department codes. Mickey probably considered this a mixed blessing. While the privacy offered a potential intruder unimpeded access to his windows, it also gave Mickey an easy means of egress. When I peered over the railing, I could see my VW below like a faithful steed, so close I could have leapt down and galloped off at a moment's notice.

All Mickey's sliding glass windows were secured. Knowing him, he'd tucked heavy wooden dowels into the inside track so the windows would only slide back a scant six inches. The lock on his front door, however, seemed to be identical to those on the neighboring apartments. The manager must have discouraged swapping out the standard model for something more effective. I studied my surroundings. The alley was deserted and I saw no signs of any other tenant. I slipped on my rubber gloves and went to work with my pick. A friend in Houston had recently sent me a keen toy: a battery-operated pick that, once mastered, worked with gratifying efficiency. It had taken me a while to get the hang of it, but I'd practiced on Henry's door until I had the technique down pat.

The door yielded to my efforts in less than fifteen seconds, making no more noise than an electric toothbrush. I tucked the pick back in my fanny pack, loosened one end of the yellow tape, and stepped over the doorsill, turning only long enough to resecure the tape through the gap before I closed the door behind me. I checked my watch, allowing myself thirty minutes for the search. I figured if a neighbor had observed me breaking in, it would take the L.A. cops at least that long to respond to the call.

The interior was dim. Mickey's curtains were drawn, and sunlight was further blocked by the six-story building across the alley. Mickey still smoked. Stale fumes hung in the air, having permeated the carpet, the drapes, and all the heavy upholstered furniture. I checked the cigarette butts that had been left in the ashtrays, along with an array of wooden kitchen matches. All were the same Camel filters he'd been smoking for years, and none bore the telltale red rim suggesting female companionship. An Elmore Leonard paperback had been left on the arm of the sofa, open at the midpoint. Mickey had introduced me to Elmore Leonard and Len Deighton. In turn, I'd told him about Dick Francis, though I'd never known if he read the British author with the same pleasure I did. The walls were done in a temporary-looking pine paneling that was nearly sticky with the residue of cigarette tars. The living room and dining room formed an L. The furniture was clumsy—big overstuffed pieces of the sort you'd buy at a flea market or pick off the sidewalk, like an alley fairy, on collection day. There was a shredder against one wall, but the bin had been emptied. In Mickey's view of the world, no scrap of paper, no receipt, and no piece of correspondence should go into the trash without being scissored into tiny pieces. He probably dumped the bin at frequent intervals, using more than one trash can, so that a thief breaking in wouldn't have the means to reassemble vital documents. No doubt about it, the man was nuts.

I moved into the dining area, past four mismatched chairs and a plain wooden table that was littered with mail. I paused, picking through the stack that was piled at one end. I was careful not to sort the envelopes, though my natural inclination was to separate the bills from the junk. I spotted a number of bank statements, but there were no personal letters, no catalogs, and no credit card bills. I had little interest in his utility bills. What did I care how much electricity he used? I longed for a phone bill, but there were none to be found. The cops had lifted those. I picked up the handful of bank statements and slipped them down the front of my jeans into my underpants, where they formed a crackling paper girdle. I'd look at them later when I was home again. None of the other bills seemed useful so I left them where they were. Best to keep the federal mail-tampering convictions to a minimum.

Off the dining area, I entered a galley-style kitchen so small I could reach the far wall in two steps. Stove, apartment-sized refrigerator, sink, microwave oven. The only kitchen window was small and looked out onto the alley. On the counter, he kept a round glass fishbowl into which he tossed his extra packets of matches at the end of the night, a road map of his journey from bar to bar. The upper cabinets revealed a modest collection of Melamine plates and coffee mugs, plus the basic staples: dry cereal, powdered milk, sugar, a few condiments, paper napkins, and two sealed bottles of Early Times bourbon. The cupboards below were packed back to front with canned goods: soups, beans, Spam, tuna packed in oil, tamales, Spaghetti-O's, applesauce, evaporated milk. In the storage space under the kitchen sink, I found an empty bourbon bottle in the trash. Tucked in among the pipes, I counted ten five-gallon containers of bottled water. This was Mickey's survival stock in case a war broke out or L.A. was invaded by extraterrestrials. The refrigerator was filled with things that smelled bad. Mickey had tossed in half-eaten items without the proper wrapping, which resulted in dark chunks of hardening cheddar cheese, a greening potato covered with wartlike sprouts, and half an air-dried tomato drawing in on itself.

I retraced my steps. To the left of the living room was the door to the bedroom, with a closet and undersized bath beyond. The chest of drawers was filled with the usual jockey shorts and T-shirts, socks, handkerchiefs. The bed-table drawer contained some interesting items: a woman's diaphragm and a small spray bottle of cologne with a partial price label on the bottom. The cologne had apparently been purchased from a Robinson's Department Store, since I could still make out a portion of the identifying tag. I removed the top and took a whiff. Heavy on the lily of the valley that I remembered from the early days of our romance. Mickey's mother must have worn something similar. I remembered how he'd lay his lips in the hollow of my throat when I was wearing it myself. I put the cologne bottle down. There was a tissue paper packet about the size of a stick of gum. I unfolded the paper and picked up a thin gold chain threaded through the clasp of a small gold heart locket with an ever-so-tiny rose enameled in the center. Not to sound cynical, but Mickey'd given me one just like this about a week into our affair. Some men do that, find a gimmick or shtick that works once—the gift of a single red rose—and recycle the same gesture with every woman who comes along.

In a cleaning bag, he'd hung two dark-blue uniforms with patches on the sleeves. I slid a hand up under the bag and checked one of the light blue patches. *Pacific Coast Security* was stitched in gold around the rim. Also hanging in the closet were a couple of sport coats, six dress shirts, four pairs of blue jeans, two pairs of chinos, a pair of dark pants, and a black leather jacket I knew very well indeed. This was the jacket Mickey wore the first time we went out, the jacket he was wearing when he kissed me the first time. I was still living with Aunt Gin, so there was no way we could go inside to misbehave. Mickey backed me up against the trailer door, the leather in his jacket making a characteristic creaking sound. The kiss went on so long we both sank down along the frame. I was Eva Marie Saint with Marlon

Brando—*On the Waterfront*—which is still one of the best screen kisses in recorded history. Not like love scenes nowadays where you watch the guy stick his tongue down the girl's throat, trying to activate her gag reflex. Mickey and I might've made love right there on the doorstep except we'd have been visible to everybody in the trailer park, which we knew was bad form, making us vulnerable to arrest.

I shook my head and closed the closet door while a sexual shiver ran down my frame. I tried the door next to it, which seemed to be an exit onto the rear gallery. The lock here was new. There was no key in the deadbolt, but it probably wasn't far. Mickey wouldn't make it easy for someone breaking into the apartment, but he'd want the key handy in case of fire or earthquake. I pivoted, letting my gaze move across the area, remembering his tricks. I knelt and felt my way along the edge of the carpeting. When I reached the corner, I gave the loosened carpet a tug. I lifted that section and plucked the key from its hiding place. I unlocked the back door and left it temporarily ajar.

I went back to the bedroom door and stood there, looking out at the living room. The cops had doubtless cruised through here once, sealing the apartment afterward, pending a more thorough investigation. I tried to see the place as they had, and then I looked at it again from personal experience. With Mickey, the question wasn't so much what was visible as what wasn't. This was a man who lived in a constant state of readiness and, as nearly as I could tell, his fears had only accelerated in the past fourteen years. In the absence of global conflict, he lived in anticipation of civil insurrection: unruly hordes who would overrun the building, breaking into every unit, clamoring for food, water, and other valuables like toilet paper. So where were his weapons? How did he intend to defend himself?

I tried the kitchen first, tapping along the baseboards for the sound of hollow spaces. I'd seen him install other "safes"—compartments with false fronts where you could tuck cash, guns, and ammunition. I started with the kitchen sink. I took out all the gallon water containers, exposing the "floor" and rear wall of stained plywood. I shone the penlight from top to bottom, side to side. I could see four screw heads, one set in each corner, darkened to match the panel. I unbuckled my fanny pack, opened my mini-tool kit, took out a battery-operated drill, and set about removing screws. A person could develop carpal tunnel syndrome doing this the old-fashioned way. Once the screws were out, the partition yielded to gentle pressure, exposing a space that was six to eight inches deep. Four handguns were mounted in a rack on the rear wall, along with boxes of ammunition. I replaced the panel with care and continued my search. I considered this a fact-finding mission. Like the LAPD detectives, my prime purpose was determining just why Mickey'd been shot. I didn't want to remove anything of his unless I had to. Better to leave the items undisturbed where possible.

At the end of thirty minutes, I'd uncovered three small recesses hollowed out behind the switch plates in the living room. Each contained a packet of identification papers: birth certificate, driver's license, social security card, credit cards, and currency. Emmett Vanover. Delbert Amburgey. Clyde Byler. None were names I recognized, and I assumed he'd invented them or borrowed them from deceased persons whose vitals he'd gleaned from public records. In every bogus document, Mickey's photo had been inserted. I left everything where it was and moved on. I'd also discovered that the back of the couch could be removed to reveal a space large enough to hide in. The paneling, while cheap, turned out to be securely fastened to the walls, but I did find tight rolls of crisp twenty-dollar bills tucked into either end of the big metal curtain rods in the living and dining rooms. A quick count suggested close to twelve hundred dollars.

In the bathroom, I removed a length of PVC, two inches in diameter, that had been set into the wall adjacent to the water lines. The pipe contained a handful of gold coins. Again, I left the stash where it was and carefully realigned the pipe in its original site. The only place I bombed out was one of his favorites, that being down the bathtub drain. He liked to drill a hole in the rubber stopper and run a chain up through the plug. He'd attach the relevant item to the chain, which he then left dangling down the drain with all the slimy hair and soap scum. This was usually where he kept his safe deposit key. I took a minute to lean over the rim of the tub. The rubber stopper was attached by a chain to the overflow outlet, but when I flashed the light into the drain itself, there was nothing hanging down the hole. Well, shoot. I consoled myself with the fact that I'd otherwise done well. Mickey probably had other secret repositories—maybe new ones I hadn't even thought about—but this was the best I could do in the time allotted. For now, it was time to clear the premises.

I let myself out the back door, using Mickey's key to lock the door behind me. I slipped the key in my pocket, stripped off my rubber gloves, and zipped them into my pack. I went downstairs and knocked at the manager's front door. I'd assumed that B & C Hatfield were a married couple, but the occupants turned out to be sisters. The woman who opened the door had to be in her eighties. "Yes?"

She was heavy through the middle, with a generously weighted bosom. She wore a sleeveless cotton sundress with most of the color washed away. The fabric reminded me of old quilts, a flour-sacking floral print in tones of pale blue and pink. Her breasts were pillowy, powdered with talcum, like two domes of bread dough proofing in a bowl. Her upper arms were soft, and I could see her stockings were rolled down below her knees. She wore slippers with a half-moon cut out of one to accommodate a bunion.

I said, "Mrs. Hatfield?"

"I'm Cordia," she said cautiously. "May I help you?"

"I hope so. I'd like to talk to you about Mickey Magruder, the tenant in Two-H."

She fixed me with a pair of watery blue eyes. "He was shot last week."

"I'm aware of that. I just came from the hospital, where I was visiting him."

"Are you the police detective?"

"I'm an old friend."

She stared at me, her blue eyes penetrating.

"Well, actually, I'm his ex-wife," I amended, in response to her gaze.

"I saw you park in the alley while I was sweeping out the laundry room."

I said, "Ah."

"Was everything in order?"

"Where?"

"Two-H. Mr. Magruder's place. You were up there quite a while. Thirty-two minutes by my watch."

"Fine. No problem. Of course, I didn't go in."

"No?"

"There was crime scene tape across the door," I said.

"Place was posted, too. Big police warning about the penalties."

"I saw that."

She waited. I would have continued, but my mind was blank. My thought process had shorted out, catching me in the space between truth and lies. I felt like an actor who'd forgotten her lines. I couldn't for the life of me think what to say next.

"Are you interested in renting?" she prompted.

"Renting?"

"Apartment Two-H. I assume that's why you went up."

"Oh. Oh, sure. Good plan. I like the area."

"You do. Well, perhaps we could let you know if the unit becomes available. Would you care to come in and complete an application? You seem discombobulated. Perhaps a drink of water?"

"I'd appreciate that."

I entered the apartment, stepping directly into the kitchen. I felt like I'd slipped into another world. Chicken was stewing on the back of the stove. A second woman, roughly the same age, sat at a round oak table with a deck of cards. To my right, I could see a formal dining room: mahogany table and chairs, with a matching hutch stacked with dishes. Clearly, the floor plan was entirely different from Mickey's. The temperature on the thermostat must have been set at 80, and the TV on the kitchen counter was blaring stock market quotes at top volume. Neither Cordia nor her sister seemed to be watching the screen. "I'll get you the application," she said. "This is my sister, Belmira."

"On second thought, why don't I take the application home with me? I can fill it out and send it back. It'll be simpler that way."

"Suit yourself. Have a seat."

I pulled out a chair and sat down across from Belmira, who was shuffling a tarot deck. Cordia went to the kitchen sink and let the faucet water run cold before she filled a glass. She handed me the water and then crossed to a kitchen drawer, where she extracted an application. She returned to her seat, handed me the paper, and picked up a length of multicolored knitting, six inches wide and at least fifteen inches long.

I took my time with the water. I made a study of the application, trying to compose myself. What was wrong with me? My career as a liar was being seriously undermined. Meanwhile, neither sister questioned my lingering presence.

Cordia said, "Belmira claims she's a witch, though you couldn't prove it by me." She peered toward the dining room. "Dorothy's around here someplace. Where'd she go, Bel? I haven't seen her for an hour."

"She's in the bathroom," Bel said, and turned to me. "I didn't catch your name, dear."

"Oh, sorry. I'm Kinsey. Nice meeting you."

"Nice to meet you, too." Her hair was sparse, a flyaway white with lots of pink scalp showing through. Under her dark print housedress, her shoulders were narrow and bony, her wrists as flat and thin as the handles on two soup ladles. "How're you today?" she asked shyly, as she pulled the tarot deck together. Four of her teeth were gold.

"I'm fine. What about yourself?"

"I'm real good." She plucked a card from the deck and held it up, showing me the face. "The Page of Swords. That's you."

Cordia said, "Bel."

"Well, it's true. This is the second time I pulled it. I shuffled the deck and drew this as soon as she stepped in, and then I drew it again."

"Well, draw something else. She's not interested."

I said, "Tell me about your names. Those are new to me."

Bel said, "Mother made ours up. There were six of us girls and she named us in alphabetical order: Amelia, Belmira, Cordia, Dorothy, Edith, and Faye. Cordi and I are the last two left."

"What about Dorothy?"

"She'll be along soon. She loves company."

Cordia said, "Bel will start telling your fortune any minute now. I'm warning you, once she gets on it, it's hard to get her off. Just ignore her. That's what I do. You don't have to worry about hurting her feelings."

"Yes, she does," Bel said feebly.

"Are you good at telling fortunes?"

Cordia cut in. "Not especially, but even a blind hog comes across an acorn now and then." She had taken up her knitting, which she held to the light, her head tilted slightly as the needles tucked in and out. The narrow piece of knitting trailed halfway down her front. "I'm making a knee wrap, in case you're wondering."

My Aunt Gin taught me to knit when I was six years old, probably to distract me in the early evening hours. She claimed it was a skill that fostered patience and eye–hand coordination. Now, as I watched, I could see that Cordia had dropped a few stitches about six rows back. The loops, like tiny sailors washed overboard, were receding in the wake of the knitting as each new row was added. I was about to mention it when a large white cat appeared in the doorway. She had a flat Persian face. She stopped when she saw me and stared in apparent wonderment. I'd seen a cat like that once before: long-haired, pure white, one green eye and one blue.

Bel smiled at the sight of her. "Here she is."

"That's Dorothy," Cordia said. "We call her Dort for short. Do you believe in reincarnation?"

"I've never sorted that one through."

"We hadn't either till this kitty came along. Dorothy always swore she'd be in touch with us from the Other Side. Told us for years, she'd find a way to come back. Then, lo and behold, the neighbor's cat had a litter the very day she passed on. This was the only female, and she looks just like Dort. The white hair, the one blue eye, the one green. Same personality, same behavior. Sociable, pushy, independent."

Bel chimed in. "The cat even passes wind the way Dorothy did. Silent but deadly. Sometimes we have to get up and leave the room."

I pointed to the knitting. "It looks like you dropped some stitches." I leaned forward and touched a finger to the errant loops. "If you have a crochet hook, I can coax them up the line for you."

"Would you? I'd like that. Your eyes are bound to be better than mine." Cordia bent over and reached into her knitting bag. "Let's see what I've got here. Will this do?" She offered me a J hook.

"That's perfect." While I began the slow task of working the dropped stitches up through the rows, the cat picked her way across the floor and jumped up in my lap. I jerked the knitting up and said, "Whoa!" Dorothy must have weighed twenty pounds. She turned her backside to me and stuck her tail in the air like a pump handle, exhibiting her little spigot while she marched in place.

"She never does that. I don't know what's got into her. She must like you," Belmira said, turning up cards as she spoke.

"I'm thrilled."

"Well, would you look at this? The Ten of Wands, reversed." Bel was laying out a reading. She placed the Ten of Wands with the other cards on the table in some mysterious configuration. The card she'd assigned me, the Page of Swords, had now been covered by the Moon.

I freed one hand and cranked Dorothy's tail down, securing it with my right arm as I pointed to the cards. "What's that one mean?" I thought the Moon might be good, but the sisters exchanged a look that made me think otherwise.

Cordia said, "I told you she'd do this."

"The Moon stands for hidden enemies, dear. Danger, darkness, and terror. Not too good."

"No kidding."

She pointed to a card. "The Ten of Wands, reversed, represents obstacles, difficulties, and intrigues. And this one, the Hanged Man, represents the best you can hope for."

"She doesn't want to hear that, Bel."

"I do. I can handle it."

"This card crowns you."

"What's that? I'm afraid to ask," I said.

"Oh, the Hanged Man is good. He represents wisdom, trials, sacrifice, intuition, divination, prophecy. This is what you want, but it isn't yours at present."

"She's trying to help with my knitting. You might at least leave her be until she finishes."

"I can do both," I said. Though, truthfully, Dorothy's presence was making the task difficult. The cat had rotated in my lap and now seemed intent on smelling my breath. She extended her nose daintily. I paused and breathed through my mouth for her. "What's that card?" I asked, while she butted my chin with her head.

"The Knight of Swords, which is placed at your feet. This is your own, what you have to work with. Skill, bravery, capacity, enmity, wrath, war, destruction."

"The wrath part sounds good."

"Not overall," Bel corrected. "Overall, you're screwed. You see this one? This card stands for pain, affliction, tears, sadness, desolation."

"Well, dang."

"Exactly. I'd say you're up poop creek without a roll of TP." Belmira turned up another card.

Dorothy climbed up on my chest, purring. She put her face in mine and we stared at each another. I glanced back at the tarot deck. Even I, believing none of this, could see the trouble I was in. Aside from the Hanged Man, there was a fellow burdened with heavy sticks, yet another fellow face down on the ground with ten swords protruding from his back. The card for Judgment didn't seem to bode well either, and then there was the Nine of Wands, which showed a cranky-looking man clinging to a staff, eight staves in a line behind him. That card was followed by a heart pierced with three swords, rain and clouds above.

By then, I'd succeeded in rescuing the lost stitches, and I reached around Dorothy to return the knitting to Cordia. I thought it was time to get down to business, so I asked Cordia what she could tell me about Mickey.

"I can't say I know all that much about him. He was extremely private. He worked as a bank guard until he lost his job in February. I used to see him going out in his uniform. He looked handsome, I must say."

"What happened?"

"About what?"

"How'd he lose his job?"

"He drank. You must have known that if you were married to him. Nine in the morning, he reeked of alcohol. I don't think he *drank* at that hour. This was left from the night before, fumes pouring through his skin. He never staggered, and I never once heard him slur his words. He wasn't loud or mean. He was always a gentleman, but he was losing ground."

"I'm sorry to hear that. I knew he drank, but it's hard to believe he reached a point where drinking interfered with his work. He was a cop in the old days when I was married to him."

"Is that right," she said.

"Was there anything else you could tell me about him?"

"He was quiet, no parties. Paid his rent on time until the last few months. No visitors except for the nasty fellow with all the chains."

I turned my attention from Dorothy. "Chains?"

"One of those motorcycle types: studs and black leather. He had a cowboy mentality, swaggered when he walked. Made so much noise it sounded like he was wearing spurs."

"What was that about?"

"I have no idea. Dort didn't like him. He was very rude. He knocked her sideways with his foot when she tried to smell his boot."

Bel said, "Oh, dear. This card represents the King of Cops . . . reversed again. That's not good."

I looked over with interest. "The King of Cops?"

"I didn't say cops, dear. I said Cups. The King of Cups stands for a dishonest, double-dealing man: roguery, vice, scandal, you name it."

Belatedly, I felt a flutter of uneasiness. "Speaking of which, what made you think I was a cop when I came to the door?"

Cordia looked up. "Because an officer called this morning and said a detective would be stopping by at two this afternoon. We thought it must be you since you were up there so long."

I felt my heart give a little hiccup, and I checked my watch. Nearly two o'clock now. "Gee, I better hit the road and let the two of you get back to work," I said. "Um, I wonder if you could do me a little favor. . . ."

Bel turned up the next card and said, "Don't worry about it, dear. We won't mention you were here."

"I'd appreciate that."

"I'll take you out the other door," Cordia said. "So you can reach the alley without being seen. The detectives park in the front . . . at least, they did before."

"Why don't I leave you a number? That way you can get in touch with me if anything comes up," I said. I jotted down my number on the back of my business card. In return, Cordia wrote their number on the edge of the rental application. Neither questioned my request. With a tarot like mine, they must have assumed I was going to need all the help I could get.

11

On the way home, I stopped off at McDonald's and bought myself a QP with cheese, an order of fries, and a medium Coke. Once I'd picked Dorothy's hair off my lip, I steered with one hand while I munched with the other, all the time moaning with pleasure. It's pitiful to have a life in which junk food is awarded the same high status as sex. Then again, I tend to get a lot more of the one than I do of the other. I was back in Santa Teresa by four-fifteen. The only message on my machine was from Mark Bethel, who'd finally returned my Monday-afternoon call at eleven-thirty Wednesday morning.

I dialed his number, taking a moment to unzip my jeans and remove Mickey's mail from my underpants. Naturally, Mark was out, so I ended up talking to Judy. "You almost caught him. He left fifteen minutes ago."

"Shoot. Well, I'm sorry I missed him. I just got back from Los Angeles. I have news about Mickey and I may need his help. I'm in for the afternoon. If he has a chance to call, I'd love to talk to him."

"I'm afraid he's gone for the day, Kinsey, but if you like you can catch him at seven tonight at the Lampara," she said, naming a downtown theater.

"Doing what?" I asked, though I had a fair idea. Mark Bethel was one of fourteen Republican candidates who'd be battling it out in the primary coming up on June 3, a scant twelve days off. I'd heard four of them had been invited to debate the issues at an event being sponsored by the League for Fair Government.

"This is a public debate: Robert Naylor, Mike Antonovich, Bobbi Fiedler, and Mark, talking about election issues."

"Sounds hot," I said, thinking, Who's kidding who? The California Secretary of State, March Fong Eu, was predicting the lowest voter turnout in forty-six years. Of the candidates Judy'd mentioned, only Mike Antonovich, the conservative L.A. County supervisor, had even a slim chance at winning. Naylor was an assemblyman from Menlo Park, the only Northern Californian in the race until Ed Zschau had stepped in. Zschau was the front-runner. Rumor had it that the *San Diego Union*, the *San Francisco Chronicle*, the *San Francisco Examiner*, and the *Contra Costa Times* were all coming out in support of him. Meanwhile, Bobbi Fiedler, a San Fernando Valley congresswoman and a seasoned politician, had had the rug pulled out from under her when a grand jury indicted her for allegedly bribing another candidate into leaving the race. The charges turned out to be groundless and had been dismissed, but her supporters had lost enthusiasm and she was having trouble recovering her momentum. As for Mark, this was his second fling at a statewide election, and he was busy pouring Laddie's money into TV spots in which he touted himself for running such a clean campaign. Like anyone gave a shit. The notion of sitting through some droning political debate was enough to put me in a coma of my own.

Meanwhile, Judy was saying, "Mark's been preparing for days, mostly on Prop Fifty-one. That's the Deep Pockets Initiative."

"Right."

"Also Props Forty-two and Forty-eight. He feels pretty strongly about those."

I said, "Hey, who wouldn't?" I pushed some papers around my desk, uncovering the sample ballot under the local paper and a pile of mail. Proposition 48 would put a lid on ex-officials' pensions. Yawn, snore. Prop 42 would authorize the state to issue $850 million in bonds to continue the Cal-Vet farm and home loan program. "I didn't know Mark was a veteran," I said, making conversation.

"Oh, sure, he enlisted in the army right after his college graduation. I'll send you a copy of his CV."

"You don't have to do that," I said.

"It's no trouble. I have a bunch of 'em going out in the mail. You know, he won a Purple Heart."

"Really, I had no idea."

While Judy nattered on, I found the comic section and read *Rex Morgan, M.D.*, which was at least as interesting. Judy interrupted herself, saying, "Shoot. There goes my other phone. I better catch that in case it's him."

"No problem."

As soon as I hung up, I propped my feet up on my desk and turned my attention to the mail I'd snitched. I picked up my letter opener and slit the envelopes. The bank statements showed regular paycheck deposits until late February, then nothing until late March, when he began to make small deposits at biweekly intervals. Unemployment benefits? I couldn't remember how that worked. There was probably a waiting period during which claims were processed and approved. In any event, the money he was depositing wasn't sufficient to cover his monthly expenses, and he was having to supplement the total out of his savings account. The current balance there was roughly $1,500. I'd found cash hidden on the premises, but no sign of his passbook. It would be nice to have that. I was surprised I hadn't come across it in my initial search. The monthly statements would have to do.

By comparing the activity in his savings and checking accounts, I could see the money jump from one to the other and then slide on out the door. Canceled checks indicated that he'd continued to pay as many bills as he could. His rent was $850 a month, which had last been paid March 1, according to the canceled check. Through the last half of February and the first three weeks of March, there were three checks made out to cash totaling $1,800. That seemed odd, given his financial difficulties, which were serious enough without pissing away his cash. The police probably had the April statement, so there was no way for me to tell if he'd paid rent on the first or not. My guess was that sometime in here he'd let his storage fees become delinquent.

By April, he was already in arrears on his telephone bill, and his service must have been cut before he had a chance to catch up. The cash he'd hidden probably represented a last resort, monies he was reluctant to spend unless his situation became desperate. Maybe his intent was to disappear, once all his other funds were depleted.

On the twenty-fifth of March, there was a one-time deposit of $900. I decided that was probably from the sale of his car. A couple of days later, on the twenty-seventh, there was a modest deposit of $200, which allowed him to pay his gas and electric bills. I did note that the $200 appeared the very day the call was made from his apartment to my machine. Someone paid him to use the phone? That would be weird. At any rate, he probably figured he could stall eviction for another month or two, at which point—what? He'd take his cash and phony documents and leave the state? Something about this gnawed at me. Mickey was a fanatic about savings. It was his contention that everyone should have a good six months' worth of income in the bank . . . or under the mattress, whichever seemed safer. He was such a nut on the subject, I'd made it a practice myself since then. He had to have another savings account somewhere. Had he put the money in a CD or a pension fund at his job? I wasn't even sure why he'd been fired. Was he drunk on duty? I sat and thought about that and then called directory assistance in Los Angeles and got the number for Pacific Coast Security in Culver City. I figured I had sufficient information to fake my way through. I knew his date of birth and his current address. His social security number would have been an asset, but all I remembered of it was the last four digits: 1776. Mickey always made a point about the numbers being the same as the year the Declaration of Independence was signed.

I dialed the number for Pacific Coast Security and listened to the phone ring, trying to figure out what I was going to say, surely not the truth in this case. When the call was picked up, I asked for Personnel. The woman who answered sounded like she was already halfway home for the day. It was close to five by now and she was probably in the process of clearing her desk. "This is Personnel. Mrs. Bird," she said.

"Oh, hi. This is Mrs. Weston in the billing department at UCLA Medical Center. We're calling with regard to a patient who's been admitted to ICU. We understand he's employed by Pacific Coast Security, and we're wondering if you can verify his insurance coverage."

"Certainly," she said. "The employee's name?"

"Last name Magruder. That's M-A-G-R-U-D-E-R. First name, Mickey. You may have him listed as Michael. Middle initial B. Home address 2805 Sepulveda Boulevard; date of birth, sixteen September 1933. Admitted through emergency on May fourteenth. We don't have a complete social security number, but we'd love to pick that up from you."

I could hear the woman breathing in my ear. "We heard about that. The poor man. Unfortunately, like I told the detectives, Mr. Magruder no longer works for us. He was terminated as of February twenty-eighth."

"Terminated as in fired?"

"That's right."

"Well, for heaven's sake. What for?"

She paused. "I'm not at liberty to discuss that, but it had to do with d-r-i-n-k-i-n-g."

"That's too bad. What about his medical insurance? Is there any possibility his coverage was extended?"

"Not according to our records."

"Well, that's odd. He had an insurance card in his wallet when he was brought in, and we were under the impression his coverage was current. Is he employed by any other company in the area?"

"I doubt it. We haven't been asked for references."

"What about Unemployment. Has he applied for benefits? Because he may qualify for medical under SDI." Yeah, right, SDI. Like we were all so casual about State Disability Insurance we didn't even need to spell it out.

"I really can't answer that. You'd have to check with them."

"What about money in his pension fund? Did he have automatic debits to his savings out of each paycheck?"

"I don't see where that's relevant," she said. She was beginning to sound uneasy, probably wondering if this was a ruse of some kind.

"You would if you saw the way his bill was mounting up," I said tartly.

"I'm afraid I can't discuss it. Especially with the police involved. They made a big point of that. We're not supposed to talk to anyone about anything when it comes to him."

"Same here. We've been asked to notify Detective Aldo if anyone even asks for his room."

"Really? They didn't say anything like that to us. Maybe because he hadn't worked here for so long."

"Consider yourself lucky. We're on red alert. Did you know Mr. Magruder personally?"

"Sure. The company's not all that big."

"You must feel terrible."

"I do. He's a real sweet guy. I can't imagine why anyone would want to do that to him."

"Awful," I said. "What about his social security number? We have the last four digits . . . 1776 . . . but the emergency room clerk couldn't understand what he was saying so she missed the first portion. All I need are the first five digits for our records. The director's a real stickler."

She seemed startled. "He was conscious?"

"Oh. Well, I don't know, now you mention it. He must have been, at least briefly. How else would we have this much?" I sensed her debate. "It's in his best interest," I added piously.

"Just a minute." I heard her clicking her computer keys, and after a moment she read off the first five digits.

I made a note. "Thanks. You're a doll. I appreciate that."

There was a pause, and then her curiosity got the better of her. "How's he doing?"

"I'm sorry, but I'm not allowed to divulge that information. You'd have to ask the medical staff. I'm sure you can appreciate the confidentiality of these matters, especially here at UCLA."

"Of course. Absolutely. Well, I hope he's okay. Tell him Ingrid said hi."

"I'll pass the word."

Once she'd hung up, I opened my desk drawer and took out a fresh pack of lined index cards. Time for clerical work. I began jotting down notes, writing as fast as I could, one item per card, piling them up as I went. I had a lot of catching up to do, days of accumulated questions. I knew some of the answers, but most of the lines I was forced to leave blank. I used to imagine I could hold it all in my head, but memory has a way of pruning and deleting, eliminating anything that doesn't seem relevant at the moment. Later, it's the odd unrelated detail that sometimes makes the puzzle parts rearrange themselves like magic. The very act of taking pen to paper somehow gooses the brain into making the leap. It doesn't always happen in the moment, but without the concrete notation, the data disappear.

I checked my watch. It was 6:05 and I was so cockeyed with weariness my clothes had begun to hurt. I turned the ringer off the phone, went up the spiral stairs, stripped, kicked my shoes off, wrapped myself in a quilt, and slept.

I woke at 9:15 P.M., though it felt like midnight. I sat up in bed, yawning, and tried to get my bearings. I felt weighted with weariness. I pushed the covers aside and went over to the railing. Below, on my desk, I could see the light on my answering machine blinking merrily.

Shit. If not for that, I'd have crawled back in bed and slept through till morning.

I pulled a robe on and picked my way down the stairs barefoot. I pressed PLAY and listened to a message from Cordia Hatfield, the manager of Mickey's building. "Kinsey, I wonder if you could give us a call when you come in. There's something we think you should be aware of."

She'd called at 8:45, so I felt it was probably safe to return the call. I dialed the number, and Cordia picked up before I'd even heard the phone ring once. "Hello?"

"Cordia, is that you? This is Kinsey Millhone up in Santa Teresa. The phone didn't even ring."

"Well, it did down here. Listen, dear, the reason I called is that detective stopped by shortly after you left. He spent quite a bit of time up Two-H, and when he finished he came right here. He seemed perturbed, and he asked if anyone had gone in. We played dumb. He was quite insistent, but neither of us breathed a word."

"Ah. Was this the tall dark guy, Detective Aldo?"

"That's the one. We're old. What do we know, with all our brain cells gone? We didn't *lie* to him exactly, but I'm afraid we did skirt the truth a bit. I told him I was perfectly capable of taking in rent checks and calling the plumber if a toilet backed up, but I don't go skulking around, spying on the tenants. What they do is their business. Then I showed him my foot and told him, 'With this bunion, I'm lucky to get around. I can't be tromping up and down.' He changed the subject after that."

"What set him off?"

"He said something was missing, though he wouldn't say what. He had a boxload of items with him and told me he'd removed the crime tape. 'For all the good it did,' is how he put it. He was sour on the subject, I can tell you that."

"Thanks for the warning."

"You're entirely welcome. Main reason I called is you're free to enter the apartment, but it won't be long. The owners are pressing to get Mr. Magruder out of there. I guess the detective notified the management company, so they know he's in a coma. They snapped right to it, taking advantage of his condition. Shame on them. Anyway, if you're interested in *renting*, you should take a look."

"I may do that. I'd like that. When would be good?"

"The sooner the better. You're only two hours away."

"You're talking about *tonight*?"

"I think you'd be smart. The owners have already served him with a three-day pay or quit, so technically the sheriff could have a new lock on the door by tomorrow morning."

"Can't we do something to prevent that?"

"Not as far as I know."

"What if I pay what he owes, plus the next month's rent? Wouldn't that cancel the action?"

"I doubt it. Once a tenant starts paying late or doesn't pay at all, the owners would just as soon clear the place out and get someone else in."

I thought about the drive, rolling my eyes with dismay. "I wish I'd known this when I was down there earlier."

"If you're coming, you best hurry. It's entirely up to you, of course."

"Cordia, it's already close to nine-thirty. If I come down tonight, I'd still have to pack and get gas, which means I probably won't arrive before midnight." I didn't mention I was close to naked.

"That's not late for us. Bel and I only need four hours sleep, so we're up till all hours. The advantage in coming now is you'd have all the time you want and not a soul to disturb you."

"Mickey's neighbors won't notice if his lights are on?"

"Nobody pays attention. Most of these folk work so they're usually in bed by ten. And if it gets too late, you can always spend the night with us. We have the only three-bedroom unit in the building. The guest room is really Dort's, but I'm sure she wouldn't mind the company. We had quite a little chat about you after you left."

I let go of my resistance and took a deep breath. "All right. I'll do it. See you in a bit."

I changed into my jeans, turtleneck, and tennis shoes, which were light and silent, good for late-night work. At least I'd been inside Mickey's place and knew what to expect. I still had the key I'd removed from his back door, but I intended to take my pick in case the need arose. Since I had no intention of driving home in the wee hours of the morning, I got out my duffel and threw in the oversized T-shirt I wear as a nightie. I routinely carry a toothbrush, toothpaste, and fresh underwear in the bottom of my shoulder bag. The remainder of the space in the duffel I filled with tools: rubber gloves, my battery-operated pick, drill and drill bits, screwdriver, lightbulbs, pliers, needle-nose pliers, magnifying glass, and dental mirror, along with two flashlights, one standard and one on a long stem that could be angled for viewing those hard-to-reach places Mickey loved so much. I suspected I'd uncovered the majority of his hiding places, but I didn't want to take the chance, especially since this represented my last opportunity to snoop. I also took a second canvas duffel bag, folded and placed inside the first. I now planned to confiscate Mickey's contraband and hold it at my place until he could let me know what he wanted done with it.

I stopped at a service station to have my gas tank filled. While the guy cleaned the windshield and checked the oil, I popped into the "refreshment center" and bought myself a big nasty sandwich—cheese and mystery meat—and a large Styrofoam container of coffee that smelled only faintly scorched. I bought a separate carton of milk, poured out some of the black liquid, and refilled the cup to the brim with milk, then added two paper packets of sugar just to make sure my brain would be properly abuzz.

I was on my way by ten past ten, the VW windows rolled down, the engine whining with the effort of maintaining a constant 60 mph. I ate as I drove and somehow avoided spilling coffee down my front. There were a surprising number of cars on the road, interspersed with semis and RVs, all of us traveling at breakneck speeds. The sense of urgency was multiplied by the darkness that encompassed us, headlights and taillights forming ever-shifting patterns. In the stretch between Santa Teresa and Olvidado, the moon sat above the water like an alabaster globe resting on a pyramid of light. Along the shoreline, the waves were like loosely churning pearls tumbling through the surf. The ancient scent of seaweed drifted in the night air like a mist. Seaside communities appeared and disappeared as the miles accumulated. Hillsides, visible in the distance by day, were reduced to pinpoints of light that wound along the slopes.

I crested the Camarillo grade and coasted down the far side into the westernmost perimeter of the San Fernando Valley. There were no stars in sight. The Los Angeles light pollution gave the night sky a ghostly illumination, like an aurora borealis underlaid by smog. I cut south on the 405 as far as National, took the off-ramp and headed east. At Sepulveda, I hung a left and slowed, finally spotting Mickey's building in the unfamiliar night landscape. I parked out on the street, taking my shoulder bag and duffel. I locked the car behind me and prayed that the chassis, the wheels, and the engine wouldn't be dismantled and gone by morning.

The lights were on in the Hatfields' kitchen. I tapped at the door, and Cordia let me in. Bel was sleeping upright in her chair, so Cordia and I had a whispered conversation while she showed me the guest room with its adjoining bath. Dorothy followed like a puppy-cat, making sure she was in the center of any ongoing discussion. I had to pause more than once to rub behind her ears. I tossed my shoulder bag on the bed. Dorothy promptly claimed ownership, using all twenty pounds to squish and flatten the contents. The last I saw, she had settled like a chicken on a nestful of eggs.

12

I went up the front stairs and along the gallery, lighting my way with the larger of my flashlights. The two apartments I passed were shrouded in darkness, the sliding glass windows open into what I was guessing were bedrooms. I continued around the corner, where I let myself into Mickey's back door, using the key I'd lifted. I debated about leaving the door locked or unlocked and decided to leave it locked. Ordinarily, I'd have opted to leave the door ajar in case I had to make a hasty exit, but I was feeling anxious and didn't like the possibility of someone coming in on me unheard. I moved through the apartment to the living room. The only light was a thin shaft coming in from the gallery between drapery panels in the dining L. I shone the flashlight beam like a sword, cutting through the shadows. Since I'd been here earlier, the fingerprint technician had been busy with his brushes, leaving powder residue on countless surfaces. I made a quick foray through the dining area and kitchen, then back through the bedroom and bathroom to make sure I was alone.

I returned to the living room and secured the openings between the drapes. I pulled on my rubber gloves. Despite the fact the cops had come and gone, I didn't want to leave evidence that I'd been in the place. I like to think I'd learned something from my little trip through Ted Rich's doggie door. I turned on the overhead light, pausing to swap Mickey's 60-watt bulb for one of the 200-watt bulbs I'd brought with me. Even a cursory glance showed Detective Aldo had been there. Kitchen cabinets stood open. All the mail was missing, and the fishbowl full of matches had been upended on the dining room table. I pictured the police sorting through the collection for clues, carefully making notes about the bars and restaurants Mickey'd frequented. In truth, only about half the matchbooks would be from places he'd been. The rest were packets other people had acquired for him while traveling, a practice left over from his youth, when he'd assembled hundreds of such covers and mounted them in albums. Who knows why kids like to do shit like that?

I got down to work, methodically emptying the miniature safes he'd created behind the electrical plates. The three sets of phony IDs, the credit cards, and the currency went into my duffel. I spent a long time in his kitchen, sorting through containers with a fine-tooth comb, checking in and behind and under drawers. Once again, I removed the five-gallon water bottles from under the sink and unscrewed the back panel. This time I lifted out the handguns from the rack he'd built and put them in my duffel with the IDs.

I went into the bedroom and took the chenille bedspread and sheets off his bed. Tacky little thing that I am, I paused to check for evidence of recent sexual excess but found none. I pulled off the mattress and checked it carefully, looking for evidence that he'd opened a seam and restitched it. Good theory; no deal. I lay on my back and hunched my way under the bed, where I peeled back the gauzy material that covered the bottom of his box spring. I shone the flashlight across the underside, but no dice. I put the mattress back in place and then remade the bed. This was worse than hotel work, which I'd also done in my day.

I crawled the entire perimeter of wall-to-wall carpeting, pulling up section after section without finding much except a centipede that scared the hell out of me. I tried the bed-table drawer. The diaphragm was gone, as were the bottle of cologne and the tissue paper packet with the enameled heart and gold chain. Well, well, well. His latest inamorata must have heard about the shooting. She was certainly quick to erase the signs of their relationship. She must've had a key of her own, letting herself in sometime between my initial visit and this one. Could she be someone in the building? That was a notion worth exploring.

I spent a good thirty minutes in the bathroom, where I lifted the lid to the toilet tank and used my dental mirror and the angled flashlight to check for items concealed behind it. Nothing. I took all the toiletries out of the medicine cabinet and lifted the entire cabinet off the wall brackets to see if he'd hollowed out a space in the wall behind it. Nope. I checked inside the shower rod, checked the cheap-looking vanity for false fronts or concealed panels. I unscrewed the heater vent and tapped along the baseboards listening for hollow spots. I removed the PVC under the bathroom sink. The gold coins were still there. I loaded those in my duffel and replaced the length of pipe. No telling what the next tenant would make of it if the fake plumbing were discovered at some future date. In the hollow core of the toilet paper roll I found a hundred-dollar bill.

I went through his closet, checking his pockets, looking behind the hanging row of clothes for the possibility of a false wall at the rear. Nothing. The numerous zippered pockets in the black leather jacket were all empty. At the back of the closet, I found his answering machine, which he'd probably unplugged once his phone service was "disconnected or no longer in service." I opened the lid, but the cops had apparently taken the tape. I found one additional stash behind the closet switch plate. In a narrow slot that ran back along a stud, Mickey'd tucked a sealed number-ten envelope. I put it in my duffel for later scrutiny.

I had one other cache to unload that I'd saved until last. I went back into the living room and turned off the overhead light. I moved from window to window, looking out at the dark. It was two-thirty in the morning and, for the most part, windows in neighboring buildings were black. Occasionally I would see a light on, but the drapes would be drawn and no one was peeking through the slit. I picked up no movement in the immediate vicinity. Traffic noises had all but died.

I unhooked the two sets of drapes and lifted down the rods. I removed the finials, flashed a light down into the hollow core, and removed the cash. I replaced the rods and rehung the drapes, moving with a sudden sense of anxiety. I lifted my head. Had I heard something? Maybe the removal of the crime tape was done to tempt me, and Detective Aldo was outside waiting. He'd be thrilled to catch me with the duffel load of burglar tools, the handguns, and the phony documents. I kept the overhead light off, restricting myself to the use of my penlight as I went through the apartment, quickly gathering my tools, checking to see that I'd left no personal traces. The whole time I had the feeling I'd overlooked something obvious, but I knew I'd be pushing my luck to go back and try to figure it out. I was so focused on escape that I came close to missing the crunch of cinders and the putter of a motorcycle as it glided to a stop in the alleyway below.

Belatedly, I realized I'd picked up the muted roar as the motorcycle passed along the street out in front. The rider must have cut the switch at the entrance to the alley, coasting the rest of the way. I went over to the rear window and opened the drapes a crack. From that angle, I couldn't see much, but I was relatively certain someone was moving along the alley. I closed my eyes and listened. Within thirty seconds, I could hear the chink of boots on the stair treads, accompanied by a jingle as each step was mounted. The guy was coming up the back way. Possibly a tenant or a neighbor. I turned off my flashlight and followed the sounds of the guy's progress as he rounded the gallery along the back of the building and came up to Mickey's front door. I had hoped to hear him pass. Instead, I heard a tap and a hoarse whispering. "Hey, Mr. Magruder. Open up. It's me."

I passed through Mickey's bedroom and headed for the rear door, fumbling in my jeans pocket for the key. My hand was steady, but every other part of me was shaking so hard I couldn't hit the keyhole. I was afraid to use my flashlight because the guy had now moved to Mickey's bedroom window, where the tapping became sharper, a harsh clicking as though he might be rapping on the glass with a ring. "Open the fuck up and get your ass out here." He had moved the few steps to the front door, where he began to knock again. This time, the pounding was of the fee-fi-fo-fum variety and seemed to shake the intervening walls.

The next-door neighbor, whose bedroom must have been contiguous with Mickey's, yelled out his window, "Shaddup, you prick! We're tryin' to sleep in here."

The guy at the door said something even worse than the F word, which I won't repeat. I could hear him jingle his way toward the neighbor's bedroom window, where I pictured him bashing through the glass with his fist. Sure enough, I heard the impact of his blow and the subsequent tinkling of glass, followed by a startled yelp from the tenant. I took advantage of this tender Hallmark moment to shine a quick light on the keyhole. I turned the key in the lock and was almost out the door when I stopped in my tracks. I'd never get into this apartment again. By morning the sheriff's deputy would arrive and the locks would be changed. While I could probably pick my way in, I didn't want to take the risk. Now that all the stashes had been cleaned out, there was only one thing of value. I set down the two duffels and returned to Mickey's closet, where I lifted the leather jacket from its hanger and shrugged myself into it, then grabbed the two duffels and eased out the back door, barely pausing long enough to lock it.

I was halfway down the back stairs when a face appeared above me. Over the wrought-iron railing, I saw shaggy corn-yellow hair, a long bony face, narrow shoulders, and a sunken chest in a blue denim jacket with the sleeves cut out. I slung one duffel over my shoulder, hugged the other to my body, and began to bound down the stairs, taking them two at a time while the guy in the jacket strode toward the landing. I reached the bottom of the stairs at the same moment he started down. I could hear every step he took because of the jingling of his boots, which must have been decorated with chains. I ran on tiptoe, keeping wide on the outside, conscious to avoid knocking into the water meters near the building.

The manager's apartment was fully dark by now, but Cordia, as promised, had left the back door unlocked. I turned the knob and opened the door to let myself in. My entrance was delayed briefly when the duffel over my shoulder got hung up on the door frame. I jerked it free and flung both duffels into the room. I was just turning to close the door when Dorothy streaked out through the narrow opening. She must have come running to see what I was up to and then couldn't resist making a bid for freedom. Once out, she stopped, astonished to find herself alone in the chilly dark at that hour. I heard a thumping noise and a resounding curse. The guy must have caught a foot on a water meter and gone down sprawling. I could hear him cussing as he recovered his gait and came limping down on us in a towering rage. If he caught up with Dorothy, he was going to wring her neck and fling her over the fence, thus forcing her return to this life in some other form. I grabbed her by the tail and dragged her backward while she struggled to gain purchase on the concrete with her outstretched claws. I hauled her, squawking, into the dark of the kitchen, closed the door, and bolted it in one motion.

I sank down on the floor, clutching her against me while my heart kept on banging and my breath came in gasps. I heard the jingling footsteps approach and come to a halt outside the Hatfields' door. The guy kicked the door hard enough to hurt himself. He must have had a flashlight with him, because a beam was soon being played across the far wall, briefly raking the kitchen table. The wand of light streaked back and forth. At one point, I could tell he'd angled up on tiptoe, trying to shine the light down into the darkened area where I was crouched. Meanwhile, Dorothy strained against my embrace and finally manage to wiggle free. I lunged, but she eluded me. She gave me a cranky look and then made a point of sashaying toward the dining room so that her path took her directly through his beam of light. There was a long, labored silence. I thought he'd break the door down, but he must have thought better of it. Finally, I heard the scritch and jingle of his boots as they receded along the walkway.

I slumped against the door, waiting to hear his motorcycle start up and go screaming away in the night. There was no such reassuring sound. I finally staggered to my feet, retrieved the two duffels, and crept through the dining room toward the guest room. The nightlight in the hallway illuminated my way. The two other bedroom doors were closed, Cordia and Belmira having slept through the uproar in the enveloping silence of poor hearing. Once in the guest room, I kicked my shoes off and lay down on the bed, still wearing Mickey's jacket. Dorothy was already on the bed. The pillow turned out to be hers so I wasn't allowed the full use of it, just a few paltry inches around the edges. The still-indignant cat now felt compelled to wash from head to toe, comforting herself after the insult of having her tail pulled so rudely. The bedroom curtains were closed, but I found myself staring at them, fearful a fist would come smashing through the glass. Dorothy's steady licking took on a restful quality. The warmth of my body activated Mickey's personal scent from the lining of the jacket. Cigarette smoke and Aqua Velva. I stopped shivering and eventually fell asleep with Dorothy's feet resting neatly in my hair.

I woke to the smell of coffee. I was still wearing Mickey's jacket, but someone had placed a heavy afghan across my legs. I put a hand above my head, feeling across the pillow, but Dorothy was gone. The door was open a crack. Sunlight made the curtains glow. I looked at my watch and saw that it was close to eight. I put my feet over the side of the bed and ran a hand through my hair, yawning. I was getting too old to horse around at all hours of the night. I went into the bathroom and brushed my teeth, then showered and dressed again. In the end, I looked much as I had when I'd arrived.

Belmira was sitting at the kitchen table, watching a talk show, when I finally made my appearance. She was a tiny thing, quite thin, so short her feet barely touched the floor. Today, she wore a white bib apron over a red-and-white print housedress. She was shelling peas, the colander in her lap, a paper bag sitting next to her with the rim folded back. Dorothy was on the counter licking butter from the butter dish.

Bel smiled at me shyly. "Coffee's over there," she said. "The sheriff's deputy just arrived with the locksmith, so Cordia went upstairs to let them in. Did you sleep well?"

"I didn't get enough of it, but what I had was fine." I crossed to the coffeepot, an old-fashioned percolator sitting on the stove. There was a mug on the counter, along with a carton of milk. I poured a cup of coffee and added milk.

"Would you like to have an egg? We have cereal, too. Cordi made some oatmeal with raisins. That's what we have. Brown sugar's in the canister if you want to help yourself."

"I think I better go on up and see if I can catch Mickey's neighbors before they go off to work. I can always have breakfast once the deputy's gone." At the door, I looked back. "Did she say anything about a motorcycle parked in the alley?"

Belmira shook her head.

I took my coffee mug with me and headed for the stairs. I could see the sheriff's patrol car parked at the curb, not far from my VW, which as far as I could tell was still intact. The day was sunny and cool, the air already fragrant with the morning's accumulation of exhaust fumes. I passed along the second-floor gallery. A few neighbors had gathered to watch the locksmith at work. Maybe for them, this was a cautionary tale about paying the rent on time. Most seemed dressed for work except for one woman in her robe and slippers, who'd also brought her morning coffee with her. Like rubberneckers passing a highway accident, they looked on, both repelled and attracted by the sight of someone else's misfortune. This was all faintly reminiscent of the fires that burned across the Santa Teresa foothills back in 1964. During the long smoky evenings, people had gathered on the street in clusters, sipping beer and chatting while the flames danced across the distant mountains. The presence of catastrophe seemed to break down the usual social barriers until the atmosphere was nearly festive.

Cordia Hatfield was keeping a careful eye on the situation, standing in the open doorway with a white sweater thrown over her shoulders. Her oversized blue-and-white checked housedress was worn ankle-length, and she sported the same pair of slippers with her bunion peeking out. She turned as I approached. "I see you found the coffee. How'd you sleep last night?"

"Dorothy was stingy with the pillow, but aside from that I did great."

"She was never one to share. Even when she came back, she insisted on having her old room. We were going to keep it closed up for guests, but she refused to use the litter box until she got her way."

Mickey's immediate neighbor, who appeared to be somewhere in his forties, emerged from his apartment, pulling on a tweed sport coat over a royal-blue Superman T-shirt. His shiny brown hair extended to his waist. He wore large metal-framed glasses with yellow lenses. A mustache and a closely trimmed beard bracketed a full complement of white teeth. His jeans were ripped and faded, and his cowboy boots had three-inch platform soles. Behind him, I could see the broken bedroom window, patched together now with cardboard and a jagged bolt of silver duct tape. He said, "Hey, Ms. Hatfield. How are you today?"

She said, "Morning. Just dandy. What happened to your window? That'll have to be repaired."

"Sorry about that. I'll take care of it. I called a glass company on Olympic, and they said they'd be out to take a look. Has Mickey been evicted?"

"I'm afraid so," she said.

The deputy clearly wasn't needed, so he returned to his car and went about his business. The locksmith beckoned to Cordia. She excused herself, and the two of them moved inside to have a consultation. The next-door neighbor had paused to watch the proceedings and he now greeted a couple who came out of the third apartment on that side. Both were dressed for work. The woman murmured something to her husband and the two continued toward the stairs. Mickey's neighbor nodded politely in my direction, acknowledging my presence.

I murmured, "Hi, how're you?"

"Good, thanks. What kind of crap is this? This dude's in a coma and they're changing the locks on him?"

"I guess the owners are pretty hard-nosed."

"They'd have to be," he said. "So how's Mickey doing? You a friend of his?"

"You could say that, I guess. We used to be married."

"No shit. When was this?"

"Early seventies. It didn't last long. I'm Kinsey, by the way. And you're . . ."

"Ware Beason," he said. "Everybody calls me Wary." He was still working to absorb the information about my marital connection to Mickey. "An ex-wife? How cool. Mickey never said a word."

"We haven't kept in touch. What about you? Have you known him long?"

"He's lived in that apartment close to fifteen years. I've been here six. Now and then I run into him at Lionel's Pub and we have a few beers. He feeds my fish if we have a gig someplace."

"You're a professional musician?"

Wary shrugged self-consciously. "I play keyboard in a combo. Mostly weekends here locally, though I sometimes play out of town as well. I also wait tables at a health food café down on National. I take it you heard about what happened?"

"I did, but it was purely by accident. I didn't even know he was in trouble until earlier this week. I'm from Santa Teresa. I tried calling from up there, but his phone was disconnected. I didn't think too much of it until a couple of detectives showed up and said he'd been shot. I was horrified."

"Yeah, me too. I guess it took 'em a while to figure out who he was. They showed up at my door about seven A.M. Monday. Big dark-haired guy?"

"Right. He's the one I talked to. I thought I better head on down in case there was something I could do."

"So how's he feeling? Have you seen him?"

"He's still in a coma so it's hard to say. I went over there yesterday and he didn't look too good."

"Damn. That's a shame. I should probably go myself, but I've been putting it off."

"Don't even bother unless you notify the cops. You can only visit with their permission, and then they keep someone with you in case you try to pull the plug."

"Jeez. Poor guy. I can't believe it."

"Me neither," I said. "By the way, what was that bunch of hollering last night? Did you hear it? It sounded like somebody went berserk and started banging on the walls."

"Hey, no shit. That was me he was yelling at. And look what he did, bashed his fist through the glass. I thought he'd dive in after me, but he took off."

"What was he so mad about?"

"Who knows? He's some pal of Mickey's; at least, he acts that way. Mickey never seemed that glad to see him."

"How often did he show up?"

"Every couple of weeks. They must've had some kind of deal going, but I can't think what."

"How long has that gone on?"

"Maybe two–three months. I should probably put it this way: I never saw him before then."

"You know his name?"

Wary shook his head. "Nope. Mickey never introduced us. He seemed embarrassed to be seen with him, and who wouldn't be?"

"No shit."

"Guy's a scuzball, a real sleaze. Every time I see that show about America's Most Wanted, I start lookin' for his face."

"Literally? You think he's wanted by the cops?"

"If he's not, he will be. What a creep."

"That's odd. Mickey always hated lowlifes. He used to be a vice detective. We worked for the same department up in Santa Teresa."

"You're a cop too?"

"I was. Now I work as a P.I."

"A private investigator."

"That's right."

"Oh, I get it. You're looking into this."

"Not officially, no, but I *am* curious."

"Hey, I'm with you. Anything I can do to help, you just say."

"Thanks. What about the scuzball? Couldn't he be the one who shot Mickey? He sounds like a nut to me."

"Nah, I doubt it. If he did, he wouldn't come around pounding on the door, thinking Mickey'd be there. Guy who shot Mickey must have figured he was dead." Wary glanced at his watch. "I better get a move on. How long you going to be here?"

"I'm not sure. Another hour, I'd guess."

"Can I buy you breakfast? That's where I'm heading. There's a place around the corner. Wouldn't take more'n thirty minutes if you have to get back."

I did a quick debate. I hated to leave the premises, but there really wasn't anything more to do. Wary might prove to be useful. More important, I was starving. I said "sure" and then took a brief time-out to let Cordia know where I was going.

Wary and I headed down the front stairs, chatting as we went. Idly, he said, "If you want, after breakfast, I'll show you where he was shot. It's just a couple blocks away."

13

I'll skip the breakfast conversation. There's nothing so boring as listening to other people get acquainted. We chatted. We traded brief, heavily edited autobiographical sketches, stories about Mickey, theories about the motive for the shooting. In the meantime, I discovered that I liked Wary Beason, though I promptly erased all his personal data. As crass as it sounds, I didn't seriously think I'd ever see him again. Like the passenger sitting next to you on a cross-country plane ride, it's possible to connect with someone, even when the encounter has no meaning and no ultimate consequence.

I did appreciate his showing me the spot where Mickey was gunned down, a nondescript section of sidewalk in front of a coin and jewelry shop. The sign in the window advertised rare coins, rare stamps, pocket watches, antiques, and coin supplies. "We also make low-rate loans," the sign said. At 3 A.M. I didn't think Mickey'd been there to negotiate a loan.

Wary remained silent while I stood for a minute, looking out at the surrounding businesses. There was a pool hall across the street. I assumed the detectives had checked it out. Also the bar called McNalley's, half a block down.

"You mentioned you used to drink with Mickey at Lionel's. Is the pub close by?"

"Back in that direction," Wary said, gesturing.

"Any chance Mickey could have been there earlier that night?"

"No way. Mickey'd been eighty-sixed from Lionel's until he paid his tab." Wary took off his glasses and cleaned the yellow lenses on the hem of his T-shirt. He held his frames to the light so he could check for streaks, and then he put his glasses on again and waited to see what I would ask next.

"Where was he, then? You have a guess?"

"Well, he wasn't at McNalley's, because that's where I was. I know the cops checked the bars all up and down the street. They didn't learn a thing . . . or so they said."

"He was out doing something, and he was doing it on foot."

"Not necessarily. I mean, just because he'd sold his car doesn't mean he hoofed it. Somebody could've picked him up and taken him somewhere. Out for drinks or dinner. Could have been anyplace."

"Back up a minute. Do you happen to remember when he sold his car?"

"Couple of months back."

"You're talking about the end of March?"

"That sounds right. Anyway, the point is, nobody even saw him leave the building that night."

"So what's your theory?"

"Well, let's just say for the sake of argument he was in someone else's car. They go out for dinner or drinks and end up closing the place down. Two in the morning, they drive back to Culver City. He—"

"Or she," I inserted, promptly.

Wary smiled. "Right. . . . The shooter could have dropped Mickey at the corner and then driven down a block like he's on his way home. Shooter parks, waits in the dark while Mickey walks the intervening block. Minute he comes abreast, the shooter steps out and—*boom!*—plugs him twice. Shooter tosses the gun and takes off before anybody figures out what's up."

"You really think it happened like that?"

Wary shrugged. "It could have, that's all I'm saying. The cops canvassed all the bars and pool halls within a ten-block radius. Mickey hadn't been in any of 'em, but they know he'd been drinking *somewhere* because he had a blood alcohol of point one four."

"How'd you hear that?"

"The detective, the dark one, mentioned it in passing."

"Really. That's interesting. What'd they make of it, did anybody say?"

"No, and I didn't think to ask. Mickey always had a buzz on. He was probably pushing point one any given day of the week."

"He was legally drunk?"

"Legally plastered is a better way to put it. For a while, he straightened up. He went on the wagon, but it didn't last long. February he went on a bender, and I guess that's when he got himself fired from his job. He tried to straighten up again, after that, but without much success. He'd go a couple days and then fall right back. I give him credit. He did try. He just wasn't strong enough to do it by himself."

I was suddenly feeling restless and needed to move. I started walking again and Wary followed, catching up with me. I said, "What about the woman he was seeing?"

He gave me an odd look, equal parts surprise and embarrassment. "How'd you know about her?"

I tapped my temple. "A little birdie told me. You know who she was?"

"Nope. Never met her. Mickey made sure."

"How come?"

"Maybe he thought I'd try to hustle her myself."

"Did you actually see her?"

"In passing. Not to recognize later. She always came up the back stairs and let herself in that way."

"She had her own key?"

"She must have. Mickey never left his doors unlocked. Some days she showed up before he got home from work."

"What about her car? Did you ever see a vehicle parked out back?"

"Never looked. I figured it was his business. Why should I butt in?"

"How often was she there?"

"I'd say every two to three weeks. Not to be gross about it, but the walls in the building are not exactly soundproof. I have to say Mickey's alcohol intake never seemed to hamper him in the performance of his duties."

"How do you know it was him? Isn't there a chance he lent his apartment to someone else? Maybe he had a friend who needed a place to misbehave."

"Oh, no. It was him. I'd take an oath on that. He's been involved with this woman for at least a year."

"How do you know there was only one? He might have had a string of women."

"Well, it's possible, I guess."

"Any chance she lived in the building?" I asked.

"In *our* building? I doubt it. Mickey would've felt hemmed in by anybody living that close. He liked his freedom. He didn't like anybody checking up on him. Like sometimes—say, he was gone for the weekend—I might ask him, you know, How's the weekend, where'd you end up? Simple shit like that. Mickey wouldn't answer questions. If you pressed, he changed the subject."

"What about since the shooting? Do you think the woman's been there?"

"I really couldn't say for sure. I go to work at four and don't get home till after midnight. She could have gone in while I was off. Actually, come to think of it, I thought I heard her yesterday. Again last night, too, before that biker geek showed up. What an asshole. Glass company says it'll cost me a hundred bucks to get that fixed."

"Wary, that was me you heard last night. I went in and pulled his personal belongings before they had a chance to change the locks. I suspected his girlfriend'd been there, because a couple of personal articles I'd seen suddenly came up missing."

We'd reached the building by then. It was time to hit the road. I thanked him for his help. I made a note of his phone number and then gave him my business card with my home number jotted on the back. We parted company at the stairs.

I watched Wary go up, and then I went back to the Hatfields to collect the two duffels. They invited me for lunch, but I'd just finished breakfast and I was anxious to get back. We said our good-byes. I thanked them profusely, including Dort in my expressions of appreciation. I didn't dare be rude in case they were right about her incarnation.

Their door closed behind me, and I was just heading for my car when I chanced to glance over at the line of mailboxes under the stairs. Mickey's was crammed with mail. I stared, transfixed. Apparently, the cops had neglected to put a hold on the mail coming in. I wondered how many civil and criminal codes I'd violated so far. Surely, one more transgression wouldn't add that much to my sentence. I felt along the bottom of my shoulder bag, extracted my key picks, and went to work on the lock. This one was so easy it would have yielded to a hairpin, which I don't happen to carry. I pulled out the wad of mail and perused it in haste. The bulk of it consisted of an oversized pulp weekly devoted to survivalist lore: ads for mercenaries, articles about pending gun legislation, government cover-ups, and citizens' rights. I put the magazine back in the box so the contents would appear untouched. The remaining two envelopes I shoved in my shoulder bag for later consideration. I'll tell you right now, they turned out to be nothing, which disappointed me greatly. I hate risking jail time on behalf of third-class mail.

• • •

When I arrived in Santa Teresa at 1:35, I snagged the morning paper from the doorstep and let myself in. I tossed the paper on the counter, set the duffels on the floor, and crossed to my desk. There were several messages waiting on my answering machine. I played them, taking notes, aware that it was probably time to get down to paid employment. In the interest of earning a living, I drove over to the office and devoted the rest of the afternoon to servicing the clients with business pending. In any given month, I might juggle some fifteen to twenty cases, not all of them pressing. Despite the fact I had money in the bank, I couldn't afford to neglect matters already in the works. I'd just spent the past three days chasing down Mickey's situation. Now it was time to get my professional affairs in order. I had calls to return and receipts to tally and enter on the books. There were numerous invoices to be typed and submitted, along with the accompanying reports to write while my notes were still fresh. I also had a few stern letters to compose, trying to collect from slow-pays (all attorneys, please note), plus bills of my own to pay.

I was checking my calendar for the days ahead when I remembered the phone call made from Mickey's number to mine on March 27. I'd never checked my office schedule to see where I was that day. As with my day planner at home, that Thursday was blank. March 26 and 28 were both blank too, so I couldn't use either as a springboard for recollection.

At five-thirty, I locked up and drove back to my apartment through the Santa Teresa equivalent of rush-hour traffic, which meant it took me fifteen minutes to get home instead of the usual ten. The sun had finally burned through a lingering marine layer, and the heat in the vehicle was making me sleepy. I could tell I'd have to atone for my late-night activities. I parked down the street from my apartment and pushed through the gate. My place felt cozy, and I was relieved to be home. The emotional roller coaster of the past few days had generated an odd mood—weariness masquerading as depression. Whatever the source, I was feeling raw. I set my shoulder bag on a bar stool and went around the end of the counter into the kitchenette. I hadn't eaten since breakfast. I opened the refrigerator and stared at the empty shelves. When I thought about Mickey's cupboards, I realized my food supplies didn't look much better than his. Absurd that we'd married when we were simultaneously too much alike and much too different.

Soon after the wedding, I began to realize he was out of control . . . at least from the perspective of someone with my basically fearful nature. I wasn't comfortable with what I perceived as his dissipation and his self-indulgence. My Aunt Gin had taught me to be moderate—in my personal habits if not in my choice of cusswords. At first, Mickey's hedonism had been appealing. I remembered experiencing a nearly giddy relief at his gluttony, his love of intoxication, his insatiable appetite for sex. What he offered was a tacit permission to explore my lustiness, unawakened until then. I related to his disdain for authority and I was fascinated by his disregard for the system, even while he was employed in a job dedicated to upholding law and order. I, too, had tended to operate outside accepted social boundaries. In grade school and, later, junior and senior high schools, I was often tardy or truant, drawn to the lowlife students, in part because they represented my own defiance and belligerence. Unfortunately, by the age of twenty, when I met Mickey, I was already on my way back from the outer fringes of bad behavior. While Mickey was beginning to embrace his inner demons, I was already in the process of retreating from mine.

Now—fifteen years later—it's impossible to describe how alive I was for that short period.

For dinner, I made myself an olive-pimento-cheese sandwich, using that divine Kraft concoction that comes in a jar. I cut the bread neatly into four fingers with the crusts intact and used a section of paper toweling as both napkin and plate. With this wholesome entrée, I sipped a glass of Chardonnay and felt thoroughly comforted. Afterward, I wadded up my dinnerware and tossed it in the trash. Having supped and done the dishes, I placed the two duffels on the counter and unloaded my tools and the booty I'd lifted from Mickey's the night before. I laid the items on the counter, hoping the sight of them would spark a new interpretation.

There was a knock at my door. I grabbed the newspaper and opened it, spreading it over the items as if I'd been reading with interest, catching up on events. I crossed to the door and peeked through the porthole to find my landlord standing on the porchlet with a plate of homemade brownies covered in plastic wrap. Henry's a retired commercial baker who now occupies his time catering tea parties for elderly widows in the neighborhood. He also supplies Rosie's restaurant with a steady line of baked goods: sandwich breads, dinner rolls, pies, and cakes. I confess I was not entirely happy to see him. While I adore him, I'm not always candid with him about my nocturnal labors.

I opened the door. We made happy noises at each other while Henry stepped in. I tried to steer him toward the sofa, hoping to divert his attention, but before I could even protest, he leaned over and closed the newspaper to make room for the plate. There sat the four handguns, the packets of phony documents, credit cards, and cash. To all appearances, I'd turned to robbing banks for a living.

He set the plate on the counter. "What's all this?"

I put a hand on his arm. "Don't ask. The less you know, the better. You'll have to trust me on this."

He looked at me quizzically, an expression in his eyes I hadn't seen before: trust and mistrust, curiosity, alarm. "But I want to know."

I had only a split second to decide what to say. "This is Mickey's. I lifted the stuff because a sheriff's deputy was scheduled to change the locks on his doors."

"Why?"

"He's being evicted. I had one chance to search, and I had to take advantage."

"But what *is* all this?"

"I have no idea. Look, I know how his mind works. Mickey's paranoid. He tends to hide anything of value. I went through his apartment systematically, and this is what I found. I couldn't leave it there."

"The guns are stolen?"

"I doubt it. Mickey always had guns. In all likelihood, they're legal."

"But you don't know that for sure. Mickey didn't authorize you to do this. Couldn't you end up in trouble?"

"Well, yeah, but I can't worry about that *now.* I didn't know what else to do. They were locking him out. This stuff was hidden in the walls, behind panels, in phony bathroom pipes. Meanwhile, he's in the hospital, completely out of it."

"What happens to his possessions? Doesn't he have furniture?"

"Tons. I'll probably offer to have things moved into storage until we see how he fares."

"Have you spoken to the doctors yet?"

"They're not going to talk to me. The cops put the lid on that possibility. Anyway, I made a big point of saying we've been out of touch for years. I can't come along afterward and ask for daily updates like I'm so distraught. They'd never believe me."

"But you said you weren't going to get involved in this."

"I know. I'm not. Well, I am a little bit. At the moment, I don't even know what's going on."

"Then leave it alone."

"It's too late for that. Besides, you're the one who said I ought to check it out."

"But you never listen."

"Well, I did this time."

"Will you listen if I tell you to butt out?"

"Of course. Once I know what it's about."

"Kinsey, this is clearly police business. You can't keep quiet about this stuff. You ought to call those detectives—"

"Nope. Don't want to. I'm not going to do that. I don't like those guys."

"At least, they can be objective."

"So can I."

"Oh, really?"

"Yes, *really*. Henry, don't do this."

"What am I doing?"

"You're disapproving of my behavior. It tears me up."

"As well it should."

I clamped my mouth shut. I was feeling stubborn and resistant. I was already in the thick of it and couldn't bail out. "I'll think about it some."

"You better do more than that. Kinsey, I'm concerned about you. I know you're upset, but this really isn't like you."

"You know what? It *is* like me. This is exactly who I am: a liar and a thief. You want to know something else? I don't feel bad about it. I'm completely unrepentant. More than that. I like it. It makes me feel alive."

A shadow crossed his face and something familiar seemed to scurry into hiding. He was silent for a moment and then said mildly, "Well. In that case, I'm sure you don't need any lectures from me."

He was gone before I could reply. The door closed quietly behind him. The plate of brownies remained. I could tell they were still warm because the air was filled with the scent of chocolate and the plastic wrap was foggy with condensation. I stood where I was. I felt nothing. My mind was blank except for the one assertion. I had to do this. I did. Something inside me had shifted. I could sense the muscles in my face set with obstinacy. There was no way I'd let go, no way I'd back away from this . . . whatever it was.

I sat down at the counter, propping my feet on the rung of the kitchen stool. I folded the newspaper neatly. I picked up the envelope and opened the seal. Inside were two passbooks for Mickey's savings accounts, six cash-register receipts, a Delta ticket envelope, and a folded sheet of paper. I examined the passbooks first. The first had once held a total of $15,000, but the account had been closed and the money withdrawn in January of 1981. The second savings account was opened that same January with a deposit of $5,000 dollars. This was apparently the money he'd been living on of late. I noticed that a series of $600 cash withdrawals corresponded to deposits in his checking account with the following discrepancy: Mickey would pull $600 and deposit $200, apparently keeping $400 in pocket change—"walking around" money, as he used to refer to it. I had to guess this was petty cash, used to pay his bar bills, his dinners out, items from the market. The six cash-register receipts were dated January 17, January 31, February 7, February 21, March 7, and March 21. The ink was faded, but the name of the establishment wasn't that hard to read: the Honky-Tonk. I was assuming he'd sold his car sometime in the third week in March because he'd deposited $900 in his checking account. The loss of his transportation might explain the sudden cessation of visits after so many regular Friday-night appearances. Why drive all the way to Santa Teresa to have a drink when there were bars in his neighborhood? I set the question aside since there was no way to answer it. Before examining the last item, I pulled out my index cards and made some notes. There's always the temptation to let this part slide, but I had to capture the data while everything was fresh in my mind.

Once I'd jotted down what I remembered, adding the cash count, credit card numbers, passbook numbers, and dates of receipts, I gave myself permission to proceed, opening the Delta ticket envelope, which really interested me. The flight coupons had been used. I removed the itinerary and the passenger receipt. Mickey had flown to Louisville, Kentucky, by way of Cincinnati on Thursday, May 8, returning late in the day on Monday, May 12. This impromptu five-day excursion had cost him more than $800 in plane fare alone.

I reached for the remaining item, a folded piece of paper, and read the brief statement, which was dated January 15, 1981. This was a simple letter agreement between Mickey Magruder and Tim Littenberg, signed by the latter, in which he acknowledged receipt of the sum of $10,000, a no-interest loan with a five-year balloon payment due and payable five months ago—January 15, 1986.

I packed up the guns and other items, hid them in a safe place, and grabbed my jacket and handbag.

14

The main drag in Colgate is four lanes wide, lined with an assortment of businesses ranging from carpet stores to barbershops, with a gas station on every other corner and an automobile dealership on the blocks between. Colgate—sprawling, eclectic, and unpretentious—provides housing for those who work in Santa Teresa but can't afford to live there. The population count of the two communities is roughly the same, but their dispositions are different, like siblings whose personalities reflect their relative positions in the family matrix. Santa Teresa is the older of the two, stylish and staid. Colgate is the more playful, less insistent on conformity, more likely to tolerate differences among its residents. Few of its shops stay open after 6 P.M. Bars, pool halls, drive-in theaters, and bowling alleys form the exception.

The parking lot at the Honky-Tonk looked much as it had fourteen years before. Cars had changed. Whereas in the seventies the patrons were driving Mustangs and VW vans painted in psychedelic shades, streetlights now gleamed on Porsches, BMWs, and Trans Ams. Crossing the lot, I experienced the same curious excitement I'd felt when I was single and hunting. Given my current state of enlightenment, I wouldn't dream of circulating through the bar scene—barhopping, we called it—but I did in those days. In the sixties and seventies, that's what you did for recreation. That's how you met guys. That's how you got laid. What Women's Liberation "liberated" was our attitude toward sex. Where we once used sex for barter, now we gave it away. I marvel at the prostitutes we must have put out of business, doling out sexual "favors" in the name of personal freedom. What were we thinking? All we ended up with were bar bums afflicted with pubic vermin.

The Honky-Tonk had expanded, incorporating space formerly occupied by the adjacent furniture store that used to advertise liquidation sales every six to eight months. There was a line at the door, where one of the bouncers was checking IDs by running them through a scanner. Each patron, once cleared, was stamped HT on the back of the right hand, the HT of the Honky-Tonk apparently serving as clearance to drink. That way the waiters and bartenders didn't have to card each cherubic patron ordering rum and Coke—the drinker's equivalent of the training bra.

Now sporting my ink brand, I walked through a fog of cigarette smoke, trying to get a feel for the age and financial status of the crowd inside. There was a large infusion of college students, fresh-faced, uninhibited, their naïveté and bad judgment not yet having come home to roost. The rest were chronic singles, the same aging bachelors and divorcées who'd been eyeballing one another since I'd first buzzed through.

There was still sawdust on the floor. Between the dark-painted wainscoting and the pressed-tin ceiling, the walls were hung with old black-and-white photographs showing Colgate as it had been sixty years before: bucolic, unspoiled, rolling hills stretching out as far as the eye could see. The images were illuminated by gaudy beer signs, red and green neon tinting the vanished grasslands and sunsets.

There were also countless photographs of local celebrities and regulars, pictures taken on St. Patrick's Day, New Year's Eve, and other occasions when the Tonk closed its doors to the public and hosted private parties. I spotted two 8-by-11 photos of Mickey, Pete Shackelford, and Roy Littenberg. The first showed them in police uniform, standing at parade rest: solemn-faced, stiff-backed, serious about law and order. In the second, they were seasoned, men who'd become cynics, guys with old eyes who now smiled over cigarettes and highballs, arms flung casually across one another's shoulders. Roy Littenberg was the oldest by a good ten years. Of the three, he was now dead and Mickey was barely clinging to life. I wondered if there was a way to conjure them up out of memories and smoke—three cops, like ghosts, visible as long as I didn't turn and try to look at them directly.

Two long narrow rooms ran side by side, lined with wooden booths. Each had its own sound system, waves of music pounding against the senses as I moved from room to room. The first held the bar and the second a dance floor, surrounded by tables. The third room, since added, was sufficient to accommodate six pool tables, all of them occupied. The guys played Foosball and darts. The "girls" trooped in and out of the ladies' room, touching up their eye makeup, hiking up their pantyhose. I followed them in, taking advantage of an empty stall to avail myself of the facilities. I could hear two women in the adjoining stall, one barfing up her dinner while the other offered encouraging comments. "That's fine. Don't force it. You're doing great. It'll come." If I'd even heard of it in my day, I'd have assumed Bulimia was the capital of some newly formed Baltic state.

When I left the stall, there were four women in line and another three in front of the mirrors. I waited for an empty place at a sink, washing my hands while I checked my reflection. The fluorescent lighting gave my otherwise unblemished skin a sickly appearance, emphasizing the bags under my eyes. My hair looked like thatch. I wore no lipstick, but that was probably just as well, as the addition would have played up the yellow cast in my aging complexion. I was wearing Mickey's black leather jacket as a talisman, the same old blue jeans, and a black turtleneck, though I'd traded my usual tennis shoes for my usual boots. Mostly, I was dawdling, avoiding the moment when I'd have to perch on a bar stool and buy myself a drink. The two young women emerged from their stall, both of them thin as snakes. The barfer pulled out a prepasted toothbrush and began to scrub. In five years the stomach acid would eat through her tooth enamel, if she didn't drop dead first.

I emerged from the ladies' room, passing the dance floor on my left. I ventured over to the bar, where I bought myself a draft beer. In the absence of available bar stools, I drank the beer standing by myself, trying to look like I was keeping an appointment. Now and then I'd glance at my watch, like I was somewhat annoyed because I didn't have all night. I'm sure many people nearby were completely fooled by this. A few guys assessed me from a distance, not because I was "hot" but because I represented fresh meat, waiting to be graded and stamped.

I deleted my ego from the situation and tried to scrutinize the place from Mickey's point of view. What had possessed him to lend Tim Littenberg the money? Mickey wasn't one to take risks like that. He kept his assets liquid even if he earned very little in the way of interest. He was probably happiest making deposits to the Curtain Rod Savings and Loan. Tim Littenberg—or his dad—must have made a hell of a pitch. Nostalgia might have played a part. Lit and his wife were never good with money. They'd lived from paycheck to paycheck, overdrawn, in debt, their credit cards maxed out. If Tim had needed a stake, they probably didn't have the cash to lend. Whatever the motivation, Mickey'd apparently made the deal. The note had been signed and payment had come due. I'd seen no evidence the loan had been repaid. Curious. Mickey certainly needed the money, and the Honky-Tonk was clearly doing good business.

Near the wall, a bar stool became vacant and I eased into the spot. My eyes strayed back to the mounted photographs and I studied the one hanging next to me. The Three Musketeers again. In this one,

Mickey, Shack, and Lit were sitting at the bar, glasses aloft, offering a toast to someone off to their left. Dixie was visible in the background, her eyes fastened on Mickey—a look both hungry and possessive. Why hadn't I seen that at the time? What kind of dunce was I? I squinted at the picture, taking in the faces, one by one. Lit had always been the best-looking of the three. He was tall, narrow through the shoulders, long arms and legs, beautiful long fingers. I'm a sucker for good teeth and his were even and white, except for one cuspid that sat slightly askew, giving his smile a boyish appeal. His chin was pronounced, his bony jaw wide at the apex. His Adam's apple danced when he spoke. The last time I'd seen him was maybe four years ago and then just in passing. His hair was thinning by then. He'd been in his early sixties, and from what Shack had said he was already in the midst of a struggle for his life.

I rotated slightly on the bar stool and scanned the area, hoping to see Tim. I'd never met Lit's son. Back when I was married to Mickey and hanging out with his parents, he was already grown and gone. He'd joined the army in 1970, and for the period in question he was off in Vietnam. In those days, a lot of STPD cops were ex-army, very gung-ho about the military, supportive of our presence in Southeast Asia. The public by then had lost patience with the war, but not in that circle. I'd seen pictures of Tim that his parents passed around. He always looked grubby and content, a cigarette between his lips, his helmet pushed back, his rifle resting against his knees. Lit would read portions of his letters in which he described his exploits. To me, he sounded reckless and defiant, a bit too enthusiastic, a twenty-year-old kid who spent his days stoned, who loved to kill "gooks" and brag about it later to his friends back home. He'd been brought up on charges after a particularly nasty incident involving two dead Vietnamese babies. Lit stopped saying much after that, and by the time of Tim's dishonorable discharge he'd fallen silent on the subject of his son. Maybe the Honky-Tonk was Lit's hope for Tim's rehabilitation.

Almost at once, my gaze settled on a guy I would have sworn was him. He was somewhere in his mid-thirties, close to my age, and bore at least a superficial resemblance to Roy Littenberg. He had the same lean face, the distinctive jaw and jutting chin. He wore a dark purple shirt and plain mauve tie under a dark sport coat, jeans, desert boots. I'd caught him in conversation with a waitress—probably a dressing down, since she seemed upset. She had straight black hair, very glossy in the light, cut at an angle, with a line of blunt-cut bangs across the front. She wore black eyeliner and very red lipstick. I pegged her in her thirties, though close up she might have been older. She nodded, her face stony, and moved away, heading in my direction. She gave her order to the bartender, fussing with her order pad to cover her agitation. Hands shaking, she lit a cigarette, took a long drag, and then blew the smoke out in a thin jet. She left the cigarette in an ashtray on the bar.

I swiveled slightly and spoke to her. "Hi. I'm looking for Tim Littenberg. Is he on the premises?"

She looked at me, her gaze dropping to my jacket and then quizzically to my face again. She hiked a thumb in his direction. "Purple shirt," she said.

Tim had turned to greet a fellow in a tweedy sport coat, and I saw him signal the bartender to comp the guy to a drink. The two shook hands and Tim patted his back in a friendly gesture that probably didn't have much depth. Roy Littenberg had been fair-haired. His son's coloring was dark. His mouth was pouty and his eyes were darker than his father's, deep-set, smudged with shadow. His smile, when it showed, never touched his eyes. His attention flicked restlessly from room to room. He must constantly estimate the status of his customers, gauging their ages, their levels of inebriation, screening each burst of laughter and every boisterous interchange for the possibility of violence. Every hour the Honky-Tonk was open, the crowd became looser and less inhibited, louder, more aggressive as the alcohol went down.

I watched him approach the bar, coming within a few feet of me. Nearby, the waitress turned abruptly with her tray to avoid contact with him. His gaze touched her and then drifted, caught mine, veered off, and then returned. This time his eyes held.

I smiled. "Hi. Are you Tim?"

"That's right."

I held a hand out. "I'm Kinsey. I knew your father years ago. I was sorry to hear he died."

We shook hands. Tim's smile was brief, maybe pained, though it was impossible to tell. He was lean like his father, but where Lit's countenance was open and sunny, his son's was guarded. "Can I buy you a drink?"

"Thanks, I'm fine for now. The place really jumps. Is it always like this?"

He said, "Thursdays are good. Revving up for the weekend. This your first time in?" He was managing to conduct our conversation without being fully engaged. His face was slightly averted, his focus elsewhere: polite, but not passionate about the need to socialize.

"I was in years ago. That's how I knew your father. He was a great guy." This didn't seem to elicit any particular response. "Are you the manager?"

"The owner."

"Really. Oh, sorry. No offense," I said. "I could see you keeping a close eye out."

He shrugged.

I said, "You must know Mickey Magruder."

"Yeah, I know Mickey."

"I heard he'd bought a part interest in the place, so I was hoping to run into him. He's another cop from the old days. He and your dad were pals."

Tim seemed distracted. "Three Musketeers, right? I haven't seen him for weeks. Would you excuse me?"

I said, "Sure." I watched him cross the room to the dance floor, where he intervened in an exchange between a woman and her date. The guy was stumbling against her and she was struggling to keep him upright. Other couples on the dance floor were giving them a wide berth. The woman finally gave him a shove, both annoyed and embarrassed by his drunkenness. By the time Tim reached them, one of his bouncers had appeared and he began to walk the fellow toward the door, using the kind of elbow grip employed by street cops and mothers with small children acting up in department stores. The woman detoured to a table and snatched up her jacket and her handbag, prepared to follow. Tim intercepted her. A brief discussion ensued. I hoped he was persuading her to take a taxi home.

Moments later, he reappeared beside me, saying, "Sorry about that."

"I hope he's not getting in a car."

"The bouncer took his keys," he said. "We'll let him chill out in back and then see he gets home in one piece. He tends to hassle people when he's like that. Bad for business."

"I'll bet."

His smile was directed somewhere to my left. He gave my arm a pat. "I better go check on him. Hope to see you again."

"You can count on it," I said.

There was only a momentary hitch in his otherwise smooth delivery. "Good deal. Anything you want, you can let Charlie know." He caught the bartender's eye and pointed at me. The bartender nodded and, with that, Tim was gone.

I waited about a minute and then set my half-filled beer glass on the bar and made my way to the pay phones at the rear exit, near the office. I wanted to make sure I knew how to find him in his off-hours. I could have hung around until the place closed and followed him home, but I thought I'd try something more direct. I hauled out the phone book and looked up his address and phone number under *Littenberg, Tim and Melissa.*

I leaned to my left and looked down the shadowy corridor, where I could see three blank doors in addition to the one leading to the office. One of the busboys came in from outside, a draft of cold air following him in. I straightened up, put a coin in the slot, and dialed, listening to a recorded female voice that apprised me of the time to the minute and the second. I said *uh-huh, uh-huh,* like I was oh-so-interested. I watched until the busboy disappeared around the corner, moving into the bar.

The area was quiet. I replaced the handset and proceeded along the corridor, opening one door at a time. The first door exposed a mop closet: brooms, gallon containers of disinfectants, kitchen linens stacked on the shelves. The second door turned out to be the employees' lounge, lined with metal lockers and two sinks, an assortment of dumpy sofas, and a lot of ashtrays, most of which were full. No sign of the drunk; I wondered where he'd gone. The third door was locked. I leaned my head against the door, listening, but there was no sound.

Tim's office was just opposite. I crossed the corridor in two steps and gripped the doorknob with care. I turned it slowly to the right and pushed the door open the faintest crack. Tim was at his desk, his back to me, talking on the telephone. I couldn't hear his conversation. I sincerely hoped he wasn't busy putting out a contract on me. I eased the door shut and peeled my hand away from the knob to avoid any rattles and clicks. Time to get out. I really didn't want anyone to find me back here. I returned to the main corridor, where I checked in both directions. There was no evidence of an alarm system: no passive infrared beams, no numbered key pad by the rear exit. Interesting.

I drove home with an eye plastered to my rearview mirror. There was no reason in the world to think Tim's call had anything to do with me. He *had* made a beeline to the office after I'd mentioned Mickey's name, but that was the stuff of B-movies. Why would he rub me out? I hadn't done anything. I hadn't said a word about the ten grand he owed. I was saving that for next time. Actually, he could have paid it back, for all I knew.

It was only 10 P.M.: lots of traffic on the freeway and none of it seemed sinister. Tim didn't know me from Adam, so he couldn't know where I lived or what kind of car I drove. Besides, Santa Teresa doesn't have any mobsters . . . at least as far as I know.

When I reached my neighborhood, I cruised the block, looking for a parking place that wasn't shrouded in darkness. I spotted only one unfamiliar car, a dark-toned Jaguar sitting at the curb across the street from my apartment. I pulled up around the corner onto Bay and waited to make sure no one had followed me. Then I locked up and walked the half block back. I was feeling foolish, but I still preferred to listen to my intuition. I knew the gate hinge would squeak, so I avoided it and approached by traversing the neighbor's yard along the wooden fence. Maybe I was being dumb, but I couldn't help myself.

When I reached the far side of Henry's garage, I lifted my head above the fence and looked. I'd left the back light on, but now my porchlet was in shadow. Henry's lights were out as well. A mist seemed to hover in the grass like smoke. I waited without moving, letting my eyes adjust to the dark. As in most cases, even the darkest night isn't without its ambient illumination. The moon was caught in the branches of a tree. Splashes of light spilled down in an irregular pattern. I listened until the crickets began to chirp again.

I divided Henry's backyard into segments and scanned them one by one. Nothing to my immediate left. Nothing near his back step. Nothing near the tree. The garage cast a triangle of blackness onto the patio so that not all his lawn furniture was visible. Still, I could have sworn I saw a form: the head and shoulders of someone sitting in one of his Adirondack chairs. It could have been Henry, but I didn't think so. I sank down below the fence. I reversed myself, easing back through the neighbor's yard to the street beyond. The leather boots I wore weren't designed for tiptoeing on wet grass, and I slipped as I crept along, hoping not to fall on my ass.

Once I gained the street, I had to wipe some doggie doo off my shoe heel, lest the odor alone make a target of me. I fumbled in the bottom of my bag until I found my penlight. I shielded the narrow beam with the palm of my hand and swept the Jaguar. All four doors were locked. I half expected the vanity plate to read HITZ R US. Instead, it said DIXIE. Well, that was interesting. I approached the backyard this time from the neighbor's property to the left of Henry's, first navigating up their driveway, then making a wide circle across Henry's yard along the rear flower beds. From this vantage point, I could see the silhouette of her tangled hair. She must have been dying to smoke. As I watched, her desire for a cigarette overrode her caution. I heard the flick of a lighter. She cupped a hand to her face and applied the flame to the end of a cigarette and inhaled with a nearly audible sigh of relief. No weapon, at any rate, unless she could wield one with her feet.

By then, I was close to the back of the Adirondack. "Gee, Dixie. Never light up. Now all the snipers in the neighborhood can get a bead on you."

She gasped, nearly levitating from her seat as she whipped her head around. She grabbed the arm of her chair and her handbag tumbled from her lap. I saw the cigarette fly off in the dark, the ember making a most satisfactory arc before it was snuffed in the wet grass. She was lucky she hadn't sucked it down her throat and choked to death. "Shit. Oh, shit! You scared the crap out of me," she hissed.

"What the hell are you doing here?"

She had a hand to her chest, trying to still her wildly banging heart. She bent at the waist, hyperventilating. I was singularly unimpressed with the possibility of heart failure. If her heart seized, she died. I was not going to do CPR on her. She was wearing what looked like a flight suit, a one-piece design with a zipper up the front. The oversized, baggy look was offset by the fact that she had the sleeves rolled midway up her arm, thus demonstrating how petite she was. She stooped to pick up her shoulder bag, which was battered leather, shaped like a mail carrier's pouch.

She tucked it under one arm. She put a hand to her forehead and then to her cheek. "I need to talk to you," she said, still sounding shaken.

"Had you thought about calling first?"

"I didn't think you'd agree to see me."

"So you wait in the dark? Are you *nuts*?"

"I'm sorry. I didn't mean to scare you. The old gentleman in the house was up when I arrived an hour ago. I could see him in the kitchen when I came around the corner, so I unscrewed the porch bulb. I didn't want him to notice and wonder what I was doing."

"What *are* you doing? I'm still not entirely clear."

"Could we go inside? I promise I won't stay long. I didn't bring a jacket and I'm freezing."

I felt a flash of annoyance. "Oh, come on," I said.

I set off across the yard. When I reached the porch, I gave the bulb a twist and saw the light come on. She followed me meekly. I took out my house keys and unlocked the door.

I took a moment to slip my shoes off. "Wipe your feet," I said crossly before I entered the living room.

"Sorry. Of course."

I pulled out a kitchen stool for her and then went around the kitchen counter and retrieved a brandy bottle from the liquor cabinet. I took out two jelly glasses and twisted the cork, pouring us both two fingers. I tipped my head back and flung the brandy to the back of my throat. I swallowed liquid fire, my mouth coming open, invisible flames shooting out. Damn, that was nasty, but it brought relief. I shuddered involuntarily the way I do when swilling NyQuil. I was calmer by the time I looked up at her. She'd chugalugged as I had, but she seemed better able to take the brandy in stride.

"Thanks. That's great. I hope you don't mind if I have a cigarette," she said, reaching into her bag as if with my consent.

"You can smoke outside. I don't want you smoking in here."

"Oh. Sorry," she said, and put the pack away.

"And quit apologizing," I said. She'd come here for something. Time to get on with it. I said, "Speak," like she was a dog about to demonstrate a trick.

Dixie closed her eyes. "What Mickey and I did was inexcusable. You have every right to be angry. I was obnoxious on Monday when you came to the house. I apologize for that, but I was disconcerted. I always assumed you'd received my letter and elected to do nothing. I guess I enjoyed blaming you for being disloyal. It was hard to give that up." She opened her eyes then and looked at me.

"Go on."

"That's it."

"No, it's not. What else? If that's all you wanted, you could have written me a note."

She hesitated. "I know you crossed paths with Eric on your way down the drive. I appreciated your keeping quiet on the subject of me and Mickey. You could have caused me a lot of trouble."

"*You* made the trouble. I didn't have anything to do with it."

"I'm aware of that. I know. But I've never been sure if Eric knew about what happened."

"He never mentioned it?"

"Nothing."

"Consider yourself lucky. I'd leave it at that, if I were you."

"Believe me, I will."

I felt myself subdivide, one part fully present, the other part watching from a distance. What she'd said so far was true, but there was bound to be more. Lacking my native talent in the liar-liar-pants-on-fire department, she couldn't help but color slightly, a bright coin of pink appearing on each cheek.

I said, "But what? You want assurances I'll keep my mouth shut from here on out?"

"I know I can't ask."

"That's correct. On the other hand, I don't know what purpose it would serve. Believe it or not, just because you 'done me wrong' doesn't mean I'd turn around and do likewise. Is there anything else?"

Dixie shook her head. "I should probably go." She picked up her handbag and began to search for her keys. "I know he invited you to dinner. Eric's always been fond of you. . . ."

I thought, *He has?*

"He's anxious to have you over, and I hope you'll agree. He might think it odd if you refused the invitation."

"Would you give it a rest. I haven't seen either one of you in fourteen years, so why would it seem odd?"

"Just think about it. Please? He said he'd probably call you early in the week."

"All right. I'll consider it, but no guarantees. It seems awkward to me."

"It doesn't have to be." She stood and held out a hand to me. "Thank you."

I shook hands with her, though I wondered in the moment if we'd made some unspoken pact. She moved to the door, turning back, her hand on the knob. "How'd you do in the search for Mickey? Any luck?" she asked.

"The day after I talked to you, a couple of LAPD detectives showed up on my doorstep. He was shot last week."

"He's dead?"

"He's alive but in bad shape. He may not survive."

"That's awful. That's terrible. What happened?"

"Who knows? That's why they drove up here to talk to me."

"Have they made an arrest?"

"Not yet. All I know about it is what they told me so far. He was found on the street a couple of blocks from his apartment. This was Wednesday of last week. He's been in a coma ever since."

"I'm . . . I don't know what to say."

"There's nothing required."

"Will you let me know what you hear?"

"Why would I do that?"

In a fragile voice, she said, "*Please?*"

I didn't bother to reply. Then she was gone, leaving me staring at the door. I resented her thinking she had equal grieving rights. More than that, I wondered what she was really up to.

15

Friday morning, I woke up at 5:58, feeling logy and out of sorts. Every bone in my body was begging for more sleep, but I pushed aside the covers and reached for my sweats. I brushed my teeth and ran a comb through my hair, which was sticking out in all directions as though electrified. I paused near the gate and did an obligatory stretch. I started with a fast walk and then broke into a trot when I reached the beachfront park that runs along Cabana Boulevard.

The morning sky was dense with cloud cover, the air hazy. Without the full range of sunlight, all the warm reds and yellows had been leached from the landscape, leaving a muted palette of cool tones: blues, grays, taupe, dun, smoky green. The breeze blowing off the beach smelled of wharf pilings and seaweed. In the course of my run, I could feel the interior fog begin to lift. Intense exercise is the only legal high I know . . . except for love, of course. Whatever your inner state, all you have to do is run, walk, ride a bike, ski, lift weights, and suddenly your optimism's back and life seems good again.

Once recovered from my run, I drove over to the gym, which is seldom crowded at that hour, the pre-work fanatics having already come and gone. The gym itself is spartan, painted gunmetal gray, with industrial carpeting the same color as the asphalt in the parking lot outside. There are huge plate-glass mirrors on the walls. The air smells of rubber and sweaty armpits. The prime patrons are men in various stages of physical fitness. The women who show up tend to fall into two categories: the extremely lean fitness fiends, who trash themselves daily, and the softer women who arrive after any food-dominated holiday. The latter never last, but good for them anyway. Better to make *some* effort than do nothing for life. I fell somewhere between.

I started with leg extensions and leg curls, muscles burning as I worked. Abs, lower back, on to the pec deck and chest press, then on to shoulders and arms. Early in a workout, the sheer number of body parts multiplied by sets times the number of repetitions is daunting, but the process is curiously engrossing . . . pain being what it is. Suddenly I found myself laboring at the last two machines, alternating biceps and triceps. Then I was out the door again, sweaty and exhilarated. Sometimes I nearly wrench my arm from its socket patting myself on the back.

Home again, I turned on the automatic coffeepot, made the bed, showered, dressed, and ate a bowl of cereal with skim milk. Then I sat with my coffee and read the local paper. Usually, as the day wears on, my flirtation with good health is overrun by my tendency to self-abuse, especially when it comes to junk food. Fat grams are my downfall, anything with salt, additives, cholesterol, nitrates. Breaded and deep-fried or sautéed in butter, smothered in cheese, slathered with mayonnaise, dripping with meat juices—what foodstuff couldn't be improved by proper preparation? By the time I finished reading the paper, I was nearly dizzy with hunger and had to suck down more coffee to dampen my appetite. After that, all it took was a big gob of crunchy peanut butter I licked from the spoon while I settled at my desk. I'd decided to skip the office as I'd dutifully caught up with paperwork the day before.

I placed Detective Aldo's business card on the desk in front of me and put a call through to Mark Bethel. I'd actually given up hope of ever speaking to him in person. Sure enough, he'd popped down to Los Angeles for a campaign appearance. I told Judy about Mickey and she went through the usual litany expressing concern, shock, and dismay at life's uncertainties.

"Can Mark do anything to help?" she asked.

"That's why I called. Would you ask him if he'd talk to Detective Aldo and find out what's going on? They're not going to tell me, but they might talk to him since he's Mickey's attorney—or at least he was."

"I'm sure he'd do that. Do you have a number?"

I recited the number and gave her Detective Felix Claas's name as well. I also gave her Mickey's address in Culver City.

She said, "I'm making a note. He should be calling when he's finished. Maybe he can touch base with Detective Aldo while he's still in Los Angeles."

"Thanks. That'd be great."

"Is that it?"

"Just one more thing. Can you ask Mark what's going to happen to Mickey's bills? I'm sure they're piling up, and I hate to see his credit get any worse than it is."

"Got it. I'll ask. He'll think of something, I'm sure. I'll have him call you when he gets in."

"No need for that unless he has a question. Just let him know what we talked about and he can take it from there."

I sat at my desk, wondering what to do next. Once more, I hauled out the assorted items I'd lifted from Mickey's and studied them one by one. Phone bill, the Delta Airlines ticket envelope, receipts from the Honky-Tonk, savings passbooks, phony documents. Emmett Vanover . . . Delbert Amburgey . . . Clyde Byler, all with trumped-up personal data and a photo of Mickey's face plastered in the relevant spots. I went back to the plane ticket, which was issued in the name

Magruder. The flight coupons were missing—I assumed, used for the trip—but the passenger receipt and itinerary were still in the ticket envelope. This was an expensive round trip for a guy with no job. What was the relevance, if any? The trip to Louisville might have been personal. Hard to know about that, since we hadn't talked in years. I laid the ticket on the desk beside the other items, lining them up in various configurations as though a story could be fabricated from the proper sequence of events.

When I was a kid, my Aunt Gin kept me supplied with activity books. The paper was always cheap, the games and puzzles designed to shut me up temporarily so she could read for an hour without my interrupting. I'd lie on the trailer floor with my big pencil and a box of crayons. Sometimes the instructions would entail the finding and circling of particular words in a gridwork of letters, sometimes a search for specific objects in a convoluted jungle picture. My favorite was dot-to-dot, in which you constructed a picture by connecting consecutively numbered points on the page. Tongue peeking out of the corner of my mouth, I'd laboriously trace the line from number to number until a picture emerged. I got so good at it, I could stare at the spaces between numbers and see the picture without ever setting pencil to paper. This didn't require much in the way of brains as the outline was usually simple: a teddy bear or a wagon or a baby duck, all dumb. Nonetheless, I can still remember the rush of joy when recognition dawned. Little did I know that at the age of five I was already in training for my later professional life.

What I was looking at here was simply a more sophisticated version of dot-to-dot. If I could understand the order in which the items were related, I could probably get some notion of what was going on in Mickey's life. For now, what I was missing were the links between events. What was he up to in the months before the shooting? The cops had to be pursuing many of these same questions, but it was possible I was in possession of information they lacked . . . having stolen it. In the rudimentary conscience I seemed to be developing, I knew I could always opt for the Good Citizen's Award by "sharing" with Detective Aldo. In the main, I don't hold back where cops are concerned. On the other hand, if I dug a little deeper, I might figure it out for myself, recapturing the thrill of discovery. There's nothing like the moment when everything finally falls into place. So why give that up when, with just a tiny bit more effort, I could have it all? (These are the sorts of rationalizations Ms. Millhone engages in when failing to do her civic duty.)

I hauled up my handbag and began to sift through the contents, coming up with Wary's phone number on the back of a business card. Maybe Mickey had said something to him about the trip. I picked up the phone and dialed Los Angeles. It was only ten-fifteen. Maybe I could catch him before he went off to breakfast. I had a vision of Wary's wire-rimmed glasses and his waist-length brown hair. Two rings. Three. When he finally answered, I could tell from his voice he'd been deeply asleep.

"Hey, Wary. How're you? Did I wake you?"

"No, no," he said valiantly. "Who's this?"

"Kinsey in Santa Teresa." Silence. "Mickey's ex."

"Oh, yeah, yeah. Got it. Sorry I didn't recognize your voice. How're you?"

"Fine. And you?"

"Doing great. What's up?" I could hear him lock his jaw in the effort to suppress a yawn.

"I have a quick question. Did Mickey say anything about the trip he made to Louisville, Kentucky?"

"What trip?"

"This was week before last. He departed May eighth and returned on the twelfth."

"Oh, that. I knew he was gone, but he never said where. Why'd he go?"

"How do I know? I was hoping *you'd* tell *me.* Given his finances,

I'm having trouble understanding why he took off for five days. The plane ticket cost a fortune, and he probably had to add meals and a motel on top of that."

"Can't help you there. All I know is he went someplace, but he never said why. I didn't even know he left the state. Dude didn't like to fly. I'm surprised he'd get on a plane going anywhere."

"Did he talk to anyone else, someone in the building he might have mentioned it to?"

"Could have. I doubt it. It's not like he had buddies he confided in. Say, you know what might help? I just thought of this. Once his phone was disconnected, he used to pop in and borrow mine. Kind of pay-as-you-go, but he was always careful to keep square. I can find the numbers, if you want."

I closed my eyes, saying small prayers. "Wary, I'd be indebted to you for life."

"Hey, cool. I'm going to put the phone down and go look on my desk."

I heard a clunk and I was guessing the handset was now resting on his bed table while he padded around, probably bare-assed naked. A full minute passed, and then he picked up the phone again. "You still there?"

"Indeed."

"I got the statement right here. They bill on the fifteenth, so this was in yesterday's mail. I haven't even opened it yet. I know some calls he made were out-of-state because he left me ten bucks and said he'd pay the difference later when the bill came in."

"Really. Did you ever hear what was said?"

"Nope. I made it a point to leave the room. I figured it was private. You know him. He never explained anything, especially when it came to his work. He was stingy with exposition in the best of circumstances."

"What makes you think this was work?"

"His attitude, I guess. Cop mode, I'd call it. You could see it in his body, the way he carried himself. Even half in the bag, he knew his stuff." I could hear him shuffling papers. Distracted, he said, "I'm still looking. Have you heard anything?"

"About Mickey? Not lately. I guess I could call Aldo, but I'm afraid to ask."

"Here we go. Okay. Oh. There was just one. This's the seventh of May. Lookit here. You're right. He called Louisville." He read the number off to me. "Actually, he made two to the same number. The first was quick, less than a minute. The longer one—ten minutes—was shortly afterward."

I was frowning at the phone. "It must have been important to him if he flew out the next day."

"A man of action," he said. "Listen, I gotta get off the phone and go take a leak, but I'll be happy to call you back if I think of anything else."

"Thanks, Wary."

Once I hung up, I sat and stared at the phone, trying to "get centered," as we say in California. Ten-twenty here . . . that would make it one-twenty in Kentucky. I had no clue who he'd called, so I couldn't think of a ruse. I'd have to make it up as I went along. I dialed the number.

"Louisville Male High School. This is Terry speaking. May I help you?"

Male High School? Terry sounded like a student, probably working in the office. I was so nonplused I couldn't think of anything to say. "Oops. Wrong number." I put the handset back. Belatedly, my heart thumped. What was this about?

I took a couple of deep breaths and dialed again.

"Louisville Male High School. This is Terry speaking. May I help you?"

"Uh, yes. I wonder if I might speak to the assistant principal?"

"Mrs. Magliato? One minute." Terry put me on hold, and ten seconds later the line was picked up.

"Mrs. Magliato. May I help you?"

"I hope so. My name is Mrs. Hurst from the General Telephone offices in Culver City, California. A call was placed to this number from Culver City on May seventh, and the charges are currently in dispute. The call was billed to last-name Magruder, first name Mickey or Michael. Mr. Magruder indicates that he never made such a call, and we've been asked to identify the party called. Can you be of some assistance? We'd appreciate your help."

"What was that name again?"

I spelled it out.

She said, "Doesn't sound familiar. Hold on and I'll ask if anybody else remembers talking to him."

She put me on hold. I listened to a local radio station, but the sound was pitched too low for me to hear what was being said. She came back on the line. "No, I'm sorry. None of us talked to anyone by that name."

"What about the principal? Any possibility he might have taken the call himself?"

"For starters, it's a she and I already asked. The name doesn't ring a bell."

I thought about the names on the phony documents and pulled them closer. "Uh, what about the names Emmett Vanover, Delbert Amburgey, and Clyde Byler?" I repeated them before she asked, which seemed to piss her off.

"I know I didn't speak to any one of them. I'd remember the names."

"Could you ask the office staff?"

She sighed. "Just a moment," she said. She put a palm across the receiver and I could hear her relay the question. Muffled conversation ensued and then she removed her hand. "Nobody spoke to any of them either."

"No one from Culver City?"

"No-oo." She sang the word on two notes.

"Ah. Well, thanks anyway. I appreciate your time." I hung up the phone and thought about it for a minute. Who did Mickey talk to for ten minutes? It certainly wasn't her, I thought. I got up from the desk and went back to the kitchen, where I took out a butter knife and the jar of extra crunchy Jif. I took a tablespoon of peanut butter on the blade and spread it on the roof of my mouth, working it with my tongue until my palate was coated with a thin layer of goo. "Hello, this is Mrs. Kennison," I said aloud, in a voice that sounded utterly unlike me.

I returned to the phone and dialed the number again. When Terry answered, I asked the name of the school librarian.

"You mean Ms. Calloway?" she said.

"Oh, that's right. I'd forgotten. Could you transfer me?"

Terry was happy to oblige, and ten seconds later I was going through the same routine, only this time with a variation. "Mrs. Calloway, this is Mrs. Kennison with the district attorney's office in Culver City, California. A call was placed to this number from Culver City on May seventh, billed to last-name Magruder, first name Mickey or Michael—"

"Yes, I spoke to him," she said, before I could finish my tale.

"Ah. Oh, you did. Well, that's wonderful."

"I don't know if I'd call it *wonderful*, but it was pleasant. He seemed like a nice man: articulate, polite."

"Can you remember the nature of the query?"

"It was only two weeks ago. I may be close to retirement, but I'm not suffering from senile dementia—not yet, at any rate."

"Could you fill me in?"

"I could if I understood what this had to do with the district attorney's office. It sounds fishy as all get out. What'd you say your name was? Because I'm making a note of it, and I intend to check."

I hate it when people think. Why don't they just mind their own business and respond to my questions? "Mrs. Kennison."

"And the reason for the call?"

"I'm sorry, but I'm not at liberty to say. This is a legal matter, and there's a gag order in effect."

"I see," she said, as if she didn't.

"Can you tell me what Mr. Magruder wanted?"

"Why don't you ask him?"

"Mr. Magruder's been shot. He's in a coma at the moment. That's as much as I can tell you without being cited for contempt of court."

That seemed to work. She said, "He was trying to track down a former Male High School student."

"Can you give me the name?"

"What's your first name again?"

"Kathryn. Kennison. If you like, I can give you my number here and you can call me back."

"Well, that's silly. You could be anyone," she snapped. "Let's just get this over with. What is it you want?"

"Any information you can give me."

"The boy's name was Duncan Oaks, a 1961 graduate. His was an outstanding class. We still talk about that group of students."

"I take it you were the school librarian back then?"

"I was. I've been here since 1946."

"Did you know Duncan Oaks personally?"

"Everybody knew Duncan. He worked as my assistant in his sophomore and junior years. By the time he was a senior, he was the yearbook photographer, prom king, voted most likely to succeed—"

"He sounds terrific."

"He was."

"And where is he now?"

"He became a journalist and photographer for one of the local papers, the *Louisville Tribune,* long since out of business, I'm sorry to say. He died on assignment in Vietnam. The *Trib* got swallowed up by one of those syndicates a year later, 1966. Now whoever you are and whatever you're up to, I think I've said enough."

I thanked her and hung up, still completely unenlightened. I sat and made notes, using the cap of the pen to scrape the peanut butter from the roof of my mouth. Was this an heir search? Had Mickey taken on a case to supplement his income? He certainly had the background to do P.I. work, but what was he doing and who'd hired him to do it?

I heard a tap at my door and leaned over far enough to see Henry peering through the porthole. I felt a guilty pang about the night before. Henry and I seldom had occasion to disagree. In this case, he was right. I had no business withholding information that might be relevant to the police. *Really,* I was going to reform, I was almost sure. When I opened the door, he handed me a stack of envelopes. "Brought you your mail."

"Henry, I'm sorry. Don't be mad at me," I said. I tossed the mail on the desk and gave him a hug while he patted me on the back.

"My fault," he said.

"No, it's not. It's mine. You're entirely right. I was being obstinate."

"No matter. You know I worry about you. What's wrong with your voice? Are you catching cold?"

"I just ate something and it's stuck in my teeth. I'll call Detective Aldo today and tell him what I've found."

"I'd feel better if you did," he said. "Did I interrupt? We can do this another time if you're hard at work."

"Do what another time?"

"You said you'd give me a lift. The fellow from the body shop called to say the Chevy's ready."

"Sorry. Of course. It's taken long enough. Let me get my jacket and my keys."

On the way over to the body shop, I brought Henry up to date, though I was uncomfortably aware that even now I wasn't being completely candid with him. I wasn't lying outright, but I omitted portions of the story. "Which reminds me," I said. "Did I tell you about that call to my place?"

"What call?"

"I didn't think I'd mentioned it. I don't know what to make of it." I laid out the business about the thirty-minute call from Mickey's place to mine in late March. "I swear I never talked to him, but I can tell the detectives didn't believe me."

"What was the date?"

"March twenty-seventh, early afternoon, one-thirty. I saw the bill myself."

"You were with me," he said promptly.

"I was?"

"Of course. That was the day after the quakes that dumped the cans on my car. I'd called the insurance company and you followed me over to the shop. The claims adjuster met us there at one-fifteen."

"That was *that* day? How do you remember these things?"

"I have the estimate," he said and pulled it from his pocket. "The date's right here."

The incident returned in a flash. In the early morning hours of March 27 there'd been a series of temblors, a swarm of quakes as noisy as a herd of horses thundering across the room. I'd woken from a sound sleep with my entire bed shaking. The brightly lighted numbers on my digital alarm showed 2:06. Clothes hangers were tinkling, and all the glass in the windows rattled like someone rapping to get in. I'd been up like a shot, pulling on my sweats and my running shoes. Within seconds that quake passed, only to be followed by another. I could hear glass crashing in the sink. The walls had begun to creak from the strain of the rocking motion. Somewhere across the city, a transformer exploded and I was blanketed in darkness.

I'd grabbed my shoulder bag and fumbled down the spiral stairs while I groped in the depths for my penlight. I'd found it and flicked it on. The wash from the beam was pale, but it lighted my way. In the distance, I could hear sirens begin to wail. The trembling ceased. I'd taken advantage of the moment to snag my denim jacket and let myself out the door. Henry was already making his way across the patio. He carried a flashlight the size of a boom box, which he shone in my face. We spent the next hour huddled together in the backyard, fearful of returning indoors until we knew we were safe. The next morning, he'd discovered the damage to his five-window coupe.

I'd followed him to the body shop and an hour later I'd driven him home. When I'd returned to my apartment, my message light was blinking. I'd hit the REPLAY button, but there was only a hissing that extended until the tape ran out. I was mildly annoyed. I assumed it was pranksters and let it go at that. Henry was standing right there and heard the same thing I did; he suggested a malfunction when the power had been restored. I'd rewound the tape to erase the hiss and had thought no more about it. Until now.

16

As soon as I got home, I put a call through to Detective Aldo, eager to assert my innocence on this one small point. The minute he picked up the phone and identified himself, I launched right in. "Hi, Detective Aldo. This is Kinsey Millhone, up in Santa Teresa." Little Miss Cheery making friends with the police.

I was just embarking on my explanation of the March phone call when he cut me short. "I've been trying to get in touch with you for days," he said tersely. "This is to put you on notice. I know for a fact you violated crime-scene tape and entered that apartment. I can't prove it for now, but if I find one shred of evidence, we'll charge you with willful destruction or concealment of evidence and resisting a peace officer in the discharge of his duties, punishable by a fine not exceeding one thousand dollars, or by imprisonment in a county jail not exceeding one year, or by both. You got that straight?"

I'd opened my mouth to defend myself when he slammed down the phone. I depressed the plunger on my end and replaced the handset, my mouth as dry as sand. I felt such a hot flash of guilt and embarrassment, I thought I'd been catapulted into early menopause. I put a hand against my flaming cheek, wondering how he knew it was me. Actually, I wasn't the only one guilty of illegal entry. Mickey's phantom girlfriend had entered the premises at some point between my two visits, making off with her diaphragm, her necklace, and her spray cologne. Unfortunately, aside from the fact that I didn't know who she was, I couldn't accuse her without accusing myself as well.

I spent the rest of the day slinking around with my mental tail between my legs. I hadn't been so thoroughly rebuked since I was eight and Aunt Gin caught me smoking an experimental Viceroy cigarette. In this case, I was so heavily invested in Mickey's concerns, I couldn't afford to have my access to his life curtailed. I'd hoped clearing myself with Aldo in the matter of the phone call would net me information about the current status of his investigation. Instead, it was clear that his trust was so seriously eroded he'd never tell me a thing.

I used the early evening hours to pick my way through a plate of Rosie's stuffed beef rolls. She was pushing *vese porkolt,* which (translated from Hungarian) turned out to be heart and kidney stew. Remorseful as I felt, I was prepared to eat my own innards, but my stomach rebelled at the notion of vital piggie organs simmered with caraway seeds. I spent the hours after supper tending to my desk at home, atoning for my sins with lots of busywork. When all else fails, cleaning house is the perfect antidote to most of life's ills.

I waited until close to midnight to return to the Honky-Tonk. I wore the same outfit I'd worn the night before since it was previously smoked on and required laundering anyway. I'd have to hang Mickey's leather jacket on the line for days. This was now Friday night and, if memory still served me, the place would be packed with feverish weekend celebrants. Driving by, I could see the parking lot was jammed. I cruised the surrounding blocks and finally squeezed into a space just as a Ford convertible was pulling out. I walked the block and a half through the darkened Colgate neighborhood. This was an area that had once been devoted solely to single-family homes. Now a full third had been converted to small businesses: an upholsterer, an auto repair shop, and a beauty salon. There were no sidewalks along the street so I kept to the middle of the road and then cut through the small employee parking lot at the rear exit.

I circled the building to the entrance, where the line of people awaiting admittance seemed to be singles and couples in roughly equal numbers. I gave the bouncer my driver's license and watched him run it through his scanning device. I paid the five-dollar cover charge and received the inked benediction on the back of my right hand.

As I moved through the front room, I was forced to run the gauntlet of chain smokers standing four deep at the bar—shifty-eyed guys trying to look a lot hipper than they actually were. The music coming from the other room was live that night. I couldn't see the band, but the melody (or its equivalent) pounded, the beat distorted through the speakers to a tribal throb. The lyrics were indecipherable but probably consisted of sophomoric sentiments laid out in awkward rhyming couplets. The band sounded local, playing all their own tunes, if this one was any indication. I've picked up similar performances on local cable channels, shows that air at 3 A.M. as a special torture to the occasional insomniac like me.

I was already wishing I'd stayed at home. I'd have turned and fled if not for the fact that Mickey'd been here himself six consecutive Fridays. I couldn't imagine what he'd been doing. Maybe counting drinks, calculating Tim's profits, and thus computing his gross. Maybe Tim had cried poor, claiming he wasn't making sufficient money to repay the loan. If Tim's bartender happened to have his hand in the till, this could well be true. Bartenders have their little methods, and an experienced investigator, sitting at the bar, can simultaneously chat with other patrons and do an eyeball audit. If the bartender was skimming, it would have been in Mickey's best interests to spot the practice and blow the whistle on him. It was equally possible Mickey's presence was generated by another motive—a woman, for instance, or the need to escape his financial woes in L.A. Then, too, a heavy drinker doesn't really need an excuse to hit a bar anywhere.

I did the usual visual survey. All the tables were full, the booths bulging with customers packed four to a bench. The portion of the dance floor I could see from where I stood was so dense with moving bodies there was scarcely any room to spare. There was no sign of Tim, but I did see the black-haired waitress, inching through the mob in front of me. She held her tray aloft, balancing empty glasses above the reach of jostling patrons. She wore a black leather vest over nothing at all, her arms long and bare, the V of the garment exposing as much as it concealed. The dyed black of her hair was a harsh contrast to the milky pallor of her skin. A dark slash of lipstick made her mouth look grim. She leaned toward the bartender, calling her order over the generalized din.

There's a phenomenon I've noticed when I'm driving on the highway. If you turn and look at other drivers, they'll turn and look at you. Maybe the instinct is a holdover from more primitive days when being the object of scrutiny might mean you were in peril of being killed and consumed. Here, it happened again. Soon after I spotted her, she turned instinctively and caught my gaze. Her eyes dropped to Mickey's leather jacket. I shifted my attention, but not before I saw her expression undergo a change.

Thereafter, I was careful to avoid her, and I focused instead on what was going on nearby. I kept picking up an intermittent whiff of marijuana, though I couldn't trace the source. I started watching people's hands, since dopers seldom hold a joint the way they'd hold an ordinary cigarette. The average smoker tucks a cigarette in the V formed between the index and middle fingers, bringing the cigarette to the lips with the palm of the hand open. A doper with a joint makes an O-ring with the thumb and index finger, the doobie at the center, the three remaining fingers fanned out so the palm forms a shelter around the burning joint. Whether the intent is to shield the dope from the wind or from public view, I've never been able to determine. My own dope-smoking days are long since past, but the ceremonial aspects seem consistent to this day. I've seen a doper ask for a joint by simply forming that O and pressing it to his lips, a gesture that signals, Shall we smoke a little cannabis, my dear?

I began to circle the bar, moving casually from table to table until I spotted the fellow with a joint between his lips. He was sitting alone in a booth on the far side of the room, close to the corridor that led to the telephones and rest rooms. He was in his mid-thirties, vaguely familiar with his long, lean face. He was a type I'd found appealing when I was twenty: silent, brooding, and slightly dangerous. His eyes were light and close-set. He sported a mustache and goatee, both contributing to the look of borderline scruffiness. He wore a loose khaki-colored jacket and a black watch cap. A fringe of light hair extended well below his collar. He carried himself with a certain worldliness, something in the hunch of his shoulders and the mild knowing smile that flitted across his face.

Tim Littenberg emerged from the back corridor and paused in the doorway while he adjusted his cuffs. The two of them, the joint smoker and the bar owner, ignored each other with a casualness that seemed phony from my perspective. Their behavior reminded me of those occasions when illicit lovers run across each other in a social setting. Under the watchful eyes of their respective spouses, they'll make a point of avoiding contact, thus trumpeting their innocence, or so they think. The only problem is the aura of heightened awareness that underlies the act. Anyone who knows either can detect the charade. Between the man in the booth and Tim Littenberg there was an unmistakable air of self-consciousness. Both seemed to be watching the black-haired waitress, who seemed equally conscious of them.

Within minutes, she'd circled and arrived at the booth. Tim moved away without looking at her. The guy with the joint leaned forward on his elbows. He reached out and put a hand on her hip. He motioned for her to sit. She slid into the bench across from him with her tray between them as though the empty glasses might remind him she had other things to do. He took her free hand and began to talk earnestly.

I couldn't see her face, but from where I stood she didn't seem relaxed or receptive to his message.

"You know that guy?" a voice said into my right ear.

I turned to find Tim leaning close to me, his voice amazingly intimate in the midst of loud music and high-pitched voices. I said, "Who?"

"The man you're watching, sitting in the booth over there."

"He seems familiar," I said. "Mostly, I was trying to remember where the rest rooms are."

"I see."

I stole a look at his face and then looked off in the other direction, deflecting the intensity with which he'd fixed his attentions on me. He said, "Remember Mickey's friend Shack?"

"Sure. We talked earlier this week."

"That's his son, Scottie. The waitress is his girlfriend, Thea. In case you're wondering," he added, with a hint of irony.

"You're kidding. That's Scott? No wonder he looked familiar. I've seen pictures of him. I take it you're still friends?"

"Of course. I've known Scottie for years. I don't like dope in my bar, but I don't want to make a fuss so I tend to ignore him when he's got a joint."

"Ah."

"I'm surprised you're back. Are you looking for someone in particular, or will I do?"

"I was hoping to find Mickey. I told you that last night."

"That's right. So you did. Can I buy you a drink?"

"Maybe when I finish this. I'm really fine for now."

He reached over and removed the beer glass from my hand and helped himself to a sip. "This is warm. Let me get you a fresh one in an icy mug." He caught the bartender's eye and lifted the glass, indicating a replacement. Tim was wearing a dark navy suit with a dress shirt that was oxblood red. His tie bore a pattern of diagonal wishbones, navy and red on a field of light blue. The musky bite of his aftershave filled the air between us. His pupils were pinpricks and his skin had a sheen. Tonight, instead of seeming restless and distracted, his demeanor was slow, every gesture deliberate as if he were slogging his way through mud. Well, well, well. What was he on? I felt a faint ridge of fear prickling up along my spine, like a cat in the presence of aliens.

I watched a frosty mug of beer being passed in my direction, hand over hand, like a bucket brigade. Tim placed the mug in my hand, at the same time resting his free hand against the middle of my back. He was standing too close, but in the press of the crowd it was hard to complain. I longed to back away, but there wasn't room. I said, "Thanks."

Again, he bent low and put his mouth close to my ear. "What's the story with Mick? This is twice you've been in."

"He lent me his jacket. I was hoping to return it."

"You and he have something going?"

"That's none of your business."

Tim laughed and his gaze glided off, easing toward Thea, who was just rising from the booth. Scott Shackelford was staring down at the table, pinching out the joint, which was barely visible between his fingers. Thea picked up her tray and began to push toward the bar, studiously avoiding the sight of Tim. Maybe she was still pissed off for what he'd said to her last night. I didn't want the beer, but I didn't see a place to set it down.

I said, "I'll be right back."

Tim touched my arm. "Where're you going?"

"To take a whiz. Is that okay?"

Again, he laughed, but it was not the sound of merriment.

I pushed my way through the crowd, praying he'd lose interest during the time I was gone. The first flat surface I saw, I put the beer glass down and walked on.

The rest room was undergoing one of those temporary lulls where I was the only person present. I crossed to the window and opened it a crack. A wedge of cold air slanted in, and I could see the smoke drift out. The quiet was like a tonic. I could feel myself resist the notion of ever leaving the room. If the window had been lower, I'd have crawled on out. I went into a stall and peed just for something to do.

I was standing at the sink, soaping my hands, when the door opened behind me and Thea walked in. She crossed to the adjacent sink and began washing her hands, her manner businesslike. I didn't think her arrival was an accident, especially when she could have used the employee's lounge around the corner. She caught my reflection in the mirror and gave me a pallid smile as if she'd just that moment noticed I was standing there. She said "Hi" and I responded in kind, letting her define the communication since she'd initiated it.

I pulled out a sheet of paper towel and dried my hands. She followed suit. A silence ensued and then she spoke up again. "I hear you're looking for Mickey."

I focused my attention, hoping she couldn't guess how very curious I was. "I'd like to talk to him. Have you seen him tonight?"

"I haven't seen him for weeks."

"Really? That seems odd. Somebody told me he was usually here on Fridays."

"Uh-uh. Not lately. No telling where he's at. He could be out of town."

"I doubt it. Not that he told me."

She took a lipstick from her pocket and twisted the color into view, sliding it across her lips. I read an article once in some glamour magazine—probably waiting for the dentist and hoping to distract myself—in which the author analyzed the ways women wear down a tube of lipstick. A flat surface meant one thing, slanted meant something else. I couldn't recall the theory, but I noticed hers was flat, the lipstick itself coming perilously close to the metal.

She screwed the lipstick back down and popped the top back on while she rubbed her lips together to even out the color. She corrected a slight mishap at the corner of her mouth, then studied her reflection. She tucked her coal-black hair behind her ears. Idly, she pursued the subject without any help on my part. "So what's your interest?" She used her tongue to remove a smudge of lipstick from her two front teeth.

"He's a friend."

She studied me with interest. "Is that why you have his jacket?"

"He's a *good* friend," I said, and then glanced down at myself. "You recognize this?"

"It sure looks like his. I spotted it when you were in here the other night."

"Last night," I said, as if she didn't know.

"Really. Did he give you that?"

"It's on loan. That's why I'm looking for him, to give it back," I said. "I tried calling, but his phone's been disconnected."

She'd taken out a mascara wand, leaning close to the mirror while she brushed through her lashes, leaving little dots of black. As long as she was wangling for information, I thought I'd wangle some myself.

I said, "What about you? Are you a friend of his?"

She shrugged. "I wait on him when he's in and we shoot the breeze."

"So nothing personal."

"I have a boyfriend."

"Was that him?"

"Who?"

"The guy in the watch cap, sitting at the booth out there?"

She stopped what she was doing. "As a matter of fact, yes. What makes you ask?"

"I was thinking to cop a joint when I saw you sit down. Is he local?"

She shook her head. "L.A." There was a pause and then she said, "How long have you dated Mickey?"

"It's kind of hard to keep track."

"Then this is recent," she said, turning the question into a statement to offset the inquisition.

I started fluffing at my hair the way she'd been fluffing hers. I leaned close to the mirror and checked some imaginary eye makeup, running the flat of one knuckle along the lower edge of one eye. She was still waiting for an answer. I looked at her blankly. "Sorry. Did you ask me something?"

She took a pack of unfiltered Camels from her jeans and extracted a cigarette. She applied a flame to the tip, using a wooden match she scratched on the bottom of her shoe. "I didn't know he was dating."

"Who, Mickey? Oh, please. He's always on the make. That's half his charm." I could picture the ashtray in his apartment, the numerous unfiltered Camel cigarette butts, along with the array of kitchen matches that looked just like hers. "He's so secretive. Jeez. You never know what he's up to or who he's doing these days."

She said, "I didn't know that about him." She turned to face me, leaning her backside against the sink with her weight on one hip.

I was warming to the subject, lies tumbling out with a tidy little mix of truth. "Take my word for it. Mickey doesn't give you a straight answer about anything. He's impossible that way."

"Doesn't that bother you?" she asked.

"Nah. I used to be jealous, but what's the point? Monogamy's not his thing. I figure what the hell? He's still a stud in his way. Take it or leave it. He's always got someone waiting in the wings."

"You live in L.A.?"

"I'm mostly here. Anytime I'm down, though, I stop by his place."

The information I was doling out seemed to make her restless. She said, "I have to get back to work. If you see him, tell him Thea said 'hi.' " She dropped the cigarette on the floor and stepped on it. "Let me know if you find him. He owes me money."

"You and me both, kid," I said.

Thea left the room. I confess I smirked when she banged the door shut. I caught sight of myself in the mirror. "You are such a little shit," I said.

I leaned on the sink for a minute, trying to piece together what I'd learned from her. Thea couldn't know about the shooting or she wouldn't have been forced to try to weasel information out of me. She must have hoped he was out of town, which would go a long way toward explaining why he hadn't been in touch with her. It wasn't difficult to picture her in a snit of some kind. There's no one as irrational as a woman on the make. She might seize the opportunity to screw around on her steady boyfriend, but woe betide the man who screwed around on *her.* Given the fact that Mickey's phone was out, she must have driven down to his apartment to collect her personal belongings. She certainly hadn't warmed to the idea that he and I were an item. I wondered how Scottie Shackelford would feel if he found out she was boffing Mick. Or maybe he knew. In which case, I wondered if he'd taken steps to put a stop to it.

17

I came out of the ladies' room and paused inside the doorway to the bar, glancing to my left. Scott Shackelford was no longer sitting in the booth. I spotted him at the bar, chatting with the bartender, Charlie. The crowd was beginning to thin out. The band had long ago packed up and departed. It was nearly one-forty-five and the guys looking to get laid were forced to zero in on the few single women who remained. The busboys were loading dirty glassware into plastic bins. Thea was now standing at the bar with Scott, using a calculator to add up her tips. I zipped up the front of Mickey's jacket. As I made my way to the front door, I became aware that she was watching me.

The chilly air was a relief after the smoky confinement of the bar. I could smell pine needles and loam. Colgate's main street was deserted, all the neighboring businesses long since shut down for the night. I cut through the parking lot on the way to my car, hands in my jeans pockets, the strap of my handbag hooked over my right shoulder. Streetlights splashed the pavement with pale circles of illumination, emphasizing the darkness beyond their reach. Somewhere behind me, I heard the basso profundo rumble of a motorcycle. I looked over my shoulder in time to see a guy on a bike turning into the alley to the rear of the bar. I stared, walking backward, wondering if my eyes were deceiving me. I'd only caught a glimpse of him, but I could have sworn this was the same guy who'd shown up at Mickey's Wednesday night in L.A. As I watched, he cut the engine and, still astride, began to roll his bike toward the trash bins. A wan light shining down from the rear exit shone on his corn-yellow hair and glinted against the chrome of the bike. He lifted the bike backward onto the center stand, locked the bike, dismounted, and rounded the building, walking toward the main entrance with a jingling sound, his jacket flapping open. The body type was the same: tall, thin, with wide bony shoulders and a sunken-looking chest.

I dog-trotted after him, slowing as I reached the corner to avoid running into him. He'd apparently already entered the bar by the time I got there. The bouncer saw me and glanced at his watch with theatrical emphasis. He was in his forties, balding, big-bellied, wearing a sport coat that fit tightly through the shoulders and arms. I showed him the stamp on the back of my hand, demonstrating the fact I'd already been cleared for admittance. "I forgot something," I said. "Mind if I go back in real quick?"

"Sorry, lady. We're closed."

"It's only ten of two. There's still a ton of people inside. Five minutes. I swear."

"Last call was one-thirty. No can do."

"I don't want a *drink*. This is for something I left. It'll only take two minutes and I'll be right out again. Please, please, please?" I put my knees together and clasped my hands like a little child at prayer.

I saw him repress a smile, and he motioned me in with an indulgent rolling of his eyes. It's perplexing to realize how far you can get with men by pulling girlish shit. I paused, looking back at him as if my question had just occurred to me. "Oh, by the way . . . the fellow who just went in?"

He stared at me flatly, unwilling to yield anything more than he had.

I held a hand above my head. "About this tall? Denim jacket and spurs. He arrived on a motorcycle less than a minute ago."

"What about him?"

"Can you tell me his name? I met him a couple of nights ago and now I've forgotten. I'm too embarrassed to ask so I was hoping you'd know."

"He's a pal of the owner's. He's a two-bit punk. You got no business hanging out with a little shit like him."

"What about Tim? What's their relationship?"

He looked at his watch again, his tone shifting to exasperation. "Are you going to go in? Because technically we're closed. I'm not supposed to admit anyone after last call."

"I'm going. I'm going. I'll be out in a second. Sorry to be such a pest."

"Duffy something," he murmured. "Nice girl like you ought to be ashamed."

"I promise I am. You have no idea."

Once inside, I dropped the Gidget act and studied the faces within range of me. The overhead lights had come on and the busboys were now stacking chairs on the tabletops. The bartender was closing out the register and the party hearties seemed to be getting the hint. Thea and Scott were sitting in a booth. Both had cigarettes and fresh drinks: one for the road, to get their alcohol levels up. I crossed the front room, hoping to avoid calling attention to myself. Good luck with that. Three single guys gave me the toe-to-head body check, glancing away without interest, which I thought was rude.

I headed for the back corridor, operating on the assumption that Duffy Something was in Tim's office since I didn't see him anywhere else. I passed the ladies' room and the pay phones and turned right into the short hallway. The door to the employees' lounge stood open, and a couple of waitresses were sitting on the couch smoking while they changed their shoes. Both looked up at me, one pausing long enough to remove the cigarette from her lips. "You need help?" Smoke wafted out of her mouth like an SOS.

"I'm looking for Tim."

"Across the hall."

"Thanks." I backed away, wondering what to do next. I couldn't simply knock on his door. I had no reason to interrupt, and I didn't want the biker to get a look at me. I glanced at the door and then back at the two. "Isn't somebody in there with him?"

"No one important."

"I hate to interrupt."

"My, ain't we dainty? Bang on the door and walk in. It's no big deal."

"It's not that important. I'd rather not."

"Oh, shit. Gimme your name and I'll tell him you're here."

"Never mind. That's okay. I can catch him later." I backed up in haste, then scooted around the corner and out the back exit. I walked forward a few steps and then turned and stared. Where the front of the building was only one story tall, the rear portion was two. I could see lights on upstairs. A shift in the shadows suggested movement, but I couldn't be sure. What was going on up there? No way to know unless I created the opportunity to pick my way in.

Meanwhile, I'd have given a lot to know what the biker was saying to Tim. From the location of Tim's office, I knew any exterior windows would have to be around the far corner to my left. I stood there, debating the wisdom of trying to eavesdrop. That corner of the building was shrouded in darkness, and it looked like I'd have to squeeze into the space between the Honky-Tonk and the building next to it. This was a feat that not only promised a bout of claustrophobia but the onslaught of hordes of domestic short-haired spiders the size of my hand. With my luck, the windowsills would be too high for peeking and the conversation too muffled for revelations of note. It was the thought of the spiders that actually clinched the vote.

I opted instead for a close-on inspection of the motorcycle. I fished out my penlight and flashed the beam across the bike. The make was a Triumph. The license plate was missing, but by law the registration should have been available on the bike somewhere. I ran a hand across the seat, hoping it would lift to reveal a storage compartment. I was in the process of the search when the rear door banged open and the two waitresses walked out. I shoved the penlight in my pocket and turned my attention toward the street, like I was waiting for someone. They moved off to my right, deep in conversation, crossing my line of vision without exhibiting any curiosity about what I was doing. As soon as they were gone, I turned off the penlight and slipped it in my bag.

Out in the street, the last of the bar patrons were straggling to their cars. I could hear doors slamming, car engines coughing to life. I abandoned the search and decided to return to my car. I jogged the two blocks, my shoulder bag banging against my hip. When I reached the VW, I unlocked the door and slid under the wheel. I stuck my key in the ignition, fired up the engine, and snapped on my headlights. I made an illegal U-turn and drove back to the Tonk.

Once in view of the place, I doused my headlights and pulled over to the right. I parked the car in the shadow of a juniper bush. I slouched down on my spine, keeping an eye on the rear exit over the rim of my sideview mirror. The biker showed up about ten minutes later. He mounted his bike, backed off his center stand, and dropped his weight down with a quick stomp that jolted his engine to life. He cranked the throttle with one hand, revving the bike until it roared in protest. He kept one foot on the ground while he pivoted his bike, the backside swinging wildly as he took off. I watched him slide through the stop sign and hang a left onto Main. By the time I could follow, he was easily five blocks ahead. Within minutes, I'd lost sight of him.

I cruised on for a while, wondering if he'd turned off on a side street close by. This was an area that consisted largely of single-family residences. The stretches of roadway between subdivisions and shopping malls were lined with citrus orchards. The Colgate Community Hospital appeared on my right. I turned left toward the freeway but saw no sign of the biker's taillight. If he'd already turned on the 101, he'd be halfway to town and I didn't have a prayer of catching up with him. I pulled over to the curb and shut off the ignition. I cranked down the driver's side window and tilted my head, listening for the distant racketing of the motorcycle in the still night air. Nothing at first and then . . . faintly . . . I picked up the rat-a-tat-tat, at a much reduced speed. The source of the sound was impossible to pinpoint, but he couldn't be far. Assuming it was him.

I started the VW and pulled out again. The road here was four lanes wide, and the only visible side street went off to the left. There was a nursery on the corner. The sign read BERNARD HIMES NURSERY & TREE FARM: *Shade Trees, Roses, Fruit Trees, Ornamental Shrubs.* The street curved along beside the tree farm and around to the right again. As nearly as I remembered, there was no other exit, and anyone driving back there would be forced to return. The Santa Teresa Humane Society had its facility toward the far corners of the cul-de-sac, as did the County Animal Control. The other businesses were commercial enterprises: a construction firm, warehouses, a heavy-equipment yard.

I turned left, driving slowly, checking both sides of the street for signs of the biker. Passing the nursery on my right, I thought I saw a flicker of light, in a strobe effect, appearing through the thicket of specimen trees. I squinted, unsure, but the darkness now appeared unbroken and there was no sound. I drove on, following the street to its dead end, a matter of perhaps half a mile. Most of the properties I passed were either entirely dark or minimally lighted for burglar-repellent purposes. Twice, I caught sight of private security vehicles parked to one side. I imagined uniformed guards keeping watch, possibly with the help of attack-trained dogs. I returned to the main road without any clear-cut evidence the biker had come this way. It was now after two. I took the southbound on-ramp to the 101. Traffic was sparse, and I returned to my apartment without seeing him again.

• • •

Mercifully, the next morning was a Saturday and I owed myself nothing in the way of exercise. I pulled the pillows over my head, shutting out sound and light. I lay bundled under my quilt in an artificial dark, feeling like a small furry beast. At nine, I finally crawled out of my burrow. I brushed my teeth, showered, and shampooed the previous night's smoke from my hair. Then I wound down the spiral stairs and put on a pot of coffee before I fetched the morning paper.

Once I'd finished breakfast, I put a call through to Jonah Robb at home. I'd first encountered Jonah four years before when he was working missing persons for the Santa Teresa Police Department. I was checking on the whereabouts of a woman who later turned up dead. Jonah was separated from his wife, struggling to come to terms with their strange bond, which had started in junior high school and gone downhill from there. In the course of their years together, they'd separated so many times I think he'd lost count. Camilla worked him like a yo-yo. First, she'd kick him out; then she'd take him back or leave him for long periods, during which he wouldn't see his two daughters for months on end. It was in the midst of one of their extended separations that he and I became involved in a relationship. At some point I finally understood that he'd never be free of her. I broke off intimate contact and we reverted to friends.

He'd since been promoted to lieutenant and was now working homicide. We remained buddies of a sort, though I hadn't set eyes on him for months. The last time I'd run into him was at a homicide scene, where he confessed Camilla was pregnant—by someone else, of course.

"What's up?" he said, once I'd identified myself.

I gave him a rundown on the situation. The LAPD detectives had filled him in on the shooting, so he knew that much. I gave him a truncated version of my dealings with them and then filled in additional details: the money Tim owed Mickey, the biker appearing at his Culver City apartment and again at the Honky-Tonk.

Jonah said, "Did you get the license plate?"

"There wasn't one. I'm guessing the bike's stolen, but I can't be sure. I can't swear he's connected to the shooting, but it seems too coincidental he'd show up in both places, especially since he's said to be a friend of Tim's. Can you ask Traffic to keep an eye out? I'd love to know who he is and how he's mixed up in this."

"I'll see what I can do and call you back," he said. "What's the story on the gun that was left at the scene? Was that really yours?"

"Afraid so," I said. "That was a wedding gift from Mickey, who purchased it in his name. Later, we switched the registration. It's a sweet little Smith and Wesson I haven't seen since the spring of '72, which is when I left. Maybe Mickey had it on him and the shooter took it away."

"How's he doing?"

"I haven't heard. I'll try calling in a bit, but the truth is, I don't want to ask for fear the news won't be good."

"I don't blame you. Scary shit. Is there anything else?"

"What's the word on the Honky-Tonk? What's going on out there?"

"Nothing that I've heard. As in what?"

"I don't know. It could be dope," I said. "I've been in there twice, and it feels *off* to me. I guess, at the back of my mind, I'm wondering if Mickey picked up on it too. I'm assuming he came up at first to bug Tim about the money owed. But why the return trips?"

"I'll ask around. It's possible the vice guys know something that I don't. What about yourself? How are you these days?"

"Doing great, considering I'm suspected of trying to kill my ex. Speaking of which, how's Camilla?"

"She's big. Baby's due July fourth, and according to the amnio it's a boy. We're excited about that."

"She's living with you?"

"Temporarily."

"Ah."

"Well, yeah. Her turd of a boyfriend abandoned her as soon as he found out she was pregnant. She's got nobody else."

"The poor thing," I said, in a tone of voice that went over his head.

"Anyway, it gives me a chance to spend time with the girls."

"That it does," I said. "Well, it's your life. Good luck."

"I'm going to need it," he said dryly, but he sounded pretty cheerful for a guy whose nuts were being slammed in a car door.

After he hung up, I dialed UCLA and asked for ICU. I identified myself to the woman who answered and asked about Mickey. She put me on hold. When she came back on, an eternity later, I realized I'd stopped breathing.

"He's about the same."

I said, "Thanks," and hung up quickly before she changed her mind.

I spent the bulk of the day in a fit of cleaning, armed with sponges and rags, a bucket of soapy water, a dustcloth, and a vacuum cleaner, plus newspapers and vinegar water for the windows I could reach. The phone rang at four. I paused in my labors, tempted to let the answering machine pick up. Of course, curiosity got the better of me.

"Hey, Kinsey. Eric Hightower here. I hope I didn't catch you at a bad time."

"This is fine, Eric. How are you?"

"Doing good," he said. "Listen, Dixie and I are putting together a little gathering: cocktails and hors d'oeuvres. This is strictly impromptu, just a couple dozen folk, but we wanted you to come. Any time between five and seven."

I took advantage of the moment to open my mail, including the manila envelope Bethel's secretary had sent. Inside was his curriculum vitae. I tossed it in the wastebasket, then took it out again and stuck it in the bottom drawer. "You're talking about tonight?"

"Sure. We've got some friends in from Palm Springs so we're geared up anyway. Can you make it?"

"I'm not sure. Let me take a look at my calendar and call you right back."

"Bullshit. Don't do that. You're stalling while you think of an excuse. It's four now. You can hop in the shower and be ready in half an hour. I'll send the car at four-forty-five."

"No, no. Don't do that. I'll use my own."

"Great. We'll see you then."

"I'll do what I can, but I make no promises."

"If we don't see you by six, I'm coming after you myself."

As soon as he hung up, I let out a wail, picturing the house, the servants, and all their la-di-da friends. I'd rather have a root canal than go to these things. Why hadn't I just lied and told him I was tied up? Well, it was too late now. I put the cleaning gear away and trudged up the spiral stairs. I opened my closet door and stared at my dress. I admit to a neurotic sense of pride in only owning that one garment, except for times like this. I took the dress from the closet and held it up to the light. It didn't look too bad. And then a worse thought struck. What if *they* were all decked out in designer jeans? What if I was the only one who showed up in a dress made of a wrinkle-free synthetic fabric that scientific tests would later prove was carcinogenic? I'd end up looking like a social geek, which is what I am.

18

I drove into the parking area at the Hightowers' estate shortly after 6 P.M. The house was ablaze, though it wouldn't be dark for another hour yet. The evening was cool, 62 degrees, according to the report on my car radio. I parked my 1974 VW between a low-slung red Jaguar and a boxy chrome-trimmed black Rolls, where it sat looking faintly plaintive, a baby humpback whale swimming gamely among a school of sharks. In a final moment of cunning, I'd solved my fashion dilemma with the following: black flats, black tights, a very short black skirt, and a long-sleeved black T-shirt. I'd even applied a touch of makeup: powder, lip gloss, and a smudgy line of black along my lashes.

A middle-aged white maid in a black uniform answered the door chimes and ushered me into the foyer, where she offered to take my bag. I declined, preferring to retain it on the off chance I'd spy the perfect opportunity to flee the premises. I could hear a smattering of conversation, interspersed with the kind of laughter that suggests lengthy and unrestrained access to booze. The maid murmured a discreet directive and began to cross the living room in her especially silent maid's shoes. I followed her through the dining room and out into the screened atrium, where some fifteen to twenty people were already standing about with their drinks and cocktail napkins. A serving wench was circulating with a tray of hors d'oeuvres: teeny-weeny one-bite lamb chops with paper panties on the ends.

As is typical of California parties, there was a percentage of people dressed far better than I and a percentage dressed like bums. The very rich seem particularly practiced at the latter, wearing baggy chinos, shapeless cotton shirts, and deck shoes with no socks. The not-so-very-rich have to work a little harder, adding an abundance of gold jewelry that might or might not be fake. I tucked my bag against the wall behind a nearby chair and then stood where I was, hoping to get my bearings before the panic set in. I didn't know a soul and I was already flirting with the urge to escape. If I didn't see Eric or Dixie in the next twenty seconds, I'd ease right on out.

A black waiter in a white jacket appeared at my shoulder and asked if I'd like a drink. He was tall and freckle-faced, somewhere in his forties, his tone refined, his expression remote. His name tag said STEWART. I wondered what he thought of the Montebello social set and sincerely hoped he wouldn't take me for one of them. On second thought, there probably wasn't too much danger of that.

"Could I have Chardonnay?"

"Certainly. We're pouring Kistler, Sonoma-Cutrer, and a Beringer Private Reserve."

"Surprise me," I said, and then I tilted my head. "Don't I know you from somewhere?"

"Rosie's. Most Sundays."

I pointed in recognition. "Third booth back. You're usually reading a book."

"That's right. I work two jobs at the moment, and Sunday's the only day I have to myself. I got three kids in college and a fourth going off next year. By 1991, I'll be a free man again."

"What's the other job?"

"Telephone sales. I have a friend owns the company, and he lets me fill in when it suits my scheduling. His turnover's fast anyway, and I'm good at the spiel. I'll be back in a moment. Don't you go away."

"I'll be here."

Halfway across the room I caught sight of Mark Bethel in conversation with Eric, hunkered beside Eric's wheelchair. Eric had his back to me; Mark was just to the left of him and facing my way. Mark's face was long and his hairline was receding, which gave him a high-domed head with a wide expanse of brow. He wore glasses with tortoise-shell rims, behind which his eyes were a luminous gray. While technically not good-looking, the television cameras were amazingly kind to him. He'd removed his suit coat and, as I watched, I saw him loosen his tie and roll up the sleeves of his crisp white dress shirt. The gesture suggested that despite his buttoned-down appearance he was ready to go to work for his constituents. It was the sort of soft-focus image that would probably show up later in one of his commercials. The thrust of his campaign was shamelessly orchestrated: babies and old folk and the American flag waving over patriotic music. His opponents were portrayed in grainy black-and-white, overlaid with tabloid-type headlines decrying their perfidy. Mentally, I slapped myself around some for being such a cynic. Mark's wife, Laddie, and his son, Malcolm, were standing a few feet away, chatting with another couple.

Laddie was the exemplary political mate: mild, compassionate, so subtle in her affect that most people never guessed the power she held. Her eyes were a cool hazel, her dark hair streaked blond, probably to disguise any early hints of gray. Her nose was slightly too prominent, which saved her from perfection and thus endeared her to some extent. Never compelled to work, she'd devoted her time to a number of worthy causes—the symphony, the humane society, the arts council, and numerous charities. As hers was one of the few familiar faces present, I considered crossing the room and engaging her in conversation. I knew she'd at least *pretend* to be attentive, even if she couldn't quite remember who I was.

Malcolm, in another five years, was going to be a knockout. Even now, he was graced with a certain boy beauty: dark-haired and dark-eyed, with a succulent mouth and slouching, lazy posture. I'm a sucker for the type, though I tend to be careful about guys that good-looking as they often turn out to be treacherous. He seemed to have an awareness of the ladies, who were, likewise, more than casually aware of him. He wore desert boots, faded jeans, a pale blue dress shirt, and a navy blazer. He seemed poised, at ease, accustomed to attending parties given by his parents' snooty friends. He looked like a stock-broker in the making, maybe a commodities analyst. He'd end up on financial-channel talk shows, discussing short falls, emerging markets, and aggressive growth. Once off the air, the female anchor, ever bull-ish, would pursue him over drinks and then fuck his baby brains out, strictly no-load with no penalty for early withdrawal.

"Excuse me, dear."

I turned. The woman to my right handed me her empty glass, which I took without thinking. While she was clearly speaking in my direc-tion, she managed to address me without direct eye contact. She was a gaunt and gorgeous fifty with a long flawless face and blown-about red hair. She wore a long-sleeved black silk body suit and blue jeans so tight I was surprised she could draw breath. With her flat tummy, tiny waist, and minuscule hips, my guess was she'd had sufficient liposuc-tion to create an entire separate human being. "I need a refill. Gin and tonic. Make it Bombay Sapphire and no ice this round, please."

"Bombay Sapphire. No ice."

She leaned closer. "Darling, where's the nearest loo? I'm about to pee my pants."

"The loo? Let's see." I pointed toward the sliding glass doors that opened into the dining room. "Through those glass doors. Angle left. The first door on your right."

"Thanks ever so."

I set her empty glass in a potted palm, watching as she tottered away on her four-inch heels. She did as directed, passing through the glass doors to the dining room. She angled left to the first door, tilted her head, tapped lightly, turned the knob, and went in. Turned out to be a linen closet, so she walked right out again, looking mildly embarrassed and thoroughly confused. She spotted another door and corrected for her error with a quick look-around to see if anyone had noticed. She knocked and went in, then did an about-face, emerging from a closet filled with stereo equipment. Well, darn. I guess I know as much about the loo as I do about high-priced gins.

I eased my way through the crowd, intercepting Stewart, who was returning with my wine. The next time I saw the woman, she avoided me altogether, but she'd probably drop a hint to Dixie about having me removed. In the meantime, a young woman appeared with another tray of hors d'oeuvres, this time halved new potatoes the size of fifty-cent pieces, topped with a dollop of sour cream and an anthill of black caviar. Within minutes, everybody's breath was going to smell like fish.

Eric's conversation with Mark had come to an end. Across the room, I caught Mark's attention and he moved in my direction, pausing to shake a few hands en route. By the time he finally reached me, his public expression had been replaced by a look of genuine concern. "Kinsey. Terrific. I thought that was you. I've been trying to reach you," he said. "When'd you get here?"

"A few minutes ago. I figured we'd connect."

"Well, we don't have long. Laddie committed us to another party and we're just about to leave. Judy passed along the news about Mickey. What a terrible thing. How's he doing?"

"Not well."

Mark shook his head. "What a shitty world we live in. It's not like he didn't have enough problems."

"Judy said you talked to him in March."

"That's right. He asked me for help, in a roundabout way. You know how he is. By the way, I did talk to Detective Claas while I was down in L.A., though I didn't learn much. They're being very tight-lipped."

"I'll say. They certainly don't appreciate my presence on the scene."

"So I hear."

I could just imagine the earful he picked up from the LAPD. I said,

"At this point, what worries me are Mickey's medical bills. As nearly as I can tell, he lost all his coverage when he was fired from his job."

"I'm sure that's not an issue. His bills can be paid from funds from Victims of Major Crimes, through the DA's office. It's probably been set in motion, but I'll be happy to check. By the way, I stopped off at Mickey's on my way back from L.A. I thought I should meet his landlady in case a question came up."

"Oh, great. Because the other thing I'm concerned about is this eviction. The sheriff's already been there and changed the locks."

"I gathered as much," he said. "Frankly, I'm surprised to see you take an interest. I was under the impression you hadn't spoken to him for years."

"I haven't, but it looks like I owe him one."

"How so?"

"You know I blamed him for Benny Quintero's death. Now I find out Mickey was with Dixie that night."

"I heard that story too, but I was never sure how much credit to attach."

"You're telling me they lied?"

"Who's to say? I've made it my practice not to speculate. Mickey didn't confide and I didn't press him for information. Fortunately, we never had to defend the point one way or the other."

I saw him glance in Laddie's direction, gauging their departure, which was imminent. Laddie had found Dixie and she was proffering regrets. Hugs, air kisses, and niceties were exchanged.

Mark said, "I better catch up. Give me a couple of days. I'll let you know about his bills. Glad we had a chance to chat." He gave my shoulder a squeeze and then joined Laddie and Malcolm, who waited in the dining room. Dixie followed them out, apparently intending to see them as far as the door.

Meanwhile, Eric had wheeled around and his face seemed to brighten at the sight of me. He pointed to a corner chair and then pushed himself in that direction. I nodded and followed, admiring his physique. His knit shirt fit snugly, emphasizing his shoulders and chest, along with his muscular arms. He looked like an ad for a fitness supplement. When he pivoted his chair, I could see the point where his thighs ended, six inches above the knees. He held a hand out to me. I leaned down and bussed his cheek before I took a seat. His aftershave was citrus and his skin was like satin. He said, "I didn't think you'd come."

"I probably won't stay long. I don't know a soul here except for Mark and his crew. The kid's attractive."

"And bright. Pity about his father. He's a waste of time."

"I thought you liked Mark."

"I do and I don't. He's phony as all get out, but aside from that he's great."

"That's a hell of an endorsement. What'd he do to you?"

Eric gestured dismissively. "Nothing. Forget it. He asked me to do a film clip for his ad campaign. Primary's only ten days off, and there's nothing like a cripple to pick up a few last-minute votes."

"Ooh, you're a cynic. You sound worse than I do. Did it ever occur to you he might see you as a shining example of success and achievement, overcoming the odds and similar sentiments?"

"No. It occurred to me he wants me on his team in hopes other Vietnam vets will follow suit. Prop Forty-two is his pet project. The truth is, he needs a banner issue because he's floundering. Laddie's not going to like it if he's trounced at the polls."

"What difference does it make? I didn't think he had a chance anyway."

"It's one thing to lose and another thing to lose *badly*. He doesn't want to look like a has-been right out of the gate."

"Easy come, easy go. They'll survive, I'm sure."

"Possibly."

"Possibly? I like that. What's that supposed to mean?"

I saw his gaze shift and glanced up in time to see Dixie return. "Things aren't always as they appear."

"The Bethels are unhappy?"

"I didn't say that."

"Incompatible?"

"I didn't say that, either."

"Then what? Come on. I won't repeat it. You've got me curious."

"Mark has places to go. He can't do that divorced. He needs Laddie's money to make it work."

"What about her? What's her stake in it?"

"She's more ambitious than he is. She dreams about the White House."

"You're not serious."

"I am. She grew up in the era of Jackie O and Camelot. While other girls played with Barbies, she was making a list of which rooms to redo."

"I had no idea."

"Hey, Mark wants it too. Don't get me wrong, but he'd probably be content with the Senate while she's longing for a place in all the history books. He won't make it this round—the competition's too fierce—but in four years, who knows? As long as he can rally support, he's probably got a shot at it one day. Meanwhile, if he starts looking like a loser, she might bump him and move on."

"And that's enough to keep their marriage afloat?"

"To a point. In the absence of passion, rampant ambition will suffice. Besides, divorce is a luxury."

"Oh, come on. Couples get divorced every day."

"Those are the people with nothing at stake. They can afford to set personal happiness above all else."

"As opposed to what?"

"The status quo. Besides, who wants to start over at our stage in life? Are you eager to fling yourself into a new relationship?"

"No."

Eric smiled. "My sentiments exactly. I mean, think of all the stories you'd have to retell, the personal revelations, the boring family history. Then you'd have to weather all the hurt feelings and the fear and the stupid misunderstandings while you get to know the other person and they get to know you. Even if you take the risk and pour yourself heart and soul into someone new, the odds are your new love's a clone of the one you just dumped."

I said, "This is making me ill."

"It's really no big deal. You put up with things. You look the other way, and sometimes you have no choice but to bite your tongue. If both parties are committed—whatever their reasons—it can work."

"And what if both aren't committed?"

"Then you have a problem and you have to deal with it."

19

I'm going to skip a bunch of stuff here because, really, who cares? We ate. We drank, and then we ate some more. I didn't spill, fart, fall down, or otherwise disgrace myself. I talked to the couple from Palm Springs, who turned out to be nice, as were most of the other folk. I listened with feigned interest to a lengthy discussion about vintage Jaguars and antique Rolls-Royces and another in which the participants told where they were when the last big local earthquake struck. Some of the answers were: the south of France, Barbados, the Galápagos Islands. I confessed I was in town, scrubbing out my toilet bowl, when a bunch of water slopped up and splashed my face. That got a big laugh. What a kidder, that girl. I felt I was just getting the hang of how to talk to the rich when the following occurred.

Stewart crossed the atrium with a bottle of Chardonnay and offered to fill my glass. I declined . . . I'd had plenty . . . but Dixie leaned toward him so he could refill hers. The collar of her silk shirt gaped briefly in the process, and I caught a glimpse of the necklace she wore in the hollow of her throat. Threaded on a gold chain was a tiny gold heart with a pink rose enameled in the center. I felt my smile falter. Fortunately, Dixie was looking elsewhere and didn't notice the change in my expression. I could feel my cheeks heat. The necklace was a duplicate of the one I'd seen in Mickey's bed-table drawer.

Now it was possible—remotely possible—he'd given her the necklace fourteen years before, in honor of the affair they were having back then. I set my glass on the table next to me and got to my feet. No one seemed to pay attention as I walked across the room. I passed through the doors into the dining room, where I spotted the same maid who'd answered the door.

I said, "Excuse me. Where's the nearest bathroom?" I couldn't, for the life of me, refer to it as the "loo."

"Turn right at the foyer. It's the second door on the right."

"I think someone's in there. Dixie said to use hers."

"Master bedroom's at the end of the hallway to the left of the foyer."

"Thanks," I said. As I passed the chair where I'd secured my handbag, I leaned down and picked it up. I moved through the living room and out into the foyer, where I turned left. I walked quickly, keeping my weight on my toes so the tap of my heels wouldn't advertise my passage. The double doors to the master bedroom stood open to reveal a room twice the size of my apartment. The pale limestone floors were the same throughout. All the colors here were muted: linens like gossamer, wall coverings of pale silk. There were two bathrooms, his 'n' hers, one on either side of the room. Eric's was nearer, fitted with an enormous roll-in shower and a wall-mounted bar to one side of the toilet. I turned on my heel and headed into the second.

Dixie's dressing table was a fifteen-foot slab of marble that stretched along one wall. There was a second wall of closets, a glass shower enclosure, a massive tub with Jacuzzi, and a separate dressing room with an additional U of hanging space. I closed the bathroom door behind me and started going through her belongings. This impulse to snoop was getting out of control. I just couldn't seem to keep my nose out of other people's business. The more obstacles the merrier. I found the cologne bottle in a cluster of ten others on a silver tray. On the bottom was the same partially torn label I'd seen at Mickey's. I sniffed at the spray. The scent was unmistakably the same.

I returned to the bedroom, where I crossed to the bed. I opened the top drawer in the first of the two matching bed tables. There sat the diaphragm case. I could hardly believe she was screwing him again . . . or was it *still*? No wonder she'd been nervous, prowling my backyard, angling for information about his current state. She must have wondered at his silence, wondered where he'd been the night she retrieved her personal items. Did she know he'd been shot? Hell, she might have done it herself if she'd found out about Thea. Maybe she was only quizzing me to determine what, if anything, I knew. I thought back to my conversation with Thea at the Honky-Tonk. Now I wondered if *she'd* seen the diaphragm et al., assuming it was mine while I'd assumed it belonged to her.

I closed the drawer and retraced my steps, emerging from the master suite just as Eric appeared, wheeling himself in my direction. I said, "Great bathroom. The maid sent me down here because the other was in use."

"I wondered where you went. I thought you left."

"I was just powdering my nose," I said, and then glanced at my watch. "Actually, I do have to go, now you mention it. I agreed to meet someone at eight, and it's almost that now."

"You have a date?"

"You don't have to sound so surprised."

He smiled. "Sorry. I didn't mean to pry."

"Could you give Dixie my thanks? I know it's rude not to do it personally, but I'd thought I'd slip out without making a fuss. Sometimes one person leaves and it starts an exodus."

"Sure thing."

"I appreciate the invitation. This was fun."

"We'll have to try it again. What's your schedule like next week?"

"My schedule?"

"I thought we'd have lunch, just the two of us," he said.

"Ah. I don't remember offhand. I'll check when I hit the office and call you on Monday."

"I'll be waiting."

Inwardly, I found myself backing away. Ordinarily, I don't imagine men are coming on to me, but his tone was flirtatious, which didn't sit well with me. I became especially chirpy as I made my retreat. Eric seemed amused by my discomfiture.

I was letting myself into my apartment some fifteen minutes later when I heard the last of a message being left on my machine. Jonah. I dropped my bag on the floor and snatched at the phone, but by then he'd hung up. I pressed the PLAY button and heard the rerun of his brief communication.

"Kinsey. Jonah here. It looks like we found your boy. Give me a call, and I'll fill you in on the nitty-gritty details. Not a very nice guy, but you probably know that already. I'm at home."

I looked up his home number and dialed with impatience, listening to ring after ring. "Come on, come on. . . ."

"Hello?"

Oh, shit. Camilla.

I said, "Could I speak to Lieutenant Robb? I'm returning his call."

"And who's this?"

"Kinsey Millhone."

Dead silence.

Then she said, "He's busy at the moment. Is this something I can help you with?"

"Not really. He has some information for me. Could I speak to him, please?"

"Just a minute," she said, not entirely happy about the situation. I heard a clunk as she placed the handset on the tabletop, then the tapping of her heels as she walked away. After that, I was treated to all the quaint, domestic sounds of the Robbs' Saturday night as they hung around the house. I could hear the television set in a distant room. Closer to the phone, one of his girls, probably Courtney, the older one, played chopsticks on an out-of-tune piano, never quite finishing her portion of the musical duet. I listened to countless repetitions of the first fifteen to twenty notes. The other daughter, whose name I forget, would chime in at the wrong spot, which caused the first girl to protest and start over again. The second child kept saying, "Stop it!" which the first girl declined to do. In the meantime, I could hear Camilla's comments to Jonah, who apparently hadn't been told there was a call for him. I could hear the sound of water running, the clattering of plates. I knew she was doing it deliberately, forcing me to eavesdrop on the small homely drama being played out for my benefit.

I whistled into the mouthpiece. I said "HELLO!" about six times, to no avail. I knew if I hung up, all I'd get was a busy signal when I tried calling back. *Clump, clump, clump.* I heard advancing footsteps on the hardwood floor. I yelled "HEY!" *Clump, clump, clump.* The footsteps receded. Another round of chopsticks was played. Shrieks from the girls. Chitchat between husband and wife. Camilla's seductive laughter as she teased Jonah about something. Once more I cursed myself for never learning how to do the piercing whistle you make when you put two fingers between your teeth. I'd pay six hundred dollars if someone could teach me that. Think of the taxis you could summon, the waiters you could signal across a crowded room. *Clump, clump, clump.* Someone approached the phone, and I heard Jonah remark with annoyance, "Hey, who left this off? I'm expecting a call."

I yelled "JONAH!" but not quickly enough to prevent his replacing the handset in the cradle. I redialed the number, but the line was busy. Camilla'd probably picked up another phone in haste, just to make certain I couldn't get through. I waited a minute and tried again. Still busy. On my fourth attempt, I heard the phone ring, only to have Camilla pick up again. This time she didn't even bother to say hello. I heard her breathe in my ear.

I said, "Camilla, if you don't put Jonah on the phone, I'm going to get in my car and drive over there right this minute."

She sang out, "Jonah? For you."

Four seconds later he said, "Hello?"

"Hi, Jonah. It's Kinsey. I just got home and picked up your message. What's going on?"

"Listen, you're going to love this. Bobbi Deems pulled your biker over last night when she saw he had a taillight out. Kid's name is Carlin Duffy, and it turns out he's driving with an expired Kentucky driver's license and expired registration. Bobbi cited him for both and impounded the bike."

"Where in Kentucky?"

"Louisville, she said. You want him, he'll be in court in thirty days."

"What about before then? Does he have a local address?"

"More or less. He claims he's living in a maintenance shed at that nursery off the 101 at the Peterson exit. Apparently, he works there part-time in exchange for rent, a claim the owner confirms. Meanwhile, Bobbi ran a background check on this crud, who's got a criminal history as long as your arm: arrests and convictions going back to 1980."

"For what?"

"Mostly nickel-and-dime stuff. He never killed anyone."

"I'm so relieved," I said.

"Let's see what we got here: wanton endangerment, criminal recklessness, theft, receiving stolen property, criminal mischief, trying to flee a halfway house where he was serving a ninety-day sentence for giving a false name to a police officer. The guy's not too bright, but he's consistent."

"Any outstanding warrants?"

"Nada. For the moment, he's clean."

"Too bad. It'd have been nice to have him picked up so I could talk to him."

"You'll definitely want to do that. Here's the best part. You ready? You want to know who his brother is? You'll never guess."

"I give up."

"Benny Quintero."

I could feel myself squint. "You're kidding me."

"It's true."

"How'd you figure that one out?"

"I didn't. Bobbi did. Apparently, Benny's name was listed as the owner on the bike registration, so Bobbi put Duffy through his paces. She'd forgotten the story, but she remembered Benny's name. Duffy claims they're half brothers. His mom was originally married to Benny's dad, who died in World War Two. Ten years later, she moved to Kentucky, where she married Duffy's dad. He was born the next year, fifteen-year age gap between the two boys. Carlin was thirteen when Benny came out to California and got himself killed."

"Is that why he's here?"

"You'd have to ask him. I'm thinking it's a good bet, unless you happen to believe in coincidence."

"I don't."

"Nor do I."

"So where is he now?"

"Well, he can't be far off if he's hoofing it."

"He could have stolen a car."

"Always possible, I guess, though outside his area of expertise. Anyway, if you decide to go looking for him, take someone along. I don't like the idea of your seeing him alone."

"You want to go?"

"Sure, I'd love it. Wait a second." He put a hand across the mouthpiece. Camilla must have been hovering nearby, listening to every word, because she squelched the idea before he even had the chance to ask. He removed his hand from the mouthpiece, addressing me again. "I'm tied up tonight, but how's Monday. Does that work?"

"Sounds ducky."

"You'll call me?"

"Of course."

"I'll see you then," he said.

As soon as he clicked off, I grabbed my handbag and walked out the door. I wasn't going to wait until Monday. How ridiculous. Duffy could be long gone; I couldn't take the risk. I stopped for gas on the way out. The nursery was maybe ten minutes away, but the needle on my gas gauge was now pointing at E, and I wasn't sure how much driving I'd have to do catching up with him.

It was twenty of nine when I finally pulled into the parking lot at the nursery. The sign out front indicated the place was open until 9 P.M. on weekends. The property must have occupied some ten to fifteen acres, the land sandwiched between the highway on one side and the side street into which I'd turned. The gardening center was immediately in front of me, a low white glass-and-frame building that accommodated numerous bedding, landscape, and house plants, seeds, gardening books, bulbs, herbs, pottery, and gifts, for "that special someone with a talent for growing."

To the right, behind the chain-link enclosure, I could see an array of fountains and statuary for sale, ceramic, plastic, and redwood planters, along with big plastic bags of fertilizers, mulches, garden chemicals, and soil amendments. To the left, I could see a series of greenhouses, like opaque glass barracks, and, beyond them, row after row of trees, a shaggy forest of shadows stretching back toward the freeway.

Now that the sun was fully down, the lingering light had shifted to a charred black, permeated by the smell of sod. The area along the side street was well lighted, but the far reaches of the nursery were shrouded in darkness. I scrounged around in the backseat and found a medium-weight denim jacket that I hoped would offer warmth against the chill night air. I locked the car and went into the gardening center with its harsh fluorescent lights shining down on banks of seed packs and gaudy indoor blooms.

The girl at the counter wore a forest-green smock with the name *Himes* embroidered across the pocket. As I closed the door, she gave the air a surreptitious fanning. She was in her teens, with dry blond hair and heavy pancake makeup over bumpy cheeks and chin. The air smelled of a recently extinguished clove cigarette.

"Hi. I'm looking for Carlin. Is he here?"

"Who?"

"Carlin Duffy, the guy with the bike who's living in the shed."

"Oh, Duffy. He's not here. The cops took his bike and locked it in the impound lot. He said it's going to cost a bundle to get it out."

"Bummer."

"He was really pissed. What a bunch of pigs."

"The worst. You two are friends?"

She shrugged. "My mom doesn't like him. He's a bum, she says, but I don't see why it's his fault if he's new in town."

"How long's he been here?"

"Maybe five or six months. He came like right before Christmas, sometime right around in there. Mr. Himes caught this other guy, Marcel? Do you know him?"

"Uh-uh."

"Marcel stole a bunch of these plants and sold 'em on the street? Mr. Himes fired his sorry butt as soon as he found out."

"And Duffy got his job shortly afterward?"

"Well, yeah. Mr. Himes had no idea Marcel was cheating him until Duffy bought a dieffenbachia off him and brought it in," she said. "I mean, Duffy's smart. He figured it's a scam right off. He only paid Marcel I guess a buck or two and there's our tag . . . like for $12.99 . . . pasted on the side."

"What about Marcel? I bet he swore up and down he didn't do it, right?"

"Right. What a dork. He acted all crushed and upset, like he's completely innocent. Oh, sure. He said he'd sue, but I don't see how he could."

"His word against Duffy's, and who's going to believe *him.* Is Marcel black, perchance?"

She nodded. "You know how they are," she said, rolling her eyes. For the first time, she assessed me. "How do you know Duffy?"

"Through his brother, Ben."

"Duffy has a brother? Well, that's weird," she said. "He told me his family's dead and gone."

"His brother's been dead for years."

"Oh. Too bad."

"What time will he be back?"

"Probably not until ten."

"Well, shoot," I said.

"Did he say he'd meet you here?"

"Nah. I saw him at the Tonk last night and then lost track of him."

"He's probably there tonight," she said helpfully. "You want to use the phone? You could have him paged. He's pals with the owner. I think his name is Tim."

"Really? I know Tim," I said. "Maybe I'll pop over there, since it isn't far. Meantime, if he comes in? Tell him I was here. I'd like to speak to him."

"About what?"

"About *what*?" I repeated.

"In case he asks," she said.

"It's sort of a surprise."

20

I cruised through the parking lot across from the Honky-Tonk and miraculously found a space about six slots down. It was not quite nine, and the Saturday-night boozers were just beginning to roll in. The Tonk wouldn't start jumping until ten o'clock when the band arrived. I crossed the street, pausing while a red-and-white panel truck idled near the garbage bins. No sign of the driver, but the logo on the side read PLAS-STOCK. I could see that second-floor lights were on in the building. Shifting shadows suggested someone moving around up there.

I continued on across the street, approaching the bar from the rear. Idly, I tried the back door, but it was locked. I guess it would be hard to insist on a cover charge out front if wily patrons could go around the back and get in for free. I moved to the front entrance. The bouncer remembered me from the night before so he waved off my ID and stamped the back of my hand. This was the third night in a row

I'd checked into the place, and I was feeling like a regular. During the period when Mickey and I were married, we were here four nights out of seven, which didn't seem odd at the time. He hung out with other cops, and that's what they did after work in those days. I was with Mickey so I did what he did as a matter of course. The Honky-Tonk was family, providing a social context for those of us without any other close ties. Looking back, I realize what an enormous waste of time it was, but maybe that was our way of avoiding each other, bypassing the real work of marriage, which is intimacy. I'm still lousy at being close, having so little practice in the past umpteen years.

I found a stool at the bar and ordered a beer. I sat with my back to the mirrored wall of glittering liquor bottles, one elbow on the bar, a foot swinging in time to whatever anonymous music played. I spotted Thea at just about the same time she spotted me. She held my gaze for a moment, her features drawn and tense. Gone was the leather vest that had exposed her long bare arms. In its place she wore a white turtleneck and tight jeans. Her belt was silver, the buckle shaped like a lock with a heart-shaped keyhole in the center. Preoccupied, she took an order from a table of four and then crossed to the bar, where she chatted with Charlie briefly before she moved toward me.

"Hello, Thea," I said. Close up, I realized she was pissed as hell. "Are you mad about something?"

"You can bet your sweet ass. Why didn't you tell me about Mickey? You *knew* he'd been shot and you never said a word."

"How'd you hear?"

"Scottie's father told us. You talked to me at least twice so you could have *mentioned* it."

"Thea, I wasn't going to walk in here cold and make that announcement. I didn't even know you were friends until you asked about his jacket. By then, I figured there was something more going on."

She shot an uneasy glance at a table near the poolroom door where Scottie was sitting, facing two men who had their backs to us. He'd apparently been watching us across the room. As if on cue, he excused himself to his companions and got out of his chair, then ambled in our direction with a beer bottle in his hand. I couldn't help but notice the change in his appearance. His mustache was neatly trimmed, and he'd shaved his goatee. He was also better dressed—nothing fancy, but attractive—cowboy boots, jeans, and a blue denim work shirt with the sleeves buttoned at the wrist. I thought he'd cut his hair, but as he drew near I could see he'd simply pulled it back and secured it in a rubber band.

Thea murmured, "Please don't say anything. He'd kill me if he knew."

"What time are you off? Can we meet and talk then?"

"Where?"

"What about that twenty-four-hour coffee shop over by the freeway?"

"Two A.M., but I can't promise—"

By then, Scottie'd reached us and we abandoned the exchange. His smile was pleasant, his tone mild. "Hi. How are you? I understand you're a friend of my dad's. I'm Scott Shackelford." He held out his right hand and we shook. I saw no indication that he was stoned or drunk.

"Nice meeting you," I said. "Tim told me who you were, but I didn't have the chance to introduce myself."

He put his left arm around Thea's neck in a companionable half nelson, holding the beer bottle just in front of her. The gesture was both casual and possessive. "I see you know Thea. How're you doin', babe," he said. He kissed her affectionately on the cheek.

Thea's eyes were on me as she murmured something noncommittal. She was clearly not all that crazy about the choke hold.

He turned back to me, his tone now tinged with concern. "We heard about Mickey. That's a hell of a thing. How's he doing?"

"He's fair. I called down there this afternoon, and the nurse said he's the same."

Scott shook his head. "I feel bad for the guy. I didn't know him well, but he used to come in here—what? Every couple of weeks?"

"About that," Thea said, woodenly.

"Anyway, it's been months."

"I heard he sold his car, so maybe he couldn't drive up as often," I said. I was trying think up a graceful excuse to extract myself. I'd only come here to find Duffy, and he was nowhere to be seen.

Scottie went on. "By the way, Tim said if you came in, he wants to talk to you."

"About what?"

"Beats me."

"Where is he?"

He looked around the room lazily, his mouth pulling down. "I'm not sure. I saw him a little while ago. Probably in his office if he's not out here somewhere."

"I'll try to catch him later. Right now—"

"Say, you know what? That's my dad and his friend at the table over there. Why don't you stop by and say hi?" He was pointing toward the two men he'd been sitting with.

I looked at my watch. "Oh, gee. I wish I had time, but I have to meet someone."

"Don't be like that. He'd like to buy you a drink. If anyone asks, Thea or Charlie can tell 'em where you're at, right, Thea?"

"I have to get back to work," she said. She eased out from under his arm and returned to the bar, where her order was waiting. She took the tray and moved off without looking back at us.

Scottie followed her with his eyes. "What's bugging her?"

"I have no idea. Look, I was just on my way to the ladies' room. I'll join you in a minute, but I really can't stay long."

"See you shortly," he said.

Scottie moved off toward the table. In retrospect, I decided he'd probably cleaned up his appearance in deference to his father. Pete Shackelford had always been a stickler about personal tidiness. I cut left toward the rest rooms. As soon as I was out of his line of sight, I headed down the corridor toward the rear exit. I had no intention of having a drink with Shack. He knew way too much about me and, as nearly as I could tell, he was already prepared to rat me out.

As I passed the short corridor where Tim's office was located, I stopped in my tracks. There was now a tarp flung across boxes stacked against the wall. Curious, I had a quick peek: ten sealed cartons with the Plas-Stock logo stamped on the sides. Clearly, this was a shipment unloaded from the panel truck currently idling outside. I dropped the corner into place. All four doors off that corridor were closed, but I could see a thin slit of light coming from under the third door on the left. That door was locked last I checked, and I couldn't help but wonder if it was locked again. I glanced around casually. I was alone in the hall and it wouldn't take but two seconds to see if it was secure. I eased to the left and placed my hand on the knob, taking care not to rattle it as I turned it in my hand. Ah. Unlocked. I wondered what was in there that required such security.

I pushed the door back, stuck my head in the opening. The floor area was only large enough to accommodate a set of stairs leading up and a padlocked door on the left, possibly a closet. I could see a dim light shining from the top of the narrow stairway. I stepped inside, closed the corridor door quietly behind me, and began to climb. It wasn't my intention to be sneaky, but I noticed I was walking on the outer edges of the treads, where there was less likelihood of creaking.

At the top of the stairs there was a landing about six feet square with a ladder affixed to one wall, probably leading to the roof. The only door off the landing was ajar, light flooding out from the space beyond. I pushed the door back. The room was huge, stretching off into the shadows, easily extending the length and breadth of the four large rooms below. The floor was linoleum, trampled in places where sooty footprints had permanently altered the color. I could see numerous electrical outlets along the walls and five or six large clean patches. The space was dense with the kind of dry heat that suggests poor insulation. The walls were unfinished plywood. There was a plain wooden table, two dozen folding chairs, a big garbage can jammed with scraps. I'd imagined cases of wine and beer stacked along the walls, but there was nothing. What had I pictured? Drugs, illegal aliens, child pornography, prostitution? At the very least, broken and outdated restaurant equipment, the old jukebox, the remains of New Year's Eve and St. Paddy's decorations from celebrations long past. This was boring.

I cruised the room, taking care to stay on the balls of my shoes. I didn't want anyone downstairs wondering who was clumping around up here. Still nothing of interest. I left the lights as I'd found them and crept back down the stairs. Again, I placed my hand carefully around the doorknob and turned it in silence. The hallway appeared empty. I exited the door, using my palm to blunt the click of its closing.

"Can I help you?"

Tim was standing in the shadows to the left of the door.

I shrieked. I flung up my hands and my shoulder bag flew out of my grasp, contents tumbling out as it hit the floor. "*Shit!*"

Tim laughed. "Sorry. I thought you saw me. What were you doing?" He was casually dressed: jeans and a V-neck knit pullover.

"Nothing. I opened that door by mistake," I said. I dropped to my knees, trying to gather up items that seemed to be strewn everywhere. "Scottie said you wanted to see me. I was looking for your office. This door was unlocked. I tried the knob and it was open so I just went on in. I figured you might be upstairs, so I called out a big *yoo-hoo.*"

"Really. I didn't hear you."

He hunkered, setting my handbag upright. He began to toss the contents back in, while I watched in fascination. Fortunately, I wasn't carrying a gun and he didn't seem to register the presence of my key picks. He was saying, "I don't know how you women do this. Look at all this stuff. What's this?"

"Travel toothbrush. I'm a bit of a fanatic."

He smiled. "And this?" He held up a plastic case.

"Tampons."

As he picked up my wallet, it flipped open to my driver's license, which he glanced at idly. The photostat of my P.I. license was in the window opposite, but if he noticed he gave no indication. He tossed the wallet into the handbag. Shack had probably already blown my cover anyway.

"Here, let me do that," I said, happy to be in motion lest he see my hands were shaking. Once we'd retrieved everything, I rose to my feet. "Thanks."

"You want to see what's up there? Here, come on. I'll show you."

"No, really. That's fine. I actually peeked at the space a few minutes ago. I was hoping you still had the old jukebox."

"Unfortunately, no. I sold that shortly after we bought the place. Great space up there, isn't it? We're thinking about expanding. We were using it for storage until it occurred to me there were better uses for that much square footage. Now all I have to do is get past fire department regulations—among other things."

"You'd do what, add tables?"

"Second bar and a dance floor. First, we have to argue with the city of Colgate and the county planning commission. Anyway, that's not what I wanted to talk to you about. You want to step into my office? We don't have to stand around out here talking in the dark."

"This is fine. I told Scottie I'd stop by his table and have a drink with his dad."

"We heard about Mickey."

"Word travels fast."

"Not as fast as you'd think. Shack tells us you were a cop once upon a time . . ."

"So what?"

Tim went right on. "We're assuming you're conducting an investigation of your own."

Thank you, Pete Fucking Shackelford, I thought. I tried to think how to frame my reply.

Meanwhile, Tim was saying, "We have a pal in L.A. who might be of help."

"Really. And who's that?"

"Musician named Wary Beason. Mickey's neighbor in Culver City."

Pointerlike, I could feel my ears prick up. "How do you know him?"

"Through his jazz combo. He's played here a couple times. He's very talented."

"Small world."

"Not really. Mickey told him we booked bands, so Wary got in touch and auditioned. We liked his sound."

"I'm surprised Wary didn't call you and tell you about the shooting."

"Yeah, we were too. We've been trying to reach him, but so far no luck. We thought you'd want to talk to him if you went to L.A."

"Maybe I'll do that. Mind if I ask you about a couple of things while I have you?"

"Sure. No problem."

"What's Plas-Stock?"

Tim smiled. "Plastic cutlery, plates, glassware, that kind of thing. We're doing a big buffet for the Memorial Day weekend. We'll comp you to it if you're interested. Anything else?"

"Did you ever pay Mickey the ten grand you owed him?"

His smile lost its luster. "How'd you hear about that?"

"I came across a reference to it in his papers. According to the note, payment was due in full on January fifteenth."

"That's right, but things were tight right about then so he gave me an extension. I pay him off in July."

"If he lives," I said. "Is that what he was doing when he came up here, negotiating the agreement?"

"Mickey's a drinker."

"I'm puzzled why he'd give you an extension when he's having financial problems of his own."

Tim seemed surprised. "Mickey has money problems? That's news to me. Last time I saw him, he didn't act like a guy with worries. You think the shooting had something to do with business?"

"I'm really not sure. I was curious why he was spending so much time up here."

Tim crossed his arms, leaning against the wall. "Don't quote me on this, especially not to Scottie, but if you want my opinion Mickey was hot to get in Thea's pants."

"What about her? Was she interested in him?"

"Let's put it this way: Not if she's smart. Scottie's not the kind of guy you mess with." I saw him lift his eyes to someone in the passage behind me. "You looking for me?"

"Charlie needs your approval on an invoice. The guy wants a check before he heads back to L.A."

"Be right there."

I glanced back. One of the other waitresses had already turned on her heel and disappeared.

Tim patted my arm. "I better take care of this. Whatever you want, it's on the house."

"Thanks."

I followed two steps behind Tim, entering the bar with another quick visual search for Duffy. Still no sign of him. Shack, at Scottie's table, caught sight of me and waved. I guessed there wasn't going to be a way to get out of this. Shack must have enjoyed the opportunity to burn me. Scottie turned to see who his dad was waving at, and then he motioned me over. I felt like a mule, stubbornly resisting even while I was being propelled in that direction.

Shack was sitting on the far side of the table, and he rose to his feet, saying, "Well, would you look who's here? We were just talking about you."

"I don't doubt that a bit."

"Sit down, sit down. Grab a seat."

The other fellow at the table rose and sank in his seat respectfully, the physical equivalent of a gent tipping his hat to a lady.

I said, "I really can't stay long."

"Sure you can," Shack said. He reached over and grabbed a chair from a nearby table, pulling it up next to him. I sat down, resigned. Shack's gaze rested on his son, his satisfaction and pride giving a lift to his normally heavy features. He was wearing a plaid wool shirt, unbuttoned to accommodate his thick neck. His companion appeared to be in his fifties, gray hair cut close, weathered complexion suggesting years of sun exposure. Like Shack, he was heavyset, bulky through the shoulders, his belly protruding as if he were six months pregnant.

Shack hooked a thumb at him and said, "This is Del. Kinsey Millhone."

"Hello."

Del nodded and then half rose again and shook my hand across the table. "Del Amburgey. Nice to meet you," he said.

We went through that "how're-you-tonight" shit while I squirmed inwardly, trying to think of something bland to say. "Are you here for a visit, or are you local?"

"I live up in Lompoc, so it's a little bit of both. I come down here now and then to see what you big-city folks are up to."

"Not much."

Shack said, "Well, that's not entirely true. This little gal was a cop back when I was in uniform. Now she's a P.I. . . ."

"What's a P.I.?" Del asked.

"A private investigator," Shack said.

I thought I was going deaf. He talked on. I watched his mouth move, but the sound was gone. I didn't look at Scott, but I was acutely aware that he was taking in the information with something close to alarm. His expression didn't seem to change, but his face shut down. Out of the corner of my eye, I could see his hands resting on the table, still relaxed, his fingers loose on the beer bottle, which he tilted to his lips. Aside from the casualness of the gesture, his body was completely still. I tuned in to Shack's commentary, wondering if there were any way to contain the damage he was doing.

". . . just about the time Magruder left the department. What was that, '71?"

"The spring of '72," I said. He knew exactly when it was. We locked eyes briefly, and I could tell blowing my cover allowed him to enjoy a moment of revenge. Whatever I was up to, he would leave me fully exposed. Better take control, I thought, get a jump on the little shit. "That was when Mickey and I split up. I lost touch with him after that."

"Until recently," Shack amended.

I looked at Shack without comment.

He went blithely on. "I guess those two LAPD detectives drove up here and talked to you. They came around my place yesterday. They seemed to think you might've had a hand in it, but I told 'em I didn't see how. You showed up at my door Monday. I didn't think you'd call attention to yourself if you'd shot him the week before. You're not that dumb."

"That was a ruse and you fell for it," I said. I was smiling, but my tone of voice was snide.

"What brings you out to Colgate?"

"Mickey lent Tim ten grand. A no-interest loan with a five-year balloon. I was curious if the money was repaid when it came due." Scottie began to tap one foot, which caused his knee to jump. He crossed his legs, trying to cover his agitation.

"When was that?" Shack asked, still enough of a cop to pursue the obvious.

"January fifteenth. Just about the time Mickey started coming in," I said. "You didn't know about the loan?"

"You ready for a drink? I'm heading to the bar," Scottie said. He was on his feet, his eyes pinned on me.

"Nothing for me, thanks."

"What about you, Dad? Del?"

"I'll go another round. My turn to buy," he said. He leaned forward, hauling his wallet from his right rear pocket.

Scottie waved him off. "I'll take care of it. What's your pleasure? Another of the same?"

"That'd be great."

"Make that two," Shack said.

Once Scottie left, Shack changed the subject, engaging me in chitchat so banal I thought I'd scream. I endured about three minutes of his asinine conversation and then took advantage of Scott's absence to slide out of my seat.

"You leaving us?" Shack said.

"I have to meet someone. It's been nice seeing you."

"Don't rush off," he said.

I made no reply. Del and I exchanged nods. I shouldered my bag and turned, scanning the crowd as I made my escape. Still no sign of Duffy, which was just as well. I didn't want Tim or Scottie to see me talking to him.

21

The outside air was chilly. It was not even ten o'clock, and the main street of Colgate was streaming with traffic, car stereos thumping. The occupants seemed to number four and five to a car, windows rolled down, everyone looking for action of some undisclosed kind. I could hear a chorus of honks, and coming up on my right I saw a long pink stretch limo bearing a bride and groom. They were standing on the backseat, their upper torsos extending through the sliding moon-roof window. With one hand, the bride clung to her veil, which whipped out behind her like a trail of smoke. With her other hand, she held her bouquet aloft, her arm straight up in a posture that mimicked the Statue of Liberty. The groom appeared to be smaller, maybe eighteen years old, in a lavender tuxedo with a white ruffled shirt, purple bow tie, and cummerbund. His hair was cut close, his ears red-tipped with cold. Numerous cars tagged along behind the limo, all honking, most decorated with paper flowers, streamers, and clattering tin cans. Their destination seemed to be the Mexican restaurant down the block from the Tonk. Other drivers and pedestrians were honking and hooting happily in response to this moving pageant.

I found my car and got in, pulling into the line of traffic behind the last of the procession. Of necessity I drove slowly, forced to a crawl as car after car turned left into the restaurant parking lot, waiting for breaks in the traffic. Glancing over to my right, I spotted Carlin Duffy walking with his head down, his hands in his jacket pockets. I'd only seen the man twice, but his height and his yellow hair were unmistakable. Had he been at the Tonk and I'd missed seeing him? He appeared to be heading toward the nursery, a distance of perhaps a mile and a half. Like a gift, the man turned, extending his right hand, his thumb uppermost.

I pulled over, leaning across the seat to unlock the passenger door. He already seemed puzzled that anyone, let alone a woman, would give him a ride at that hour. I said, "I can take you as far as the 101 at Peterson. Will that do?"

"That'd be good."

Spurs jingling, he slid into the passenger seat and slammed the door. He looked back over his shoulder with a snort of derision. "You see them beaners? What a bunch of Pacos. Groom looks like he's thirteen. Probably knocked her up. He shoulda kept his pecker in his pocket."

"Nice talk," I said.

He looked at me with interest. At close range, his features seemed too pinched for good looks: narrow-set light eyes and a long thin nose. He had one goofy incisor that seemed to stick straight out. The rest of his teeth were a snaggle of overlapping edges, some rimmed with gold. The yellow in his hair was the result of peroxide, the roots already turning dark. He smelled funky, like wood smoke and dirty gym socks. He said, "I seen you before."

"Probably at the Honky-Tonk. I was just there."

"Me too. Took a bunch of money off some niggers playin' pool. What's your name?"

"I'm Kinsey. And you're Carlin Duffy. I've been looking for you."

He flashed a look in my direction and then stared out the windshield, his face shutting down. "Why's that?"

"You know Mickey Magruder."

He seemed to assess me and then looked out the side window, his tone dropping into a range somewhere between sullen and defensive. "I didn't have nothing to do with that business in L.A."

"I know. I thought we'd figure out what happened, just the two of us. Your friends call you Carlin?"

"It's Duffy. I'm not a fruit," he said. He looked at me slyly. "You're a lady cop, ain't you?"

"I used to be. Now I'm a private eye, working for myself."

"What d'you want with me?"

"I'd like to hear about Mickey. How'd the two of you connect?"

"Why should I tell you?"

"Why shouldn't you?"

"I don't know nothin'."

"Maybe you know more than you think."

He considered that, and I could almost see him shift gears. Duffy was the sort who didn't give anything away without getting something in return. "You married?"

"Divorced."

"Tell you what. Let's pick us up a six-pack and go back to your place. We can talk all you want."

"If you're on parole, an alcohol violation's the last thing you need."

Duffy looked at me askance. "Who's on parole? I done my bit and I'm free as a bird."

"Then let's go to your place. I have a roommate and I'm not allowed to bring in guests at this hour."

"I don't have a place."

"Sure you do. You're living in the maintenance shed at Bernie Himes's nursery."

He kicked at the floorboard, running an agitated hand through his hair. "Goddang! Now, how'd you know that?"

I tapped my temple. "I also know you're Benny Quintero's brother. Want to talk about him?"

I had by then passed the entrance to the nursery, heading across the freeway toward the mountains.

"Where you goin'?"

"To the liquor store," I said. I pulled into a convenience mart in a former gas station. I took a twenty from my shoulder bag and said, "It's my treat. Get anything you want."

He looked at the bill and then took it, getting out of the car with barely suppressed agitation. I watched him through the window as he went into the place and began to cruise down the aisles. There was nothing I could do if he cruised right out the side door and took off on foot. He probably decided there wasn't much point. All I had to do was drive over to the nursery and wait for him there.

The clerk at the counter kept a careful eye on Duffy, waiting for him to shoplift or maybe pull a gun and demand the contents of the cash drawer. Duffy removed two six-packs of bottled beer from the glass-fronted cooler on the rear wall and then paused on one aisle long enough to pick up a large bag of chips and a couple of other items. Once at the counter, he paid with my twenty and tucked the change in his pants pocket.

When he got back in the car, his mood seemed improved. "You ever try licorice and beer? I got us some Good and Plentys and a whole bunch of other shit."

"I can hardly wait," I said. "By the way, what's the accent, Kentucky?"

"Yes, ma'am."

"I'll bet it's Louisville, right?"

"How'd you know?"

"I have an instinct for these things."

"I guess so."

Having established my wizardry, I drove back over the freeway, turned right onto the side street, and pulled into the lot for the nursery. I parked in front of the gardening center, which was closed at this hour and bathed in a cold fluorescent glow. I locked my car, hefted my bag to my shoulder, and followed Carlin Duffy as he made his way down the mulch-covered path. This was like walking into a deep and well-organized woods, wide avenues cutting through crated and evenly spaced trees of every conceivable kind. Most were unrecognizable in the dark, but some of the shapes were distinctive. I could identify palms and willows, junipers, live oaks, and pines. Most of the other trees I didn't know by name, rows of shaggy silhouettes that rustled in the wind.

Duffy seemed indifferent to his surroundings. He trudged from one darkened lane to the next, shoulders hunched against the night air, me tagging along about ten steps behind. He paused when we reached the shed and fumbled in his pocket for his keys. The exterior was board-and-batten, painted dark green. The roofline was flat, with only one window in view. He snapped open the padlock and stepped inside. I waited until he'd turned on a light and then followed him in. The shed was approximately sixty feet by eighty, divided into four small rooms used to house the two forklifts, a mini-tractor, and a crane that must have been pulled into service for the planting of young trees. Anything more substantial would have required larger equipment, probably rented for the occasion.

The interior walls were uninsulated, the floor dirt and cinder crunching under our feet. One of the rooms had been hung with tarps and army surplus blankets, draped from the ceiling to form a tentlike substructure. Inside, I could see a canvas-and-wood cot with a rolled-up sleeping bag stashed at one end. We moved into the shelter, where illumination was provided by a bare hanging 60-watt bulb. There was also a space heater, a two-burner hot plate, and a mini-refrigerator about the size of a twelve-pack of beer. Duffy's clothes were hung on a series of nails pounded into the side wall: jeans, a bomber jacket, a wool shirt, black leather pants, a black leather vest, and two sweatshirts. Being fastidious by nature, I had to ponder the absence of visible clean underwear and a means of bathing and brushing his teeth. This might not be the sort of fellow one would want to have a lengthy chat with in a small unventilated space.

I said, "Cozy."

"It'll do. You can set on the cot and I'll take this here."

"Thanks."

He placed the brown paper bag on an orange crate and removed the six-packs. He liberated two bottles and put the balance in his mini-refrigerator, leaving several on top. He reached in his pocket, took out a bottle opener, and flipped the caps from two beers. He set his bottle aside long enough to open the bag of chips and a can of bean dip, which he held out to me. I grabbed a handful of chips and put them in my lap, holding onto the can so I could help myself to dip.

"You want a paper plate for that?"

"This is fine," I said.

Having cleared the orange crate, he used it as a stool on which he perched. He opened his box of candy-coated licorice and tossed two in his mouth, sipping beer through his teeth with a little moan of delight. Before long, his teeth and his tongue were going to be blacker than soot. He leaned over and turned on the small electric space heater. Almost immediately, the coils glowed red and the metal began to tick. The narrow band of superheated air made the rest of the room seem that much colder by contrast. I confess, there was something appealing about this room within a room. It reminded me of "houses" I made as a kid, using blankets draped over tabletops and chairs.

"How'd you find me?" he asked.

"That was easy. You got pulled over and cited for a defective taillight. When they ran your name through the system, there you were in all your glory. You've spent a lot of time in jail."

"Well, now, see? That's such bullshit. Okay, so maybe sometimes I do something bad, but it's nothing *terrible.*"

"You never killed anyone."

"That's right. I never robbed nobody. Never used a gun . . . except the once. I never done drugs, I never messed with women didn't want to mess with me, and I never laid a hand on any kids. Plus I never done a single day of federal time. It's all city and county, mostly ninety-day horseshit. Criminal recklessness. What the fuck does that mean?"

"I don't know, Duffy. You tell me."

"Accidental discharge of a firearm," he said contemptuously. The crime was apparently so bogus, I was surprised he'd mention it. "It's New Year's Eve . . . this is a couple years now. I'm in this motel in E-town, having me a fine old time. I'm horsin' around, just like everyone else. I pop off a round, and the next thing you know, bullet goes through the ceiling and hits this lady in the ass. Why's that my fault?"

"How could it be?" I echoed, with equal indignance.

"Besides, jail's not so bad. Clean, warm. You got your volleyball, indoor tawlits, and your color television set. Food stinks, but medical care don't cost you a cent. I don't know what to do with myself half the time anyway. This pressure builds up and I blow. Jail's kind of like a time-out till I get my head on straight."

I said, "How old are you?"

"Twenty-seven. Why?"

"You're getting kind of old to be sent to your room."

"Probably so, I guess. I intend to straighten up my act, now I'm out here. Meantime, it's fun breakin' rules. Makes you feel free."

"I can relate to that," I said. "You ever hold a real job?"

He seemed mildly insulted that I'd question his employment history. "I'm a heavy equipment operator. Went to school down in Tennessee and got certified. Scaffolds, cranes, forklifts, dozers, you name it. Graders, backhoes, hydraulic shovels, boom lifts, anything Caterpillar or John Deere ever made. Ought to see me. I set up there in the cab and go to town." He spent a moment shifting gears with his mouth, using his beer bottle as a lever while he operated an imaginary loader.

"Tell me about your brother."

He set the empty bottle at his feet, leaning forward, elbows on his knees, his face animated. "Benny was the best. He looked after me better than my dad and momma. We done everything together, except when he went off to war. I was only six years old then. I remember when he come home. He'd been in the hospital and then rehab, on account of his head. After that, Momma said, he changed. She said he's moody and temperamental, kind of slow off the mark. Didn't matter to me; 1971, he bought the Triumph: three-cylinder engine, twin-style clutch. Wasn't new at the time, but it was hot. Nobody hardly fooled with Harley-Davidsons back then. None of them Jap bikes, neither. It was all BSA and Triumph." He motioned for me to hand him the chips and the can of bean dip.

"What brought him to California?"

"I don't know for sure. I think it had to do with his benefits, something about the VA fuckin' with his paperwork."

"But why not in Kentucky? They have VA offices."

Duffy cocked his head, crunching on potato chips while he wiped his lips with the back of his hand. "He knew someone out here he said could cut through the red tape. Hey, I got us some nuts. Reach me that bag."

I pushed the brown bag in his direction. He pulled out a can of peanuts and pulled the ring. He poured some into his palm and some into mine. I said, "Someone in the VA?"

"He never said who it was, or, if he did, I don't remember. I'se just a kid back then."

"How long was Benny here before he died?"

"Maybe a couple weeks. My momma flew out, brought his body back for burial, and had his bike shipped home. I still go to see him every chance I get. They got this whole section of Cave Hill Cemetery just for veterans."

"How much was she told about the circumstances of his death?"

"Some cop punched him out. They scuffled at the Honky-Tonk and Benny wound up dead."

"That must have been hard."

"You got that right. That's when I started havin' problems with the law," he said. "I did Juvie till I was finally old enough to be tried as an adult."

"When did you get out here?"

"Five–six months back. My dad died September. He had emphysema, smokin' three packs a day. Even at the end, he'd risk blowing hisself up, puffing on butts while he's hooked up to oxygen. Momma died a month later. I guess her heart give out on her while she was out rakin' leaves. I'd been over to the Shelby County jail on a DUI. Now that was bullshit for sure. I blew—what, point oh two over the limit? BFD is what I say. Anyway, once I finished out my time, I hitched my way home and here's the whole house is mine, plus furniture, motorcycle, and a bunch of other junk. Took me a long time to get the bike fixed up."

"Must have felt strange."

"Yeah, it did. I wandered around the place doing anything I felt like, though it wasn't any fun. I got lonesome. You spend time in jail, you get used to havin' other people near."

"And then what?"

"Well, Momma always kept Benny's room just like it was. Clothes on the floor, bed messed up the way he left it the day he come out here. I went through the place, just a cleanin' and sortin' and throwin' stuff out. Partly I was curious and partly I just needed me a little somethin' to do. I come across Benny's lockbox."

"What kind of lockbox?"

"Gray metal, about so-by-so." With his hands, he indicated a box maybe twelve inches by six. "It was under his bed, tucked up in the box springs."

"You still have it?"

"Naw. Mr. Magruder took it, so he probably hid it someplace."

"What was in the box?"

"Let's see. This press pass, belonged to a fellow named Duncan Oaks. Also, Oaks's dog tags and this black-and-white snapshot of Benny and some guy we figured had to be Oaks."

Duncan Oaks again. I wondered if Mickey'd put the items in a safe deposit box. Mentally, I made a note. Next time I was down there, I'd have to try again if I could pick my way in. So far, I hadn't come across a safe deposit key, but maybe another search would yield results. "Tell me about your relationship with Mickey."

"Mr. Magruder's a good dude. I like him. He's a tough old bird. Once he knocked me on my ass so bad I won't never forget. Popped me smack in the jaw. I still got a tooth loose on account of it." He wiggled an incisor to demonstrate his point.

"Why'd you come out to California, to track him down?"

"Yes, ma'am."

"How'd you find him? He moved to Culver City fourteen years back. He's cagey about his phone number and his home address."

"Hell, don't I know? I got that from Tim, guy owns the Tonk. I tried the bar first because that's where the fight between him and my brother took place. I figured someone might remember him and tell me where he was."

"What was your intention?"

"To kill his ass, what else? I heard he's the one who punched Benny's lights out. After we talked, I begun to see things his way."

"Which was what?"

"He figured he was framed, and I'd agree with him."

"How so?"

"He had him an alibi. He was bonin' this married lady and didn't want to pull her into it, so he kept his mouth shut. I talked to this cop said he saw the whole thing. Mostly, insults and pushing. The two never even struck a blow. I guess somebody come along later and beat the crap out of Benny. What kilt him was havin' that metal plate in his head. Blood seeped into his brain, and it swelled up like a sponge."

"Do you remember the cop's name?"

"Mr. Shackelford. I seen him at the Honky-Tonk earlier tonight."

"What about the snapshot in the box?"

"Two guys out in the boonies, gotta be Veetnam. Sojers in the background. Benny's wearin' fatigues and his big old army helmet he's decorated with this peace symbol. You know the one. Looks kind of like a wishbone with a thing stickin' out the end. Benny's got this shit-eatin' grin and he's flung his arm around the other fellow, who's bare to the waist. Other fellow has a cigarette hangin' off his lip. Looks like the dog tags he's wearin' are the same as the ones in the box."

"What's he look like?"

"You know, young, unshaved, with these big old dark brows and a black mustache: dirty-looking, like a grunt. Hardly any chest hair. Kind of pussyfied in that regard."

"Any names or dates on the back of the photograph?"

"No, but it's Benny clear as day. Had to be 1965, between August tenth when he shipped out and November seventeenth, which is when he got hit. Benny was at Ia Drang with the two/seven when a sniper got him in the head. He shoulda been medevacked out, but the choppers couldn't land because of all the ground fire. By time he got out, he said the dead and wounded was piled on each other like sticks of firewood."

"What was Mickey's theory?"

"He didn't tell me nothin'. Said he'd look into it is all I heard."

"Where's the lockbox now? I'd like to see the contents."

"Said he had a place. I learnt not to mess with him. He's the one in charge."

"Let's go back to Duncan Oaks. How does he fit in?"

"Beats me. I figure he's someone in Benny's unit."

"That's what Mickey was looking into. I know he placed a call to a high school in Louisville—"

"Manual, I bet. Benny went to Manual, played football and everything."

"Not Manual," I said. "It was Louisville Male High. He talked to the school librarian about Duncan Oaks. The next day, he hopped on a plane and flew east. Did you talk to him later, after he got back?"

"Never had a chance. I called a couple times. He never picked up his phone so I finally went down. I's madder than shit. I figured he's shining me on."

"You didn't know he'd been shot?"

"Uh-uh. Not then. Some guy down there told me. Fellow lived next door. I forget his name now, something queer."

"Wary Beason?"

"That's him. I busted out his winda, which is how we got acquainted." Duffy had the good grace to look sheepish about the window. He still didn't seem to realize I'd been on the premises that night.

I found myself staring at the dirt floor, trying to figure out what the hell was going on. How did the fragments connect? Tim Littenberg and Scott Shackelford were both in Vietnam, but the timing was off. Benny Quintero was there early in the war and then only briefly. Tim and Scottie went later, in the early seventies. Then there was Eric Hightower, whose second tour was cut short when he stepped on a mine and had his legs blown off. Again, that was long after Benny'd been shipped home. And why was any of it relevant to Mickey's being shot? I knew Mickey well enough to know he was on to *something*, but what?

"You with me or gone?"

I looked up to find Duffy staring at me with concern. I set aside my beer. "I think I'll butt out for now. I need time to absorb this. At the moment, I don't have a clue how any of it fits . . . or if it does," I said. "I may talk to you later when I've had a chance to think. You'll be around?"

"Here or the Tonk. You want me to walk you out?"

I said, "Please. It's dark as pitch out there."

22

I let myself into my apartment at eleven-fifteen, surprised to realize my entire conversation with Duffy had only taken an hour. I set up a pot of coffee and flipped the switch, letting it brew while I stretched some of the kinks out of my neck. I felt a faint headache perched between my eyes like a frown. I was longing for bed, but there was work to do yet. While the information was fresh, I opened my desk drawer and pulled out a new pack of lined index cards. Then I retrieved, from their hiding place, the various items I'd snitched from Mickey's.

I sat in my swivel chair, jotting down everything I could remember from the evening. Activities at the Honky-Tonk were turning out to be less sinister than I'd imagined. Maybe, as Tim had said, Mickey simply went there to drink and hustle Thea. I had to admit philandering would have been in character for him.

When the coffee was done, I got up from my chair and poured

myself a mug, adding milk that seemed only mildly sour. I returned to my desk, where I remained on my feet, idly pushing at the index cards. There were still countless minor matters that didn't fit the frame: Mickey's being shot with my gun, the long hissing message on my answering machine. That had originated from his apartment the afternoon of March 27. Who'd called me and why? If Mickey, why not leave a message? Why let the tape simply run to the end? If it wasn't Mickey, then what was the purpose? To imply contact between us? It had certainly made me look bad in the eyes of the police.

I sat down at my desk and began to play with the cards. I had to assume Mickey was on the track of Benny Quintero's killer. That question would nag at him as long as he lived. Benny's death had never been officially ruled a homicide, but Mickey knew he'd been blamed, despite the fact that charges had never been filed. In light of his checkered history with the department, his involvement in the matter had called his credibility into question and further damaged his already tainted reputation. As he saw it, his only choice was to abandon the profession he'd loved. His life after that had never amounted to much: booze, women, a shabby apartment. He couldn't even hold on to the sorry job he'd found: Pacific Coast Security with its faux-cop uniform and dime-store badge. He must have dreamed of escape, creating a way out with his caches of money and his phony IDs. I turned over a few cards, making a column, sorting facts in no particular order.

Idly, I set two index cards on edge, using the weight of each to support the other. I added a third, leaving the right side of my brain in neutral while I constructed a maze. Building card houses was another way I'd amused myself as a kid. The first floor was easy, requiring patience and dexterity but not much else. To add a second story to the first, you had to append a flat layer of cards, deftly floating a "ceiling" on the substructure until the whole of it was covered. Then began the real work: starting again from square one. First balance two cards atop the structure below, using the pair for their mutual support. Then add a third at an angle to the first two. Then add a fourth, then a fifth. At any point in the process, as the overall dimensions increased, there was always the danger that the whole of it would collapse, tumbling in on itself like—well, a house of cards. Sometimes, perversely, I'd even done this myself, snapping a corner with my finger, watching as the cards deconstructed in slow motion like a demolition project.

I glanced at the card in my hand, reading the note on it before I added it to the pile. Carefully, I added another card to the maze. I paused to remove it, reading the datum again. I experienced a jolt of insight and felt myself blink. I'd seen a connection, two index cards suddenly appearing in conjunction. What a dummy I was that I hadn't seen it before! A name showed up twice and I could feel my perception shift. It was like the sharp dislocation of a temblor, coming out of nowhere, fading away soon after. What I spotted was the name Del Amburgey, the man to whom Shack had introduced me at the Tonk. Delbert Amburgey was also the name on one of Mickey's packets of fake IDs: California driver's license, credit cards, social security card.

I set the index cards aside, pulling out the documents with Mickey's face laminated on top of what were probably Delbert's vital statistics. I swiveled in my swivel chair and studied the effect. Did these documents belong to Delbert or had his identity been lifted? Was the date of birth real or bogus, borrowed or invented, and how had it been done? I knew credit card scammers often got into "Dumpster diving," coming up with charge slips or carbons, even credit card statements discarded once the monthly bills had been paid. The information on the statements could be used to generate additional credit. The scammer would apply for cards based on lines of credit previously established by the individual in question. Any number of new accounts might be opened in this way. With a name, address, and social security number, ATM cards could be obtained, along with blank checks or proceeds from insurance policies. The scammer would supply the credit company with a substitute address, so the owner of the card remained unaware that goods and services were being charged to his or her legitimate account. The cards could also be milked through a series of cash withdrawals. Once the credit limit was exceeded, the scammer could either make the minimum payment or move on, fencing items or selling them at a discount and pocketing the profits. Actually, counterfeit documents like those in Mickey's possession were worth money on the open market, where felons, illegal aliens, and the chronically bankrupt could buy a brand-new start in life with thousands of dollars of fresh credit at their disposal.

I went back to Mickey's financial statements. I studied his savings passbook, beginning to understand the regular withdrawals of six hundred dollars on dates that corresponded with his trips to the Tonk. I thought about Tim and the conversation we'd had about the second floor, where he was claiming he might add tables. In retrospect, I marveled at how carefully I'd been duped. He'd offered me the bait—the unlocked door—and the subsequent glimpse of what had appeared to be undeveloped floor space. I'd seen the bouncer scan the driver's licenses of those granted admission to the bar. Since the bar retained a copy of each credit card transaction, the numbers would have been easy enough to match to the driver's license data. I couldn't guess at the whole of it, but there were people who'd know.

I looked at my watch again. It was 1:55. I said, "Oh, shit." I'd told Thea I'd meet her as soon as she got off work at two. I leapt up, shoved all the cards in my desk drawer and locked it, put Mickey's phony IDs back in their hiding place. I grabbed my jacket and car keys. Within minutes, I was on 101, driving north again toward Colgate, restraining the temptation to put the gas pedal to the floor. Traffic was light, the freeway virtually deserted, but I knew this was the hour when the CHP would be out. I didn't need a traffic stop or a speeding ticket. I found myself talking out loud, encouraging the VW's performance, praying Thea would wait for me at the coffee shop until I arrived. The restaurant shared a parking lot with the bowling alley next door. Every slot was filled and I groaned as I circled, looking for a place. Finally, I left my car in a moderately legal spot. I cut the lights and the engine as I opened the car door and emerged. It was 2:13. I locked the car and then did a run/walk to the restaurant, pausing for breath as I hauled the door open and started looking for her.

Thea sat at a back booth, smoking a cigarette. The harsh fluorescent lighting washed all the lines from her face, leaving her expression as blank as Kabuki makeup.

I slid into the seat across the table from her. "Thanks for waiting," I said. "I was caught up in paperwork and lost track of the time."

"Doesn't matter," she said. "My life's rapidly turning to shit anyway. What's one more thing?"

She seemed curiously withdrawn. My guess was she'd had too much time to reconsider. At the Honky-Tonk earlier, I could have sworn she'd confide. People with problems are generally relieved at the chance to unburden themselves. Catch them at the right moment and they'll tell you anything you ask. I was kicking myself I hadn't had the opportunity to take her aside then.

I said, "Look, I know you're pissed off because I didn't own up to who I was—"

"Among other things," she said acidly. "I mean, give me a break. You're a private detective, plus you're Mickey's ex-*wife?*"

"But Thea, get serious. If I'd said that up front, would I have learned anything?"

"Probably not," she conceded. "But you didn't have to lie."

"Of course I did. That was the only means I had of getting at the truth."

"What's wrong with being straight? Or is that beyond you?"

"Me, straight! What about you? You're the one screwing Mickey behind Scott's back."

"You were screwing him too!"

"Nope. Sorry. Wasn't me."

She looked at me blankly. "But you said—"

"Uh-uh. You might have leapt to that conclusion, but I never said as much."

"You didn't?"

I shook my head.

She started blinking, nonplussed. "Then whose diaphragm was it?"

"Good question. I just got the answer to that myself. It looks like dear Mickey was screwing someone else."

"Who?"

"I think I'd better keep mum, at this point."

"I don't believe you."

"Which part? You know he was seeing someone. You saw the evidence yourself. Of course, if you weren't systematically betraying Scottie, you wouldn't have to worry about these things."

Her gaze hung on mine.

I said, "You don't have to look quite so glum. He did the same thing to me. That's just how he is."

"It's not that. I just realized I didn't mind so much when I thought it was you. At least you'd been married to him, so it didn't feel so bad. Is he in love with this other woman?"

"If he is, it didn't stop him from picking up on you."

"Actually, *I* pursued *him.*"

"Oh, boy. I hate to say this, but are you nuts? The man's a barfly. He's unemployed, and he's older by—what, fifteen years?"

"He seemed . . . I don't know . . . sexy and protective. He's mature. Scottie's temperamental, and he's *so* self-involved. With Mickey, I felt safe. He loves women."

"Oh, sure. That's why he betrays us every chance he gets. He loves each one of us better than the last, often at the same time but never for long. That's how mature *he* is."

"You think he's going to be okay? I've been worried to death, but I can't get the hospital to say a word."

"I hope so, but really I have no idea."

"But you're hooked in, aren't you?"

"I guess. What feels strange is I'd put him out of my mind. Honest, I hadn't thought of him in years. Now that he's down, he seems to be everywhere."

"I feel the same. I keep looking for him. The door at the Tonk opens and I think he'll walk in."

"Why'd he keep coming back? Was it you or was something else going on?"

"Don't ask. I can't help you. I mean, I care about Mickey, but not enough to put my life on the line."

"Isn't it possible Scottie knows?"

"About Mickey and me?"

"That's what we're discussing," I said patiently.

"What makes you say that?"

"How do you know it wasn't Scott who shot Mickey?"

"He wouldn't do that. Anyway, his dad told us Mickey was gunned down two blocks from his apartment. Scottie doesn't even know where Mickey lives."

"Well, that's weak. I mean, think about it, Thea. Where was Scottie a week ago last Wednesday?"

"How should I know?"

"Was he with you?"

"I don't think so," she said. She stared at the table, going over it in her mind. "Tuesday, I was off. I wasn't feeling good."

"Did you talk to Scott on the phone?"

"No. I called and he was gone, so I left a message and he called me back the next day."

"In other words, he wasn't with you that Tuesday night or early Wednesday morning. We're talking May fourteenth."

Thea shook her head.

"What about the next day? Did you see him then?"

She stubbed out her cigarette. "I don't remember every single *day*."

"Start with what you do remember. When did you see Scottie last?"

Grudgingly, she said, "Monday. He and Tim had a meeting on Sunday. He drove up for the night and then left for L.A. the next day. I didn't see him again until the weekend. That was Saturday a week ago. He drove up here yesterday and goes back to L.A. tomorrow."

"What about you? Were you with Mickey at all on the night he was shot?"

She hesitated. "I went down to his apartment, but he was gone."

"Couldn't Scottie have followed you? He could have hung out in town. Once you got in your car, all he had to do was tail you to Mickey's."

She stared at me. "He wouldn't have done that. I know you don't like him, but that doesn't make him bad."

"Really. You told me he'd kill you if he ever found out."

"When I said he'd kill me it was . . . what do you call it—"

"Figurative."

"Figurative," she repeated. "Scottie wouldn't actually *shoot* anyone."

"Maybe his motive was something more serious."

"Like what?"

"A scam."

Thea's face underwent a shift. "I don't want to talk about this."

"Then let's change the subject. The first time I came in, Thursday of this week, Tim was pissed off at you. What was that about?"

"That's none of your business."

"Are Tim and Scottie partners?"

"You'd have to ask them."

"What kind of business?"

"I don't have a comment."

"Why? Are you involved in it too?"

"I gotta go," she said abruptly. I watched as she gathered up her jacket and her purse. She studiously avoided looking at me as she slid out of the booth.

It was 2:45 when I finally crawled into bed. I woke at 6 A.M. from long habit, nearly rolling out for my jog until I remembered it was Sunday. I lay for a moment, looking up at the skylight. The sun must have been close to rising because the sky was growing lighter as though a dimmer were being turned up. I felt oddly hung over for someone who'd drunk so little. It had to be the smoky bar, the conversation with Duffy, and tension between me and Thea, not to mention the late-night theorizing and driving around at all hours. I got up and brushed my teeth, took two aspirin with a big glass of water, and then returned to bed. In less than a minute, I was sleeping again. My bladder woke me at 10. I did an inner body survey, checking for symptoms of headache, nausea, and weariness. Nothing seemed to be amiss and I decided I could face life, but only with the promise of a nap later on.

I went through my usual morning routine: showered, donned my sweats, and made a pot of coffee. I read most of the Sunday paper, then wrapped myself in a quilt and settled on the couch with my book. Turned out to be nap time at 1 P.M. and I slept until 5. I climbed up the spiral stairs and checked myself in the bathroom mirror. My hair, as I suspected, was mashed flat on one side and sticking up in clumps on the other like dried palm fronds. I stuck my head under running water and emerged moments later with a more refined arrangement. I stripped off my sweats and pulled on a turtleneck and jeans, gym socks, my Sauconys, and Mickey's jacket. I picked up my shoulder bag, locked the door behind me, and crossed the patio to Henry's, where I tapped on his back door. There was no immediate response, but I realized the bathroom window was open a few inches, and I could hear sounds of a shower. Steam wafted out scented with soap and shampoo. I knocked on the window a familiar rat-a-tat-tat.

From inside, Henry yelled, "Yo!"

"Hey, Henry. It's me. I'm on my way to Rosie's for supper. Want to come?"

"I'll be there in a jiffy. Soon as I'm done in here."

I walked the half block to Rosie's, arriving at five-thirty, just as she was opening for business. We exchanged pleasantries, which in her case consisted of abrasive comments about my weight, my hair, and my marital status. I suppose Rosie's a mother figure, but only if you favor the sort that appear in Grimm's fairy tales. It was her avowed intention to fatten me up, get me a decent haircut, and a spouse. She knows perfectly well I've never met with success in that department, but she says *eventually* (meaning when I'm old and dotty, demented, and infirm) I'll need someone to look after me. I suggested a visiting nurse, but she didn't think that was funny. Then again, why should she? I was serious.

I sat down in my usual booth with a glass of puckery white wine. It's hellish to learn the difference between good wine and bad. Henry wandered in soon after, and we let Rosie browbeat us into a Sunday night supper that consisted of *savanyu marhahus* (hot pickled beef to you, pal) and *kirantott karfiol tejfolos martassal*, which is deep-fried cauliflower smothered in sour cream. While we mopped up our plates with some of Henry's homemade bread, I filled him in on the events of the past few days. I must say, the situation didn't seem any clearer when I'd laid it out to him.

"If Mickey and Mrs. Hightower are having an affair, her husband had as much reason to shoot him as Thea's boyfriend," he pointed out.

"Maybe so," I replied, "but I got the impression Eric had made his peace with her. I keep thinking there's more, something I haven't thought of yet."

"Can I do anything to help?"

"Not that I know, but thanks." I glanced up as the door opened and the waiter from the Hightowers' party came in with a hardback book under one arm. He wore a tweed sport coat over a black turtleneck, dark trousers, and loafers polished to a fare-thee-well. Having seen him in his white jacket serving drinks the night before, it took a moment to come up with his name.

I turned to Henry as I rose. "Can you excuse me for a minute? There's someone I need to talk to."

"Not a problem. I've been itching to finish this," he said. He brought out a neatly folded copy of the Sunday *New York Times* crossword puzzle and a ballpoint pen. I could see he was half done, completing the answers in a spiral pattern, starting at the edges and working toward the center. Sometimes he wrote in the answers leaving out every other letter because he liked the way it looked.

Stewart was passing the booth when he caught sight of me. "Well, hello. How are you? I wondered if you'd be here."

"Can I talk to you?"

"Be my guest," he said, gesturing toward the booth where he traditionally sat. I gave Henry's arm a squeeze, which he barely noticed, given his level of concentration. Stewart waited till I was seated and then sat down across from me, the book on the seat beside him.

"What's the book?" I asked.

He picked it up, holding the spine toward me so I could read the title, *The Conjure-Man Dies* by Rudolph Fisher. "I usually read biography, but I thought I'd try something new. Detective novel written in the early thirties. Black protagonist."

"Is it good?"

"Haven't decided yet. I'm just getting into it. It's interesting."

Rosie appeared. She stood by the table, her eyes fixed on the far wall, avoiding the sight of us. I noticed she was wearing slippers with her bright blue cotton muumuu.

Stewart reached for the menu and said, "Good evening, Rosie. How're you doing? Any specials I should hear about?"

"You tell him is good, the pickled beef," she said. Rosie can speak in perfect order the English when it suits her purposes. Tonight, for some reason, she was behaving like someone recently admitted to this country on a temporary visa. She seldom addresses men directly unless she's flirting with them. A similar inhibition applies to strangers and women, children, the hired help, and people who pop in and ask directions of her. She might answer your question, but she won't look.

I said, "The pickled beef is great. Fabulous. And the deep-fried cauliflower is not to be believed."

"I think I'll have that," Stewart said, setting aside the menu.

"What to drink?" she asked.

"Try the white wine. It's piquant. The perfect compliment to pickled beef," I said.

"Sounds good. I'll try it."

Rosie nodded and departed while Stewart shook his head. "I wish I had the nerve to order something else. That Hungarian stuff is for the birds. I come here because it's quiet, especially on Sundays. I go home with indigestion keeps me up half the night. Now what can I do for you?"

"I need to ask you about the Hightowers."

"What about them?" he asked, with a caution that didn't bode well for me.

I took a deep breath. "Here's the deal," I said. "My ex-husband was shot in Los Angeles. This was in the early morning hours, May fourteenth. He's currently in a coma, with no clear indication he'll pull out of it. For various reasons too complicated to go into, I'm trying to figure out what happened. Obviously, the cops are too." I was watching his eyes: intelligent, attentive, giving nothing away. I went on. "Both the Hightowers know Mickey, and I'm trying to determine if there's a link."

"What's your question for me? Because some things I'll tell you and some I won't."

"I understand. Fair enough. What's your job?"

"My job?"

"Yeah, what do you actually do for them?"

"Chauffeur, handyman. I wait table sometimes."

"How long have you been there?"

"It'll be two years in June. Same as Clifton. He tends bar at parties like the one they had last night. Otherwise, he manages the house and handles general maintenance. All the major repairs are hired out, but it seems like there's always something broken or in need of adjustment."

"What about Stephanie? Does she work for both of them or just Dixie?"

"She's Mrs. H's personal assistant. She comes in Mondays and Thursdays, noon to five or five-thirty. Mr. H takes care of his business on his own. Phone calls and letters, personal appointments. He keeps it all up here," he said, tapping his head.

"I take it there's a cook, as well?"

"Cook and cleaning crew. There's two women do the laundry and another one does flowers. Plus the gardeners, the pool guy. I wash the cars and Mr. H's van. Clifton and the cook—her name's Ima—both live on the property. The rest of us live out and come in as needed."

"Which is when?"

"It varies. I'm usually not there during the week. Fridays and Saturdays I'm always on call, especially if the two of them are going out. Other times Mr. H prefers to drive himself. Mrs. H likes the car. They have a six-passenger limo she enjoys."

"Did you drive either one of them to Los Angeles last week?"

"I didn't, but that doesn't mean they didn't go down on their own."

"You know Mickey Magruder? Good-looking guy, in his fifties, an ex-cop?"

"Doesn't sound familiar. What's his connection?"

"We go way back, the four of us. More than fifteen years. Mickey and Dixie were having an affair back then. I have reason to believe they've rekindled the flame. I'm wondering if Eric knew."

Stewart thought briefly; then he shook his head. "I don't carry tales."

"I can appreciate that. Is there *anything* you can tell me?"

"I think you'd do better asking one of them," he said.

"What about the marriage? Do they get along okay?"

Again, Stewart paused, and I could see the conflict between his knowledge and his reticence. "Not of late," he said.

23

That was as much as I was able to get from him. I must say I admired his loyalty, though it was frustrating. The evening wasn't completely unproductive. Henry's point was well taken. If jealousy was the motive for the shooting, the number of suspects had just increased. Eric Hightower was in the mix and Thea was another candidate, though not a particularly strong one. She'd risked a lot for Mickey, and while she professed her care and concern, that might have been laid on for my benefit. Dixie was another possibility. What would she have done if she'd discovered Mickey's affair with Thea?

The problem was, it all seemed so melodramatic. These people were grown-ups. I found it hard to picture any of them lurking in the shadows, plugging away at Mickey with my gun. It's not like you don't read about such things in the daily paper, but the scenario left too many things unexplained. For instance, who was Duncan Oaks? How was he related to events? Was Mickey on the trail of the person or persons responsible for Benny's fatal beating?

We left Rosie's at eight, Henry and I, walking home in the dark without saying much. Once back in my apartment, I sat down at my desk yet again and reviewed my notes. Within minutes, I realized my heart wasn't in it. I made a pile of cards and shuffled, dealing myself a tarot reading of the data I'd collected. No insights emerged, and I finally packed it in. Maybe tomorrow I'd be smarter. There was always the outside chance.

Six A.M. Monday morning, I rolled out of bed, pulled on sweats, brushed my teeth, and went for a three-mile jog. The predawn light was gorgeous: the ocean luminous blue, the sky above it orange, fading to a thin layer of yellow, then a clear blue sky beyond. Along the horizon, the oil rigs sparkled like an irregular line of diamond scatter pins. The absence of cloud cover eliminated any special effects when the sun finally rose, but the day promised to be sunny and that was sufficient for me. When I finished the run, I headed over to the gym, where I variously stretched, curled, extended, crunched, hyperextended, pressed, pecked, pushed, shrugged, raised, pulled down, and pulled up weights. At the end of it, I felt keen.

I went home and showered, emerging from the apartment at nine in my jeans, ready to face the day. I drove my car north on 101, taking the off-ramp that put me in range of the county offices adjacent to the VA. I parked and went into the Architectural Archives, where I gave the Honky-Tonk's address and asked to see whatever drawings and blueprints they had on hand. I was given a set of progress prints showing the vicinity plan, site plan, demolition plan, foundation and framing plans, elevations, and electrical legend. It didn't take me long to find what I was looking for. I returned the prints and headed for the parking lot where I'd seen a pay phone.

I dialed directory assistance and asked for the number of the Secret Service in L.A., the offices of which were actually listed as part of the U.S. Treasury Department. In addition to the L.A. number, I was given a telephone number for the agency in Perdido. I charged the call to my credit card, punching in the Perdido number. The phone rang once.

"Secret Service," a woman said.

How secret could it be if she was willing to blurt it out that way?

I asked to speak to an agent and she put me on hold. I stared out across the parking lot, listening to the sibilant ebb and flow of traffic on the highway. The morning was clear, the temperature in the 50s. I imagined by afternoon that would warm to the usual 70s. The line was picked up moments later, and a flat-voiced gentleman introduced himself. "This is Wallace Burkhoff."

I said, "I wonder if you can help me. I'm calling because I suspect there's a credit-card scam being operated from a bar in Colgate."

"What kind of scam?"

"I'm not sure. A friend of mine—actually, my ex-husband—bought some phony documents from a fellow up here. I think the owner of the bar might be running a regular manufacturing plant." I told him about the Honky-Tonk: the scanning device for drivers' licenses and my guess about the matching of credit-card charge slips to names on licenses. On the surface, it sounded thin, but he listened politely as I talked on. "A couple of days ago I saw a truck on the premises. Ten cartons had been unloaded and stacked in the corridor. The boxes were marked Plas-Stock, which the owner told me was plastic glassware and cutlery."

"Not quite." Burkhoff laughed. "Plas-Stock specializes in commercial equipment for manufacturing plastic cards and blank card stock for medical ID cards and health club memberships."

"Really? My ex has three sets of fake IDs in his possession, including drivers' licenses, social security cards, and a fistful of credit cards. I'm reasonably certain some of the data came from a regular bar patron, because I was introduced to the guy, and the name and approximate date of birth are the same."

"What's his interest in acquiring phony IDs?"

"He's a former vice detective, and I think he picked up on the operation three or four months back. I mean, I can't swear this is true, but

I have the receipts he kept from a series of visits to the place and I also have the phony documents with his picture plastered all over them."

"Would he be willing to talk to us?"

"He's currently out of commission." I told Agent Burkhoff about Mickey's condition.

"What about yourself?"

"Hey, I've already told you as much as I know. This is outside my area of expertise. I'm just making the call. You can do with it as you please."

"Where's their base of operation?"

"I think it's somewhere in the building. Yesterday, the owner set it up so I had a chance to see the second floor. It was empty, of course, but I did spot a number of electrical outlets. I don't know what kind of equipment would be in use—"

"I can tell you that," he said. "Optical scanners, encoding machines, shredders, embossers, tippers—that's what puts the gold on the newly embossed numbers—laminators, hologram punch devices. You see anything like that?"

"No, but I suspect they were operating in the space until a couple of days ago. I checked with the local architectural archives and took a look at the plans submitted when the owner applied for building permits. The structure's one of the few in town with a basement and my guess is they moved the operation down there."

"Give me the particulars and we'll check it out," he said.

I gave him the name and address of the Honky-Tonk and Tim's name and home address. I added Scottie's name to the mix, along with the dates Mickey'd been there and the names on the assortment of phony documents he had. "You need anything else?"

"Your name, address, and phone."

"I'd prefer not," I said. "But I'll make copies of the IDs and put those in the mail to you."

"We'd appreciate that."

I hung up, hauled out the telephone book, found my travel agent's number, and put a couple of coins in the slot. I told her I needed plane tickets for Louisville and gave her my budget limitations.

"*How* much?"

I said, "Five hundred dollars?"

She said, "You're joking."

I assured her I wasn't. She tapped the information into her computer. After much silence, many sighs, and some additional clicks, she told me the best she could do was an airline that had been in business for less than two years and was offering a no-frills flight to Louisville out of LAX with only two connections, Santa Fe and Tulsa. There was no advance seat assignment, no movie, and no meal service. She assured me the company hadn't filed for bankruptcy (yet) and hadn't reported any major flaming crashes to date. The point was I could get there for $577.

I had her book me on an early morning flight, leaving the return ticket open since I really had no idea how long my inquiry would take. Basically, I'd make it up as I went along. In addition to the plane fare, I reserved a rental car at the airport in Louisville. I'd find a motel when I got there, preferably something cheap. At the end of this, if nothing else, my debt of guilt with regard to Mickey would be paid in full. I went home, packed a duffel, and chatted briefly with Henry, letting him know I'd be gone for some indeterminate period. I also put a call through to Cordia Hatfield, telling her of my arrival later in the afternoon.

I stopped by the travel agent's and picked up my ticket, then drove over to the office, where I spent the balance of the morning getting life in order in case I didn't make it back. The drive to Culver City was uneventful, and I parked in the alley behind Mickey's building at 4:55. I left the duffel in the car, not wanting to seem presumptuous about staying overnight. Cordia had extended an invitation, but she hadn't seemed that thrilled.

I knocked on the Hatfields' door, wondering if they'd hear me over the blare of the TV set. I waited a moment and then knocked again. The sound was cut and Cordia opened the door.

I'd last seen the two sisters on Thursday, only four days before, but something in her manner seemed different. She stepped back, allowing me to enter. The apartment, as before, was uncomfortably warm, the temperature close to 80, windows fogged over with condensation. Steam curled from a pot simmering on the stove. The bubbling liquid was cloudy, and a collar of scum had collected on the surface. The air smelled of singed pork and something else, unfamiliar but faintly dunglike. The TV had been muted, but the picture remained: the late afternoon news with its steady diet of calamities. Belmira seemed transfixed. She sat at the kitchen table, tarot deck in hand, while under her chair, Dorothy chewed on a bony bundle of something crunchy and dead.

"Is this a bad time?" I asked.

"As good as any," Cordia said.

"Because I can come back later if it's more convenient."

"This is fine." She wore a long-sleeved cotton housedress in shades of mauve and gray with a smocklike apron over it, trailing almost to the floor. She turned to the stove, reaching for a slotted spoon that she used to adjust ingredients in the boiling water. Something floated to the surface: heart-shaped skull, short body, not a lot of meat on it. I could have sworn it was a squirrel.

"How have you two been?" I said, hoping for an answer that would clue me in.

"Good. We're fine. What can we do for you?"

Abrupt, to the point, not entirely friendly, I thought. "I'm on my way out of town, and I need to check Mickey's for something someone left with him."

Her tone was aggrieved. "Again? You were just up there last night. We saw lights on till close to midnight."

"At Mickey's? Not me. I was in Santa Teresa all weekend. I haven't been here since Thursday morning."

She looked at me.

"Cordia, I swear. If I'd wanted to get in, I'd have asked for the key. I wouldn't go in without permission."

"You did the first time."

"But that was before we met. You've been very helpful to me. I wouldn't do that behind your back."

"Suit yourself. I won't argue. I can't prove it."

"But why would I be here now if I'd already been in last night? That doesn't make sense."

She reached into her pocket and took out the key. "Return it when you're done and let's hope this is the last of it."

I took the key, aware that her manner was still stony and unyielding. I felt terrible.

Belmira said, "Oh, my dear!" She'd turned over four cards. The first was the Page of Swords, which I knew now was me. The remaining three cards were the Devil, the Moon, and Death. Well, that was cheering. Bel looked up at me, distressed.

Cordia moved quickly to the table and snatched up the cards. She crossed to the sink, opened the cabinet under it, and tossed the deck in the trash. "I asked you to quit reading. She doesn't believe in tarot. She told you that last week."

I said, "Cordia, really—"

"Go on up to the apartment and be done with it," she snapped.

Belmira's misery was palpable, but she didn't dare defy Cordia. Nor did I, for that matter. I tucked the key in my pocket and let myself out. Before the door closed behind me, I could hear Bel protesting her loss.

I unlocked Mickey's front door and let myself in. His drapes were still closed, blocking the light except for a narrow gap between panels where the late-afternoon sun cut like a laser, warming the interior. The air was dense with dust motes and carried the moldy scent of unoccupied space. I stood for a moment, taking in the scene. With no one to clean the place, many surfaces were still smudged with fingerprint powder. If someone had been in the apartment the night before, there were no obvious signs. I skipped the rubber gloves this time and did a quick walk-through. On the surface, it was just as I'd seen it last. I paused in the bedroom door. A small gauzy piece of cloth trailed out from under the bed. I got down on my hands and knees, lifted the bottom of the spread, and peeked under the bed. Someone had systemically removed the fabric covering the bottom of the box spring, and it lay on the carpet like a skin shed by a snake. I knelt by the bed and lifted one corner of the mattress. I could see a line where the fabric had been scored by something sharp. I lifted the bulk of the mattress, turning it over with the sheets still in place. The underside had been gutted, slit the entire length at ten-inch intervals. Stuffing boiled out, cotton tufts protruding where the thickness had been searched. There was something both sly and savage in the evisceration. I did what I could to restore the bed to a state of tidiness.

I checked the closet. Mickey's clothing had been slit in a similar fashion: seams and pockets slashed, linings ripped open, though the garments had been left hanging, apparently undisturbed. To the casual observer, nothing would appear amiss. The damage probably wouldn't have been discovered until Mickey returned or his belongings were moved to storage. I went back to the living room, noticing for the first time that the cushions on the couch appeared to be out of alignment. I turned them over and saw they'd been sliced open as well. Along the back of the couch, the fabric had been picked open at the seam. The damage would be apparent the first time the couch was moved, but, again, the vandalism wasn't evident on cursory inspection.

I checked both of the heavy upholstered chairs, getting down on the floor so I could squint at the underside. I lifted the chairs one at a time, tilting each forward to inspect the frames. On the bottom of the second chair, there was a rectangular cut in the padding. I removed the wedge of foam rubber. In the hole there was a gray metal box, six inches by twelve, like the one Duffy'd described. The lock had been badly damaged and yielded easily to pressure. Gingerly, I opened the lid. Empty. I sat back on my heels and said, "Mickey, you ass."

What a dumb hiding place! Given his ingenuity and paranoia, he could have done better than this. Of course, I'd searched the place twice and hadn't found the damn thing on either occasion, but *somebody* had. I was sick with disappointment, though there was clearly no remedy. I hadn't even heard about the lockbox until Saturday night. At the time, it hadn't occurred to me to drop everything and hit the road right then. Maybe if I had, I might have beat "somebody" to the punch.

Ah, well. It couldn't be helped. I'd simply have to do without. I could find a picture of Duncan Oaks in his high school yearbook, but I would have liked the dog tags and the press pass Duffy'd mentioned to me. There was something about an authentic document that served as a talisman, a totem object imbued with the power of the original owner. Probably superstition on my part, but I regretted the loss.

I returned the box to its niche, tilted the chair back into its upright position, and let myself out the front door, locking it behind me. I went down the steps and knocked on Cordia's door. She opened it a crack and I gave her the key. She took it without comment and closed the door again. Clearly, I wasn't being encouraged to spend the night with them.

I crept out to the alley, got in my car, and drove to the airport. I found a nearby motel, offering shuttle service every hour on the hour. I ate an unremarkable dinner in the nondescript restaurant attached to one end of the building. I was in bed by nine and slept until five-forty-five, when I rose, showered, threw on the same clothes, left my VW in the motel parking lot, and took the shuttle to LAX, where I caught my 7 A.M. plane. The minute the nonsmoking sign was turned off, all the passengers in the rear set their cigarettes on fire.

It was in the Tulsa airport, while I was waiting between planes, that I made a discovery that cheered me up no end. I had an hour to kill so I'd stretched out in a chair, my legs extended into the aisle in front of me. The position, while awkward, at least permitted a catnap, though later I'd probably require hundreds of dollars' worth of chiropractic adjustment. In the meantime, I was using Mickey's leather jacket as a pillow, trying to ease the strain on my neck. I turned over on my side, not easy to do while sitting upright. As I did so, I felt something lumpy against my face—metal zipper tab, button?—I didn't know what it was, except that it added an unacceptable level of discomfort. I sat up and checked the portion of the jacket that was under my cheek. There was nothing I could see, but by pinching the leather I could feel an object in the lining. I flattened the jacket on my lap, squinting at the seam where I could see an alteration in the stitching. I opened my shoulder bag and took out my nail scissors (the same ones I utilize for the occasional emergency haircut). I picked a few stitches loose and then used my fingers to widen the opening. Out slid Duncan Oaks's dog tags, the black-and-white snapshot, and the press card. Actually, the hiding place made perfect sense. Mickey'd probably worn this very jacket when he made the trip himself.

The dog tags bore Duncan Oaks's name and date of birth. Even all these years later, the chain was crusty with rust or blood. The snapshot was exactly as Duffy had described it. I set those items aside and studied the press card issued by the Department of Defense. The printing around the border said: LOSS OF THIS CARD MUST BE REPORTED AT ONCE. PROPERTY OF U.S. GOVERNMENT. Under the line that read *noncombatant's certificate of identity* was Duncan Oaks's name, and on the left was his picture. Dark-haired, unsmiling, he looked very young, which of course he was. The date of issue was 10 Sept. '65. Four years out of high school, he was no more than twenty-three years old. I studied his face. Somehow he seemed familiar, though I couldn't think why. I flipped the card over. On the back, he'd pasted a strip on which he'd written, *In case of emergency, please notify Porter Yount, managing editor, Louisville Tribune.*

24

My plane arrived in Louisville, Kentucky, at 5:20 P.M., at a gate so remote it appeared to be abandoned or under quarantine. I'd been in Louisville once before, about six months back, when a cross-country romp had ended in a cemetery, with my being the recipient of an undeserved crack on the head. In that case, as with this, I was out a substantial chunk of change, with little hope of recouping my financial losses.

As I passed through the terminal, I paused at a public phone booth and checked the local directory on the off chance I'd find Porter Yount listed. I figured the name was unusual and there couldn't be that many in the greater Louisville area. The high school librarian had told me the *Tribune* had been swallowed up by a syndicate some twenty years before. I imagined Yount old and retired, if he were alive at all. For once my luck held and I spotted the address and phone number of a Porter Yount, whom I assumed was the man I was looking for. According to the phone book, he lived in the 1500 block of Third

Street. I made a note of the address and continued to the baggage claim level, where I forked over my credit card and picked up the keys to the rental car. The woman at Frugal gave me a sheet map and traced out my route: taking the Watterson Expressway east, then picking up I-65 North into the downtown area.

I found my car in the designated slot and took a moment to get my bearings. The parking lot was shiny with puddles from a recent shower. Given the low probability of rain any given day in California, I drank in the scent. Even the air felt different: balmy and humid with the late-afternoon temperatures in the low 70s. Despite Santa Teresa's proximity to the Pacific Ocean, the climate is desertlike. Here, a moist spring breeze touched at newly unfurled leaves, and I could see pink and white azaleas bordering the grass. I shrugged out of Mickey's jacket and locked it in the trunk along with my duffel.

I decided to leave the issue of a motel until after I'd talked to Yount. It was close to the dinner hour, and chances were good that I'd find him at home. Following instructions, I took one of the downtown off-ramps, cutting over to Third, where I took a right and crossed Broadway. I drove slowly along Third, scanning house numbers. I finally spotted my destination and pulled in at a bare stretch of curb a few doors away. The tree-lined street, with its three-story houses of dark red brick, must have been lovely in the early days of the century. Now, some of the structures were run-down, and encroaching businesses had begun to mar the nature of the area. The general population was doubtless abandoning the once-stately downtown for the featureless suburbs.

Yount's residence was two and a half stories of red brick faced with pale fieldstone. A wide porch ran along the front of the building. Three wide bay windows were stacked one to a floor. An air conditioner extended from an attic window. The street was lined with similar houses, built close to one another, yards and alleyways behind. In front, between the sidewalk and the street, a border of grass was planted with maples and oaks that must have been there for eighty to a hundred years.

I climbed three steps, proceeded along a short cracked walkway, and climbed an additional six steps to the glass door with its tiny foyer visible within. Yount's residence had apparently once been a single-family dwelling, now broken into five units, judging from the names posted on the mailboxes. Each apartment had a bell, connected to the intercom located near the entrance. I rang Yount's apartment, waiting two minutes before I rang again. When it became clear he wasn't answering, I tried a neighbor's bell instead. After a moment, the intercom crackled to life and an old woman clicked in, saying "Yes?"

I said, "I wonder if you can help me. I'm looking for Porter Yount."

"Speak up."

"Porter Yount in apartment three."

"What's the time?"

I glanced at my watch. "Six-fifteen."

"He'll be down yonder on the corner. The Buttercup Tavern."

"Thanks."

I returned to the sidewalk, where I peered up and down the street. Though I didn't see a sign, I spotted what looked like a corner tavern half a block down. I left my car where it was and walked the short distance through the mild spring air.

The Buttercup was dark, cloudy with cigarette smoke, and smelling of bourbon. The local news was being broadcast at low volume on a color TV set mounted in one corner of the room. The dark was further punctuated by neon signs in a series of advertisements for Rolling Rock, Fehr's, and Stroh's Beer. The tavern was paneled in highly varnished wood with red leather stools along the length of the bar. Most of the occupants at that hour seemed to be isolated individuals, all men, all smoking, separated from each other by as many empty stools as space allowed. Without exception, each turned to stare at me as I came in.

I paused just inside the door and said, "I'm looking for Porter Yount."

A fellow at the far end of the bar raised his hand.

Judging from the swiveling heads, my arrival was the most interesting event since the Ohio River flooded in 1937. When I reached Yount, I held my hand out, saying, "I'm Kinsey Millhone."

"Nice meeting you," he said.

We shook hands and I perched on the stool next to his.

I said, "How are you?"

"Not bad. Thanks for asking." Porter Yount was heavyset, raspy-voiced, a man in his eighties. He was almost entirely bald, but his brows were still dark, an unruly tangle above eyes that were a startling green. At the moment, he was bleary-eyed with bourbon and his breath smelled like fruitcake. I could see the bartender drift in our direction. He paused in front of us.

Yount lit a fresh cigarette and glanced in my direction. He was having trouble with his focus. His mouth seemed to work, but his eyeballs were rolling like two green olives in an empty relish dish. "What'll you have?"

"How about a Fehr's?"

"You don't want Fehr's," he said. And to the bartender, "Lady wants a shot of Early Times with a water back."

"The beer's fine," I corrected.

The bartender reached into a cooler for the beer, which he opened and placed on the bar in front of me.

Yount said peevishly, "Give the lady a glass. Where's your manners?"

The bartender set a glass on the bar and Yount spoke to him again. "Who's cooking tonight?"

"Patsy. Want to see a menu?"

"Did I say that? This lady and I could use some privacy."

"Oh, sure." The bartender moved to the other end of the bar, accustomed to Yount's manner.

Yount shook his head with exasperation and his gaze slid in my direction. His head was round as a ball, sitting on the heft of his shoulders with scarcely any neck between. His shirt was a dark polyester, probably selected for stain concealment and ease of laundering. A pair of dark suspenders kept his pants hiked high above his waist.

He wore dark socks and sandals, with an inch of shinbone showing. "Outfit okay? If I'd knowed you was coming, I'd've wore my Sunday best," he said, deliberately fracturing his grammar.

I had to laugh. "Sorry. I tend to look carefully at just about everything."

"You a journalist?"

I shook my head. "A private investigator. I'm trying to get a line on Duncan Oaks. You remember him?"

"Of course. You're the second detective to come in here asking after him this month."

"You talked to Mickey Magruder?"

"That's the one," he said.

"I thought as much."

"Why'd he send you? He didn't take me at my word?"

"We didn't talk. He was shot last week and he's been in a coma ever since."

"Sorry to hear that. I liked him. He's smart. First fella I met who could match me drink for drink."

"He's talented that way. At any rate, I'm doing what I can to follow up his investigation. It's tough, since I don't really know what he'd accomplished. I hope this won't turn out to be a waste of your time."

"Drinking's a waste of time, not talking to pretty ladies. What's the sudden interest in Oaks?"

"His name's cropped up in connection with another matter . . . something in California, which is where I'm from. I know he once worked for the *Tribune*. Your name was on his press pass, so I thought I'd talk to you."

"Fool's errand if I ever heard one. He's been dead twenty years."

"So I heard. I'm sorry for the repetition, but if you tell me what you told Mickey, maybe we can figure out if he's relevant."

Yount took a swallow of whiskey and tapped the ash off his cigarette. "He's a 'war correspondent'—pretty fancy title for a paper like the *Trib*. I don't think even the *Courier-Journal* had a correspondent back then. This was in the early sixties."

"Did you hire him yourself?"

"Oh, sure. He's a local boy, a blueblood, high society: good looks, ambition, an ego big as your head. More charisma than character." His elbow slid off the bar, and he caught himself with a jerk that we both ignored. Mentally, he seemed sharp. It was his body that tended to slip out of gear.

"Meaning what?"

"Not to speak ill of the dead, but I suspect he'd peaked out. You must know people like that yourself. High school's the glory days; after that, nothing much. It's not like he did poorly, but he never did as well. He's a fellow cut corners, never really earned his stripes, so to speak."

"Where'd he go to college?"

"He didn't. Duncan wasn't school-smart. He's a bright kid, made good grades, but he never cared much for academics. He had drive and aspirations. He figured he'd learn more in the real world so he nixed the idea."

"Was he right about that?"

"Hard to say. Kid loved to hustle. Talked me into paying him seventy-five dollars a week—which, frankly, we didn't have. Even in those days, his salary was a pittance, but he didn't care."

"Because he came from money?"

"That's right. Revel Oaks, his daddy, made a fortune in the sin trades, whiskey and tobacco. That and real estate speculation. Duncan grew up in an atmosphere of privilege. Hell, his daddy would've given him anything he wanted: travel, the best schools, place in the family business. Duncan had other fish to fry."

"For instance?"

He waved his cigarette in the air. "Like I said, he wangled his way into a job with the *Trib,* mostly on the basis of his daddy's influence."

"And what did he want?"

"Adventure, recognition. Duncan was addicted to living on the edge. Craved the limelight, craved risk. He wanted to go to Vietnam and report on the war. Nothing would do until he got his way."

"But why not enlist? If you're craving life on the edge, why not the infantry? That's about as close to the edge as you can get."

"Military wouldn't touch him. Had a heart murmur sounded like water pouring through a sluice. That's when he came to us. Wasn't any way the *Trib* could afford his ticket to Saigon. Didn't matter to him. He paid his own way. As long as he had access, he's happy as a clam. In those days, we're talking Neil Sheehan, David Halberstam, Mal Browne, Homer Bigart. Duncan pictured his byline in papers all across the country. He did a series of local interviews with newlyweds, army wives left behind when their husbands went off to war. The idea was to follow up, talk to the husbands, and see the fighting from their perspective."

"Not a bad idea."

"We thought it had promise, especially with so many of his classmates getting drafted. Any rate, he got his press credentials and his passport. He flew from Hong Kong to Saigon and from there to Pleiku. For a while, he was fine, hitching rides on military transports, any place they'd take him. To give him credit, I think he might have turned into a hell of a journalist. He had a way with words, but he lacked experience."

"How long was he there?"

"Couple months is all. He heard about some action in a place called Ia Drang. I guess he pulled strings—maybe his old man again or just his personal charm. It was a hell of a battle, some say the worst of the war. After that came LZ Albany: something like three hundred fellas killed in the space of four days. Must have found himself caught in the thick of it with no way out. We heard later he was hit, but we never got a sense of how serious it was."

"And then what?"

Yount paused to extinguish his cigarette. He missed the ashtray altogether and stubbed out the burning ember on the bar. "That's as much as I know. He's supposed to be medevacked out, but he never made it back. Chopper took off with a bellyful of body bags and a handful of casualties. Landed forty minutes later with no Duncan aboard. His daddy raised hell, got some high Pentagon official to launch an investigation, but it never came to much."

"And that's it?"

"I'm afraid so. You hungry? Ask me, it's time to eat."

"Fine with me," I said.

Porter gestured to the bartender, who ambled back in our direction. "Tell Patsy to put together couple of Hot Browns."

"Good enough," the man said. He set his towel aside, came out from behind the bar, and headed for a door I assumed led to Patsy in the kitchen.

Yount said, "Bet you never ate one."

"What's a Hot Brown?"

"Invented at the Brown Hotel. Wait and see. Now, where was I?"

"Trying to figure out the fate of Duncan Oaks," I said.

"He's dead."

"How do you know?"

"He's never been heard from since."

"Isn't it possible he panicked and took off on foot?"

"Absence of a body, anything's possible, I guess."

"But not likely?"

"I'd say not. The way we heard it later, the NVA were everywhere, scourin' the area for wounded, killing them for sport. Duncan had no training. He probably couldn't get a hundred yards on his own."

"I wonder if you'd look at something." I hauled up my bag from its place near my feet. I removed the snapshot, the press pass, and the dog tags embossed with Duncan's name.

Yount tucked his cigarette in the corner of his mouth, examining the items through a plume of smoke. "Same things Magruder showed me. How'd he come by them?"

"A guy named Benny Quintero had them. You know him?"

"Name doesn't sound familiar."

"That's him in the picture. I'm assuming this is Duncan."

"That's him. When's this taken?"

"Quintero's brother thinks Ia Drang. Benny was wounded November seventeenth."

"Same as Duncan," he said. "This'd have to be one of the last pictures of Duncan ever taken."

"I hadn't thought of that, but probably so."

Yount returned the snapshot, which I tucked in my bag.

"Benny's another Louisville boy. He died in Santa Teresa in 1972: probably a homicide, though there was never an arrest." I took a few minutes to detail the story of Benny's death. "Mickey didn't mention this?"

"Never said a word. How's Quintero tie in?"

"I can give you the superficial answer. His brother says he went to Manual; I'm guessing, at the same time Duncan went to Male. It seems curious he'd end up with Duncan's personal possessions."

Porter shook his head. "Wonder why he kept them?"

"Not a clue," I said. "They were in a lockbox in his room. His brother came across them maybe six months back. He brought them to California." I thought about it for a moment, and then I said, "What's Duncan doing with a set of dog tags if he was never in the service?"

"He had them made up himself. Appealed to his sense of theater. One more example of how he liked to operate: looking like a soldier was as good as being one. I'm surprised he didn't hang out in uniform, but I guess that'd be pushing it. Don't get me wrong. I liked Duncan, but he's a fella with shabby standards."

A woman, probably Patsy, appeared from the kitchen with a steaming ramekin in each of her oven-mitted hands. She put a dish in front of each of us and handed us two sets of flatware rolled in paper napkins. Yount murmured "thanks" and she said, "You're entirely welcome."

I stared at the dish, which looked like a lake of piping-hot yellow sludge, with a dusting of paprika and something lumpy underneath. "What *is* this?"

"Eat and find out."

I picked up my fork and tried a tiny bite. A Hot Brown turned out to be an open-faced sliced turkey sandwich, complete with bacon and tomatoes, baked with the most divine cheese sauce I ever set to my lips. I mewed like a kitten.

"Told you so," he said, with satisfaction.

When I was finished, I wiped my mouth and took a sip of beer. "What about Duncan's parents? Does he still have family in the area?"

Yount shook his head. "Revel died of a heart attack a few years back: 1974, if memory serves. His mother died three years later of a stroke."

"Siblings, cousins?"

"Not a one," he said. "Duncan was an only child, and his daddy was too. I doubt you'd find anyone left on his mother's side of the family either. Her people were from Pike County, over on the West Virginia border. Dirt poor. Once she married Revel, she cut all ties with them."

He glanced at his watch. It was close to 8 P.M. "Time for me get home. My program's coming on in two minutes."

"I appreciate your time. Can I buy your dinner?"

Yount gave me a look. "Obvious you haven't spent any time in the South. Lady doesn't buy dinner for a gent. That's his prerogative." He reached in his pocket, pulled out a wad of bills, and tossed several on the bar.

At his suggestion, I spent the night at the Leisure Inn on Broadway. I might have tried the Brown Hotel, but it looked way too fancy for the likes of me. The Leisure Inn was plain, a sensible establishment of Formica, nylon carpet, foam rubber pillows, and a layer of crackling plastic laid under the bottom sheet in case I wet the bed. I put a call through to the airline and discussed the options for my return. The first (and only) seat available was on a 3 P.M. flight the next day. I snagged it, wondering what I was going to do with myself until then.

I considered a side visit to Louisville Male High, where Duncan had graduated with the class of 1961. Secretly, I doubted there was much to learn. Porter Yount had painted an unappealing portrait of the young Duncan Oaks. To me, he sounded shallow, spoiled, and manipulative. On the other hand, he was just a kid when he died: twenty-two, twenty-three years old at the outside. I suspect most of us are completely self-involved at that age. At twenty-two, I'd already been married and divorced. By twenty-three, I was not only married to Daniel but I'd left the police department and was totally adrift. I'd *thought* I was mature, but I was foolish and unenlightened. My judgment was faulty and my perception was flawed. So who was I to judge Duncan? He might have become a good man if he'd lived long enough. Thinking about it, I felt a curious secondhand sorrow for all the chances he'd missed, the lessons he never learned, the dreams he'd had to forfeit with his early death. Whoever he was and whatever he'd been, I could at least pay my respects.

At ten the next morning, I parked my rental car on a side street not far from Louisville Male High School, at the corner of Brook Street and Breckinridge. The building was three stories tall, constructed of dark red brick with white concrete trim. The surrounding neighborhood consisted of narrow red-brick houses with narrow walkways between. Many looked as if the interiors would smell peculiar. I went up the concrete stairs. Above the entrance, two gnomelike scholars were nestled in matching niches, reading plaques of some kind. The dates 1914 and 1915 were chiseled in stone, indicating, I supposed, the year the building had gone up. I pushed through the front door and went in.

The interior was defined by gray marble wainscoting, with gray-painted walls above. The foyer floor was speckled gray marble with inexplicable cracks here and there. In the auditorium, dead ahead, I could see descending banks of curved wooden seats and tiers of wooden flooring, faintly buckled with age. Classes must have been in session, because the corridors were empty and there was little traffic on the stairs. I went into the school office. The windows were tall. Long planks of fluorescent lighting hung from ceilings covered with acoustical tile. I asked for the school library and was directed to the third floor.

The school librarian, Mrs. Calloway, was a sturdy-looking soul in a calf-length denim skirt and a pair of indestructible walking shoes. Her iron-gray hair was chopped off in a fuss-free style she'd probably worn for years. Close to retirement, she looked like a woman who'd favor muesli, yoga, liniments, SAVE THE WHALES bumper stickers, polar-bear swims, and lengthy bicycle tours of foreign countries. When I asked to see a copy of the '61 yearbook, she gave me a look but refrained from comment. She handed me the *Bulldog* and I took a seat at an empty table. She returned to her desk and busied herself, though I could tell she intended to keep an eye on me.

I spent a few minutes leafing through the *Bulldog*, looking at the black-and-white portraits of the senior class. I didn't check for Duncan's name. I simply absorbed the whole, trying to get a feel for the era, which predated mine by six years. The school had originally been all male, but it had turned coed somewhere along the way. Senior pictures showed the boys wearing coats and ties, their hair in brush cuts that emphasized their big ears and oddly shaped heads. Many wore glasses with heavy black frames. The girls tended toward short hair and dark gray or black crew-neck sweaters. Each wore a simple strand of pearls, probably a necklace provided by the photographer for uniformity. By 1967, the year I graduated, the hairstyles were bouffant, as stiffly lacquered as wigs, with flipped ends sticking out. The boys had all turned into Elvis Presley clones. Here, in candid class photos, most students wore penny loafers and white crew socks, and the girls were decked out in straight or pleated skirts that hit them at the knee.

I breezed by the Good News Club, the Speech Club, the Art Club, the Pep Club, and the Chess Club. In views of classes devoted to industrial arts, home ec, and world science, students were clumped together pointing at wall maps or gathered around the teacher's desk, smiling and pretending to look interested. The teachers all appeared to be fifty-five and as dull as dust.

At Thanksgiving of that year, the fall of 1960, the annual Male–Manual game was played. Male High was victorious by a score of 20–6. "MALE BEATS MANUAL 20 TO 6, CLINCHES CITY & AAA CROWNS," the article said. "A neat, well-deserved licking of the duPont Manual Rams." Co-captains were Walter Morris and Joe Blankenship. The rivalry between the two high schools had been long and fierce, beginning in 1893 and doubtless continuing to the present. At that time, the record showed 39 wins for Male, 19 for Manual, and 5 games tied. At the bottom of the page, in the accompanying photograph of the Manual offense, I found a halfback named Quintero, weighing 162.

I went back to the first page and started through again. Duncan Oaks showed up in a number of photographs, dark-haired and handsome. He'd been elected vice president, prom king, and class photographer. His name and face seemed to crop up in many guises: the senior play, Quill and Scroll, Glee Club. He was a Youth Speaks delegate, office aide, and library assistant.

He hadn't garnered academic honors, but he had played football. I found a picture of him on the Male High team, a 160-pound halfback. Now that was interesting: Duncan Oaks and Benny Quintero had played the same position on opposing teams. They must have known each other, by reputation if nothing else. I thought about Porter Yount's comment that these were Duncan's glory years, that his life after this never approached the same heights. That might have been true for Quintero as well. In retrospect, it seemed touching that their paths had crossed again in Vietnam.

I turned to the front of the book and studied the picture of Duncan as prom king. He was wearing a tuxedo: shorn, clean-shaven, with a white boutonniere tucked into his lapel. I turned the page and studied the prom queen, wondering if they were boyfriend/girlfriend or simply elected separately and honored on the same occasion. Darlene LaDestro. Well, this was a type I'd known well. Long blond hair pulled up in a swirl on top, a strong nose, patrician air. She looked classy, familiar, like girls in my high school who came from big-time money. Though not conventionally pretty, Darlene was the kind of girl who'd age with style. She'd come back to class reunions having married her social equal, still thin as a rail, hair streaked tastefully with gray. Darlene LaDestro, what a name. You'd think she'd have dumped it the first chance she got, called herself Dodie or Dessie or—

A chill swept through me, and I made an involuntary bark of astonishment. Mrs. Calloway looked up, and I shook my head to indicate that I was fine . . . though I wasn't. No wonder Darlene looked familiar. She was currently Laddie Bethel, alive and well and living in Santa Teresa.

25

I postponed my return, moving the reservation from Wednesday afternoon to a morning flight on Thursday to give myself time to compile some information. I'd combed copies of the 1958, 1959, 1960, 1961, and 1962 yearbooks for reference to Mark Bethel but had found no mention of him. If Laddie'd known him in those days, it wasn't because he'd attended Louisville Male High. I made copious copies of the yearbook pages where Laddie and Duncan were featured, both together and separately, going all the way back to their freshman year. In many candid class pictures, the two were standing side by side.

I placed the stack of yearbooks on Mrs. Calloway's desk. I left the high school, driving through the area until I found a drugstore, where I bought a pack of index cards and a city map to supplement the simple sheet map I'd acquired from Frugal Rents. In the rental car again, I circled back to the public library, which was not far away. I inquired at the desk and was directed to the reference department. Then I got down to work. By cross-checking past city directories with past telephone books, I found one LaDestro and made a note of the address. The 1959, 1960, and 1961 business directories indicated that Laddie's father, Harold LaDestro, had owned a machine shop on Market and listed his occupation as precision machinist and inventor. Because of Laddie's poise, her elegance, and her aristocratic airs, I'd assumed she came from money, but perhaps I was wrong. In those years, her father was a tradesman, and there was no hint whatever that his business interests extended beyond the obvious. From the yearbook, I knew she'd graduated with honors, but the list of her achievements made no mention of college plans. She might have enrolled at the University of Louisville, which was probably not expensive for local residents. It was also possible she'd attended a nearby business college, taking a secretarial course so she could work for her dad. That was the sort of thing a conscientious daughter might have done in those days.

But where had she met Mark? On a whim, I pulled out the 1961 phone book, where I found listings for twenty-one families with the last name of Bethel and four with the last name Oaks. There was only one Revel Oaks, and I made a note of that address. As for Bethels, I had another idea how to pin down Mark's family. I ran off copies of the phone book listings and pages from the relevant city directories, adding them to the copies I'd made of the yearbook information. I wasn't sure where I was going, but why not follow my nose? I'd already spent the money for plane fare to get here. I was stuck until flight time the next morning. What else was there to do?

I fired up the rental car and did a quick driving tour, starting with the Oaks family home on Fourth Street, still in the downtown area. The house was impressive: an immense three-story structure of stucco and stone, probably built in the late 1800s. The style fell midway between Renaissance and Baroque, with cornices, fluted columns, curved buttresses, a balustrade, and arched windows. The exterior color was uncommon: a dusky pink, washed with brown, as if the facade had been glazed by age to this mournful shade. From the sign on the lawn, the building was now occupied by two law firms, a court reporting firm, and a CPA. The property was large, the surrounding stone wall still visible, as well as the original gateposts. Two majestic oak trees shaded the formal gardens in the rear, and I could see a carriage house at the end of a cobbled driveway.

The LaDestros' address was less than two miles away, within a block of the university on a narrow side street. I checked for the number, but the house was gone, evidently razed to make way for expanding campus facilities. The remaining houses on the street tended to be elongated one-story boxes sheathed in dark red asphalt siding. Depressing. I couldn't imagine how Laddie'd been catapulted from these grim beginnings to her current wealth. Had she been married before? In those days, a rich husband was the obvious means by which a woman could elevate her social standing and improve her prospects. She certainly must have been eager to bail herself out of *this.*

While I was still in range of the central city, I located the Jefferson County clerk's office in the courthouse between Fifth and Sixth Streets on West Jefferson. The fellow at the desk couldn't have been more helpful when I told him what I needed: the marriage certificate for Darlene LaDestro and Mark Bethel, who I believed had been married in the summer of 1965. I couldn't give him the exact date, but I was remembering the line I'd picked up from Mark's secretary, Judy, who told me he'd enlisted in the army right after his college graduation. What would have been more natural than to marry Laddie that summer, before he went overseas? I was also operating on the theory that Laddie (aka Darlene LaDestro) was an obvious choice for one of Duncan's interviews. She was young, she was lovely, she was local. She would have been easy to approach, since they lived in the same town and he'd known her for years. Duncan's press credentials were dated September 10, 1965. If he'd talked to Laddie at all, it was probably sometime between her marriage, Mark's departure, and his own flight to Vietnam soon afterward.

Fifteen minutes later, I experienced one of those exhilarating moments of satisfaction when, sure enough, the clerk found the marriage record.

"Oh, wow. This is great. Isn't this *amazing*?" I said.

The clerk's look was jaded. "I'm completely stunned."

I laughed. "Well, I like being right, especially when I'm flying by the seat of my pants."

He leaned on the counter, his chin on his hand, looking on while I took out my cards and jotted down the information embedded in the form. The license was issued on June 3, 1965. Assuming it was good for thirty days, the wedding must have taken place within the month. Darlene LaDestro, age twenty-two and working as a bookkeeper, was the daughter of Harold and Millicent LaDestro and resided at the address listed in the 1961 telephone book. Mark Charles Bethel, age twenty-three, occupation U.S. Army, was the son of Vernon and Shirley Bethel with an address on Trevillian Way. Neither the bride nor the groom had been previously married.

Idly, the clerk said, "You know who he is, don't you?"

I looked up at him with interest. "Who, Mark Bethel?"

"No, LaDestro."

"I don't know a thing about him. What's the story?"

"He was awarded the patent for some kind of widget used on the Mercury space flights."

"And that's how he made his money?"

"Sure. He's still famous around here. Self-taught, eccentric. He didn't even have connections to the aerospace industry. He just worked on his own. I saw a picture of him once, and he looked like a pointy-headed geek. He'd been tinkering all his life without making a dime. In hock up to here, living in a dump. Everybody wrote him off as a nut, and then he comes along and aces out McDonnell-Douglas for the rights to the thing. He died a rich man. I mean, *very very* rich."

"Well, I'll be darned," I said. "What was it, the thing he patented?"

"Some doodad. Who knows? I heard it's in use to this day. The world is full of guys who design gizmos they never get credit for. LaDestro hired a patent attorney and took the big boys down."

"Incredible."

"His daughter sure lucked out. I hear she lives in California now on some fancy estate," he said. He pointed to the license. "You want a copy of that?"

"How much?"

"Two dollars for regular, five for certified."

"Regular's fine," I said.

I drove from Jefferson to Third, then hung a left on Broadway, driving east until it angled into Bardstown Road. I followed Bardstown Road through an area of town known as the Highlands. Once on Trevillian, I found the house where the Bethels had once lived. The white frame house looked comfortable, not large but well-maintained in a solid middle-class neighborhood, certainly superior to the one where Laddie'd grown up. I parked in front of the house, traversed the long sloping walk, and climbed the stairs to the porch. No one was home, but a simple check of the mailbox revealed that a family named Poynter now occupied the house. This was Donna Reed country: green shutters on the windows, pansies in the flower boxes, a tricycle on the sidewalk, and a dog bone lying in the yard. All the windowpanes sparkled, and the shrubs were crisply trimmed. As I looked on, a lean gray cat picked her way carefully across the newly cut lawn.

I returned to the car, where I sat and studied my map. Gauging the proximity of schools in the area, I decided Mark probably attended Highland Junior High and then Atherton or St. Xavier, the Catholic high school on Broadway. He might have gone to private school—I wasn't sure about that—but he struck me as the sort who'd take pride in his public school roots. Now what?

I leafed through the pages I'd assembled, letting my mind wander. I'd added a number of dots, but I still couldn't see all the lines connecting them. Duncan Oaks seemed pivotal. I sensed his presence like the hub of an enormous wheel. I could trace the hometown relationship between him and Benny Quintero. Contemporaries, two high school athletes who had played the same positions on opposing football teams, their paths had crossed years later on the bloody soil of

Ia Drang. After that, Duncan Oaks had vanished but Quintero had survived, keeping Duncan's dog tags, his press credentials, and a snapshot. I could also tie Duncan Oaks to Laddie Bethel, born Darlene LaDestro, who'd attended high school with him. And here's where the machinations became more intricate. Laddie was now married to the attorney who'd represented my ex-husband, a suspect in Benny Quintero's beating death seven years later. If Duncan Oaks was the hub, maybe Mark Bethel was the axle driving subsequent events.

I started the car and headed back to my motel. Even without the links, a picture was forming, crude and unfocused, but one that Mickey must have seen as well. The problem was I had no proof a crime had been committed all those years ago, let alone that it had sparked consequences in the here-and-now. It simply stood to reason. *Some* combination of events had resulted in the killing of Benny Quintero and the shooting of Mickey Magruder. I had to fashion a story that encompassed all the players and made sense of their fates. If life is a play, then there's a logical explanation, an underlying tale that pulls the whole of it together, however clouded it first appears.

Before my plane the next morning, I put in a call to Porter Yount, asking if he could lay his hands on the columns Duncan Oaks had written before he went to Vietnam. Much hemming and hawing, but he said he'd see what he could do. I gave him my address and a great big telephone kiss, telling him to take care, I'd be in touch with him.

The flight home was uneventful, though it took up most of the day: Louisville to Tulsa, Tulsa to Santa Fe, Santa Fe to Los Angeles, where I shuttled to the motel, picked up my VW, and drove the ninety minutes home. Between the actual hours in the air, the wait between planes, and the commute at the end, I arrived in Santa Teresa at 4:30 P.M. I was feeling irritable: tired, hungry, flat-haired, oily-faced. I was also dehydrated from all the nuts I'd eaten in lieu of meals that day. I had to slap myself around some to keep from whining out loud.

The minute I got home, I sat down at my desk and removed Mark

Bethel's curriculum vitae from the bottom drawer where I'd tucked it Saturday. On the front page, he'd listed his date and place of birth as Dayton, Ohio, August 1, 1942. He'd graduated with a BA from the University of Kentucky in 1965. Under military experience, he listed U.S. Army, modestly omitting mention of his Purple Heart. I'd call Judy in the morning, my palate smeared with peanut butter, pretending to be a journalist so I could pin that down. If Mark had been at Ia Drang, I'd be one step closer to completing the picture, which was almost done.

I stripped, showered, and shampooed my hair. I brushed my teeth, got dressed again, and trotted down the spiral stairs.

My first thought was to have a conversation with Carlin Duffy, conveying a condensed version of what I'd learned in Louisville, though at this point I still didn't know quite what to make of it. I'd restrict myself to the facts, leaving out the speculations and suppositions I was still playing with. The contact was largely a courtesy on my part. He hadn't hired me. He wasn't paying me and I didn't feel I owed him an explanation. I was hoping, however, that he'd have something to contribute, some piece of the puzzle he hadn't thought to share. More to the point, I remembered Duffy's rage and frustration the night he'd shown up at Mickey's. I didn't relish a repeat performance and this was my way of protecting myself. Duffy's brother had died, and he had his stake in the matter.

I headed out to the nursery, where I found a parking slot in front of the gardening center. I prayed Duffy was on the premises instead of at the Honky-Tonk. The bar was open at this hour, but I didn't dare go back. I thought I'd better keep my distance in case Tim and Scottie realized I was the one who'd blown the whistle on them. It was close to five-thirty, still light out, and I made my way easily along the tree-lined paths. I could see the roofline of the shed at the rear of the lot, and I mentally marked my route. There was no direct passageway, and I angled back and forth between the crated trees.

When I reached the shed, I saw a compact yellow forklift parked in the entrance. Several large bags of mulch were stacked on the forks in front. Tall and boxy, the vehicle was an overblown version of the

Tonka toys I'd played with when I was six. The phase had been short-lived, tucked somewhere between Legos and the demise of the baby doll I'd flattened with my trike. I moved into the shed, pushing aside the blanket Duffy'd hung to eliminate drafts. He'd passed out, lying shoeless on his cot. His mouth hung open and his snores filled the enclosure with bourbon fumes. He cradled an empty pint of Early Times against his chest. One sock was pulled half off, and his bare heel was exposed. He looked absurdly young for a fellow who'd spent half his life in jail. I thought, shit. I found a blanket and tossed it over him and then placed the dog tags, the press pass, the snapshot, and a note on the crate where he'd see it when he woke. The note said I'd be in touch the next day and fill him in on the trip. I backed out of the shed, leaving him to sleep off his drunken state.

I walked back to the car, thinking how often I identified with guys like him. As crude as he was with his racist comments, his tortured grammar, and his attitude toward crime, I understood his yearning. How liberating it was when you defied authority, flouted convention, ignoring ordinary standards of moral decency. I knew my own ambivalence. On the one hand, I was a true law-and-order type, prissy in my judgment, outraged at those who violated the doctrines of honesty and fair play. On the other hand, I'd been known to lie through my teeth, eavesdrop, pick locks, or simply break into people's houses, where I snooped through their possessions and took what suited me. It wasn't nice, but I savored every single minute of my bad girl behavior. Later, I'd feel guilty, but still I couldn't resist. I was split down the middle, my good angel sitting on one shoulder, Lucifer perched on the other. Duffy's struggle was the same, and while he leaned in one direction, I usually leaned in the other, searching for justice in the heart of anarchy. This was the bottom line as far as I was concerned: If the bad guys don't play by the rules, why should the good guys have to?

I drove back into town. It was now 5:50 and I was starving, of course, so I made a quick detour. I pulled up to the drive-in window at

McDonald's and asked for a QP with cheese, a large order of fries, and a Coke to go. I was fairly humming with excitement as I waited for my bag of goodies. I'd go back to my apartment, change into my jammies, and curl up on my couch, where I'd watch junk TV while I ate my junk food. While I drove home, the car smelled divine, like a mobile microwave oven. I found a great parking place, locked the car, and let myself in through the squeaking gate. I rounded the corner, all atwitter at the notion of the pleasures to come. I stopped dead.

Detectives Claas and Aldo were standing on my front porch. This was a replay of our earlier encounter: same guys in their late thirties, the one dark, the other fair, same sport coats. Claas carried the briefcase, just as he had before. Gian Aldo chewed gum. He'd had his dark hair trimmed short, but his eyebrows still met like a hedge across the bridge of his nose. I longed to fall on him with a pair of tweezers and pluck him bald.

I said, "What do you want?"

Detective Claas seemed amused. Now *that* was different. "Be nice. We drove all the way up here to have a chat with you."

I walked past him with my keys and unlocked the door. Detective Claas wore a hair product that smelled like a high school chemistry experiment. The two followed me in. I dropped my shoulder bag on the floor near my desk, taking a moment to check my answering machine. No messages.

I held up my McDonald's bag, the contents getting colder by the minute, as were my hopes. "I gotta eat first. I'm half dead."

"Have at it."

I crossed to the kitchen, moving around the counter to the refrigerator. I took out a chilled bottle of Chardonnay and sorted through the junk drawer until I found the opener. "You want wine? I'm having some. You might as well join me."

The two exchanged a look. It was probably against regulations, but they must have thought I'd be easier to get along with if I were all likkered up.

"We'd appreciate that. Thanks," Claas said.

I handed him the wine bottle and the opener, and he got to work while I set out three glasses and a paper plate. I dumped the fries out of the carton and fetched the ketchup bottle from the cabinet. "Help yourself," I said.

Detective Claas poured the wine and we stood there, eating lukewarm french fries with our fingers. They were completely limp by now, and we dropped them in our beaks like a trio of birdies eating albino worms. Ever gracious, I cut the QP into three equal parts and we gulped those down, too. After supper, we walked the six steps into the living room. This time I took the couch and let them settle into my director's chairs. I noticed Detective Claas kept his briefcase close at hand as he had before. I knew he had a tape recorder in there, and it made me want to lean down and address all my comments into the opening.

"So now what?" I said, crossing my arms against my chest.

Detective Aldo smiled. "We have some news we thought you might want to hear firsthand. We picked up a partial print on the Smith and Wesson and matched it to some prints that showed up in Magruder's place."

Claas said, "You remember a gray metal box concealed in the bottom of a chair?"

I could feel my mouth go dry. "Sure." No sound. I cleared my throat and tried again. "Sure."

"We got a real nice set on the inner rim of the lid, like someone pulled it open with their fingertips."

I was going to call his attention to the matter of subject-pronoun agreement, but I held my tongue. Instead, I said, "Who?" Was that an owl I heard?

Aldo spoke up again, clearly enjoying himself. "Mark Bethel."

I stared at him, blinking. "You're kidding. You gotta be *kidding*."

"He went in there Sunday night and left prints everywhere."

"That's great. I love it. Good for him," I said.

"We're not sure what he was looking for—"

I held a hand up. "I can tell you that," I said. I gave them a hasty summary of the work I'd done, including the discovery of Duncan Oaks's credentials in Mickey's jacket lining. "I can't believe he was dumb enough to leave his fingerprints. Has the man lost his mind?"

"He's getting desperate," Claas said. "He probably saw the print dust on all the surfaces and figured we were done."

"You dusted again?"

"Tuesday morning," Aldo said.

"But why? What possessed you?"

"We got a call from Cordia Hatfield. She'd seen lights on Sunday night. You swore it wasn't you, so she suspected it was him," Claas said.

"But how'd he get in?"

"With the key she'd given him. He'd stopped by last week and introduced himself as Magruder's attorney. He said he'd be paying Mickey's bills till he was on his feet, and he was hoping to pick up insurance policies and bank deposit slips. She gave him a key. Of course, he returned it later, but probably not before he'd had a copy made for himself," Claas said.

Detective Aldo spoke up. "I don't think the computer would have caught the match without the fresh set he left. Of course, we wasted a *lot* of time eliminating yours."

I could feel my cheeks heat. "Sorry about that."

Aldo wagged his finger, but he didn't seem all that mad.

Claas said, "We can also place Bethel in the area at the time of the shooting."

"You guys have been busy. How'd you do *that*?"

Claas was clearly pleased with himself. "On the thirteenth, Bethel was in Los Angeles for a TV appearance. The taping finished at ten. He checked into the Four Seasons on a late arrival and then went out again, returning in the early hours of the fourteenth. He might have slipped in unnoticed, but as it happened the valet car park was a supporter and recognized his face."

"Tell you what else," Detective Aldo said. "We got somebody saw them together that night."

"No."

"Oh, yes. We went through a bunch of matchbooks Magruder kept in a fishbowl. We found seven from a dive on Pico near the Pacific Coast Security offices. A gal at the bar remembered seeing them." Detective Aldo sat back, the wood and canvas chair creaking perilously under his weight. "What about you? What'd you pick up back east? Your landlord told us you made a trip to Louisville."

"That's right. I just got back today."

"Learn anything?"

"Actually, I did. I'm just piecing this together so I can't be sure, but here's what I know. Laddie Bethel went to high school in Louisville with a guy named Duncan Oaks. They were the prom king and queen in '61, the year they graduated. At some point, Laddie met Mark. They married in the summer of 1965, after he graduated from the University of Kentucky. Mark enlisted in the army right around the time Duncan Oaks was doing a series for the *Louisville Tribune.* I suspect Mark served in Vietnam, but I haven't pinned that down—"

"We can help on that. We haven't been exactly idle." Claas reached into his briefcase and removed a manila folder, which he opened, leafing through the contents. "Alpha Company, First Battalion, Fifth Cavalry."

"Well, great," I said. "I don't have a clue how it ties in, but maybe we'll figure that out. At any rate, Duncan had an idea for a series and began interviewing the soldiers' wives. His intention was to talk about the war from their differing perspectives, one off in Vietnam, the other stuck on the home front. I think Duncan and Laddie had a brief affair. Pure conjecture on my part. Within weeks, Duncan Oaks went to Vietnam. He and Mark must have crossed paths. In fact, Duncan probably sought him out for the second half of the interview."

"And?"

"That's as far as I can go."

Aldo said, "Maybe Mark fragged him. That's what it sounds like to me."

"Fragged?"

"You know, offed. Eliminated. Kilt him deader than a doornail. I mean, how hard could it be with bullets flying? It's not like the medics run ballistics tests."

I thought about it for a moment. "That's probably not a bad guess. Especially if Mark found out about the relationship between Duncan and his wife. . . ."

"Assuming there was one," Claas said.

"Well, yeah."

"Anyway, go on. Sorry for the interruption."

"I start faltering here and have to resort to waving my hands. I mean, I can put some of this together, but I don't have proof. Benny Quintero was another Louisville boy. I know Duncan and Benny were at Ia Drang together because I saw a picture of the two. According to my information, Duncan Oaks was wounded—by Mark, friendly fire, the NVA—we're never going to know, so we might as well skip that. In any event, he was loaded on a chopper filled with the wounded and the dead. By the time the chopper landed, he'd disappeared without a trace."

Aldo spoke up. "Maybe Mark's on the chopper and shoves him out the door. The guy falls—what? six to twelve hundred feet, landing in the jungle? Trust me, in two weeks there's nothing left but bones. From what you say, Oaks wasn't even in the army, so it's perfect. Who gives a shit about a fucking journalist?"

I said, "Right. The point is, I think Benny knew and that's why he held on to Duncan's ID. Again, I don't have proof, but it does make sense. Maybe he thought of a way to turn a profit on the deal."

Claas said, "What happened to Benny?"

"He was wounded by sniper fire and ended up with a metal plate in his head. In 1971, he came out to California; that much we know. Mickey and Benny got in a shoving match. A day later, someone beat Benny senseless and he ended up dead." I went on to detail Mickey's history of misbehavior and why he'd looked good for the beating when Internal Affairs stepped in.

Claas said, "I don't see the relevance."

"Mark was Mickey's attorney. He's the one who advised him to leave the department to avoid questioning."

"Got it."

Aldo leaned forward. "Speaking of which, how'd Bethel end up with your Smith and Wesson? That seems like a trick."

"I think Mickey sold it to him. I have a record of a deposit in March for two hundred dollars. Mark told me Mickey called and asked for money. I know Mickey better than that. I know he'd hoarded a stash of gold coins and bills, but that was probably not something he would have dipped into. He sold his car about then and he was probably off-loading his other possessions, trying to make ends meet. The minute Mark bought the gun, he must have seen his way clear, because it was on that same trip he made the phone call from Mickey's apartment to my machine. All he had to do was distract Mickey's attention, dial the number, and let the tape run on when my machine picked up."

"What if you'd been there?"

"Sorry wrong number, and he tries the call later. He knew Mickey and Duffy were as thick as thieves by then. Whatever his faults, Mickey's always been a hell of a detective. Mark must have known it was only a matter of time. He had a gun registered to me. He'd established a connection to me on Mickey's telephone bill. I'd be implicated anyway as soon as the gun registration came to light."

Aldo snorted. "Fuckin' devious."

Claas rubbed his hands together, then stretched his arms out in front of him, his fingers laced with the palms turned outward until I heard his knuckles crack. "Well, boys and girls, I've enjoyed the bedtime stories. Too bad none of this'll fly in court."

"Oh, yeah. Which brings us to the next step," Aldo said, chiming in on cue. "Shall I tell her the plan?"

I said, "I don't like this. It sounds rehearsed."

"Exactly," Claas said. "So here's what we thought. Forget Vietnam. We're never going to get him for whacking Duncan Oaks. No weapons, no witnesses, so we're out of luck on that score."

Aldo said, "Quintero's another one. I mean, even if you prove it, the best you can hope for is a manslaughter bust, which is strictly bullshit."

I said, "Which brings us to Mickey."

"And to you," Claas said. He reached in his briefcase and pulled out the tape recorder. He held it so I could see.

I said, "I knew that was in there."

"But did you know how well it works?" He pressed REWIND and then PLAY, producing a clear, unobstructed recording of the conversation we'd just had. "We figure you can put this in your handbag, trot yourself off to Bethel's, and maybe help us out."

"You have an eavesdropping warrant?"

"No, we don't."

"Isn't that illegal? I thought you needed a court order. Whatever happened to the Fourth Amendment?" This from Kinsey Millhone, upholder of the Constitution.

"What you'd be doing is called a consent recording. It's done all the time by informants and undercover cops. As long as you're only taping comments someone makes to you, the court doesn't have a problem. Worst-case scenario—assuming what you get is juicy—you use the tape to refresh your own memory when you testify in court."

"Now I'm testifying?"

"If Mickey dies, you do. Right?"

I could feel my attention shift from Aldo to Claas, who said, "Look at it this way. We're building a case. We gotta have something concrete for the DA."

Aldo leaned forward. "That's what we're in business to do, get this cocksucker nailed, if you'll excuse my Greek."

"And Mark won't guess what I'm up to? He's not a fool," I said.

"He's Mickey's *attorney.* You're back from Kentucky with a shitload of information and you're filling him in. How can he resist? He wants to know what *you* know so he can measure the depth of the hole he's in. Of course, if he figures you're on to him, he'll want to pop you next."

"Thanks. That helps. Now I'm really feeling good about all this."

"Come on. It's no sweat. He's not going to do it in his own living room."

Aldo moved to the phone, holding the receiver out. "Give him a call."

"Now?"

"Why not? Tell him you have some stuff you want to talk to him about."

"Yeah," I said cautiously. "And then what?"

"We haven't made that part up yet."

26

The Bethels' estate was on the outer edges of Montebello, perched on a bluff overlooking the Pacific Ocean. I'd spoken to Laddie on the phone and she'd given me directions to the house on Savanna Lane. Mark was out, but she said he'd be returning shortly. It worried me she hadn't voiced greater surprise or curiosity about the reason for my call. I'd mentioned the trip to Louisville, that I had something to discuss, preferably with the two of them, though I'd certainly value the opportunity to talk to her alone first. If she was alarmed about such a conversation, she gave no indication.

At seven on the dot, I pulled in at the gate. Detectives Claas and Aldo had followed me in their car, and they were parked in a grove of eucalyptus trees about a hundred yards off. I had the tape recorder in my bag, but I wasn't wired for sound so there was no way they could monitor the conversation once I was inside the house. No one (meaning them) seemed to think this would present a problem since I'd be in the Bethels' home with other people (meaning servants) on the premises. Our plan—if that's what you want to call it—was for them to hover on the sidelines, falling in behind me when I left the estate. Then we'd go back to my place, listen to the tape, and see if what we'd picked up constituted probable cause. If so, we'd find a judge who could sign a warrant for Mark's arrest on charges of assault with a deadly weapon and attempted murder in the shooting of Mickey Magruder. If not, we'd move to Plan B, on which we'd never quite agreed. On reflection, even Plan A seemed a bit half-assed, but I was there at the gate and I'd already pressed the button.

I expected to hear someone on the intercom asking for my name. Instead, there was silence. The gates simply swung open, allowing me entrance. I waved to the "boys" and put the car in gear. The driveway was long, curving off to the left. The land on either side was barren except for the grasses bending under the offshore winds. Occasionally, a tree broke the line of the horizon, a stark silhouette against the milder dark of the sky. I could see the lighted windows of the house, dazzling yellow and white, set in a bulky block of dark stone. I parked out in front on an enormous apron of gravel. I shut off the engine and sat taking in the sight of the house through the driver's side window.

The structure was curiously reminiscent of Duncan Oaks's house in Louisville. Despite the appearance of age, I knew construction had been completed only five years before, which might explain the absence of mature trees. The exterior was stone and stucco. Landscape lights washed the facade with its glaze of dusky pink underlaid with brown. In theory, the style was Mediterranean or Italianate, one of those bastard forms that Californians favor, but the arches above the windows seemed remarkably similar to their Kentucky counterpart. The front door was recessed, sheltered in a portico flanked by fluted columns. Even the balustrade was kindred in design. Was Laddie conscious of what she'd done or had she mimicked Duncan's house inadvertently? What is it that prompts us to reenact our unresolved issues? We revisit our wounds, constructing the past in hopes that this time we can make the ending turn out right.

The carriage lights on either side of the door came on. Reluctantly, I reached for my bag. I'd left the zippered compartment open, the tape recorder in easy range of my hand. I emerged from the car, crunched my way across the parking pad, and climbed the low front steps. Laddie opened the door before I had time to ring the bell. "Hello, Kinsey. How nice of you to drive all the way out here. I take it you had no trouble finding the place."

"Not at all. It's beautiful."

"We like it," she said mildly. "Can I take your jacket?"

"This is fine for now. It's cold."

She closed the door behind me. "Come on into the living room. I've got a nice fire burning. Will you have a drink? I'm having wine," she said. She was already walking toward the living room, her heels clicking smartly against the highly polished marble floors.

I followed her, saying, "I better not, but thanks. I had wine with dinner and that's my limit."

We stepped down into the living room, with its twelve-foot coffered ceiling. One entire wall of French doors looked onto a patio. The room was surprisingly light, done in shades of cream: the twenty- by twenty-four-foot area rug, the walls, the three plump matching love seats arranged in a U in front of the fireplace. There were touches of black in the throw pillows and lampshades, Boston ferns providing spots of green here and there. Maybe I could snitch some ideas for my spacious abode. The coffee table was a square of three-quarter-inch glass resting on three enormous polished brass spheres. A second wineglass sat near a bottle of Chardonnay in an insulated cooler. Laddie'd made quite a dent for someone drinking alone. I flicked on the tape recorder during the momentary lull as she picked up her wineglass and settled on one of the sofas that flanked the fireplace. The hearth was a glossy black granite that reflected the blaze. Really, I was taking notes—I had to have one of those.

I sat down opposite her, wondering how to begin. These transitions can be awkward, especially when you're trying to shift the discussion from niceties to the subject of murder.

She said, "What were you doing in Louisville? We used to go for the Derby, but it's been ages."

A maid came to the door. "I left Mr. Bethel's plate in the warming oven. Will there be anything else?"

"No, dear. That's fine. We'll see you in the morning."

"Yes, ma'am," the woman said, and then withdrew.

I said, "Actually, I went to Louisville on a research trip. Do you remember Benny Quintero, the fellow who was killed here a few years ago?"

"Of course. Mark represented Mickey."

"Well, as it happens, Benny was from Louisville. He went to Manual the same time you were at Louisville Male High."

Her lips parted in expectation. "What kind of research *was* this? I can't imagine."

"I keep thinking there's a connection between Benny Quintero's death and Mickey's being shot last week."

Laddie's frown was delicate. "That's quite a leap."

"Not really," I said, "though it does seem odd. Here the four of you come from the same hometown—"

"Four?"

"Sure. You, Mark, Benny, and Duncan Oaks. You remember Duncan," I said.

"Of course, but he's been gone for years."

"My point exactly," I said. Gee, this was going better than I'd thought. "During his stint in Vietnam, Mark was at Ia Drang, right?"

"You'd have to verify that with him, but I believe so."

"Turns out Benny was there too."

Laddie blinked. "I'm not following. What does any of this have to do with me?"

"Let me back up a step. Didn't Duncan Oaks interview you for the *Louisville Tribune*?"

She said, "Kinsey, what *is* this? I don't mean to be rude, but you're skipping back and forth and I'm confused. I really don't see the relevance."

"Just hear me out," I said. "Duncan was doing a series for the local paper. He interviewed army wives, like you, who'd been left behind—you know, talking about the war from their perspective. His idea was to tell the same story through the eyes of the husbands off fighting in Vietnam."

Laddie shook her head, shrugging. "I guess I'll have to take your word for it."

"At any rate, he did talk to you."

She took a sip of wine. "It's possible. I don't remember."

"Don't worry about the date. I've asked his editor to send a copy of the article. We can pin it down from that. Anyway, Duncan's editor says he flew to Vietnam in September of '65. He ran into Mark and Benny at Ia Drang, which was where Duncan disappeared." I was doling out pure theory, but I noticed she'd stopped offering much in the way of objections. "Seven years later Benny shows up in Santa Teresa with Duncan Oaks's ID. The next thing you know, Benny's been murdered. You see the link?"

"Benny wasn't *murdered.* You're overstating the situation. As I remember, Benny had a subdural hematoma, and his death was the result of an arterial bleed. Given the nature of his injury, it could have happened any time. Even the coroner's report said that."

"Really? You're probably right. You have quite a memory for the details," I said.

"Mark and I discussed it at the time. I suppose it stuck in my mind."

"Mickey's another link. He went off to Louisville on Thursday, May eighth. He came back on Monday, and in the wee hours of Wednesday morning he was shot, as you know."

Laddie's smile was thin. "Not to sound superior, but you're committing what's called a post hoc fallacy. Just because one event follows another doesn't mean there's a cause-and-effect relationship."

"I see. In other words, just because Benny knew something doesn't mean he died for it."

"Is this what you wanted to discuss with Mark?"

"In part."

"Then let's leave that. I'm sure it's more appropriate to wait till he comes in."

I said, "Fine. Could we talk about your relationship with Duncan?"

"I'd hardly call it a relationship. I knew him, of course. We went all through school together."

"Were you pals, confidants, boyfriend/girlfriend?"

"We were friends, that's all. There was never anything between us, if that's what you're getting at."

"Actually, it is," I said. "I thought since you were the king and queen of the senior prom, you might have been sweet on each other."

Laddie smiled, her composure restored. This was something she'd thought about; her version of the story was preassembled and prepackaged. "Duncan wasn't interested in me romantically, nor I in him."

"Too bad. He looked cute."

"He was cute. He was also extremely narcissistic, which I found obnoxious. There's nothing worse than a seventeen-year-old kid who thinks he's hot stuff."

"You don't think he was charismatic?"

"*He* thought he was," she said. "I thought he was conceited—nice, funny, but such a snob."

"What about your father?"

She looked at me askance. "My father? What's he have to do with this?"

"This is peripheral and probably none of my business—"

"None of this is your business," she said, bridling.

I smiled to show I hadn't taken offense. "I was told he was awarded a patent that earned him a lot of money. I gather, before that, he was considered a bit eccentric."

"If he was, so what? Make your point."

"I'm just thinking his fortune must have changed people's perception of you. Duncan's, in particular."

She was silent.

"Yes? No?"

"I suppose," she said.

"You went from being one down to one up where he was concerned. He sounds like the type who enjoyed a conquest—to prove he could do it, if nothing else."

"Are you trying to build a case for something?"

"I'm just trying to get a feel for what kind of guy he was."

"A dead one."

"Before that. You never had a fling with him?"

"Oh, please. Don't be silly. We never had an *affair.*"

"Hey, an affair is six weeks or more. A fling can be anything from one night to half a dozen."

"I never had a fling with him, either."

"When did Mark leave for Vietnam? I know you married him in June. His orders came through . . ."

"July twenty-sixth," she said, biting off the words.

"The way I read the situation, Duncan was in Louisville after Mark shipped out. There you were, a young newlywed with a husband off at war. I'm sure you were lonely . . . needy. . . ."

"This is offensive. You're being extremely insulting, not only to me but to Mark."

"Insulting about what?" Mark said from the corridor. He shrugged out of his overcoat and tossed it over the back of a chair. He must have come in through the kitchen. His high forehead and receding hairline gave him an air of innocence, the same look babies have before they learn to bite and talk back. Laddie got up to greet him. I watched the two of them as he bussed her cheek.

He said, "Hang on a minute while I make a quick call." He crossed to the phone and dialed 9-1-1.

Laddie said, "What's going on?"

Mark raised a finger to indicate the dispatcher had picked up. "Hi, this is Mark Bethel. I'm at Four-forty-eight Savanna Lane. I've got a couple of guys parked in a car near the entrance to my gate. Could you have a patrol car cruise by? I really don't like the looks of them. . . . Thanks. I'd appreciate that." He replaced the handset and turned to Laddie and me with a shake of his head. "Probably harmless, a lovers' tryst, but just on the off chance they're casing the place. . ." He rubbed his palms together. "I could use a glass of wine."

I tried to picture Detectives Claas and Aldo busted by the local cops on a morals charge.

Laddie poured Chardonnay in a glass, holding it by the stem so as not to smudge the bowl. The trembling of her hand caused the wine to wobble in the glass. Mark didn't seem to notice. He took the glass and sat down, giving me his full attention. "I hope I didn't interrupt."

"We were talking about Benny Quintero," Laddie said. "She's just back from Louisville, where she did some research."

"Benny. Poor guy."

I said, "I didn't realize you were all from the same town."

"Well, that's not strictly true. I was born in Dayton. My family moved to Louisville when I was six. I lived there till I went off to U of K."

"And you knew Benny then?"

"I knew *of* him, just as he must have known about me from football games."

"I didn't realize you played football."

"More or less," he said ruefully. "I went to Atherton, which was all girls for years. School didn't go coed until 1954. Even then, we seldom won a game against Manual or Male. Mostly, the players knew each other by reputation. I remember there was a guy named Byck Snell at Eastern. . . ."

"So Benny came to California and looked you up," I said.

"Right. He must have heard I was a lawyer and somehow got it in his head I could help him with his VA benefits. I mean, it's like I told him: just because I'm an attorney doesn't make me an expert. In those days, I knew next to nothing about the Veterans Administration. Now, of course, I'm educating myself on the issues because I can see what a difference I can make—"

I said, "Sounds like a campaign speech."

Mark smiled. "Sorry. At any rate, I couldn't seem to convince Benny of my ignorance. The whole thing was ludicrous, but I couldn't get him off it. The guy started stalking me, appeared at the office, appeared at the house. The phone started ringing at all hours of the night. Laddie was getting nervous, and I couldn't blame her. That's when I asked Mickey to step in and see what he could do."

"Meaning what?"

I could see him hesitate. "Well, you know, Mickey was a tough guy. I thought he could put the fear of God in him. I'm not saying Mickey meant to hurt him, but he did make threats."

"When?"

"During the incident in the Honky-Tonk parking lot."

"You talked to Benny after that?"

"Sure. He called me and he was furious. I said I'd talk to Mickey. I made a few calls but never managed to track him down, as you well know."

"Because he and Dixie were together," I said, helping him along.

"So they claimed. Frankly, I've always wondered. It seemed pretty damn convenient under the circumstances."

"So you're saying Mickey went back to Benny and beat the shit out of him."

"I'm saying it's possible. Mickey always had a temper. He hated it when some punk got the best of him."

"I hardly think Benny got the best of him. Shack says it was a shoving match with no blows exchanged."

"Well, that's true. Actually, I heard the same report from the other witnesses. The point is, Mickey came off looking bad, and for a guy like him that's worse."

"You know, this is the second time you've implicated Mickey."

"Hey, I'm sorry, but you asked."

"Why didn't you ever mention you knew Benny back in high school?"

"When did I have the chance? In those days, you barely spoke to me. And since then, believe me, I've been acutely aware you're not a fan of mine. We run into each other in public, you practically duck and hide, you're so anxious to avoid contact. Anyway, that aside, you weren't speaking to Mickey either, or he'd have told you the same thing."

I felt myself color at his accuracy. And here I thought I was so subtle. "Can I ask one more thing?"

"What's that?" Mark took a sip of his drink.

"After you joined the army, you were sent to Vietnam. Is that correct?"

"Absolutely. I'm proud of my service record."

"I'm sure you are," I said. "Benny Quintero was there and so was Duncan Oaks." I went on, giving him a hasty summation of what I'd learned from Porter Yount.

Mark's face took on the look of a man who's trying to pay attention while his mind is somewhere else. I could tell he was thinking hard, composing his response before I'd finished what I was saying. His resulting smile held an element of puzzlement. "You have to understand there were hundreds of guys who fought at Ia Drang. The one/five, the one/seven, the two/seven, the Second Battalion Nineteenth Artillery, the Two-twenty-seventh Assault Helicopter Battalion, the Eighth Engineer Battalion—"

"Got it," I said. "There were lots of guys. I got that, but Duncan was a journalist and he went out there specifically to talk to you because of the series he was writing. He must have told you he talked to Laddie. My guess is you'd felt threatened by him for years. He and Laddie were tight. She was poor in those days and never good enough for him, but I'll bet her classmates would tell me she'd had a crush on him, that she'd have given her eyeteeth for his attention—"

"That's absurd. That's ridiculous," Laddie interjected.

Mark made a motion with his hand that told her to hush, the sort of command you teach a dog in obedience training. She closed her mouth, but the significance of the gesture wasn't lost on her. Mark was clearly annoyed. "Let's get to the bottom line. What are you suggesting?"

"I'm suggesting the three of you connected up. You and Benny and Duncan Oaks."

Mark was shaking his head. "No. Wrong."

I said, "Yes. Right. I have a snapshot of the two of them, and you're visible in the background."

Laddie said, "So what?"

"I'll take care of this," he said to her. And then to me, "Go on. This is fascinating. Clearly, you've cooked up some theory and you're trying to make the pieces fit."

"I know how they fit. Duncan interviewed Laddie for the paper after you shipped out. By then, her daddy had money and Duncan couldn't resist. After all, a conquest is a conquest, however late it comes. The two had a fling and you found out about it. Either she 'fessed up or he told you himself—"

Laddie said, "I don't want to talk about this. It's over and done. I made a mistake, but it was years ago."

"Yeah, and I know who paid," I said caustically.

"Laddie, for God's sake, would you shut your mouth!" He turned back to me again, his face dark. "And?"

"And you killed him. Benny Quintero saw it and that's why he was hounding you. You set Mickey up. You killed Benny and made sure Mickey took the rap for it."

Mark's tone was light, but it wasn't sincere. "And you're saying what, that I shot Mickey too?"

"Yes."

He held his hands out, baffled. "Why would I do that?"

"Because he'd put it together the same way I have."

"Wait a minute, Kinsey. Duncan's body was never found, so for all you know he's alive and well. You think you can make a charge like this without evidence?"

"I have the snapshot. That helps."

"Oh, that's right. The snapshot. What crap. I think I better call your bluff. You have it with you?"

"I left it with a friend."

Mark snapped his fingers. "I forgot about Benny's brother. What's his name again? Duffy. Carlin Duffy. Now, there's a bright guy."

I said nothing.

He went on. "My sources tell me he's living in a shack at Himes Nursery. With his criminal history, it should be easy enough to put the screws to him."

"I thought you weren't worried."

"Call it cleanup," he said.

"Really. Now that you're running for public office, you have to bury your misdeeds, make sure the past won't rise up and bite you in the butt when you're least expecting it."

He pointed at me. "Bingo."

"Did you hate him that much?"

"Duncan? I'll tell you what pissed me off about that guy. Not so much that he screwed Laddie the minute my back was turned, but he showed up at Ia Drang, trying to pass himself off as a grunt. I had buddies—good friends, young guys—who died with valor, brave men who believed in what we were doing. I saw them die in agony, maimed and mutilated, limbs gone, gut-shot. Duncan Oaks was a sleaze. He had money and pretensions but not an ounce of decency. He deserved to die, and I was happy to help him out. Speaking of which, I'd like to have his personal effects."

"Effects?"

"Press pass, dog tags."

"I can't help you there. You'd have to talk to Duffy about those things."

From the depths of my shoulder bag, there was a small but distinct click as the tape ran out and the recorder shut itself off. Mark's gaze flicked down and then flicked up to my face. His smile faded, and I heard Laddie's sharp intake of breath. He held his hand out. "You want to give me that?"

"Hey, Dad?"

The three of us turned in unison. The Bethels' son, Malcolm, was standing in the door to the dining room.

"What is it?" Mark said, trying not to sound impatient with the kid.

"Can I take your Mercedes? I've got a date."

"Of course."

Malcolm continued to stand there. "I need the keys."

"Well, get a move on. We're in the middle of a conversation here," Mark said, waving him into the room.

Malcolm shot me a look of embarrassment as he entered the room. Impatiently, Mark removed his keys from his pocket, twisting the key from the ring as he separated it from the others. Meanwhile, I was staring at the kid. No wonder the photographs of Duncan Oaks had seemed familiar. I'd seen him . . . or his incarnation . . . in Laddie's son. The same youth, the same dark, distinctly handsome looks. Malcolm, at twenty, was the perfect blend of Duncan at seventeen and Duncan at twenty-three. I turned to Laddie, who must have known the final piece of the puzzle had fallen into place.

She said, "Mark." He glanced at her, and the two exchanged a quick piece of nonverbal communication.

"Where're you off to, Malcolm?" I said, ever the chipper one.

"I'm taking my girlfriend to a kegger out on campus."

"Great. I'm just leaving. I think I'll follow you out. I got lost coming in. Could you steer me in the right direction?"

"Sure, no problem. I'll be happy to," he said.

I kept a careful eye on the rear of Mark Bethel's black Mercedes as Malcolm drove slowly down the driveway ahead of me. In my rearview mirror, I saw another set of headlights come into view. Mark had apparently made a scramble for Laddie's BMW, a sporty red model perfect for a hit-and-run fatality or a high-speed chase. In front of me, Malcolm had just reached the gates, triggering the automatic mechanism buried in the drive. Slowly, the gates swung open. Out on the road, I spotted two Santa Teresa Sheriff's Department cars pulled onto the berm, lights flashing. Four deputies were in conversation with Detectives Claas and Aldo, who were just in the process of identifying themselves. Malcolm turned left onto Savanna and I followed in his wake. Detective Aldo caught my eye, but there was no way he could help until the deputies had finished with them. So much for Plan A.

I checked the rearview mirror. Mark was so close on my tail, I could see the smirk on his face. I hugged the back end of the Mercedes, figuring Mark wouldn't ram me or shoot as long as Malcolm was close by. Maybe I'd accompany Malcolm and his girlfriend to the kegger out on campus, have a beer, shoot the shit, anything to avoid Mark. We passed a cemetery on the left and slowed at the intersection by the bird refuge. Malcolm tapped his horn and gave a final wave, turning left on Cabana while I turned right and headed for the freeway.

I took the 101 north, keeping my speed at a steady 60 mph. I could see Mark keeping pace. Traffic was light. Not a cop on the road. I groped through my bag, fumbling among the contents with one hand while I steered with the other. I popped the used tape out, leaned over and opened the glove compartment, tossed the tape in, and closed it. I pulled a fresh cassette from the packet on the passenger seat and inserted it in the tape recorder. I didn't have my gun. I'm a private investigator, not a vigilante. Most of my work takes place in the public library or the hall of records. Generally speaking, these places aren't dangerous, and I seldom need a semiautomatic to protect myself.

Now what? I had, of course, invented the bit about Mark's being in the snapshot, visible as a backdrop to Duncan and Benny's reunion. If such a picture existed, it certainly wasn't in my hands . . . or Duffy's, for that matter. I winced. The very notion had put Mark on a tear, thinking we had evidence of their association. Big damn deal. Even if we had such a picture, what would that prove? I should have kept my mouth shut. Poor Duffy didn't have a clue as to what misery was bearing down on him. The last time I'd seen him he was drunk as a coot, passed out on his cot.

I took the Peterson off-ramp and turned left at the light. I didn't bother to speed up or make any tricky moves. Mark didn't seem to be in any hurry either. He knew where I was going, and if I went somewhere else, he'd go to Himes anyway. I think he liked the idea of this slow-paced pursuit, catching up at his leisure while I was frantically casting about for help. I turned right onto the side street and right again into the nursery parking lot. Mine was the only car. The garden center was closed. The building's interior was dim except for a light here and there to discourage the odd burglar with a green thumb or an urge for potted plants. The rest of the acreage was blanketed in darkness.

I parked, locked the car, and headed off on foot. I confess I ran, having given up all pretense of being casual about these things. Glancing back, I could see the headlights of the Beamer as it eased into the lot. I was waiting for the sound of the car door slamming, but Mark had bumped his way across the low concrete barrier and was driving down the wide lanes between the crated trees. I cut back and forth, holding my shoulder bag against me to keep it from jostling as I increased my pace. Idly, I realized the maze of boxed trees had shifted. Lanes I remembered from earlier were gone or rotated on an axis, now shooting off on parallel routes. I wasn't sure if trees had been added, subtracted, or simply rearranged. Maybe Himes had a landscape project that required a half-grown arbor.

I yelled Duffy's name, hoping to alert him in advance of my arrival, but the sound seemed to be absorbed by the portable forest that surrounded me.

Mark was still barreling along behind me, but at least the narrow twists and turns were slowing him down. I felt like I was stoned, everything moving at half speed—including me. I reached the maintenance shed, heart thumping, breath ragged. The yellow forklift was now blocking the lane, parked beside the shed with a crated fifteen-foot tree hoisted on the forks. The shed door was open and a pale light spilled out on the path like water.

"Duffy?" I called.

The lights were on in his makeshift tent, but there was no sign of him. His shoes were missing and the blanket I'd laid over him was now crumpled on the floor. A cheap saucepan sat on the hot plate filled with a beige sludge that looked like refried beans. A plastic packet of flour tortillas sat, unopened, on the unused burner. The pan still felt warm so maybe he'd stepped out to take a leak. I heard the BMW skid to a halt.

"Duffy!"

I checked the top of the orange crate. Duncan Oaks's press pass, his dog tags, and the snapshot were still lying where I'd left them. Outside, I heard the car door slam, the sound of someone thumping in my direction. I gathered Duncan's things in haste, looking for a place to hide them before Bethel appeared. Quickly, I considered and discarded the idea of hiding the items in Duffy's clothes. The shed itself was crude, with little in the way of furniture and no nooks or crannies. In the absence of insulation, I was looking at bare studs, not so much as a toolbox where I could stash the stuff. I shoved the items in my back pocket just as Mark appeared in the doorway, a gun in his hand.

"Oh, shit," I said.

"I'd appreciate your handing me the tape recorder and the tape."

"No problem," I said. I reached in my shoulder bag, took out the tape recorder, and held it out to him. While I watched, he tucked the tape recorder up against his body, pressed the EJECT button with his free hand, and extracted the cassette. He dropped the tape recorder on the dirt floor and crushed it with his foot. Behind him, I caught a flicker of movement. Duffy appeared in the doorway and then eased back out of sight.

"I don't get it," I said. I focused on Mark, making sure I didn't telegraph Duffy's presence with my eyes.

"Get what?" Mark was distracted. He tried to keep his eyes pinned on me while he held the gun and cassette in one hand and unraveled the tape with the other, pulling off the reel. Loops of thin, shiny ribbon were tangled in his fingers, trailing to the floor in places.

"I don't understand what you're so worried about. There's nothing on there that would incriminate you."

"I can't be sure what Laddie said before I showed."

"She was the soul of discretion," I said dryly.

Mark smiled in spite of himself. "What a champ."

"Why'd you kill Benny?"

"To get him off my back. What'd you think?"

"Because he knew you killed Duncan?"

"Because he saw me do it."

"Just like that?"

"Just like that. Call it a flash of inspiration. Six of us were loaded with the body bags. Duncan was pissing and moaning, but I could tell he wasn't hurt bad. Fuckin' baby. Before we could lift off, the medic was killed by machine-gun fire. Benny seemed to be out of it. I'd been shot in the leg, and I'd taken a load of shrapnel in my back and side. Up we went. I remember the chopper shuddering, and I didn't think we'd make it under all the small arms fire. The minute we were airborne, I crawled over to Duncan, stripped him of his ID, ripped the tags off his neck, and tossed 'em aside. All the time the chopper lurched and vibrated like a crazy man was shaking it back and forth. Duncan lay there looking at me, but I don't think he fully understood what I was doing until I hoisted him out. Benny saw me, the shit. He pretended he'd passed out, but he saw the whole deal. By then, I was light-headed and rolled over on my side, sick with sweat. That's when Benny took the tags and hid 'em. . . ."

"I take it he pressed you too hard."

"Hey, I did what I could for him. In the end, I killed him as much for being dumb as trying to screw me over when he should have left well enough alone."

"And Mickey?"

"Let's cut the chitchat and get on with this." He snapped his fingers, pointing to the bag.

"I don't have a gun."

"It's Duncan's tags I want."

"I left the stuff sitting on the orange crate. Duffy must have taken it."

Mark snapped his fingers, gesturing for me to hand him the bag.

"I lied about the snapshot."

"GIVE ME THE FUCKIN' BAG!"

I passed him my shoulder bag and watched while he searched. His holding the gun necessitated working with the bag clamped against his chest. This made it tricky to inspect the interior while he kept an eye on me. Impatiently, he tipped the bag upside down, dumping out the contents. Somewhere nearby, I heard the low rumble of heavy equipment and I found myself praying, *Please, please, please.*

Mark heard it too. He tossed the bag to one side and motioned with the gun, indicating I should leave before him. I was suddenly afraid. While we talked, while we stood face-to-face, I didn't believe he'd kill me because I didn't think he'd have the nerve. My own fate had seemed curiously out of my hands. What mattered at that point was knowing the truth, finding out what had happened to Duncan and Benny and Mick. Now the act of turning my back was almost more than I could bear.

I moved toward the door. I could hear the deep growl of a diesel motor, some piece of machinery picking up speed as it advanced. My skin felt radiant. Anxiety snaked through my gut like summer lightning. I yearned to see what Mark was doing. I wondered if the gun was pointed at my back, wondered if he was, even then, in the process of releasing the safety, tightening his index finger on the trigger, speeding me to my death. Most of all, I wondered if the bullet would hit me before I heard the sound of the shot.

I heard the crack of sudden impact and glanced back, watching with astonishment as the shed wall blew in, boards splintering on contact as the tractor plowed through. Duffy's cot was crushed under the rolling track, which seemed to have the weight and destructive power of a moving tank. The front-mounted bucket banged into the space heater and sent it flying in my direction. I ducked my head, but the heater caught me in the back with an impetus that knocked me to my knees. As I scrambled to my feet, I looked over my shoulder. The entire rear wall of the shed had been demolished.

Duffy threw the tractor in reverse and backed out of the flattened structure, doing a three-point turn. I ran, emerging from the shed in time to see Mark jump into the BMW and jam the key in the ignition. The engine ground ineffectually, but never coughed to life. Duffy, in the tractor, bore down on the vehicle. From the grin on his face, I had to guess he'd disabled the engine. Mark took aim and fired at Duffy, perched high in the tractor cab. I was caught between the two men, and I paused, mesmerized by the violence unfolding. My heart burned in my chest and the urge to run was almost overpowering. I could see that Mark was corralled in the cul-de-sac formed by the wreckage of the shed, a row of crated trees, and the tractor, which was picking up speed again as Duffy accelerated. I was blocking his only avenue of escape.

Mark started running in my direction, apparently hoping to blow by me in his bid for freedom. He fired at Duffy again and the bullet zinged off the cab with a musical note. Duffy worked the lever that controlled the lift arm as the tractor bore down on him. I started running at Mark. He veered off at the last minute, reversing himself. He jumped up on one of the crates, hoping to crash through the trees to the aisle just behind. I caught him midair and shoved him. He bungled the leap, toppled backward, and fell on me. We went down in a heap. As he scuttled to his feet, I reached out and snagged his ankle, holding on for dear life. He staggered, half-dragging me into Duffy's path. Duffy stomped on the accelerator. I released Mark and rolled sideways. The tractor lurched forward, diesel engine rumbling, the bucket lever screeching as Duffy maneuvered it. Mark pivoted, trying to launch himself in the opposite direction, but Duffy bore down on him, the bucket extended like a cradle. Mark turned to face the tractor, gauging its momentum in hopes of dodging its mass. He fired another round, but it clanged harmlessly off the bucket. He'd badly misjudged Duffy's skill. The metal lip banged into Mark's chest with an impact that nearly lifted him off his feet, driving him back against the side wall of the shed. For a moment, he hung there, pinned between the bucket and the wall. He struggled, his weight pulling him down until the lip of the bucket rested squarely against his throat. Duffy looked over at me, and I could see his expression soften. He propelled the tractor forward, and Mark's neatly severed head thumped into the bucket like a cantaloupe.

It wasn't *quite* Plan B, but it would have to do.

Epilogue

The bust at the Honky-Tonk didn't come down for another six months. A federal grand jury returned a fifteen-count indictment against Tim Littenberg and a twelve-count indictment against Scott Shackelford for manufacturing counterfeit credit cards, which carries a minimum five-year prison term and a $250,000 fine for each conviction. Both are currently free on bail. Carlin Duffy was arrested and charged with voluntary manslaughter and he's awaiting trial in the Santa Teresa County jail, with its volleyball, indoor tawlits, and color television sets.

Mickey died on June 1. Later, I sold his handguns, pooling the proceeds with the cash and gold coins I'd lifted from his apartment. Mickey'd never bothered to change his will and since I was named sole beneficiary, his estate (including some pension monies he'd tucked in a separate account, plus $50,000 in life insurance) came to me. Probably out of guilt, Pete Shackelford made good on the ten grand Tim Littenberg owed Mickey, so that in the end, there was quite a substantial sum that I turned over to the Santa Teresa Police Department to use as they saw fit. If he'd survived, I suspect Mickey would have been one of those miserly eccentrics who live like paupers and leave millions to charity.

As it happened, I sat with him, my gaze fixed on the monitor above his bed. I watched the staggered line of his beating heart, strong and steady, though his color began to fade and his breathing became more labored as the days went by. I touched his face, feeling the cool flesh that would never be warm again. After the rapture of love comes the wreckage, at least in my experience. I thought of all the things he'd taught me, the things we'd been to each other during that brief marriage. My life was the richer for his having been part of it. Whatever his flaws, whatever his failings, his redemption was something he'd earned in the end. I laid my cheek against his hand and breathed with him until the last breath. "You done good, kid," I whispered, when he was still at last.

Respectfully submitted,
Kinsey Millhone